# THE DARK *Series*

BOOKS 1-3

**The Dark Series Boxset (Books 1-3)**

*Lilly & Rhys's Complete Story*

*Boxset (3nd) Edition*

This edition contains the first three books in The Dark Series: In the Dark, Out of the Dark, and Of Light and Dark.



Editor: Tanya Keetch | The Word Maid, Jenn Lockwood | Jenn Lockwood Editing

Proofreader: Mary | On Pointe Digital Services

Cover Design Background: Covers by Jules

Cover Design Title: Danah Logan

Interior Formatting: Danah Logan

ISBN: 979-8-9851796-6-8 (e-book )

ISBN: 979-8-9851796-4-4 (paperback)

# A NOTE FROM THE AUTHOR

It is important to me, as the author, to be up front with my readers. To avoid any misconception regarding this trilogy, **please continue reading to ensure this story is for you**.

**Each book in The Dark Series is unique to its main characters. They write the story; I'm just along for the ride. As they get older, their characters grow throughout the series, make mistakes that can have you either relate to, like, or dislike (possibly even hate) them. They are raw and flawed, but we love them anyway.**

*Trust Lilly and Rhys.*

Lilly & Rhys's story is a dark, **forbidden**, new adult, romantic suspense trilogy consisting of *In the Dark*, *Out of the Dark*, and *Of Light and Dark*.

The books are labeled dark due to the themes that may be considered **TRIGGERS** for some, including, but not limited to, the **adopted/step siblings** trope. **None of the characters entering a relationship (in any of my books) are related.** Lilly and Rhys's connection *(why Lilly is able to feel the way she does)* is explained throughout the trilogy.

**If you do not enjoy dark, forbidden themes, this book is *not* for you.**

While the entire series is intended for **MATURE** (18+) readers, please be aware the trilogy is a **SLOW BURN**.

*(For a more detailed list of potential triggers and tropes in this book, scan the below QR code.)*

*For my readers.*
*You gave Lilly and Rhys a chance*
*when I was a brand new author.*
*Thank you from the bottom of my heart.*

xoxo
Danah Logan

# PLAYLIST

Scan the barcode below to listen to
*The Dark Series Trilogy* Playlist.

# IN THE DARK

book 1

## PROLOGUE

### HIM

*I WALK INTO HER ROOM FOR THE NIGHTLY CHECK, EXPECTING THE usual crying and pleading to let her go home, but when I open the door and hear nothing, I know something is wrong. I rush to her small form on the bed, calling her name, but she is not responding. I shake her, but she's completely limp in my arms. Checking her pulse, I sigh in relief. She's alive. What have I done? I scoop her up and race outside to my car which, thankfully, is still in the driveway from my earlier errand. Making sure she is secure in the backseat, I break every speed limit to the nearest emergency room. I can't lose her, too. Making sure my hat is low, hood covering my hair and most of my face, I race inside the double doors and nearly throw her at the first nurse I can find. "HELP HER!"*

*Back in the car, I lean my forehead against the steering wheel and try to catch my breath, chanting, "She will be fine. She will be fine. She will be fine. I'll get her back."*

# CHAPTER ONE

## LILLY

It's mid-November, and everyone is talking about the upcoming Thanksgiving break. Denielle and I sit with Emma and Sloane at our usual lunch table. Our cafeteria is a huge, rectangular hall located in the center of where the three wings of Westbridge High meet. Two sets of double doors lead in from the east and west wings. The south wing is connected via two walkways to the east and west wings. Technically, it is its own building, not a wing, but since it's south of the main complex, everyone calls it the south wing. I'm sure someone put *a lot* of thought into it before making that decision, or it was just the most logical, who knows. The south wing also leads to the parking lot and houses the administration offices, health office, and all of the art-related classrooms—best lighting and all.

Our lunch table is in the heart of the room, next to floor-to-ceiling windows overlooking the outdoor seating area and green space. We have the perfect view of everything and everyone. When I'm not required to pay attention to my friends, I tend to just stare outside at the trees framing the school grounds. We are the only mixed table of gymnasts and cheerleaders. Emma and Sloane are the cheerleaders. Denielle and I are on the school's gymnastics team and train at the local academy during our off-season. The rest of the cheerleaders flock around the far corner table by the east exit, and the rest of the gymnasts are spread over different tables on the west side. It's like an unspoken agreement, but since the four of us have been friends since middle school, we refused to conform to that rule when we entered high school. The jocks claim three of the middle tables and are the center of attention, no matter where in the room you are—you can't miss them. This includes my brother, Rhys, quarterback of the school's football team as well as reigning wrestling champion, and his best friend, Wes.

I'm chewing on my turkey-avocado wrap, tempted to let my gaze wander outside and stop listening to Den going on incessantly about her boyfriend, Charlie. They have been together for two years, and this will be the first time he's coming home since he left for college in August. I peer at my watch—twenty-three minutes and counting. I quietly sigh to myself but try to be a supportive best friend and pay attention. Denielle and I have been friends since my family moved back to Westbridge, Virginia four years ago. We lived here when Dad did his tour at the Pentagon, but he ended up taking command in North Carolina for three years, so we moved again. When he retired from the Marine Corps after twenty-some years, he took a government contractor position. His new job requires him to travel, so he doesn't care where we live. Mom has been a corporate attorney with the same firm for as long as I can remember. She is able to commute between her local office and the firm's main office in Alexandria easily. Living in North Carolina, she had to travel for days at a time, and she never liked leaving us kids for that long—especially when Natty, our little sister, was younger. But it wasn't just that. Both my parents had lived in the Virginia area when they went to school, which was where they met, and a lot of their college friends are still here. Rhys had immediately voted for Westbridge, as you would've thought he'd lost a limb when we left there three years earlier and he had to say goodbye to Wes. The two had been inseparable since Rhys's first day at Westbridge Elementary. My brother had dropped his lunch, and Wes shared his grilled cheese sandwich with him. The bond they formed over two pieces of bread resulted in a lifelong friendship. With so many ties to Virginia, my parents figured moving back was a win-win for everyone. Oh, and of course there is Butler Gymnastics Academy where I had trained for years before we moved.

I've done gymnastics my entire life, so it was a no-brainer to rejoin Butler's as soon as my boxes were unpacked. I kept up with it in North Carolina, but it wasn't the same. Every academy has its individual training method, and I remember being so nervous that I wouldn't make the cut. Denielle took one look at me during my first practice session and flashed me a grin. "I like you. I think we'll be best friends." And that was it. Luckily for us, we also attended the same middle school, and she's been by my side ever since. There was never a question we would compete for spots on the school team as soon as we started high school.

I FINISH MY WRAP, and Denielle is coming up on thirty-four minutes. My attention is fading quickly. My mind drifts again, and I remember the second week of our freshman year when Charlie literally ran Denielle over. He was coming out of the cafeteria, late for his next class, and we were about to enter for our lunch period. His head was turned, talking to one of his buddies, when he plowed her down. It was comical; her books went flying, and the contents of his opened backpack went everywhere. Den was about to let him have it when their eyes locked. Both of them just stared at each other, slack-jawed. They went on their first date the following weekend and have been together ever since. They have one of those relationships you only read about—*the perfect couple*. They complement each other in every way: where she is spontaneous and temperamental, he is calculated and level-headed. Even their fights make you want to gag at how perfect they are. Sometimes, I wonder how they make it work. Anyway, Charlie left for college this summer, and they are working their way through a long-distance relationship. So far, it's been going well, but Thanksgiving will be the first time he's been back, and to say Den is excited would be like saying the sun is *kinda* warm.

"HE'LL REGRET SENDING me all these naughty texts and then not acting on them."

Emma and Sloane laugh at Denielle's comment, and I just roll my eyes. "You are so full of it. First of all, how could he act on it, being three states away? And second, the minute you two are alone, you'll jump his bones."

Den grins at me sideways. "Wasn't that what I was referring to?"

I just shake my head and gather my things. "Grab your stuff. I don't want to be late for journalism again. Mr. Davey said we'd get our research assignment today."

"Geek."

"Love you, too. Get your ass moving."

"You have until after break to finish your paper. We've talked a lot about the news in the last few weeks—how subjectively things are being presented based on the presenter. I want you to pick a current news topic. It can be anything from economics, politics, even a recent criminal case, and research the entire subject. What is being reported and how is it presented versus what you believe is being left out and why."

Mr. Davey mentioning a criminal case immediately intrigues me. Economics and politics have never really interested me. I'm more a math and computer science kinda girl. Plus, our household is composed of an attorney and a former Marine. Heated discussions over politics are a given, which is a reason I stay clear of it as much as I can. Criminal case it is.

## RHYS

I glance toward the table by the windows where Lilly and her friends had taken up residence during the first week of freshman year. As much as the three middle tables are ours, that one is *property* of Denielle, Sloane, Emma, and Lilly, with the occasional visit from a random student. Lilly is staring out the window while Sloane and Emma hang on Denielle's every word. I press my lips together to hide the smile that wants to creep across my face from seeing Lilly's bored expression. I wonder what the topic of Den's monologue is that evokes such an opposite reaction in Lilly versus her two friends. Not that I would ever dare ask. If I did, the answer wouldn't extend beyond Denielle's middle finger. Turning back to my table, a chuckle escapes me at the visual in my mind, and Wes gives me *the eyebrow*. Purposefully ignoring my best friend, I shove another forkful of the disgusting *and* cold spaghetti in my mouth. How the cafeteria folks can fuck up something simple like spaghetti is beyond me.

THE LAST TWO classes are dragging. All I can think about is today's practice since Coach decided to jam extra sessions in before break. I walk between Wes and Jager toward the gym when my girlfriend appears in front of us. Kat gives my friends her usual sultry eye flutter before she wraps her arm around mine and pulls me toward the guys' bathroom we just passed.

"Excuse us, guys. I need Rhys to take care of something for me *really* quick."

She gives me a sidelong glance, and I know exactly what goes through my best friend's and teammate's heads.

*Awesome.*

Wes fist bumps me as I'm being dragged away, and Jager hoots loudly. However, before we get to the bathroom door, I stumble into someone, which is followed by, "What the fuck, McGuire?"

*This is getting better by the minute.*

I turn toward the voice and come nose to nose with Lilly's best friend and *my* archenemy. With her four-inch heels, Denielle is almost at eye level with me, and we stare at each other—neither of us budging. I put my most bored expression on, one I have mastered over the last few years, but before I can say anything, Kat sneers from my side, "Watch where you're going. You're holding us up."

Kat intimidates ninety-nine percent of the school's female population, but not Denielle Keller. She just raises an eyebrow and looks between her and me before settling on Kat.

"Oh, you mean now you have to finish him off in three minutes versus five?" Her gaze travels to me, and with a smirk, she continues, "I think you'll be fine. From what I've heard, you two never need more than two."

Instead of walking around me, she bumps her shoulder into mine with as much force as she's able to gather in the short distance between us.

As I follow Den's retreating form, a hiss comes from Kat that sounds something along the lines of *bitch*, but instead of engaging, Den just flips her the finger and keeps walking. I bite the inside of my cheek not to burst out laughing and let Kat drag me the rest of the way into the bathroom.

After ensuring we're alone, she rounds on me. "You've been ignoring me this week."

*She can't be serious.*

This time, I don't even have to pretend to be bored. "What are you talking about?"

"During lunch *and* practice!" With both fists on her hips, all that's missing is her stomping a foot to complete the temper tantrum.

The urge to turn and walk out is overpowering, but after a calming inhale and exhale, I simply say, "I've had extra practice, and you know that. What do you want from me? Walk you to the other end of the gym in the middle of everything so that we're seen together?" I almost expect her to say yes, but instead, she switches gears altogether.

"Don't forget Emma's party on Friday. I expect you to be there."

It's not like I have anywhere else to be—like home.

"I will."

My answer pacifies her, and she presses a quick kiss on my cheek. "That's my boyfriend."

I sigh inwardly. Yes, it is.

## CHAPTER TWO

### LILLY

Thanksgiving break is finally here.

Emma is throwing a party at her new stepdad's house tonight, and Denielle has been spamming me with texts since we separated at the parking lot earlier.

**U HAAAVE to come. Jake will be there. I told u about him. He REEEAAALLY wants to meet u.**

*What's with the elongated spelling?*

I can't remember the last party where Den didn't want to hook me up with a guy, but this is exaggerated even for her. I love her for trying, and every once in a while, I indulge her, but all the guys are just missing something. It gets old quick.

I respond with the only thing that will make her stop.

**It's a cheer party. I have no desire to run into them, and u know she'll be there, which means he will be too.**

A few minutes later, my phone lights up again.

**Sigh!**

Bingo! Internal fist pump. I grin until I see her next text, and my feeling of satisfaction fades.

**Babe, you need to get over this shit. It's been over 2 yrs. Ur brother is a dick and I have ur back, but u can't avoid

**every party where the Wicked Bitch will be because u don't
want to run into him.**

Now, it's my turn to sigh.

**Ugh. Ur right. But not tonight, k? I just don't want a
repeat of the end of summer party.**

**That was months ago, but ok. Call me if you change your
mind. Love you, babe.**

**K. Love you 2.**

FEELING SOMEWHAT RESIGNED, I put my phone down next to my
laptop. I'm sitting at my desk, which is positioned between the two
windows facing the backyard, and I peer over at the small, framed
photo of Rhys and me.

My brother is a year older—actually, ten and a half months, to be
precise, which has been cause for quite some fertility jokes about
our mom over the years.

Slightly taller, he has his arm draped around my shoulder, grinning at the camera while I beam up at him. It was taken at Woodland Park right after we moved to Westbridge the first time, ten
years ago. Rhys and I used to be so close; we did everything
together. And then it all changed a little over two years ago—*he*
changed.

After a year of attending different schools—Rhys at Westbridge
High and me still in middle school—we were going to finally be in
the same place again. He was so busy his freshman year that I saw
him less and less. In my mind, we would carpool, and Rhys, Wes,
and I would get to hang out again. I had it all planned out in my
mind and couldn't wait for school to start. They were both gone for
camp over the summer, and despite spending most of my time with
Denielle, I missed them a lot. Wes had been Rhys's best friend for
eight years, but he was one of my closest friends as well. Though,
when they got back, Rhys had changed even more. He was
completely withdrawn. Wes tried to assure me that it had nothing
to do with me; Rhys was just busy. But I knew better. By the time
school had officially started, my brother was full-on ignoring me. I
tried several more times, but he just became more irritated. When I
entered a room, he would turn and leave. I had lost my best friend

over something I didn't understand. Then, he started dating Katherine Rosenfield, the head cheerleader, and I gave up trying to fix the unknown. The quarterback and the cheerleader—the perfect couple. Gag.

Shaking my head, I turn away from the picture. I've put it away several times, but something always compels me to place the frame back on my desk.

I pull up the search engine on my computer and start looking for a topic for my journalism paper. The quicker that's done, the quicker I can enjoy the break. Maybe Denielle will even disentangle herself from Charlie long enough to spend some time with me.

I've been browsing different news websites for the past hour when I come across a headline that piques my interest. *Seven-Year-Old, Rose Ashbaugh, Discharged from Local Hospital After Missing for Two Weeks.* I click on the article and am immediately sucked in. This little girl is the fifth victim. She was taken at a local park she visited with her mother regularly. The mom was talking to another parent and didn't notice Rose was gone until it was too late. They kept getting regular updates from the perpetrator with pictures showing her healthy and taken care of. No demands were made, and a couple of weeks later, she just turned up at a random hospital. What the hell?

I read every article I can find linked to this one. Most of them are from the same freelance reporter, a guy named Lancaster, who seems to have made this story—case—his sole purpose in life. It's all he writes about. I look up the other victims, and not one girl could give a decent description of the kidnapper. They were being kept tranquil, but not fully sedated, just *kind of* drugged. All they could tell the authorities was the man was tall, *white*—so, Caucasian—and *nice.* Nice? What the—? He talked to them, read with them, played games, made them their favorite foods, etc. The hairs on my arms stand up while reading this. The girls were taken from all over the U.S. There is no rhyme or reason to the timeline; all they have in common is their appearance: slender with long blonde hair, hazel eyes, and fair skin.

*I think I've found the topic for my paper.*

I decide to go through the articles victim by victim and compare the coverage. Other news outlets followed the first reporter's lead and mentioned a possible connection between these cases. I take notes from each article and bookmark sites. My phone buzzes a few times, but I ignore it. I don't have the patience for party gossip right now. I'm on the second article for victim number three, Meredith Scagliotta, when my gaze wanders back to the picture of Rhys and me. Suddenly, something about the picture feels off, but I can't pinpoint what. I rub my eyes and peer over my left shoulder at my queen-size bed—anywhere but the photo. I recently got a new light-gray, upholstered wingback headboard. My old one was a hand-me-down from the guest bedroom set in our last house, and I'd been begging for a room makeover for years. Mom finally caved when she found this one on sale at the local furniture store. After spending some of my own money on a white pin-tuck duvet set and some gray and purple throw pillows, my new bed has become my sanctuary when I'm at home. It's the one place I can fully relax and feel at peace. The rest of the house always keeps me on edge because there is a chance of Rhys showing up. He pretends I'm invisible yet can't stand to remain in the same room as me for more than a few minutes. Not that he ever does, though—show up, that is. I focus back on my screen and the photo of the little girl displayed on the website, but my eyes are drawn to the white picture frame next to it. I was so happy in the picture. Still in the memory of when my brother slung his arm around me, laughing, a stabbing pain assaults my head. Squeezing my eyelids shut, I dig the heels of my palms into my eyes, trying to make it go away.

*Shit, that hurts.*

That's when I see myself—no, my *kid* self, maybe six or seven years old. The reflection stares back at me, surrounded by a white ornate wooden frame—a mirror. My pale skin enhances the dark circles under my eyes—God, *so* pale. The throbbing between my temples slowly subsides, and I blink against the light of my desk lamp.

*What. The. Hell. Just. Happened?*

I read once that you can see flashes with migraines. But number one, I have never had a migraine in my life, and two, this didn't feel random. It was more like a déjà vu or...a memory. Though, I know for a fact I never had a mirror like that, so it *can't* be a memory.

*So weird.*

The alarm clock on my nightstand shows it's almost one in the morning, and I automatically stifle a yawn. Shrugging, I chalk this whole thing up to being overtired and having overindulged in too many unsettling news reports.

I call it a night and decide to continue tomorrow.

### RHYS

I'M STANDING with Wes in Emma's kitchen. Her stepdad owns Iron Moore Construction, a local company specializing in underground services, tunneling, and electrical power. A few years ago, he landed a big contract in the city, and his empire exploded from there. When he and Emma's mom hooked up, they moved into his ostentatious Westbridge mansion within weeks.

The party is in full swing. Everyone holds either a red Solo cup or bottle of *something* in their hand—the liquids' colors ranging from clear to amber to red. People are laughing and shoving each other in the cramped space, hence why I've parked my ass against the countertop in the corner. I'm on my second beer, questioning again what the fuck I'm doing here. Oh yeah, avoiding home and making sure my girlfriend is happy. Kat is somewhere in the living room, holding court over her cheerleader minions and making sure she is appropriately admired. The occasional kiss and endearments keep her appeased these days—as long as everyone and their mother sees it, of course. Kat and I have been together for almost two years, but it's *never* been about love for us. Sure, she's hot with her long blonde curls, killer body, big...uh, eyes, and when she wears that *tiny* uniform—well, you get the picture. We had fun in the beginning—*a lot* of fun. But all she cares about is her image and being the head cheerleader dating the school's quarterback. She's known from the start that we're not happily-ever-after material, and she's never asked me what my motives are, which is perfectly fine. But lately, it's getting harder and harder to keep up the act. It's fucking exhausting.

Wes keeps talking when I spot Denielle weaving through the crowd. I heard Charlie is coming home this weekend, and she probably wants to party before holing up with him for the week. Her long, dark-brown hair is curled at the ends, and she is dressed to kill in black skinny jeans, a lacy red top, and black heels—the ones with the red soles that cost a fortune, which is also something I know from dating Kat. If she weren't basically married to her boyfriend, I would think she's trying to get laid. Though, no one would dare say that to her face. I keep following her with my eyes, searching for her best friend. They are usually a package deal and easy to spot with Den's dark hair and Lilly's blonde head, but I've noticed that for the last few months, Lilly's been avoiding parties where I'd be. Can't say I blame her.

Being busy with practice, I haven't seen Denielle since our run-in earlier this week, and when she catches my eye, she gives me the usual death glare that has been solely reserved for me. Maybe not solely, but I definitely get the nastier ones, which still makes me feel a *little* special. I hold my beer up in greeting, but she just flips me off and keeps walking. Yup, she's clearly mastered the flip-the-dickhead-brother-off gesture. Taking a swig from my beer, I hide my amusement. If they only knew.

"Dude, are you even listening?"

I blink and look over at my best friend. "Huh?"

"Yeah, that's what I figured," he huffs. "Are you training with Spence tomorrow?"

Oh, he's still going on about our workout plans. The school gym is closed this weekend for *deep cleaning*, whatever that means, so we need to change our usual plans.

"Uh, no. Lilly is training with him Saturday. I'm meeting him Sunday. You should know that by now; we work out together *every* freakin' week." I barely manage to keep the irritation out of my voice. We go through the same spiel every single Friday. Sometimes I question Wes's long-term memory.

"Okay, cool. Then let's go at eleven and grab lunch after."

*Wonderful.* That's in the middle of Lilly's session, but I just nod. Why he insists on making plans is beyond me. I'm sleeping on his couch. It's not like we'll miss each other taking a piss in the same bathroom.

I switched the days of my training sessions with Spence, one of our dad's Marine Corps buddies, so I could avoid Lilly. She kept the Saturdays, and I moved to Sundays and started working out in the school's weight room when Lilly is at the gym.

"I still don't get why you stopped sparring with Lil. The two of you are lethal together."

*Why. Does. He. Not. Shut. Up?*

Tightening the grip on the bottle in my hand, I grit out, "Let it go, man."

He's right on that account, though. When Lilly and I had worked together with Spence, we always used to push each other. I miss sparring with her, but I would never admit that. Instead, I add, "It was time to change it up."

Wes has learned over the years to not push me on that topic once I reach a certain point, and he switches to angling his bottle at Amber Jennings' ass. Apparently, it's shaped like a ripe peach in her jeans.

*Who the fuck talks like that?*

I take that as him moving on now that he and Kimberly are done. Time for me to zone out again. Another hour and I'll have fulfilled my obligation.

# CHAPTER THREE

### LILLY

I meet Spence at the gym. He and Dad have known each other forever, and he's been training Rhys and me on and off for the past ten years in mixed martial arts. At first, I didn't get why our parents were so adamant for us to learn self-defense. I had gymnastics and didn't want to do anything else. But it only took a few sessions for me to fall in love with it—like, I-want-to-do-this-every-day in love. When we moved to North Carolina, I missed it so much that Spence would come down once a month to train us. Since we're in gymnastics season, I only have time for one session a week until March, and I make sure I don't waste a single second of it. Spence pushes me for the whole two hours, without a break, and I'm drenched from head to toe when he announces we're done.

He chuckles. "You look like you took a dip in the pool. You did great today!"

He's right; my hair is plastered against my scalp like I just stepped out of a shower. Despite being completely exhausted, I feel exhilarated, adrenaline from our last round still rushing through my body.

His praise makes me grin from ear to ear. "I have a decent trainer."

Spence winks, giving me a quick side hug. "I'll see you next week, kiddo."

I grab my things and wave goodbye on my way to the locker room.

WALKING TO MY CAR, I see Wes's red 4Runner in the parking lot, and sure enough, two spots down is Rhys's black Defender. What are they doing here? They usually work out at the school's gym on Saturdays—something else Rhys started doing after he moved his sessions to Sundays.

Dad has had the Defender longer than we've been alive, and to everyone's surprise, he gave it to Rhys for his eighteenth birthday this year. Not that I was jealous—well, maybe a little bit. I love my white, four-door Wrangler, and despite the *situation* between Rhys and me, I was happy for him. He's been in love with that car since he could see over the steering wheel, and he spent hours sitting in it, pretending to drive. It matches his personality; they both dominate their surroundings wherever they go—or drive. I sigh in relief as I get into my Jeep, glad I didn't run into either of them.

Determined to work on my paper and find out more about this case, I make my way home.

BY SUNDAY AFTERNOON, my eyes are burning from staring at the computer screen. I have no idea where my glasses are since I rarely use them. Note to self: find glasses or get new ones. My eyes are killing me. I've cataloged each article by victim and am making good headway on my paper. Every reporter has his or her theory, and it's making the assignment almost laughably easy. What keeps me glued to the screen, however, is the tightness in my chest. I don't understand where it comes from, and even though it makes me shift in my chair every few minutes, I keep reading and researching. The facts are almost the same for all the girls. They are taken during a brief moment of distraction on the caregiver's side. The families receive some sort of footage of the girls every day, showing they are well, but the authorities are unable to trace the footage back to its source. Then, the girls turn up in a different part of the state; all have been given something to keep calm, but they are well cared for. What is even more disturbing is that, despite being held against their will, all the girls say the man had only been kind to them. The websites talk about five victims; however, I can't find any decent information about the first. My paper is done, but I have an overwhelming urge to keep looking. I *have* to find out more.

I SPEND most of the week at home, doing one of two things: lounging on my bed with my favorite books or doing more research on the case. I get to see Denielle for a few hours on Tuesday. She *graces* me with her presence after Charlie got called home so his mom also gets to see him during break. She catches me up on Charlie's college life, how busy his classes keep him, and we watch several episodes of our favorite TV show. I don't mention the case to her. Something keeps me from sharing it with my best friend.

The day before Thanksgiving, I stumble across a video this Lancaster guy recorded after the fourth victim. It's only available on his personal website; I'm not sure it was ever officially broadcasted by a news outlet. He recaps the kidnappings, and what he says next makes my blood run cold.

"After Ava Conway and Meredith Scagliotta, Chloe Lynn is the fourth victim of the unknown perpetrator. After extensive research, I have concluded that these three girls were used as placeholders by the offender for the first victim. The unknown six-year-old girl was recovered at a hospital in Northern California after she was dropped off anonymously at the emergency room with a potential drug overdose and was unconscious for several days. The hospital staff was unable to identify the girl, as no missing person reports were found matching the description. After the girl's recovery, she was removed from the hospital without leaving a trace. The name of the girl was never released, nor was the hospital staff able to give us any further information. I believe the overdose was not intentional by the kidnapper and was the reason she was brought to the emergency room. He seems to have revised his method since, as the other girls were monitored very carefully and have shown no signs of extensive sedation."

I pause the video and let the information sink in. Placeholders?

But why? That doesn't make any sense. I peer over at my six-year-old self in the photo and, without warning, feel like someone is shoving shards of glass in my eyes.

Accompanying the stabbing pain, I see a white bed canopy hovering above me.

*Why am I on my back?*

By the time the agony subsides, I am bent forward in my desk chair. My head is almost between my knees, and I'm clutching it with both hands. Something is definitely wrong here—with me.

THANKSGIVING COMES AND GOES, and we all watch football most of the day. Dad and Rhys are in deep discussion about the games—Rhys actually bothered coming home. Mom and Natty are playing Monopoly, and my little, ten-year-old sister is draining Mom's money fast with all her hotels. I try to pretend to be interested in all of it when, in truth, I want to hide in my room and figure out what's happening to me.

BY THE TIME I am back at school on Monday, I have had two more *migraines*, as I call them now. The thought of calling them memories scares the crap out of me. I mean, I don't actually remember any of it. And visions? I'd rather think that I'm going plain old crazy.

The first happened when I walked out of the bathroom Friday evening. I was on my way to the closet to drop my gym clothes in the hamper when, mid-step, my head exploded. That time, I saw a white bergère chair with pale-green cushions and a well-loved stuffed bunny sitting in one corner.

The second one blindsided me in the kitchen on Sunday when Rhys walked in from the garage and stopped in the doorway. He was dressed in black sweats and a matching hoodie that emphasized his broad build. With his chocolate-brown hair recently buzzed short for wrestling season and his permanent scowl, he could scare the shit out of anyone who didn't know him.

We rarely run into each other because we internalized the other's routine a long time ago and do everything possible to avoid a confrontation. But I was downstairs later than usual to make myself a cup of herbal tea with the hope it'd help me sleep.

Seeing him standing there, I experienced the most disturbing migraine yet: the silhouette of a man standing in a doorway, staring back at me. Because of the light coming from outside, all I could make out was that it was a man, but no face. My heart was beating in my throat.

As my vision cleared and the invisible glass shards disappeared from my eye sockets, I saw Rhys was right in front of me. His hands lifted up as if he were going to touch me, but then he stopped himself. His head cocked to the side, and he looked...concerned? Something I hadn't seen directed at me in a long time.

"Are you okay?" He even sounded worried.

*Interesting.*

I shook my head, taking a step back. "Yeah, I'm fine. Just a headache."

Before he could call me out on the lie, I sidestepped him and made my way to the sink to fill up the kettle. He was too close, and I needed to put distance between us. When I turned back around, Rhys was standing in the same spot, shoulders slumped, and I almost felt guilty for brushing him off. Almost.

*Screw it; he did it first.*

We used to tell each other everything. A few years ago, I would've confided in him in a heartbeat. One day, we were best friends, and the next, we weren't. He didn't want anything to do with me.

I'M on my way to deposit some books in my locker and then hand in the journalism assignment to Mr. Davey. He said we could drop it off at his desk at any point before his class this week, and to be honest, I want to get rid of the paper. I forced myself to stick to the facts—the way the press reported the case—and not let my emotional reaction bleed into my analysis.

I wade through the sea of students without really paying attention to my surroundings. Sleep has gotten less and less since this whole thing started.

Suddenly, an arm slings around my shoulder from behind. My

mind has lost its ability to think logically, and I react on instinct. Spinning around, I start pushing the assailant into the lockers with my forearm against their throat. Thankfully, the brain fog clears, and I realize that I am not being attacked, but greeted, by my best friend. What I was about to do dawns on me before I completely embarrass myself in front of everyone—or worse, hurt Denielle.

Hands in front of herself, Den gawks at me with wide eyes. "Whoa, babe! What's going on with you?"

*Shit. Crap. Shit!*

I mumble, "Uh...nothing, sorry. Just tired."

I try to turn away, but she grabs my arm and moves me to face her again. She has her typical that's-bullshit-and-you-know-it glare: head tilted slightly, one eyebrow lifted, lips pursed. "Wanna try again?"

She wouldn't be my best friend if she didn't see through my lame excuse, but I don't want to talk about it—I can't. I have no idea what's going on with me, and I'm not ready to share my concern about potentially losing my mind over a homework assignment.

"I just didn't sleep well." She doesn't believe me, but she doesn't press any further. She would never do that to me in the middle of the school.

## RHYS

*WHAT THE FUCK JUST HAPPENED?*

I was watching Lilly from the other end of the hallway when Denielle came up from behind and hugged her. Lilly could've done some serious damage.

Spence has been working on that move with her during self-defense lessons. During a sparring session, she once almost crushed my windpipe with that maneuver. I hurt for two days.

Being briefly distracted by the memory, I catch myself before a grin shows on my face. Lilly appears to be your stereotypical high school girl. The years of gymnastics and martial arts have given her an athletic build. Her long blonde hair and minimal makeup just enhances the innocent look, but behind the five-foot-four girl hides a lethal weapon.

· · ·

I WANT to know what's going on, but when I take a step in their direction, Kat puts her hand on my arm. "Where are you going, sweetie?"

I peer down at her and exhale slowly, forcing a smile on my face. "Nowhere."

I fucking loathe her pet names for me, and lately, everything with her just annoys me. I put my good-boyfriend face on and pretend to listen to her conversation with Jenny, one of my teammate's girlfriends, about some new boots she has to have and her dad refuses to buy her because they cost more than a small used car. I have the urge to bang my head into the nearest locker.

*Make. Her. Stop.*

Taking another glance in Lilly's direction, I notice them walking away now.

I think of Sunday and the way she looked at me when I came home from the gym to grab my clothes for the week. All my clothes at Wes's were dirty, and I hadn't had time to wash them yet.

I didn't expect her to be in the kitchen that late. One second, she stared at me, and the next, she held onto her head, eyes squeezed shut. I dropped my bag and took two long strides toward her, but I stopped myself from touching her at the last moment. I wanted to grab her shoulders, demand to know what was wrong, but her eyes opened, and she instantly shut down. This is all my fault. She used to tell me everything, and something is obviously wrong with her. These days, she would rather swallow her tongue than talk to me.

*Understandably.*

I need to find out what's going on.

# CHAPTER FOUR

## LILLY

Over the next week and a half, I'm convinced I am losing my mind.

The school team often uses Butler's gym for practice sessions so we don't have to share the gym with all the other teams at school. After our mandatory practice session on Wednesday, I procrastinate in the shower, and everyone is gone by the time I walk to my Jeep. I'm almost at the driver's side door when I glance over to the small park across the street. Just a small, fenced-in playground with two slides, some swings, and a merry-go-round. It's freezing. Yet, kids are still playing there, bundled up in snowsuits and oblivious to the cold, while their parents or sitters look beyond miserable. A little girl is running toward a woman who catches her, and the girl squeals in delight when she spins her in a circle.

Thankfully, I've already reached my car when it hits me. I lean against the side, knowing what comes next, and wait for the agony to subside. This one confuses me more than the previous migraines.

I'm running toward a woman. Who is she? I'm wracking my brain, trying to remember if I have ever seen her. She seems to be in her early thirties, long blonde hair, fair skin. She is dressed in jeans, a white cap-sleeve blouse, and sandals. I come up blank. Maybe a friend of Mom? But why would I run toward her like that?

. . .

THE FOLLOWING SUNDAY, Dad knocks on my door, peeking his head in. "Wanna go to the range with me?"

*Hell yeah!*

A broad grin spreads across my face. We haven't gone in a few weeks due to Dad's travel schedule, and I've missed our unusual daddy-daughter dates.

Rhys and I were nine and ten when he first sat us down and showed us his .45. He talked for over an hour about gun safety rules, what it means to handle a firearm responsibly, and eventually, he started taking us to the range. By the time I turned fifteen, I was able to hit my mark up to twenty-five feet.

Spending the morning with Dad takes my mind off everything else, and when he suggests going to eat lunch at our favorite diner, I jump up and down, clapping my hands like Natty when Mom surprised her by telling her we were going to Disneyland a few years go. I have no desire to be back home yet.

I have just scooted into the booth when the sledgehammer hits again.

*Not now!*

I grab my temples and squeeze my eyes shut. Here we go. I'm sitting in a booth similar to this one. Across from me, a couple is talking to each other, the man smiling at me in between their conversation. It's the same woman from the park, but like last time, I have no recollection of her. The man next to her has black hair and seems to be around the same age. His arm is wrapped around her shoulders.

When my vision clears, Dad looks at me with concerned eyes. "Everything okay, sweetheart?"

I smile tightly, still waiting for the remaining pain to subside. "Yes, I've been having some headaches lately. Probably need to get my eyes checked; I can't find my glasses."

*Nice save, Lilly.*

I want to pat my own back for that one.

He nods in understanding. "That's a good idea. You may need new glasses with all the screen time you have. It's not good that you stare at your computer all day and not use your glasses."

I nod and divert the conversation by asking about the upcoming weekend trip with Mom. Every few months, they go away for a weekend to make up for all his traveling. This time, he is whisking her away to New York, but Mom doesn't know yet. He got them Broadway tickets with a super-fancy dinner beforehand. She'll be ecstatic; she's been talking about seeing that show forever, but the opportunity hasn't come up.

EARLY MONDAY MORNING, Dad leaves for his last overseas trip before Christmas, Mom is busy with Natty and her upcoming Christmas recital, and Rhys and I don't talk as it is, which makes it easy for me to just hole up in my room when I'm not in school or at practice.

I start avoiding my friends because I'm scared of when the next migraine could hit. I don't want to deal with potential questions. Denielle throws sidelong glances my way whenever she thinks I don't see it, but she doesn't press the issue. She knows me. If she'd push for more details than I'm willing to give, I'd simply shut down. It was the same when the whole Rhys thing first went down. I wouldn't talk to anyone for weeks. If Den finds out that I think I'm losing my mind, she'll make me tell my parents, and I'm not ready for that.

THE NEXT THREE days pass without any further incidents, and I let hope creep in that the migraines are gone.

*I was wrong.*

Thursday evening, Mom announces we are having family dinner together. Dad is not back until tomorrow morning, but for some unknown reason, Rhys is home. I don't remember the last time he was home for dinner during the week—on a non-holiday weekday. Mom takes it as a sign and makes spinach lasagna—Rhys's favorite. Most guys go for pizza or burgers, but not my brother; he takes anything veggie over junk food.

We sit down at the kitchen dining table Mom bought a few months ago on a whim from the same furniture store my headboard is from. It's a distressed gray trestle table made from salvaged wood.

She took that as an opportunity to give the kitchen a redesign. She had new gray Carrara marble countertops put in and painted the walls in the palest turquoise-green color. I have no clue what the actual color is called, but that's how I describe it when someone asks. A matching bench replaced our old wooden kitchen chairs on one side of the table, and diamond-tufted chairs in a similar color as the walls were on the remaining three sides. With the white cabinets and gray-ish wooden floor, the new color scheme made the kitchen become my second favorite room in the house—besides my own.

Dinner passes relatively smoothly. Rhys keeps eyeing me but doesn't say anything. He gives me the same look as Denielle, and it's getting annoying.

*Who's he to act all worried?*

He participates in Mom and Natty's conversation about her next dance lesson and when she has to go for her costume fitting. For a brief moment, I see the old Rhys, the one who was home for meals, played board games with us in the evenings, talked to us about his practice, and always inquired about what was going on in our lives— in my life.

I start gathering my empty plate, taking another look at everyone before getting up. That's when the fireworks explode behind my eyes.

*No, no, no, no.*

I drop my plate and press my palms into my eyes, trying to control my breathing. A similar rectangular dining room table appears in front of my mind's eye. A young Rhys sits next to me, laughing and throwing a fry at my face. I squeal and grin at him. Dad sits at the head of the table, and Mom is to the right of him, deep in conversation with someone else. Oh. My. God. It's the couple from the diner migraine.

*Who the hell are these people?*

I slowly lower my hands and blink. Once. Twice. Mom's and Natty's blurry forms start to come into focus, both staring at me, wide-eyed, while Rhys is on his feet next to me, ready to act.

"Dad told me you're having headaches. Did you make an appointment for your eyes yet?" Mom asks, concerned, head slightly tilted to the side as if she's assessing my physical well-being.

Heart pounding in my throat, I recover from the shock and shake my head. "Not yet. I'll call tomorrow."

"Okay, make sure to call first thing in the morning. Now go take some Tylenol and lie down."

Unable to face my siblings, I nod at Mom and crouch down to pick up the broken plate. Rhys squats next to me, and our hands briefly touch as he takes the pieces from me. I experience a flutter-like sensation in my chest, which shocks me deep to the core.

*What the hell was that?*

"I'll take care of that." We're hidden underneath the table, and I stare up at him. Even when he squats, he's taller than I am. His voice is so tender and concerned. One look at him and it's clear he doesn't buy the headache excuse. Shaking my head, I don't allow myself to think of him as the old Rhys. I stand up without another word and head to my room. I need to be alone. I need to think.

## RHYS

I'VE BEEN WATCHING Lilly all week—whenever I could without bringing attention to myself. She has withdrawn from her friends. Physically she is with them, but she doesn't participate in conversations and mostly stares off into space. She's also wearing less and less makeup as the week progresses, and her usually styled hair hangs either flat or is up in a messy bun. The looks Denielle gives her tell me that her best friend also doesn't know what's going on, which makes the pit in my stomach expand by the day. Lilly tells her everything since I've *stepped* out of the picture. Before that, it was me she confided in.

I contemplate asking Den directly, but I'm not sure she would tell me even *if* she does know something.

THURSDAY WAS the first day I didn't have practice, and I decided to go home in the evening.

After what happened during dinner, I text Wes that I'm sleeping at home tonight. Within two seconds, he sends me an emoji with raised eyebrows.

*Fucking great.*

For the past two years, I'd have rather slept on his hard-as-a-rock couch than my own bed, which has one of the most comfortable memory foam mattresses ever made. He's not stupid, but I'm not going to elaborate. Not until I figure it out myself.

I plant my ass on my bed, leaning against the headboard, with the door slightly open. From here I have a direct line of sight to Lilly's room across the hall. I'm determined to confront her.

Natty's room is at the other end of the hall by the stairs, and Mom and Dad's bedroom takes up the entire third floor. Mom is already upstairs, and I'm not too concerned about checking up on Lilly. If Dad would've been home, I probably wouldn't have risked it, but Mom doesn't care. At least I don't think she does. I'm pretty sure she hates this fucked-up situation as much as I do.

The light shines under Lilly's door until well after midnight, but she doesn't come out. Resigned, I go to bed.

*I need to get her alone.*

WHEN I SEE Lilly during lunch the next day at school, she seems even worse than the previous days. She has dark circles under her eyes, wears zero makeup, and her messy bun looks like she slept in it. Add boyfriend jeans and an oversized hoodie to the mix, and she looks like a mess. Wait a sec, that's *my* old hoodie. What the—? She'd never voluntarily wear that thing if she were in her right mind.

Denielle's eyes meet mine across the cafeteria, and for the first time in years, there is no distaste directed toward me. I see my concern reflected back at me, and she gives me a sad nod.

I HAVE a wrestling match tonight and won't be home until late, but the only thing on my mind is finding out what has put Lilly so on edge—and keeps her there. I'm obsessing over it to the point of losing a match. Kat is getting annoyed with my lack of attention, and in true *mature* fashion, I ignore her more. At one point, her face is almost as red as her Christmas-themed lipstick, steam basically coming out of her ears. But none of that phases me. I don't give a fuck about her games anymore. I have more important things on my mind—someone more important.

DAD'S PLANE landed early Friday morning, and Mom and Dad left in the afternoon for their weekend getaway. Natty is staying with her friend Olivia until Sunday. I almost cancel my weekend workout session with Wes but then decide against it to not cause any more unwanted attention. We meet *every* Saturday, and Wes would be up my ass with a million questions.

The entire morning, he goes on and on about tonight's party. Jackson is apparently throwing *the* party. Every party is *the* party, but Kat has also been on me for the past two weeks to make sure we're seen there together. I've neglected to tell either of them that I have no intention of showing up. The last thing I want to do today is watch my classmates get hammered and subject myself to Kat's constant need for validation. It's not like her confidence needs any more boosting; it already sucks enough oxygen out of a room to inflate a hundred egos.

I GET HOME around noon and see Lilly's car has not moved an inch. The branch I purposefully placed against her rear tire for that reason is still in the same spot. She didn't train with Spence today.

*Shit.*

My pulse increases the longer I stare at her Jeep. She never misses her session. I climb the stairs, finding her door closed. It's been closed whenever I've been home for the past few weeks. It never used to be closed. Usually, it was my door that was closed—to avoid running into her.

Suddenly feeling nervous about just barging in and demanding answers, I chicken out and take another shower. I already showered at the gym, but this seems like a plausible reason not to knock right away.

Afterward, I keep pacing back and forth in my room. What am I doing? Why am I so fucking on edge? Oh, yeah, I've been a complete dick to her for over two years, and she hates me.

*She's never going to tell me what's going on.*

I pace some more. Sit down on my bed. Turn on the TV. Turn it back off. Throw the remote back on the bed. Fuck! Back to more pacing.

I waste a whole hour with that.

When I end up sitting on my bed yet again, I put my head in my hands. I'm losing my mind. I haven't worried about Lilly like this in a very, *very* long time. I've carefully maintained my distance for over two years. I built this nice, solid wall in my head, making sure to keep her at arm's length until she finally stopped talking to me. When that day came, it hurt. Fuck, how it hurt. I stayed at Wes's for two days, hiding from home, and have pretty much been there since. But I deserved it; I hurt her first.

"FUCK IT!" I stand up.

I'll deal with the consequences later.

I WALK ACROSS THE HALL, hesitating one last time. I take a deep breath and knock. No answer. She's home, so I knock again. When she still doesn't respond, I ease the door open and slowly walk in.

Lilly sits in the middle of her bed, facing away from the door. Her laptop is open to the right of her, and what looks like hundreds of printouts and notes are scattered on her white duvet. Two of our old family photo albums are in front of her.

My blood runs cold.

*FUUUCK!*

I'm starting to understand what this is about. Fuck, crap, fuck. I rake my hands through my hair, which prompts Lilly to turn, and I notice her headphones.

Her eyes widen, followed by her expression changing to wariness. I'm sure she wants to know what I'm doing here. Heck, I almost wish I hadn't come. The first piece falls out of my once nice, solid barrier toward Lilly.

*Shit.*

After what seems like an eternity of us staring at each other, she softly says, "Hi?"

---

# CHAPTER FIVE

---

**LILLY**

Earlier, I decided to search our old family photo albums for the mystery couple. The old albums are all in my parents' room upstairs, and we rarely go up there unless it's an emergency. Not that we're not allowed to; it just happens to be that way since everyone usually congregates on the first floor during the day, and Mom and Dad are only upstairs at night.

The king-size bed is to the right between two large windows. Across from the door, on the opposite wall, is a small sitting area with a short bookshelf. The doors to the massive walk-in closet and bathroom that Mom had completely remodeled upon buying the house are to the left. The entire room is mid-century modern. Chic and classy, but still cozy. Mom has phenomenal talent in arranging a room. Stepping into their closet, there is another wall of shelves that holds old photo albums and important binders and files. It feels like I'm violating their privacy, but I quickly shake the thought—I need answers.

I'm comparing some of my notes again when something moves in my peripheral vision. My heart immediately beats in my throat since

I *assumed* I was alone in the house. But there is Rhys, standing in the middle of *my* room.

*What the—?*

I stare at him. He hasn't been in here in years. I'm confused. "Hi?"

"Hi." Is that reluctance in his voice?

Instead of asking the obvious—what is this mess on my bed?—he points at my phone. "What are you listening to?"

*Is he for real?*

"Uh, Freedom Call?" My answer sounds more like a question.

"Which album?"

What. The. Heck? "*Legend of the Shadowing*."

"'Tears of Babylon' or 'A Perfect Day'?"

Why does he care? I used to listen to this album on repeat for months, but I didn't think he'd remember my two favorite songs. I try to hide my irritation. "'A Perfect Day.'"

The corner of his mouth tilts up. I haven't seen that directed at me in forever, and something inside of me flips in a somersault —a sensation that I used to experience all the time until he *left* me.

"You always made me listen to that one when we were sparring with Spence."

I bite my lip, stopping the grin that wants to spread across my face. "I didn't think you'd remember."

I don't like this and try to compose myself. With my change in demeanor, his smile falters. His next words are spoken so softly that I think I must hear him wrong. "I would never forget that. It *was* a perfect day."

I'm speechless. We have barely spoken in years. He *hates* me.

Rhys realizes his blunder and schools his features. The mask I've seen for years is back in place. He nods toward the chaos on my bed. "So...what's all this?"

I glance down, as if confirming everything is still here, and back up at him. Enough with this game; I'm too exhausted. "Why are you here?"

"I'm worried about you."

I snort sarcastically. "Yeah, right. You haven't given two shits about me in years."

The mask slips again, his expression changing to something mirroring...heartbreak?

"It's more complicated than that."

I cock my head. I feel like I'm in an alternate reality. Who is this guy in front of me?

Rhys slowly lowers himself onto the edge of my bed. "Calla, what's going on with you?"

Being the emotional mess I am these days, hearing him call me by the nickname he used to have for me causes tears to instantly well up in my eyes. "You haven't called me that in forever." I don't want to cry in front of him.

*Not him!*

"I know. I'm sorry." Rhys's gaze falls onto my necklace, a small silver calla lily blossom on a delicate silver chain. "You're still wearing it."

Unconsciously, I reach up and say, "You gave it to me," before I can stop myself.

Four years ago, we visited a botanical garden during a family trip, and I was obsessed with calla lilies after that. I thought they were the most beautiful flowers ever. That year, Rhys took his savings, bought me the necklace for my birthday, and started calling me Calla. It became the nickname only he used, and the first time he called me Lilly again, I knew something between us was broken. I cried for hours that night.

Having Rhys sitting in my room and remembering old times is too much. I don't want to fall back into old habits. I have barely slept since the migraines started. I'm so tired and confused. I wipe my nose, trying to keep it together.

All of a sudden, Rhys moves closer and reaches out for me, putting his hand on mine. Before I can think logically, all my bottled-up emotions rush to the surface, and I launch into his arms. I can't hold the tears back any longer and completely fall apart, my fists balled into the front of his t-shirt. Everything—not just the past three weeks, but the past two-plus years—is coming out, and I cry for what feels like hours.

Rhys just keeps his arms wrapped around me, rocking back and forth. When I finally have no tears left, I disentangle myself from his arms but don't move away. His hands are still resting on my forearms, which are now laying in my lap, and I focus on them as I whisper, "I think I'm going crazy."

Rhys gently lifts my chin up with his index finger, forcing me to look into his eyes. "Talk to me, Calla." His voice is shaky, but his smile tells me this is not a game for him.

I am scared to open up to him; he's been distant for so long. I missed him so much until I finally accepted that I couldn't fix the unknown. I moved on; he was no longer a part of my life, and I was no longer part of his. If I invite him back in, he'll either think I'm crazy, or by Monday, he'll ignore me again. Neither is a road I want to go down in my current, potentially crazy, mental state.

Still holding on to me, he whispers, "Please tell me. You're scaring me."

His concern is genuine. I am terrified, but I also have to admit to myself that I can't do this alone anymore. I take what feels like the longest, deepest breath of my life. "I keep seeing things."

## RHYS

I DON'T KNOW if I am holding on to Lilly for her sake or for my own. She keeps seeing things. What the fuck does that mean? I don't trust my voice, and my next question comes out in a strangled rasp. "What do you mean?"

She doesn't look directly at me. Her eyes are focused on my shirt, and I can see her internal struggle. Then, she finally focuses on my face. "I have these headaches, like migraines, and—and I see things." She pauses for a moment. "Things I don't remember but *feel* real."

I'm gonna throw up; the need to put some distance between us overwhelms me. I move backward until I'm settled against the headboard of her bed and take that moment to collect myself. Her expression mirrors something resembling loss when I move away from her, but I need to stay in control. If I touch her, all bets are off.

"Why don't you start from the beginning?" My voice doesn't give away how wound up I am inside.

Lilly settles back in the middle of her bed and plays with her headphones, wrapping them around her fingers, untangling them again, and starting over.

I nod, signaling her that I'm listening whenever she's ready.

"We got this assignment for journalism. A research paper." She pauses as if figuring out if she wants to continue. "We could choose whatever topic we wanted, and I went with a criminal case. You know how I feel about economics and politics." She briefly smiles to herself, and I chuckle—because I do.

"I found this article about a girl that went missing here in Virginia and was recently found. She was the fifth victim. I decided to use this case for the assignment, and the more I read, the more I got this feeling—"

*Mother f— There's a fifth victim?*

I had no clue. I stay quiet, scared that if I speak, my voice will betray me this time.

"I kept researching; I read every article I could find on all the girls. I felt anxious and scared, but not just because it's such a horrible incident. Something felt...off. It was like I had to find out more. Then, I read an article about the third victim." She points at her desk. "I looked at our picture—it was like I was drawn to it— and when I focused back on the computer, I got this stabbing pain in my head. I saw myself—*my kid self* from our picture—staring back, framed in a white mirror."

Her eyes jump back and forth between mine, and she says, with total conviction in her voice, "I never had a white mirror. You know that." The next words are spoken softer. "I was so scared."

I'm not sure how much longer I can keep my composure, but Lilly continues, not noticing that I'm close to hyperventilating.

"Then it happened again."

*Jesus Christ.*

This time, I have to say something. "What did you see?" I stop myself from using the word *remember*.

"I was lying on a bed, looking up at a canopy above me."

*Don't throw up! Don't fucking throw up.*

I swallow several times before I can form the words. "How many times has this happened?"

"A few."

*A few?*

For fuck's sake. No wonder she's been such a mess.

Lilly keeps telling me about the other migraines, as she calls them, and I can't believe what I'm hearing. She finishes with, "Am I going crazy?"

I am barely holding on to a thread. This is insane. After ten years? I have no clue what to do. I promised. Bile starts to rise in my throat.

I do the only thing I can manage at this point. I bolt from her room.

As soon as my door closes, all strength leaves my legs, and I sink to the floor. I don't bother with a chair or my bed; I have nothing left. I need to get my breathing under control, or I am really going to puke. Putting my head in my hands, I close my eyes and slowly count my breaths. At seventeen, the sour taste in my throat has subsided, and I can swallow again without the feeling of being choked.

I promised Mom and Dad to never tell her. I even pushed her away, my best friend for as long as I can remember, because of that promise. This is different, though. I can't leave her like this. She thinks she is losing her mind, for fuck's sake. Even if I talk to Mom and Dad on Sunday, letting her think that something is wrong with her—no matter for how long—is cruel. Not when I can give her *the truth*.

My wall has officially crumbled, the remnants of it in ruins, and I have to come clean—with everything. Her secret and mine. Even if it means she may never speak to me again.

I stand up with resolve and open the door, coming face to face with Lilly. One look, and I see that she is going to demand answers. She's smart; she knows I'm hiding something.

"Let's talk."

## CHAPTER SIX

**LILLY**

Okay, then. I just poured my heart out to the one person I trust the least, and he runs out of my room?

Wonderful. *Just. Wonderful.*

Weirdly enough, though, Rhys's reaction makes me actually feel better. He didn't laugh or dismiss me. It was written all over his face how much my confession unsettled him.

I turn and look at Rhys's closed door through my still open one. I see a shadow under it and realize he is sitting right there.

Wracking my brain about what could have him so worked up, I stare for several minutes.

I slam my fists on the comforter. Whatever it is, he's shit outta luck. I've let him determine the rules of our relationship for the past two-plus years. He has never bothered to tell me what I did to make him hate me so much. *This* time, he is going to talk, even if I have to beat it out of him—*in the ring, of course.*

He knows something, no question there. Bawling out all my bottled-up emotions has calmed me enough to focus, and I'm even more determined to find out the truth.

I stand up and march toward his door, prepared to force it open with him sitting behind it. But before I can reach for the doorknob, it swings inward, and we lock eyes. He's resigned.

Whatever he's going to tell me will change everything.

I FOLLOW him without a word down the stairs to the family room. Rhys sits down on the middle piece of the large, U-shaped monstrosity Mom calls our *couch*, and I slowly lower myself onto the left arm closest to the door. Despite my need for answers, an urge to flee is also present.

Leaning with his forearms on his thighs, Rhys stares at his clasped hands. His chest is heaving like he just ran practice sprints. I watch him closely, and if I didn't know better, I would say he is scared. No, not scared—terrified. But Rhys is neither of those emotions. *Ever.*

"You are not crazy." The words are spoken so low that I'm not sure I hear him right at first. Before I can make sure, he continues, "You're remembering."

I feel like someone has punched me in the gut, and I suck in a breath.

*I'm what?*

I heard what he said, but my mind has already gone into denial. He's wrong. He's playing a cruel joke on me after all. Finally, my brain-to-mouth connection is somewhat reestablished, and I rasp out, "Remembering what?"

"The, uh—incident."

"Huh?" My mind is racing through possible scenarios. I'm trying to make sense of it, but I come up with absolutely nothing.

"I don't know where to begin. I promised." Rhys looks pale, and I can see him breathing erratically.

"Promised who? What?"

"Mom and Dad...to never tell you."

Cold starts building in my core. Mom and Dad? What the hell is going on here? When I speak, my voice sounds calmer than I feel. "Rhys, what is going on? It can't be that bad if I'm not going crazy."

*Makes sense, right?*

He rubs his palms across his face and mumbles, "You have no idea."

I have *never* seen him like this. I'm more confused than ever. I do want my answers, but for a brief moment, I forget the last few years. I push all the hurt he has caused away and scoot over to his side of the couch. After a moment of hesitation, I pull his hands away from his face and try to hold on to them.

Rhys flinches away from my touch and looks at me with pure anguish. "I can't lose you again."

I'm on an emotional rollercoaster. *He* can't lose *me? Again?* Anger replaces the coldness. I put some distance between us and stare. Who does he think he is? He left me two years ago. He stopped talking to me and never bothered to tell me why. I try to contain my temper, but I can't stop raising my voice. "EITHER YOU START TALKING, OR I'M OUT!" A little calmer, I continue, "You turned your back on me, and now you play the victim? I'm the one seeing people while my head threatens to burst open! SCREW YOU!"

My last words make him flinch, but he just keeps staring at his lap. I've had enough. After the last three weeks, I have no patience left. I'm exhausted, and his behavior is just too much.

I stand up and take two steps when he whispers, "I love you."

*Uh—what?*

I stop in my tracks and turn. He doesn't look at me.

"I love you, too." Because despite everything that has happened between us, I do.

"No, I love you. Like *I. Love. You.*" His voice is barely audible, but he emphasizes every word.

I just stand there, dumbfounded. "Huh?"

*I mean, that's a very valid response, right?*

He finally faces me, and our gazes lock. His eyes mirror everything from agony, to embarrassment, to love. "I'm not your brother." After a brief pause, he adds, "But you were never supposed to know."

*Uh.*

He takes another breath. "I've loved you my entire life. For as long as I can remember. But then you became my sister ten years ago, and you were never supposed to find out."

I plop ungracefully back onto the couch. My legs don't support my weight, and when my lungs start to burn, I realize I'm holding my breath. All I get out is a rasp, "I don't understand."

*I truly don't.*

Rhys drops his eyes again. "You're remembering. Those migraines you have are memories."

The next pause is endless, and I begin to think he is not going to say anything else.

"You were kidnapped."

*KIDNAPPED?* A voice in my head screeches. I must have misheard him. There is no freaking way one forgets something like that. I'm pretty sure my eyebrows are somewhere in my hairline.

"They never told me all the details. I was too young. I can tell you what I've pieced together over the years."

"Okay." My voice sounds detached, not at all like my own.

"You were taken during a field trip to the San Diego Zoo. You were gone for about a month before you were found at a hospital in Northern California. We had just moved to Virginia a few months before. Mom went back to San Diego a few times to be with your parents. From what I overheard, there were no cops involved at all, no authorities. Even back then, I thought that was fucking weird." Rhys laughs, unamused. "Then, one day, you pop up at an ER in Northern California. You were sick, and scared, and the hospital couldn't figure out who you were until you told them days later."

My vision gets blurry. This can't be true.

Rhys looks at me with a sad expression. "Do you want me to keep going?"

I wring my hands together. *Do I?* "Yes."

"Grandma Ruth flew in and stayed with me. Mom and Dad left as soon as you were found. I never figured out what happened while they were gone, but a few weeks later, you became my sister, and I was to never tell you the truth."

Rhys's entire body is tense when he finishes. He's waiting for my reaction to the bomb he just dropped on me.

"Who am I?"

He seems to have expected a different question, but simply states, "You're Lilly. That has never changed."

Okay, so at least I know my name.

"Who are my parents?"

He hesitates a second. "Your biological parents' names are Emily and Henry Sumner. You were born as Lilly Sumner. Emily and Mom had been best friends forever. I knew you from the day you were born. We were always together."

*I guess that explains all the childhood pictures of us.*

"Where are my parents?"

Rhys hangs his head. "I don't know; I'm sorry. I've searched for them online a few times over the years, but nothing recent ever came back."

We're both quiet. I'm trying to process what I just heard. I was kidnapped. My parents are not my parents. I'm not related to any of the people I live with. Oh. My. God. I was kidnapped. And why don't I remember any of this? My heart is about to explode out of my chest.

I lean forward, rest my head on my knees, and wrap my arms around my thighs. I mumble, "Why don't I remember any of this?"

"I have no fucking clue. They never told me shit." His voice is hard. "I was seven, and my best friend needed me. For the first few years, I didn't question Mom and Dad. I was happy you were back with me. I had missed you after the move. When I was old enough to ask questions, they simply said to me that they couldn't tell me."

I let this sink in more. Rhys has frustration and disappointment written all over his face. He thinks he's let me down. I was kidnapped, and I don't remember anything.

Then, another thought hits me. "Is *this* why you stopped talking to me?"

His eyes fling up to me, and he rakes his hands through his hair—something he does when he is nervous or stressed.

"No! Shit no." He pauses and fully turns to me. "When we moved back to Westbridge, uh...Wes was all over you. He would always hang around, and"—Rhys takes a deep breath—"I got jealous. Fuck, I sound like such an idiot." He laughs at himself. "Dad saw it and made it clear that I couldn't have these types of feelings for *my sister.* You met Denielle and started spending most of your time with her, which helped, but it got harder and harder to play along. When I started high school, it was my chance to start over—to move on from you." Rhys averts his eyes. "Our schedules were different for the first year, which made it easier, but then you started WH. Dad caught me looking at you all the time, and I knew I had to make drastic changes to maintain my façade. One evening, he came to my room and told me I had to get a grip, or he and Mom would need to figure something else out. He never said what they would do, but he basically insinuated sending one of us away. Which wasn't a fucking option for me."

My blood pressure is through the roof. I don't know which revelation has shocked me more. I guess you'd assume the fact that I was kidnapped and don't remember a thing, but I thought I knew my brother. No, he isn't my brother. But we were so close.

"Well, you seem to have successfully moved on." My voice sounds dry and sarcastic. The feeling of utter betrayal starts spreading through every cell of my body.

Rhys snorts. "I guess I'm a better actor than I thought."

"Katherine?"

Now, his voice sounds hesitant. "Kat and I are..." I can see him trying to find the right words. "An arrangement. We give each other what the other needs: an image. I've still been watching over you, even though you haven't noticed. I try to stay far enough away so no one will notice, but I've been there."

*Awesome, so he abandoned* and *stalked me.*

WE SIT THERE IN SILENCE. I see Rhys glancing over at me every so often, but he doesn't say anything. He's waiting for me to make the next move.

I feel like I've been put through an emotional wringer. I'm not crazy. Relief. I was kidnapped. Terror. I don't have any memory of it. Anxiety. Rhys doesn't hate me after all. Relief again, maybe even happiness. I've been lied to—by everyone. Betrayal.

I need to sort through all of this in my head. Alone. Standing up, I blurt out, "I need to be alone right now."

I'm racing out of the room to grab my keys and purse before Rhys can say much. All I hear is, "Okay."

# CHAPTER SEVEN

## LILLY

I leave the house and drive around for a while. It's already getting dark, and the streets are empty. Today is one of the coldest days of this winter, which seems fitting for how I feel: cold and alone. They've kept me *in the dark* for ten years.

I don't want to run into any of my friends. Not knowing where else to go, I end up in the school parking lot.

I park at the end of the lot closest to the football field and turn the lights off. Back here, I'm invisible from the street. I scroll through my playlists and play one random song after another. I try to find something that fits my mood, but thanks to the tornado that just wrecked through what I thought was my life, nothing seems right. I just keep flipping through playlists, then albums, then artists. Eventually, I settle on "A Perfect Day" by Freedom Call, and gut-wrenching sobs instantly start wracking through my body. I cry for everything I just lost—including the knowledge of who I am.

I think about the couple from my migraines. My parents. Shit, what kind of people deposit their daughter with friends after she was kidnapped? My throat constricts. How could my parents keep this from me for ten freaking years. No, I remind myself, they are not my parents. Heather and Tristen? Natty and Rhys's parents? What the hell do I call them now? I slam my palms against the steering wheel. The tears have dried up, but now I have the urge to scream.

Why did the kidnapper pick me? What makes me so special? Based on my research, that means I'm victim number one. The one all the others are placeholders for. Oh God, I was kidnapped. *I'm* the reason these poor girls were taken.

My breathing becomes erratic. The car is all of a sudden way too small—I have to get out. I didn't bring a jacket during my escape, and the temperature has dropped below freezing, but I don't care. Crouching next to my car, I gulp in the freezing air and wait for the panic to subside.

When my entire body begins to shake from the cold, I get back in the car and crank up the heat. I lean my head against the headrest. What am I going to do? I can't just move on like nothing ever happened. I'm not losing my mind, but I don't belong in this family. I have no idea who I am anymore. And if it's true what the news says, the kidnapper will keep going until he's caught, or he gets what he wants—*me*. My heart rate accelerates again.

*Breathe.*


I SIT in the parking lot for another hour until I force myself to drive back home. The house is mostly dark except for the track lighting in the kitchen, which shines into the hallway. I make my way up the stairs without turning on any of the other lights. Reaching my room, I notice a gleam under Rhys's door. Huh? I don't remember the last time he was home on a Saturday night. I know for a fact there is a party tonight; the whole school has been buzzing about it all week.


I DECIDED in the car that I want to talk to Rhys more, but I'm not ready. I'm freezing despite having the heater blasting hot air at me ever since I got back into the Jeep. The bone-chilling cold inside of me is not from the outside temperatures anymore, but it also won't go away. I've heard that shock could do that to a person. It's probably fair to say that I'm in some state of shock after tonight's revelations.

I opt for a hot shower before facing the boy I believed to be my brother and best friend for years.

Procrastinating, I slowly dress in my PJs—gray sweats and a white, long-sleeve Henley. I stare at the chaos on my bed. Everything is where I left it, but the pile of notes and printouts is no longer a big question mark to me. It's part of who I am. It's all connected to me.

With one last breath, I walk across the hall to Rhys's door and knock softly.

"Come in."

## RHYS

IT TAKES every ounce of strength not to follow Lilly. The urge to make sure she is safe is driving me fucking crazy, but I know that with one wrong move I'm going to lose her forever.

*If I haven't already.*

I stay in the family room, channel surfing for a while, but nothing holds my interest. Back in my room, I see that I have three missed calls from Kat and several texts from her, Wes, and other guys from the team.

Kat: **Sweetie, I'm here. Where are you?**

Kev, from the football team: **Dude, this party is lit. Just saw Nora topless in the hot tub.**

Kat: **Where are you?**

Jager: **We have 4 kegs. U on ur way?**

Wes: **Dude, where r you? Your gf is LIVID.**

Kat: **WHERE THE FUCK ARE YOU?**

That fucking party. I glance at the timestamps. Did they start at what? Three in the afternoon? They're going to be plastered by eight. *Idiots.* I don't respond and put my phone back down. I'll deal with that tomorrow.

Grabbing the laptop from my desk, I sit down against the headboard. My bed is positioned opposite the door, and my gaze sweeps over the room. It's similar in size to Lilly's, but mine faces the front of the house—not that it matters since we live on a quiet street that ends in a cul-de-sac. The size is where the similarities to Lilly's room end, though. Where hers is neatly put together with its lavender paint and matching décor, my room still has the white walls from the day we moved in. My furniture is mismatched victims of Mom's remodeling projects. The most modern items are my media setup and mattress, both of which I have barely used in the last few years due to my constant absence.

I haven't looked into *Lilly's case* in a while, and had no idea another girl had gone missing. When it comes to watching the news, Lilly and I have always been on the same page. Sitting through endless debates between Mom and Dad during mealtimes has conditioned us for the future. Unless it's sports related, I stay clear of any type of news show.

I pull up the most recent article my search engine returns to me and work my way back to when the girl was first reported missing. After I finish reading a few of the articles, I lean my head back and stare at the wall above my flat screen. I've felt lost for so long. Playing my part, I'd watched Lilly get hurt from my actions over and over, but nothing compared to the shock and betrayal that played across her face when I came clean today.

*It'll be a miracle if she talks to me at all.*

I'm so deep in thought that the knock on my door startles me. There is only one other person in the house this weekend, and my stomach is immediately in knots.

Sitting up straight, I call out, "Come in."


LILLY PEEKS INTO MY ROOM, and her eyes zero in on me. She seems reluctant to come in, and I can't read her at all. Her face is completely blank. I've always prided myself on being able to read her, no matter what. This is not good.

She hesitantly smiles, and some of the knots in my stomach loosen.

"Hi."

Try to look *casual* and not like the guy who basically just took her life and threw everything she knew out the window. "Hey."

Seeing her in her PJs, my mind instantly wanders. Even in sweats, she looks breathtaking. I've missed her so much. Out of self-preservation, I didn't allow myself to linger in the same room with her—unless necessary. I didn't trust myself to keep up my charade. This was also the reason she and everyone else started to think I disliked her—hated her. And I never corrected them. I always made sure to be cool and curt, although I wanted the exact opposite. And because of all that, Mom and Dad let me do whatever I wanted. I've had the *ultimate* freedom since I was sixteen. Only so the fucking secret could be maintained. Mom has never been happy with my constant absence, but she accepts it. She knows I'm hurting just as much—if not more.

I mentally shake my head; this is not the time to focus on that. My feelings are not important; I'll deal with that another day. Lilly is here, and she needs a friend more than anything else.

When she still doesn't come in, I attempt to make her more at ease. "How are you?"

"Um, not sure." She thinks before continuing. "Relieved, betrayed, angry, scared, happy?"

The last one is more of a question.

"Happy?"

"For not being crazy," she clarifies quickly.

"I guess that's a valid feeling." I try to sound reassuring. What other reason would she have to be happy? Not because her best friend who dumped her and treated her like shit has finally come clean so his own conscious is lighter.

*Selfish prick.*

Finally, Lilly steps into my room and sits down in the armchair, tugging her legs underneath. Facing me, she says, "Before getting to the reason I came, I want to ask you something."

Her tone worries me. She sounds like a recording, lacking emotion. "Uh, okay."

She takes a deep breath and levels me with a serious expression. "Are you going back to ignoring me tomorrow? Or Monday? Or—"

I fully straighten from the bed and interrupt her before she can even finish. "No! I'm done with the secrets." I put all the conviction I have behind my words. Unless she asks me to, I don't give a flying fuck anymore. This secret has been suffocating me for too long. I'm done.

She gives a brief nod and expels a sigh. Her simple reaction to my reassurance releases the remaining tension in my core. She doesn't hate me—or at least she's still talking to me. I think?

*When did I become such a fucking pussy?*

"So, um...I would like your help in finding out what happened to me."

I can't stop the grin that automatically spreads across my face. I turn my laptop for her to see the different case articles displayed on my screen.

SINCE EVERYTHING IS ALREADY SPREAD out in Lilly's room, we go there, and she shows me her notes and research.

*Holy crap, how much time has she put into this?*

Something is off about her, though. She talks like herself, but not. I can't put my finger on it. She is different. But who wouldn't be in her situation, right?

We go over her migraines more, and I've just started reading her notes when her stomach informs us it is way past dinner time.

We both turn toward the alarm clock on her nightstand. With raised eyebrows, she states, "Well, that would explain why I am starving." It's past nine, and neither of us has eaten since before noon.

"I'll order pizza," I say as I get up to get my phone.

I walk into my room and find my phone already lit and buzzing with an incoming call—Kat. *Great.* I stare at it, waiting. When it finally stops ringing, I see I have eight missed calls from her. Eight? (Not counting the ones I ignored earlier.) Fuck. Me. I'm in deep shit.

I contemplate for a second and hit the callback option. Let's get this over with.

I'm greeted with, "Where the fuck are you?"

*Yup, she's pissed.*

"I'm not coming."

"You better be joking! *Everyone* is here. Do you have any idea how that makes me look? Get your ass in your car and—"

"No!" She needs a serious attitude adjustment, and it's my own fault for staying with her for so long.

"Excuse me?" I can hear the disbelief in her voice. I don't think I've *ever* told her no.

"You heard me. NO! I'm busy." I hang up.

When I turn, Lilly stands in the doorway. "You need to go?"

But instead of her being angry, or disappointed, or even relieved, there is nothing. It's like a switch was flipped; she went from being *my* Lilly to someone I don't even recognize. A cold shiver runs down my spine.

"Nope, all good," I say with false cheer. I know she heard the exchange. "Ordering pizza now."

"You can go." This time I can hear a hint of panic in her voice.

"Calla, I am exactly where I want to be. I'm not going anywhere. You still eat pepperoni and sausage?"

She nods, and I grin brightly. "Cool. Let me make the call, and I'll be right back."

THE PIZZA ARRIVES forty-five minutes later, and we're sitting on the floor in her room, eating, when she peers at me through her lashes. "What were my parents like?"

I finish chewing to buy myself time.

"Emily was a writer. I don't remember for what, though. We could probably find that out. Mom knew her since kindergarten, I think. I'm not sure where she met Henry. I think they were married for a few years before you were born—or at least together for a few years. He was an architect—traveled a lot." Those are all facts, not really what she asked for, so I add, "They were nice. I liked them. Henry was awesome. He always played with us when he was around, instead of hanging out with the other adults."

I purposefully don't call Emily and Henry her mom and dad. In my mind, my parents are *her* parents. They have raised her for most of her life and made sure she was safe as well as loved. To me, that's what constitutes them as Lilly's parents, not the blood relation.

Lilly squeezes her lips together for a moment, contemplating something. "What was I like?"

I smirk, remembering. "You were...*you*—always on the go; still are. You were sweet and funny. We lived close by, so there were a lot of barbecues and shit. You were somewhat of a tomboy. When you were five, you beat me up with a stick."

She looks up with a shocked expression. "Nuh-uh!"

I burst out laughing at her face. "We were playing pirates in the yard, and you refused to be the damsel in distress. You took my sword"—I make air quotes around the word sword—"and started hitting me with it, yelling I can be the girl."

Lilly barks out a laugh, and it feels so good to hear that sound coming from her. It's the first genuine expression she's shown all evening. Then, all the color drains from her face. "Why don't I remember that?"

*Why indeed?*

That memory is not related to the incident or her parents. "I don't know."

I sound just as defeated as she does.


WE SIT and talk for a long time. I tell her more stories from our childhood. We look at some of the pictures in the photo album, and I remember other things about her parents: places we went to, family outings we had. Some things she remembers, others she doesn't. Eventually, Lilly's face grows somber, and she stares off into space. She is starting to withdraw, so I suggest that we watch more news videos. Not that this topic is any better, but once she retreats into her head, I can't get her back out for a while.

We just finished another video, and I say, "That one didn't have any new information." When she doesn't respond, I turn and see that she has fallen asleep, leaning against her throw pillows.

I scan her face; her features are relaxed for the first time in...I don't know. It feels so surreal to sit here with her. I've wanted to be able to talk to her about everything for so long but never dared to hope I would actually get the opportunity. What are the chances that she'd find the one case for a homework assignment that triggers her memory?

I take the blanket from the bottom of her bed and drape it over her. After one last glance, I head to my own room but leave both doors open.

# CHAPTER EIGHT

## LILLY

I'm slightly disoriented when I wake up; I'm not under my covers. Shifting up on one elbow, I realize I'm covered with my purple throw blanket that is usually draped over the foot of my bed. Then, everything from yesterday assaults my brain at once, and I let myself fall back into the pillow, pressing the heels of my hands into my eyes. Oh. My. God.

*Did that really all happen in the last twenty-four hours?*

I put more pressure on; maybe if I press hard enough, the memories will disappear. Three, two, one—*nope, still there*. It was worth a try.

My alarm clock shows a little after nine a.m. Holy cow, I slept for more than seven hours. For the first time in weeks, I feel somewhat rested. I haven't slept more than two or three consecutive hours since my first migraine. When I get up, I notice that my door is open, and so is Rhys's. Confused, I walk over and partially see his sprawled-out form in his bed. Despite the torrent of emotions already rising back to the surface, after the blissfully blank few hours of sleep, a smile tucks on my lips. Our doors haven't been open at the same time in forever. I peer across the hall one more time before I close mine and retreat to take a shower.

When we moved here, I chose this room because of the adjoining bathroom. All the bedrooms have a bathroom attached, but whoever owned the house before had remodeled this one. The standard one-piece bathtub was replaced with a massive custom shower with a gorgeous white subway tile and gray mosaic border. The glass doors make the shower even grander. Since I never take baths, I left no room for negotiation that this room would be mine.

Standing under the hot spray, I try to separate my feelings.

Against all logic, the happy feeling of not being crazy makes the other revelations almost tolerable. *Almost.*

It's like every single emotion a human is capable of has been thrown in a blender and deposited inside of me.

I was kidnapped as a child and held for weeks. My breathing immediately increases. Why me?

My parents handed me over to their best friends and dropped off the face of the earth. Confusion and disappointment come to the forefront. Who does that? To their *only child*. What could have happened for them to take such actions? And where the hell are they? Are they dead? What other answer is there for abandoning your child for ten years?

As for my parents—no, Heather and Tristen!—I decided last night that using their first names—even if it's just in my head—makes the most sense. They are not my biological parents, but what do I call the people I've been living with for most of my life? This causes more confusion—with a side of betrayal. They've kept this huge secret from me and had me think that I was their daughter. The conclusion following this thought makes my fists ball in anger. *They* are the reason I lost my best friend. *They* made Rhys walk away from me. It's. All. Lies.

Something or someone messed with my memory prior to seven years old, and the memories I have are jumbled. I don't know what is real and what is not. My anger turns to rage, and my entire body starts shaking. They violated me. They invaded my mind. What the hell did they do to me? And how? A tear slips down my cheek, and I quickly wipe it away. I refuse to cry anymore. I've cried too much already.

If this reporter was correct, these poor girls have been kidnapped and taken from their families because of me. I feel at fault for their trauma and scared for any little girl that could still be taken.

Rhys is back in my life. That fact makes me happy, but I can't shake the feeling of deception. Until yesterday, I thought I was okay with him no longer being a part of my life, but when he said he would not *abandon* me again, it felt like a smothering blanket had finally lifted. I haven't allowed myself to miss him for so long. But he lied. He was supposed to be my best friend, even if he was never my brother.

And then, there is the other *revelation*. He loves me. We both ignored that tidbit for the rest of the night and just focused on the case. I exhale slow and long. He. Loves. Me. A groan escapes me. What am I supposed to do with that? I guess we do have to talk about that fact eventually.

I sink to a crouch in the shower and put my head in my hands. Maybe I'll just stay here and ignore the world for a while. That sounds like a decent plan. I let the water run over my body, scorching my skin in the hot stream. The burn allows me to block everything else out.

But after a few minutes, I stand up and shake my head. I'm not this person. I don't want to hide—not anymore. I've been lied to for the better part of my life, in addition to Rhys letting me believe that I did something for him to hate me. I took it all without a fight, accepted it without question. No more! I clench and unclench my fists. I let the rage and betrayal take over. It prevents me from feeling weak. I can handle this mess, also known as my life. No more self-pity!

Looking at my pruned hands, I realize I spent way more time in the shower than I had planned. With a new sense of purpose, I turn the water off and grab my big white towel from the hook.

I dry off and dress in black yoga pants, a black Y-top, and wrap myself in my favorite gray duster cardigan. For the first time in weeks, I'm blow-drying my hair. Self-care was not a priority when I thought I was crazy, but now I have a goal and the urge to feel like myself again, even if it's just the appearance. I will never be myself again.

*Time for some caffeine.*

I'm SITTING at the kitchen island, eating my usual breakfast of steel-cut oats with almond butter and banana, scrolling through my social media sites. I've been going over everyone's posts from last night's party to distract myself. My emotional self-scan in the shower has left me raw. Anger and betrayal are simmering under the surface, exactly where I want it. But I also need to control both in order to accomplish the other part of my new plan. No one can know that I'm no longer in the dark.

The party seems to have been a good one. Den wasn't there, but I wouldn't have gone one way or the other. I haven't been to a party that Katherine or Rhys has attended in months. Not after what happened over the summer. But I had also gotten tired of the looks people gave me. Poor Lilly will always be in her brother's and Katherine's shadows.

*Yeah right, if they only knew.*

When Rhys slouches in, his eyes are barely open. I tilt my head, assessing if he's even fully awake. He's wearing a navy-and-yellow hoodie with the school's mascot on the front and matching sweats. He walks straight to the coffee machine and grumbles, "I guess you're still not a coffee drinker?"

I arch my eyebrows, not that he sees it from his angle.

"Good morning to you, too." I keep chewing my oatmeal and add, "And no, I still think it tastes like shoe leather."

Rhys snorts. "I just hoped for a cup right now."

"I'm sure you can manage on your own." I let the sarcasm drip from my voice but grin to myself. I enjoy our easy banter. Watching as he gets busy with the coffeemaker, it feels comfortable. But at the same time, I'm unsure how to act toward him. The whole *love confession* complicates the already arduous situation even more.

Anger and betrayal—that's my focus.

With his coffee in hand and two freshly toasted waffles from the freezer, Rhys settles down on the barstool next to mine. "So, what are we doing?"

"You're still helping?" I can't keep the doubt out of the question.

He eyes me from the side. "I told you I would."

"Yeah, you said that...I just..." I trail off and shift my focus to my half-empty tea.

"I understand you don't trust me. I kept this from you for ten years and then also treated you like shit for the last two, but I swear, that's over. It's you and me against the world again. If you can forgive me...one day."

The last words are spoken quietly. I press my lips together to keep from smiling at the reference to something we used to always say when we were little.

*But forgive him?*

I ignore the whole part and blurt out, "I don't want anyone to know." I hadn't planned on announcing it like that, but it's out now, so I might as well keep going. "Not yet, anyway. Mom and—" I stop. "I mean, Heather and Tristen..." I trail off again, and my frustration is obvious.

He stares at his half-eaten waffle.

"They may not be your biological parents, and they have kept a lot of secrets from you, but they've still raised you for most of your life. They've kept you safe, and they love you like their own," Rhys says in a gentle tone.

He's right, but the betrayal is so overwhelming that I want to scream. I've always been a rational and level-headed person; emotions never get the best of me. Even with everything that went down between us, I leaned on the logical side and didn't let the hurt get the best of me. I ignored it, and then I focused on other things: school, gymnastics, and training with Spence.

But since last night, that's all out the window. As long as I stay busy, going over my research with Rhys or reading my friends' social media posts, I can keep a lid on it. But as soon as there is a break, it all rushes back.

I shake my head, and I blow out a huffed breath. "I just feel so confused."

Rhys awkwardly pats my back. "I know. We'll figure it out. Together."

*Together.*

That gives me the opening I need to ask the other question swirling around in my head. "What are we? I mean, you said you..." I trail off, feeling weird saying it out loud.

"I love you." He doesn't hesitate one bit. He's a whole new person. It's like this enormous weight is off his shoulders. At that moment, I understand that he *is* the old Rhys again. The one before everything went down the crapshoot. Before Tristen told him he can't be around me if he can't control his feelings. Before his arrangement with Katherine. He has been living a lie himself. That knowledge almost knocks the air out of me, and I cock my head, looking at him again. I truly see him for the first time in years. The Rhys I used to know is back—*my* Rhys.

Oblivious to my epiphany, he adds, "We are friends...I guess? I won't even attempt to understand what's going on in your head, and I'm not going to ask you for anything else. Like we used to be."

Does he mean before the *incident*, as he's been calling my kidnapping, or after, when I thought he was my brother and also best friend? I leave his sentence hanging and simply reply, "Thank you."

I glance over and can't stop myself this time. "I did miss you." Because it's true; I missed him a lot. Part of me felt lost. Maybe because I never knew why, maybe because he was my best friend for so long, who knows?

He smiles genuinely at me. "Me too, Calla."

Instinctively, I move to hug him, but a voice in my mind reminds me: *he lied to you. They all lied to you.* And I squash the urge like a bug.

I'm happy there are no more secrets between us, and I understand now why, but I can't turn off the whisper in my head. If he truly was my best friend, he should've told me.

One could say I feel slightly schizophrenic with the emotional back and forth. I'll probably need years of therapy to understand everything going on inside my head.

## RHYS

After breakfast, we sit back in Lilly's room, each of us individually reading different articles on our laptops, when a thought comes to mind. "So, if you don't want anyone to find out, how do we explain us?" I point back and forth between us.

Lilly looks up from her screen with raised eyebrows. "Us?"

"Yeah, I mean, we haven't talked to each other in years, and all of a sudden, we do? People will notice, especially Mom and Dad."

Her mouth forms a brief O, and she looks toward the other side of the room, debating what I just pointed out. When she turns back, her face, once again, has an unreadable expression. "We won't talk then. It's time I have my own secret."

The last part is so full of contempt that I cringe.

"Cal, I get you are pissed and hurt and whatnot, but they just tried to protect you. They did what they were asked to do—*and* more. They love you."

Lilly presses her lips together and grumbles, "Why do you always have to be so reasonable?"

"I'm just telling you how it is. You only get the truth from me."

"Except for when you stopped talking to me," she snarls.

*Well, if that wasn't a kick straight to the balls.*

I can hear the hurt in her voice, but in a knee-jerk reaction, I can't stop myself from snapping back. "That was a fucking cheap shot. You know damn well I had no choice."

Her eyes widen at my sharp response. It sounded harsher than I intended, and I take a deep breath, softening my tone. "You have no idea how often I came this close to telling you. This shitshow has been eating me up for years, and I couldn't do anything about it."

She averts her eyes, whispering, "I'm sorry."

"I know I was a dick to you, and you have every right to be pissed. So, let's come up with a plan about how we're going to pull this off." I mean it; I want to help her in any way possible. Lilly is in charge. It's her life that has been turned upside down.

In the end, we decide to keep going as before. The thought of having to continue ignoring her in public doesn't sit right with me, but I respect her wish—for now.

LATER, Lilly sits on her bed with her papers and notes, and I'm on the floor, watching more news videos with my headphones on, when all of a sudden, a mass of paper rains down on me.

*What the fuck?*

I turn around, and Lilly is sitting in the middle of the bed with tears in her eyes and her fists balled into her cardigan. Getting up, I cautiously sit on the edge.

My hands are raised like I'm trying not to startle a feral animal. "Cal?"

"This isn't getting us anywhere," her voice cracks. "We've read every single article five times. There is no new information." She lets go of the sweater and slams her flat palms onto the comforter.

She's frustrated; I can deal with that. When I saw the tears, my initial thought was that she had another migraine. Seeing it twice was more than enough for me, especially knowing what it is.

We sit in silence for several minutes. Lilly is breathing heavily and trying to regain control. I want to comfort her, but I don't know how.

While she struggles to calm herself, I have an idea. "Let's take a different approach."

Her eyes swivel to mine with a big question mark.

"Instead of only listening to what the media reported, why don't we look at it from your point of view?"

"What do you mean?"

I try to explain, "Well, so far we've been looking at it from other people's points of view—everyone who ever reported about the kidnappings. No one knew anything about you, except that you were the first and you were dropped off at the ER anonymously. Let's start with your migraines again. You were in a room—a nice room, at that. Think about what you've seen in those memories."

Lilly gets up and digs through a pile of papers on the floor. She pulls out the one containing the notes she made of her migraines, settles back on the bed, and closes her eyes. After a few deep inhales and exhales, she starts talking in a low voice—more to herself than to me. "Mirror, canopy, the stuffed bunny, and...the man."

She shudders, and instinctively, I reach over and grab her hand. Realizing what I've done, I try to pull away again, but she holds on to me. I'm stunned at my body's reaction to this simple contact. I meant to comfort *her*, but when she doesn't let go, it has the same effect on me. An instant calm settles over my mind, and everything else vanishes. It's just the two of us.

"Let's focus on the first three. Can you remember anything else?

Like what color were the walls or the bedding? Where was the bunny?" I ask her.

She takes several more breaths, and then she's quiet for what feels like an eternity. I can see her eyes move underneath her eyelids.

"The white mirror has an old look to it. It has these ornate carvings. It stands out against the wall." She pauses. "The walls are pale lavender. I remember thinking that I liked the color."

I sweep her room. She still does. She's always liked everything purple. Pillows, throw blankets, accents in purple, lavender, heather, and periwinkle are everywhere. Yup, I know what periwinkle is—don't judge. I have a mother who is obsessed with interior design when she isn't knee-deep in a legal battle, so we were dragged to Home Depot and Lowe's our entire childhood.

I lightly squeeze her hand. "You're doing great. Keep going."

She remains still. "The canopy is white. It matches the bedding. But the bedding also has patterns on it—butterflies, I think, in different colors."

I wait for her to continue; my thumb strokes the knuckles of her hand.

"The bunny sits on an armchair. It's also white, with pale-green cushions. It's one of those bergère chairs. Everything in the room looks antique, but it's not...old." She opens her eyes. "Does that make sense?"

I think for a second. "Yeah, I guess. The furniture or room was probably made to look antique. Like a specific style or theme."

Lilly nods and straightens, pulling her hand away from me. The loss of contact hits me more than I would've expected. She's immediately distant. Is she purposefully putting space between us?

I ignore it and say, "You did good. You were in a nice and well-furnished room. Whoever it was wanted you to be comfortable."

She snorts and gives me a *"Yeah, right"* look.

I hold up my hands. "Let me finish my train of thought for a sec. Whoever it was didn't just take you and toss you in a cell or locked room. He wasn't a child molester, and he didn't lay a hand on you otherwise. This was planned and had a reason. Now, we have to figure out what that reason was."

"I don't know if that makes me feel better or worse," she huffs.

We keep throwing ideas back and forth, but none really make sense. Why did this person choose Lilly, and why is she the one he still wants?

I peer at the clock and realize it's already four in the afternoon. Reality comes crashing back, and I almost beg her to tell Mom and Dad just so this torturous charade can finally be over. I don't want to leave. But instead, I force myself to sound nonchalant as I say, "They'll be home soon. I should probably head out. Otherwise, they'll know right away that something is up."

Lilly nods, and her face falls slightly. She composes herself quickly, but not before I see the change in her. "Okay, yeah, you're right. Where are you going?"

"Wes's."

She pauses and then asks, "What about Katherine?"

*Good point.*

I haven't talked to her since I hung up last night, and not hearing from her means I'm on her shit list. But that's none of Lilly's concern. "She's probably shopping for Christmas presents somewhere."

She just nods at me, and I squeeze her shoulder on my way out.

# CHAPTER NINE

### LILLY

WHEN RHYS TAKES MY HAND, THE TOUCH STARTLES ME, YET I hold on like a lifeline. The emotional turmoil instantly fades away, and I'm able to stay in control, concentrate on the task at hand. It's almost as if he...*anchors* me?

The soothing motion across my knuckles calms the anxiety that had started to rise to the surface as soon as I thought about the room. But when I open my eyes, my first thought is he knew this happened to me, and he didn't say a word for ten years! I pull my hand away, and for a fraction of a second, hurt flares in his eyes. Having perfected not letting anyone see his *real* face, he smoothes his features and immediately pretends like nothing happened. But I *did* see it.

THE REST of the afternoon is easier. We stay busy, and I get comfortable being around him. I don't have time to think any further than the case and searching for answers.

So, when he leaves later, I'm surprised about the feeling of loss settling inside of me. It's been only twenty-four hours, and I shouldn't just fall back into our old relationship. Scratch that, I can't go back to that—since he's not my brother. But even as friends, he kept my past from me, for goodness' sake. I can't just ignore that. I don't like how I'm already used to him being around. It opens me up to get hurt, and I refuse to let that happen. I force the anger to rise back to the surface, and instantly feel more in control.

HEATHER AND TRISTEN come home around five-thirty. In my head, I call them by their first name, even though Rhys is right and they are my parents, blood relation or not. It's self-preservation. I need to figure out what really happened to me, and for that, I need distance. I can't let them distract me with their love for me.

I spend some time downstairs. They tell me about their trip, and Natty is chatting about her weekend with Olivia and their friend Adelyn, who also slept over. I smile and nod when appropriate and then excuse myself under the pretense of finishing homework. I'm drained. Getting a slight glimpse into Rhys's life, I'm starting to understand why he'd rather stay away. Keeping up a façade is exhausting.

I sleep better than I have in the last few weeks, but not as good as the night before. I'm restless. I haven't seen Rhys since he left this afternoon.

MONDAY MORNING, I automatically search for Rhys's Defender in the school parking lot but don't see it anywhere. That's strange, he usually is here early for some sort of practice—wrestling, football, whatever is going on at the time.

I don't see him all morning or during lunch. Without thinking, I ask Denielle, "Have you seen Rhys today?"

Den looks at me like I sprouted a third eye and sneers, "Why?"

*Dumb, dumb, dumb.*

I haven't asked her that in years. We have a silent agreement to ignore everything involving Rhys, ever since the day she found me crying in a girls' bathroom stall. The week before, Rhys had started to call me Lilly, but I kept telling myself he was just distracted. Then, during one of my first days at WH, I had run up to Rhys, excited to tell him something, and he completely brushed me off. As I was walking away, I heard him laughing and making a comment to his friend, Kellen Jager, about how his life is over now that his little *pest* of a sister is here. That was also the day I officially stopped talking to him.

I look back at Den. "Oh, um..." *Think, damn it.* "Uh, Mom wanted me to tell him something because she missed him this morning."

*Missed him?* Jesus, I need to shut up. Denielle is fully aware that Rhys doesn't sleep at home, but thankfully, she ignores that fact. Instead, she narrows her eyes at me. "Why doesn't she just text him?"

*Crap.*

I don't think I can dig my hole any deeper. I set myself up for that one. I shrug and ask, "So, when is Charlie coming home again?"

She barks out a laugh. "Dude, you suck at this," she says but lets it go. "Next week. He says he has a surprise for me."

And with that, we speculate the rest of the day what it could be.


FOR THE REMAINDER of my classes, I debate if I should text Rhys to see where he is. We didn't talk about staying in touch when we're not at home, but I kind of *want* to know. He is finally back in my life.

Then, the voice in my head reminds me: *He lied to you. If you let him back in, he could hurt you again.* It works until I check my phone again—still no message from him.

The anger and betrayal keep me going, but Rhys grounds me in a way that I can't explain. I need both to stay in control, and I don't like it. As if I don't already have enough conflicting feelings, it's like a tug of war for sanity in my head.


I SIT in the Jeep and pull out my phone. The voice screams at me to stop and put the phone away. I hesitate one more time. Screw it. Scrolling through my contacts, I realize I still have the picture of Rhys from our last family trip as his profile picture; a smile tucks on my lips at the memory. I haven't had a reason to text or call him in so long that I had forgotten about it.

We were at the Grand Canyon, and he made me take picture

after picture, trying to capture himself jumping in the air with the Grand Canyon as the backdrop. We did get the shot eventually, but his profile picture is one of the outtakes. He jumped, realized he miscalculated, tripped during the landing, and spread-eagled on his stomach in the dirt. I took the picture right after he pushed himself into a sitting position and was flipping me off for laughing so hard that I had tears running down my face.

Selecting the text option from his contact, I start typing.

**Haven't seen u all day.**

I hit send. Okay, I've done my sisterly—uh, friendly—duty.

*God, what a cluster fuck.*

I put my phone away and drive to Butler's. I have gymnastics practice every day this week, which will hopefully keep me distracted. But despite all the physical activity, I'm already looking forward to Saturday when I meet with Spencer. He promised we would start incorporating some new moves, and I could use that type of training for my emotional state.

AFTER PRACTICE, I check my cell and see a response from Rhys.

**@Georgetown with Kat & Wes. Back later 2NTE. Everything ok?**

My jaw clenches as a pang of annoyance hits me. This past weekend has altered both our lives in ways no one else could ever relate to, and him going back to his old habit of not talking to me is...frustrating? Disappointing? I have no idea how to categorize this. But then, why would Rhys tell me? I insisted we keep going as before. Plus, I don't want to fall back into my old habit of depending on him. I can't. Why would I expect something different from *him*? I start typing a response and then think better of it. Before saying something I may regret, I pocket my phone and head home. Our relationship is so complicated, and with everything else, I need to focus on myself and what happened to me. He says he's helping me, but until I know the truth of what happened ten years ago, do I really want to let someone else in? Even if it's Rhys?

. . .

I'M SITTING IN BED, re-reading some articles, when I hear a soft knock on my door, and Rhys comes in. My eyes widen. Heather and Tristen are home.

*What the hell is he doing?*

I try to glance around him to make sure no one sees him.

"Mom and Dad already went upstairs, and Natty is sleeping," he says while closing the door quietly.

Him being home by itself would raise questions, but I just nod, not sure what to say. I'm still annoyed with him and, at the same time, mad at myself for caring. I really don't need to add any more irrational feelings to my already confused mental state.

Rhys hesitates for a moment by the door before walking toward my bed and sitting down on the edge. "You didn't respond. Everything okay?"

"Yeah, all good."

He arches an eyebrow. Of course, he knows it's not all good. I grind my teeth.

"You're mad at me." Not a question, but a statement.

"No, yes, no—gah! I don't know." I throw my hands up. I. Don't. Want. To. Care.

*But you do,* the voice whispers in my head.

"You're mad that I didn't tell you about Georgetown." Another statement.

*I'm going to have a cramp in my jaw soon.*

"How do you always know everything?" Sarcasm drips from the question.

Rhys grins smugly at me, and I want to sucker-punch him.

"Not everything, Cal. Just you."

*Right, I forgot; he has spied on me for the past two years.*

I press my lips together in an attempt to hide my smile and remain angry, but it's not working. He's always had the ability to pull me back from any sort of emotional cliff. So much has happened between us, but he still knows me that well. I'm not sure how that makes me feel.

"I'm sorry I didn't tell you. It didn't occur to me to text you. I'm glad you did, though." He genuinely smiles at me.

I sigh. "Okay. Just..." I try to think of the right words, and something clicks. "I can't do this alone." I gesture at the papers. As much as I don't want to let him in, I need his help, which scares me almost as much as the reason *why* I need him.

Rhys understands the meaning. "We can message during the day. You can tell me what you're up to, and I can text you when I'm home. We can meet up after everyone goes to bed and work on things."

I frown. "Um, what are you going to tell Heather and Tristen about coming home all of a sudden?"

He shrugs nonchalantly. "Nothing. Not my problem what they think."

"Rhys!" My pulse increases; he promised not to act any different.

"Calla!" he mimics my tone. "Calm down, if they ask—which they won't since you and I will still ignore each other—I'll just say Wes is sleepwalking again. He confuses the couch for the bathroom, and I don't enjoy getting pissed on every other night. It'll be fine. I promise." Without blinking an eye about the ridiculous lie, he switches gears and gestures to the articles. "What are you doing?"

I snort. "Not so fast. First of all, that's the most unbelievable story I have ever heard come out of your mouth—and that's saying a lot after last weekend. And second, what about Wes?"

Rhys rolls his eyes. "You're overthinking this. I haven't had to explain myself to anyone in years. If it makes you feel better, I'll tell Wes I'm staying at Kat's."

*No, that doesn't make me feel better.*

Not satisfied with his answer, but refusing to analyze why the excuse of him sleeping at his girlfriend's house causes a red haze to settle over my vision, I frown at the paper still in my hand and admit, "I was hoping something would trigger another migraine, something that can give us a hint as to where to start looking."

He looks concerned now. "Nothing?"

"Nothing," I huff.

WE'RE BOTH SO busy during the week with our individual routines that, twice, I fall asleep before Rhys gets home.

Thursday, I finally remember something. We go over the room I was in, and I try to outline where everything is when I recall a small bookshelf with lots of used children's books and a small dresser on the other side of the door that contained clothes—all around my size.

*So creepy.*

It all points even more toward *the incident* being planned and thought out.

Why did he pick me?

## RHYS

ASIDE FROM LILLY remembering more furniture, we've made zero progress. It's getting late, and she sits cross-legged, leaning against her headboard, laptop on her lap. I sit at the foot of the bed, facing her, and sift through notes.

"I feel like there has to be something in this house."

Lilly glances over her screen, trying to stifle a yawn. "What do you mean?"

I shrug. "Like adoption papers, medical files, whoever erased your memory about Emily and Henry. I don't know. *Something*. I mean, you have my last name; there must be a paper trail for that."

Lilly doesn't flinch anymore when I mention Emily and Henry. I've told her everything I remember about them, which, unfortunately, isn't a whole lot. After all, I was seven when everything went down. But I do remember that they seemed to be good people. Good parents. I make sure to emphasize that to Lilly. I want her to understand that not everyone in her life is—or was—bad.

Her internal battle is obvious. She is angry, and I do my best to understand. She refers to Emily and Henry by their first names, instead of *her parents*, and also starts doing that with my parents. It hurt the first few times, but I get it—she is protecting herself.

Lilly tucks a strand of her blonde hair behind her ear, a gesture she does when she's thinking something over, and it makes her look freaking adorable. She stares off toward the other end of the room, and I use the opportunity to gawk at her openly. She is wearing her usual gray PJ sweats, but instead of a Henley, she has my old hoodie on. The navy blue is so faded that it appears more gray than blue. I had given it to her a few months into my freshman year. I had bulked up from practice and had to get a bigger one. I'm surprised to see her in it tonight. I was sure the one day she had worn it to school was a mistake, and now I wonder if she did it on purpose or if she hasn't given it a thought at all. Either way, seeing her in my clothes stirs something deep inside of me.

I'm completely distracted when she speaks. "*If* there is something in the house, it's probably in the office. Maybe the safe? I don't think they would just keep it anywhere, like their bedroom."

Her words make me snap out of my internal debate about the hoodie. "I agree, but I'm not sure how we can search for it properly with Mom and Dad around."

Lilly taps her pointer finger against her lips.

*God, she is so sexy when she does that.*

I all but drool at the sight. When she looks back at me, I avert my eyes quickly.

*Get a grip, dude.*

"We're allowed to leave during lunch; one of us could drive home."

"That could work. You think you can do it without anyone asking questions?" I say, thinking that if I disappear, either Kat or Wes will notice immediately.

She thinks for a second. "Yeah, I can always say I forgot something."

# CHAPTER TEN

## RHYS

The next day, after lunch, I'm sitting in English Lit when my phone vibrates in my back pocket. Miss Cipriano is reading something from the book we're currently discussing, so I take a chance and pull it out. Both Kat and Wes are in this class with me, which means it's most likely Lilly, and she wouldn't text me unless it's important. None of my other friends text in the middle of class; we've all gotten into trouble for it over the years. The school has had a no-cell-phones-in-class policy ever since a group of seniors, a few years ago, somehow used their phones to cheat during several exams. It was never released what they did exactly, but if someone gets caught with a phone out in class, you can kiss it goodbye for the rest of the day. None of us are willing to risk that twice—except for me right now.

I swipe across Lilly's name on the screen.

**Got something.**

My heart immediately hammers in my throat. Got what? A migraine? Did she go home? I didn't think she would try so soon, but I'm not surprised. Neither of us can claim patience as one of our redeeming qualities, and she's been dealing with this much longer.

I keep my reply short to not attract attention: **?**

With my phone on my thigh, I wait for the vibration so I don't have to look at it constantly. I can't help myself, though, and take a peek. I see the three little dots on the screen, but it seems like an eternity until I feel the familiar sensation on my leg.

**Went home during lunch. T never changed combination to safe, but there were only family documents, passports, etc.**

I am about to respond when she types again. The next message makes the blood pound hard in my ears.

**Still had time. Looked through T's desk. Found folder taped to bottom of middle drawer with a discharge form for a Jane Doe from a hospital in Santa Rosa, CA and a copy of my passport. With my REAL name.**

*Holy fuck!*

My adrenaline level is through the roof before I finish reading, and I'm close to jumping out of my seat. Lilly has to be back in school by now, and I have the desperate need to go searching for her.

When I glance toward the front at Miss Cipriano, I see Kat studying me with a raised eyebrow.

*Shit.*

I'm drawing attention. Kat will interrogate me later about who I was texting.

Unable to let it go, though, I type **U okay?**

When no three dots appear, I put my phone away. She's probably back at school.

*I hope.*


I DON'T SEE Lilly after class, and she hasn't responded to my text, which keeps me in a state of complete distraction during the meeting with my coach for tonight's wrestling match. He yells at me twice, and Wes gives me a *what-the-fuck* glare.

*So much for keeping a low profile. That makes twice today.*

Tonight's match is against our main rival, and everyone's eyes are glued to the mats. I'm up next. When I walk onto the mats toward Jeff Convoy, one of the best on the other team, I notice familiar blonde hair near the side of the bleachers. I turn my head slightly, and sure enough, my gaze zeros in on Lilly. She's chewing on her thumbnail and lifts her other hand in a small wave, clearly trying not to draw attention. I do that all on my own. *Again.*

I stop mid-step and stare at her. What is she doing here? Is something wrong? She hasn't been to a game or match since...since before. I try to compose myself, nod at her, and continue to my mark. I assure myself that if something were wrong, she would've texted me. But *why* is she here?

Lilly watching gives me an adrenaline spurt like never before. All I can think of is that I *have* to win. Yes, total caveman reaction, but what can I say?

Fortunately, I also have the advantage of years of private MMA lessons over most opponents. I'm good at anticipating the next move—very good, actually. Not to boast—well, maybe a little—but the match is over in no time.


Kat instantly gets up when I walk off the mats. She usually greets me with a big show—winning or losing, anything that gives her attention—but I don't care for her theatrics tonight. Instead of heading toward her, I veer to the edge of the bleachers. Lilly's eyes widen when I approach, and she takes a step back. She looks like she wants to hide under the bleachers. I briefly regret my decision, but she didn't respond all afternoon. I need to make sure she is okay, not giving a fuck that all eyes are on us.

I stop right in front of her and keep my voice low. "Everything okay?"

She seems confused for a second. "Yes, why?"

"You didn't text back."

*I'll take 'Lovesick Moron' for one hundred, Alex.*

Realization hits her. "Oh! Yes, crap, I'm sorry. I wasn't alone until I decided to come here."

"Why are you here?" Not that I'm complaining; I'm probably reading into it way too much.

Lilly glances over my shoulder and then shrugs as if she is not sure herself. Or she doesn't want to answer my question. Before I can prod further, she remarks dryly, "You better go back before Katherine's head explodes."

I'm sure she's foaming at the mouth, but that doesn't impact Lilly.

"She'll get over it." *I hope.* "See you later?"

When Lilly nods, I turn and head over to my usual spot. Sure enough, I can see Kat internally fuming.

*Fan-fucking-tastic.*

I'm going to pay for that when we're alone, but in front of everyone else, she throws herself into my arms and chokes me with her tongue. *Really?* I will never understand how tongue-fucking me in public is helping her image.

By the time I can disentangle myself from Kat and the catcalls have stopped, Lilly is gone. At least that seems to have distracted everyone from *my little sister*, who I haven't spoken to in years, showing up.

## LILLY

AFTER GYMNASTICS PRACTICE, Denielle meets her parents for dinner, but I can't bring myself to go home after what I found today. Not that it is a major breakthrough; however, it's the first true proof that Heather and Tristen have been lying to me all these years. The longer I let the feeling of betrayal fester, the tenser I grow. I'm close to the point of snapping. The little bit of rational thinking that's left reasons to stay away from my *pretend* parents until I can think straight again.

I DRIVE AROUND and briefly consider going to grab food, but when I pass the school, I spontaneously pull into the already packed lot. I haven't been to one of Rhys's matches in years, and I'm too worked up to think about how it could be perceived.

As I push through the gym's double doors, a guy named Matt, or Mark, or something like that is in the middle of his match. He's holding his own from what I can see, and I scan the room for Rhys. He sits on the bottom row of the bleachers on the far end, talking to someone I recognize but don't remember the name of. Wes is a few seats down and raises his eyebrows when he spots me.

*Shit.*

I should leave before I draw more attention, but somehow, being here calms me. Maybe there is more to my anchor theory than I thought? I remain at the edge of the bleachers and try to hide in the shadows, but Rhys immediately spots me on his way to his mark and falters mid-step. Before he can compose himself, Katherine's eyes snap up and zero in on me. Her head slightly cocked to the side, she narrows her eyes.

*Crappity crap.*

I finally make my exit after Rhys openly approaches me after his win. What was I thinking? Oh right, I wasn't. Everyone knows that Rhys and Lilly McGuire don't talk to each other.

*Shit. Fuck. Shit.*

And on top of that, I've started cursing like my best friend.

I AVOID Heather and Tristen when I make it home. Back in my room, I'm waiting to show Rhys the copies I made earlier. I never thought I'd be so happy about Tristen's insistence of us needing this massive fax/printer/scanner contraption that can basically do everything but make me dinner. Earlier, I copied both papers and stashed them back where I had found them.

Leaning against my headboard, laptop propped up in my lap, I type in the name of the nurse that signed the discharge papers in the search engine window: Madeline Cross. Nothing useful comes back—nothing of use to me, that is. I get a bunch of random entries for social media sites and other stuff, but nothing that can be tied back to a nurse in Santa Rosa ten years ago. Well, so much for that.

I keep looking at my phone, and by two a.m., I decide to give up. My anger is under control, but I'm frustrated that Rhys didn't come home. I can guess where he is—damage control. Which means I shouldn't be frustrated with him. But he is the only one I can talk to about this, and I *want* his input. This is our first clue.

*Our clue?*

I guess I have to accept that he is in this with me. Even though I was the one kidnapped, manipulated, and lied to, he's part of this. Always has been, to an extent.

My inner battle is causing havoc inside of me. I don't want to be dependent on him. Being dependent means he has the ability to let me down, hurt me. But I don't want to be alone, either. My feelings are getting more jumbled by the day.

I need sleep. I need to shut my brain off for a while. Though, before falling asleep I decide that it's time to change my approach. No more waiting for more migraines. I'm going to the source.

Rhys won't be happy with my newfound plan.

# CHAPTER ELEVEN

## LILLY

SPENCE PUSHES MY TRAINING SESSION THIS WEEK TO THE afternoon. So, instead of being at the gym Saturday morning, I'm in the kitchen, helping Natty with her science project. Helping is actually code for her doing it and explaining it to me in the process. At the moment, she is building a waterwheel out of a cork, a few plastic pieces, a skewer, a funnel, and a two-liter bottle to demonstrate the power of water for her school's winter science fair. I could be considered biased, but Natty is one of the smartest and kindest humans I've ever encountered. She looks like Rhys's mini-me with her dark-brown hair and green eyes; she even laughs like him.

I always tease her that she's ten going on thirty-two. When she is not with her two best friends, or at a tap or ballet lesson, she is holed up in her room, studying or with her head in a book. Her favorite books are *Wuthering Heights* and *Jane Eyre*. How she can read that over and over is beyond me. I tried reading both books once, but I didn't make it past page fifteen. Natty is more grown up than I am most of the time. She is the last person I ever expect to give Heather or Tristen trouble. She'll go places one day—that much Rhys and I always agreed on.

. . .

RHYS WALKS in through the garage around noon, lingering by the door. I glance over and see guilt written all over his face. He obviously didn't plan to stay out all night and mouths, "I'm sorry."

I lightly touch Natty's arm. "I'll be right back, okay? I need to talk to Rhys."

Engrossed in her project, she just nods.

Even during the past few years of Rhys and me avoiding each other, we had a silent understanding not to let it interfere with our relationship with Natty. Whenever all three of us were in the same room, which wasn't often, we were a *normal* family.

Natty won't think twice about this, but if Heather and Tristen had been here, my statement would've immediately attracted attention.

I stand up, walk out of the kitchen, and up the stairs without saying another word. Rhys follows quietly, probably thinking I'll lay into him as soon as we're upstairs. I feel sorry for him. As if Katherine isn't bitchy enough for all the females in Westbridge and surrounding towns—no, make that states. I decided last night that I won't say anything about him *not* coming home. One, I refuse to look weak and needy, even though I did want him with me—to talk about my find. And second, I'm nothing like Katherine, and I don't ever want to be. She is an evil bi—uh, witch who needs constant attention and validation. She has been manipulating everyone in school for years, and whoever doesn't follow her mighty rules will be outcast. I saw it happen a few times, and it was never pretty. One girl even transferred to a private school one town over. I know for a fact that she doesn't like me, but so far, she hasn't tried to touch me either. I'm not sure if it's because of being Rhys's *sister* or because of my own social standing in school. I'm not at the top of Westbridge High's food chain by any means—that would be Katherine and Rhys with their respective BFFs—but I'm definitely not at the bottom, probably even higher than the middle. I do my own thing, stick to my friends, and try to be polite to everyone, which has worked just fine for me—until now.

It's beyond me how no one sees how fake she is, which was another reason why it hurt so much two years ago. Rhys replaced our friendship—our bond—with *her*.

· · ·

Instead of going to my room, I walk straight into Rhys's and close the door as soon as he's over the threshold.

Eyebrows furrowed, he asks, "Where are Mom and Dad?"

"Lunch with someone from Heather's firm."

He avoids making eye contact.

I suppress a laugh and get straight to the point. "I'm going to California."

Now his gaze snaps to me. "Wha—? When? What happened?"

"Not sure yet. Soon." I shrug like I just told him I'm going down the street to grab dinner. "We won't find anything new here. I need to go where it started."

The wheels in his head are turning, and I'm preparing myself for a fight when he says, "When are we leaving?"

*He wants to come with me?*

"Umm..."

Scanning my stunned face, Rhys chuckles. "Cal, I told you we are doing this together. I've known you your entire life, and if you set your mind on something, you won't change it. You're more stubborn than a mule, and if someone tries to push you one way, you run the opposite direction as fast as you can—no matter the consequence. So, when are we leaving?"

I've gone through every possible argument with him in my head since waking up this morning, and none of them resulted in...this. I was prepared to fight, to yell, and to defend my decision. Anything to not feel weak or dependent. But his simple statement has me tearing up. The cold feeling of betrayal is slowly being replaced by something else. Something I can't decipher yet. Trust? At that moment, I follow my instinct and wrap my arms around his waist.

"Thank you," I whisper into his chest.

Rhys must've expected a different reaction as well because he goes rigid at the physical contact. Though, after a moment, he relaxes and hugs me back, resting his chin on my head, saying, "Always, Cal."


Heading back down to Natty, I hear Rhys's shower turn on and him rummaging around in his room for a while. A little later, I see my phone light up on the kitchen island, and while I walk over, Rhys races through the kitchen to the garage.

"Bye, girls!" he shouts and disappears.

On my screen is a text from him: **Heading to Wes's for a bit. See you later. PROMISE.**

## RHYS

AFTER THE MATCH, the team and several of the girlfriends go out to eat. I focus on the guys, we joke around, discuss the match and the team we're going up against next. Kat is busy with the girls, but as soon as we are alone in the Defender, she lets me have it. After the first five minutes of her going on and on about how I made her look like a fool by not immediately coming to her, I tune her out. At some point, she starts ripping into Lilly and the *audacity* of her showing up the way she did. It takes all the self-control I can muster not to pull over and physically kick her out of my car. I focus on breathing in and out while keeping my mouth shut, which gets harder with every venomous word that comes out of hers.

*Why the fuck have I put up with this shit for so long?*

Am I really that pathetic, instead of just sucking it up and dealing with my feelings for Lilly? The answer is simple: yes. I took the coward's way out, and now I'm paying for it.

We stop in front of the entrance that leads to Kat's gated community. She turns with an expectant look when I make no indication of keying in the code.

"Rhys?"

*First name, huh?*

"Not today." I can't pretend tonight.

"I see." Her tone has turned to ice, and with one ferocious push, she is out of the car and slams the door shut.

I expel all the air I held in my lungs, put the car in drive, and leave Kat standing at the curb. She can walk the last half mile to her house.

I planned to go home, but I am too worked up. I drive to Wes's and let myself in through the side door as I've been doing for years. Wes walks out of the bathroom when I enter his room. His eyebrows raise with an unspoken question, but I just head to the couch that already—or still, I should say—holds my pillow and blanket. Without a word, he turns off the light, and we both settle for the night.

Wes is still asleep when I leave his house the next morning.

GOING HOME to shower and change, I had planned to come clean about where I was all night. Guilt has been constricting my throat since waking up. I should've texted Lilly that I was staying at Wes's. Not that I owe her an explanation, but I'm sure she has the wrong assumption about my whereabouts, and that simply bugs me. Her new plan, however, completely distracts me from explaining what happened. She wants to go to California. Well, fuck me. What am I supposed to do? She can't go alone—that much is clear.

*I guess we're going to the golden state.*

FOLLOWING MY USUAL PATTERN, I am leaving again, but I quickly regret my decision to go back to Wes's.

When Mrs. Sheats opens the front door, she gives me a questioning look. She wears her usual outfit of black leggings and flowy tunic. Today's color of choice is turquoise. I don't think I have ever seen her in anything different, no matter what time of day. Her blonde hair is tied in a low ponytail. A lot of people mistake her for Wes's older sister. She had Wes when she was just eighteen, and with her natural youthful look, that perception makes sense. I've fucked with Wes many times, saying how hot his mom is. Not that I would ever go there, but the way he gets riled up from the comments is hilarious.

"Uh, is everything okay, Rhys? Since when do you use the front door?"

*Good question.*

I don't think I've done that since...no idea. Lilly's decision has me completely distracted.

I put on a nonchalant grin and give her a peck on the cheek. "Just trying out something new, Mrs. S."

Her eyebrows are still up in her hairline, and she grunts, "Mm-hmm," with a smirk before closing the door behind me. Wes's house has been more my home than my parents' house since I was sixteen. I think his mother eventually accepted my constant presence here, and I became like her second son.

I head to the family room where I'll find Wes at this time of day. We're lounging on the large sectional, playing video games, when Wes casually announces, "I saw Lil last night." He leaves the sentence hanging.

Of course he noticed her. I'm an idiot for thinking he wouldn't have. *Everyone* saw her. He wants me to elaborate, especially after my unexpected appearance at his house last night; Friday nights are usually reserved for Kat.

"Yup." I hope he'll let it go, but I know better. Three, two,...

"Dude, Lilly came to *your* game, and that's all you got?" He's annoyed, and I'm scrambling for a logical explanation without telling the truth.

I opt for a half-truth. "We made up."

Wes pauses the game and scowls at me. "Care to elaborate?" When I keep staring at the screen, he continues, "I still have no freaking clue what the fuck happened in the first place. Lilly *was* one of my closest friends. I had to choose between you two."

My head whips around, and I stop myself at the last moment from calling him out on his bullshit. I never made him choose.

With a lot of restraint, I manage not to snarl at him. "I can't go into it. We've made up. Leave it at that, okay?"

"Seriously? You're not giving me shit? Why the hell did you end up on my couch last night?" Wes sneers back.

Now I'm getting irritated. "When was the last time I had to explain myself to you?"

Wes glowers, nostrils flared, but then starts the game back up.

I'm grateful that he's my best friend on so many levels. I'm not stupid; I can see he's livid—who wouldn't be? But where others would keep pushing, he knows that I'll tell him when the time is right—it just hasn't been. Wes was pissed for weeks after I shut Lilly out, but eventually, he let it go. It had to have been something serious for me to *leave* Lilly, which was reason enough for him. He still talked to her on occasion, but he was my best friend first, and that probably hurt Lilly just as much. She didn't just lose me. I took Wes with me.

He's yet another person who got involuntarily pulled into this scheme and had to pay the price with his friendship to Lilly. I probably owe him an apology—one day. For *all* of it.

LILLY IS SITTING on her bed, reading, when I walk in around eleven. She genuinely smiles, and I can't help the feeling of warmth spreading through me.

"How is Wes?"

I settle myself next to her against the headboard of her bed with one leg on the mattress and the other hanging down. I make the split-second decision to not mention our argument to her; she has enough going on. "Good. He asked about you."

Lilly closes the cover of her e-reader and tilts her head.

"He saw you last night."

"I shouldn't have come. I was so angry at Heather and Tristen and couldn't make myself go home." She balls her fists into the comforter.

I don't want her to regret coming. It was the best part of the entire evening for me. "It's fine. Wes is fine. I told him we made up."

Alarm flickers in her eyes. "You what? What does he know?"

"Nothing. I never told him anything. He knew it had to be something major for me to act the way I did. He was up my ass for weeks, but eventually, he let it go. He's a good friend, Cal. I think we can trust him—when you're ready."

Lilly's face goes blank for a second, and then she nods. "Yeah, maybe."

WE SIT IN SILENCE, and I play with the fringe of one of her throw pillows in my lap when I reveal, "I have an idea about how we can pull off our trip to California."

That piques Lilly's interest, and she looks at me expectantly.

"But before I get to that, have you reconsidered talking to Mom and Dad? If they knew, maybe they would fill in the blanks."

"No!"

It comes out so forcefully that I lift my hands defensively, not pushing further. "Okay," It was worth a try. "I was going on a ski trip with a bunch of people from school and—"

"The one Den and Charlie are going on? After Christmas?" Lilly interrupts.

"Yeah, I'm going with Wes. Anyway, what if you come *with* us"—I make air quotes around 'with'—"and you and I head to California instead?"

She frowns. "Heather and Tristen will never let me go. You remember what happened when I was supposed to go on the field trip to D.C. freshman year."

It was a three-day trip, and Mom and Dad found every possible excuse under the sun to not let her go. Of course, Lilly didn't get why. A lot of tears and yelling were involved, and in the end, Lilly didn't talk to anyone for almost four days.

"I remember, but that was a few years ago. Den and Charlie will be there, and so will Wes and I. We can figure something out." I *try* to sound confident.

"How do you explain to Wes that you're not going? And how would they cover for us unless we tell them? And how would we explain to Heather and Tristen that *you* would look out for me? We don't talk to each other." She's right. I didn't think about all of that. We sit quietly for several minutes.

Lilly is the first to speak again. "I can get Den to cover for me." She sounds convinced. "I'll ask Heather and Tristen to go with her, and when they start saying no, I'll bring up that you and Wes are there as well. I mean, you would keep me safe, no matter how we"—she gestures between us—"are with each other."

*That approach could work.*

"What are you gonna tell Den?" She is as nosy as they get, but I don't say that out loud.

Lilly taps her finger against her lips, and once again, I ogle her like a cheeseburger while I'm on my strict-as-fuck, wrestling-season nutrition plan.

*God, why does she keep doing that?*

"I'm not sure yet. Probably part of the truth?"

I arch an eyebrow, waiting for her to continue.

"You and I have to go to California, and I'll fill her in on every-thing when we get back. I'm just not ready yet."

"And you think she'll be cool with that?" I'm skeptical. Denielle Keller hates my guts.

"Yes, she's my best friend, *and* she trusts me."

I sit up. "Okay then, let's give it a try."

# CHAPTER TWELVE

**LILLY**

ONCE RHYS GOES TO BED, I TEXT DENIELLE TO ASK IF SHE WANTS to go Christmas shopping in the morning. As expected, she's still up and immediately replies: **Um, duh! :-P**

WE MEET SUNDAY MORNING, and Den drags me from one store to the next. Four hours later, she has thirteen shopping bags. *Thirteen*! I glance down to my hands—two. A book for Natty, and the other bag is for Rhys, but Den doesn't know that. I was getting new shin guards when I saw a set of black gel shock quick-wraps and spontaneously decided to get them for him as a Christmas present.

Since the hug, I've had a hard time keeping the anger barrier up. He's not forgiven, but he is slowly breaking down my defenses. He is giving up his ski trip to help me with something that could just as well be a useless endeavor.

While I trail Den through the shops, I go through possible ways on how to broach the subject, bumping into her several times when she stops to pick something up and I'm too far in my head to notice. After the third time, she gives me the raised eyebrow, and after the fifth, she exclaims, "Really? What's going on with you today?"

By the time we sit down for lunch, I'm a hot mess. She is my best friend, but despite what I told Rhys, I'm worried she'll press for more information than I am willing to give.

We go to our usual lunch spot, a small sushi restaurant. We've just ordered, and the waitress is walking away when Den leans forward, arms on the table, and says, "Okay, I've waited long enough. Spill!"

Almost spitting out my water, I set the glass down slowly, avoiding direct eye contact. I love this girl to pieces. She'll always have my back, but at the same time, she can intimidate the crap out of me.

"What do you mean?" I finally glance up from the red-and-white checkered tabletop.

She gives me a *don't-try-to-play-dumb* look. "Something has been going on with you for weeks, and I want to know what it is."

*Shit.*

Sometimes, it's a disadvantage that she can read me so well.

"Umm...well...I did want to talk to you about something," I stammer.

Den stares blankly and waves her hand in a motion for me to continue.

I grab a napkin from the dispenser and start shredding it.

*How small can I make the pieces?*

I take a deep breath. "I need you to cover for me."

"I don't follow." She squints at me.

"The ski trip over the New Year; I need you to cover for me with my parents—that I am there. With you."

Her scowl turns into a shit-eating grin. "Ohhhhh, who is the lucky guy?"

Okay, here it goes. "Rhys."

Her eyes bulge out. "Come again?"

I snicker. My best friend is rarely at a loss for words.

"Rhys and I need to go...*somewhere*, and our parents can't find out." I almost said *his* parents. Before she's able to interject, I add quickly, "I swear I'll tell you everything when we're back, but I'm not ready. I need you to trust me. Please," I all but plead.

Den thinks it over. And thinks some more. I'm holding my breath until my lungs start to burn. The wait is excruciating, even though the wall clock above the neighboring table shows that it's less than two minutes before she speaks.

"Does this have to do with why you've been acting like a paranoid zombie on coke for the last few weeks?"

*Well, if she put it like that.*

I nod.

"It's something serious, isn't it?"

Another nod. I'm unable to form a response without blurting out *the secret*.

"Are you going to be safe? With Rhys, I mean? He's not going to leave you stranded somewhere, right?"

A smile tugs at my lips at her protectiveness. "Yes, things have changed." I look at her with what hopefully constitutes as a serious but convincing face.

*Or I could just appear constipated.*

The silence drags out another minute and a half before Denielle sighs, almost resigned. "Okay, but I want to know what's going on with you when you get back. You're freaking me out."

I reach across the table to hug her. "Thank you!"

"Anything for you, babe."


I'M SITTING at the dinner table, peeking at Heather and Tristen through my lashes. It's the first time I've been in the same room with them for more than five minutes since Friday. Heather made salmon with roasted asparagus, which I usually love, but today it's like chewing paper. We're eating in silence, and once again, I am sorting through the emotions in my head.

They're my parents. They're all I remember. But I can't bring myself to call them Mom and Dad. The hurt was written all over Rhys's face when I started calling them Heather and Tristen, but he didn't say anything to correct me.

I sneak glances when they're not paying attention to me. How can they just pretend day in and day out? Or has this farce gone on for so long that they believe it themselves?

Rubbing my palms against my pants, I fight the urge to shout at them. Why am I here? Why did you take me in? Why have you been lying to me for ten years? WHY?

My breathing increases, and my eyes gloss over. A feeling of being manipulated is taking over my senses, and I focus down at my plate, inwardly counting backward from thirteen. Don't ask me why thirteen. It's a technique Spence taught us early on in our training to focus. I've been using it ever since.

Once I'm back in control, I unclench my fists under the table. I wonder if I'll be able to forgive them one day. Probably? I don't know—maybe? As long as my emotions go haywire when we're in the same room, I am not ready. For now, I need to figure out what really happened.

I push the same piece of salmon around on my plate for the fourth time, and Heather examines me with a quizzical yet knowing look. She can see that something is going on, but wants me to tell her what it is. She has used this technique many times over the years, and usually, it works for her.

Sitting down for dinner, I was prepared to have a hard time controlling myself. I'm nowhere near as good as Rhys in putting on a show for everyone, but I decide to use it to my advantage. While Heather still tries to figure out what's wrong with me, I blurt out, "Denielle asked me to come with her on the ski trip over the New Year."

It's a gamble, and I wait for them to call me out on the real reason. Subconsciously, children always think that their parents have built-in bullshit detectors, right?

*But they are not your parents*, the voice reminds me.

I hold my breath.

Heather's hand has stopped halfway to her glass of white wine, and her gaze ping-pongs between Tristen and me. Tristen is the first to react. "The ski trip Rhys is going on? After Christmas?"

*Why does he immediately bring Rhys up?*

I shrug. "No idea. I'm not sure who all is going?" I phrase it more like a question and hope I come across like I don't care one bit. Plus, technically, I wouldn't know since Rhys and I don't talk or run in the same circle.

Heather wears her typical frown when she is debating something. "I don't know." Looking at Tristen, she asks, "What do you think?"

Their internal struggle is apparent. They don't want me to go, and logically, I get it. They are scared and want me safe but can't give away why.

I decide to push a little bit. "I'm almost eighteen. Den will be there, and so will Charlie. Please?" With that, I shove some of the papery salmon in my mouth to stop myself from revealing anything that could mess it up.

I finish two more bites before one of them speaks up. They keep silently communicating with each other. Eventually, Tristen clears his throat and declares, "I'll talk to Rhys."

*What? That's it? What does that mean?*

"Um, okay."

I leave dinner somewhat defeated. My trip to California—to my past—relies on them letting me go.

## RHYS

Lilly is talking to Denielle this morning, so I tell Wes to meet me at the gym after my session with Spence—to get it over with. He is confused that I asked him to come today, but he agrees.

When I finish with Spence, Wes is already on the treadmill a good two miles into his usual five-mile run. I walk up and lean against the equipment next to his, waiting for him to slow down.

When he's at a brisk walk, I rip off the Band-Aid. "Hey, man, I need you to do me a favor."

No reason to drag this out and make it more painful.

"Sure, what do you need?" He takes a big gulp from his water bottle.

"I'm not going to make it on the ski trip, but if anyone asks, I'm going. Especially my parents."

Wes wiggles his eyebrows. "You and Kat taking some alone time?"

"No, Lilly and I are."

He hits the emergency stop button and turns to me. "Your sister Lilly? *Our* Lilly?" He gestures back and forth between us.

I stare back at him. *My Lilly*, a growl reverberates in my head. I compose myself before answering. After all, that was what got me into this mess in the first place—my jealousy toward Wes. "Yes, I can't tell you more right now. I need you to trust me."

His face turns from surprise to annoyance. "That seems to have become a pattern between us."

I can't fault him. This is the second time in two days. But then he switches to concern. "Are you guys okay? What's going on?"

"Lilly needs my help, but until we're back, it's better for you not to know. Plus, it's not my place to tell. It's Lilly's decision. She'll fill you in when she's ready. But she needs more time."

*Cryptic much?*

When Wes hesitates, I ask him flat out, "Can I count on you?"

I'm holding my hand out toward him. I am forcing my luck.

He deliberates for another moment. "Yeah, of course." He slaps his palm in mine. "I'm just...curious. And worried. I mean, Lilly? You haven't spoken ten words to her in years."

I sigh. "You'll understand soon enough."

He cocks his head to the side. "What about Kat?"

I shrug. "What about her?"

"Uh...won't she want to know about this?"

Wes is as oblivious as everyone else about how it is between Kat and me. I've never felt the need to elaborate.

"Nah, she's fine. She's gone with her family."

Wes nods and starts running again. "Come on, you're two miles behind me."

*Moving on.*

IT'S ALMOST midnight by the time I enter Lilly's room. Dad caught me when I got home around eight, and we *chatted* for over an hour before he retreated to his office until eleven-thirty. Not taking any risks, I stayed in my room until I heard his footsteps going up the stairs.

When I slowly ease Lilly's door open, her lights are off, and she is facing away. The blackout curtains are open, and in the dim light, I can see her long hair fanned out on the pillow. I close the door behind me and walk around the bed, gaping at her. I inwardly laugh at myself. I can't remember one time I had that reaction toward

Kat, not even when she would fuck my brains out. I never would just stare at her, marvel at how beautiful she was. Lilly is the complete opposite. She is gorgeous inside and out, and I could watch her for hours.

Lilly looks peaceful; there is no concern, no anger, and *no* blank mask on her face. The mask is what has thrown me off more than the other emotions this past week. It fucks with my head when I can't read her, makes me feel helpless.

I squat down, bringing myself to the same level. "Hey, Cal?"

A grumbled, "Hmm," comes from her sleeping form.

I smirk. "I talked to Dad. We're all set."

Her eyes pop open, and she jerks straight up. "Are you serious?"

The abrupt motion scares the shit out of me, and I land ungracefully on my ass. *Ouch.* I peer up at her expectant face. "Yup, we're going to California." I can no longer suppress my ear-to-ear grin.

She turns her bedside lamp on, fully facing me. "What did he say? I can't believe they're letting me go."

I return to my squatting position. "It was touch and go for a bit, but in the end, I convinced him."

Exasperation drips from her voice. "Rhys! What. Did. He. Say?"

I kind of enjoy keeping her hanging, but it's not fair—not with this.

"Dad was waiting for me in the kitchen. Scared me half to death. I wasn't even through the door when he barked at me that you had asked to go on the ski trip and wanted to know if I had heard about it. I played dumb. I mean, how would I? He announced that they were against you going because they didn't want to risk anything."

Lilly inhales sharply, waiting.

"I said that I get it, but that in a few months you'll be eighteen, and they won't be able to stop you anymore. Dad thought that over and then asked how *I* felt about you being there."

I roll my eyes as I continue. "It was pretty obvious what he was fishing for. I mean, he is the fucking reason I don't talk to you."

I'm still squatting, my forearms resting on my thighs, and I realize my fists are balled. Anger is an understatement for the emotional onslaught I'm experiencing. I haven't thought about that night for a long time for exactly this reason. The night he pulled me aside and told me I couldn't feel that way toward Lilly and I had to do something about it. Resentment and fury surge through me, and I want to punch something...someone. Lilly was not the only one who lost her best friend. I missed her so much at the beginning that I almost told her twice—screw the consequences.

I remind myself that that's over now. Lilly waits patiently for me to continue, watching me fight for composure. Where someone else might have gotten impatient, she knows when to let me work it out in my head. My insides warm at the realization.

Finally, I say, "I told him that I didn't care if you'd be going. You'd probably just hang out with Den anyway. But if anything came up, Wes and I would be there. He thought that over for a few minutes and then gave *his permission* under the condition that we check in every day. I have to keep tabs on you, and I'm to bring you home at the slightest sign of anything unusual."

Lilly rolls her eyes. "What does he think will happen? If my kidnapper hasn't found me here, he won't find me at a random ski resort."

*Not that we're actually going there.*

I hate how casually she mentions that psychopath. Most people would break down and shit their pants under this pressure, but not Lilly; she takes it on headfirst. I always knew she was strong, but I realize that I have underestimated her. She doesn't comprehend how unique she is.

I slap my hand on her comforter. "Let's get some sleep. We have a trip to plan and one more week of school."

Lilly settles back into her pillows. "Thank you!"

"For what?"

"Everything."

I stand and walk toward the door. "Goodnight, Cal."

Before the door closes, I hear, "Night."

---

# CHAPTER THIRTEEN

---

### LILLY

THE NEXT EIGHT DAYS DRAG ON FOR-EV-ER. I'VE BEEN ON EDGE all week. Christmas lost all its appeal, and all I want is to leave for California.


IT TAKES us two days to arrange everything, and by Tuesday evening, we have a plan. We have ten days and contemplate flying versus driving. In the end, we decide to take the Defender. That way, we won't have to leave it at the airport with our *pretend* ski gear and won't have to rely on cabs or Uber when we get to our destination. The goal is to push it and make the drive in three days, which gives us three days to find out what happened to me.


I DO my best to stay busy. I spend almost every night at Denielle's house to avoid being around Heather and Tristen. Mrs. Keller often travels with her husband to conferences he's speaking at, but since it is the week before Christmas, she's deep in holiday preparation. She's absolutely delighted with my intrusion in her house. I had made myself scarce over the last month, and she caters to Den and me with snacks and drinks like we're back in middle school having a sleepover.

*I love it.*

Emma and Sloane join us twice, and I enjoy being around my friends. I've avoided them for the most part because I never knew when a migraine would hit.

I have to let Denielle in eventually, especially after she covers for me, but for now, I push that thought out of my mind. Staying busy is top priority, and thankfully, she doesn't pressure me.

The first few times Rhys and I text when I'm at her house, she assesses me carefully. She was the one who picked up the pieces two-plus years ago, and I can't fault her for being suspicious. Toward the end of the week, though, she must realize that since I am okay, she can be as well. I gotta love my best friend for always watching out for me and having my back. I know how rare it is to have such a genuine friend in life and how lucky I am.

On Christmas Eve, I am a nervous wreck. Rhys keeps throwing me *keep-it-together* looks all day. I'm waiting for Heather and Tristen to call us out.

We have our traditional Christmas dinner of turkey, cranberry sauce, stuffing, mashed potatoes, corn, and green beans. Every year, Heather makes a tri-color gelatin mold in the shape of a Christmas tree. White, red, and green, but no one ever eats the white. She mixes nuts in it to make it appear like Christmas lights. Red and green are spared the disgrace as the nuts wouldn't be adequately visible, according to her. Rhys and I always say that this is just plain wrong. Why would anyone ruin perfectly good Jell-O with nuts? Heather doesn't care, though; her mom made it that way, and so does she. That doesn't stop us from making fun of her all night.

At one point during dinner, Heather starts talking about a Christmas party when Rhys and I were little. Heather laughs at Tristen but talks to me. "Rhys chased you with a fake snake through the house. Who gave him that thing again?"

Tristen is focused on Rhys, but he only shrugs, keeping his face expressionless.

No idea if he does or doesn't remember.

She snaps her finger. "Rob Drager!" When she notices the question mark on everyone's face, she adds, "He used to live a few houses down. He worked at the zoo. Don't you remember, Tristen?"

Tristen just mumbles between bites, "Uh, yeah. I think so."

*I doubt he does.*

"Anyway..." The attention is back on me. "You come around the corner and run straight into the camping table that was set up next to the kitchen. The table folded down on itself, and you were covered in vanilla pudding and cranberry sauce. You were so upset that you ruined everyone's evening. Rhys was laughing like a hyena, and I had to send him to his room." She winks at Rhys.

Then, she adds with a bright smile, "Only the Jell-O mold survived."

I glance over at Rhys next to me, who watches me carefully, before I ask softly, "When was this?"

His eyes widen; he understands immediately. I don't remember any of this.

Heather looks at Tristen thoughtfully. "Hmm, I think that was our last Christmas before moving to Virginia. Tristen?"

He nods in agreement. "Sounds about right."

My entire body goes rigid. They are talking about the Christmas *before* everything happened. When I was *not* part of their family. And yet they talk about it as if it were the most normal thing ever. Like I lived there.

I'm being choked by the rage that instantly starts building inside of me. How. Dare. They. Trying to control my breathing, I count backward, but it's not working.

Then, Rhys touches his leg ever so slightly against mine under the table, and I gain control again. Heather and Tristen keep talking, oblivious to what just happened here. When my breathing has evened out and the red haze lifts, I return Rhys's gesture to let him know that I'm okay.

I remain silent for the rest of dinner. I am terrified I'll say something that gives away that I know. At the same time, I also try to figure out why Rhys seems to be the person who can always make me *come back*. Without him, I wouldn't have been able to keep up the pretense. Another layer of the wall of betrayal and distrust toward Rhys has been chipped away tonight.

. . .

AFTER THE TABLE is cleaned up, the dishes are in the dishwasher, and the leftovers are in the fridge, we watch *A Christmas Story* together. I purposefully position myself at one end of the couch and pull Natty down next to me when she walks in. Rhys is at the other end of the sectional, as usual when we do something as a family. We keep as much space as possible between each other. That leaves the middle for Heather and Tristen. Before settling down, Heather grabs my favorite navy-blue throw blanket from the back of the couch and drapes it over Natty and me, smiling down at us.

I mumble, "Thank you," avoiding eye contact. Rhys observes me; he's probably waiting for me to snap. Only Natty, Heather, and Tristen don't notice anything.

My little sister cuddles against me, and the movie keeps me semi-distracted until I can escape to my room.


THANK goodness Christmas Day goes by fast. We open presents after breakfast, and I focus on Natty the entire time. We retreat to the couch where she immediately starts reading the book I bought her during my shopping trip with Denielle. I get a play by play while she is skimming through. For a ten-year-old, this child can read incredibly fast. Heather is on the phone with her mother and sister, and Rhys keeps Tristen involved in random sports conversations. I wonder if he's doing it on purpose.

After lunch, I head upstairs to finish packing. I hear a soft knock on my door, and before I can say anything, Rhys slips into my room, quickly closing the door.

"They're *Skyping* with Aunt T, so I figured it's safe."

I nod and turn back to my suitcase. Aunt T is Tristen's older sister, Teresa, and once she starts talking, it'll be hours before Heather or Tristen can get off the phone. I have one pile of clothes I need for the fake ski trip, just in case Heather or Tristen end up checking my luggage or closet and find my ski gear there, and one pile that I actually plan to wear. I stash the ski clothes on top of the less-insulated outfits and turn back to Rhys.

He is leaning against the door, watching me.

I raise my eyebrows, waiting.

Taking a step away from the door, he pulls a small square, purple box out of his back pocket. The ribbon—in the same color as the box—is slightly smashed from where it was stashed.

"What is this?"

He hands it over. "Open it."

He is careful not to show any emotion, but for a fraction of a second, I see the eagerness in his eyes. My palms suddenly begin to sweat. Glancing between Rhys and the small box one last time, I pull on the ribbon. When I lift the lid, I find a tiny purple pouch nestled inside. I don't dare to glance up. Shaking the contents of the pouch into my palm, it's a small silver bracelet with a thin bar in the middle of a dainty chain. At closer inspection, I notice that it has coordinates engraved in it. This time I do raise my eyes back up and wait for Rhys to explain.

"They're the coordinates of the house you grew up in. I wanted you to be able to have something from your past, even if you don't remember it." With a cheeky grin, he adds, "Merry Christmas, Cal."

I'm speechless. I wipe away the tear that's running down my cheek. This is by far the best gift he could've given me, and with that, another layer of the wall is gone. He either knows what he is doing, or I have completely misjudged him.

A hiccupped laugh bubbles up. "I—I don't know what to say. Now my gift doesn't feel very original. Thank you so much."

"You got me a present?" Rhys says it so softly that it's barely audible.

"Uh, well...yeah. You got me something."

He just shrugs, staring at his feet, and I take that as my cue to head into my closet to retrieve the gift bag I hid between my winter and rain boots.

When Rhys pulls out the quick wraps his entire face lights up. "No way! I've been looking at these. This is fucking awesome, Cal! How did you know?"

I blush at his excitement. I didn't think they would be that special. "I, uh, saw them when I was buying new shin guards and thought of you. Spence told me once you complained about your old wraps. They're supposed to be one of the best," I babble.

Rhys grins from ear to ear. "They are!" With one step, he's across the room and has me in a bear hug. "Thanks, Cal!"

It feels natural to return the embrace, and for a moment, we're just us again. Rhys and Lilly. No secrets. No lies. *No baggage.*

It's almost dark when we put the last of our bags into Rhys's car. The street is quiet, and I scan the other houses while I wait for Rhys. Lights are on in about half of them. In some, you can see the Christmas tree in the window, and it gives the entire street a peaceful feel.

Rhys parked in the driveway so I could move the Jeep into the garage and it wouldn't be outside while we're gone. Rhys's car is the one that usually needs safekeeping. No one cares how my car withstands the weather. I get it, though. I would probably tuck my car in every night and sing it a lullaby if the roles were reversed.

Rhys maneuvers another one of the bags around when I say, "I still can't believe Tristen gave you his baby for your birthday. I admit I was a bit jealous."

Rhys is finally satisfied with the luggage arrangement in the back and turns toward me. One would think he is playing a real-life version of Jenga instead of loading the car.

He winks. "You got your dream car for your sixteenth birthday. I had to wait a lot longer."

"Well, *my* dream car didn't cost a small fortune," I shoot back, smiling. "You can't compare the two. The Defender was Tristen's baby *long* before you came along."

That gets me a chuckle.

"Ha, very true. I was actually saving for a used Bronco when Dad came up with that idea."

"I think it's great. She suits you." Rhys's Defender is a girl, you see. However, I've never asked *how* he determined that. "With the eight-cylinder engine and four-wheel drive, you just run over everything in your way, exactly like in every other part of your life."

I genuinely enjoy that we can banter again like we used to. The small voice in my head that has continuously reminded me of Rhys's part in the betrayal has lessened. It still perks up, but not as frequently anymore.

His eyes crinkle, and he bumps my shoulder. "No wonder guys are scared of you. You know your cars, you're a black belt, and you can hit your mark with Dad's .45 better than anyone I know—*including me.*"

Now I roll my eyes, but my cheeks heat, nonetheless. His compliment makes me self-conscious. I don't think I'm anything special; I like what I like. And that includes gymnastics, martial arts, cars, and being on the range.

I don't want him to see how his words affect me, so I just return the shoulder bump, saying, "Whatever," and walk into the house without turning back.

Tomorrow morning, we leave on our trip, and if everything goes well, I will find out what happened to me.

## RHYS

Lilly disappears to her room after dinner with the excuse that she needs to talk to Denielle about the schedule for the next few days. She's avoided making eye contact with me since I complimented her by the car.

I'm aware that I made her uncomfortable but couldn't stop my stupid mouth before the words came out. Damn brain-to-mouth connection went offline as it usually does when I get too comfortable with her. I contemplate if I should say something. Apologize? But in the end, all I did was tell her the truth. Most guys in school tuck their tails and run when it comes to her. And that's not because she's *the QB's little sister*. She may not realize it, but she can be pretty intimidating all by herself. Add Denielle to the mix, and you get a recipe for "don't fuck with us." Denielle is fiercely protective of Lilly, which earned her the nickname "Bulldog" a few years ago—not that I'd call her that to her face. She's scary as fuck to anyone who is not in her inner circle. No one without a vagina voluntarily approaches her. Not that I'm complaining, either. That way, I don't have to worry about potential boyfriends. I'm a possessive dick when it comes to *my girl*—sue me.

It was bad enough when I saw Scott Grier, one of Charlie's friends, tongue-diving in her mouth at Sloane's end-of-summer party. Let's just say that night did not end well for anyone involved. I almost blew my cover. The urge to beat the shit out of the asshole was overwhelming. It also didn't help that none of us were sober. When Scott stumbled into me on his way to the patio, I had my opening. I ended up getting a good punch in, but Kat was livid. *Her boyfriend does not behave like a pubescent Neanderthal.*

*Yes, ma'am.*

It was one of the few times we fought. Usually, I just let her rant and move on. But that night, I yelled back and stormed away like a little bitch. Not my most manly moment, but I was also pissed at myself for dropping my act. Immediately after my embarrassing exit, I ran into Lilly in the hallway to the downstairs bathroom. Still amped up from sucker-punching the little tongue fucker, followed by getting ridiculed by my pretend girlfriend, I lost it on her. Asking if she enjoyed having Scott's tongue down her throat in front of everyone like a cheap cheerleader was probably the low point of our relationship. Her eyes had widened, and that was the last I'd seen of her at a party I attended.

*Yup, I think I need to apologize to her—at least for that stunt.*

I'M FINALLY in bed by ten, after Dad gives me another lecture on how to keep Lilly *safe* as if I am still the sixteen-year-old boy he told to stay away from *his sister.* When he is satisfied that I understand all his instructions, I'm *dismissed.* It takes a lot of self-restraint not to salute him. I wonder if he'll ever get that I'm not one of his little soldiers. I want to remind him that he's freaking retired from the Marine Corps, and I'm his son. His. Son. Not his Marine. But that probably wouldn't go over well, so I swallow my retort and leave, closing the door a little bit more forceful than necessary. My bad—not.

IT'S 3:47 A.M., and my alarm is set for four. I've barely slept all night. I rotate through my three pillows and change positions for the hundredth fucking time, but nothing helps. At one point, I'm so frustrated that I hurl my comforter off the bed but start freezing almost immediately—not surprising when one has the window open in the dead of winter. I pick it back up with a sigh.

I can't stop thinking about Lilly, about what we'll potentially find and how it'll impact her life. I seriously question if we're making a mistake going to California. Mom and Dad have been paranoid for ten years, and there has to be a reason for it. Then, there is the fact that we'll be spending a lot of time in close quarters. I hope I can keep it together and not dry hump her in my sleep —that wouldn't be weird at all, nope. It's been fairly easy to stay in control since we can't be seen together, but that'll change as soon as we hit the road. Ten days, here we come.

*I. Can. Do. This.*

My little pep talk done, I throw my covers off and disable the alarm.

The coffeemaker takes unusually long this morning; at least, that's how it seems while I wait. I need caffeine—a lot of caffeine— if I want to make it through the fifteen-hour drive.

While waiting for my fix, I decide to make Lilly her usual morning drink: Earl Grey tea, no sugar or anything. I have no clue how she can drink that.

Lilly walks in around four-fifty and smiles broadly when she sees me holding out her white Yeti travel mug which she bought to match her white Jeep. To say that she has a fixation for color coordination is an understatement.

She is wearing black yoga pants with a white tank and a black— what I'm told is a Barre sweatshirt over it. Don't ask me what a Barre sweatshirt is, but Kat had a whole ten-minute lecture for me when I had called something similar a *sweater* a few weeks ago. Lilly has a massive scarf wrapped around her neck and her chocolate-brown UGGs on. The entire outfit is casual, but the way it accentuates her toned body, I have to pick my jaw up off the floor. Holy shit, this trip is going to test my self-restraint.

She grabs the mug, and her fingers brush against mine ever so slightly. "Let's do this!"

*Something* stirs in my pants at the contact, and I readjust myself as soon as she turns away.

*Fuck, I'm never going to make it ten days.*

She sounds a lot more confident than I feel, but I decide this is about her—and her only. I'm here to help and support her, and that's what I'll do. I can do this.

We're on the way out the front door when Dad appears at the foot of the stairs. He rubs his eyes and squints against the kitchen light that I was just about to switch off.

"I was just going to see you kids off." He gives me a hard look, and I hold his gaze.

*Really?*

He extends his arms out to Lilly, and, after a glance in my direction, she crosses the distance and lets him hug her. She has avoided any type of physical contact with either of my parents since the secret came out. I can see how stiff her posture is.

"We gotta get going if we want to meet up with the others on time, Lil-ly." I emphasize her name and try to sound annoyed that I got stuck chauffeuring her.

She takes a step back and plays along perfectly. "Caaalm. Dooown. We're fifteen minutes ahead of schedule, thanks to you stomping around like an elephant this morning."

I'm so proud of her for sounding like a massive brat that I have to press my lips together to hide my grin. She turns toward me and is also struggling to keep her composure. At that moment, we're just two kids conspiring against their parents, and my body buzzes with excitement.

Dad gives us one more lecture on driving safe and checking in daily before he lets us walk out the door.

# CHAPTER FOURTEEN

### LILLY

Leaving town, we're the only ones on the street. Most houses are still dark, and I'm watching the barely visible landscape go by as I relax into the leather seat. We're on the road for over an hour before Rhys speaks. "I think we should cover as much ground as possible and then stop somewhere for the night."

I take a sip from my tea and nod. "Yeah, makes sense. What were you thinking?"

"Well, we left early enough. If we trade off, we could make it to Des Moines by tonight."

I stare at him. "Iowa? That's what, over a thousand miles?"

Rhys barks out a laugh. "Yes, Calla, Des Moines, Iowa. You do realize we're on a time crunch."

Ugh, he's right.

"What if this entire trip is useless and we don't find anything?" I hate voicing my doubt; after all, he gave up skiing for this.

His face sobers, and the elongated silence makes me shift in my seat. "Then we tried our best, and we'll find another way to get the information."

His encouraging words make my doubts feel a little less dooming.

. . .

THE QUIET IN the car is beginning to get to me. I think about walking into the hospital where I was found, which causes the usual tsunami of emotions to build up. I need a distraction.

"What kind of music do you want to listen to?"

"I don't care, plug your phone in," he responds, concentrating on the road.

Before Tristen handed the Defender over to Rhys, he had a new sound system installed, and instead of the old cassette deck, we can now connect our phones. When he presented the change to us, I informed him, outraged, that this was sacrilege; he totally ruined the car. The cassette deck was part of *her*.

*I guess I agree with Rhys that the Defender is a girl.*

I scroll through my playlists and smirk to myself. Hitting play, "Fear of the Dark" by Van Canto comes through the also newly installed speakers.

Rhys gawks at me incredulously before returning his eyes to the road.

"Very appropriate," he deadpans.

I grin broadly. "I figure it's time to lighten the mood a bit. Why not with some good music?"

He chuckles. "You're the only girl I've ever met that would listen to this *and* Brantley Gilbert in the same playlist."

I shrug, trying to look serious but failing. "Your point?"

He is smiling to himself, focused on the road. I watch him a moment longer before turning my head toward the passenger window. I feel tears well up in my eyes but don't want Rhys to see it.

Why did I never notice that we don't look anything alike? That I don't look like any of them. I should've seen it ages ago. Rhys and Natty both have wavy brown hair. You can't see it nowadays because Rhys keeps his hair so short. Tristen's hair is almost black, and not counting Heather's highlights, hers is dark as well. All four have a natural tan—even in the winter. I, on the other hand, am on the complete other end of the spectrum. I have spaghetti-straight, light-blonde hair and have to buy the lightest foundation there is for my complexion.

It takes me a while to get myself under control. Thankfully, it's just now getting light outside, and I'm able to hide the tears in the darkness.

We're both deep in thought, but eventually, I have to voice the question I've been pondering for a while. "Can I ask you something?"

"Sure." He is so focused on driving that he doesn't notice the quiver in my voice.

I eye him sideways. I'm too chicken to face him straight on. "Was it weird for you when I moved in?"

That gets his attention. His lips form a thin line, and he's trying to figure out how to answer the question. Rhys has always been honest with me—well, with everything except who I am and why he stopped talking to me. Okay, scratch that, maybe not always, but I knew he would be with this, and until now, I wasn't sure I was ready to hear his answer.

"Maybe a little." He pauses, taking a breath. "I mean, we had hung out for as long as I can remember. I think it was weirder that, all of a sudden, Emily and Henry were out of the picture and you acted like nothing ever happened. Before, you always cried when you stayed with us for a few hours by yourself. It was kind of...I don't know...creepy. It took some time to get used to you calling Mom and Dad *not* Heather and Tristen. I kept waiting for you to snap out of it, but you never did."

*I was creepy.*

How does one respond to that? I can only whisper, "I'm sorry."

He scowls and briefly looks over. "Huh? What for?"

What indeed? It's not like any of this is my fault. But I can't shake the feeling of being the cause of so many people's cruel fates: Rhys, Heather, Tristen, the girls that got kidnapped because I *disappeared*.

"I feel like all I've done is cause trouble."

He frowns. "Don't be ridiculous, Cal. None of this is your fault. If anyone is at fault, it's the psycho who took you." Once again, he knows exactly what I'm thinking. Then, the crinkles between his eyebrows disappear, and he looks almost sad. "I'm sorry, too."

I stare at him with an expression that must look to him like a big question mark, because he continues, "For treating you like shit the last few years, and also for how I sprung everything on you. I was a selfish asshole and just wanted the secrets to be over."

I let that sink in for a moment and realize something fundamental. "I understand." *I do.* "I mean, why you did it. I'm not mad anymore. I don't know what I would have done. If I could have been as strong as you..." I trail off.

Rhys's mouth tilts upward, but it doesn't reach his eyes. "I was *far* from strong. I've done a lot of things I am not proud of to forget you and distract myself. Though, nothing has worked; all I could do was try to stay as far away as possible but still be able to watch out for you. When you told me about your migraines, I just couldn't stand by anymore. It was my chance at coming clean...with everything." He pauses before adding, "Like I said...selfish."

I'm swept up by a flash flood of emotions. Confusion about what Rhys has done that he's not proud of. Sadness and guilt that he had to go through all this because of me. Happiness for having him back in my life and not being alone on this journey. With this short exchange, the last bit of the wall that separated us is gone. I thought I would be terrified when it happened. I didn't want him having the power to hurt me again, but instead, I'm...calm. There is no fear, just contentment about having my friend back.

WHEN I BLINK my eyes open, I am blinded by the glare from an SUV's windshield parked across from us.

*When did I fall asleep?*

We're at a gas station, and my neck is stiff from being slumped sideways for who knows how long. The sun is high in the sky, and I glance at my watch; it's almost two in the afternoon. Holy cow, I slept for hours. That clearly explains the sharp pain when I first moved my head.

The driver side door opens, and Rhys climbs in, putting two cellophane-wrapped sandwiches, a bag of chips, and two apples in the middle.

He hands me a water. "One turkey, and one ham and cheese. And I called home. I told Dad we made it, and you're checking out the slopes with Den. *You're* to call them tomorrow." Rhys apologizes as if it's his fault.

I nod, thankful to him for making the call, but not looking forward to tomorrow's conversation. Maybe I'll call Heather's cell instead of the house phone; that way, it's less likely that I'll get Tristen. I'm convinced he'd immediately call me out on not being where I say I am. When he showed up at the foot of the stairs this morning, I was close to confessing everything myself.

"Why don't I drive for a bit? You can use the rest."

*And I won't be able to think.*

Rhys sighs gratefully.


## RHYS


I'M PHYSICALLY EXHAUSTED, but when I can't fall asleep, I start messing around with my phone. After a few miles, Lilly suggests, "Let's play a game!"

"A game?" She sounds a little too cheery, and I scowl suspiciously.

"Yeah! Let's play twenty questions!"

My scowl deepens. What are we? Twelve?

Lilly glances over excitedly. "We have over two years to make up for, and it's not fair that you were secretly part of my life, but I missed everything that happened in yours."

She genuinely wants to get to know me again. She's not taking a stab at me to make me feel guilty. This could be fun. *Or fucking disastrous.*

"This should be...interesting. Let's do it." I attempt to sound as cheery as she is. Her entire face lights up, and all trepidation about the potential consequences of playing this game evaporates. Seeing her happy is so worth it.

"Okay, let's start easy. Favorite movie in the last two years?" She all but bounces in the seat.

Maybe this *is* going to be enjoyable. "That's easy. *Captain America: Civil War*. Yours?"

She chuckles, eyes never leaving the road. "Ha, I probably could've guessed that one. Let me think...It's a close tie between *Resident Evil: The Final Chapter* and *Underworld: Blood Wars*."

I make a mock shocked face. "You're over *Blade: Trinity*?"

She had forced me to watch that movie so many times, because she had a girl-crush on Abigail Whistler, that it became a running joke. I could recite half the movie at one point. My favorite quotes were obviously from Hannibal King; he's freaking awesome. "*I just have two things to say to you. One, your hairdo is ridiculous. And two, I ate a bunch of garlic and I just farted. Silent but deadly.*"

Did I mention that Hannibal is hi-lar-i-ous?

Lilly pulls me out of the memory when her eyes flick to me briefly and she looks appalled. "Never. I would never cheat on Whistler, but we're talking the last *two* years here."

"Point taken. Okay, my turn." I try to come up with the next question. "What's the song you've listened to most in the last few months? Not counting anything Nightwish, Freedom Call, or Van Canto."

"Excluding my favorites is not fair! Well…" She pauses, opens her mouth, and closes it again before answering, "Probably 'Helsinki' by The National Parks. Yours?"

Without hesitating, I say, "'Good Goodbye'."

Lilly does a double-take. "Linkin Park's 'Good Goodbye'?"

She smoothes her expression so quickly and concentrates back on the road that I can't figure out what she is thinking.

"Yes, why?"

"Nothing." Her answer comes a little too quickly.

That was…odd. We're quiet for a moment, and I take in the flattening landscape; we have officially entered the Midwest.

Lilly continues, "What are you going to do next year? I mean, where do you plan to go to school?"

Ah, the topic I've been avoiding for months. I've received partial scholarships to two schools, but I don't want to be away from Lilly—I just got her back. Even before I told her the truth, I didn't want to leave her. Call me lovesick…or co-dependent—or both.

Attempting to sound neutral, I mumble, "I'm not sure; I want to stay close by. I have the option of an athletic scholarship for South Carolina or Georgia, but I'm hoping for something closer." *To you,* I mentally add. "I also applied to Virginia Tech and VMI." VMI is Dad's alma mater, and in a way, I had hoped it would improve our relationship. We used to be super close until the day he pulled me aside and told me I had to get a grip on my feelings or he'd *figure* something out. Figure out my ass. His ultimatum basically made me move out. Since that day, our conversations have been nothing but surface level. Mostly because I let resentment rule our relationship, but deep down, I still want my father to be proud of me.

"VMI? Since when are you interested in the military?" Lilly's eyes widen in surprise, and I focus back on our conversation.

"I'm not. I guess I was trying to make Dad happy." I pretend it's not a big deal. Though, her raised eyebrows tell me that she knows better.

"Didn't you also just visit Georgetown? Heather's alma mater?"

She doesn't press the VMI topic, and I appreciate it. I expected the Georgetown question. Lilly is perceptive, and Mom did go to law school there. I'm facing the window. "Yeah, but that was more for Kat than me."

"I see," is Lilly's response.

Peering over, I notice her suddenly tense posture. Her playfulness is gone.

"Have you decided what you want to do yet?"

"No, not really. I'm thinking of something with math or computers. I have another year to figure it out."

A selfish thought crosses my mind, and I give her a grin. "Virginia Tech?"

Her eyes crinkle. "Maybe." Then, she looks like she's about to add something but stops herself and presses her lips together.

"What is it, Cal?"

Her gaze flicks to me for a fraction of a second.

"I, uh...I've kind of started playing with the idea of going back to the West Coast. Going back to where I'm originally from, you know?" She avoids eye contact, and I can't read her at all.

"That, uh...yeah, I mean, that's kinda understandable." My stomach clenches.

*God, I'm so screwed.*

She quickly adds, "We'll see; I have other priorities now." She's probably misinterpreting my unenthusiastic reaction.

After a while, we continue the game, asking questions back and forth. Anything from favorite book, to the top five places we would want to visit, to if you could speak one other language fluently, what would it be?

Lilly is not surprised when I tell her that I want to visit Rome. The Colosseum, gladiators—what else could you want, right?

However, I did not anticipate her desire to speak Latin. I would've expected Italian, or even something like Mandarin. She already takes Spanish and French in school, but she says Latin is a classic language. It provides the root words for all of the modern sciences.

When I remain quiet, she explains, "Every type of science has its own vocabulary: biology, chemistry, astronomy, even computer science. We think of it all as individual, but essentially, all the specialized words are derived from the classical languages, Latin or Greek. Computer comes from the Latin word computo, to count. Or here is another example: the vernal equinox is the one day of spring when day and night are equal. Vernal comes from the Latin word for spring: ver, veris. Like pasta prima*vera*...spring pasta, get it?"

*What the—?*

I am completely stunned by the speech she just delivered. I gape at her, resembling a goldfish.

She laughs out loud. "You didn't expect that, huh?"

"Uh." I still can't form a coherent sentence.

"Yeah, I developed a slight fascination with it after we had a short lecture in history last year."

*Slight?*

It sinks in that there is so much I have missed the last few years, and a wave of irritation that my parents have kept me from sharing all this with Lilly crashes through my body.

I END up napping for about an hour between questions ten and eleven. The game makes the time fly by, and we reach our destination a little after nine o'clock. We pick a motel close to the interstate to not lose too much time in the morning.

The room is simple. The bathroom is off to the right, the two beds are covered with floral quilts that have seen better times, and a small window is exactly opposite the entrance. Across from the beds is a desk and a dresser with a TV on it. The TV is the most modern thing in the entire room, even though it seems to be older than Natty. But it appears to be clean, which is all I care about for tonight.

We take turns in the bathroom, and I flop onto my bed, not even bothering with the cover. I'm about to doze off when I hear Lilly. "Rhys?"

"Hmm?"

"Thanks. For being here, I mean."

I smile into my pillow. "I wouldn't want to be anywhere else."

# CHAPTER FIFTEEN

## LILLY

RHYS'S ALARM GOES OFF AT FIVE, AND WE'RE BACK ON THE ROAD by six. Seven hours of sleep is more than I've gotten most nights lately, but I am still grateful that we stop for caffeine before we hit the interstate.

Rhys takes the first shift driving, and I gaze out of the side window into the dark. My mind keeps replaying yesterday's twenty question game. It was fun to get to know him *again* and also see his reaction to some of my answers. His face was priceless when I explained why I would want to speak Latin.

I could've guessed maybe a quarter of his answers; the rest I had no idea. His response to his favorite song caught me off guard, though. When picking my song, I was between "Helsinki" and "Good Goodbye," and when Rhys said Linkin Park, I experienced this fluttery feeling in my belly. But I mean, it's just a song—no big deal.

THE MORNING STRETCH goes by pretty quickly, and Rhys tells me this story about Wes dating a girl from another school that has me in tears—the laughing kind.

"She was cute and actually really nice—not like some of the other chicks he'd been seeing, where all that counted was their ass or the size of their rack." Rhys rolls his eyes. "Anyway, he tries to surprise her and sneak in her window one night; he'd done it before. But he doesn't know that her grandmother is staying with them for the week, and the girl is bunking with the little sister across the hall. He ends up waking up the grandmother, who screams bloody murder and beats him with her cane until he just jumps out of the window and takes off running for a good five blocks. His car was still at the house." Rhys is cracking up while he talks, and by the time he finishes, I have tears running down my cheeks.

That could only happen to Wes. He could have almost any girl by merely snapping his fingers. With his naturally bronze skin and shaggy blond hair, he looks like he belongs in a surf ad. This year, he showed up with a mohawk on the first day of school, which gave him an *Abercrombie-model-turned-bad-boy* vibe. Every girl in a thirty-foot radius stopped what they were doing and instantly started drooling—well, besides Den and me. But even Denielle admitted that he looked smokin'—her words, not mine. Don't get me wrong, Wes is absolutely gorgeous, but I've known him most of my life. I'm probably one of the few females that doesn't want him *that* way. He's been Rhys's best friend for a decade, and he was a good friend to me, even during the last two years. Though, I don't think Rhys is aware of that. When we first moved back, years ago, he had started flirting with me, but I'm positive it was never anything serious. However, I can now see how it could've pushed Rhys in ways I *never* anticipated. Long story short, Wes and me—not going to happen.

I pull down the visor and see that I have raccoon eyes. I try to fix my mascara as much as possible without having my makeup bag in reach.

We talk about our sessions with Spence. Rhys explains how Spence has been incorporating wrestling moves into the sparring lessons, and I'm intrigued. Spence and I have been mostly working on defense moves, and now I realize that this must have been on purpose. I'm supposed to learn how to defend myself against an assailant. But I'm not sure if that means Spence is in on the secret or if he just follows Tristen's orders. Either way, I don't like it. That's another part of my life that was manipulated. My teeth automatically clench.

I wish I had already called home. Now I have to make sure to sound calm and like someone who's having the time of her life on her first real trip away with her best friend. I'm going to need mental prep time. And I'm definitely calling Heather's cell; there is no way I can pretend with Tristen.

Rhys pulls me out of my internal rant. "Maybe we could start training together again sometime?"

The idea makes me smile. "I'd like that."

I really would; our joined sessions were always fun. We could spin it in a way that I need a different opponent whose moves I'm not used to.

*Not anymore.*

WE STOP at a small Mom-and-Pop diner attached to the local gas station for lunch. It's almost noon, and between bites of my chicken sandwich, I suggest that we should push it as far as possible again. Rhys pulls up the route on his phone, and we settle on Salt Lake City. That'll make the last day only around ten hours if everything goes smoothly.

We trade off every few hours, which allows both of us to nap some throughout the afternoon. As before, we settle on a motel close to our route, and the entire setup is similar to last night. Rhys gets ready for bed first today, and I use the time to dial Heather's phone. I make up a story about Charlie tripping as we got off the lift and Den faceplanting in the snow. Heather laughs, and the entire check-in takes less than five minutes. Yet, it drains the last bit of energy I have left.

Rhys suggests ordering something from the room service menu. Well, menu is an overstatement. It's a piece of paper with three items scribbled on it and has been copied one too many times. We settle on grilled cheese and scrambled eggs with bacon. The menu must be for all three main meals.

While we wait, I take a shower and change into my flannel pajama pants. I throw on an oversized Henley that was on top in my bag and realize that it's not mine. I look down at myself. I must've grabbed Rhys's shirt from last night when I threw everything into my bag this morning. I can't go back out since this is the only top I have with me in the bathroom. The shirt I wore all day smells like I ran a marathon. I guess this will have to do. It's comfy and, taking a whiff of the armpit area, doesn't stink.

Rhys hollers through the door, "Dinner is here."

I step out of the bathroom, and his eyes go wide, followed by him scrambling for the remote.

Thanks to the shower, I'm awake enough to eat my grilled cheese.

## RHYS

SEEING Lilly walk out of the bathroom, my eyes widen, and my breath hitches in my throat. I choke on my saliva and start violently coughing.

*Holy fuck!*

Heat shoots through my body. Never in a million years could I have imagined seeing one of my *fantasies* come to life, and definitely not *here*. When I checked my bag, I thought I had left that shirt at the last hotel, which sucked since it was one of my favorites.

I can't stop gawking and stifle a groan. Blood is traveling to places it definitely should not be. I shift around to find a less...constricting position. Even though my shirt is way too big on her frame, the way the neckline slides down to reveal the top of her right shoulder is sexy as hell. It is by far the hottest thing I have ever seen.

My palms are sweating, and I'm fighting the urge to grab her, push her against the wall, and devour her mouth with mine. This is not good. Not. Good. At. All.

I need something to distract myself, something to snap myself out of staring like a complete perv. I fumble for the remote and turn the TV on. I start scanning the channels like a maniac—there has to be something. I stumble upon an old episode of Baywatch.

*I didn't realize they're still showing reruns.*

Half-naked chicks are so not helping my current dilemma. I

shift again for some subtle rearrangement in the groin region and press the channel button. Bingo! It's the History Channel. It looks like it's a show about hairy dudes living in the back country somewhere.

*Much better.*

I settle down on my bed and shove a forkful of eggs into my mouth. Crisis averted.

When I'm fully in control, I peer over at Lilly and notice she's asleep with her plate still sitting next to her. I remove the plate, put it on the nightstand, and cover her with the blanket she, thankfully, already pulled back. I don't know if my self-restraint would've lasted if I had to touch her to move her under it. I need to get back to the bearded dudes. Like. Right. Now.

I WAKE UP COMPLETELY DISORIENTED. It's pitch black, and the alarm clock by my bed displays three-twelve.

*What the fuck?*

*Still* trying to figure out why I'm awake, I hear it and bolt right up. My eyes have adjusted to the dark, and I can make out Lilly curled up in the middle of her bed, covers tangled, and whimpering.

I jump out of bed but stop with my shins pressed against her mattress, hesitant to move any closer. I'm not sure what to do. Long strands of her pale hair are plastered against her forehead and cheeks. Even in the dark, I can see she is drenched in sweat. I don't want to scare her, but when her whimpering starts back up and she mumbles, "*No, no, no,*" I can't watch any longer. I carefully lower myself down onto the edge of her bed with my hand hovering above her. The whimpering turns into something resembling a strangled animal, and I gently put my hand on her back, trying to soothe her. "Calla? Cal, wake up. You're dreaming."

*How original, dude.*

It takes a few more attempts of rubbing her back and calling her name before she jolts upright and scans the room wildly. She zeros in on me, eyes wide, and scoots to the far end of the bed, pulling her knees to her chest.

*Shit, that's exactly what I didn't want to happen.*

I'm turned toward her, one leg on the bed, the other still on the floor, and I hold my hands up. "Cal, it's me."

She blinks once, twice. "Rhys?" Her voice sounds so unsure.

"Yes, you're safe." I slowly lower my hands to my leg on the bed.

She briefly closes her eyes before she launches herself into my arms and starts sobbing.

*Holy fuck, what is going on?*

I'm completely helpless. My arms wrap around her, and I rub her back, rocking her back and forth. "Shhhh, it's okay. You're safe. I won't let anything happen to you, babe."

*Babe?*

I want to smack my forehead. The last thing she needs right now is her horny, adopted-brother-slash-friend making a move on her.

After a while, she calms down, and I risk asking, "What happened?"

But she shakes her head against my chest.

Eventually, her breathing slows, and she is falling back asleep. I maneuver her back under the covers, and I stand up to go to my bed when her hand shoots out, grabbing my wrist.

"Don't go!"

I glance back at her. She looks so small.

"You need rest, Lilly." I consciously use her name this time; I don't want another slip-up.

"I know." She pauses. "Please stay." The last two words are barely audible.

I freeze at her request, heart pounding in my chest. She makes room but remains propped up on her elbow, holding my wrist with her other hand. I shouldn't, but this may be my only chance to be close to her. My head is telling me to go to bed, she'll be okay, but my heart wants to stay and comfort her. I stare down at her, and neither of us makes a move.

*Fuck it.*

I climb in and pull the cover over both of us. Without a word, she curls into my chest, and only seconds later, her breathing evens out. She is tucked under my chin, and I can smell remnants of her coconut shampoo. Carefully wrapping my arm around her, I make sure it's above the covers to avoid something inappropriate happening in my sleep.

*At this point, anything is possible.*

As I start to drift off, I think about how I'm going to give in to my selfish side only this once, but before I even finish that thought, I know deep down that's not true.

If she asks me again, I'll cave.

# CHAPTER SIXTEEN

**LILLY**

I'M IN THE FOGGY STATE BETWEEN SLEEP AND AWAKE. THAT POINT when reality slowly seeps in but you're technically still asleep. When the fog starts lifting, awareness crashes down on me with lightning speed. I can't move.

*What the—?*

Arms are wrapped around me, and instant panic sets in. I'm about to fight when I get a whiff of Rhys's signature shower gel scent, and the events from last night come flooding back. My body immediately goes still.

*The nightmare.* No, not nightmare—memory. I'm sure of it. The most vivid—*and worst*—one yet.

I remember when I came to, all I saw was *him* sitting on my bed again. I had to blink several times to comprehend it was Rhys in front of me, not him. My clothes were drenched in sweat, and I had no control over the violent tremors wracking through my body. Not wanting to be a victim anymore, I fought the urge to cry, but at that moment, I was six years old again. All I wanted was my best friend —exactly like it was ten years ago, which this memory revealed to me as well.

After my flood of tears subsided, I felt calmer, but then Rhys attempted to go to his bed, and my insides were gripped with terror.

*I can't be alone. I don't want to be alone* kept running through my head. Instinctively, my arm shot out and locked onto his wrist. "Don't go!" I'm sure he could hear the quiver in my voice. The internal struggle was visible on his face even in the dark, but then he slid into bed next to me, and...I was safe.

Lying here like this, wrapped in this safety cocoon, my head tells me I should be embarrassed. I shouldn't have asked him to stay. I should've been stronger. Rhys has a girlfriend—maybe a fake one, but a girlfriend. The voice in my head hurls one accusation after the other at me, and I cringe inwardly. It's all true, but when I am honest with myself, for the first time in weeks, I feel completely and utterly safe.

I relish that sensation a moment longer before I slowly ease out of his arms, and Rhys flops on his stomach. I look down at him, grateful for his presence on this trip, and head to the bathroom to wash last night's grime off my body.

As I step out of the shower, I hear the alarm go off and Rhys scrambling out of my bed to his phone. I finish getting ready and step back into the hotel room, finding Rhys sitting on his bed. His arms are resting on his thighs, head hanging low, and shoulders visibly tense. My steps slow.

"Good morning." I announce my entrance tentatively, hoping he doesn't feel weirded out after last night. I broke down in his arms for the second time in three weeks. We never established new boundaries after his love declaration. I've been too preoccupied with myself and have completely ignored his feelings.

"Hey." He looks slightly more at ease when he sees me, and his posture relaxes, but there is still a wary undertone. I brace myself for him to say something about what happened, to ask questions, but all he does is get up and duck into the bathroom. "Let me get ready, and we can hit the road."

*Avoidance it is. Works for me.*

We've been driving for two hours in complete silence when Rhys finally asks the question I've been waiting for.

"Do you want to talk about it?" He keeps his voice at a whisper as if not to scare me.

I've been facing the window, thinking about exactly that since we left the hotel. Do I? Since last night, all the rage and betrayal has been replaced by the desperate need for safety. The safety I felt waking up this morning. I know this can't last. I need the other emotions to see this through, not to be a victim. But at this moment, the need to be anchored wins. I take a deep breath. "I had a nightmare." After another long inhale and exhale, I turn toward him and add, "I think."

Rhys draws his eyebrows together. "You think?"

"It wasn't *just* a nightmare. I think it was a memory." I sound hoarse.

The car is slowing down. "What do you mean?" His gaze keeps switching between the road and me.

Blood pounding in my ears and hands shaking uncontrollably, I know I have to tell him. I rush it out before changing my mind. "I was back in that room. I was so scared. The man was in the room with me, and he, uh...he was talking to me."

Rhys slams on the brakes and moves over to the side of the road, ignoring the car behind us honking ferociously. As soon as the car comes to a stop, he turns to me. "Did he hurt you?" His face is chalk white.

"No!" I force my mind back to the memory, trying to recall his words. "He was sitting at the foot of the bed. He kept saying things like, 'I had no idea you existed. I'm so happy I found you after losing Audrey. You'll be happy. We're family.' He didn't threaten me or anything, but..." Panic rises back up, and I try to calm my breathing. "I could *feel* how confused and scared I was. The fear of not seeing my parents again. Or you."

Rhys is rigid, and his eyebrows shoot up almost to his hairline. "Me?"

I look at my hands in my lap, heat creeping up my face. "Yeah, I, uh...I remembered wishing you'd be with me and that you'd...um, come and take me home."

Rhys's hand is over mine, interlacing our fingers, and he gives my hand a gentle squeeze. "You're safe now. Did he say anything else?"

I contemplate if I should tell him the next part. He's already way too worked up. But if not him, who else?

"He..." Deep breath. "He gave me something—drugged me." I keep talking to our joined hands, and the more I say, the more Rhys's hand tightens on mine.

"I think it was in the water. I kept telling him I didn't want it, but he said that until I trusted him, it'd be safer for me. He didn't want me to hurt myself again."

Rhys goes completely rigid; my hand is in a vise in his, and he rasps, "Again?"

A whimper escapes me, and he releases his death grip. Instead, he latches onto the steering wheel.

"I don't remember being hurt. What does this mean? Rhys, who is Audrey?" Not that he would know any of that. If it is even real. I mean, that guy was crazy, right?

I watch Rhys closely as he works on gaining control again. The color slowly returns to his face, and his white-knuckle grip on the steering wheel loosens. Taking a deep breath, he says, "I don't know, but we've got more clues. This is good." His voice sounds disconnected, and he won't make eye contact. He puts the car back in drive and pulls out onto the road without another word. I don't like it.


THE ONLY SOUND during the next few hours is the radio. Neither of us connects our phone. It's like the wall has reappeared. He only asks what I want to eat when we stop at a gas station and then goes back to driving. He doesn't give me a turn either. I can't read him, and I'm starting to freak out. I haven't done anything wrong, but he has completely withdrawn. The distance between us brings the loneliness back. Fear and anxiety start churning deep in my core. The safety I felt this morning has evaporated, and I need to fix this. Whatever *this* is.

Finally, I can't take it anymore. "Rhys, talk to me. What did I do?"

His gaze flicks over to me. "Huh?" The wheels start turning, and I wait. Then it clicks, and the light comes on. "Uh. Oh! Fuck." He expels a long breath. "I'm sorry, Cal. This just...I've been thinking.

What you said earlier...I asked, but hearing it...what happened to you. Fuck." He shakes his head. "You were scared, and you wanted me to save you. ME! I feel like someone gutted me. I let you down."

*What?*

I thought he was angry, but instead, he believes he failed me? I'm at a loss. The fluttery feeling in my belly is back, but instead of trying to decipher the stir, I attempt to reassure him. "You were a child. There is no way you could've done anything, even if you'd been there."

He nods but still sounds dejected. "I can't help it."

He resembles a little boy, and I act on instinct. I reach over and grab the hand closest to me from the steering wheel, interlacing our fingers. Rhys's eyes widen for a fraction of a second, but he doesn't look away from the road. All the tension leaves his body, and he squeezes my hand back. He may not have been the one taken, but I understand more and more that his life changed that day as well. We're in this together, no matter what I've been telling myself.

AFTER WE CLEARED THE AIR, Rhys is more relaxed, and the crease between his brows has disappeared. He connected his phone to the car a little while ago, and one of his favorite rock playlists replaced the radio. The uncomfortable tension is gone, and I lean my head back, watching the landscape pass by. I didn't realize how wound tight I was myself and suddenly feel completely worn out. I let the music fill my brain and block everything else out. I pretend to be a regular girl on a road trip. Just for a little while, I want to forget about all the chaos and questions in my life.

## CHAPTER SEVENTEEN

### LILLY

WE'RE ABOUT AN HOUR OUT OF SANTA ROSA, AND I'M A WRECK.
*Again.* My earlier relaxation is gone, including the girl from this
morning that was ready to take this whole disaster of a life head-on.
It's like she stayed behind somewhere along the way.

I can't stop flipping my fingers against my thumb. Back and
forth, back and forth. It's a tic I've had forever and a tell for
everyone who knows me. Rhys has already asked three times if I'm
okay, and I think if I hear the question one more time, I may lose it.
I grind my teeth together.

"Should we go straight to the hospital or wait until the
morning?"

*Oh, thank God he's not asking if I'm okay again.*

However, his new question turns my stomach to knots. I peer at
my watch. It'll be close to five by the time we get there.

"Let's give it a shot," I say before I lose my barely existing
courage.


WE ARRIVE at the hospital that was listed on my discharge papers
at ten to five. It's not huge but larger than I anticipated for a place
like Santa Rosa.

*I'm so close to potentially getting answers.*

But when I climb out of the Defender, I'm a mess. The need for answers that has kept me going for the last two-plus weeks has exited, and a sour taste in my mouth makes it hard to swallow. Do I really want to know? What if I'm making a mistake? Maybe I should've waited longer? Should I have talked to Heather and Tristen after all?

I'm convinced any shrink would diagnose me with some type of mental instability at this point. Though, would that be a surprise for someone who was kidnapped and had her memory erased? I can't keep track of all my contradicting emotions, let alone keep them in check. I go from betrayal and anger to rage, to feeling safe, to fear and anxiety, to happiness, to uncertainty, back to anger, and now...dread.

*What am I doing here?*

Saliva is pooling in my mouth, which accompanies the nausea and cold sweats that started when we left the interstate ten minutes ago. Is this what a panic attack feels like? My breathing is erratic. Yup, I'm having a panic attack. All I can think is *so much for no longer being the victim*. Who am I kidding? I'm six years old.

*Oh God, I'm going to pass out.*

I'm next to the car, staring at the pavement, as the black spots appear in my vision. I brace myself for the impact with the ground, but instead, I find myself in a bear hug. My face is pressed against soft fabric.

I inhale deeply. Rhys! One arm is wrapped around my waist, the other holds the back of my head; I'm held immobile.

*When did he get so strong?*

His voice tells me to breathe, and I do as I'm told. In, out, in, out.

The nausea slowly subsides, and I lift my arms to return the embrace.

"There you are, babe. You scared me there for a minute."

*Babe?*

That's the second time. Whatever. I'm safe.

We stand like this in the middle of the parking lot for several minutes until I'm back in control. I should be embarrassed by my breakdown, but as if Rhys can read my thoughts, he leans back so he can look me in the eyes, and all I see is understanding.

"You and me, remember?" he whispers, and I nod.

Without another word, he starts walking toward the entrance, and I fall in step beside him. That's it. He knew what I needed, and as soon as it was over, it was time to move on. I marvel at how he does that time and time again—after years of being apart.

W E  STEP  through the rotating door into the foyer, and I stop abruptly. "Where do we go?"

Rhys turns toward me. "I figured we'd start with patient services or the admin department, whatever it's called in a hospital."

That makes sense. "Okay."

He navigates us to the correct door before I can search for a map of this maze. I raise my eyebrows at him as we step off the second-floor escalator opposite two glass doors, but he just shrugs as if to say *I did my research*.

With shaking hands, I push through, and Rhys murmurs from behind, "I'll be back here if you need me."

By the time I glance over my shoulder, he's leaning against the wall next to the door. His arms are crossed over his chest, and one foot is up against the wall. He isn't wearing anything special, just a gray hoodie, faded blue jeans, and his worn black Frye Bowery Chelsea boots he bought years ago. However, his entire posture emanates confidence and strength. I've seen this abrupt change in him many times from afar in school. This is why the entire school puts him on a pedestal and follows his every command. He knows how to take over a situation, and currently, he's giving me the strength to do this on my own. Some of my old confidence returns as I slowly move into the room.

A lone woman in her late twenties sits at one of the four desks. She glances up, and I immediately see that the last thing she wants to do so close to the end of her day is deal with me.

My mouth goes dry as I approach her desk hesitantly. "Excuse me?"

She looks up again, and up close, I can see that she is probably in her early thirties, not twenties. She has wavy red hair which is styled immaculately. So are her makeup and manicured nails. She doesn't belong in a hospital. I glance at her nametag. Nina Farley should be in an ad for shampoo or some sort of beauty product, but not here.

When she waits for me to continue, I clear my throat. "Hi, uh...I'm looking for a nurse who signed my discharge papers ten years ago. I, um...I want to thank her for everything that she did for me back then."

Yeah, that sounds like utter bullshit even to my ears, and Nina is not dumb. Her eyes flick back and forth between Rhys and me.

Her tone is cool when she says, "That is confidential. We don't give out employee information."

I rub my upper arms and fight the urge to find Rhys in the back. I can do this. "I don't need information on her. *I know her name.* I just want to talk to her." I'm not asking for her social security number, just to tell me where to find my nurse.

For a second, I think Nina will help me, but then her gaze flickers to the clock on the side wall, and she repeats again, "I'm sorry, I can't help you."

I'm dismissed. "Please, I—"

I'm ready to plead when two hands land on my shoulder. "Thank you for your time."

What? I turn my head to argue with Rhys, but his expression leaves no room for negotiation. Without another word, he places a hand on my lower back and steers me out into the hallway.

My eyes start to gloss over. We've wasted three days in the car for nothing. We're back to square one. Here comes the waterfall.

*I'm so tired of crying.*

## RHYS

I GUIDE Lilly toward the food court I saw on the map I studied during our quick lunch stop this afternoon. This outcome was a possibility, but nothing had prepared me for the defeat on her face.

She doesn't say anything and lets me lead her to a booth. The bright-red linoleum upholstery and yellow tables are out of place for a hospital. Someone either tried to make this place bright and happy and failed miserably, or they stole the furniture from the McDonalds down the street. Either way, the whole vibe is fucking disturbing.

Lilly stares at her hands, and I grab us two waters and a Coke before settling into the seat across from her.

We sit like this for half an hour. She's in her head, and I wait. There is no point in forcing a conversation. She's dealing.

Our relationship has changed in the last twenty-four hours. It's grown beyond what it used to be—before I turned into an asshole on her. I don't know what we are or what she feels toward me, but my urge to protect her has reached a new high. The strong and confident fighter let me see her vulnerability last night. She asked for my comfort. Even when I first stopped talking to her, she never let me see how much I had hurt her. Her recalling her memory immediately caused a red haze to form over my eyes. How could anyone have done this to an innocent child? And she wanted me. Me! Her words were like continuous front kicks in the gut. She's right; there was nothing I could've done, but still—what would you feel if the girl you love tells you that shit? I need to do something to help her—or at least try.

After she still hasn't said anything thirty minutes later, I come to a decision. "Be right back."

I make out a small nod from her and add, "Keep your phone on you, okay?"

Another head bob.

*Okay then.*

I LEAVE the food court and walk back to the department we left earlier. The lights are off, and the doors are locked. So much for giving that another try.

Next, I head to the emergency department. Thankfully, it's a slow evening. Otherwise, I probably wouldn't have found anyone to talk to. I approach a younger nurse in blue scrubs that comes out of the nurses' station.

"Excuse me?"

Her eyes are glued to a piece of paper in one hand, and she's scribbling on it with the other. How people can do that while walking amazes me. I can't write one freaking word without a stable surface underneath. When she realizes I'm talking to her, her eyebrows shoot up, and she slowly scans me up and down. Yup, I'm aware of the effect I have on females, which was another reason I approached her instead of the older nurse that's on her heels. No, I'm not arrogant. It's just how it's always been. It's not like I use it to my advantage—well, except for maybe right now.

"Can I help you?"

Deep breath. "Yes, uh..."—I glance at her embroidered nametag—"Beth, hi. My name is Rhys McGuire. I was wondering if I could ask you a quick question?" Do I need to give her my name? Nope. But I learned a long time ago that when you want to gain something from a conversation, bringing it to a personal level helps. Having an attorney for a mother has taught me a trick or two.

"Is this regarding a patient?" Her tone is wary, and the older nurse is now right behind Beth. I focus on Beth and try to be as charming, yet not creepy, as possible.

"No, well—actually yes. You see, my sister was in this hospital a long time ago, and we came here to talk to the nurse that took care of her back then. It's a long story, but my sister doesn't remember much from that time, and we just found out the nurse's name, and we wanted to talk to her." I'm rambling. "Her name is Madeline Cross—the nurse, not my sister—anyway, do you know her? I tried the patient services place on the second floor, but they're closed."

*No need to tell her they already said no.*

Both nurses' eyes resemble manholes; neither probably expected me to deliver such a speech. The older nurse stares at me but clears her throat to give Beth a hint.

Beth jumps at the sound. "Oh, uh..." She turns around and locks eyes with the other woman before she faces me again. "I'm sorry, I'm not familiar with that name. I've only been here for two years and..." She trails off when understanding hits that she shouldn't even have told me that.

Well, fuck, but it was worth a try. I thank her and turn back the way I came. I don't want to leave Lilly alone for too long, otherwise, I would scour more units and ask around. They'd probably kick me out at some point, but I'd do anything to help *my girl.*

. . .

LILLY IS STILL in her seat when I slide into the red clown bench across from her.

"Are you hungry?"

She glances at the wall behind me, and her eyebrows knit together. "Is that clock right?"

"Plus or minus a few minutes, yeah."

"I've been sitting here for that long? Why didn't you say anything?" She sounds incredulous.

"Because you needed time to collect yourself."

Her cheeks turn pink. "Oh."

She's adorable when she's embarrassed, and I have to press my lips together not to make a comment about how stunning she looks.

*Not the time or place, horndog.*

"Let's eat and then find a place to crash. We'll regroup tomorrow."

We go to the hot bar, and I can't stop staring as Lilly puts the most random shit on her plate. A scoop of mac and cheese, three Brussels sprouts, a pancake that looks like it's been sitting there for about twelve hours, a few leaves of lettuce, and a grape. *One* grape. I'm about to make a dumb joke when I bite my tongue. If she wants to eat that, who am I to judge? After the day she's had, she can do what she wants, and I will cheer her on, imaginary pom-poms and all.

We've just finished, and I put my fork down when a swarm of nurses in different color scrubs comes from every direction and descends on the food court.

*What the ever-loving—?*

Lilly sees my expression and barks out a laugh. It's the first genuine laugh I hear from her today. At least I've accomplished that tonight.

"It's probably shift change." She smirks, plopping the lone grape in her mouth.

I playfully smack my forehead at my stupidity when a shadow falls over our table.

I turn and face a wall of blue. My gaze travels upward, and I meet the eyes of the older nurse from the emergency department.

Lilly's gaze flickers from me to the woman and back.

Without a word, the nurse, whose nametag reads Margery, hands me a folded piece of paper.

*Uh.*

I slowly grab the note, and right before she turns to leave, she scans Lilly up and down. Her whole expression softens.

"You've grown into a beautiful woman."

With that, she's gone.

Lilly's mouth hangs open, and I'm mirroring her stunned expression, trying to comprehend what just happened. My hand is still suspended mid-air when Lilly plucks the note out of my hand. Her motion is so quick I can't even react. Instead, my hand hangs there empty.

Slowly, she unfolds the paper. Once. Twice. I see her eyes scan the words, and then her hands fly to her mouth as she drops it. I snatch it up before it can land on her remaining mac and cheese.

Tears are pooling in her eyes, and she whispers, "What did you do?"

*Huh?*

Finally, I look at the note in my hand.

*Madeline Cross*

*Angelwood Medical Center*

*Saint Louis*

# CHAPTER EIGHTEEN

## LILLY

RHYS DOESN'T SAY ANYTHING. HE FOLDS THE PAPER BACK UP AND tucks it in his pocket. After he cleans up our table and returns the trays to their station, he stops next to me, holding out his hand. I'm in a daze, unable to move. What. Just. Happened?

When I don't make a move, he takes charge, grasps my hand, and pulls me out of the booth. Rhys only lets go of my hand when he deposits me into the passenger seat of the Defender and takes his place behind the wheel. His hand is back in mine as soon as we pull out of the parking spot.

I glance over, unsure what to make of all this. I'm so confused. How did this woman find us? All I can come up with is that Rhys did something when he disappeared for a while.

WE CHECK INTO A HOTEL, one of those chain places with free Wi-Fi and breakfast. I don't pay attention to the name as Rhys handles all the logistics. The room is nicer than the motels from the last few nights. The beds have crisp white sheets. There is a double seater couch under the window on the far wall, and a big flat-screen TV across from the beds that is positioned on top of two adjoining dressers.

He leads me to the bed by the couch and gestures for me to sit. He still hasn't said a word and just plops down across from me.

His elbows are resting on his thighs, and he rubs his hand over his face before finally looking at me. I mean, really looking at me. "We did it, Cal." His voice is low.

It feels weird to talk out loud after so much silence, and my question is no more than a whisper. "What did you do?"

He tells me about how he went to the ER, and how he left empty-handed, how he wanted to help me because he saw how upset I was. He didn't think twice about the nurse that showed up at our table until...well, until she showed up at the table.

Rhys's flight out of the hospital had me so distracted that I haven't thought about what this note means for us—for me. There's actually a chance to get answers.

"So, uh...this is good, right? Why are you acting so weird?" It should be good news, but his strange behavior also is starting to scare me.

His next words are more to himself. "It is, yeah. We know where to find Madeline Cross, but we also made your presence known. I guess, um...I guess my parents' paranoia has rubbed off on me. I just have this weird feeling."

We lock eyes, and that sends a chill through my entire body. He is really worried.

*Did we make a mistake?*

Our evening routine is completed in silence. We're both deep in thought, and Rhys is already in his bed when I walk out of the bathroom. He's turned toward my side, the white comforter pulled up to his ears and his eyes closed. His facial features are tense, a clear indicator that he's awake.

"Rhys?"

"Mhmm?" His response is mostly grumbled, and he doesn't open his eyes.

I squat down right in front of him. My shadow falls over his face, and his eyes pop open, immediately zeroing in on mine.

I smile sheepishly and move back an inch. "Sorry."

Rhys raises one eyebrow in a *perfect* semi-circle. It's fascinating how he does that. I either raise both eyebrows or neither, but he has complete control of his features, and it makes him even more expressive. My cheeks heat at that thought.

*Change of subject.*

"I, um...without you, we'd be going home with nothing, but now we actually have a chance to talk to Madeline. So, uh, thanks."

His lips curve in a small smile, and he says softly, "I'd do anything to help you."

This entire trip, he's been very careful to give me space, and not once has he mentioned his feelings for me. Besides the two *babes*, that is. You'd think he is simply a good friend. But this response says it all. No more words are needed, and the fluttery sensation I'm starting to get familiar with stirs inside of me again. I move back to sit on my bed and take one more look. He has closed his eyes again, but this time, he is relaxed. I crawl under the covers and turn the light off before mirroring Rhys's position.

THE NEXT MORNING, we enjoy the complimentary breakfast and are on our way to St. Louis by ten. Rhys has his phone plugged in, and various Linkin Park albums are playing over the speakers. I watch the landscape go by and think about the nurse, Margery. Was she there when I was brought in? Did she treat me? She clearly knew me and where I could find Madeline. The more I think about it, the more I understand why Rhys raced us out of there. But did she recognize me because Rhys mentioned Madeline, or did she recognize me for...well, me? He's right; Heather and Tristen have made sure to keep me under the radar for so long, but this one encounter surely hasn't caused any harm. Has it?

I'm still distracted when Rhys asks, "What do you want to do about New Year's Eve? The chances of us finding your nurse that day are probably pretty slim."

I totally forgot about the date. It's December twenty-ninth, and we won't make it to St. Louis until the first. Dejected, I say, "Yeah, you're probably right. I don't know. What do you think?"

"We have to be home by Friday afternoon. We can make it in fourteen hours with breaks from St. Louis. So, we have to leave sometime Thursday. That would give us at least two days there. Three, if we push it."

Listening to him list off our options, my throat constricts with guilt. Rhys is missing the ski trip with his best friend, and to top it off, he'll spend New Year's in some random hotel instead of hitting the slopes and partying.

Averting my eyes out the passenger window, I say, "You're usually at a party." It really is more of an observation. I don't expect a reaction to my statement, but when he doesn't say anything for several minutes, I can't stop myself from glancing over. His face is somber.

"Rhys?"

His eyes flick to me, and for a second, I see shame in them. What the—?

"Do you remember what I told you a few days ago? That I've done a lot of things I regret?" He speaks in such a monotone voice that he sounds nothing like his usual self.

"Yes?"

His Adam's apple bobs, and he gazes at me again. "Well, the partying and what comes *along* with that, for example. It's not me, I mean. It's what Kat wants, what's expected with my...social status. Hell, this past year I've been fake drinking half the time. But before that..."

When he notices my confusion, he explains further. "The first year after I, uh...*walked away*, I did pretty much everything as long as I could ensure it wouldn't get me kicked off the team. But even that was not a good enough excuse during my low points—when I needed to forget." The last sentence is no more than a whisper.

"Forget what?" I have an idea but can't stop myself from asking.

He doesn't respond right away, and just when I assume he won't, he rasps, "You."

"Oh." I don't know what to say. This is another reminder of how his life was impacted by what happened to me. Sure, there could be worse things than being *forced* to party, but he's insinuating that he's done extracurricular and recreational *stuff* I never would've expected —not from health-conscious Rhys. My chest tightens, and I press my fist against my sternum.

I've heard a lot of stories about *them*—Rhys and Katherine, the reigning couple—but no one ever mentioned the things he just admitted. Denielle knows not to talk about him, but others have always given me detailed recaps of the parties he'd gone to with Katherine. My mind starts to wander to some of those stories. Sex in the pool or a bathroom is nothing unusual, but hearing that about my brother was always...ugh. Now that he is no longer my brother, it's—*nope, not going there.*

"It's not your fault. You had no idea." His tone is gentle, and he mistakes my pained face for the initial guilt, not the memory of Sloane giving me a play by play about Katherine's shouts from the first-floor bathroom at Kellan Jager's pool party. I shake my head.

The corners of Rhys's mouth tilt up. "I'd rather spend New Year's in a hotel room watching a movie than be at a party with a ton of people I hardly know or *like*, watching them get wasted, and most likely waking up with a hangover from hell myself."

My lips tighten in a forced smile, but I can't refrain from asking the question I've conveniently avoided since we left Westbridge. "What did you tell Katherine? I mean, about where you are?"

He doesn't speak right away; his face just turns blank.

"Nothing."

## RHYS

"Nothing?" Lilly asks in disbelief.

I peer at her several times. Something is going on inside her head, but I can't figure out what. I slow the car to be able to better assess her. "Cal, what are you thinking?"

She blushes and squeezes her lips together.

Oh no, she's not clamming up on me. I just admitted one of my darkest secrets to her, something I never intended for her to find out, but I swore to myself that I'd no longer keep anything from her, either. "Cal?" My tone has a warning note to it. She is going to talk to me. My gut tells me it has something to do with me and is probably nothing good.

"Can we please let it go?" She sounds exasperated and flustered at the same time.

"No!"

"Ass," she grumbles, and the shade of her face resembles an overripe tomato.

"Come on, spill it! What has you so worked up?"

*This is going to be interesting.*

"Fine," she harrumphs. "I just...I was wondering if the image thing is why you always have public sex? I would want to know where my boyfriend is—I mean, if he were traveling with another girl. Not that I'm just any girl; I'm your sister, but I'm not. But they think I am, but I'd still want to know. We're friends, and if my boyfriend was traveling with a female, I'd want to know. Right, I already said that. So why didn't you tell Katherine?"

*Uh...what?*

She rambled that off so fast that I have to replay it in my head. Public sex. Wait, what? We're friends. Does that mean she has forgiven me? At the same time, she completely jumped over the *thing* I just admitted to her.

I open my mouth and close it again. I have no idea where to begin. Finally, I manage to say, "I didn't expect you to forgive me." I drop the whole sex thing. *What the fuck?* We'll get back to that later.

"Yeah, me neither." She's attempting to suppress a smile. I guess she hadn't planned to word vomit all that.

"I'm glad." I force my voice to remain steady. My entire body has just come alive, and I want to grin like a fool. I rake a hand through my hair and glance over. Lilly watches intently for my reaction, and I feel like a little boy with his first crush. *Pathetic.* Well, technically, she is my first crush. There has never been a second. And Lilly knows how I feel, but that doesn't mean I want her to see *how much* this affects me.

*I do have some pride left.*

I wiggle my eyebrows at her. "And all it took was finding the nurse that helped you ten years ago. Piece of cake."

She catches on, and just for that, I want to kiss her. She could've busted my balls for being all emotional, but that's not her. She changes the subject.

"You didn't answer my question."

"Huh? Oh, which one?"

"What did you tell her?"

"Oh yeah, I didn't tell her anything. She doesn't know I'm not skiing. I honestly don't even remember if she knew I was going in the first place."

"Why?" I don't expect her to remotely understand what Kat and I are. We don't have a relationship in the traditional sense; we don't *share*. I'm not proud of that. It's exhausting to always pretend in front of everyone.

I explain, "I didn't tell Kat because she wouldn't have cared. She's in Florida, enjoying the sun, probably banging some rich country club dude and heir to the next big business empire."

"What? That's awful. Why would you be with someone like that?" Lilly exclaims, disgusted.

I sigh. "I told you before that Kat and I have a silent arrangement. We've never officially talked about it; it is simply understood. We give each other an image, something I needed to save face when it came to my feelings for you. She has never been faithful to me—not when she's traveling. And she knows I know, but she probably just assumes I'm one of those dumb jocks who jump everything with a pussy."

"Crass much?" Lilly shakes her head. "Is that why you always have sex in public? The image?"

*Ah, we're back to that.*

Still baffled, I ask, "When did I have public sex?" I'm honestly curious. I generally don't pay attention to the gossip or whatever Kat tells people. I mean, we used to have sex—a lot, actually, in the beginning, since my main goal was to work Lilly out of my system, and Kat *is* hot as fuck. But that never worked, and over time, the sex became less and less. I don't even remember the last time. Definitely weeks, if not months.

"Uh...um...Kellan's party. Sloane heard you guys in the bathroom."

"Kellan?" I rack my brain. "Oh, Jager's pool party."

*We fucked there?* Not that I remember, and I wasn't hammered enough to forget that. Then it clicks, and I burst out laughing. I can't stop, and Lilly glares with her lips pursed.

I finally gain control and declare, "That wasn't me."

"But Sloane saw you and Kat go in the bathroom."

She's right, we did go in there together, but I never touched her. I left through the adjoining bedroom and out the patio doors. I have no idea what Kat did after I left. A laugh bubbles up as I try again. "Oh God, that is priceless."

"WHAT?" Lilly is growing impatient. She thinks I'm making fun of her.

I explain, "Kat was in rare form that night. She was already smashed by the time I got to Jager's, and she kept dry-humping me to make a public statement or some shit. You know her—well, the *public* her. Anyway, she dragged me into the bathroom with the intent of what you *think* happened. But there was no way I'd touch her in that state. She was all sloppy and—whatever, that's not important. She got pissed that I wouldn't comply, so I left through the bedroom and out the patio doors. I went home from there. I had no clue she put on a one-woman show." And with that, I howl with laughter.

Lilly gawks at me, perplexed. "You're saying she *pretended* to have sex? Alone? In the bathroom?"

"I guess so." I wipe a tear from my eye.

"That is...wow. I mean, I don't even know what that is."

Every so often, one of us randomly giggles. I can't wait to tell Wes about that when we get home. Maybe I'll even text him later; I haven't checked in with him since we left.

When "Good Goodbye" comes on, I see Lilly shiver out of the corner of my eye. She has her legs pulled up, and her chin is resting on her jean-clad knees. Her head is tilted toward me, and her face heats when she realizes I'm watching. I want to question her what this is about, but instead, I focus on the road, concentrating on singing along to my favorite song.

"I almost named that one as my favorite," Lilly mumbles.

Even though her voice is low, it startles me, and our eyes meet before I focus back on the road.

"Uh...what?"

*Why does my voice sound all raspy?*

She turns forward but can't hide her embarrassment. "'Good Goodbye'. When you asked me about my favorite song, this was the first one that popped into my head, but I changed my mind to 'Helsinki'."

Oh. This is...What is this? Is she embarrassed about it?

I'm confused and elated at the same time. Does her odd behavior mean there is...more? Otherwise, why would she be so weirded out by us liking the same song? I don't allow myself to hope; after all, she just admitted that we're friends again. I'm not going to push my luck.

"Well, you have good taste." I make light of it instead of feeding into the awkward tension, and it works. Lilly visibly relaxes and starts singing herself.

# CHAPTER NINETEEN

**HIM**

*I loathe business dinners. The clients always expect to get wined and dined on the most crazy expensive items on the menu and then get shitfaced. All on my money. So predictable. I'm bored, but Hank says I have to be in this meeting. It's for our current project in Florida, and they have questions only I can answer. We're halfway through the project already. Why we couldn't have done this over the phone I have no clue. I take a sip from my Chateau Petrus Pomerol—also the client's choice—when my phone vibrates with an incoming email. I glance down at the device on the white tablecloth, and my hand with the wine glass freezes mid-air. The email came to the account I only use for one purpose.* Her.

*I excuse myself from the table and receive a pointed look from Hank, but I don't care. I walk to the nearest restroom and into the closest stall. Away from prying eyes, I open the email and stare. I haven't thought about this particular watcher in forever. Years ago, I installed a program in the Santa Rosa hospital system that watches only one file: Jane Doe, 22105017_0217. It's just one small routine, undetectable unless one specifically looks for it and the reason why I have left it there for so long. Someone accessed Jane Doe's file tonight. Her file. That can't be a coincidence. It's been over ten years. And to think that I almost didn't reinstall it four years ago when they switched to the new patient system.*

*I send a quick text message to Hank with a bogus excuse and instructions* to reschedule the meeting. I run this project, and I have to get home to my computer.

Fuck the client.

*An hour later, I read the log file for the third time. Someone looked up the file at 7:02 p.m., but why? I haven't had the need to hack into a surveillance feed in a while, and it takes me longer than it used to. I need to brush up on that skill. Once in, I easily find what I'm looking for. Pressing play, I watch the Emergency Room feed beginning at six p.m. Six different camera angles run simultaneously on my screen, and I scan them all meticulously. At 6:47, I pause the feed. There! Two nurses are talking to a young guy; his back is to two of the cameras and one partially shows his face. He can't be more than nineteen. I press play again. The conversation doesn't last more than a few minutes, and then he turns and walks out. The younger nurse leaves as well, and only the older one remains. I pause again and do a double-take. She's about ten years older and probably twenty pounds heavier, but I have no doubt about who it is: Margery. She's been an ER nurse for over twenty-five years and was the person I handed* her *to before sprinting out of the hospital.*

*Sure enough, Margery walks back into the nurses' lounge and to a computer. So, she was the one accessing the file. The timestamp matches my log file.*

*Who is the boy?*

*I start accessing other feeds throughout the hospital but can't find him anywhere. FUCK! I'm about to start over at an earlier time before he showed up at the ER when I watch the camera in the lobby. The timestamp shows 7:36, and there he is again. He is leading a girl with long blonde hair, by the hand, out of the sliding doors. No! My breath hitches. It can't be.*

*My fingers feverishly fly over the keyboard until I find the right angle. There she is. My little Lilly—just not so little anymore.*

# CHAPTER TWENTY

### LILLY

WHY THE HELL DID I ADMIT TO HIM THAT I LIKE THE SONG? I'VE been asking myself that for the last two days. But even more importantly, why does it bother me so much that we like the same song? I can't shake this weird, indistinguishable gut feeling. Maybe I'm not over him lying to me after all? I'm starting to wish I could talk to Den. Well, I could, but not without telling her about the minor detail of being a kidnapping victim *and* having lost part of my memory. Yeah, no—I'm not ready for that conversation. I need to figure out as much as possible before bringing anyone else into this.

WE SPEND New Year's Eve in another chain hotel near Kansas City. We cover as much ground as possible and still get a few solid hours of sleep. From here, the last leg is not more than a couple of hours.

The room is a similar setup to the place in Santa Rosa, clean and comfortable. Rhys even pays extra for a living area and kitchenette. It's like a little apartment, and curling up on the couch feels completely natural.

Rhys gets nostalgic and suggests a *Blade* marathon. How can I say no to that? Finishing this year with my all-time favorite movies and Rhys probably reciting Hannibal King word for word—I grin from ear to ear.

Smiling, I think of how Denielle makes fun of me whenever she gets the chance. "Those movies are older than you!" Followed by her famous eye roll. I've seen her intimidate girls and guys alike with that, but I just shrug her off with, "It's a classic. You don't know what's good." And then I make fun of her for her *Friends* addiction.

*I miss my best friend.*

We've texted a few times, but mostly things like: **How r u? Wish u were here! Can't wait to see u next week.**

I'm sitting on the couch and watch as Rhys somehow connects his laptop to the TV. When I question him about why he carries around the exact connectivity cables in his backpack, all he says is, "I'm a guy."

How does that explain it. Whatever.

We start the first movie late in the afternoon, and after *Blade II,* Rhys says he needs a break. He wants to shower and change before we keep going, which is fine with me. I showered this morning before we left, so while he is in the bathroom, I put on my PJs and resume my position on the couch.

Rhys is taking forever, and after checking my social media and sending Denielle a "Happy New Year's Eve" text, I move over to the small table where we left the pizza we ordered earlier.

I bite into another piece when I realize he has opened the bathroom door to let some of the steam out. Through the opening, I see him in front of the sink. Shirtless. His blue-and-green plaid pajama pants riding low on his trim hips. My mouth stops chewing, and I can't avert my eyes. Is it warm in here? He is washing his face, and with every move, the muscles in his broad back flex. I get glimpses of his incredibly toned arms moving back and forth, scrubbing his face, and my lips part, heart pounding in my chest. Holy—has he always been this, uh...defined? I drop the pizza and rub my suddenly sweaty palms against my flannel pants.

*Oh great, now I have grease stains on my pants.*

I look up at the precise moment that Rhys turns toward the door and pulls a fresh navy t-shirt over his head. My eyes trail his chest down to his abs, and I gulp, choking on the pizza I forgot was still in my mouth.

The way his taut muscles move with every motion, I can't take my eyes off of him. Once his head is through the opening, he pulls the rest of the fabric over his body, and I jerk myself around. I can barely control my rapid breathing.

*What is going on?*

He's my bro—adopted brother. This is all kinds of wrong.

RHYS WALKS THROUGH THE DOOR, and I quickly stuff more pizza in my mouth, afraid if I have to talk, my voice will betray me.

He drops his dirty clothes on top of the suitcase and then comes over to get another slice himself. When he leans over me, our arms brush against each other, and my entire body stiffens. I hold my breath as his clean scent causes a whole new wave of sweat to pool in my palms.

*Please don't let him notice anything.*

But Rhys just grabs his pizza and walks back to the couch. "You coming?"

I keep my eyes trained on the tabletop and finish chewing. "Mm-hmm."

THE ENTIRE NEXT MOVIE, I am so distracted by my physical reaction that I pay zero attention. Rhys busies himself, reciting Hannibal as expected, and since I know it by heart, I can answer and comment on any question as soon as I glance at the screen.

We watch until right before midnight, then switch to the New Year's countdown, and toast with our water bottles. Rhys leans over and gives me a tight hug that lingers a little longer than just regular friends. But we have history—a lot of history. I tell myself that it's nothing out of the ordinary.

Thankfully, my body doesn't have a mind of its own this time, and when he releases me, I'm finally able to relax. We're done right before 1:30 a.m. I stumble to my bed and am asleep before my head hits the pillow.

## RHYS

I WAKE UP BEFORE LILLY. I glance at her sleeping form, covers pulled almost over her head.

*Best New Year ever!*

I meant what I said in the car; the partying is not me—never has been. It's fun, sure, and in the beginning, it was a vice to numb myself. A way to not deal with my feelings toward Lilly or the guilt that consumed me for treating her like shit. As time went on, I realized the numbing only worked temporarily. Once it wore off, everything came flooding back tenfold, and I felt worse than before, because then it was not just my head that was messed up. About a year ago, I quit the extra *stuff* for good. Some days, I still use the parties and my social status as an excuse to get piss-drunk and forget, but the majority of the time, I fake it—not that anyone notices. Well, Wes does catch on at times. He gives me the squint-eye when I hold the same beer for three hours, but I simply mirror his expression. Within seconds, he's back to charming his way into the pants of the next chick who glances in his direction.

I don't like the person I have become to maintain the secret—both secrets, my parents' and mine—allowing Kat to parade us around as if we are the perfect couple, feeding into the fucking pretense she loves so much, and just nodding when some guy tells me how lucky I am to *bag* Katherine Rosenfield. I just want to respond with, "*Have at it*," but I can't. People see what they want to see: a smoking-hot cheerleader that's at the top of the high school food chain and her athlete boyfriend. Not once in two years has Kat asked me how I'm doing—not once. And again, I just play along. I don't call her out on it. My life is a big. Fat. Farce.

Until now, that is. Now that Lilly knows, I can finally be myself, even if it's just with her. But that's all that counts. And if she ends up telling Denielle and Wes the truth, I don't have to put up a front with them anymore, either. Maybe Den will stop with the death glares. I'm a selfish prick for hoping. The reason we're here is to find answers for Lilly. It's her life, her past, and her future. *Her safety*.

I shake myself out of the depressing mood. We had a great evening. I hadn't enjoyed myself that much in a long time, and using New Year's as an excuse, I gave in to my urge to be close to her.

We'll make it through this trip and then figure out where to go from there.

. . .

LILLY STIRS AROUND NINE-THIRTY. I've been scrolling through my social media for the past hour but don't see anything worth mentioning. Kat is enjoying the Florida sun. Wes posts almost hourly videos of himself attempting some snowboarding stunt—most of them failing. They are the usual Christmas break updates.

I also check Lilly's account, but there is nothing to see. Mom and Dad have gone through rigorous security measures. All the family accounts—if they even exist—are locked down. The audience is strictly controlled, and my parents regularly check that there are no pictures of Lilly anywhere. And I mean regularly. They use Dad's military career and now contractor position as the main reason for their cyber paranoia, but in truth, it's all about keeping Lilly hidden. I wonder if she's caught on to that yet.

Lilly eventually opens her eyes and squints. We didn't close the blackout curtains, and the window is facing east. Once her eyes have adjusted, she gives me a sleepy, "Good morning."

My worries are forgotten. "Morning yourself."

"How long have you been up?"

"Not long."

She sees my phone in my hand. "Anything I should know?"

"No, same old." I place my phone on the nightstand.

Lilly lets her head plop back onto the pillow, and I add, "Maybe we can swing by the hospital and at least figure out when Madeline is working."

That makes Lilly perch herself up on one elbow. "You think they will tell us?"

I shrug. "Let's try. We'll have to come up with a less questionable reason, though."

After calling home—on speakerphone—and wishing Mom and Dad a Happy New Year with some more fake stories about what Wes and Den are up to, we take our time getting ready and hit the road after we find an open Starbucks to load up on caffeine.

. . .

It's early afternoon when we arrive at Angelwood Medical Center. It's small, no more than three floors, which hopefully works to our advantage this time.

We walk through the double doors, and Lilly's pinkie brushes against mine. I see her stiffen for a fraction of a second, but she composes herself quickly. That was...weird. She's probably on edge about Madeline.

The center is built around an atrium with lots of planters and bright, comfortable sitting areas, which gives the whole place an almost welcoming feel. Definitely not like a hospital. There is a small reception area straight ahead. The hallway to the left leads to the emergency department, based on the layout I saw when we parked. The right side seems to be offices, maybe administration.

We approach the desk manned by an elderly woman whose nametag reads Maria Adelstein. Her graying hair is tied in a bun at the back of her neck, and she is dressed impeccably in a crisp, white blouse. I let Lilly take the lead and stand slightly back.

"Hi. Happy New Year."

Maria Adelstein genuinely smiles at us. She doesn't seem to mind being here on New Year's Day at all. "Hello, and Happy New Year. How can I help you?"

Lilly takes a deep breath. "I'm looking for Madeline Cross, but I'm not sure if she's working today. We're just passing through and wanted to say hi. I can't remember which station she is at now."

Complete bullshit, but we figured if we make it personal, it'll be less suspicious.

The woman places both hands on her heart. "Oh my, how wonderful. Young people nowadays rarely take the time to visit anyone in person with all that technology. In my day, we visited all the time." She sounds like she's talking about the early nineteen hundreds. I worry she's launching into a whole story, but then she continues, "We are such a small hospital. I know pretty much every-one's schedule." She beams at us.

Lilly glances over her shoulder at me, and I can see the relief in her eyes.

When she faces forward again, Maria says, "Maddie is such a wonderful nurse, especially with the kids. Everyone loves her. She is currently out for the holiday, but she is working the night shift tomorrow evening."

Lilly reaches back and takes my hand. Her touch is like a jump-start for my pulse. I squeeze her hand in an attempt to let her know I'm here for her.

Maria watches our exchange closely and gushes, "You are such a sweet couple."

Lilly lets go of my hand immediately and stammers, "Oh, uh...no. We're just friends."

Ouch. I try to hide my disappointment, despite feeling as if I were just sucker punched.

But Maria just winks at us. "If you say so."

She gives us instructions to come back here at eight p.m. tomorrow, and she will let the evening receptionist know to provide us with directions to Madeline's station.

## CHAPTER TWENTY-ONE

### LILLY

WE ARRIVE AT THE HOSPITAL A LITTLE AFTER EIGHT, AND THE night receptionist directs us to the east wing of the second floor. It's the longest elevator ride in the history of elevator rides. When was this thing made? I envision someone manually pulling us up. I start flicking my thumb against my fingers again, and Rhys gives me a knowing sideways glance but remains mute.

The number on the display finally switches from one to two, the doors open, and my stomach contracts into a tight ball. We find a middle-aged woman at the nurses' station, and I hesitantly approach her. Is she Madeline?

"Excuse me?" My voice sounds weak.

She looks up from her computer. "Yes?"

I take a breath and try to steady my voice. If I sound like Minnie Mouse on helium, no one will believe I'm here to pay a visit to an old family friend. "I'm looking for Madeline Cross. We were told we could find her here."

The nurse scans me up and down. She's skeptical, but then she points to the right and says, "Why don't you head over to the family room? I'll let her know you are here. What's your name?"

"Lilly McGuire."

The woman nods and starts talking into a walkie-talkie-looking thing pinned to her scrubs. We're dismissed. I turn and head in the direction she pointed.

The family room doesn't look like a hospital either—a waiting area, yes, but not a hospital. It contains similar planters to the ones downstairs with two beige couches positioned in an L along two walls. Under the window is a small shelf with various books and magazines. It's cozy.

I sit down on the farthest couch, and Rhys lowers himself onto the other one. His ankle is crossed over his knee, and his arms are spread over the back of the couch, radiating calm and relaxation. I'm pretty sure that it's for my benefit. For a while, it works, but after thirty minutes, I can't sit still anymore and start pacing. Rhys remains still the entire time, which eventually starts feeding into my restlessness.

Another fifteen minutes later, I am ready to go back to the nurses' station. Maybe she didn't tell Madeline we're here after all. I start for the door when it swings open, and I come face to face with a woman in her mid-forties. She's petite with a heart-shaped face, wearing light-green scrubs. Her short blonde hair is tied in a pony-tail, and she wears little makeup. Her eyes are exhausted.

"I'm sorry, I was held up and—" Madeline's gaze sweeps the room, and when she locks on mine, she stops in her tracks. Her eyes grow wide, and neither of us looks away. *I remember her!* An imme-diate sense of peace fills me. I trusted this woman. Tears start to well up, and her expression mirrors mine.

"You were such a beautiful little girl, but you have grown up into a stunning young woman," she whispers in awe.

My hands fly to my mouth, and I can't contain the sniffle that has bubbled up inside of me. Rhys is now directly behind me. I feel his presence without turning, and he murmurs, "You okay?"

I nod but talk to Madeline, "I remember you."

My ears register a sharp intake of breath, but I can't distinguish if it comes from Rhys or Madeline.

"Why don't we sit down?" She gestures toward the couches.


I TAKE the couch Rhys previously occupied, and he sits down beside me. He resumes the same position as before, arm spread behind me, but this time, it's not calmness that comes over me in waves—it's protectiveness. Whatever this woman is going to tell us, he'll make sure I'm safe. I fight the urge to lean back into his arm.

Madeline takes the other couch. "How did you find me?"

I expected that question, so I hold out the copy of the discharge form I found in Tristen's office. She glances down and hands it back. "That was a very long time ago. Where did you get this?"

I glance at Rhys, and even though his face is expressionless, he gives me the slightest of nods. This is my show until I need him to take the stage.

I talk mostly to my hands folded in my lap. "A few weeks ago, I started remembering...that something happened to me. At first, I thought I was going crazy, but Rhys told me the truth—or, well...what he knew happened."

This is the first time Madeline focuses on Rhys. She studies him for what feels like an eternity. "You're Heather and Tristen's son."

Rhys's expression briefly turns into shock, but he smoothes his features out immediately and drawls, "You know my parents?"

I'm stunned by how his *cool-and-collected* persona just snaps into place. I haven't seen that side of him up close since he walked into my room three weeks ago. He's been one hundred percent himself when he and I are together. He's mastered putting on a show for people; he lets them see what he wants them to see. At this moment, he's the alpha who runs the show. And it works.

Madeline moves her head up and down. "I met them briefly when they arrived at the hospital." She looks at me again. "You also called out his name at night." After a pause, she amends, "During your nightmares."

*I did?*

My breathing becomes erratic, and words won't form. Rhys studies me for a second and takes over, giving me the time to collect myself. It's like we rehearsed this, but he simply knows.

"I told Lilly everything I remember. But I was young, and my parents never told me any details. That's why we're here. We found the discharge paper in my parents' office. Whoever took Lilly is still doing it, and we found information that Lilly was the first. Why was her name never released?"

Madeline takes a deep breath. "That is a lot of questions. Do your parents know you're here?"

"No." His voice is hard and determined.

"I see." She pauses. "I'm not sure I should be talking to you."

My head snaps up. "What? No! I have to know what happened to me. I've been lied to for ten years. I have the right—" Madeline holds up her hands, and I stop.

"Yes. Yes, you do. I figured that one day this would come back to haunt me, and I guess the day has come." Then, she smiles tightly and says, "Just let me tell my co-worker that I'll be taking my break early."

## RHYS

WE'RE face to face with Madeline. The whole situation is surreal. I can see how Lilly is trying to remain in control of her emotions. I'm having a hard time myself. When she whispered, "I remember you," my heart went into overdrive.

While Madeline is gone, Lilly starts pacing again. It was easy to have my shit together toward the nurse, to portray the arrogant jock. She's a stranger, and the other persona is second nature to me. But watching Lilly walk the length of the room over and over makes me feel helpless.

"Cal?"

"Mm-hmm?" She increases her speed.

"What can I do?"

That makes her halt, and she turns, confused. "Huh?"

I don't want to fuck this up. Changing positions so my elbows rest on my thighs and my hands are clasped together, I look up at her. "I feel pretty helpless here. What do you need from me?"

Her mouth forms an *O*.

I almost chuckle at her surprised expression but can remain serious. "I just want to do the right thing."

Her features soften, and she smiles. When she walks over, sits down, and covers my clasped hands with hers, I'm the one who does the *O*.

"You're doing exactly what I need. You're here."

Without thinking, I pull one hand out and flip the other palm side up. Lilly doesn't hesitate to intertwine our fingers, and the familiarity of this motion makes my heart skip a beat. She sits and holds my gaze when Madeline comes in.

IF THE NURSE thinks anything about our position, she doesn't give it away. She settles back on the other couch, and Lilly and I straighten up. Lilly angles herself toward Madeline and pulls her hand out of mine but doesn't move away. Our legs still touch.

The woman sitting across from us is clearly having an internal struggle. Her lips are pressed in a hard line, and she keeps picking at the hem of her scrubs. Finally, she looks at both of us several times before settling on Lilly. "Some of what I'm going to tell you may not be easy to hear. Are you sure?"

Lilly nods.

"Well, okay..." She takes one more deep breath. "You were dropped off anonymously at the ER. No one knew where you came from. You were unconscious. We couldn't figure out who you were. There weren't any missing person reports matching your description. At the time, we didn't know if a caregiver had neglected you or if something *else* had happened to you. You didn't have any physical injuries. The tox screen showed that your condition was due to an extremely high amount of sedatives. Every person's body reacts differently to different dosages, but you were so small and were given too much. We assumed that it was the reason you were *brought in*."

While we listen, Lilly seeks out my hand again, never breaking eye contact with Madeline. I interlace my fingers with hers and rest both our hands on my thigh. This time, the butterflies in my stomach remain at bay. I need her touch as much as she needs mine to listen to this. Madeline's eyes briefly flicker to our joined hands, but she doesn't pause.

"You were unconscious for several days. Physically, you should've woken up, but we believed it was your mind's way of protecting itself. You shut yourself off from the outside world. I took care of you whenever I was scheduled to work, and I was there the day you opened your eyes. You were scared and confused. It took me over twenty-four hours of almost constant talking before you told me your name. I just talked to you about myself, my dog Harvey, my sister and her kids, anything and everything. But you wouldn't tell anyone what had happened to you, and no one was able to go near you. Your attending physician and I were the only people you let come close, and you only let him when I was in the room during the checkups. I didn't leave the hospital for almost forty-eight hours to stay by your side."

Madeline takes a drink of water. "After you told me your name, the hospital was able to locate your parents quickly, and they arrived the same day. They drove all the way from San Diego. You had just had another episode—a nightmare—and I was about to take a quick break when they walked in. I knew at first glance who they were; you and your mother looked so much alike. Same fair skin and light hair.

"Of course they wanted to see you right away, but we had to follow procedure—take both to a different room to figure out what happened and brief them on your condition. Social services was assigned at that point.

"The attending physician gave his medical report. Your father was barely holding on when he heard about the sedatives. I explained to them what had happened since you woke up. You didn't say much while you were awake, but you had nightmares every time you fell asleep. You cried a lot in your sleep. Called out for your father—and Rhys."

This is the first time Madeline looks at me longer than just a quick glance, as if she wants to say something, but then continues. "After I mentioned the nightmares, your father broke down and had to leave the room. Your mother informed us what happened to you. You were taken on a school field trip, and the kidnapper black-mailed them into keeping quiet so that you wouldn't be harmed. They received daily updates with photos, videos, and timestamps until the day you were brought to the hospital. She showed them to us. Your father wanted to involve the authorities at that point, but your mother refused. I assume out of fear for your life—it wasn't my place to make assumptions.

"Your father had just returned to the room when your mother's phone signaled an incoming message." Madeline shudders at the memory.

Her next words are spoken very softly as if she purposefully tries not to frighten us. "The message contained a picture of the three of us. It showed me leading them to the room we were still in. All it said was, 'You cannot hide.'"

"Your mother said they had received another message while they were on their way with a picture of one of the surveillance cameras from the hospital that said that *he* would get you back. Whoever this person was, they knew what they were doing."

By now, Lilly's grip on my hand is so tight that I have to untangle my fingers from hers and, instead, clasp her hand between both of mine. Madeline watches us like she is studying something under a microscope. I don't like it.

"You wouldn't let your mother near you for the first few hours; it was heartbreaking. At some point, your mother received another message. She didn't let me see it, but it deeply unsettled them. I overheard some phone calls with your parents. They had just landed in California." She focuses on me. "From what I gathered, they suggested taking Lilly and hiding her from the kidnapper."

This time, it is me squeezing Lilly's hand. For whatever reason, I always assumed that Lilly's parents initiated all this, and my parents were just friends helping out. My parents suggesting to hide Lilly makes my stomach churn. Why would they do that? Couldn't Emily and Henry have protected her?

"I suggested a specialist to help you cope with your memories. In the state you were in, you wouldn't have been able to have a normal childhood for a very long time. In that short period, I grew very fond of you. I was worried for you. After that last communication from the kidnapper and when they got off the phone with Heather and Tristen, your mother came to me. She asked to talk in private and begged me to help her. There were things your father apparently wasn't aware of, and she wouldn't tell me either, but she wanted to check you out immediately. No one could know you were there. She wanted no trace of you found. She even offered me money to help her." *Money?* Madeline pauses to take another sip of her water.

"I could see how scared she was. She trusted me with your life.

We'd had several victims from a large car accident come in just prior to your parents' arrival, and with everyone being busy, you were still listed as Jane Doe in the system. Of course, we had verified that your parents were who they claimed to be. Besides the obvious resemblance, they had your birth certificate and pictures. But I never updated the record, and neither did the charge nurse nor attending physician. I called in *a lot* of favors and was able to keep it that way until you were discharged. You remained Jane Doe in the hospital system."

Until now, neither Lilly nor I have spoken, but her last statement sparks a deep sense of anger in me that I can't contain.

"*You* suggested the specialist? He obviously did more than just help her cope. Lilly forgot everything. Even her parents." My pulse is racing, and Lilly jumps at my outburst. She tightens her grip on my hand, and her gentle reminder calms my nerves. I squeeze back, silently thanking her. I'm baffled by the realization that I need her touch as much as she seems to need mine.

Madeline squeezes her lips together in a sad smile. "Yes, it seems he did. And from what I saw in the brief time I spent with you and then your parents, I believe they did what was best for you at the moment to keep you safe and give you a chance of a normal life." Her tone is professional—detached, even—which is probably due to years in her profession.

Lilly speaks for the first time, her voice so soft that it's barely audible. "Do you know what happened to my parents?"

I scan Madeline's face carefully, and her eyes widen in surprise ever so slightly. If I hadn't looked for a reaction, I probably would've missed it.

"I do not, I'm sorry. I never heard from your parents again after you were discharged. As much as I wanted to know if you were okay, I also knew that reaching out in any way could bring you back in harm's way. I saw the news reports of the other girls, and I do believe that you are the one he wants. If he gets back on your trail, he will find you."

WE SIT in silence for a long while, no one speaking. Everyone is lost in their own thoughts. Lilly shudders, and I wrap my arms around her. I don't care anymore about keeping up appearances. This has freaked both of us out.

Lilly stares at her now folded hands, her body shivering every so often. I'm starting to worry she is going into shock and look up at Madeline, who is in her own head.

"Can you tell us the name of the specialist?"

She thinks for a moment before speaking carefully. "No, I only suggested seeing a specialist. I believe your father"—she looks at me—"was somehow involved in finding the right person. Maybe it's time to talk to them?"

That brings a reaction out of Lilly. She locks eyes with Madeline. "Thank you for everything you have done for me."

Madeline genuinely smiles at the girl in my arms. "I would do it again. Take care of yourself, Lilly." Then, she looks at me, still smiling, but with a serious gaze. "And you take care of her also."

This woman truly cares about Lilly, and I am grateful for that.

"I intend to. Thank you." I nod at her.

THE DRIVE back to the hotel is quiet. Lilly hasn't said a word since thanking Madeline, and I am back to feeling lost.

We've finally gotten some answers, but those have also sparked more questions. Madeline's last words haunt me. *If he gets back on your trail, he will find you.*

In the hospital, Lilly let me hold her. She needed me, but I can't assume that she still wants that even if I need her touch just as much. This is such an emotional cluster fuck. I remind myself that I can't mistake her need for comfort for anything else; it's just a need for support. Denielle would've done the same thing for her.

WE GET ready for bed in silence. Lilly is changing in the bathroom, and when she is done, I go to brush my teeth.

Her bedside lamp is turned off when I return, and she is facing away from me. For a second, I stand there, no clue what to do. Should I say something?

I decide to give her time and wait until morning. I settle in my own bed and turn the light off, but sleep won't come. I have flashbacks from the night before we left for this trip. My mind is racing. I think about everything we found out today, my feelings for Lilly, our situation at home. I stare at the ceiling as if it holds the answers. Turning one way, then the other, I reposition my pillow about a hundred times. If Lilly weren't in the room, I'd hurl the fucking thing across the room out of frustration.

## CHAPTER TWENTY-TWO

### HIM

*My phone buzzes with incoming texts and calls all night. Hank wants to know what the fuck happened. This was an important meeting for the expansion project, and I blew it. Whatever. It's not like I need the money. I have enough to live ten lifetimes. The sole reason for this is to build relationships, and if my projects make them money, they're happy and bring me more business. I text back that I'll call the guy in the morning and to not get his panties in a wad. I imagine Hank's beet-red face reading my reply, and a smirk forms on my lips. Tonight, I have other priorities.*

*After downloading the hospital surveillance footage to my local server, I back out of the system. No reason to be in there longer than necessary. I watch the videos several times and find a few more angles to get a good look at Lilly and the guy with her. She has grown up, and I can't deny that she looks stunning. Lilly looks healthy and strong, like she's been working out a lot. I remember that she used to like gymnastics as a little girl. I wonder if she still does.*

*Next, I scan the guy with her. He is tall with short, dark hair and broad shoulders. I can see the muscles moving in his arms and back while he drags Lilly out of there. He must be important because I can't imagine just anyone being with her there. I grind my teeth; it will take some time to track them, and I'm not very patient at the moment. Maybe I'll try a different angle to get to the information I need.*

*I pull up Margery's file. Over the years, I have been tracking everyone that had come in contact with Lilly while she was in the hospital. Most nurses have moved on to other hospitals, including the one that mainly took care of Lilly, but Margery stayed put. Little does the rest of the staff know, Margery has been struggling since her back surgery five years ago. Every few months, she takes a detour to the pharmacy after her shift and stocks up on fentanyl. Granted, I was a little shocked when she moved on from morphine about two years ago, but I noticed that she is stocking up less, which means she makes it last longer. How she gets it is none of my concern; if she's stealing it or bribing someone, that fact is not important to me.*

*How to do it? How to do it? Email, text message, or phone call. I tap my index finger against my chin. I decide on a quick phone call. I've wanted to use my latest voice-distortion software forever, and for a simple prank call to Margot or Julian, it's too expensive. Plus, Margot would be up my ass for days.*

*It's almost four in the morning, which will hopefully also help my cause. I set everything up and dial Margery's cell number. Just for fun, I don't go with the creepy voice but a stuffy British female accent. Being on call all the time, she has to answer her phone.*

*"This is Margery." She sounds sleepy.*

*"Hello, Margery."*

*"Who is this?" She is already more alert.*

*"That's not important, dear Margery. What is important is that I know your little secret."*

*"Wha— How— Who?" she splutters.*

*Oh, this will be even easier than I thought.*

*"Oh, Margery, I was so sorry to see you resort to such measures after your back surgery, but I do understand that you can't allow the pain to get the best of you. Not in your line of work."*

*She understands my insinuation, and when Margery doesn't say anything, I continue.*

*"You had a visitor tonight."*

*That gets a reaction, and I hear her sharp intake of breath.*

*"So, my dear, as I see it, we have two choices."*

*"What do you want?" She sounds strangled.*

*"Well, you see, I've been waiting for this day for a very long time, but unfortunately, I need you to fill in some blanks for me. Unless, of course, you*

*would like Human Resources to get an anonymous email about your whereabouts after your shift on December second."*

*Oh yes, I know exactly when she stocked up last. I did my homework.*

*"No!" She is fully awake now.*

*"Very well, then. So why don't you tell me about your visitor, my dear?" I smile to myself.*

*"Why can't you just leave that poor girl alone?" Her question is no more than a whisper. She knows who I am and is afraid. Rightfully so. I may not harm anyone physically, but with today's technology, you don't need physical harm to destroy someone.*

*"That is not your concern." I struggle to keep my voice calm. "Just tell me what happened."*

*"The boy was talking to one of my nurses. He was asking about Maddie. He said she took care of his sister a long time ago. Beth is new. She never met Maddie and told him that."*

*Sister? That's interesting; but why did they race out of the hospital if that was all?*

*"Margery," I chastise, "you are not telling me everything."*

*"Really! That's all they talked about." She is almost pleading.*

*"Margery, you and I both know that you are holding something back. Do I have to remind you again what's at stake?"*

*I can hear her take slow breaths which I assume are to calm herself.*

*"I gave them Maddie's information. I didn't talk to them, but I gave them a note with her new hospital."*

*"Ahhh. Now, was that so difficult, my dear? Now, one last thing, did they mention any names? Besides Madeline Cross."*

*I have searched for Lilly for years, but her name hasn't popped up anywhere.*

*"He only said his sister; he didn't mention her name." Listening closely to the way she rushes it out tells me there is more.*

*"Margery, dear, are you certain this is all he said?" I make sure to lace my tone with a warning undertone.*

*"Yes," she croaks. She doesn't want to tell me but knows she has no choice. However, she is trying, which is commendable since she's seen what I could do ten years ago.*

*"I'm growing impatient, Margery. Nathalie is working tonight, and I'm sure she'll check her emails at some point." Nathalie Rehn is the charge nurse*

*who's on duty tonight and also a strict rule follower. She would have Margery reported within the hour.*

*"He said his name was McGuire. Rhys McGuire." There we go.*

*"Well, thank you, Margery. That wasn't so difficult, now was it?"*

*"Will you tell anyone?" She is terrified of losing her job.*

*"No, not at this point. Your little problem has not harmed anyone, but the day it does, I will happily take action."*

*I don't wait for a reply and hang up.*

*Rhys McGuire, who are you and what do you have to do with my Lilly?*

*I'm about to start my search when my phone rings, and Margot's name and picture lights up the screen. She chose the picture. Margot doesn't leave anything to chance. It was taken at a gala we attended a few months into dating. She wore a strapless black gown which emphasized every curve of her body. Her normally curly blonde hair was impeccably styled in one of those fifties-style up-dos, no doubt by her personal stylist. She looked truly stunning that night.*

*If she calls me at this hour, it means something has happened, and not answering is out of the question.*

*"Margot? What's wrong?"*

*"Oh, darling, Marco quit and left me stranded at The Club. He just left; can you believe it? How am I going to get home now?" she wails into the phone. Oh boy, Marco was her most recent driver, and I don't even bother questioning why this one quit.*

*"I'm on my way," I sigh.*

*Rhys McGuire has gotten one more night of peace.*

# CHAPTER TWENTY-THREE

## LILLY

I wake up exhausted. I couldn't sleep for the longest time, and neither could Rhys from what I heard from his side of the room. I think I finally drifted off around four.

Propping myself up to glance at the alarm clock on the other side of Rhys's bed, I see it's only nine. Five hours—that explains why I'm so tired. Rhys is still out, probably just as worn out as I am.

Plopping back onto my pillow, I stare at the ceiling. Holding Rhys's hand during Madeline's recollection kept me calm. In the last few weeks, I've let anger and betrayal run my life with Rhys as my anchor. But it's a new day, and instead of rage or betrayal, I'm consumed with a different emotion—fear. It has completely taken over. I was kidnapped, drugged, stalked, abandoned, and brainwashed. Bile starts to rise in my throat, and I scramble out of bed to the bathroom, where I empty the remnants of my stomach into the toilet.

I cling to the white porcelain. My skin is clammy, and I have no control over the shivers rolling through my body. After the second wave, I feel a wet washcloth against my forehead.

*God, that feels good.*

Once I make no indication of a third wave coming on, Rhys pulls me back against him. We sit in the middle of the small bathroom. He is leaning against the tub, his legs on either side of me and my back against his chest. With one hand, he holds the cold fabric to my forehead, while the other is wrapped around my waist, pinning me in place. Both of my arms automatically wrap around the arm holding me. It takes several minutes for my breathing to even out, and I fully slump against him. I'm spent.

Rhys hands the washcloth to me and wraps both his arms around me. "Let's go home."

All I can do is nod.

*Home.*


WE GET ready and hit the road mid-morning. Rhys is driving, and I watch the landscape flying by. My stomach has settled, and the urge to spew my guts out has subsided, but I can't shake the cold feeling that has taken hold in my chest.

"What if we made a mistake?" It's just a whisper, but Rhys hears me.

I turn toward Rhys. His knuckles turn white as he grips the steering wheel harder, but besides that, he shows no reaction, and I amend what we both refuse to voice out loud. "What if he is still after me?"

His mouth is set in a hard line, and I'm about to ask what he thinks when he reaches over and holds out his hand, palm up. I glance between his face and his hand but place my palm in his. He squeezes my hand in a comforting gesture. "Then we'll deal with it. You are no longer a helpless girl. You're a fighter. You've been training with Spence for years, not taking into account the training Dad has put both of us through."

He's talking about the weekends at the range, which now all make sense. Warmth spreads through my body. Heather and Tristen have taken every precaution to protect and prepare me. It doesn't fully negate the lies, but it helps me understand their motives.

After another pause, he adds, "And you have me."

With this simple action and words, the courage and need for answers that I thought I expelled this morning into the toilet slowly returns.

"Thanks."

He's right. I am no longer six years old. I've been training for a decade—a whole freaking decade. I might not have known for what, but I do now. I will work even harder. I refuse to let this define my future. The rage that has kept me going still simmers deep in my core. I don't think the feeling of betrayal will completely go away until I know the truth. But I'm also not ready to confront Heather and Tristen. Logically, I should, but I don't trust that they would be completely honest with me.

It's a gut feeling, but that's all I have for now.

THE DRIVE IS UNEVENTFUL. We ignore the ginormous elephant in the room, aka my past and everything we've learned. Instead, we banter about music and what to eat. We end up spending another night at a motel by the interstate and arrive home early Thursday.

The Defender hasn't fully come to a stop in front of the open garage door when Heather tears into the garage. With Natty also being on break and us "skiing," she took the holidays off work to be with her youngest.

"What happened?" Her eyes scan both of us frantically, and I understand her thought process. She is not too far off, but Rhys and I agreed on a stomach bug before we left this morning. Seeing how tired I look, Heather doesn't ask any more questions and begins fussing. She smoothes the hair back from my face, and I see her lips moving, but all I can focus on is Rhys's retreating form. Before he clears the threshold to the kitchen, he turns, and our eyes lock. Glancing at his mother's back and then at me, Rhys briefly closes his eyes before turning and leaving me alone in the garage. No, not alone—I'm with Heather—but why does it feel like I'm alone all of a sudden?

FOR THE ENTIRE DRIVE, I did my best to prepare myself that I'd have to face one—if not both—of my adoptive parents. But as soon as Heather is in front of me, all the pep talks were for shit. My throat constricts. I have the urge to flee and cry in her arms all at the same time. I excuse myself to my room under the pretense of lying down and unpacking.

I send a quick text to Denielle, telling her that we're home and the change in the story.

Her response is almost immediate: **U ok?**

I type back: **Yes and no.**

I still don't know how much I want to reveal to her. She is my best friend. But, for one, do I want to burden her with all this? And second, am I *ready* to talk about it?

**We'll be back Fri afternoon. I cleared my Sat and u r finally going to spill what the fuck is going on.**

I guess Den has made the decision for me.

BIDING MY TIME UNTIL SATURDAY, I hide in my room. Natty comes in a few times and tells me about everything I missed. I was so preoccupied with the entire trip that I didn't realize how much I missed her little face. The first time she walks in, I jump up and hug her so tight that she pats my back. "Ca-n't brea-the."

Laughing, I let her go. This little girl *is* my sister, my family—no matter what.

Rhys checks on me via texts, and on Friday, he even calls when I don't respond immediately.

"What's wrong? Why aren't you answering?"

"I was in the shower," I deadpan, clamping my phone between my shoulder and ear so I don't lose my towel.

"Oh."

I chuckle at his reaction. We chat for a few minutes before I hear Wes in the background, yelling for him to get moving. As soon as we hang up, I stare at the blank screen. It happened again. When his picture lit up on the screen, my heart started pounding double-time, the same way as in the hotel room. My mind is racing, searching for a logical explanation. It can't be what my brain tells me it is. It. Just. Can't. Swallowing hard, I resign myself to the fact that I may have to let Den in on *everything*.

ALL EVENING, I go over my conversation with my best friend. How it all started, what I've learned this last week, and the second elephant in the room—my adopted brother's feelings. Around midnight, I force myself to go to bed. I've bitten all my nails down to the nailbed—something I have never done in my life. I don't even like chipped nail polish. Now they look...I don't have words.

I've just turned off the light and settled on my pillow when there's a soft knock at my door. The fluttery sensation in my stomach returns full force.

*No, no, no.*

The few times I ventured downstairs, Rhys was nowhere to be seen. This would be the first face to face since he left me with Heather in the garage yesterday. I turn away from the door, clutching my hands to my stomach under the covers, and squeeze my eyes shut. Maybe he'll just go away, but of course, the door slowly swings open, and I hear a few muffled footsteps. I hold my breath.

*Go away! Go away! Go away!*

I can't take any more weirdness in my life, and my physical reaction definitely is—weird, that is. Eventually, the door closes again, and I exhale a long shaky breath.

I think I sleep for about two hours that night.


I MEET Denielle at Magnolia's, our favorite little café. It's located downtown. The entire street is lined with older, historic houses that have been restored to their original state. All the buildings are painted in pastel colors, and Magnolia's exterior is no exception with its soft pink. I often wonder which came first: the name or the paint color. The inside is cozy with rustic-looking chairs and benches. Everything is mismatched and gives the entire place an intimate feel. People hang out here for hours to work or just read.

Den beat me here this morning, which has never happened in the entire time I've known her. Usually, I have to tell her to be somewhere at least thirty minutes earlier if I want her there no more than fifteen minutes late. I'm barely through the door when she barrels into me and envelops me in a bear hug. Her favorite perfume immediately surrounds me, and I take in the familiar scent of florals, exotic spices, and Moroccan incense. Pulling back slightly, she gives me a once-over with her eyebrows knit together. "Babe, you look like shit."

Here we go already. I try to brush it off. "Sugarcoat much?"

"You know I call it as I see it. That's why you love me."

I give her another squeeze and say into her ear, "True."

Complete and utter honesty has always been the foundation of our friendship. We don't talk around things to make the other feel better. We say it as it is.

I watch her walk to our table while I order my usual tea and bagel. This time, it's my eyebrows that narrow. What the—? Den rarely dresses casual outside of the house, but today she is wearing black leggings paired with a bright-red, long-sleeve workout shirt, and a massive blanket scarf wrapped all around her. And when I say massive, I mean king-size-blanket big. The outfit accentuates every curve. She totally pulls it off, but I wonder what has brought this on? She usually chews me out when we meet up and I wear anything less than casual jeans.

"Your friend has quite the...presence," a deep voice drawls into my ear.

I turn and come face to face with a guy I've never seen here before. I know most of Magnolia's regulars, and he's not one of them. And he is way too close in my personal space. I take a step back, bumping into the bar in the process. My elbow knocks over the pile of lids for the to-go cups, and they go flying everywhere.

*Shit.*

I start picking up the little plastic disks when a hand lands over mine. "Let me help. I didn't mean to startle you." His tone is low as if he has to force himself to sound...friendly?

I instinctively pull away and take a closer look. Despite his semi-clean appearance, something is off. He is probably in his mid to late forties, tall, with dark curly hair sticking out in every direction. This close, his eyes have an eerie glow to them; the blue is so light it's almost white. His clothes have a musty smell that envelopes me, and I force myself to not take another step back. I can't put my finger on it, but his outfit doesn't fit right, like he usually doesn't wear these clothes.

"It's okay," I mumble, but I hear Madeline's voice in my head. *If he gets back on your trail, he will find you.* The urge to get away from the guy becomes almost too much to keep me in place.

Thankfully, the barista puts my order on the counter at that moment. "Here you go, Lilly."

I grab everything and turn toward our table when the stranger whispers, "Bye, Lilly."

The hairs on my neck stand in all directions.

I SETTLE into my chair across from Denielle and chance a peek at my best friend. Her face is expressionless. She seems to have missed my exchange with the creep at the bar, and I have no desire to rehash it.

"What's with the casual outfit?" I'm genuinely curious.

My friend looks down at herself and back up at me, shrugging. "Kelly gave it to me for Christmas. I spent the night at Charlie's since he's leaving tomorrow. I thought I'd wear it."

I plaster an exaggerated grin on my face and touch my hand to my chest. "Awww, you went against your every instinct to make your future mother-in-law happy."

She grumbles, "Shut up," but she can't keep a straight face either.

"So, how was the trip?" I try to draw out the inevitable conversation with her for a little longer.

Her right eye twitches ever so slightly as she crosses her arms over her chest. I'm stalling, and she knows it. The question is, will she play along?

After a moment of deliberation, she smirks. "It was great. I wish you would've *actually* been there, but we had a good time. It's probably better you didn't have to share the room with Charlie and me." She winks. "Oh, and you should've seen Wes face-plant into the snow the first day. Oh my gosh, I haven't laughed that hard in forever."

She digs in her purse, followed by sliding her phone across the table. A picture of Wes is on the display. He's *literally* sticking head-first in the snow, his neon-green snowboard pants and matching board up in the air. She makes a hand motion, and I swipe. The next picture is Wes flipping Denielle off, his entire head covered in snow. I crack up, and Denielle joins in. We both laugh until tears run down our faces, and I realize how much I've missed my friend these last few weeks. Until now, I wasn't sure what I would tell her, but sitting here with her, I feel lighter already.

Den and I have a special connection. We understand each other, similar to what Rhys and I had in the past—have again? Telling her is the right decision.

I exhale slowly. "What I am going to tell you can never leave this table. You cannot tell anyone. Not Charlie. No one."

Denielle stares at me, almost like she's trying to figure out if I'm messing with her. "Babe, I've watched you the last few weeks. I know some serious shit is going on. You've not been yourself, and then, out of the blue, you make up *and* take off with the enemy. What the fuck is going on?"

My pulse feels like it's somewhere in the one-eighty range, and I blurt out the first thing that comes to mind, my entire rehearsed speech forgotten. "Rhys is not my brother."

Den's eyes widen. "Excuse me?"

Stalling, I take a sip of my tea. Setting the cup down, I chuckle at the absurdity of this entire situation. "And that's not even the biggest piece of news." I snort.

My gaze is met with a blank stare. "Umm...o-kay?"

Another sip. "It all started with our journalism assignment."

She frowns at me. "The criminal case one you got the A for?"

I nod.

"Lilly McGuire, that was *before* Thanksgiving! Are you telling me you've been carrying whatever this is around for the past six weeks?"

She's fuming. I didn't anticipate that, which was bad judgment on my part. I should've known she'd be disappointed with me. I nod again, not looking at her.

"Go on," she orders in a cool tone.

*Crap.*

A flush creeps across my cheeks, and I dip my chin. "So...uh, my paper was about a string of kidnappings. Little girls that have been kidnapped all over the country and then turn up a few weeks later at random hospitals. It's been going on for over ten years, and I stumbled across the most recent victim when I was looking for a topic. It caught my interest, so I kept looking up the other victims. I read every article I could find, and I..." God, this is harder than I thought. Deep breath. "I started getting this feeling."

I finally make eye contact, and she just nods at me to continue. I wipe my palms on my pants.

"The more I researched, the stronger the feeling got, and then I started, uh...I started remembering."

She inhales sharply but still doesn't say anything. She lets me get it all out, and I'm grateful for that.

"At the time, I didn't know I was remembering. I thought I was losing my mind. Eventually, Rhys noticed that something was off and confronted me."

"I knew it! That's why he kept looking at you more than usual!"

*More than usual?*

My eyebrows are somewhere in my hairline, and I just stare at Denielle.

"Sorry, keep going." Of course she won't elaborate on what she means by that.

Shaking my head, I continue, "I told him that I thought I was going crazy. I was remembering things that were not part of my life —not the life I do remember, anyway. I told him everything, and he...got up and left."

Now Den's eyebrows shoot up, and she opens her mouth, but I hold my hand up.

"The way he acted, I just knew he was hiding something. So, I confronted him."

That gets me a smug smile; she is proud of me, and I sit up a little bit taller.

"The first thing he said to me was he loves me."

Denielle interprets it the same way I did. "Aww, that's sweet."

I grin at her reaction. "No, he *loves* me."

I wait. The wheels are turning, and then it clicks. Her eyes turn to saucers, and she opens and closes her mouth several times until it remains shut. Seeing my best friend speechless is a rare sight.

"Yeah, that was pretty much my reaction, too. Anyway, that wasn't the biggest shock of the night."

"Um..." She still can't form a coherent sentence, so I keep going. The faster I get everything out, the sooner I can, hopefully, get my heart rate under control. I'm pretty sure otherwise I'll have a heart attack soon.

I word vomit the next part. I had no clue I was capable of

speaking *that* fast. "He told me that I wasn't going crazy. I was kidnapped when I was six. I was held for several weeks and then eventually turned up at a hospital in Northern California. Rhys didn't know a lot of details either since he was just a kid himself when it happened. From what I know now, I was so traumatized that I wouldn't let anyone near me, and whoever had me kept threatening my parents. So, they decided to hide me and make me forget."

Time to breathe.

After what feels like an eternity, Den finally bursts out, "Holy shit! I mean...Holy. Fucking. Shit!"

I smile tightly as she interlaces her hands around her coffee mug and stares at her hands. We sit, and the silence elongates.

Eventually, she looks up. "You found all this out by coincidence? Because of our assignment?" Her tone is matter of fact.

I nod. Again.

*So much nodding this morning.*

"Whoever had me has been taking girls for the past ten years. I found the most recent victim, and the more I dug, the more I found and also remembered."

Denielle briefly glances to the ceiling. "Okay, so let me get this straight. You were kidnapped, got your memory erased, were implanted in a fake family, and your brother—well, fake brother—is in love with you?"

Oh Lord. I cackle out a laugh. "Only you could make this sound like a terrible soap opera."

My statement is met with a smirk and a one-sided shoulder shrug.

I try to explain. "My parents—I mean, Heather and Tristen— had been friends with my biological parents forever. My birth mother and Heather went to kindergarten together or something. Rhys and I pretty much grew up together, even before."

I tell her about our trip to California, how we ended up in Saint Louis, and the blanks Madeline filled in.

This time, Denielle snorts, "THAT. IS. SERIOUSLY. FUCKED. UP." She enunciates every word. "So, where are your real parents? What are their names?"

I hadn't expected to feel this relieved once everything is out in the open. But then, she knows me almost as well as Rhys. We've been friends for years. I think about her questions for a second before answering.

"Their names are Emily and Henry. I haven't figured out where they are. Rhys has been helping me piece the information together. He helped me remember more, but there is no trace of my parents anywhere."

"Heather and Tristen don't know either?"

I mumble, "We haven't told them that I know."

"WHAT? Why?"

My constant slow simmer of anger all of a sudden turns to a boil, and I snap, "Because they lied to me for ten freaking years." A little calmer, I manage, "I'm not ready to confront them."

"Wow. I, um...I'm seriously speechless right now. And that rarely happens."

I smile at her sadly.

All of a sudden, there is a spark in her eyes. "Okay, but wait; why is there nothing about you in the media? I mean, when you researched the case?"

"That's another thing my nurse told us. Whoever had me was blackmailing my parents, and they never filed a missing person report. That was why it also took so long for the hospital to identify me. They had no idea who I was until I told them. I was in the system as Jane Doe. Madeline helped my parents make me disappear. My real name never showed up in the hospital system. The media knows *of* the first victim, but not who it was. That's also why some speculate that the other girls are just placeholders."

Den's entire face scrunches together while she lifts the coffee mug to her lips. "Placeholders for what?"

"Me."

A spray of coffee explodes over the table, and Denielle frantically grabs napkins from the dispenser. People in the café turn at the commotion while we hastily clean the mess. I'm patting my bagel dry when she whisper-shouts, "Are you telling me that this freak is still looking for you?"

"We think so, yes."

She grasps my hand on the table. "Why are you so fucking calm?"

Rhys's response echoes in my mind. "I am scared, but I'm also not a helpless little girl anymore. Heather and Tristen made sure of that over the last ten years."

She nods in understanding.

My stomach growls loudly, and I finally take a bite of my bagel. We eat in silence, and it's visible that Den is mulling all the information over in her head. Before I can shove the last piece in my mouth, she levels me. "Can I ask you something?"

I tilt my head to the side. "Sure."

She pauses, so I eat my last piece of bagel. "So, Rhys loves you?"

"Hm-mm." I'm still chewing.

"Why has he been ignoring you for years?"

Ahh, the question I haven't elaborated on. Yet. Den was there to pick up the pieces and loathe him for me until I got over the hurt and to the loathing stage myself.

I swallow. "Tristen figured out that he was in love with me and made it clear that he could not act on it. He could never tell me. So, Rhys did the only thing he could think of."

She throws her hands in the air and lets her palms smack on the table. "Well, now I can't hate him anymore for you. I almost feel sad for him."

A chuckle escapes me. "Almost?"

"Well, he still made the choice to date the Wicked Bitch."

"Oh." My tongue suddenly feels like sandpaper.

"Speaking of...what is happening now? I mean, he came clean. Is he going to keep whoring himself out to her?"

I take a big gulp of the now almost cold tea, hoping to get rid of the dryness in my mouth. But it just feels like I've swallowed a stone that is now settling in my stomach. I haven't thought about that. Will he? He loves *me*. But why would I care? I shouldn't, right?

I shrug. "I guess. I mean, no one can know that I know. It's really his choice."

My best friend doesn't buy my brush off. "But how do *you* feel about it?"

*Am I that easy to read?*

"I don't know. Things have changed." I want to tell her about the sweaty-palm pizza incident at the hotel and the phone call flutters, but I chicken out. This is too weird. So, instead, I say, "I understand why he did it—all of it. He's been gone a lot since we got back, so I don't know what his plan is. If we change our behaviors, Heather and Tristen will know something is up, but..." I pause. I don't want to admit to myself that it does bother me that he's been gone the entire time. But then, *I* also avoided *him* last night.

We sit quietly.

Finally, she says, "Are you sure you don't want to tell Heather or Tristen? Or the police?"

"I'm sure." Instantly, all my defenses are back up, and I have to force myself to not snap at Den.

She sighs, resigned. "Then you need to be careful. If that freak is really still looking for you, don't let your guard down."

I'm glad she lets the Rhys topic go for now and doesn't push the other. "I won't. Maybe he isn't even looking anymore."

But while I say it, we both know that neither of us believes it.

I AVOID Rhys successfully for the rest of the weekend. I respond to his texts, but every time he comes in at night, I pretend to sleep. And every time, my body reacts the same way. He's gone when I venture downstairs in the morning, and with every passing day, I grow almost resentful. His life is back to normal while mine is...well, not. Not anymore. I know, logically, it's not his fault. I'm ignoring him, and he has to keep up the show, but still. A little bit of the betrayal creeps back into our newly built friendship.

# CHAPTER TWENTY-FOUR

**RHYS**

I haven't talked to Lilly in person since we got home four days ago. She's avoiding me, and I'm at a loss. When I text her, I get one-word answers. Every time I attempt to check on her at night, she pretends to sleep. I see the glow of the nightstand lamp under the door, but as soon as I knock, it turns off. The trip has changed everything. I thought I'd missed her before, but since we've gotten back and I've been hiding at Wes's, I realize *how much* I need her in my life.

Kat came home yesterday. We briefly spoke on the phone, and as usual, she hasn't asked how my holidays were. I also have no desire to volunteer information. That's our relationship. Unless it benefits her in some way, she doesn't care. Not that I care, either.

*What does that say about me?*

One more day and we're back in school. Everyone will once again think we're *the perfect couple*. She will grope me every opportunity she gets, make a big freaking show of it, and I...I'll let her. Because no one can fucking know that I've been in love with another girl my entire life.

. . .

W ES HASN'T SAID anything about my presence at his house since he got back, but the questions are written all over his face. He deserves answers. He covered for me—for us. However, unless Lilly gives her okay, I can't give him what he wants. It's her life and her decision. And since she won't talk to me, I have no choice but to divert Wes's attention whenever we get close to the topic.

Lilly moved her training with Spence to Sunday to meet with Denielle on Saturday. That much I got out of her via text message, but how it went, I have no idea. I annoyed the shit out of Wes until he agreed to meet at the gym Sunday morning—the same time Lilly scheduled her session. That's how low I have sunk to get a glimpse of her.

I get there about twenty minutes early just so I can see her spar with Spence. The room we always use is free for anyone to use when there are no group exercise classes scheduled. But the owner is an old friend of Spence's, and we always get dibs before anyone else. A perk I can't deny I enjoy. Two sides of the room are glass, which made Lilly super uncomfortable in the beginning. She hates being the center of attention, and when she trains, people stare. The petite, five-foot-four blonde beating up the six-foot-four Marine used to be the talk of the gym. Eventually, everyone got over it. The other members got used to our regular sessions, and Lilly learned to block them out.

Denielle sits cross-legged on the side, watching, and despite my best intention of just getting a brief glimpse, I stop mid-step and gawk. I haven't seen her spar in a while, and she is good. Like, *really* good. Spence is wearing pads, and Lilly is going at it. My jaw hits the floor, and I all but drool.

*Holy fuck, what a turn-on.*

I'm really glad I chose my looser workout pants today; sliding my hand into the pocket, I adjust myself as inconspicuous as possible. I have the urge to get in there and trade places with Spence, pushing her like I used to. At that precise moment, Spence glances up and spots me. His eyes widen briefly; I haven't been here at the same time as Lilly in years, but then his entire demeanor changes, and I know he's up to something. He stops Lilly and says something to her. Her whole body goes rigid, and both Lilly and Denielle swivel toward me. Denielle presses her lips together in a failed attempt to hide a grin, and Lilly looks like she's about to throw up. What the—? Then, Spence points at me and beckons me over.

*Fuck.*

Lilly holds my gaze, and very slowly, I put one foot in front of the other.

*Has the glass door always been this heavy?*

With every step, my pulse increases. Did Spence turn the heat up? I swear the room feels like one of those hot yoga studios. Coach made us take one of their sculpt classes once to prove his point that it's not all about heavy weight training and sprints. The entire team was nearly in tears at the end of the hour.

Getting closer, it's like I see Lilly for the first time in years, not four days. Finally in front of her, I'm able to tear my eyes away and look at Spence.

"Rhys." He is enjoying himself.

"Spence." I will my voice to sound calm and collected. My eyes flicker between all three of them.

"I didn't expect you until this afternoon."

Huh? Oh. "Uh, yeah. I'm meeting Wes in a few."

"Mm-hmm."

I narrow my eyes at my trainer. Spence peers over at Lilly, who is clearly uncomfortable, before addressing me again.

"How about a match between my two best fighters?"

"Wha—?" she squeaks.

"Uh..." is all my brain comes up with.

Lilly and I stare at him, both mirroring equal expressions of shock and disbelief, and Denielle is covering her mouth with her hand. Well, at least one of us is enjoying the show.

"You heard me. Suit up."

*He can't be serious.*

When we don't comply, Spence puts on his Marine face. "MOVE!"

That gets us both in action. I follow Lilly to her bag in the corner, and when I drop mine, she turns and hisses, "What are you doing here?"

*What the fuck is her problem?*

I'm starting to get irritated by her attitude. I have done nothing but help her in the last few weeks.

I drawl, "I guess fighting you." Two can play that game, and I've been playing it *much* longer.

Her nostrils flare, and there is a spark in her eyes. She is letting the fighter out, and a jolt of electricity flows through my body. The thought of fighting this girl ignites a whole other level of yearning inside of me.

"TODAY, YOU TWO!"

I grab my gear that's always in my gym bag, including the new gel pads Lilly gave me for Christmas, and get ready. Ten minutes later, Lilly and I are facing off in the middle of the room. Denielle is sitting up straight against the wall, and out of the corner of my eye, I see some of the older gym members stop what they're doing. People used to see us spar all the time, but not in the last few years. We've just become zoo animals.

*Fucking great.*

I let my gaze turn to tunnel vision. Focus on Lilly. She is doing the exact same, already in her fight stance. No distractions. Not that looking at her isn't already distraction enough. *Ugh, get a grip, or you'll get your ass handed to you*, I silently yell at myself.

In the back of my mind, I hear Spence go over the rules. As if we don't know.

"GO!"

This. Is. It. Lilly's eyes narrow, and she is waiting for me to make the first move. I don't think I should be this excited, should I? When I don't attack, Lilly takes over and launches herself at me with a cross punch followed by a hook. I block both, and a wide grin spreads across my face.

*Game on, baby.*

Her eyes widen ever so slightly. She knows I'm not going easy on her—never have—and this is no exception.

"My turn," I taunt. And with that, I drop low and go for her legs. Everyone else I would've swept off their feet, but Lilly simply jumps and brings her elbow down on my back.

"Umpf."

"Stop playing around," Spence barks at both of us.

Lilly cocks her head, and a wicked gleam enters her eyes. She's enjoying this as much as I am. I nod, silently telling her I'm all in, and a slow smile spreads across her face, showing her baby-blue mouthguard. When she dips her head as well, I let all hesitation go. It's just the two of us in the room, and I lunge. She blocks my punches and kicks as if it's second nature and counters each move with one of her own. I don't know how long we're at it, but my eyes are starting to burn from the sweat, and Lilly doesn't look much better. She's breathing heavy, loose strands of hair plastered against her face, but Spence makes no move to stop us. He's standing against the wall, arms crossed over his chest. Next to him are Denielle and Wes.

*When did he get here?*

This brief moment of distraction is all Lilly needs. She sweeps her foot, and I'm flat on my back. But she doesn't stop. She drops on top of me, wraps one arm around my neck and, oh no, she's not —yup, she is. *Crap.* She grabs the inside of her sleeve with the arm that is under my neck, immobilizes my head with hers, and then sneaks the forearm of her still free hand between her head and my throat, applying pressure. Sleeve Choke. I tap out, and I hear someone clapping slowly in the background. Lilly loosens her grip and inches back so our eyes meet. We're both breathing heavily, neither of us saying anything. I can't decipher her expression, but I'm glad she still has me pinned down. My gaze dips to her mouth, and I stifle a groan as her tongue swipes across her bottom lip. If I could move, I don't think I would be able to fight the urge to slam my mouth onto hers right here and now. My dick enjoys the close proximity between us as well, and my pulse speeds up again. It's a miracle she hasn't shown any indication of noticing my hard-on pressing against her. This was hotter than all the sex of the past two years combined.

*I wonder what actual sex with her would be like...*

Lilly is lifted off me before I can finish the thought, and a hand appears in front of my face. Spence no longer looks smug, but proud. Slapping my palm into his, he pulls me up and claps my back.

"Good fight, buddy!"

I just nod because I can still feel Lilly pressed on top of me. Now I'm also grateful for choosing this particular shirt earlier, as it covers a certain body part below my belt that has not gotten the *we-are-in-public* memo.

Lilly is next to Denielle, who says something that makes them both crack up, and Wes punches my shoulder. "What the fuck, man? I walked in here and thought I was tripping. That was AWE-SOME!"

Then, he adds with a whisper, "And seeing Lilly hand you your ass was fucking hot!"

That snaps me out of it, and a snarl erupts out of my throat.

He holds up his hands and grins. "Sorry, man!"

Of course, Wes thinks it's because of the handing-me-my-ass part, not him referring to *my* Lilly as hot.

During my interaction with Wes, Lilly grabs her bag and leaves the room with Denielle without saying a word. And that easy, my excitement turns back to irritation.


LILLY AND DENIELLE run through their workout routine while Wes and I are in the free weight section which is tucked in the back of the gym. I sneak a glance whenever I can, and twice, Lilly's eyes meet mine, but she averts her gaze immediately. I know we're not supposed to like each other in public, but really?

It's Wes's turn on the bench press when I sweep the gym again. The girls are on the other side of the treadmills, stretching and laughing. I'm about to focus back on my best friend when something catches my eye. One of two guys by the farthest leg press—the one closest to Lilly and Denielle—is openly watching them. His buddy is busy with the machine and doesn't notice that his friend is not paying any attention while he's chatting away. My eyes narrow, and I scan both of them. I haven't seen either of them before. The one on the leg press has black hair and somewhat of an Asian look to him; the other one is as Caucasian as it gets. And I don't like one bit how he's ogling the girls.

"Your turn." Wes making room for me on the bench snaps me out of my thoughts, and I shake my head. I need to get a grip, or there is no way I will make it through school tomorrow. Maybe having to *endure* Kat will actually be a good distraction.


WE FINISH, and Wes insists on going over to Lilly and Denielle, who are now sitting at a table by the protein and juice bar. We're almost at their table when Denielle points at something, and sure enough, I follow her gaze and land on the two guys. They have moved on to pull-ups, and this time, I get a better look at them. They're both older, late twenties I'm guessing, and definitely new here. The dark-haired guy is shorter than his friend, but both are well over six feet and built, like those guys that work out for a living. Asian dude notices the girls watching and winks at them. Fucking winks. Wes sees me staring and mutters something I can't understand because of the blood rushing inside my ears.

I've seen Lilly flirt before. I've seen Lilly kiss before. But despite my drunken tantrum at Sloane's party, I always knew it was nothing serious. That was before. Before we spent day and night together for almost ten days. Before I held her in her sleep, before I held her hand when she needed comfort, and before she was flat on top of me just an hour ago.

We reach their table, and I stand back, biting my tongue. I have no right to act like the jealous boyfriend, but I can't stop my hands from balling into fists. Lilly has avoided me for days. The closeness *I know* she felt during our match and now these flirting fuckers are too much.

Lilly stands up to hug Wes.

"What's up, beautiful? I didn't get to congratulate you earlier for beating your brother's ass."

LILLY BLUSHES, and her gaze flickers to me.

Den smirks devilishly. "What's up, snow face?"

Both girls burst out laughing, and Wes frowns. "Not cool, D."

Which makes them laugh even harder. I raise my eyebrows.

Wes catches my eyes and just grumbles, "Let it go."

Before I can stop myself, I blurt out, "I haven't seen you at home."

That brings three sets of eyes to me. Lilly's turning cold. "That's because you haven't *been* at home." Her words are like someone dumped a bucket of ice water over my head.

*Is* that *why she is so mad at me?*

Den cocks her head knowingly, Wes looks puzzled, and Lilly stands up, brushing past me. "Den knows."

*Wha—?*

She's walking away fast, and I call, "Everything?"

Lilly keeps going without a backward glance. Denielle slowly gets up to follow.

"Everything." She almost sounds sorry when she responds, which confuses me even more. She's been my biggest detractor for years.

FAN-FUCKING-TASTIC.

The girls are gone, and we drop our asses into their discarded chairs. Wes raises his eyebrows at me, waiting.

"Dude, I can't."

He presses his lips in a white slash, but he doesn't push me.

# CHAPTER TWENTY-FIVE

### HIM

*Almost two days. That was how long it took before I finally found Rhys McGuire. But it didn't actually take me that long to find the boy. The majority of the time, I spent finding Margot a new driver and chauffeuring her around. Who the fuck would've expected that it was that hard to find a new personal driver in a city with four million people? It was like Margot's previous employees had banned together and warned everyone in the business about her.*

*This afternoon, I finally found someone who either didn't know about my fiancée's eccentrics of not walking more than ten feet from the car to wherever she is going or didn't care because I doubled the salary. Two more days of driving her and I would've tripled it.*

*Now, I'm sitting at my desk, three monitors in front of me, reviewing all the information about Rhys McGuire I was able to dig up in an hour. I was a little surprised to find very little about him. He has two social media accounts, but none of the information is public. I have to dig into some not-so-easily-accessible records to figure out that he lives in Westbridge, Virginia with his parents and two sisters.*

*Another thirty minutes into it and I'm looking at a picture from last year's yearbook of Westbridge High's gymnastics team. I almost can't believe it, but there she is, more beautiful than ever. Under the picture, I scan the name for the third time: Lilly McGuire.*

*I marvel at how much she has grown up. A lot of her features are the same, her light-blonde hair untouched, no high or lowlights like every other girl or woman out there. Her hazel eyes sparkle with life. She is a natural beauty.*

*Besides this picture, there are only two more in the entire yearbook. One is of her and a girl from the gymnastics team, Denielle Keller. They're hugging in front of a banner that reads: Congratulations, WHS Gymnastics! District Champs! The other picture is her yearbook picture. Her hair is draped over one shoulder, and she smiles at the camera, though it's not the same natural smile as in the other two.*

*Over the next seven hours, I track everything I can find in Lilly McGuire's minuscule online presence. The clock at the top of my screen reads 5:12 a.m. My eyes are burning, but I stare, satisfied, at the results displayed in front of me.*

*Ten years ago, I wasn't aware of Heather and Tristen McGuire or their relationship to Lilly and her parents. From what I know now, they moved two months before Lilly entered my life, and back then, I didn't bother with her past. A mistake that has made me miss ten years.*

*Besides her new parents, she has a brother—hello again, Rhys—and a little sister, Natty. Neither of them looks anything like her. I wonder how no one ever asked questions. It is so obvious.*

*I compile a list of her friends, as well as what I can find out about the remaining McGuire family members' acquaintances, occupations, and hobbies. Thankfully, besides Lilly's immediate family, most of them have a very well-documented social media presence, which makes that part of my research, once again, laughably easy. You gotta love people and their need for validation; the more likes the better, and the more they post. Especially that Katherine girl I found connected to her brother, Rhys.*

*I do wonder if the minimal online activity from all the McGuires has to do with Heather and Tristen's careers, or in fact, because they were hiding Lilly from the world—from me. I'll find out soon enough.*

*Leaning back in my chair, I take one last look at everything before dialing Hank's number.*

*"This better be good. I'm still pissed at you," he grumbles half asleep into the phone.*

*"I'll fund the project myself. Let's expand the Virginia operation."*

*That wakes him up. "I thought you wanted to move to Chicago next. More options and shit."*

*"Changed my mind," I drawl. "Figure we'll see how that goes and then maybe add a few more to the mix."*

*"Well, um, okay. You want me to come with?"*

*I think that over for a moment. "Nah, I'll conference you in from there. You keep an eye on the west coast for now."*

*"Sounds like a plan."*

# CHAPTER TWENTY-SIX

## LILLY

THE FIRST WEEK OF SCHOOL PASSES PRETTY UNEVENTFULLY. Everything is back to pre-Thanksgiving break. Well, as much as it can be after the revelation that my entire life is a big fat lie.

I haven't figured out my next steps. Despite Denielle hounding me, talking to Heather and Tristen is still out of the question. I go back to my old routine: hang out with Denielle and the girls, go to practice, and get my schoolwork done. Den rarely leaves my side, and the sidelong glances tell me this whole thing has unsettled her as well. But no more Rhys—not at home, and barely at school, which is a relief and a letdown at the same time. His texts have stopped since our match on Sunday, and by Tuesday, I no longer check. I may or may not have chucked my phone across the room when the realization hit—only into the pillows on my bed, of course. I'm not a *complete* twit.

AT SCHOOL, I see Rhys in passing between classes, but he is either with his friends or Katherine—usually both, since her tongue seems to be permanently attached to his. Every time I see them together, her hands are somewhere under his clothes, and my teeth automatically clench. Midweek, I have a perpetual cramp in my jaw, and I turn the opposite direction as soon as I spot either of them, which makes me late to class twice. It's like two years ago all over again.

I've just pulled into our driveway on Friday when Denielle's name appears on my screen.

**Sloane and I are going to Magnolia's. U in?**

I don't want to be home, but I am physically and mentally drained from this week.

**Not today. Going to stay in. See u tomorrow?**

**:)**

*My sanctuary* has become more crucial now since I can barely stand to be in the same room as Heather and Tristen for an extended period of time. I don't get tunnel vision anymore, but the urge to flee is as strong as ever. They were the ones to suggest taking me away from my parents. Who does that?

It's late, and I'm curled up under my throw blanket, reading, when I hear the garage door open and close. Rhys is home. My stomach does its fluttering thing again, and I squeeze my eyes shut.

Why? Why? Why?

Last I checked, Tristen is still up, and it's confirmed by muffled voices from below.

All of a sudden, the noise level rises. "WHAT DO YOU CARE?!"

I sit up straight in bed, my dread about the fluttering immediately forgotten. Footsteps pound up the stairs, and the door across from my room slams shut.

*What the hell?*

I bite my lip and clasp my hands in my lap. I don't remember the last time Rhys shouted at Tristen. Not even...uh, nope, not even two years ago. He just disappeared.

I fist my throw blanket, forcing myself to stay put. Why would I check on him? He's made his choice to move on with his life. Slowly, my grip on the blanket loosens through its own volition, and my legs slide off the bed. Opening my door, I notice the light coming from the first floor, but when there is no movement, I tiptoe across the hall.

I don't bother knocking. Despite the only illumination coming from the streetlamps outside his window, the outline of Rhys sitting at the edge of his bed is clear as day. His shoulders are hunched, head hanging low, hands resting on his legs.

"Go away, Cal."

*Cal, not Lilly.*

I halt for a second, but there is no backbone in his words. My heart aches, and after closing the door behind me, I cross the distance between us. Getting closer, I see he is in black sweats with a matching black hoodie, and his hair is still wet. He looks like he came from the gym. It's late on a Friday night; why is he here?

Unsure what to do, I lower myself down next to him and tentatively wrap my arm around his shoulder. Rhys's body goes rigid, but after a shuddering breath, he melts into my side. His arms wrap around my midsection, and his head nestles into the crook of my neck. Feeling his breath against my skin makes my entire body go ablaze, and I close my eyes.

This is not about me or my messed up physical reactions; I'm here for him. I squash the urge to flee to my room and pretend I never heard the exchange between Rhys and Tristen. Instead, I return his embrace and realize I'm...home. No words are spoken. We just sit, and he clings to me.

I'm not sure how much time passes, but I hear footsteps moving around downstairs, and Rhys stiffens at the same time. He untangles himself. "You need to go!"

"But—?"

"NOW!" he hisses.

He pulls me up and, after a quick peek down the hall, pushes me toward my room and closes his door immediately, without another word. The light in the kitchen turns off, and the bottom step creaks. That's my cue to move. My door shuts when I see Tristen's head appear near the top of the stairs.

Heart pounding, I stand in the middle of my room and expel all air from my body.

*I should've gone to Magnolia's.*


THE NEXT FEW days continue the same: I hide at Denielle's or in my room, school, homework, practice with the occasional gymnastics meet, repeat. Rhys has been absent once again. Heather and Tristen act like it's the most normal thing in the world that their son doesn't come home, which adds to my irritation.

Tuesday, I get the first glimpse of Rhys. I'm on my way to third period when I spot him standing down the hallway. Wes's head is inside his locker as he digs around like a stoner hunting for his stash before a random drug search. Not that health-obsessed Wes would ever do drugs—he doesn't even do caffeine, though he makes people believe he's coffee addicted. Anyway, Katherine gropes Rhys per usual, one hand under his shirt and clearly on its way down the backside of his pants. But that's not what stops me in my tracks. It's Rhys's posture. He is as stiff as a board and doesn't return her touches at all. Hands stuffed deep in his front pockets, his features are blank while he stares at Wes's backside. As if sensing me, his head swivels in my direction, and I quickly step behind a group of freshmen. I'm wracking my brain if he's been like that the entire time and I was too focused on Katherine's actions that I didn't notice it.

Swallowing a lump in my throat, I turn and head the other way.

## RHYS

AFTER THE FIRST few nights back, I start keeping a second bag of clothes at Wes's. That way, I barely have to go home. I stopped texting Lilly on Sunday, and I haven't seen or talked to her in days. Not true, I've seen *plenty* of her retreating form in the hallways, and I'm not a fucking idiot to not catch on to what she's doing. After all, *I* invented the avoidance tactic in the McGuire family.

Now, it's Friday, and I head home to repack a new bag when I run into Dad. He's up later than usual, which I didn't take into account. Everyone went bowling tonight since there is no party, but I decided on my *third* workout for the day.

Wes is mad as fuck. I'm camping out on his couch but refuse to tell him shit. And now I also make up excuses to not hang out with him and our friends. I would be pissed at me as well.

*Whatever. I'd rather wallow in my self-pity alone.*

Despite being used to Wes's couch for years, I sleep like crap.

Constantly seeing Lilly speed in the opposite direction has me wound up tighter than a two-dollar watch. When I walk through the door, Dad's simple, "How are you?" makes me snap. He looks at me with a mixture of concern and understanding after my outburst, which makes black spots appear in my vision. It is his mother-fucking fault that I'm in this mess. With balled fists, I head upstairs to cool off. Another confrontation wouldn't end well. I'm smart enough to recognize that, even in my current state.

AFTER HERDING Lilly out of my room, I retreat to my bed and grab the nearest pillow. Biting down on it, I let out the primal scream that has been building up the entire week. When I'm done, I call Wes and let him know that I'll be back at his place in a few. My voice is no more than a croak, and I have to assure him three times that everything is fine. Of course, nothing is fine. He knows it, and I know it, but he stops asking. Holding Lilly for those few minutes...that can't happen again. I need to stay away.

Looking around my room, I draw in a deep breath and come to a decision. Grabbing a third bag, I pack almost my entire wardrobe. I'll start washing my clothes at Wes's or the laundromat—anything to not have to come back here.

KAT HAS, thankfully, been completely absorbed with cheer practice, and I only have to play *the part* while we're in school.

Two of her girls broke something on the ski trip, and she's had to train the replacements personally. No one else is good enough—her words, not mine. I can barely contain my relief when she tells me on the first day of school with a pout on her face, making sure everyone sees it.

# CHAPTER TWENTY-SEVEN

## LILLY

THE DAYS TURN INTO A WEEK, THEN ANOTHER, AND BEFORE I realize it, it has been four weeks since we returned from our trip. I've perfected my route between classes to avoid the daily grope session—at least, I thought I did. This weekend is our first invitational at home, and the entire team is buzzing with excitement. The last two invitationals went better than any of us had expected with the freshman that joined the team this year. Some are already talking about the Senior Showcase Invitational. I'm focused on Den discussing a fumble with one of the new girls and don't pay attention that we are exiting through the west wing doors, not the east wing doors—my *new* route to class.

"BAAABYYY, THERE YOU ARE!"

My eyes snap up, and there he is. Shit! With perfecting my route, I thought I had also perfected the not caring *again*, but as soon as my eyes land on Rhys, the freaking flutter is back.

*Wonderful, I have a first-row seat for today's show.*

Katherine is dressed in her blue-and-yellow cheer uniform. I swear, she has taken at least two inches off the skirt. Her hair is styled impeccably; her elaborate ponytail is curled to precision with a ginormous bow in matching colors, and even the loose strands around her face have been manipulated to appear unintentional. As soon as she reaches Rhys, she jumps into his arms, and he *has* to catch her under her ass, or she would've slid down him like a greased stripper pole. Sadly, for some reason, I can actually see that becoming her reality if she doesn't find a rich heir and become his trophy wife. It's like watching one of those terrible reality shows. You are fully aware that you shouldn't watch it, but you can't turn it off because you've somehow gotten emotionally invested despite your better judgment. She immediately shoves her tongue down his throat. The guys standing with them are starting to whistle and hoot. I feel bile rising in my throat, but I can't move.

I absently feel a hand on my arm, but it's like I have tunnel vision. Rhys lets Kat slide down, and as soon as she hits the floor, he steps away. Wes materializes next to him and nudges his elbow, looking at me. Rhys's eyes flick in my direction and widen when he realizes what—or more likely who—Wes is pointing out.

Locking eyes with him is like someone pouring a bucket of water over my head, and it becomes clear what I'm doing. My jaw hurts, and I can feel the imprints of my fingernails in my palm. Rhys takes a step toward me, and my entire body goes ablaze.

*Crap.*

I turn and walk toward the nearest bathroom as fast as I can without breaking into a full-on sprint. Inside, I lean with my hands on the sink and stare at my reflection in the mirror.

*Breathe.*

The door opens behind me. Denielle steps in, crossing her arms, and leans with her hip against the sink next to mine. "Uh, what was that?"

My breathing is still ragged, and I snap, "WHAT?"

She gestures toward the hallway with her head. "That! I thought you were going to jump the Wicked Bitch out there."

"Did she really have to maul his face like that in public? It's gross," I pretty much shout.

*I need to get a grip. What am I doing?*

I look at my best friend through the mirror, and my gaze is met with a raised eyebrow. "Is there something you haven't told me?"

I frown at her. I don't like where this is going—exactly where I have *refused* to go since the first flutter.

"Let's get to class. We're late." I turn, pull the door open, and walk out without giving her a chance to respond.

THAT NIGHT, I literally run into Rhys while coming out of my room and am too stunned to say anything. I don't remember the last time he was home this early—or in general. He must've come straight from practice.

We're in a standoff until he clears his throat. "Cal, uh, about today..."

Oh no, he's not going there. I look past him at the wall, feeling my ears heat. I notice movement out of the corner of my eye. Natty and Heather are coming out of Natty's room.

"There is nothing to talk about." It's not more than a hissed whisper.

His shoulders slump, but I am in self-preservation mode. The whole encounter has me unsettled enough, especially with Denielle eyeing me for the rest of the day. I turn on my heels and go back to my room. I can't face anyone. Leaning against my closed door, I sink to the floor, no longer able to hold my tears back. Slamming my fists against the floor, I *almost* wish I had never found out about my past. I was content with my pre-Thanksgiving-break life.

## CHAPTER TWENTY-EIGHT

### LILLY

My alarm goes off at six-thirty. I stay in bed, digging the heels of my palms into my eyes and letting out a low growl. We're hosting today's invitational. We've been practicing more than usual all week, and my body feels like I've been run over by a car which then backed up and repeated the motion about twenty-three times. I'm pretty sure my face is blotchy, and no amount of concealer will erase the hours of tossing and turning.

After my run-in with Rhys last night, I sat on the floor for an hour until the constant flow of moisture dried up. I'm so tired of Rhys's presence messing with me. I have enough to deal with, trying to figure out who Lilly McGuire—or rather, Lilly Sumner—is. I don't need my body to have weird physical reactions that make no logical sense.

*Something needs to change.*

It's my turn to drive, and I pull into Denielle's driveway at seven-fifteen. I haven't bothered with a shower since my hair goes up in a tight bun anyway and I'm just going to smell like before within the hour. I spend all of the time on my makeup, and thanks to the new foundation Denielle made me get months ago, I am semi-presentable.

We're stretching on the far end of the gym when Denielle mutters, "What the fuck is she doing here?"

I slowly follow her gaze and freeze in my straddle. Katherine Rosenfield, head cheerleader and self-proclaimed gymnastics-is-for-girls-who-didn't-get-on-the-cheer-team hater is here. All my senses go into overdrive.

"WHAT. THE. FUCK!" I clamp a hand over my mouth. I rarely use the f-bomb.

Denielle snickers beside me, and I throw her a glare that hopefully conveys, *Whose side are you on?*

I scan the gym, and sure enough, there he is. A knot forms in my stomach. Rhys is standing by the doors, talking to Camden Sewall, another senior, who's probably here to support his girlfriend, Grace.

*This can't be real.*

My eyes swing back to Katherine. She is talking to a girl I don't know, wildly gesturing with her arms like Miss Howard, our crossing guard in middle school. Katherine's uber-cheery demeanor doesn't meet her eyes. It's obvious she's enjoying being here as much as I enjoyed my first gynecological exam.

I'm still in my stretch, and my upper body drops forward, resting my forehead on my arms. The pounding in my ears makes it hard to concentrate.

I lift my head and peer at my best friend. "Unbelievable!"

Den gazes at me sideways, lips pinched together, but she doesn't comment.

For the next few hours, I avoid Rhys's general direction. I don't have to see him, my body is automatically aware of where in the room he is. There is a constant buzz in my veins with the occasional flutter in the stomach region. I go through the motions, but my performance is a joke. I can't clear my mind. I fumble during my back handspring, which almost lands me on my ass. As the morning progresses, the low buzz is replaced by a roaring in my ears.

I need to call Spence when this is over to schedule a training session ASAP.

Our team, overall, makes second place, which is at least something, but I can't take any credit for that. We pack up, and Denielle and I walk toward the locker room when Rhys steps in my way. I try to walk around him, but he follows my movement and blocks me. The tunnel vision returns. How *dare* he show up here? With her! I'm exhausted and frustrated with my performance. My entire body tenses. I'm itching for a fight.

Den puts a hand on my forearm, and I force my eyes to meet Rhys's.

"Hi." He sounds hesitant.

We stare at each other. I'm unable to form a coherent thought.

He opens his mouth to say something, but something inside of me snaps, and I sneer, "Why are you here? With *her* of all people!"

"Because you won't talk to me at home."

*Is he for real?*

"ARE YOU KIDDING ME?" I stomp my foot like a five-year-old throwing a temper tantrum, knowing how ridiculous I must look, but I can't help it. "ARE. YOU. FUCKING. KIDDING. ME?"

Eyes swivel toward us. I'm making a scene. I take a deep breath to regain some restraint and seethe, "You have not talked to me since we got home. You went back to your normal life with your perfect, fake relationship while I sit at home. *Alone.* My life is a big fucking farce. I live with people who have lied to me for ten years. TEN YEARS, Rhys. And you go back to banging your cheerleader whore who cheats on you at every opportunity and who you don't even *like*. And then you have the audacity to rub it in my face. Do you have any idea what that does to me?" My chest is heaving, and I can't stop the moisture from building in my eyes. My hand clamps over my mouth for the second time today.

*Where did that come from?*

Denielle is frozen with her hand still on my arm, and Rhys gapes at me with an open mouth.

Mortified, I glance around. People are still watching, but I'm pretty sure no one heard my rant. At least I had the foresight to lower my voice. However, that doesn't change the embarrassment factor.

Almost lightheaded, I shrug Denielle off and dart around both of them to the locker room.

*Oh God, oh God, oh God.*

"I'll talk to her," Denielle tells Rhys before I'm out of earshot.

THE LOCKER ROOM is bustling with girls in various stages of changing. I pass everyone, ignoring the ones calling my name, and head to the far end. Between the showers and the last row of lockers is an unused nook, probably because the drain back here always smells like sewage and the school has never been able to fix the issue. I sit on the floor with my forehead resting on my knees and arms wrapped around my shins when my best friend sinks next to me.

Denielle bumps my shoulder. "Umm...babe?"

I turn my head to look at her, letting my temple rest on my knees. "Don't say it. I don't know what happened out there." My voice sounds strangled.

She frowns at me and sighs, "I'm pretty sure I do."

I scan her face. Huh?

She wraps one arm around my shoulders and squeezes. "From what I have seen these past few weeks, Rhys's feelings are not one-sided."

*She really went there.*

"Den, he's my brother. Crap, no. He's my friend. At least, I thought he was while we were gone. But he just went back to his old life as if our trip never happened. As if nothing has changed. At. All." My heart starts pounding in my chest.

That gets me another squeeze. "Babe, first, he is *not* your brother, nor has he ever been. And second, I think you guys are way past the friend stage. You may have been running the opposite direction every time you saw him anywhere, but he saw you too. And the look on his face said it all. He doesn't think anyone notices, and I might not have if you hadn't filled me in on this fucked up situation. I can tell you...he most certainly has not gone back to his old life. His feelings for you are written all over his face. It's obvious."

I'm about to tell her that this is not news; he admitted it himself, but Denielle holds up the hand that is not wrapped around me.

"Don't think I haven't watched you too since you told me. You are just as gone as he is."

*What?*

My eyebrows scrunch together. I can't be. That's...I just can't.

After a pause, she adds, "And you know what...in its own twisted way, it probably makes sense."

I rub my forehead. "Uh. Huh?"

Den chuckles. "Okay, let me make it clearer. Babe, when you and I met, the two of you were joined at the hip, with an occasional Wes on the other side. You were closer than any brother-sister relationship I'd *ever* seen. When Rhys stopped talking to you, you were distraught. And not just in an *I-had-a-fight-with-my-brother* kind of way. It was as if you got broken up with, like you lost the other half of your soul. I didn't understand it at the time. I mean, I love my brother, but if Oli stopped talking to me over a fight or whatever...oh well, I'd get over it. But you didn't. Even when you started *functioning* again, you never were the same. Now it all makes sense."

"Huh?" is my very profound response once more.

"Whatever that memory doctor did to you, he didn't fully erase what you and Rhys already had before the you-know-what. I've thought about it a lot, and I think it's always been there. Now that he's come clean, and with everything you guys went through together on your trip...well, you can finish that sentence."

"Huh?" I'm convinced I have a uni-brow by now.

"Oh, come on, you're not that dense. Wes maybe, but not you," she chastises. "Or are you in denial?" She squints and scans my face. "Oh my gosh, YOU ARE!"

Her outburst makes me jump. I turn away, and I narrow my eyes at the blue locker across from me, replaying everything Den just said. What Rhys and I had before I got kidnapped and had my memory erased. That I acted like I had lost my other half. My mind wanders to the hotel room. The butterflies in my stomach. The sparring a few weeks ago. And despite my initial anger at Spence for putting me in that situation, it was the happiest I'd been since we got back. The fluttery feeling in my stomach. *Butterflies.* I blink. Oh! Oh. My. God.

"I'm in love with him," I say in a strangled whisper. I rub my hands over my eyes. I can't be. It's wrong.

I'm scared to look at Denielle, at what I'm going to see in her face. Pity? Revulsion? Disappointment? I chance a glance and am shocked for the second time. She genuinely smiles at me, and all I see is understanding and happiness. But for what?

"Why are you not disgusted?" I rasp out.

*This is all just so wrong.*

"Huh?"

I have to laugh. I guess I'm not the only one here who doesn't have the most intelligent way of expressing confusion.

"He's my brother. This should disgust you. Gross you out," I clarify my statement.

"Oh." She purses her lips and looks away for a second. Meeting my eyes again, she says, "Why would I be? You are my best friend, and your feelings are important to me. But even more importantly, he is *not* your brother. He never was. Besides being a bit slow, you have done nothing wrong. None of this is your fault."

"I doubt anyone else will see it that way. It's wrong."

"No, it's not. Fuck everyone else. Who gives a shit?"

My insides warm at her outburst. Denielle has always had my back. I couldn't wish for a better best friend. For the first time, I look around to make sure no one is listening to our conversation.

"What am I going to do? I mean, it's not like we can be together."

There is a sour taste in my mouth, and I feel like someone has deposited a fifty-pound weight on my chest.

"Well, as I see it, it's whatever you two make of it. It can be nothing. You can keep going as it is: he dates the Wicked Bitch, and both of you are miserable, *or* it could be everything for the two of you."

"But we can't be together." She doesn't get it. To everyone else, we're blood-related. That's incest.

Denielle moves so she is facing me head-on and puts her hands on each side of my face to force me to look at her.

"Yet," she says with a stern tone. "This will not last forever. Eventually, you'll have to come clean to Heather and Tristen, and one day, this whole cluster-fuck will be cleared up. That's when you can officially be together. But it's *your* choice."

*My choice*.

My forehead tilts forward to rest on hers. "Thank you."

She moves her hands, gives me a kiss on the cheek, and stands up, holding out her hand. "Let's hit the shower and go find your soulmate."

# CHAPTER TWENTY-NINE

## LILLY

APPROACHING THE LOCKER ROOM DOORS, MY HEART RATE TRIPLES with every step. I fight the urge to dig my heels into the ground, and Denielle pretty much pushes me through the double doors.

I scan my surroundings, but Rhys is nowhere in sight. A sigh of relief *and disappointment* escapes me, which makes Denielle cackle at my side. In the shower, I asked to spend the rest of the weekend at her house, and she just doubled over laughing. I'm so glad my best friend finds my situation hilarious. I just can't face anyone until I figure out what I want to do about my newest revelation. I'm in love with Rhys.

I send Heather a text that I'm staying at Denielle's and prepare myself for some sort of argument since I've always had to plead in advance before I was allowed to spend the night there.

**Have fun, sweetie. Dad is taking Natty and me to the museum tomorrow. We'll be back after dinner.**

I read the message twice before tilting the screen toward Denielle. "Umm...does she have the wrong child? She has to have confused me with Rhys, right?"

Den shrugs. "I don't think Rhys would even tell them if he wasn't coming home."

*Fair point.*

We're in Denielle's room, lounging on her king-size bed while her 60-inch flatscreen is showing reruns of one of the CW's vampire shows. Usually, I would be totally into it, but not today.

A lump forms in my throat. When I go home tomorrow, I'll have to face Rhys alone...unless I wait until the evening, which is the coward's way out.

*Why is it all of a sudden so hard to breathe in here?*

Before we go to bed, I text Spence that I need a training session ASAP. I hope that a good workout will help me clear some of the fog in my mind, and maybe I'll have an epiphany about what to do about Rhys. My phone vibrates not a minute later.

**No problem, kiddo. Your brother canceled his session tomorrow. Meet around 9?**

Rhys canceled his session? Why would he do that? Unless he is waiting for me to come home.

*Oh great, the butterflies in my stomach made room for hornets on steroids.*

I WALK into our usual training room at eight fifty-five with Denielle on my heels. She has not stopped muttering obscenities at me since I dragged her out of bed an hour ago.

She just settled in her usual spot on the floor against the far wall, steaming vanilla-caramel latte in hand, when she whispers, "Ohhh, he's back."

Huh? One arm across my chest, stretching out my shoulder, I look at her questioningly. She nods her head toward the other side of the room, and I try to subtly look over my shoulder. However, what I don't expect is my eyes colliding with a pair of hazel ones right on the other side of the glass wall. It's the friend of the Asian guy who winked at us the other day. Personally, I thought that was pretty sleazy. I mean, who winks these days? This guy is tall—taller than Rhys's six-one—with light-blond, shaggy hair. His eyes are striking, even from a distance, no question there. I can't determine if the brown or green is more dominant. It's almost as if his eyes are changing color right in front of me—it's captivating. This close, there is also no denying that he is in shape. Like, *really* in shape. His broad shoulders are emphasized even more by the wifebeater he's wearing paired with gray sweats. His sweats are loose-fitting, but I can see that his lower body is just as defined as his upper body. My eyes wander back to his face, and his mouth quirks up on one side with an eyebrow raised. Heat creeps up my cheeks, and I spin around, squeezing my eyes shut.

*Oh God, how embarrassing.*

A sudden knock on the glass makes me stiffen, and I glance down at Denielle, who is peering around my legs, wiggling her fingers with a seductive smile. I swivel on my heels. Another set of eyes has joined the first. Asian guy is standing next to his friend and is intently staring at Denielle. As Wes once phrased it, he is *eye-fucking* her.

"Den!" I hiss.

Spence chooses that moment to walk in the room and lets the glass door fall shut.

"Let the fun begin!" He grins broadly.

*Oh, thank goodness.*

I fight the urge to hug Spence. Who knows what would've transpired otherwise? Denielle loves Charlie, but she flirts like there's no tomorrow. I once asked Charlie about it, and he just said, "That doesn't bother me." Nothing else.

"Get your wraps."

I'm pulled out of my thoughts and grin.

*YES!*

Spence is in full-body armor as if he sensed what I needed. He pushes me hard, and for ninety blissful minutes, I forget everything. Nothing matters, and I am just me. No kidnapping, no lack of memories, no brother turned *lover*. I'm at peace, punching and kicking my trainer in whatever body part he commands.

Denielle and I sit at our usual table with our usual post-workout shake when I tell her, "I'm going home."

I can't avoid Rhys forever. Well, I probably could, but do I want to?

She just nods as if she knew all along.

*She probably did.*

. . .

I PULL up to the house in the early afternoon. Pushing the button on my visor, the garage door slowly lifts, and as expected, Tristen's car is gone. However, Rhys's car is not. I swallow hard. I wipe my hands on my borrowed pants since my overnight stay hadn't been planned.

I'm still unsure what I'm going to do. I can't avoid him all day—maybe a little bit longer.

Sounds resembling an action movie are coming from the family room, and I duck past the opening without looking and sneak up the stairs.

I showered at the gym, so I only have to change into my own clothes: my go-to home attire of black yoga pants and a long-sleeve, crew-neck shirt. I grab the first shirt I find, which has a gray herringbone pattern. Good enough.

That didn't take nearly enough time to calm my nerves. I feel like such an idiot. My body gave me all the signals, and I refused to acknowledge them. I smack my hand to my forehead. Den is right. Logically, I haven't done anything wrong. Rhys and I aren't blood related, but the thought of what others will think makes my stomach churn.

Pacing the length of my room about a dozen times, I eventually stop and take a deep breath. I can't stall any longer before it becomes ridiculous. Rhys knows I'm up here. Our house isn't that soundproof.

*I can do this.*

I'm halfway down the stairs when my phone vibrates in my hand with an incoming text message. I glance at my screen and stop with one foot in the air. The sender is listed as UNKNOWN. What the —? I swipe and stare at a picture of myself with Denielle at Magnolia's. It's from the morning I told her everything and ran into that weirdo. I scroll down, and the next picture shows me walking to my car after school. I'm bundled up, which tells me it's also recent. The last picture is me at the gymnastics meet yesterday. I had just finished and am walking toward my coach. With every picture, my throat constricts more. After the last photo is a short message, and my throat completely closes up.

**I can't believe it's really you.**

My hands fly to my mouth, and I watch my phone clatter down the stairs.

## RHYS

I SHOULDN'T HAVE GONE to Lilly's meet—and most definitely not with Kat. What was I thinking? Oh right, I wasn't. After it sank in that she actually cares about me, possibly the same way I care about her, all I could think about was that I wanted to be near her. Screw the consequences.

I had just put my car in reverse when Kat texted to meet her for breakfast—a demand, not a question. I contemplated ignoring her, but she'd just call, so I sent a quick text back.

**I'm busy. On my way to Lilly's meet.**

About to pocket my phone, another message appeared on my screen.

**Pick me up. I'll wait outside.**

*FUCK.*

I knew if I argued it'd just result in a massive fight, and to be honest, I didn't intend to pay any attention to Kat, so whatever. But in my hormonally-guided, eighteen-year-old guy brain, I didn't even consider how Lilly would take me showing up with her.

Dumb. Dumb. Dumb. I want to kick myself in the balls for my stupidity.

*Maybe I'll have Wes do it. I deserve it.*

When Denielle left me to hurry after Lilly, I went to find Kat. Leaning against my car, she was typing furiously on her phone, looking up when I approached.

"Why are we here, Rhys?"

*Oh joy, first name.*

"Because I wanted to support my sister." I forced myself to show no emotion—not how Lilly's reaction had unsettled me and not how much Kat's entire presence annoyed me.

She gave me one more glare before her entire demeanor changed. "Don't forget Meghan's party tonight. We're all meeting at Chop's Diner at seven and then heading over to her place."

*Uh, what?*

I just stared at her. *Maybe she has ADHD?* Something I'd considered before, because how can one person switch topics *or* personalities that quickly? Or she doesn't give a shit about me. The party, however...I knew Meghan had been Kat's rival for cheer captain for a while, and I was sure she had something planned.

"Yeah, sure." I was too exhausted to argue or let her know that I would *most definitely* not be there. I planned to be at home, hopefully talking to the girl I love.

MY PHONE HAS BEEN BUZZING since six, but every time I see it's neither Lilly nor Denielle, I put it back down, not bothering to read the messages.

When there is still no sign of Lilly by eight, I head downstairs and *casually* ask Mom. She holds my gaze a little longer than usual before replying, "Lilly is staying at Denielle's."

Without another word, I turn on my heel and make my way back upstairs. I don't have it in me to put on a show. Lilly is hiding at her friend's house. What am I supposed to make of that? My chest tightens. I rake my hands through my hair and grab my jacket from my bed. Halfway toward the door, a voice in my head chastises me. *What are you doing? Running off to a chick you can't stand because your girl doesn't immediately come home and throw herself at you?*

Not knowing what's going on with her makes me ball my fists, and I fight the urge to kick my desk chair across the room. Is this how Lilly felt two years ago? My anger and frustration instantly deflate, and I put my jacket back down.

*Another sleepless night is ahead of me.*

IT'S early afternoon when I hear the garage door open and close, and *someone*—insert air quotes here—is trying to quietly sneak upstairs. She's here. Mom and Dad are gone, and we could finally figure it all out, but she remains upstairs. I try to concentrate on my movie, but my gaze keeps wandering to the ceiling. We have to talk eventually; she can't avoid me forever. Okay, maybe she can. I managed it pretty good for two years.

*I hope she's not that good.*

Finally, I hear footsteps coming down the stairs, and my body starts tingling all over. But the footsteps halt. She's making a run for it again. *Fuck.* Then, something falls down the stairs in a loud clatter, and I'm instantly off the couch.

I skid to a halt at the bottom step. Lilly is halfway up the stairs, pale as a ghost, with her hands in front of her mouth. Her eyes are wide. The last time I saw this look on her face was in the middle of the night in our hotel room. Every rational thought leaves me, and I take two steps at a time until I reach her. Without thinking, I pull her into my arms, and she returns my embrace without hesitation, shaking like a leaf. I feel my blood turn to ice. Something is seriously wrong. Her face is pressed against my chest, and she holds on for dear life. I have one arm wrapped around her back, and the other holds the back of her head. My thumb is moving back and forth, trying to soothe her.

"Babe, what happened? What's wrong?" I murmur.

Lilly clutches even tighter, it's almost painful. She mumbles something that sounds like, "He's back," but my brain doesn't comprehend her words.

I pull back to frame her stricken face with my hands. Tilting her head upwards, I search her eyes. "He who?"

All she does is glance toward the bottom of the stairs where I now see her phone.

*That's what made the sound.*

I guide her to sit on the step and disentangle myself to retrieve the phone. I settle down on the same step and hold it out for her to unlock it. Without paying attention, she presses her thumb on the button, and a text message appears on the screen. I look at each picture until I get to the caption at the end and finally understand.

*He is back.*

"Fuck!"

I PULL Lilly upright and lead her to my room where we both sink down onto the bottom of the bed. She pulls her legs underneath herself, and I lean forward with my forearms on my thighs, head low, staring at the floor. I have no clue how much time passes. I'm scared shitless, and the same thought runs through my head over and over.

*This is my fault. I shouldn't have let her go to California. This is all my fault.*

"You called me babe." Her voice startles me.

My eyes snap up to Lilly, who is staring at her hands. I did? A chuckle escapes me at the absurdity of the situation. "Yeah, I guess I did."

"I liked that."

*Wait, what?* We just discovered that the psycho who kidnapped her ten years ago is back, and she *likes* that I called her babe? I must have misheard.

"Umm..." Smooth, way to play it cool.

Lilly glances at me through her lashes. Her eyes shine with an emotion I never thought I'd see her direct at me.

"Say something," she whispers.

"Uh..." I'm still too stunned to form a coherent response.

That's when she reaches over and interlaces her fingers with mine. The contact gives me the jolt I need to snap out of my stupor. Holy. Fucking. Hell. She *reciprocates* my feelings. It hits me like a sledgehammer. For a fraction of a second, I forget everything that happened just minutes ago, and I want to pound my chest like a damn caveman. Before I can relish the feeling, though, reality comes crashing back.

He is back.

I squeeze her hand, and she leans her forehead against my shoulder. "I'm scared."

I let go of her hand and wrap my arm around her shoulder. "Me, too." And I am. I feel like the seven-year-old boy all over again. Completely helpless.

Lilly wraps both of her arms around my waist, and we sit there. I'm the most terrified and—at the same time—the happiest I have been in years.

I am holding *my* girl in my arms. But I also can't shake the feeling that this is all my fault.

## CHAPTER THIRTY

**HIM**

Exactly one week after receiving the email alert, I'm getting off the plane in Virginia. I had to stay through the New Year since Margot and I were hosting this year's party. Hank and I used the remaining time to iron out the details for the expansion project. Stepping off the bottom step of the company jet, it feels like I'm in fucking Antarctica. Snow covers the ground, and with everything occupying my mind, I didn't think to pack the appropriate attire. I stare at my brown Ferragamo loafers, no socks. Well, shit, guess I'm going shopping before settling in my suite.

I had called Margot from the plane, and she was displeased, to say the least. She knew I was leaving on a business trip, but I had neglected to tell her for how long since I had no idea myself. Next week is the annual charity event for Shelter for Kids, and it had completely slipped my mind. As vain as Margot can appear to an outsider with all her shopping and eccentrics, this is one of three charities she is one hundred percent dedicated to. When I first met her, it was one of the reasons that drew me in and made me want to get to know her beyond the casual hookup—which may have been the first reason, if I'm completely honest.

I promised to fly back for the event and to double my usual contribution. Not that that would've been necessary, but it also reduced some of my guilt. I do care for the charity as well; I just got...sidetracked.

. . .

I SETTLE *into my top-floor penthouse suite in the city before picking up a rental car at a no-name place on the outskirts. The rental car is for the sole purpose of driving to Westbridge and back. For everything business related, I will continue using the car service I hired to pick me up from the airport. I emailed the company my schedule, and they assured me that a car would be waiting downstairs every time.*

*It's late afternoon on a weekday when I first drive into Westbridge, Virginia. Seeing the city limit sign, all my senses intensify. I scan my surroundings and take everything in as I pass the high school, Butler's Gymnastics Academy, and a local coffee shop named Magnolia that several of Lilly's friends have checked into on social media. This is where Lilly has spent the last ten years, with the exception of a brief stay in North Carolina. I take a deep breath and go through a mental list of things to do. My focus at home was the expansion project, which left me little time to prepare for the other reason for this trip. I am in no way ready, which is not like me. I plan— extensively. I calculate. I wait for the right time, and* then *I execute. But not this time, so now I have to do the planning locally. I have to get everything right, and that will take time. At least I have enough work to do that the waiting hopefully won't be too excruciating.*

I'D ARRIVED *during winter break, but as soon as school starts back up, I learn Lilly's routine quickly. She does the same things every day. School, practice, home, with the occasional meeting of friends. On the weekends, she goes to a local gym with her friend Denielle, who has rarely left her side since I arrived. She seems to be a good friend to Lilly, and that pleases me. She only deserves the best.*

*Back in my suite, I load today's pictures and carefully scan all of them. I was surprised to see Rhys at Lilly's gymnastics meet, and from her look in some of the pictures, Lilly wasn't very happy about her brother's show of support. Skipping through the pictures faster, it's apparent that Lilly is distracted. She has a scowl in almost every photo. What has you so bothered, Lilly? The last picture makes me stop. Lilly looks like she's yelling at her brother. His face is in complete shock, and from Denielle's hand on Lilly's arm, it looks like she's comforting her. Interesting.*

. . .

LAST NIGHT, *I spent several hours carefully choosing the three pictures I am now looking at. They are the perfect selection from the last few weeks. She just arrived home. I didn't want to do this while she was out and risk something happening to her. It's time to make contact. I hit send and lean back in my chair, fingers interlaced behind my back, smiling at the screen.*

*Soon we'll meet again.*

# CHAPTER THIRTY-ONE

**LILLY**

Ever since reading the caption at the bottom of the text message, I'm paralyzed. My brain-to-body connection has been severed, and my legs won't obey my command to run and hide.

Sitting on Rhys's bed, I focus on the one thing that distracts me from *him. Psycho-kidnapper him, not Rhys him*.

I can't help the embarrassment of not admitting it to myself sooner. The signs were clear as day, but I simply couldn't fathom how I could be *in love* with my brother—well, not my brother, but my best friend since birth. But he was my *brother* longer—at least on the surface. Perhaps Den is right and the memory doctor didn't do his job all the way. Maybe he left some old connections in place that eventually surfaced again? I just chose to ignore it, listening to the logical side of my brain instead of my heart.

Unfortunately, the distraction doesn't last very long, and the bone-chilling fear grips me again. Holding onto Rhys is what's keeping me from completely losing it. My head is nestled against his side, and I inhale his familiar scent. Safe.

I lose track of time when Rhys suddenly whispers against my hair, "Let's get out of here."

I pull far enough away to see his face. "Where are we going?"

His gaze settles somewhere over my shoulder, and he shrugs. "I don't know. Out. I don't want to be here when Mom and Dad come home."

My breathing instantly doubles. "What if he follows us?"

Rhys stiffens but wraps his arms around me again. "We'll be careful."

He puts up a front, but anxiety is coming off him in waves. He is as freaked out as I am. Though, I have to agree with him; I don't want to be here either when Heather and Tristen come home. The whole charade would tumble down faster than the cheerleaders' pyramid during last year's homecoming game when Katherine forced the new girl to do back handsprings in the front row, and the poor girl knocked over two of the guys holding everyone up. Needless to say, the whole thing didn't end pretty.

I'm pulled out of the memory when Rhys stands up and drags me with him by the hand. He doesn't let go until we reach the garage.

RHYS'S CAR is inside as usual, and I parked in front of Heather's spot outside of the garage. Neither of us has to be out in the open for us to leave. Rhys leads me to the passenger side door and waits until I'm settled before walking over to his side. As soon as the dome light is off, he reaches over and interlaces our fingers together again. He hits the garage door button and slowly backs out into the driveway. The street is quiet, but instead of its usual peaceful feel, the hair on my arms stands up, and I'm scanning our surroundings feverishly. Rhys makes sure the garage door is closed before he fully pulls out into the street. He squeezes my hand, never looking away from the road.

WE DRIVE FOR SOME TIME, not letting go of each other's hands. Rhys absentmindedly strokes my hand with his thumb. His fingers are calloused from years of training, but despite the rough texture, the touch is gentle and sends tingles through my body. I relish the feeling of safety it evokes inside of me. We stop at a small café a few towns over. When no other car pulls into the parking lot for ten minutes, we deem it safe and exit the Defender. I pick the table farthest from the windows and door while Rhys get us something to drink. He puts a steaming paper cup of Earl Grey tea in front of me, lid placed on a napkin on the side. Warmth rushes through me like a big wave. He still remembers my quirks.

We don't talk, both just holding onto our respective cups. I notice Rhys staring at my fingers. His thumb is moving back and forth against his coffee cup like he is still caressing my hand. I ache with the need to feel his touch again and intensify the grip on my tea harder, fighting the urge to reach out to him.

Eventually, Rhys breaks the silence. "Do you want to tell Mom and Dad?"

I look up. His face is deadly serious, but I don't have to think about my answer. "Not yet." Logically, we should. Any sane person would, but every fiber of my being screams at me that it's not time *yet*.

He nods, lips pressed together as if he is keeping himself from saying something else. I continue, "So far, we only know that he is back, but not what his end game is—besides that he wants me."

Rhys's posture goes rigid, and he almost crushes the paper cup. Without thinking, I reach over and cover his hands with mine. His eyes dart to my face, and I realize what I've done, pulling back immediately. We're in public.

"I think we should wait and see if he makes contact again. We can tell Heather and Tristen at any point, but I'm not ready yet. They'll freak out and do God knows what, probably pack up the house and move us in the dead of night." I have to grin at the visualization of that, but then another thought occurs. I add, my tone somber, "And it opens too many other doors I don't want to deal with."

Rhys immediately understands. "Your parents?"

It still blows my mind how he always seems to read my mind. I nod. "And us."

His expression turns into surprise. Almost like he doesn't expect there to be an *us*.

I blush. "Well, once they find out, everything will change.

Tristen was very clear in his stance about your feelings for me. What if they make one of us leave? I'm not eighteen yet, so it would be you!" With every word, my breathing gets more ragged, and the thought of Rhys leaving me, voluntarily or not, has me close to hyperventilating. I can't handle any more changes at this point.

Rhys sees my distress, and after a quick scan of our surroundings, he pries my hand from my cup and interlaces our hands. He angles his body so his back is to the room and our hands are hidden from view.

"I don't think they would take such drastic measures, but you're right, there'd definitely be changes." He chuckles, mostly to himself. "They'd probably put a lock on your room—or mine—from the outside."

I try to pull my hand away, but he holds on tight. "Not funny."

That gives me a genuine laugh. "I'm sorry, babe. I'm just trying to lighten the mood a bit. Bad timing."

Babe. There it is again. How can one word already feel so right?

*Is that why it hasn't bothered me the two times he slipped?*

Rhys grows serious, and his eyebrows draw together. "I do want you to tell Denielle. I want one of us with you at all times. And I think Wes deserves to know."

"I'll talk to Den tomorrow. If you think we can trust Wes, tell him." Wes has been a loyal friend for years.

He nods and visibly relaxes.


By the time we're back in the car, it's almost eight, and we drive home in silence, not touching this time. When we pull into the driveway, the first floor is brightly illuminated. They're home. Rhys opens the garage door but doesn't pull in. I figure he's leaving the car outside for some reason and reach for the door. When he keeps his hands on the steering wheel, staring forward, I turn back and look at him questioningly. Without averting his eyes from the front of the house, he whispers, "You and me?"

Huh? It takes me a moment to understand what he is asking. What is he doing? I'm confused but put my hand on his forearm and say with full conviction, "You and me."

His eyes find mine, and he nods. "I have to go do something."

"Uh...okay." But then it clicks; he is going to Katherine. My stomach immediately drops. Why does he have to go to her? Now of all times?

He must see my panicked face. "I'll come home tonight; I won't go to Wes's."

I force myself to answer. "Okay."

## RHYS

It's well past midnight by the time I get home. I've just spent the last three-plus hours getting yelled at by a furious cheerleader. Of course, her main concern was what *the school* would think. Who the fuck cares? When the yelling didn't help, she went for tears, but she forgot that I've seen it all before. I've witnessed her tactics for years, and just because I played along or chose to ignore it, doesn't mean they work on me. Eventually, she kicks me out, and I'm glad to leave. Lilly probably thinks by now that I've changed my mind, and I prepare multiple speeches in my head to convince her that she is the only one for me.

The house is quiet, and Lilly's room is dark. I curse at myself for letting Kat go on for so long. I have to shower and change first before I can go to Lilly. At one point, Kat started throwing random stuff, one of which was a flower vase with disgustingly old water. Once I'm sure I no longer smell of rotten plants, I creep over to Lilly's room.

As soon as I open the door, I can see the light of her e-reader on the far end of the bed. She waited for me, which makes me pick up my pace. I walk to her side and kneel down. In the dim light, I can see her questioning look, and I take one of her hands away from the device and fold it between mine. "It's done."

"Wh-what is done?" She is nervous, and I press my lips together. I feel like a piece of shit now for not explicitly telling her what I was going to do.

I exhale slowly. "I told Kat that we're over."

Lilly whispers, "You were gone for a long time."

I squeeze her hand and sigh. "She didn't take it well. I'm hurting her social standing." I have to snort. "We knew from the start that it was never true love for us. All she ever cared about was how we, or more likely *she*, looked to everyone else dating me."

Lilly looks me straight in the face. "You told me that you dated her for appearances, but I still don't understand. Why her? She is so—"

"Evil?" I finish the sentence for her with a smirk.

"I guess. That's one word to describe her." She gives me a one-sided shrug.

I squeeze her hand. "That's easy. She is the opposite of *you*, and I needed that to function."

Lilly exhales sharply. "Oh."

We look at each other for a long moment, and then her eyes gaze at the alarm clock. It's almost one in the morning. She puts her e-reader on the bedside table, and I stand up, getting ready to leave. That's when she scoots to the middle of her bed and says, "Stay."

My breath hitches, and I don't think I've heard her correctly. "Uh..."

I can't see her face anymore, but I swear she's smiling when she responds, "You and me."

These three words are spoken with raw emotion, and there is no question anymore. I'm hyperaware of the proximity between us as I settle on top of her comforter. Despite everything that has brought us to this point and everything we're going to have to deal with come morning, I'm pretty sure if I slide under the covers with her, I'll lose the last bit of self-restraint I have. We lie facing each other, and I take both her hands between mine.

"This is going to be hard." I nuzzle her hands to my face and press them against my lips.

"Huh?" Lilly doesn't understand what I mean.

"You being mine, but..." I take a resigned breath. "No one can know."

My eyes have adjusted to the darkness, and I can make out her features again. She places one hand on the side of my face, and the touch sends all my senses into overdrive. My heart is hammering in my chest.

She gazes at me with such love that I can barely breathe. "We'll figure it out."

All I want is to kiss her so bad, but it's not the right time. Everything is too fresh, and we still have the issue of her kidnapper being back. Instead, I settle my hand over hers and lean into the touch.

I wake with a start around four a.m. I don't remember falling asleep and stare at her sleeping form for several minutes before finally forcing myself to leave. Once in my room, I send Wes a text.

**We need to talk.**

I'm surprised when he responds right away. It's the middle of the night.

**Time and place?**

Best to get it over with.

**600 @ gym.**

Might as well get a workout in before class.

Since it doesn't make sense to go back to sleep, I take a shower and head out around five. The school gym is always open for team members, which has been my safe haven when avoiding home for years. Now, I'd rather be home, but it's not like I can be with Lilly anyway.

Wes walks in around five-thirty. I'm sitting on one of the bench presses, scrolling through my phone. "You're early."

Wes gives me a chin nod. "If you text me at four in the morning, I figure it has to be important."

I press my lips in a tight smile.

He throws his bag on the floor and settles on the bench across from mine. "So? Talk."

Straight to the point, but I guess I can't expect anything else since I've left him hanging for weeks—years, if I'm one hundred percent honest.

I take a long breath. Where to start? "This is about Lilly."

He raises his eyebrows as if to say *no shit,* and I continue, "Okay, so..." I pause again. God, how did Lilly tell Denielle? This whole thing is fucking insane. I should've asked her for specifics before texting Wes.

Another breath. "Lilly is not my sister." There, that's number one. I got that out. "And she is being stalked by a guy who kidnapped her as a child." Number two. "And we're together. I think. Either way, I'm in love with her." Number three.

*See, wasn't so hard.*

Wes just stares at me. And stares. And then bursts out laughing. "You're shitting me, right?"

I guess I could've expected that reaction; this entire scenario is freaking ridiculous. "Nope."

He stops abruptly, mouth pressed in a flat line. "Anything else I should know while we're at it?" His tone has turned to stone, and I guess when you're dropping a bomb like this on your best friend who thought he knew you, he has every right to be pissed.

I should probably explain it more. "Lilly and I have known each other our entire lives. We grew up together in San Diego. Our parents were friends. Shortly after I moved here with my parents, she was kidnapped on a school field trip. She was missing for several weeks but eventually turned up again. The gist is, the freak wanted her back. He stalked Lilly and her parents, who then decided to have her memory manipulated and hide her with my parents. That's when she moved in with us—as my sister."

Wes scans me up and down, deliberating whether I am not messing with him after all. Eventually, his expression changes, and all he says is, "That's fucked up!"

"That's not all of it."

He remains silent, and I continue, "I've loved her my entire life."

Wes interrupts me. "Uh, dude, you've been dating Kat for years."

I sigh and hold my hands up. "I'm getting to that. You've grown up with us. You know we've always been close. But over time, it became more to me, and my dad saw it. That's when I started dating Kat. He said I was never to act on my feelings since Lilly had no clue she wasn't my sister—and neither did anyone else, for that matter. Kat was an easy out for me. You know her; she never cared about me." I leave out the part where I was jealous as fuck of him and his friendship with Lilly.

He nods in understanding. "What's next?"

"Lilly started remembering around Thanksgiving last year."

"That's when she started acting all weird?"

I nod. "You noticed?"

"Sure, man. I've been around you guys most of my life. It was obvious, but it wasn't my place to do or say anything. I figured if it was serious enough, you'd step in no matter what was going on between the two of you. I've seen you watch her over the years, though I never expected *this*."

I hadn't anticipated him being this observant.

"Anyway, I, uh, watched her for a while and finally confronted her mid-December. She told me she thought she was going crazy because of memories that weren't hers. That was when I saw my chance to finally come clean with her."

Wes whistles through his teeth, and I keep talking. I tell him everything about her memories, our trip, what we found out, and about the message she received yesterday. I finish with, "And I broke up with Kat last night."

My best friend is visibly stunned and is processing everything in his head. He stares at his shoes for what feels like an eternity. Finally, he exhales and looks at me. "Dude, this is seriously fucked up."

I guess that's an appropriate statement. "Tell me about it." I press my lips together.

"So, what are we doing now?"

*We.* That's exactly what I would've expected Wes to say. I could always count on him. "I'm not sure, man. Lilly doesn't want Mom or Dad to know, but I'm pretty freaked out about the text. The only other person she was willing to tell was Den. That's why I told her I want you in. I want one of us with her all the time."

He holds his fist toward me, and I bump it with mine. "You got it."


It's almost seven when we finish talking. Wes asks more questions and even wants to know how Lilly and I ended up together—I'm fairly certain we are together. She hasn't admitted her feelings yet, and I'm curious what changed. With the text message, we never talked about why she was on her way downstairs.

Other guys from the team start filing in, and we start working out. When we leave the locker room for our first class, Wes says, "Kat will not go down easily."

I sigh. "I know."

# CHAPTER THIRTY-TWO

### LILLY

My alarm goes off at six-thirty. Rhys is gone, and I lie under my down comforter, digesting everything that has happened in the last twenty-four hours. Shaking my head, I cover my eyes. I am dating my adoptive brother—*I think*. What am I doing? The voice in my head still says it's wrong, but in my heart, it couldn't feel more right.

I reach over and grab my phone. Rhys has sent multiple texts, ranging from 4:06 to 5:32 a.m.

**Didn't want to leave. :(**

**Heading to the gym to meet Wes.**

**@ gym. If anything happens, CALL ME!**

A slow smile creeps across my face, and my stomach somersaults. Then, the initial burst of giddiness subsides as confusion with a side of apprehension sets in again. What do I respond? Are we officially an unofficial couple? He broke up with Kat, but what does that make *us*? Things are changing so quickly.

**Will do. Tell Wes hi.**

I guess that covers the latter two messages. I chew on my lip, type, and hit send before I can chicken out.

**See you later?**

When no response comes, I head to the shower. They're probably still talking.


I ARRIVE at school twenty minutes early. Denielle is already waiting near my usual parking spot, and I'm not fully out of the car yet when she's hovering next to my door, looking worried.

"Why is *your brother* texting me at five in the morning to make sure I talk to you before school?"

I'm glad Den is keeping up the charade—not that that statement alone wouldn't raise suspicion. Den hasn't talked to Rhys for as long as I haven't—hadn't. I'm convinced if it were just the two of us, she would've made some sort of torturous comment about my new love life, so I'm grateful to be in public for the moment.

I climb out of my Jeep. "Something happened."

Her eyebrows furrow, waiting for me to continue, but I shake my head. "Not here."

We walk toward the south wing, and Den keeps up the small talk like it's a typical Monday morning. We pass student masses making their way through the halls to their destination and head to the east wing bathroom, which is rarely used at this time of day since it's the farthest from everything.

I squat low without my hands touching the floor, my inner germaphobe on full alert, glancing under the stalls to make sure we are, indeed, alone. Pulling out my phone, I hand it over, and Denielle starts scrolling. She goes utterly still, and her hand is basically strangling the device. Her gaze jerks between the screen and me, finally settling on my face. "Holy. Fucking. Shit. Please tell me you told Heather and Tristen? Called the police?"

I shake my head. "Neither." My voice is more a whisper, and I don't know why I sound like I'm guilty of doing something wrong. This is *my* life for goodness' sake—*my* decision.

She looks at me in disbelief. "You're insane. This dude kidnapped you and now has photos of us! Of YOU!" Her voice raises, and I shush her, expecting someone to come in and check what's going on.

When it remains closed, I sigh. "I'm sorry you got dragged into this."

My best friend crosses her arms. "Oh, for fuck's sake, I don't care about that. I'm worried about *you*. *You*'re the one he wants. *You* had your whole life turned upside down over the last three months."

I give her a blank stare, unsure of what to say. My life has been turned upside down. My kidnapper found me because my need for answers put me back on his radar. Not to mention, I'm in love with my adopted brother slash former best friend, a person I would've never considered for that role. I'm so far out of my element.

My chest constricts, and I press my fist against it. I mumble, "Rhys says we'll figure it out."

Den's eyebrows shoot up to her forehead.

*How is that anatomically possible?*

"We?" Denielle's voice faintly registers with me, and I snap out of my ADD moment.

Shrugging, I look at my feet.

Denielle's hands fly to her mouth. "Oh my gosh, are you dating your brother?"

My eyes widen, mortified, and she cackles, "I'm sorry, but this whole situation is too good to not make a joke about it."

I punch her in the shoulder. "You're a bitch."

That gets me a bear hug. "Forgive me?" Then she pulls back. "So? Are you guys..." She trails off.

Another shrug. "I have no idea. He broke up with Katherine last night. But we never talked about it—about us," I stammer like an idiot.

"He broke up with the Wicked Bitch? I have to hear this." She looks at her watch. "We have ten minutes before class starts; I can make it to mine in two. Start talking!"

She won't leave me alone until I tell her, so I relent and repeat everything that happened after we parted ways at the gym. "I wanted to apologize for being such a bitch and explain why. But I didn't know how. And then the text came." I pause for a second and tell her about Rhys finding me on the stairs, our drive, how he left me at the house after we got back, and then when he came back from Katherine's. I conclude with, "I asked him to stay."

Denielle's eyes are about to pop out of their sockets. "Uh, who are you, and what have you done with my best friend?"

My lips twitch with a smile; she doesn't judge me. I still wait for her to be grossed out about the whole thing, but she's actually excited for me.

"She got her life turned upside down." I shrug with a smirk.

She slings her arm over my shoulders. "Well, *I'm* also in this with you."

"Thanks. I'm going to need your help. I am at a total loss when it comes to Rhys," I confide.

She has a devious grin on her face. "Rhys can handle the psycho, and I can help with your love life."

I dramatically smack my palm to my forehead. "What have I done?"


MY PSYCHO-STALKER-KIDNAPPER IS BACK, and I have no idea what status Rhys and I are, but I can't help the bounce in my step all morning. I get sidelong glances everywhere, and I want to roll my eyes. Have I been that mopey and depressed the last few years?

Rhys's classes are mostly on the second floor, so I don't expect to see him until later. Denielle and I are headed to lunch when I get my first glimpse of him. My entire body immediately starts buzzing, and my mind wanders to last night when he was lying in bed with me. Nothing happened besides holding hands, but the small contact was so intimate my cheeks heat at the memory. The instant he laid down, I felt safe. *Home*.

I'm being jerked by the elbow, which brings me back to reality—I was about to smack nose-first into an open locker. Now my face is really on fire, and I fight the urge to cover it with my hands. Looking up, Rhys's eyes crinkle in amusement, but to everyone else, he radiates boredom. He has mastered the stone façade over the years, but I can see past it, and his eyes send a *completely* different message. He is as affected as I am, and his eyes jump between mine and...my lips. Is he thinking about kissing me? I can't go there right now; I'd probably trip over my own feet.

"Keep it together, babe. You're drooling," Denielle hisses beside me.

I force my gaze away from the gorgeous boy ahead of me and focus on my destination—the cafeteria. Instead, I find Katherine standing at the end of the hallway. Her emerald-green eyes are zeroed in on Rhys's back, and my stomach turns into a tight knot. She's been with him for years, and he broke up with her for me, not caring how it'd look to the rest of the world, also known as Westbridge High. As if she heard my thoughts, her gaze snaps to mine. *Does she know I'm the reason?* No, she can't, I chastise myself. She's always disliked me for one reason or another, but now she emanates outright hostility.

We get within earshot of Rhys and Wes, and Denielle hollers, "Hey, Wes, how's the snow today?"

I'm so startled that I break out of my stare-down with Katherine. Den winks at me, and I understand. She intended exactly that. I love my best friend.

Wes flips her off. "Fuck off, D."

Both can barely contain a knowing grin, and even Rhys's stony mask cracks a tiny bit as he gives my best friend a barely visible nod. She dips her head in acknowledgment, and a secret message passes between them. Despite my heart still racing in my chest from my standoff with Katherine, I feel pure joy. I have *all* my friends back in my life. No more secrets, no more hiding. The four of us can finally be *us* again.

For the first time in—actually, for the first time ever, I'm skipping practice. I was in a fog of happiness and dread during the rest of my classes. The people that have meant the most to me in the past are all back in my life, but I can't tell anyone. I have to pretend that I despise Rhys, that Wes and I don't talk, and that Den is my only close friend. Sure, Sloane and Emma are my friends, but I wouldn't confide in them. Maybe trivial things like a *random* boy crush, yes, but not with what's really going on in my life. And then there is the matter of the text message. Every time my phone vibrates, I feel like I'm being choked, and I can't breathe until I see it's not *him*. So, instead of going to practice, I'm heading home to hide in my sanctuary. I need some time to collect myself and figure out how to play my part in all of this.

I'm about to back out of my parking spot when I stop and send Rhys a quick text: **Heading home.**

The three dots immediately start dancing on the display.

**Everything ok?**

Of course he'd be worried since I never skip practice.

**Yes, just need to be alone for a bit.**

**K. Be careful.**

Before I can put my phone away, another message from Rhys comes in: **PS: Netflix and chill tonight?**

I nearly drop the device, and my thumbs hover over the digital keyboard.

*Is he serious?*

I'm about to type a reply when another bubble pops up: **Just kidding, babe. Can't wait to be alone with u though.**

I grin at the screen like a loon, and the hornets in my stomach go haywire. This is unreal—all of it.

My happiness fades as I back out of Rhys's text, and the "UNKNOWN" sender jumps out at me.

*What do you want with me?*

WHEN I GET HOME, the house is eerily quiet. It has never struck me as weird being alone at home, but walking from the garage through the first floor, the hair on the back of my neck stands up. I eye the windows.

*Are you out there right now?*

It's almost four. Rhys is at practice, Heather is with Natty at ballet, and Tristen left for another two-week trip this morning.

After a very long and scorching shower, I dress in my favorite gray cotton harem lounge pants, loose white shirt knotted in the front, and my go-to duster cardigan, completing the comfy look with some fuzzy socks. Settling at my desk, I pick up the picture of Rhys and me and hold it in both hands. What would have happened if I'd never been kidnapped? Would we still be in touch? Live close by? I would be with my birth parents and have a *normal* life. Would I be happy? I shake my head. No point in thinking about what-ifs— it happened.

With a sigh, I pull up the file with my case research on my laptop and lay my phone with the text message next to it. I start a new page in the document, writing out everything I notice in the pictures. Date, time, place, who was with me, angle, and location from where they were taken. I'm not super familiar with photography, despite taking journalism. I have no clue how far away the photographer could have been in the outdoor shots. He must've been in the audience for the gymnastics one. I briefly wonder if anyone might have caught him on camera in their own pictures, but for that, I would have to start asking around, and that's not an option.

I obviously put him back on my trail when we went to California. But how? And then, another thought hits me: did he find me through my research? Anything is possible with today's technology, right? I recall what Madeline said about the emails and the photos my birth parents received. She said they were from the hospital's surveillance camera. A cold shiver runs down my spine. If that's the case, who knows what this freak is capable of?

I slowly close my laptop and take stock. I'm scared, yes, but shouldn't I be freaking out? Like, losing-my-mind freaking out? Hiding in my closet panicking? Or at least wanting to tell Heather and Tristen? But I am not. I have the subliminal knowledge that he doesn't want to *harm* me. But why? I have no clue how I know, but I do.

*Is this another half-erased memory?*

Why me? What makes me so special? Instead of finding the answers in California, I have more questions than ever. They seem to be piling up by the day.

I DON'T FEEL like reading, and I have no more homework left. I could study for the chemistry quiz on Friday, but instead, I wander down to the family room and turn the TV on. I have thirteen episodes of various shows to catch up on. I haven't relaxed in front of the TV since this all started. Plopping down in the middle of the couch, I prop my feet on the round ottoman and grab the remote. A CW drama is exactly the distraction I need today.

Around five-thirty, Heather and Natty walk in through the garage, and I hear Heather start prepping dinner shortly after.

I've avoided spending long periods of time with either of my adopted parents since we got home. Sitting here now, listening to her opening and closing the fridge and cabinets, I wonder if either of them has noticed my absence. I have no idea how to act around them, and being constantly paranoid I'll let something slip, I've stayed away. For the first time since it all started, I crave being near Heather, being with my mom. The need hits me like a punch in the gut. After weeks of being driven by rage and resentment, I've relented to no longer being mad at them. I am unable to forgive them, *yet*, but I also understand their motives better. They have kept me safe for ten years. I owe it to them and myself to try.

I stand in the doorway to the kitchen and watch Heather buzz around. She is a born multi-tasker. I witness her manning the stove with three pots on it while reading a work document propped on the cookbook stand and helping Natty who is sitting at the island with her homework. The scene fills me with warmth. Heather has just started cutting an onion next to the stove, and she hasn't seen me yet. I walk up from behind and wrap my arms around her waist, burying my face in her back.

"Oh my gosh, sweetie!" She is startled by my unusual assault. "Is everything okay?"

"Hmm-mmm. All good," I mumble into her back. Standing there, I realize that, besides the brief hugs from Denielle and the comfort Rhys has given me during the trip, this is the first physical contact I have initiated in weeks. It feels good.

"Well, okay then." I hear her smile. "Want to help me prep dinner?"

Do I want to? My heart rate picks up, and I experience a brief moment of panic. This means spending time with her. Am I ready to put myself in this situation? What if I slip up? Or what if she says something that ignites my anger again and *then* I slip up? I take a deep breath. I can do this. With all the new developments in the last two days, I want to be around my family. I want a little bit of normality, even if it technically is just a pretense.

We chat about school and the invitational last weekend. I conveniently neglect to mention that Rhys was there. I tell her about Denielle and Charlie and how they deal with their long-distance relationship. Heather loves both of them and always wants to know how they are.

"Denielle might visit him during spring break. Since Charlie has come home twice, she wants to see his life there."

Heather nods. "That'll be fun."

I'm stirring the tomato sauce when Rhys announces his entrance by dropping his gym bag in the middle of the kitchen with a loud thud. My back is toward the room, and my body goes on high alert, which almost makes me lose my grip on the spoon.

"Honey! I didn't expect you home this early. Why aren't you at Wes's? Or Katherine's?" Heather's tone is pure delight.

I don't turn, knowing my flushed skin will betray me. I need time to compose myself. As if my embarrassing behavior in school wasn't enough today. God, I hope it's not going to become a pattern whenever he's around.

"Wes is at home, and I broke up with Kat."

Rhys's reply is as casual as if he were talking about what he had for lunch.

I'm so shocked by his response that I drop the whole oregano container into the sauce. "Shit!"

"Everything okay, sweetie?"

I still make no move to face the room, and I hear Rhys chuckle. That ass.

"Um, yeah, it just slipped out of my hand."

The next question is directed at Rhys again. "What happened?" Heather doesn't sound upset or broken up about it. I know she never liked Kat very much.

*You and me both, Heather.*

I fish out the oregano, and I swivel on my heels, wanting to see Rhys's face when he answers.

He gives a one-sided shrug. "It just wasn't right. Hasn't been for a long time."

And with that, the topic is closed. Heather nods in understanding and moves on. Did she know that his relationship was all for show? I guess a happy dance would be inappropriate, right? Even though I'm pretty sure all of us think about doing it for different reasons.

"Are you eating with us?" The question slips out before I can stop myself.

Three sets of eyes are trained on me, two in various expressions of surprise. Yes, I know I haven't openly talked to Rhys in years, but *come on*. I try not to scowl at their looks and raise my eyebrows instead...waiting.

"Umm...sure?"

Ha! Rhys's cheeks have turned bright pink, and I give him my biggest Cheshire grin once Heather's back is to me.

He shakes his head, smiling, and walks out of the room with his gym bag draped again over his shoulder. My phone vibrates in my sweater pocket, and after glancing at Heather, who is pulling plates out of the cabinet, I sneak a peek.

**Just wait until later. ;)**

And with that, I resemble a red traffic light again.

DINNER IS, thankfully, uneventful. Natty monopolizes the mealtime conversation with stories of her ballet lessons and what her teacher has planned for class next time. A few times, I chance a peek at Rhys, and every time, his eyes are focused on me. His eyes sparkle with the earlier threat, and heat ignites in places I've never experienced before. I press my lips together to prevent myself from grinning.

I'm putting the dishes in the dishwasher when Rhys excuses himself upstairs, and Heather calls after him, "I'll see you in the morning. I'm going to turn in early since I got up with Dad this morning."

"'Kay, night," he calls back and disappears.

# CHAPTER THIRTY-THREE

## RHYS

I can't get out of the kitchen fast enough. Whenever Mom is busy talking to Natty during dinner, I risk a glance at Lilly, and every single time, her hazel eyes immediately snap to mine. It's like she senses my gaze. Add to that the unspoken emotions in her eyes—ones I never thought I'd see directed at me—and it takes every ounce of self-restraint to not *claim* her right there—on top of the kitchen table. I groan inwardly.

*Yeah, that would go over well.*

Natty would be scarred for life, and Mom probably would have a heart attack. No matter how hard I try, I can't prevent the heat in my core from spreading further every time we lock eyes. By the end of the meal, my pants are so tight I'm sure I'll have to do the penguin walk upstairs to not blow from the friction in my jeans. I need a cold shower—very cold.

At one point, I'm so deep in my head, envisioning myself exploring Lilly's graceful neck with my mouth down to her collarbone, that Lilly kicks me under the table.

*Yup, I'm fucked.*

. . .

I STAY under the freezing spray until I'm shaking uncontrollably and the last bit of *heat* has left my body. Busying myself in my room, I put on sweats and a fresh t-shirt, pick up stuff here and there, and scroll through my social media. Eventually, I hear Natty's door close followed by Mom's footsteps upstairs. Lilly's door is ajar with the light off, which means she's downstairs. Alone. This time, the fire remains at bay. Instead, a knot forms in my stomach, and my hands start trembling. It's like being fourteen again, playing Seven Minutes in Heaven with Mandy Chamberlain. I slump down onto the foot of my bed and put my head in my hands. Deep breaths. Logically, I know I'm being ridiculous. I'm far from being a virgin. If sex were an Olympic sport, I'd have earned the gold medal the first year Kat and I dated. But this is Lilly, and I have no clue how to act. We're not just your average high school couple falling in love. There is a moving truck full of baggage attached to each of us.

I ROUND the corner to the family room and find Lilly covered under a throw blanket, watching one of her favorite shows. I stop at the sight. She hasn't done that in forever, and it brings back a feeling of normality. She is cuddled up in the corner while I remain in the doorway, watching *her*.

Without glancing away from the TV, she says, "You sitting down or what?"

*Busted.*

She's smirking to herself as she speaks, and I huff out a laugh. I can always tell when Lilly is around, even if I haven't seen her yet. It's weird. It seems like she has developed the same skill, because I am sure I didn't make a sound coming down.

Since she is cuddled in the corner, I sit down in the middle of the couch. I don't want to assume, but I don't want to sit too far away from her in my usual spot at the other end either. Crossing my arms over my chest, I have no clue what else to do with them—the urge to pull her on top of me makes my fingers twitch. We watch in silence, and I peer over at her whenever I think she's not looking. Her posture is stiff, and I'm convinced she is paying as much attention to what's on the screen as I am.

Lilly shifts, her feet touching my thigh through the blanket. It's like I've touched a live wire, and I instinctively jerk my leg away. My heart starts racing, and I'm pretty much panting. Not to mention what's going on in my sweats—again. I need to get out of here, or this time, I am going to jump her.

I bolt from the couch, mumbling something along the lines of, "Be right back," and escape to the kitchen. Opening the fridge, I let the escaping air cool my skin.

*That's better.*

I stare inside the fridge for a good five minutes before I grab two water bottles and make my way back with the best intention of keeping it together.

Handing one of the bottles to Lilly, our fingers brush when she takes it, and her eyes widen at the contact. She lets her fingers linger for longer than necessary before settling back onto the couch. Maybe I'm not the only one affected here? But despite her body language, her voice is calm, almost nonchalant, when she lifts the edge of the blanket. "Sitting down?"

My eyes bounce between her face, her raised hand, and the spot on the couch a few times.

"Rhys?" Her eyes twinkle with mischief.

Uh, wha—? God, I need to get a grip. If someone looked up "horny as fuck" right now, I'm pretty sure my picture would be there.

I settle down, and she drops the blanket over my lap. That's when I notice—fuuuuuck. Instead of angling away from me with her feet on my side, her feet are now in the opposite direction, and she slowly starts leaning into me. Here we go again: heartbeat from zero to one-eighty in 0.1 second. I shift to release some of the sudden constriction in my pants.

*I didn't realize my sweats were this small.*

Long inhale, four, three, two, exhale. Nope, not working, still sporting a tent. I'm between sprinting back to the fridge and pressing her into the couch cushions. How am I supposed to be *good* with her this close?

Ah, fuck it. What's the worst that can happen? Besides her shooting me down and our life becoming more awkward than it already is? Yeah, no big deal. I slide my left hand toward her under the throw blanket until our pinkies touch, holding my breath. Without hesitation, she intertwines our fingers.

Holy sh— With this one touch, all anxiety leaves my body, and I'm...*home*. The other part of my anatomy also calms, even though I would've expected the opposite, given the skin-to-skin contact. For the first time tonight, I'm able to relax and actually watch some of the show still playing on the screen.

"Rhys?"

"Hmmm?" I'm so freaking content with her hand in mine.

When she doesn't say anything else, I turn my head. "What is it, Cal?"

Not looking at me, she takes a deep breath like she is deliberating. "What are we?"

Huh? My eyebrows knit together while I attempt to decipher what she is asking.

She squeezes my hand. "This. I mean..." She hesitates, pink staining her cheeks. "We can't be together."

*What the hell is she talking about?*

My chest constricts, and I fully angle my body toward her. "What are you talking about, babe? Why not?" I clutch her hand; a different type of anxiety now slowly builds up.

She pulls her hands away from mine and starts wringing them together in her lap. "Because to everyone else, we are related."

Oh. Ohh. That's what she's worried about. And I thought she was going to break up with me before we even started dating. I take her hand back in mine and try to sound calm and reasonable. "But we're not. Never have been. We're doing nothing wrong."

She finally makes eye contact. "I know, but we are the only ones that know. Besides Den and Wes, I mean..." Another pause. She tilts her head to the side. "By the way, what did you tell Wes?"

I turn one of her hands over and start rubbing my thumb over the heel of her hand, slowly massaging the fleshy part. Her entire body relaxes under my touch, and she melts into the couch with her head leaning against the back of it.

"I told him the truth. What happened to you, why you're here, how I feel, and that...*he* is back. Wes knew that something was up.

He noticed the change in you, too." I laugh to myself. "I guess our friends are more perceptive than we gave them credit for."

She smiles and turns to me as I continue. "As for what we are...that depends on you. I told you how I feel, and that won't change. But I understand if you are not ready or would rather not —"

"I love you."

I'm about to launch into a full-length explanation that I understand if this is all still too weird for her. I mean, it's only been two months since she found out that we're not related. *Wait.* What she said sinks in, and I stare, open-mouthed. Her look changes to something resembling concern. "Say something!"

All I can do is mumble, "You love me?" I'm gobsmacked. Never in a million years would I have expected those words to come out of her mouth. Sure, there has been hope that maybe one day...

Lilly must see that I'm having a hard time believing that I heard her right, because she repeats herself more confidently. "I love you!"

She loves me. Holy fuck. She. Loves. Me. My grin spreads so far my cheeks start hurting. I pull her into my arms. "Come here."

She moves to her knees next to me, wrapping her arms around my neck. Her head is burrowed in my shoulder, holding on tight while I nuzzle her neck. The scent of vanilla and coconut makes every nerve ending in my body come alive. I whisper into her hair, "God, you have no idea how long I have waited for this."

The cocky horndog has officially left the stage, and the whipped lovestruck fool has entered. If Wes were to see me right now, I would hear about it until the end of time.

I feel her smile. "You still haven't answered my question."

I chuckle. My arms wrap around her waist and squeeze tight. "You are mine. You always have been—even if you didn't know it at the time—and always will be. And if you want to put a label on it...Lilly Ann Calla McGuire Sumner, will you be my girlfriend? Please check one of the below three boxes. Yes, no, maybe." I pretend to write on my palm to make light of the situation—and to not feel like a complete pussy.

Lilly makes a sound between a laugh and a squeal and almost chokes me in her hold. This girl has some serious strength. She gives me one last squeeze and settles back to sit beside me, smiling to herself. I lift my arm, and she cuddles into my side, holding my other hand between hers.

Before turning back to the TV, she glances up with flushed cheeks. "I'd like that."


We must've fallen asleep, because the next thing I know, I blink open my eyes, and the clock on the wall reads 11:12 p.m.

We're slumped together on the couch, covered with the throw blanket. Lilly's arm is hooked around mine, our hands interlaced, with her head resting against my shoulder and my head on top of hers. Realization of where we are shoots through me, and a flood of adrenaline makes my heartbeat increase. Thank God Dad is gone, and Mom usually never comes back down once she's settled for the night.

I slightly lift my head from hers and, without thinking, place a kiss on her hair. "Babe? I think we need to get you to bed." *Before anyone finds us.*

Lilly grumbles something incoherent and snuggles closer, angling her face upward. My eyes immediately zero in on her pink lips. I stare. And stare some more. That's when I notice the change in her breathing, and her lips part. I move my gaze upward and see her looking back and forth between my eyes and mouth.

My breath hitches; this is it. I can't hold back any longer. With my pulse thrashing in my ears, I slowly inch closer, continually flipping between her eyes and lips, making sure I'm not missing any sign that she doesn't want this, giving her every opportunity to move away.

She peers back at me with hooded lids. I take one last deep breath and close the distance.

*Finally.*


## LILLY


Oh my God, oh my God, oh my God. My heart is about to burst out of my chest. I'm holding my breath, afraid to move. Still in a sleepy haze, my eyes meet Rhys's, and I know he is going to kiss me.

There's nothing but raw desire in his eyes—an emotion I'm sure my own are reflecting. I would be lying if I said I haven't thought about it—a lot.

He touches his lips to mine, and stars explode behind my eyes. He is tentative at first, giving me the chance to move away, but I'm gone. Every cell in my body has come alive, and I can't get close enough. Moving to my knees, I end up straddling his lap and taking his face between my hands. Rhys reciprocates by pulling me closer, his hands moving up my back beneath my shirt, burning my sensitive skin with his cool touch.

His lips are soft and firm at the same time. Until now, the kiss was careful, a gentle exploration, but the moment his hands make contact with my bare skin, something ignites in both of us. I rock myself into him, and a sound between a moan and growl reaches my ears. Was that me or him? Our mouths start moving together, and the kiss turns frantic. I've made out with guys before, but this... My lips part over his, and his tongue slides in without hesitation. Rhys nips at my bottom lip, and in return, I press my entire body into his, the friction bringing my core to life. His hands glide up my spine, and I have the urge to clench my thighs together. We're both panting, and I don't want this kiss to stop. Ever.

But as soon as I think that, Rhys pulls back, and I hear myself whimper, trying to kiss him again. He touches his forehead to mine, taking a long, steadying breath.

"We need to stop." There is no backbone in his words.

"Why? What's wrong?"

*Was it that terrible?* I know I don't have a ton of experience, but—

He shifts, and his hard length pushes against me. "Babe, if we keep going, I won't be able to stop myself. And apart from the fact that we are in the living room, I want to do this right."

"Oh." My reply is no more than a breath. Relief replaces the paranoia. I didn't do anything wrong.

*Why am I so insecure?*

Rhys continues in a low tone, "I have never felt this way with anyone, and after this, I doubt I'll ever get enough of you. Not now that I've had a taste." He gently nips at my lower lip again, and his voice holds a promise that makes my body grow hot all over.

Still in his lap, a girlish giggle escapes me. I barely recognize myself, but I've also never felt this giddy. I wrap my arms around his neck and place a kiss right behind his ear.

Rhys shudders. "That's what I'm talking about. How am I supposed to act like we don't speak to each other when all I want to do is this?"

And with one swift move, he tightens the hold on my waist and flips me over. My heart races as my back is pressed into the couch cushion, and he hovers above me, propped up on one elbow. An even louder giggle escapes me, and my hands fly to my mouth, trying to muffle the sound. We both look to the ceiling, waiting to hear movement, but when nothing happens, our gazes lock again. His eyes shine with glee. He is completely carefree at this moment, and I relish that I did that to him.

We stare at each other. Hiding a grin, I say, "We'll have to be strong and do our best to ignore each other. Otherwise, I'll do..." I let the sentence trail off, and Rhys looks at me with raised eyebrows.

I let the internal, mischievous grin appear on my face, and his eyes widen when I grab his face between both of my hands, wrap my legs around his midsection, and use my entire weight to pull his mouth to mine again. He lands on me with an "oof" sound but immediately opens. When our tongues start moving together this time, a deep groan escapes him. His reaction makes me wanton. I arch up, pressing my chest against his, and he rolls his hips against me in return. Heat pools in my core. *Oh, my God.* Still propped up on one arm, he caresses my thigh with his free hand, moving up my side and rib cage. I want him to touch me everywhere.

We continue for what seems like hours, and I can't get enough. Rhys makes me forget all the drama and angst my life consists of these days. I lose myself in the moment. Right here, right now, we're just a girl and a boy in love.

When the clock announces midnight, Rhys hesitantly pulls back. "I think we both need to get some rest, or we won't fool anyone very long."

He has moved away, sitting on the edge, and I push myself up into a sitting position, pouting.

He barks out a laugh and places a kiss on the tip of my nose. "My dick is not happy at the moment, believe me. He wants to be inside of you bad." He glances down to his lap and back up to my face with a cheeky grin; my breathing instantly increases as a visual forms in my head. He continues, "All I care about is making this work for us. I've waited too long, and we need to figure out the *other* situation first."

The other situation. That's a nice way of putting it. What other new couple deals with a child-kidnapping stalker and the whole world believing your boyfriend is your brother? He is right. It'll take a lot for us to make this work, not just being head over heels in love.

I huff and nod. "We'll figure this out together."

He takes my hand and places a kiss on the inside of my palm. "Together."

AT THE TOP of the stairs, we let go of each other, but before I can reach my door, Rhys pulls me toward him and places a soft kiss on my lips. "Good night, babe."

"Good night, boyfriend."

A wide grin spreads over his face, and I close my door after taking one more look at him. I lean against my door and touch my fingers to my lips. I can't stop smiling.

## CHAPTER THIRTY-FOUR

**RHYS**

I skipped my workout. I haven't missed a pre-school workout in...no idea. I couldn't fall asleep until after three. My mind kept wandering to a certain blonde girl across the hall. The taste of her lips, the smoothness of her skin, how her legs were wrapped around me, that hot-as-fuck little whimper she made when I pulled away. The list goes on. I had to take my second cold shower of the day after we parted in the hallway. But even after my body finally settled down, I was unable to fall asleep.

Waking up from a much-too-short night, I'm exhausted. My eyes burn like the time I helped Mom chop jalapenos and rubbed my eyes without washing my hands—fun stuff. None of that can put a damper on my ridiculously good mood, though. I catch myself humming in the shower—talk about being a lost cause. I bang my forehead against the tiled wall while letting the water run down my face.

At the same time...I. Don't. Care. I would've never in a million years expected those three words to come out of her mouth. Her mouth...A groan instantly escapes me. All I want is to kiss her senseless, the taste of her tongue...My body's entire blood flow is immediately redirected below the naval, and I glance down. Fucking great. I turn the lever back to cold and hang my head.

*How on earth am I going to make it through school?*

I'M PUTTING on a white T when someone knocks on the door and opens it an inch.

"You decent?" Mom's voice comes through the small gap.

I bark out a laugh. "Depends on what you call decent. All the *important* parts are covered." Boxers and t-shirt are in place; I haven't gotten to the rest yet.

The door swings in, and Mom's head appears. "Why are you still at home?"

*Shit.*

"Uh, Wes wasn't feeling it this morning. He had a late night." I give her a significant *you-can-fill-in-the-blanks* look. "I figured I could sleep an extra two hours for once."

Blame it on the best friend. Why not? Note to self: make sure Wes knows about *his* late night.

Mom cocks her head, lips pursing. The woman has a bullshit detector that's better than any polygraph. She knows that Wes skipping a workout has never stopped me, but for whatever reason, she drops the topic. "I'm heading out. Natty and I are picking up Gemma this morning. Her mom has an early client meeting."

Gemma's mom is an architect, specialized in restoring the old houses in this area to their original state but adding a modern touch. She's responsible for most of the shops and condos on Main Street, including Magnolia's—Lilly's favorite hangout.

"Okay, cool." I try to act as nonchalant as possible while stuffing random shit in my backpack.

Mom starts closing the door. "Don't be late. Love you."

"Love you, too."

When she is gone, I take in the contents of my backpack. Fan-fucking-tastic. I just shoved pretty much every book from my desk in there, including a leftover paper coffee cup, my stapler, and Natty's stuffed monkey that she left here approximately three years ago to keep me safe. I slump down in my desk chair. There is no way in hell we can pull this off. Not at this rate.

. . .

THIRTY MINUTES LATER, I walk into the kitchen while Lilly is pouring hot water into her travel mug, the usual tea bag hanging out to the side. Her back is to me, and for the first time, she doesn't seem to have noticed me yet. We're alone in the house. Mom left about twenty minutes ago, and I can't help myself. I sneak up to her, wrap my arms around her waist, and settle my chin on her shoulder, whispering, "Good morning, beautiful."

She squeals, dropping the kettle.

*Whoops.*

She spins around and whisper-shouts, "What are you doing?"

Her flustered expression has me bursting out laughing. "Mom and Natty already left. Didn't you hear them? She needs to pick up Gemma."

Lilly sinks against the counter, covering her eyes, while I rest my hands on her hips. "No, I didn't. I just came down. Don't ever do that to me again!" She's trying to calm her breathing.

I pull her fully into my arms. "I'm sorry, babe. Come here, I want to kiss my girlfriend good morning."

With that, she winds her arms around my neck and sinks into the embrace. She smirks up at me before pressing her lips to mine. "Hmmm...good morning."

LILLY PARKED her car inside yesterday, so I left mine in the driveway. Walking in, I press the opener next to the kitchen door to let myself out through the garage.

We stop next to her Jeep. I don't want to let go of her, but the automatic door is almost up, and we can't risk being seen by any nosy neighbors.

I slowly pull away, taking a step back. "What are your plans today?"

"Practice, maybe grab something to eat with Den. Why?"

I feel myself relaxing a bit. "Okay, good. I don't want you alone until we know what that psycho has planned." The thought of her anywhere by herself has me all fidgety. I can't be around most of the time, but that's why I wanted our best friends to be filled in on the situation. One of us should be with her. "Maybe Wes and I can join you?"

Lilly is in the process of climbing into her car and stops with one foot in the air. "You think that's smart? I mean, it's one thing that they know, but if we start making public appearances together..."

She's right, but fuck if I care. I just give her my typical crooked grin. "Just let me handle it; you worry too much."

She exhales slowly, deliberating. "Okay."

I REVERSE out of the driveway while Lilly is still getting situated. That'll give me a good ten-minute head start. I know my girl—she drives like Grandma Ruth. Scratch that, Grandma Ruth drives faster than Lilly.

Pulling into my usual spot in the senior corner of the parking lot, I'm briefly distracted, replaying the previous night, when a shadow appears at my driver's side door. Turning, I come face to face with Kat, staring at me with her resting bitch face commonly reserved for her female enemies.

"Jesus Christ!" I drop my backpack on the passenger seat. "What the fuck, Kat?" There goes my good mood. I stare at her incredulously before exiting the Defender.

"I want to talk to you."

*I don't.*

Better get this over with; she won't take no for an answer. I gesture with my hand for her to go ahead.

I follow Kat toward the side entrance that leads directly to the art studios. From across the lawn, Wes tracks my movement, giving me a *what-the-fuck* look, and I shrug.

When we reach the building, she takes a step back, as usual, expecting me to open the door for her. I don't have it in me to argue; I want this over as quickly as possible. Kat ducks under my arm as I make room for her. Her hand brushes along my abdomen in the process, right above the waistband of my jeans, as she disappears inside. It's a gesture that, at the beginning of our relationship, got me ready and going; now all it does is make me feel cold and dirty.

Before trailing after her, I scan the parking lot and immediately zero in on a set of furious hazel eyes. With her stance wide and hands balled into fists, Lilly is planted next to Denielle, staring back at me. She shows zero emotion on her face, but I can see the hurt written all over it.

*FUCK. Shit. Fuuuck.*

I don't want to follow Kat. I want to go over to Lilly to ensure she doesn't interpret this as anything it isn't. But I can't. I can't act differently.

Wanting to slam my fist into the brick wall of the building, I give her one last look.

*I hate this.*

Kat waits for me with her arms crossed, and we make our way to one of the smaller art studios a few doors down.

"What do you want?"

She saunters closer, sliding her hands up my stomach to my chest. "I want you, baby. You're just confused for whatever reason, but deep down, you know that we need to be together. I'll forgive you for your momentary lapse in judgment."

*Is she serious?*

I have no patience for her games. Plus, doesn't she realize that I know all of them? We were together for years.

"Need?" I raise an eyebrow. "You mean *you* need *me* to keep your position at the top," I say, deadpan.

That gets a reaction out of her, and she moves a step back, looking at me in disbelief. Yeah, I guess I really never talked back to her. I never needed to.

Her green eyes blaze with something I recognize immediately. Fury. She doesn't like not getting her way.

"What the fuck is going on with you? Are you doing this because of your sister?"

*Wha—?*

I feel myself pale but am able to compose myself—I think. "What does Lilly have to do with this?"

She puts her hands on her hips and snarls, "First, she shows up at your match, and you *talk* to her. I don't hear from you at all over Christmas break. You drag me to her idiotic gymnastics meet, followed by you breaking up with me. Oh, and don't forget that you didn't go on the ski trip as planned, and no one saw you *or your sister* during that time. Notice a pattern here?"

Why does she have to start paying attention all of a sudden? She hasn't given two shits about what I've done for years.

"How— She is my sister; we talk." *Amongst other things*, but she doesn't need to know that. "You and I do our own thing during breaks. Since when did that change?" I catch myself before I question how the hell she knows about the ski trip. I don't remember talking to Kat about my plans before Christmas break at all.

"How do I know?" Of course, she doesn't let it go. "Do you really think I don't make it my business to know where *my* boyfriend is?"

I want to laugh in her face. I'm ninety-nine percent sure she has banged someone else during every break we didn't spend together, and she's pulling the boyfriend card?

"You always texted, even during breaks." She stomps her foot and looks like a little girl. I almost feel bad. Almost.

I try the reasonable route. "Kat, I can't do this anymore. We were never about the happily ever after. It was about convenience, and you know that. We would've parted ways anyway once the year is over." I'm almost pleading. She has to acknowledge this.

"So? You found someone more convenient?"

*I have, but that's none of your business.*

I sigh. "No, I'm simply tired of pretending we're something we're not."

"You will regret this! We had plans." The venom drips from every word. No one dismisses Katherine Rosenfield, and I just did.

After one more glare, she spins around and storms off.

Well, fuck me. Now we have a psycho stalker *and* a psycho ex to deal with.

## LILLY

THE BURNING SENSATION in my chest won't go away all morning. I wait for Rhys to text me, tell me what Katherine wanted, and that everything is fine. We're not even together for twenty-four hours, and the drama already starts. That's what you get when you start a secret relationship with your adopted brother. I have enough problems with my psycho stalker. Do I really need this kind of drama? Of course I do; this is Rhys. What am I even thinking? Jealousy is an ugly trait and not something I've experienced before.

*Add that to the list of things to discuss with my future therapist.*



I DON'T SEE or hear from Rhys until lunch. Denielle and I sit at our usual table, still waiting for Sloane and Emma, when Wes and Rhys walk up. Wes plops down at the table while Rhys remains standing behind his best friend, hands in his pockets, acting bored—his school persona on full display.

"D, we're grabbing something to eat after practice tonight. You guys want to join?"

I am focused on my tray like it holds the most delicious meal in the world and not a slice of soggy cheese pizza. Out of the corner of my eye, I see Denielle silently asking me what she's supposed to do, but I don't react. It takes all my concentration not to show any emotion toward Rhys.

Finally, she clears her throat. "Umm, sure. Text me when and where." She decided for me.

"Cool. Talk to you later."

Wes starts pushing out of the chair but stops when Rhys makes no indication to move.

*Don't look up, don't look up,* I chant over and over in my head. If I make eye contact, I won't be able to keep a neutral face.

*Why hasn't he texted?*

I have not once cared when a guy didn't message me; I simply moved on. But this is different. My feelings, my entire frame of mind—and not just because of the other *thing* going on in my life. Rhys is different. I care about him. No, I love him, and I don't want to lose him. *Again.* How do I know that my stalking kidnapper won't harm me, but Rhys talks to his ex, and I go off the deep end?

I stifle a groan.

"Seems like the Wicked Bitch still has her claws in you." My eyes snap to Denielle, who is glaring directly at Rhys. What is she doing?

Rhys swears under his breath. He talks to Den, but his answer is directed toward me. "She wanted to talk."

"If you say so," Denielle says coolly. She's in full-on guard dog mode.

Rhys finally glances at me. "Cal?"

I still don't trust myself to speak.

"Not here," Denielle hisses disapprovingly. She makes him understand that this is not the time or place, and I could kiss her for that.

Wes takes over, almost a little too loud. "Dude, let's grab some food. I'm starving." Then, he basically manhandles Rhys toward the lunch line.

As soon as they're gone, I lift my head, and my gaze collides with Katherine's, who is standing near her usual table, openly glaring at me. She must have followed the entire exchange. This is getting better and better.

"Babe?" Den bumps her leg against mine, and I focus on her.

I mumble an embarrassed, "Thanks." One word to convey that, without her and Wes taking over the situation, I either would've thrown a jealous tantrum or broken down in tears.

Before she can reply, my phone next to my tray lights up with a text from Rhys. I swipe, and Denielle leans in to read it as well.

**I SWEAR nothing happened. It's over. She wanted to talk. I'll explain.**

Next to me, Denielle chuckles and bumps my shoulder. "I believe him. He looks like he's about to puke. Put him out of his misery."

I pretend to grab something from my bag on the floor and glance back to where Rhys and Wes are standing in line. Den is right. He has a greenish tint, and the anxiety that has been buzzing through my body all morning evaporates. I've been overreacting.

I take my lip gloss out of my bag and carefully apply it. I'm fully aware that Katherine's still watching me, so I take my time before grabbing my phone.

**I believe you.**

I haven't put it down yet when another bubble appears.

**ILY**

Den barks out a laugh. "Oh my, he's got it bad. Poor guy."

That puts the first smile since arriving at school on my face.

# CHAPTER THIRTY-FIVE

### LILLY

WES TEXTS DENIELLE SOMETIME DURING PRACTICE. WE'RE meeting the guys at Bones, a local BBQ place that serves everything on the bone. It's far enough out of town that not many high school students go there during the week, which I'm sure is why they picked it.

I drop my car off at home and ride with Den, figuring I'll either drive back with her or Rhys. Rhys's and Wes's cars are both already in the parking lot when we pull in, and Denielle lets out a string of curse words.

"Why do they have to pick the one place with a gravel parking lot? If I find one scratch on my paint, I'm going to kill Wes."

Denielle drives a brand-new, shiny, gray Audi Q3, which she got for her seventeenth birthday. I shouldn't have been surprised since her previous Audi was a hand-me-down from her brother, Oliver, when he left for college, and was already *two* years old. Of course she needed a new one. At least, that's how her mom justified it. But then, this is pocket money for Mr. Keller, who is a neurosurgeon in the city. Every so often, I'm still surprised how down-to-earth my best friend is compared to some of the others with parents on the wealthier side.

Before exiting the car, I turn to Denielle. "Is this weird?"

She peers at me questioningly.

"That we're all having dinner together? I mean, now that Rhys and I..." Heat creeps into my cheeks.

Denielle smirks. "Oh, you mean because you are sucking face with your brother?"

"Den!" I scowl at her.

That makes her laugh even harder. "I'm sorry, babe, I can't help it. I understand what you're asking, and the answer is, I have no idea."

My stomach clenches. I'm glad she's honest with me, but it doesn't make me feel better.

"I've known both of you forever, but as I told you before, you guys have never been the *typical* brother-sister pair." She makes air quotes around typical. "I guess what I'm trying to say is, we'll have to wait and see. It's not like this is a normal, everyday situation. Probably no one could say at this point how they'd feel about it?" She phrases it more like a question and shrugs her shoulders.

The elongated silence in the car is starting to get uncomfortable when she slaps one hand on my thigh. "Let's go. Don't let your guy wait any longer."


THE BOYS ARE in a booth farthest from the entrance and windows. The inside of Bones is dark. There is no other way to put it. The tinted windows don't let a lot of natural light in, and the walls have wood paneling probably last replaced sometime in the seventies. The brown and beige tile-looking linoleum floor, same era, is paired with brown linoleum chairs and bench seats around more beige tables. I don't think I have to worry about being spotted in here with Rhys. I can barely make out anything myself. The majority of the light comes from the various neon beer signs and random phrases the owner has collected over the years. Definitely not from the pendant lights hanging over the individual tables, whose light bulbs seem to have been installed at the same time as the wood paneling.

Both look up as we approach the table, and Wes stands, letting Denielle and me scoot in. Den waits for me to move next to Rhys, and I don't know if I should be excited or embarrassed. This whole situation is...awkward.

No one says anything, and I begin to feel like this was a bad idea when Wes clears his throat. "So, Lil...am I correct to assume there isn't a chance anymore?" He gestures with one finger between him and me with a ridiculous grin plastered all over his face, eyebrows wiggling suggestively.

Rhys scowls at him. "What the fuck, man?"

Wes just shrugs as if saying it was worth a shot. I have to laugh at his attempt to break the ice. He accomplished what he set out to do; the weird tension is gone. Denielle rolls her eyes, and I smile. "Sorry, I'm taken."

I reach for Rhys's hand under the table, and he immediately interlaces our fingers, giving it a squeeze.

*I'm home.*

Wes places a hand over his heart and sighs dramatically in mock disappointment. We're all cracking up at this point. He holds out his fist to Rhys but looks at me. "Too bad. But I get it. If I would swing that way, I would totally go after his tight ass."

I turn when Rhys bumps his fist to Wes's and find him looking down at me. He has a goofy grin on his face, and I hear Denielle on the other side, "Awwww!"

I blush but allow myself that one moment to pretend we are a normal couple. I lean into Rhys, resting my head against his shoulder and close my eyes.

Dinner passes as if it has always been this way. We joke, reminisce about old times, talk about the guys' upcoming matches and our invitationals. Everyone is at ease, and it feels so good to be able to be myself around my friends. We don't talk about the elephant in the room, also known as my past, but I'm sure it will come up eventually. For now, I simply let myself enjoy the moment.

As we walk toward the cars, I pull Denielle aside. "Is it okay if I ride with Rhys?" The awkward feeling is back.

She genuinely smiles at me. "Sure thing, babe. I'll see you in the morning."

She gives me a side hug and joins Wes, a few paces ahead, who is still talking to Rhys. They separate and go to their respective cars while I join Rhys at his Defender.

. . .

## **RHYS**

How did it go from kissing Lilly good morning and feeling on top of the world to being completely fucked up within five hours? Standing in the lunch line, I see Kat eyeing her—this is not good.

Wes leans in. "Kat is going to make your life hell, dude. Or more like Lilly's. She suspects something but can't put her finger on it."

I haven't told him yet what Kat said to me this morning. He's perceptive and definitely correct on that account. Kat has become a problem.

"I know."


As I hold Lilly's hand under the table, everything falls back into place. I spent the entire day looking over my shoulder, expecting my ex to stalk me.

Finally alone with her in the car, I exhale a long breath. As soon as the dome light turns off, I reach for Lilly's hand and say, "I swear that nothing happened with Kat."

She angles her body toward me.

"I know." Her voice is soft, and her thumb gently strokes back and forth over our intertwined fingers. "I...I was just...I'm not good at this."

She sounds embarrassed, and I give her hand a squeeze. If she knew what a fucking mess I was, she wouldn't feel that way.

In a low tone, she asks, "What did she want?"

I press my lips together briefly before speaking. "She kind of tried to change my mind."

Lilly turns her face forward, and I can see the hard lines around her eyes.

"Not because she loves me or wants to be with me; it's all about her image. She had this whole thing about prom and whatnot planned out in her head, and I screwed that up for her." I'm not sure if I'm making the situation better or worse. I neglect the fact that Kat has some suspicion about Lilly having something to do with all of it. Logically, I should tell her, but I want to protect her so badly. I may not be able to hide her from her stalker again, but at least I can keep Kat's craziness away from her. *I hope.*

Hesitantly, Lilly turns back. "What did you respond?"

"That I'm done pretending. We're over." Without intending to, my tone is hard, almost angry.

"I bet she didn't take that well," Lilly says cheekily. My confident girl is back, and I'm so relieved I could cry.

*Yes, I'm man enough to admit that.*

"She did not. She's used to getting what she wants." My amused tone fades, and I add, "We need to be careful around her."

Lilly huffs out a breath and looks away from me.

"Cal?"

"Hmm-hmm?"

"You're it for me." She has to get that.

Lilly's face is illuminated red from Bones' neon sign. She stares ahead for several heartbeats then shifts toward me, placing both hands on my cheeks. "I know. I do. It's just a lot right now. Everything is so new, and I'm not used to this relationship stuff—to being jealous or insecure when it comes to a guy."

Her hands fall to the middle console, and I take them in mine. "Me, neither, babe."

THE REST OF THE WEEK, Lilly and I fall into a routine. First school, then practice, and because Dad is still out of town, Lilly spends the evenings with Mom and Natty. I'm glad she is making an effort, because even if Mom hid it well, she did notice the shift in her daughter.

Once Mom and Natty are in bed, I sneak across the hall, and for a few hours, it's the two of us. We're in our own world where we don't have to pretend. That time is spent with *a lot* of making out. And fuck, she is good at it. I can't get enough of this girl. Never in my wildest—extremely graphic—dreams did I imagine the feel of her lips on mine being this mind-blowing. On more than one occasion, I have to stop us from going further, which always ends with Lilly's grumbled whimper of protest. Not that I want to put the brakes on. Hell, I think, at this point, I'm more acquainted with cold showers and my hand than any guy should ever be, but I need to do this right. I've waited too long for this—for her. Then, there is our double truckload of baggage we need to work through if we want this to work long-term.

Coach is at a conference, so I don't have practice on Friday. Looking forward to a few hours alone with Lilly before Mom and Natty get home, I head to my car and come to a dead stop when I spot Kat leaning against it.

My steps slow until I'm right in front of her. "What do you want?"

She saunters toward me, hips swaying, and places one hand against my abdomen as if my icy tone was an invitation to grope me. "I just want to see if you have reconsidered yet?"

I take a step back, breaking the contact. "There is nothing to reconsider. I told you we're done."

I know the look in her eyes. She is set on convincing me—at all costs. What she doesn't understand is that there is nothing she could offer me that would make me turn my back on Lilly. But I can't tell her that.

Kat pushes forward so she's flush against me. Her hands pushing into my jacket and around my waist, we're nose to nose. Her lips hover over mine, not touching, but I feel her breath. The next words out of her mouth make my blood run cold. "I have no idea what weird thing you have going on with your sister, but I intend to find out. And I promise you, you will come back to me when I'm through with her."

With that, she puts her sweet but fake smile on and walks away as if nothing happened.

Fuck.

# CHAPTER THIRTY-SIX

**LILLY**

By the time I meet with Spencer on Saturday, I am completely fidgety.

I've been on cloud nine all week. No more texts from my psycho stalker; besides a few stolen glances, I've been able to keep it together at school; after almost a year of practice, I finally mastered the double back; and to top off my good mood, Rhys and I spend our nights holed up in my room—just the two of us. Wednesday and Thursday night, I fell asleep in his arms, and he stayed until the alarm went off at four a.m. It was the best sleep I've had in months.

The voice that initially kept telling me how wrong all this is has subsided. Being with Rhys has turned out to be more natural than anything else in my life.

Then, Friday happened. Rhys was supposed to meet me at home after school, but he didn't show up. At five, I got a text that something came up with Wes, and he'd be home late. The whole thing felt off, but after the incident with Katherine earlier this week and me going all insecure-jealous girlfriend on him, I wanted to give him the benefit of the doubt. He came to my room around eleven-thirty. I was half asleep when he slid into bed behind me and wrapped his arms around my waist. He was holding on so tight, nuzzling my hair as if I'd disappear at any moment. His behavior intensified my suspicion that my initial gut feeling was correct after all. But I have to believe that he would tell me if something was bothering him.

SPENCE MUST SENSE what I need, because five minutes into the warm-up, he announces we're sparring instead of working on specific moves. And sparring we are. He disappears for a few minutes and comes back with body armor for both of us, including a *full* face shield.

"Holy cow, are you going to beat me up?" I raise my eyebrows at him.

"I got these babies a few weeks ago and have been dying to try them out." He sounds giddy like a little boy.

By the time my hour is up, I am a sweaty mess and riding on an endorphin high. I take the shield off, and my hair looks like I just stepped out of the shower. I grin from ear to ear, which in return makes Spence's face shine with pride. Despite being so much older, he's been a good friend and mentor to me for years, and I enjoy spending time with him.

Leaving the workout room, I feel lighter and more relaxed than when I walked in. I head to the general area Denielle and I always meet up at when someone falls in step beside me. I'm so startled that I trip over my own feet, and an arm shoots out to steady me. I instinctively pull away and take a step back. After the incident with Den a few weeks ago, I try to suppress my impulse to defend first and think later until I actually assess the danger.

When I turn, I meet familiar hazel eyes, and my mouth falls open. Up close, he's even more striking than from afar or behind glass. The blond guy Denielle had pointed out to me before, and later had watched me train, is smiling down at me genuinely. "Sorry, I didn't mean to startle you."

"Uh." He is indeed an inch or two taller than Rhys, and I have to crane my neck to get a good look at him.

I compose myself and put some distance between us. "No, it's okay. I just didn't expect, uh...anyone." No reason to tell him that I have a psycho kidnapper stalking me, and I'm on constant high alert. I start walking again, and he matches my stride easily.

After a few steps, he says, "I wouldn't want to meet you in a dark alley."

That brings me to a dead stop once more. "Excuse me?"

He laughs at my confused look. "I watched you sparring. You're good."

His compliment catches me off guard, and my cheeks heat. "Oh, um, thanks, I guess?"

"I'm sorry, I didn't mean to make you uncomfortable. I just admire when a girl knows how to handle herself."

Is he flirting with me? I cock my head to the side and look him up and down. No, I don't think so. He doesn't give off a flirty vibe, just polite small talk.

I eye him skeptically, and he reaches his hand out. "I'm Nate Hamlin."

I take it. "Lilly." I omit my last name on purpose—trust issues and all.

"It's nice to meet you, Lilly."

Still holding my hand, he glances toward the treadmills. "Your friend is staring."

I follow his line of sight, and sure enough, Denielle is standing there with her water bottle halfway up to her mouth, gaping.

I smirk. "Ha, my best friend has no shame."

Nate snorts. "That's probably why Todd is so attracted to her."

Ah, so his friend's name is Todd. I'm sure Denielle will like to know that fact. I turn back to Nate and smile. "I gotta go. It was nice to meet you."

Nate nods at me and starts moving backward. "I'll see you around."

WHEN I REACH DENIELLE, she has lowered her water bottle but still stares at me like I sprouted a third eye.

"Who are you and what have you done with my best friend?"

I shrug. "What?"

She hooks her arm around mine, and we start toward our usual treadmills. I swear, whenever Den is around, people scatter from the equipment as soon as we approach. She is the female version of Rhys, commanding the room the second she enters.

"Well, for starters, you have not had interest in the opposite sex for, um, EV-ER. Then, you score the hottest guy in school, and now this dude—what did he want?"

"Eww." The thought of her insinuating anything with Nate makes me shudder. "Nothing; he complimented me on my session with Spence and introduced himself." I have the urge to tell her that there is absolutely nothing flirty between Nate and me, but she probably wouldn't believe it.

"He introduced himself. What's his name?"

"Nate." *Shit, what was his last name?* "Hamin? No, Hamlin."

Denielle pulls her phone out and starts typing. She clicks and scrolls around until she puts her phone away, and I raise my eyebrows. "What's the verdict?"

She shrugs. "Nate Hamlin, born in New York, grew up between New York and Los Angeles, and works at the new hotel in the city —the one that rich dude opened up a few months ago. Remember the article we discussed in journalism? Anyway, nothing juicy. Kind of a bummer; he's so hot." Her disappointment is apparent. She's a sucker for gossip, and whenever there is a new face around—one that is this handsome—it could mean there is an interesting backstory.

I wrap my arm around her shoulder. "Aww, I'm sorry the new guy doesn't live up to your expectations. Now let's go, we have a few miles to cover today." I purposefully omit the fact that I know the friend's name. Den would totally make me search for Nate to get Todd's last name.

We've reached the treadmills, and I put my headphones in, hit the quick start button, and end the conversation.

Sunday morning, I walk into the kitchen to Natty helping Heather pack a small cooler.

"What are you guys up to?"

Natty turns to me, beaming. "We're going to the museum with Gemma and her mom."

Her excitement is contagious, and I can't help but grin back at my little sister. "That sounds awesome. You'll have so much fun."

"Mark is on a business trip, and Nathalie asked if we wanted to join her and Gemma since Dad is gone as well. Make it a girls' day," Heather explains.

"He's gone more than usual, isn't he?" I remember Heather mentioning another business trip the other night when we cooked together, and from what I remember, Gemma's dad is a financial advisor at one of the banks in town. Since when do they travel so much?

Heather frowns. "Yes, Nathalie is not happy."

I leave it at that. I don't feel like gossiping about one of Natty's friend's parents—especially in front of Natty. Who knows what's going on there?

I busy myself with heating water in the kettle when Heather comes from behind and hugs me around the waist. "You want to join us?"

Several things register at once in my mind. Her touch does not make me flinch. I don't have the urge to pull away anymore. I would actually enjoy a day with Heather and Natty. We haven't done that in a long time, even before my life was turned upside down. But the next thought is what makes me almost drop my tea mug—Rhys and I will be alone in the house. All. Day. My mouth turns dry, and I swallow several times.

"Um, uh, I think I'll lay low at home today. I still have eight episodes to catch up on."

*Not counting the ones I have to re-watch because I made out with* your son.

Oblivious to the beads of sweat starting to appear on my forehead, Heather places a kiss on my temple. "Sounds good. If you see Rhys, let him know we'll be back around seven. It's so nice having him home more these days."

"Will do," comes out as a squeak. Does she know anything? Oh my gosh, I might as well hold a neon sign with rotating blinking lights that reads *I'm making out with my adoptive brother* over my head.

Thankfully, Heather's attention is back on Natty. They finish packing, and I move to the living room with my tea, turning on the TV.

ONCE THEY'RE out the door and I hear her pull out of the garage, I glance toward the ceiling. Rhys is still sleeping. We're alone in the house. I could walk upstairs and join him in his bed without anyone noticing.

Why is my mug all of a sudden so slippery? And did Heather turn the heat up before she left? I shimmy out of the sweater I slept in. The cool air feels good on my flushed skin.

I've made out with guys, but I've never let it go further. If a guy pushed for more, I would put on the brakes, and that was that. I never had the urge to go to the next level, but with Rhys, I'm actually *entertaining* the thought. We've made out whenever we were alone in my room. A lot. Hands wandered, but our clothes—most of them—always remained in place; Rhys made sure of that. My mind starts drifting again. His calloused fingertips gliding under my tank top, cupping my—ugh, I need to stop before I'm forced to fully strip down in the living room or risk my body spontaneously combusting.

I place my empty mug in the sink and slowly make my way up the stairs, taking one last look at my sweater draped across the back of the couch. At the top of the stairs, I take a few calming breaths and wipe my palms on my pajama pants before easing Rhys's bedroom door open slowly.

Rhys is sprawled diagonally across his bed. He's on his back, one hand behind his head, the other one on his stomach. His comforter is hanging half off the bed, and his shirt is all twisted, the lower part of his taut abdomen peeking out. My breathing immediately accelerates at the sight, and I bite my bottom lip. I can't seem to look away from his abs and have the urge to slowly trace each muscle with my tongue.

*Has his room all of a sudden gotten hotter as well?*

Once I get a grip on myself again, I slowly move into the room toward his bed. For a few heartbeats, I marvel at how this boy is mine and that there could have been a chance of me never knowing.

I carefully lower one knee onto the mattress, followed by my trembling hands, until I'm on all fours. Rhys shows no sign of waking up, and I crawl until I am right next to him. Lowering myself down, I make sure not to startle him. When he *still* doesn't move, I exhale a shaky breath. Inching closer, I nuzzle my head in the crook of his neck, wrap my arm around his waist, and place a kiss underneath, slightly behind his ear. The remnants of his shower gel invade my nose, and I inhale. His scent alone makes my core come to life.

*That* gets me a reaction, and he mumbles, "Cal?"

Rhys's head is angled toward me, and I take the opportunity and capture his mouth with mine. His eyes pop open immediately, and he pulls back an inch, glancing between me and the still-open door. "Uh...am I dreaming?"

I grin deviously at him. "Does it feel like a dream?"

"Umm..." His eyes dart to the door and back to my face again. "No?"

My poor guy is still half asleep. I place my hand on his face, slowly sliding it to his neck while pulling him slowly back to me. One leg hooked over his, I'm halfway on top when I say, "Then let me kiss you good morning already."

I have no clue where my bravado comes from; I barely recognize myself. Walking in his room and seeing him there, sprawled out, mine for the taking, all hesitation has left my body, and a new sense has taken over—unrestricted desire. I want him.

Rhys smiles against my lips, and I can feel his body responding to mine. He pulls on me until I'm draped on top of him and mumbles against my lips, "Mhmmm...I like that kind of wake-up call."

## RHYS

LILLY TAKING what she wants from me is such a turn-on that I can't stop myself from pulling her on top of me and deepening the kiss. When her lips part ever so slightly, all bets are off, and my primal instincts take over. My tongue invades her mouth, and she reciprocates in kind. I can taste the bergamot orange on her tongue. She's already had her tea.

*When did kissing become better than sex?*

If kissing her is this good, I can't even think of—that's when she nips on my lower lip, and a guttural groan escapes me. With one move, I reverse our position, and she's under me, caged between my forearms resting on each side of her head. My hips press against her center and, moaning, her eyes roll back. Focusing back on me, she holds my gaze and slowly slides her hands under my shirt, up my back. Her soft fingertips ignite my skin, and I can feel the path she is making burning all the way into my muscles. My dick is already painfully hard, and I can't stop myself from rocking into her. The whimper escaping her confirms that she can feel my hard-on pressing against her core. I can barely contain the urge to strip her. But maybe some dry humping?

*No, stop that right there.*

When Kat and I had started our *arrangement*, it didn't take more than three days before we ended up in the back of my car together. And the entire school knew about it the next day. Kat made sure of that. Even at the stage of wanting to forget everything about Lilly, I knew that it was wrong. It felt wrong. But this...Lilly, even mostly clothed, gives me more than the wildest sex in my past. And the difference is...I love her.

When she braces her feet against the mattress and presses herself against my throbbing cock, I finally pull back. We're both panting, and if we keep this up, I'll have to get a clean pair of briefs soon. I see another cold shower in my near future and groan inwardly.

Breathing heavily, I touch my forehead to hers and huff out a laugh. "Babe, what are you doing to me? Who are you?"

Lilly blushes. "Honestly, I'm not sure."

"You're killing me."

"Sorry?" She shrugs. But she's not.

I peck her nose. "Do you have any idea how much I want you right now? Fuck, you interrupted a pretty R-rated dream of yourself when you attacked me."

The daring gleam returns to her eyes. "Oh yeah? Do tell."

That makes me shake my head. And I thought I couldn't be any crazier about her. "Uh, no, I already need a cold shower. I don't want to add to the pain by talking about what we did in the car."

"The car, was it?" She wiggles her eyebrows.

*Fuck me and my stupid mouth.*

I burrow my face in the crook of her neck. "Cal, I want to do this right, but if you tease me any more, I will strip you, and all bets are off."

Her body tenses, and I draw back, leaning on my elbow. She is staring at the ceiling, and my heart sinks.

"And if that's what I want?" The question is just a whisper, but it's like she's stuck a knife in my gut. I never want her to think that I don't want her. I'm ninety-nine percent sure she's never had sex before.

With my free hand, I turn her face until she is forced to look at me. "Calla, I love you. I want to do this right."

The corners of her mouth pull up ever so slightly. "I love you, too." She's not convinced.

I gather her against my chest, and she wraps her arms around me. We hold each other for a long time before I say in a low tone, "Babe, you have so much going on in your life. That's why I'm trying to take *that part* slow. I want to be able to take you on a real date before...you know..." I actually blush. I don't think I've ever blushed talking about sex. Hell, last year, a guy from the team caught Kat giving me head in the locker room after a game, and I simply saluted him while she kept going. Word spread fast, and I just grinned, shrugged it off with a fist bump to everyone who commented.

Lilly tilts her head up and places a well-aimed kiss on my neck, right underneath my ear. She's already learned that this is my weak spot, and I growl at her.

This earns me a genuine laugh. In a teasing voice, she says, "Won't that get boring for you?" My mind immediately goes to the locker room incident again. I'm sure she caught wind about it, too. Bile rises in my throat at the thought of all the shit Lilly must've heard about me.

I swallow and try to find the right words in my mind.

"No, it won't get boring for me. Do I want to see you naked? Hell yes." The implied *duh* is obvious. My enthusiasm makes both of us laugh, and I continue, "But we are a lot more than a make-out session and a quick fuck. We have a past *and a future*. Does that make sense?"

I feel her shrug. "I think so, yeah."

I breathe in her shampoo, let the smell take over my senses, and murmur into her hair, "And we can do a lot of other stuff besides me dipping my dick inside of you."

*I'm not a monk.*

Lilly cackles at that. "Oh, yeah? What do you have in mind?"

It's my turn to smile deviously at her. In one swift movement, I have her on top of me again and run my hands under her shirt and up her spine. Lilly shivers under my touch.

"Like this," I tease.

With my pulse speeding up, I reverse the motion and slowly ease my fingers under the waistband of her pajamas and cup her firm, round butt.

"Or like this."

Lilly rocks into me, moaning against my mouth, and I capture her lips with mine.

*Maybe we can push the make-out boundaries a little more than I planned.*

W**E** **SPEND** most of the morning in bed, and the boundaries definitely get pushed farther than I intended. In the end, my shirt is off, and Lilly's pajama pants are somewhere near the bottom of the bed. We're covered in a sheen of sweat, and I'm pretty sure I came in my boxer briefs at one point. Okay, I totally did. But in my defense, so did she. There is only so much dry humping two people can do before it gets messy.

I take in Lilly sprawled in *my* bed, only wearing a thin gray tank top and black boy shorts. Her hair is all mussed, and anyone walking in would be convinced we'd gone at it like rabbits. Though, I'd probably knock out anyone before they could get a good look at her.

I mentally shake myself. What am I even thinking? I'm still waiting to wake up and find that everything is back to before. Before Thanksgiving. Before Lilly started to remember.

We're in a stare-down, Lilly with her back on the mattress and me kneeling to the side of her. The challenging gleam in her eyes tells me that she is not done yet. Challenge accepted.

I lower myself down and slowly kiss from her ear to her neck, letting the tip of my tongue slide across her flesh between nips and kisses. She shudders every time my lips make contact with her flushed skin, and my need to take care of her consumes every cell of my body. At her collarbone, I place a soft kiss on the small birthmark she has there and continue my trail to the valley of her breasts, pausing there to give each of them the appropriate attention even with the layer of fabric in between. Lilly is writhing underneath me, and I move on to her flat stomach, hooking my thumbs inside her tank top. Beginning to slowly push it up, my tongue continues the expedition of her body downward, placing a kiss on each of her defined and sexy-as-hell abs.

When Lilly moans and arches into me *again,* my last bit of self-restraint is lost. My fingers move from the edge of her shirt to the waistband of her shorts. When she doesn't protest, I pull further until her hip bones are exposed. My own breathing has become labored at this point. God, she is so fucking sexy. She has no intention of stopping me, and I'm not sure I still can or even want to. Wanting her is overpowering all my senses.

*So much for my earlier speech.*

At that precise moment, her stomach growls so loudly that her eyes widen, and we both burst out laughing. I put my forehead to her stomach and murmur, "That's a sign."

She places a hand on my head and gently strokes my hair.

*I'm in heaven.*

I move next to her on the bed and say, "Let's get your physical needs fulfilled first before we continue anything else."

Lilly raises her eyebrows, and I repeat in my head what I said. I slap myself against the forehead, and we both grin like idiots.

"Let's go, or I'm going to strip you all the way, and you won't get anything to eat for a long time." True statement.

She pretends to pout but doesn't resist me.


WE END up on the living room couch, both of us holding a steaming mug. Lilly's contains her usual tea versus mine which is filled to the brim with coffee. She balances a plate of muffins on her lap while I have my arm around her. I've turned one of her shows on, and we just sit together. Content.

At one point, I glance over at Lilly and notice that she is staring out the window, deep in thought.

"What's going on in your head, babe?"

Her eyes snap to mine, and she smirks. "I think I knew all along."

I narrow my eyes in confusion. "Knew what?"

"That I love you." Her focus is back out to the yard.

"Oh?" My pulse accelerates, like every time she says those three words.

She is sorting through her thoughts, and I wait. "The more I think about it, the more I'm convinced they forgot to rewire some parts of you in my head. Otherwise, it wouldn't have hurt so bad two years ago."

My insides turn to knots, and when she sees my expression, she rushes on, "I don't mean to make you feel guilty. I've just been thinking a lot about everything."

I tighten my arm around her, and I press a kiss to her forehead. "I know, babe. You have no idea how sorry I am. There were many times where I was so close to telling you the truth, but I was terrified you would never look at me again because I kept this secret from you."

Her lips tighten, and she remembers the night I came clean. "I did feel betrayed. For a while, I wasn't sure if I could forgive you."

Her honesty is brutal, but what did I expect? "But you did?" I know she has. She's told me as much, but I need to hear her say it out loud again.

Lilly must sense that and turns to me, placing a hand on my neck. "I have. You only did what you were asked to do—keep me safe. The past is the past. Let's move forward?"

She can feel my racing pulse under her hand. I slowly move toward her, and before placing my lips on hers, I say, "Forward."

## CHAPTER THIRTY-SEVEN

### LILLY

OUR FREEDOM IS GOING TO END. WHENEVER TRISTEN TRAVELS, Heather makes sure to give one hundred and ten percent to Natty, which means she is busy all day, retires early, and Rhys and I can be *in our little bubble* for the rest of the evening. I'm not sure if Heather notices the change in us and turns a blind eye or if she's too busy. My gut tells me she knows. She's our—well, Rhys's—mother, after all. At the same time, the thought of it freaks me out. What if she tells Tristen, and he takes the *necessary steps* he threatened Rhys with so long ago?

WHEN IT'S the two of us, Rhys is the attentive and loving boyfriend every girl dreams of, but at school, he doesn't spare me a second glance. Something has changed over the past week. Up until Friday, when he didn't come home as planned, our gazes would meet, and even in that fraction of a moment before he'd avert his eyes, the underlying promise of what *he'd do to me later* was as clear as day. Now...there is nothing. His face is expressionless, and the heavy blanket of the past, of not knowing why he's changed, starts settling over me again. I'm so over this. I'm tired of being a puppet for everyone to play with as they please. At the same time, I can't say anything; we're not supposed to talk or make eye contact in public.

I try to catch a glimpse of him every chance I get. My Rhys radar is stronger than ever. I'm aware of his presence as soon as he enters a hallway or the cafeteria without searching for him. However, besides the initial acknowledgment paired with an impassive look of boredom, he won't pay attention to me. Katherine, however, gets the opposite. At first, I thought I had imagined it, but by Wednesday, I'm positive that Rhys is watching her. He's assured me that I'm *it* for him, and deep down, I believe him, but something is going on between those two, and he's keeping me in the dark. Katherine, in return, tracks me like a hawk, and whenever our gazes meet, she gives me a smug smile that makes my blood run cold before she throws a significant look in Rhys's direction as if to tell me *he's mine, you'll see.*

Most of the time, I'm able to shrug it off as misplaced paranoia. There haven't been any more messages from my psycho stalker in almost two weeks, but the chance of everything being back to *normal* is just too far-fetched.

TRISTEN WILL BE BACK early tomorrow morning. Today was the gymnastics league championship, and I'm beyond exhausted. We placed second, so we didn't get the bragging rights of being league champs, but to be honest, I was relieved. Not that I would admit that to the team or even Denielle. With what's been going on the last few weeks and the fact that Rhys will go back to staying at Wes's, I can't focus on it.

Heather, Natty, and I are downstairs watching a movie together when the garage door opens, and my body immediately starts buzzing with anticipation. Rhys is home. He marches into the kitchen and abruptly stops in the doorway to the living room when he notices us lined up on the couch. "What are you guys watching?"

Before I can turn, Natty flips around and beams at her big brother. "It's the new Disney movie. The one I told you about this week. Mom rented it for us." She's bouncing up and down like she's on a trampoline, and I snort a laugh. Rhys's eyes snap to mine, and the laughter dies in my throat. In the past, it would've been because we couldn't stand each other. We didn't interact—ever. But that's not the case anymore. It's because my throat closes up and my mouth turns dry. My mind is instantly upstairs in bed with him hovering above me, tracing my body with his tongue while his hands roam freely under my clothes. My eyes widen, and Rhys is pressing his lips together in an attempt to remain expressionless. He knows exactly where I just went, and the gleam in his eyes is assurance of him doing exactly *that* later. I fight the urge to cover my face with my hands, and when I peek at Heather, she is watching me closely.

*Crap.*

My adrenaline level increases even further—and not in a good way. Does she know?

"I'm gonna crash. I'm meeting Wes early tomorrow before my session with Spence." Rhys's voice snaps me out of the stare-down with his mother, and we both turn.

"Sounds good, honey. Have a good night." Her voice doesn't betray anything, and I wonder if it's all just in my head.

He leaves, and we resume the movie as if nothing happened. Natty comments enthusiastically on various scenes, but my interest went with Rhys.

As soon as Tristen arrives home, Rhys moves back to Wes's, and the nights become endless. In our short time together, I've gotten used to sleeping in his arms. I keep replaying our last night over and over—Rhys fulfilled his promise and spoiled my entire body until he snuck back to his room in the early morning hours.

But he's not here anymore. It's been a week, and as if on cue, the nightmares are back. It's always the same dream, ever since the very first time on the road trip. Sometimes *he* just talks to me; other times, he *anxiously* forces me to drink something that makes me sleepy. But I never see his face. I wonder if I have *ever* seen it. If the memory doctor erased it, or if my subconscious is suppressing it. Whatever it is, when the dream ends, I wake up with a stifled scream, racing heart, and am covered in sweat—every single time.

Rhys texts me, asking if I'm okay, and I assure him that I'm good and just miss him. It seems to appease him—or he's humoring me. I don't know.

. . .

I DON'T WANT to dream anymore. On Friday—day six of the never-ending cycle—I manage to stay awake until one-thirty. That's the last time I glance at my alarm clock. Next thing I know, I wake up with a start, sitting in bed, every limb shaking.

*Not again.*

I crave Rhys's voice and having him assure me that I'm safe, but it's four in the morning, and I can't bring myself to call him. He'd be over here in minutes, and that would instantly raise questions with the parental units sleeping upstairs.

Slowly, I pad into my bathroom to wash the cold sweat off. Closing the door behind me, Rhys's hoodie, which is hanging on the back of it, comes into view. Without thinking, I strip out of my sweat-soaked clothes, wash off the grime, and pull it over my head. He gave it to me freshman year, right before we completely stopped talking, and for the longest time, I had it stuffed in the bottom drawer of my dresser. But when the migraines started, something made me dig it out. I think I even wore it to school one day, as out of it as I was.

*No wonder I've drawn attention.*

The sleeves have always been too long, and there is a hole under one of the arms where the seam has come undone, but I don't care. I cover my face with my hands hidden inside the fabric and inhale deeply. Rhys wore the sweatshirt the other night, making fun of me for still having it. It was way too tight *and* short, revealing his lower abs. He looked like the Hulk about to burst out of his clothes. He explained that he wanted it to smell like him, which at the time made me laugh, and I replied how cheesy he sounded. Now, in the middle of the night, I'm beyond grateful for this small piece of him.

IN THE MORNING, I cancel my session with Spence and text Denielle that I don't feel up for a workout. Her response is immediate.

**What's wrong?**

Sometimes I hate that she knows me so well. I don't cancel a workout—not unless I'm deathly ill. Putting my phone down, I debate what to type back. I don't want to tell her about the nightmares. I haven't even mentioned them to Rhys. I'm sick of being treated like the victim.

**I'm just tired.**

**Try again.**

Ugh.

**I haven't slept well since Rhys has been staying at Wes's.**

When Den doesn't respond, I plug the phone back in its charger and take a shower. I only washed up last night and still feel gross.

Emerging an hour later with my hair smelling of my new favorite shampoo, slightly curled, and some light makeup, I feel semi-normal. Checking my phone, my best friend texted at some point to come to her house at eleven instead of meeting at the gym. Her parents are gone for the weekend—a spontaneous ski trip or something like that.

*I can do that. Hanging out and watching TV.*

I'm on my way to Denielle's when a message from Sloane lights up the screen. We had been texting about a potential shopping trip with Emma and Den last night, and she probably wants to iron out the details. I plan to respond when I get to Denielle's since I refuse to text and drive. I have to admit that I used to do it. But then a senior from WH got in a horrible accident last year because he was texting and spent weeks in the hospital. It was a wakeup call for a lot of us, and I haven't done it since.

When I pull into the drive, I hit the brakes. A spike of adrenaline makes my pulse increase, and I grip the steering wheel. Rhys's Defender is parked in front of the garage, and I can't get out of my car fast enough. He's here. By the time I ungracefully scramble up the front steps, the front door is already open, and I fly into his arms.

*Home.*

Catching me under my butt, he lifts me up like I weigh nothing. My arms and legs are wrapped around his body like a monkey, and he opens his mouth to say something when I capture his lips with mine. God, how I've missed this. He hums in approval, and I'm about to pull a Katherine when someone clears their throat behind us.

Denielle's voice penetrates my foggy mind from far away. "Maybe we should take the welcoming scene inside?" She doesn't sound upset, more amused.

I pull back from my Rhys as he walks back into the house with me in his arms, and the door closes. Den is behind me, and when I scan the foyer, Wes is standing on the bottom step of the wide staircase. Arms crossed over his chest, leaning with his hip against the rail, Wes grins like a loon. I wonder if Rhys has been just as mopey as me. He's done a one-eighty and is moving us toward the kitchen. I tighten my hold, resting my chin on his shoulder. Zeroing in on Den, I mouth, "Thank you!" I can't stop smiling.

Her eyes crinkle, and she gives me a nod. Her mission is accomplished.

Not letting go, Rhys deposits me on the kitchen island. He pulls me forward until my chest is flush against his, and we're at eye level.

"I missed you." The three words are spoken in a murmur as his lips flutter over mine. Inhaling the smell of his minty toothpaste in combination with his own scent that is all Rhys, my body heats to an almost uncomfortable level, and I can't stop the moan escaping my throat. Instinctively, I roll my hips forward, and he lets out a groan.

"Ohhh-kaaay, you two, take it upstairs before I start making out with Wes to alleviate all the sexual tension you two are emanating." Den's words make me pull away and bury my face into Rhys's chest, hiding my flushed face.

## RHYS

WE STAYED up way too late again, but this video game is addicting, and it is the only reason I can tolerate being here.

Dad came home Sunday and gave me the oddest look as soon as he noticed me standing in the kitchen. So, I packed my duffels—all three of them—and left with the comment that I'd be staying at Wes's. Of course, he didn't even blink. Camped out with his computer and files on the kitchen table, he barely acknowledged me before lowering his gaze back to the screen. Mom was prepping lunch, and despite her initial glance toward her husband, she didn't try to stop me either.

Unclenching my fists, I force one foot in front of the other before I give in to the urge to haul his fucking laptop against the wall. Keeping Lilly safe is one thing, but cutting your son loose over it—who the hell does that?

THIS MORNING I wake up to a text from Denielle.

**Call me.**

My hand tightens around the phone. Something is wrong with Lilly; there is no other reason for Den to message me this early—or at all. Wes is still snoring, but I don't give two shits if I wake him up. Den picks up on the second ring, and before she can say hello, I blurt out, "What's wrong with her?"

She sighs, "Good morning, Rhys. I'm good. Thanks for asking."

"Den, don't fuck with me. You've never asked me to call you. What. Is. Wrong. With. Her?" I'm shaking at this point, and Wes has opened his eyes, staring at me, alarmed.

"Dude, chill. She's fine. I think."

*She thinks?*

"YOU THINK?" Great, now I'm shouting.

"Lilly canceled our workout this morning."

That's all I need to hear. I'm off the couch that I've called my bed for the past week, scrambling to find my pants.

"Hold your horses. I'll send you a screenshot."

There is silence on the other end, and then my phone vibrates against my ear. I pull it away and read the short text message exchange. Fuck. Me. How did I not consider the nightmares when I chose to stay away like a freaking pussy?

When I don't speak, Den says, "I'm going to tell her to come over. My parents are gone this weekend. You guys can all stay here 'til Monday."

Two days with Lilly. Alone. No hiding. My lower region immediately stands at attention—no need to think about what I'm going to do. "What time?"

"Eleven. Be here before that."

The small alarm clock on Wes's bedside table shows ten-fifteen.

"Give me twenty." Den lives only a few blocks from Wes's house. Twenty minutes gives me plenty of time to shower and drive over.

Before I hang up, Denielle says, "Bring Wes, since I'm safe to assume that I won't see much of you *or* my best friend for the rest of the weekend." Her tone is light, and all the tension leaves my body.

"Den?" My voice is soft.

"Yeah?"

"Thank you." And I mean it.

She chuckles. "Anything for our girl."

AFTER LILLY'S best friend all but threatens to make out with Wes, I pick Lilly up and throw her over my shoulder, smacking her butt.

"Rhyyyys!" she squeals and swats at my ass.

Ignoring the laughter following us up the stairs, I make my way to the first guest room I can find.

At least I hope it is a guest room.

Inside, I can't kick the door shut fast enough and almost lose my balance in the process.

Lilly giggles at my haste. "Slow down, big guy. I'm not going anywhere."

Turning, I lower her as gently as I can with the raging boner trying to break through my pants. My jeans need to go. Fast. As soon as her feet hit the floor, I walk her back against the door and nuzzle my nose in her neck. My hands find her hips, and I squeeze. My body buzzes as if I just chugged several energy drinks. Having my fingers on her after being apart for days, I have to force myself to slow down.

A sigh escapes her, and my tongue darts out, licking the skin underneath her ear. Lilly fists her fingers into my shirt just as mine make their way into the back of her pants.

*Fuck, it feels so good having her back in my arms.*

She moves her hands up, leaving a tingling sensation in their wake. She cups my face between both and guides it to hers. Immediately diving in, her lips part, and her warm tongue meets mine. She tastes like bergamot and orange, a flavor that's all Lilly, and I never thought it would have the ability to drive me crazy, wanting to strip her then and there. Her arms intertwine behind my neck, and she hikes up one leg. Taking that as an invitation, I grab her under her ass, and she wraps both legs around me again. Grinding myself against her core, Lilly nips at my bottom lip, and all bets are off. I need her out of those clothes. Hell, I need to get out of mine. I pull her away from the door and carry her over to the queen bed where I let us both drop on the mattress.

"You don't get to do that and not pay the price." I smirk down at her.

Her eyes widen in mock horror before a devilish grin spreads across her features. "I'm good for the money," Lilly declares in a sultry tone that makes my dick even harder—if that's possible.

Without another word, I clasp the hem of her top as she grasps for my belt buckle. Within less than a minute, the only barriers left are my briefs—which will probably have a hole in them soon with the way I'm tenting—and Lilly's white lace boy shorts with matching bra. I would stare at her splayed out like that all day if I didn't have a major blood-flow issue in my lower half to alleviate.

I don't break eye contact as I lower my face to the swell of her breast. Bringing my lips to her soft skin, moisture floods my mouth, and I lick her above the hem of her bra. Lilly's breathing becomes more labored, and she arches into the touch. "God, yes."

With my mouth already on her, I let the hand that's not holding me up explore other parts of her body.

A moan escapes her, and she reaches for my dick.

I pull back slightly. "Let's make sure the underwear stays on, 'kay?"

"Wha—? Why?" She's truly confused, and the wrinkle between her brow makes me chuckle.

"I refuse to have our first time in one of the Kellers' spare bedrooms, babe. Believe me, I want you." I glance between us where she cups me. "As you can see. And feel." I drop my forehead to hers. "But not here."

Disappointment is visible on her face, but she nods in agreement. "Okay."

We spend the rest of Saturday holed up in the room until Wes bangs against the door. "Get your horny asses downstairs. We ordered pizza."

My face is currently nuzzled into the crook of Lilly's neck with one hand palming her breast, pinching her nipple, while she, in return, clutches my biceps, arching up to give me better access—her bra came off a while ago. We both groan in frustration, but we've been in our bubble for the last, uh...I peer at the clock on the nightstand...six hours, and I know we're shit friends if we remain up here any longer. Not that *I* care, but Lilly does.

Trudging into the kitchen ten minutes later, we find two big boxes of steaming pizza on the white marble island that could seat an entire football team. Lilly's hand is securely in mine, and no one seems to think that it's weird anymore.

I grin at our friends. "Is it safe to say that Wes lost a bet, and that's why *he* came to get us?"

Denielle is getting plates out of the cabinet and smirks. "Of course. He sucks at rock, paper, scissors."

"You cheat!" Wes now hollers from somewhere in the back hallway.

"Do not," Den growls.

Lilly eases away from me and walks over to her best friend. Denielle puts the plates on the island and turns to my girl, who wraps her arms around her and says, "Thank you."

I swear I can see Denielle's cool exterior crack the tiniest bit as she returns the embrace and mumbles, "Love you, too, babe."

I smile to myself, thinking how all our lives have changed in the last few months, not just Lilly's. Even though her change is obviously the most dramatic *or traumatic* one. Denielle and I have never been close. Before I "chose" to walk away from Lilly, it was usually the two of them and me and Wes. We never hung out together. Then, I became the enemy, and Denielle was like a pit bull, protecting Lilly from me—the person who did all this to keep her safe in the first place. Despite the resentment that grew over the years from watching them be so close and me being forced to remain on the outside, Denielle gained my deepest respect for how she cared for Lilly. Now, for the first time, it's all four of us together, and it feels completely natural. Like it was always supposed to be this way.

. . .

THE ENTIRE WEEKEND is fucking amazing. There is no other way of saying it. Lilly calls Heather at one point, asking to stay at Denielle's since her parents are gone, and Wes and I simply...stay. We watch movies in Denielle's parents' ostentatious twenty-person theater room. Who needs a movie room for that many people? Or a movie room period. We eat more fast food than any of us has in a year, and I spend two nights wrapped in Lilly's arms. Okay, there was also a lot more making out involved, but we did sleep, too. Some.

By Monday morning, Lilly is like a new person. Her skin is no longer pale, and the circles under her eyes have vanished. She radiates happiness.

My good mood lasts until I get to school.


WALKING down the senior hallway with Wes by my side, I pay no attention until Kat steps right in front of me.

"Rhys," she purrs.

I look down, wary of what I see in her eyes. "Kat."

Wes cocks his head at me, and I give him a nod. *Go ahead.*

Once he's halfway down the hall, Kat hooks her arm around mine, holding onto my bicep. The gesture is similar to what Lilly did this weekend, but the emotion it stirs in me is so very opposite. I fight the urge to dislodge her hand from my arm but don't want to cause a scene with half our class around.

Tucked away in a nook that leads to a supply closet, she lets go and faces me. I slip my hands into my front jean pockets and wait.

"I've been watching you." Unlike last time, she doesn't try to grope me, which I'm grateful for, but her tone hints of a deeper meaning.

"Okay," I drawl, appearing bored with this exchange.

"You're doing a much better job, but your little sister is slipping." Her voice is sweet and taunting, dripping venom at the same time. She is planning something, and knowing her, it is nothing good. I lean back on my heels and raise my eyebrows.

*Do. Not. Show. Weakness.*

"Nothing? Well, let me put it this way. The creepy eye-fucks your little sister is throwing your way all the time are dis-gus-ting. What do you think will happen when others start noticing?" The question is spoken with a malicious smile on her face that makes me want to throttle her.

Deep breath.

"Kat, I have no clue what you *think* you're seeing, but I wouldn't spread rumors you can't back up." My tone is controlled, but I make sure to put as much force behind it as possible. We're on the same level when it comes to social hierarchy in school, and she knows it.

That makes her smirk even more. "Oh, sweetie, I have no intention of spreading *rumors*."

With that, she walks around me, dragging her hand across my pecs, and disappears into the crowd.

I remain tucked in that corner until well after the bell rings, trying to get my racing pulse under control.

# CHAPTER THIRTY-EIGHT

## HIM

IT'S BEEN OVER THREE WEEKS SINCE I SENT LILLY THE TEXT MESSAGE. *I did not anticipate still being in Virginia. After flying home for the Shelter for Kids charity event, I was called to the Florida location to check on the remodel—something Hank easily could've done without me, but had I not gone, it would've raised questions with my nosy-as-fuck partner. I keep telling myself that I've waited ten years for this; a couple more days won't make a difference. I'm methodical. I plan. But I'm growing impatient.*

*TONIGHT, I'm sitting in my penthouse suite, propped up by three pillows on the king-size bed, computer in my lap, reviewing some of the pictures and footage again. I want one more picture for my next message to Lilly. Scanning the school surveillance footage, an idea starts forming. The school has made it easy for me to track all the key players with the obscene number of surveillance cameras they installed two years ago after an unnoticed bullying incident. The parents of the targeted kid were—unfortunately for the school —very influential and very connected residents of Westbridge and, for lack of a better term, raised hell. Now, something that was installed to protect the students has given me access to information I probably would've missed otherwise.*

*Lilly spent this weekend at her friend Denielle's house together with Rhys and their other friend, Wes. I found he is a close friend to both McGuires' but was Rhys's friend first. Over the last week, Rhys has gone back to staying at Wes's house, and I assume it has to do with Tristen McGuire being back in town after a two-week business trip. I'm itching to find out what's going on behind the walls of Lilly's current home, but Tristen and Heather seem to be almost as paranoid as I am when it comes to protecting their family. There is nothing to be found besides the official public records. Nothing on a personal level. It fills me with pride and curiosity that Lilly has been kept safe under their roof for so long.*

*THANKS to a few perfectly timed photos and the school's video, I now understand why Rhys was the one to show up with Lilly in California. Though, the only other people that officially know seem to be the two best friends. Add to the mix Rhys's absence at home whenever Daddy Dearest is in town, and I am convinced that this is (A) a new development and (B) Heather and Tristen are not aware of or agree with it.*

*All these things make my new plan almost laughably easy. I do have some reservations executing it this way. I don't like seeing Lilly hurt, but I don't see another way to isolate her and get her home. The timing has to be perfect, though, so once again, I can't rush things.*

*I'M ABOUT to put together the next message for Lilly when my personal phone rings. Checking the caller ID, I'm relieved that for once it's not Hank with any more work issues, but Margot. I haven't talked to her since yesterday, and I expected her call this evening.*

*"How was your day, sweetheart?"*

*"Darling, I'm glad I caught you. I wasn't sure if you were still working." Not that that has ever stopped my fiancée before from demanding my attention.*

*"I'm just looking over some information for the current project." Not a lie.*

*"Oh good. Do you think you'll be back in two and a half weeks? Celeste is having a party for her twenty-ninth birthday." Twenty-nine? Didn't she celebrate that three years ago? Though, that's a question I most definitely won't ask.*

*Celeste is my buddy Julian's fiancée. Julian is one of the few friends I've kept around and who doesn't care about my past. It also helps that we enjoy the same things. Cars, motorcycle, airplanes, anything fast—and women. We both had our fair share before settling down. It'll be good to see him; with my travel, it's gotten difficult to get together regularly.*

*"I should be back by then. Tell Celeste to let Julian know that I refuse to let him win this time."*

*"Darling," she chastises. "You know how I despise when you two do that. What if something happens?"*

*"I know, sweetheart, but we are extremely good at what we're doing. Nothing will happen."*

*That just gets me a sigh. "I know I won't be able to stop you."*

*"No, you won't," I chuckle. Just the thought of the little competition we carry out whenever we get together makes my pulse race.*

*We disconnect after a few more minutes of catching up, and I place my phone on the nightstand.*

*Back to bringing Lilly home.*

## CHAPTER THIRTY-NINE

### LILLY

It's been five nights since I slept in Rhys's arms, and I am yet again in a state of *The Walking Dead*. Sunday can't come soon enough. Tristen has to go back to his most recent job site for a follow-up, and Rhys has promised to sleep at home. Between school and practice for the district championship, I haven't spent more than five minutes alone with him, and the ache in my chest is growing stronger.

The same way Rhys started coming to the gym on Saturdays, I am going to the gym on Sundays. That also works out in my favor for the training sessions with Spence whenever I miss my Saturday session due to an invitational or, like this weekend, the district championship.

Between districts and Spence deciding to do a full hour sparring session after I already ran five miles on the treadmill with Denielle, I can barely walk straight when I come home on Sunday. My giddiness that I'll be in Rhys's arms in a few short hours immediately disintegrates, like the dried flower petal I attempted to pick up from the kitchen counter the other day, when I enter the kitchen and find Heather, Tristen, and Natty having lunch together.

*He was supposed to have left by now.*

As if he's reading my mind, Tristen informs me that he moved his flight to early Monday morning. I'm fighting the urge to burst into tears on the spot. Rhys won't be coming home.

MONDAY SEEMS TO NEVER END. Classes are dragging, and I can't concentrate. I'm either about to fall asleep or am too jittery to pay attention due to the amount of caffeine coursing through my veins. In both scenarios, I'm only semi-functioning and can't answer one question when the teachers call on me.

Relieved I've finally made it through my last class, Denielle and I have just exited the west wing when my phone vibrates in the back pocket of my jeans. My stomach immediately does a flip with a cartwheel followed by a back tuck because Den is walking next to me, and that means it's Rhys—until I pull it out and glimpse at the screen. *UNKNOWN.*

*No, no, no.*

Denielle takes a couple more steps before she realizes I'm not beside her. Turning, her gaze falls to my phone with a frown. "Babe?"

Sometime between me reading the sender's name of the incoming message and my best friend noticing I wasn't following her, my entire body started trembling. I'm struggling to hold on to the small rectangle. She seems to understand what's happening, because she's at my side with two long strides. Grabbing my phone, she sticks it in her coat pocket and leads me by the arm to my car. I stumble along like I've had one too many drinks—*which in my case would probably be just half of one.* Without stopping, she fishes the keys out of my leather jacket, unlocks the Jeep, and deposits me in the passenger seat.

I didn't even notice that she led me to this side of the car.

Joining me on the driver's side, she holds the phone out once settled inside. "Do you want me to read it, or do you want to?" Her tone is gentle like she's worried I'll break down at any moment, which *is* a possibility.

I take the phone from her and swipe the message open. I can

feel Denielle watching me. One more deep breath and I look down at the screen.

The first photo is from the evening we all met at Bones. It's grainy, but you can recognize everyone in the picture. Rhys is fist-bumping Wes across the table, Denielle is laughing, and I'm cuddled into Rhys's side with my eyes closed. The whole exchange took maybe five seconds. I remember clearly that I didn't allow myself to linger any longer on Rhys's shoulder, but the picture is perfectly timed.

The second is of Nate and me at the gym, the morning he introduced himself. And once again, the timing is impeccable. He is shaking my hand, and we're both smiling at each other, which makes the scene appear way more intimate than it was.

The third one is of Rhys and Katherine. It's taken from an angle above. A school surveillance camera? They're tucked in some corner. Kat's hand is on his chest, and a smug smile is on her evil face. What. The. Hell? My sight is starting to fog, but I keep scrolling to the last picture and want to throw up. Dropping the device, it clatters to the floor, facing up—the photo of Denielle and me walking out of the school displayed on the screen. She is wearing her new camel pea coat—the one she bought this past weekend—and I'm wearing my black leather jacket. The picture is not fifteen minutes old. The caption underneath reads *See you soon*.

"He's here." My voice is hoarse, and I can't seem to take a breath.

"WHAT?" Denielle sounds the opposite, loud and shrill. She climbs over the middle console and bends down with her head half in my lap to retrieve the phone. I can't move. Scrolling through the message and muttering several curse words, she opens the door and jumps out.

That snaps me out of my paralysis. "Where are you going?"

Her muffled voice seeps into the inside of the Jeep as she walks around the car to open my door and pulls me out. "We're going to find Rhys and Wes."

"Wha—NO!" I dig my heels in the ground, but it's no use.

*When did she become so strong?*

"We can't. He has practice. With the cheerleaders." Katherine will be there. He met with her behind my back. The thought slams into me like lightning hitting a tree.

"I don't give a flying fuck about that. That fucker was here. At school! FUCK!" Den even stomps her foot to emphasize her level of *fucked*-up-ness.

"Can you not say fuck so much?" I mumble as she drags me down the path leading to the field house and gymnasium.

"Babe, fuck is a very appropriate expression for the current situation."

*I guess it is.*

WES SEES US FIRST. We enter on the opposite end of the gym from where the cheerleaders practice, and Rhys and Wes are doing some sort of warm-up drill at the other end.

All I can do is stand there, because Denielle does her usual thing. She commands the attention of the entire room, and I pray the ground opens up and swallows me on the spot. I have no clue how she manages that, but everything stops. The chatter coming from the girls dies down, and out of the corner of my eye, I'm aware of almost all of them staring at us.

Wes nudges Rhys, who's facing away, whispering something to him, and his head whips around. He blinks once, twice as if to make sure I'm really here and then flicks his gaze to Denielle. They exchange some sort of unspoken message, and Rhys's entire demeanor turns menacing, yet his eyes shine with worry. I know this boy's face like my own, and he's putting up a front for everyone in this room but asks me at the same time what's wrong.

Both Rhys and Wes say something to their coach, grab their things, and march over, ignoring the gawking cheerleaders. No one speaks. Den turns on her heel and leads me out of there, away from the building and possible prying eyes. Rhys and Wes are close on our heels. I feel the heat radiating off Rhys's body, but he doesn't touch me.

We don't stop until we're back in the parking lot. Denielle hands over my phone to Rhys, who immediately starts scrolling.

*Which one of them unlocked my phone? I seriously have no privacy in my life.*

Wes is peeking over Rhys's shoulder, his eyes threatening to pop out of their sockets. He glances over to Denielle and me and then mumbles, "The last one is from today."

That gets Rhys's attention, who has moved back to the picture of Nate and me. He zeros in on Denielle, then me, then the picture.

"Fuck."

*Is that the only word they have in their vocabulary?*

## RHYS

"Uh, dude, your sister just walked in."

Huh? My sis— Oh. I peer over my shoulder and instantly know something is wrong. Apart from the fact that neither Denielle nor Lilly *ever* show up during practice, Denielle has her guard-dog face on full display. Her hand is protectively around Lilly's upper arm, anchoring her to the spot, and Lilly is pale as a ghost.

My gaze flickers over to the left, and not surprisingly, Kat has noticed them as well. Everyone has. At that moment, Kat's eyes meet mine, and she raises one perfectly plucked eyebrow, her mouth set in a devious smile: *See, I told you she doesn't do a good job.*

SKIPPING THROUGH THE MESSAGE, my mind is stuck on the second picture. Lilly is talking to the tall blond from the gym, and he's grinning down at her like...I don't even know. When did that happen? And why hasn't she told me about it? A growl echoes in my mind.

"Down boy," penetrates the red haze. I recognize Denielle's voice.

*Did I growl out loud?*

"—from today." Today? What? Moving to the last picture and taking a better look at Lilly and her best friend beside me, I only come up with one word. "Fuck."

"We should get out of here," Wes speaks up, and I couldn't agree more.

"Let's go to my place," Denielle offers. Her parents are still gone, so we won't risk being interrupted.

I try to catch Lilly's eyes, but she focuses on everything but me.

Wanting to get her alone, I say, "Okay. Lilly and I will meet—"

"No." Her voice is low but stern. She finally turns to me, and her expression sends chills down my spine.

"Babe?" I whisper, not wanting anyone to overhear but also unable to keep my emotions in check any longer.

"Wes can drive me in my car. You can take him to get his later." Turning to her best friend, she adds, "We'll meet you at your house." And with that, she plucks her keys from Denielle's fingers, hands them to Wes, and marches off. My mouth hangs open, and so does Denielle's.

*What just happened?*

"Uh..." Wes is as stunned as I am, but I shrug, and he jogs after *my* girl.

I BEAT everyone to Denielle's house and am waiting impatiently in the driveway when first Lilly's Jeep and then Denielle's Audi pull in. Watching my best friend behind the wheel of my girlfriend's car with her seated next to him makes me ball my hands into fists. There is nothing going on that would justify the black spots appearing in my vision, but deep down, I know that something has shifted, and it's easier to blame Wes than myself.

We follow Denielle into the kitchen, who then disappears down the back hallway, coming back with a bottle of Macallan 30 and four glasses. As Wes and I eye the bottle, she smirks. "From my dad's collection. He won't notice; he has like eight of them."

"Uh. O-kay then."

Den fills each glass with a double and hands them to us. "Drink up."

I'm still staring at my glass when Lilly puts her empty one back on the counter. I gawk at her, unable to form words.

"Well, now that that's settled." Lilly's voice is icy and disconnected until she levels me. Her tone changes to something I've only ever known from Kat: sarcastically sweet and full of rage. "Do you want to explain the picture of you and your ex getting all cozy?"

"Uh oh," chuckles Wes.

My eyes briefly flicker over to him, and he wipes the smirk off his face. I'm fuming.

Instead of explaining the situation to her, I snarl, "How about *you* explain the picture of the Abercrombie douche *to me*."

"Wha—?" Lilly's eyes narrow.

"He did not just go there." Denielle sighs.

Wes fake-coughs into his fist, "Shut up."

The tension in the room grows from awkward to uncomfortable as hell.

"I have nothing to explain to you. I did not make out with my ex in the middle of school!"

"What the fuck?" The guilt of keeping this from her makes me lash out. I should just come clean about my psychotic ex's threats, but I can't bring myself to admit I've not been one hundred percent honest with her the last few weeks. Lilly is perceptive, and I've been lying to myself about her not noticing.

"Don't *what the fuck* me, *Rhys*! I have eyes. Were you really at Wes's all last week?" The way she spits out my name is like a slap in the face.

"You're one to talk, *Lilly*!" A voice in my head screams at me, *Abort! Shut up immediately!* but it's out of my mouth before I can stop myself. "I've seen you flirt with the guy."

Her eyes bulge, and she opens her mouth to counter-attack, but Denielle steps between us, holding up both hands as if to prevent us from physically going at each other, which is not too far-fetched at this point, I guess.

"STOP! BOTH OF YOU!" She glares first at me and then at Lilly before continuing. "Don't you realize that this is what *he* wants? He wants to create a rift between you."

Lilly blinks before switching her gaze between Denielle and me. Her words sink in. What am I doing attacking her like a possessive asshole? I interlace my hands on top of my head and draw in a breath before looking at Lilly.

"I'm sorry, babe. I don't know what just happened there."

The rage in her eyes disappears and is replaced by tears slowly escaping down her cheeks. I open my arms, and she dives at me, clinging to my shirt, sobbing.

Denielle and Wes quietly exit the kitchen to give us time, and I simply hold Lilly in my arms while she lets it all out. It crushes me to see the strong girl I love more than I can put into words crumble in front of me, and there is nothing I can do.

LATER, we find Denielle and Wes in the living room with their heads bent together. I lower myself onto the couch and pull Lilly down next to me. She drapes her legs over mine, and with my arm wrapped around her shoulder, she leans into my chest, clasping my other hand between hers.

I haven't spent much time in Denielle's house until recently. I knew her parents were loaded, but I never realized how loaded. The entire house is high-end, a perfect combination of rustic chic and modern. The massive gray sectional we currently occupy is made of some sort of wool material but looks state-of-the-art and is paired with a low, rustic, espresso-colored chest serving as a coffee table. An assortment of pillar candles is perfectly arranged on a tray in the middle of the chest—the staged look completed with a massive orchid next to it.

Wes is sitting opposite from us in a matching armchair, his arms resting on his thighs. "So, what are we going to do now?"

All eyes turn to Lilly, but she doesn't say anything.

"Let's go over the pictures?" I suggest.

Lilly stiffens in my arms, and I start rubbing circles on her back. Slowly, she pulls her phone out of the back pocket of her jeans and opens the text message.

## CHAPTER FORTY

### LILLY

FOR THE PAST THREE WEEKS, I'VE LIVED IN COMPLETE OBLIVION. Being in love can do that to you. I admit I had forgotten about my psycho-stalker-slash-kidnapper. I've let my guard down. That cannot happen again. And looking at the pictures now, it's even more apparent that he is *everywhere*. He even managed to get a picture of me at Bones. Nineteenth-century gas lanterns provide more light than the lamps inside of the place, yet he managed to get a fairly clear picture of me cuddling with Rhys. If this picture leaks—I don't even want to think about it. A knot starts forming in my stomach, and my hand trembles as I move on to the next picture. Rhys stiffens underneath me, and I hear the edge in his voice, even though he's trying to hide it. "When was this?"

Next to us, Denielle raises her eyebrows, and I turn the phone to her.

"Oh, that."

Rhys's hand stops circling my back; of course, he's caught on that she knew about my interaction with Nate. Before he can come to more false conclusions, I mumble, "She was there."

Denielle adds, "It was after Lilly's session with Spence the other day. The two were beating the shit out of each other. The entire gym was watching. He caught up with her when she was on her way to me. He complimented her on the fight."

"That's it?" Rhys doesn't seem convinced. Why is he acting this way? He behaves like I'm the biggest flirt ever. I haven't had one serious relationship at seventeen, for crying out loud. The thought makes the wall I assumed was gone snap into place inside of me.

"That's it." I refuse to justify myself any more on this.

Denielle has taken the phone from me and moves to the third picture. Flipping it toward the room, she addresses Rhys, "What about this one?"

He exhales slowly, and his breath tickles my neck. "She's still trying to *persuade* me to start our arrangement back up."

Rhys's hand is circling my back again, and I pull away slightly to get a better look at him. He is omitting something. I'm sure he's telling the truth. I can definitely see Katherine trying to convince him, but there is more, and he is not sharing that with us—*with me*.

Den seems to have the same suspicion, because she presses, "What exactly did she say?"

There is a brief pause, his eyebrows pull together, and he averts his eyes downward for a fraction of a second. The entire change in demeanor is over before it starts, but that's all I need as confirmation that he is hiding something from me. The wall grows taller.

"She's been talking about prom. We had plans. She wants to keep her image up."

Both Denielle and Wes narrow their eyes at him. Seeing Wes unconvinced makes the breath catch in my chest.

"Let's talk about the fact that the freak was at school earlier." Wes diverts the topic, and there is now a line drawn between Rhys and the rest of us. He just lied to us.

"This picture could have been taken from anywhere as long as he has the appropriate lens. He doesn't have to be too close if he has a clear line of sight, and there isn't anything blocking the view to the school's west entrance apart from a few trees." Denielle and I are both in the same journalism class, but she knows more about photography than I do. Her aunt owns a photography studio, and Den helps out every once in a while.

"That does not make the situation any better," I grumble.

"I'm sorry, babe. I'm just providing the facts here."

I look at my best friend. "I know." She's right, and I'm grateful that she's not sugarcoating it. I don't think I could handle that right now.

Rhys has been quiet during the exchange, and the rubbing of my back has stopped.

"I want you to tell Mom and Dad."

My head whips around. "NO!"

Rhys speaks quietly, almost detached. "It's getting too dangerous. They need to know."

My heartbeat increases. I know he's right, but the thought of them knowing makes bile rise in my throat. "I'm not ready."

"Cal, we don't have a choice anymore. This guy made it clear with these pictures that he is everywhere. That he can get to you *everywhere*."

"He's right," Denielle says softly, and Wes nods as well.

*Shit.*

"Okay." It's just a whisper. I can't bring myself to raise my voice above that. "But we wait until Tristen gets back."

That gives me forty-eight hours.

"Fine," Rhys concedes.

The air is thick, and I can't take it anymore. Untangling myself from Rhys, I say, "I'm heading home."

"I'll come with." Rhys stands to follow, but something inside me cringes at the thought. For the first time since the night he revealed the secrets to me, I don't want Rhys anywhere near me. I don't know if it's because he is keeping something from me or if I need to process everything on my own.

"No, it's okay. I, uh...I think I need to be alone for a bit. Mom and Natty will be home." I walk out without a second glance. I feel three sets of eyes trained on my back and pick up my pace.

On the short drive home, I spy the Defender in my rearview mirror and can make out two figures in it. Rhys and Wes are following me home. This should make me feel safe, but there is...nothing.

Again, Rhys doesn't come home that night.

• • •

TUESDAY MORNING, I am in a daze. My mind is foggy from another sleepless night, and Denielle simply shows up at my car, walking with me. She follows me to my locker and first period classroom before she makes her way to her own class. I don't pay attention to my surroundings, and my first period passes in a blur. By my second class, I'm a little more alert, and by the third, I know for certain that I'm being *watched*. And not just watched. Conversations stop when I enter the classroom, heads turn when I pass, and that's when it hits me. *They know*. I'm not sure what, but they know something.

*How?*

I settle down in my usual window seat in the second row when several things happen at once: Denielle bursts into the classroom, searching for me, Mr. Hayworth is calling my name, followed by a frantic Rhys coming through the back door of the classroom.

*What the—?*

"Miss McGuire, you're requested in the principal's office."

Both Den and Rhys stand in either doorway, staring at me. I slowly stand up, putting my book back in my bag, unsure of what to do.

"Why?" comes out as a croak when I focus on my teacher.

But Mr. Hayworth addresses Rhys instead. "*Mister* McGuire, this is not your classroom; please return to your floor." He speaks in a curt tone, but Rhys doesn't budge. Mr. Hayworth is one of the nicest teachers in school. Even when someone gets out of line, he has never used that tone before.

"I need to talk to Lilly."

"I think you have done enough. If you don't leave this classroom, I will call campus security."

*What is going on?*

Sweat starts trickling down my spine. My gaze jumps back and forth between my teacher, Denielle, and Rhys. And while all this is going down, every other set of eyes in the room is locked on me. I slowly take inventory. Two guys in the back are leering at me, two cheerleaders to the left stare with a mixture of disgust and malicious joy, and a group of girls that I barely know glare with pure contempt. The bottom of my stomach plummets.

I walk toward the front of the room and pass Denielle, who immediately hooks her arm around mine and steers me down the hall to the nearest bathroom. Stragglers are still in the hall, and I'm met with the same variety of expressions. All I can do is let Denielle drag me along. I'm faintly aware that Rhys is following.


THE DOOR CLOSES BEHIND RHYS, who leans against it, and Denielle checks every stall before turning to me.

"Babe, I'm so sorry." She appears small and distressed when she addresses me. Denielle is anything but those two attributes. She always stands straight, radiating confidence; that's how she commands every room. But right now, she looks like a little girl, and it sends tremors through my body.

"What's going on?" I rasp out the question. Deep down, I know, but I need one of them to confirm it.

"Kat knows," Rhys speaks up behind me. I turn and take in his slumped shoulders under his black V-neck sweater, his hands stuffed deep in the pockets of his faded jeans. He won't make eye contact with me.

"Knows what exactly?" I try to sound calm. I mean, that's a valid question; there is not just one secret surrounding me. My gaze ping pongs back and forth between them as I wait for one of them to speak up.

Without a word, Denielle holds out her phone, and I'm looking at Katherine's social media profile. Smack in the middle is a picture of Rhys and me. But not just any picture. The photo is taken from a side angle. I'm wrapped around Rhys, my arms around his neck, my legs around his middle, and his hands on my butt. We're kissing. It's the day he surprised me at Denielle's house.

I swallow several times. There is too much saliva in my mouth. A sheen of sweat begins to build on my skin as I keep staring, but no matter what, I can't stop it. I thrust the phone back to Denielle and lurch to the nearest stall. I didn't eat much today, so there is not really anything to expel from my stomach, but the retching won't stop.

I don't know how long I hover over the not-so-white porcelain, and at some point, someone holds my hair back. When I'm finally done and sit back, Denielle helps me up.

After cleaning myself up, I take a deep breath. "What else is there?"

Denielle looks at Rhys before meeting my eyes again. Rhys is still in the same position, and a feeling of dread starts spreading through my body. Our eyes meet for the first time since coming in here, and what I see knocks the wind out of me. His voice is low when he speaks. "Kat has suspected something for a while. She's as smart as she is cunning. I underestimated her."

"YOU KNEW?" I can't keep the shrillness out of my voice. If possible, he shrinks even further.

"She saw the change in our pattern. We were talking. You came to my match. I went to your meet. Then, I broke up with her. She saw how I looked at you and how you looked at me. She was just waiting for proof, and then—" Rhys breaks off and drags in a ragged breath.

"Kat posted it this morning. I didn't hear about it until the middle of second period. I couldn't get a hall pass, otherwise, I would've come to you sooner. I texted you, but you never check your phone during class," Denielle explains. "My guess is the school must've gotten wind of it, too." My best friend's voice is full of remorse as if any of this is her fault.

She holds her phone out to me, and I read the caption under the picture. "*It looks like 'Sister' Lilly has a very special relationship with WH's QB.*"

"I was supposed to go to the principal's office as well," Rhys confirms Den's assumption.

Bile is rising again, but I'm able to force it down. Katherine purposefully put the focus on me. Not Rhys. Me! He is probably going to get high fives from his buddies versus I'll get the incestuous slut title. And Rhys knew.

*He. Fucking. Knew.*

Something that I haven't felt since the day he came clean surges up inside of me like a geyser. My body buzzes with rage.

"WHY DIDN'T YOU TELL ME?" I don't bother remaining quiet. It's all out anyway; why worry about it now?

"I..." He trails off for a moment before continuing in a whisper. "I wanted to protect you."

*Is he serious?*

"ARE YOU SERIOUS? Protecting me when I have a crazy stalker monitoring my every move? Don't you think this piece of information about *your psychotic ex*"—I enunciate each of the three words clearly—"also stalking me would have been something I should know?"

I register pain in my palms and realize I've been clenching my fists so tight that my nails have left deep indentations on the insides of my hands. A voice in my head tells me that he meant well, but the flight sensation is too overpowering. I need to get away from Rhys. I need to put as much distance as I can between me and the boy I love so much that it hurts.

I push Rhys out of the way with all the force I'm physically capable of and take off down the hall. I vaguely realize that the halls are crowded. It's the middle of third period. Everyone should be in their classrooms. Then, someone steps in front of me, and I halt, coming face to face with Katherine Rosenfield, head cheerleader and *Queen Bitch* of Westbridge High.

"Lilly, I was waiting for you," she sneers at me.

"Katherine." I refuse to cower to her, but the initial adrenaline rush is over, and my strength is draining rapidly. Out of the corner of my eye, I notice the group around us increasing in size.

This time when Katherine speaks, she's addressing me, but really, she's talking to the spectators that keep multiplying.

"Well, we are all curious about how this little incestuous relationship came to be. Or maybe it started a long time ago, and Rhys just took a break from *his sister* when he met me—"

"Kat, that's enough," Rhys growls directly behind me.

Before the logical side of my brain has any time to interject, I ball my fist and let it fly, straight into Katherine's jaw. Right before the impact, she realizes what's happening, her eyes widen, and her perfectly glossed lips form an O. Katherine's head wheels to the side, and she falls into Wes, who had just pushed his way through the masses. A collective gasp runs through the crowd, and I realize what I've done. Not only am I the incestuous slut, but I also physically assaulted the queen of WH.

Holding her jaw, Katherine's eyes draw to slits as she faces me again and hisses, "You little slut. It's not enough for you to fuck your brother, now you also assault his girlfriend?"

*She is not only evil, but also deranged.*

Her gaze moves behind me and changes into something resembling a helpless doe. "Rhys, do something!"

I can't believe what's happening here. I turn on my heels and come face to face with my boyfriend. But all he does is look at me wide-eyed. There is nothing. No defending me, no telling Kat to stop spewing lies. Nothing. He is, for all intents and purposes, *frozen*. And with that, it's as if he just hit me in the face with a cross punch.

I'm done. Screw them all. I wrap my arms around my stomach and shoulder past Rhys through the crowd. I don't bother stopping at my locker; I have my bag with my wallet, phone, and keys. That's all I need.

HALFWAY TO MY CAR, I hear Rhys yelling my name behind me. Glancing over my shoulder, I see him push through the front door, followed by Denielle and Wes.

I start running. I'm fast, and with my head start, I make it to my car before them. Cutting across the lawn, I'm inside my Jeep with locks engaged when Rhys reaches my door.

"Cal! Babe, open up!" His voice is laced with panic. He doesn't lower his volume. Anyone in the vicinity can hear him.

Denielle and Wes are in front of my hood on the sidewalk, displaying mirrored expressions of concern, and across the lawn, more and more students spill out of the doors, even a few teachers.

WHAT I SHOULD'VE DONE IS THINK about this first.

What I should've done is tell them that Rhys isn't my biological brother.

What I should've done is get out of the car and hear Rhys out.

What I should've done is let my best friend take me home.

What I should've done is calm down before putting my car into reverse and speeding out of the parking lot.

I did none of those things.

Right before I exit the school's parking lot, I see Rhys and Wes sprinting to the Defender in my rearview mirror, but I keep going. The voice in my head is screaming at me to drive. Fast.

Tears are running down my face. Tears of anger, tears of embarrassment, tears of frustration, tears of betrayal, and tears of self-pity.

*Why me?*

I NEED TO BE ALONE. Just driving through town, being surrounded by the people who go about their lives is too much. I end up driving past Magnolia's, a place that used to be welcoming and a second home; now it fills me with dread. As I pass the café, the guy who approached me weeks ago steps out of the entrance, and our eyes lock. The instant feeling of something being off about him returns. His eyes are...lifeless. Finally, breaking out of the stare-down, I have to slam on the brakes. I'm about to run straight into the side of a car in the process of parallel parking.

*Shit.*

The driver gives me a *what-the-fuck* look, and I just sit there, too mentally exhausted to apologize. It seems like he purposefully takes forever to complete the maneuver. Getting irritated, I peer in the rearview mirror to check that Rhys has not caught up to me. Instead of the Defender, I see the creep standing in the middle of the street, staring at me. A shiver runs down my spine, and I hit the gas. The slow parker is almost in his spot, and I only have to move halfway into the opposite traffic to get around him. The oncoming car beeps at me, but I keep going. Two more turns and I'm finally on the back road to Fallsbrook. Not that I have any intention of stopping there, but it's a start.

I'M on the way out of town when an SUV shows up in my rearview mirror—*not* the Defender. At first, I don't think anything of it, but then it comes closer. Not too close, but close enough that I can make out the driver—or more accurately, *not* make out. He is wearing a baseball hat and glasses, paired with a hoodie that covers most of his face.

It's *him*.

I push the gas pedal to the floor, and my Jeep roars to life. The SUV accelerates as well but remains several car lengths away. I'm speeding down the narrow road, a field on one side and the West-bridge Forest Preserve on the other. If I just make it to Fallsbrook, I'll be good. I can take Main Street back home. Heather is working from home today because Natty's school has teacher conferences. I'll be safe there.

Just as I finish that thought, something shoots out of the field and across the road. Of course, I do the one thing you're not supposed to do in that situation—I yank on the steering wheel. I immediately feel how my Jeep tilts too far to one side and—

SLOWLY COMING TO, my head is pounding, and something is digging into the crook of my neck and shoulder—the seatbelt. I'm upside-down.

I try to turn my head, but it hurts. All I can do is focus out the front of my cracked windshield. I notice red speckles on it but can't make out if they're on the inside or the outside. Are they from whatever I hit, or are they from...me?

Something is moving toward me—no, not something...someone.

I start struggling against the seatbelt, but excruciating pain shoots through my shoulder, and that's when everything goes black.

*I should've stayed in bed this morning.*

---

# EPILOGUE

---

**HIM**

WE'RE HOME.

I'M STANDING *in the doorway to Lilly's new room, watching her curled up on the top of the white comforter. She is still wearing the clothes she wore to school yesterday, which are now dirty and bloodstained from the cut on her forehead caused by the airbag and me dragging her out of the wrecked Jeep. I'm grateful she was driving such a sturdy car. This was definitely not part of the plan. When I saw the fox run across the road, followed by Lilly losing control and the car rolling twice before it came to a halt on its roof, I was close to a panic attack. Not again!*

*Getting her out of there and home was more difficult than I had planned. I had to adjust my meticulously organized trip.*

*I made sure she wasn't seriously injured and patched up her cut before we left Virginia but didn't dare change her out of her clothes. That would have been a violation of privacy. Well, not that I haven't violated her privacy in other ways, but still—touching her that way just wouldn't be right. Not if she can do it herself when she wakes up. Plus, time was of the essence. I had to pull a lot of strings to get the plane ready on such short notice.*

*I'm still in thought when I notice small movements on the bed. She is waking up. My heart starts pounding, and I'm actually...nervous. I wait, not daring to move. She slowly moves one limp arm after the other, like she's taking stock of her injuries. A groan escapes her, and I hold my breath. I hope she is not in too much pain. That's when her eyes open. She blinks a few times against the light of the small bedside lamp and moves her head side to side. When she seems satisfied with her assessment, she pushes herself into a sitting position. I had purposefully added more pillows to the bed earlier, so she is automatically propped up.*

*Still squinting, she scans the room. Her gaze settles on me, and her eyes widen.*

*"You!"*

# OUT OF THE DARK

book 2

## PROLOGUE

**LILLY**

IT'S DARK. MY HEAD IS POUNDING, AND MY EYES WON'T OPEN. Why won't my eyes open? I swallow, and a metallic taste registers in my brain—blood. Why am I swaying? More awareness seeps in. I'm being carried. Arms are placed under my legs and back. It's him. I just know. The sound of my heartbeat is thrashing in my ears. I need to fight, but my body doesn't obey. My arms won't move. My eyes still won't open. My lungs constrict as a primal scream builds, but no sound comes out. Suddenly, my body connects with a flat surface, and a sharp pain shoots through my shoulder. A whimper escapes, but it's just the whisper of a sound compared to the cry echoing inside my head. I feel a prick in my upper arm, then...*blank*.

AGONY. That's the only word that comes to mind when the fog clears. I hurt. Everywhere. What the—? Oh God, the accident. He was there. He took me. *Again.* Everything starts slowly coming back. My heartbeat instantly accelerates, but I force myself to lie still, keep my eyes closed, and take stock. I'm on a soft surface; the fabric under my fingertips feels smooth—a comforter or duvet? Not important—yet. I wiggle my fingers, followed by rotating one arm ever so slightly, then the other, and—stars explode behind my eyelids. Shit, that hurts. The sensation is excruciating yet numbing at the same time. Like someone held a hot blade against my skin for so long that my body shut off its pain receptors. Pressing my lips together, I keep from crying out. Next, come the legs. I'm able to bend my knees and slowly move them left to right. I'm not paralyzed; a crushing weight lifts off my chest. However, my entire body is sore, and something is definitely wrong with my shoulder.

I blink my eyes open. A small light next to me hurts, and it takes several minutes for my vision to adjust. I'm in a bedroom. It looks familiar, but not. I force myself to inhale and exhale through my nose to calm my rapid breathing.

*I can't fight when I'm hyperventilating.*

Slowly I turn my head to the side. When I can't get a decent overview, I slowly push myself up with my uninjured arm until I'm in a sitting position. The walls are the same shade of lavender that I remember, almost the same I have at home—this is beyond weird. All the furnishings are white and antique-looking; my gaze travels over a familiar chair. The. Chair. Out of the corner of my eye, I register a doorway to the left. Subconsciously, I know what I'm going to see next—who I will see next.

Closing my eyes, I inhale through my nose—three, two, one. Exhaling—three, two, one. I open my eyes.

The door is wide open, and I meet familiar hazel eyes. Eyes I thought were familiar when I first saw them. Now I understand why.

"You!"

"Hello, Lilly."

## CHAPTER FORTY-ONE

**RHYS**

FOUR DAYS. THAT'S HOW LONG SHE'S BEEN GONE. I CAN'T EVEN utter her name in my head. The first day was a complete shit show; everyone was yelling at everyone, though Dad directed his anger mostly at me. I can't even fault him for that. She's gone because of me.

At the end of day two, he sent me to my room because I wouldn't stop cursing out the cops and, later, the agents who turned our kitchen into their command center. The FBI replaced the local cops when they officially linked Lilly to the missing girls. But the motherfuckers can't find a trace of her. They're the fucking FBI and can't find her. Nothing. What use are they?

*See, cursing a lot.*

WES LEFT THIS MORNING; I guess he couldn't take being around me anymore either. I don't blame him. I'm either swearing, throwing shit, or vegetating; not to forget the few times I went across the hall and sobbed on her floor like a goddamn baby. My best friend has been with me since we found her car—or, as the federal morons call it, "the scene of the accident." She was kidnapped, for fuck's sake;

she didn't just drive into a ditch and decide to take a spontaneous vacation without telling anyone.

She. Is. Gone.

It's almost six in the evening, and I'm sitting on the floor at the foot of my bed, legs bent, arms resting on my knees, replaying Tuesday once again in my head. I've done nothing else for the past seventy-two hours, but I can't stop either.

BY THE TIME Wes and I got to my car, Lilly's Jeep was already out of sight. She turned right, which could get her anywhere: the highway, Glen Meadow, and Fallsbrook. Both towns are just about four miles, depending on if you take Main Street or 52nd Street out of town, and then there are the back roads. The back roads! Somehow, I knew that she'd take one of them instead of the main roads. She'd want to be alone, and that included cars and people as well. I was about to reverse out of the parking spot when Denielle stopped me by slapping her hand on the hood of my Defender.

"Not now," I growled under my breath.

"Where are you going?" I heard her muffled voice as she walked to the passenger side.

Wes lowered the window so I could respond, "I'm going to find my girlfriend."

*What kind of question was that?*

"Do you think that's smart?" Her voice was so full of disdain; it still makes my skin crawl.

"What are you trying to say?" I snapped back at her, driven by my guilt in all of this.

She inhaled deeply before saying more calmly, "You lied to her. You just stood there when your psycho ex humiliated her in front of half the school. She feels betrayed. Do you really think she wants you to find her right now?"

Denielle got her point across; I royally fucked up. I knew she was right. But there was no question; I had to go after Lilly. The thought of losing her over this threatened to suffocate me, and deep down, something was telling me that I would if I didn't at least try to find her. Though, I didn't realize how literal it'd be.

"I have to go," was all I replied.

She leveled me with a hard look and nodded. "Okay." With that, Den opened the back door, got in, and settled in the middle of the backseat. Slapping her palm on my headrest, she commanded, "Let's go."

*Who put her in charge all of a sudden?*

I glanced at Wes, and then Den through the rearview mirror, before finally pulling out of my spot. As I put the car in drive, I looked over to the school's main entrance, a direction I purposefully avoided until this point. As expected, a large group of students lingered on the steps leading up to the two sets of double doors, openly following the show. I even saw a few teachers who attempted to guide everyone back inside but were completely ignored. And to no one's surprise, Kat stood front and center, arms crossed, and eyes fixed on me.

*How could I've ever been with someone like her?*

My gaze turned into tunnel vision, and a red haze forming in front of my eyes briefly replaced the panic about finding Lilly. The urge to get out of my car, walk over, and throttle my psychotic ex was overpowering my senses.

"Rhys!"

Denielle's barked tone snapped me out of the stare-down with Kat, and my focus immediately was back on what was important. Finding Lilly.

THERE ARE three back roads between the surrounding towns. One is not paved and can barely be called a road. I doubted she'd take that one. So, we had a fifty-fifty chance. I took the wrong one. I chose the wrong fucking road.

*Did I already mention that I'm dropping a lot of F-bombs lately?*

My error cost us twenty-five minutes, and when we finally drove down the other road, I immediately saw the flashing lights. My hands tightened around the steering wheel to the point that the stretched skin over my knuckles started to burn. Denielle leaned forward between the seats with her hands covering her mouth, eyes wide. Next to me, Wes expelled a string of curse words while gripping the door with one hand and the side of his seat with the other. I pushed the pedal to the floorboard until we came to a screeching halt behind another car. I was out the door before Wes could unbuckle his seatbelt. Sprinting around the other vehicle, I passed an older couple standing in the middle of the road. There, halfway in the field, was Lilly's Jeep. It was flipped upside down, and I could see the deflated airbags. My knees threatened to buckle at the sight.

*No, no, no.*

I frantically started to look around, hoping to find some trace of her, but deep down, I already knew. The doors to the ambulance were wide open—the back empty—and the pit in my stomach deepened even further. Cruisers were half blocking the road on either side of the scene. Without thinking, I started forward and came face to face with one of the cops. The top of his head didn't even reach my nose, but he outweighed me by probably a hundred pounds—not muscle.

"Where do you think you're going, buddy?" he asked me in a nasal tone.

*Buddy?*

The blood was rushing in my ears, and I could barely make out my voice when I responded through gritted teeth, "This is my girlfriend's car. I need to get to her!"

The man's entire demeanor changed from *I'm-a-cop-what-do-you-think-you're-doing-here* to something I couldn't decipher. He peered at his partner, who was slowly walking over. I noticed faintly that Wes and Denielle had taken position on either side of me.

"Um, son, what's your name?"

*What the fuck?*

I was about to tear past them when Denielle touched my forearm ever so slightly. I glanced to the side, and she mirrored the cop's expression.

"What?" My gaze jumped back and forth between them.

The second cop cleared his throat. "Son, there is no one in the car. It was empty when we got here."

With that, my legs gave out, and I crumbled to the ground, head in my hands. "No, no, no, noooooooooo!" My scream echoed in my head long after my voice gave out.

I remember that Wes and Denielle dragged me back to the Defender, and Den sat in the backseat with me, holding my shaking hands, silently crying until my mother arrived. Her blood-curdling scream will be etched into my brain until the day I die. After that, everything was a blur until Dad came home later that night.

I can't shake the feeling that it's my fault. If I had just told Lilly about Kat. But my brain-to-mouth connection was completely severed when my ex cornered her, and my gorgeous girl retaliated in the form of a right hook. I didn't see the attack coming, but I wasn't surprised either. When Lilly gets pushed too far, her instincts take over. Years of training have drilled that into my brain as well. The corner of my mouth lifts, recalling Kat's stunned face. No one had ever dared lift a hand against her, not even when she slapped Rebecca Corbin in junior year for accidentally spilling water on her. But the whole time, I was rooted to the spot. I willed my body to move, take a stance, but it wouldn't obey. And then she was gone.

Lilly. I make myself think her name, and it reverberates in my mind. My insides constrict, and I wrap my arms around my midsection, bending forward, swaying back and forth. If I could hold her one more time and tell her how sorry I am, how much I love her. Tears are running down my face again, and I don't care to wipe them away.

It's how I still sit when my phone begins to vibrate on my desk. I ignore it as I have for the past four days. People stopped calling. This is the first time in—fuck, I have no clue. Lilly was reported missing on Wednesday, but for all I know, the official version is that she took off after the showdown in school. I haven't bothered asking, and my friends learned pretty quickly not to mention anything related to Lilly around me.

The vibration starts back up. I ignore it again and then a third time. What. The. Fuck? I push myself up on the bed with one hand and reach my desk right when it stops ringing. My screen is lit and shows three missed calls from "UNKNOWN". Bile rises in my throat. It starts ringing once more, and I squeeze my eyes shut. Maybe it's all a dream? The sound of the vibration on the wooden top of my desk is like a jackhammer in my ears. I know who will be on the other end, but I can't bring myself to move. The caller hangs up, or my voicemail takes over, I'm not sure. I. Can't. Fucking. Move. Again. When I think this is it, the screen lights up once more, and this time, my body obeys. I dive for my phone. My hands shake so badly that it slips out of my grasp twice before I can get a hold of it. After drawing in one last breath, I swipe across the screen and hold it to my ear. My voice won't cooperate.

"Rhys?"

That voice. A sob escapes my hoarse throat.

"Are you there?" Her tone is low as if she is trying not to startle me. I thought I'd never hear that voice again.

"Yes." It's barely a whisper.

"Hey." This one word settles over me like a soothing blanket, and I hear the smile in Lilly's voice.

"Cal, I'm so sor—" But I can't finish the sentence. My throat constricts, and I swallow several times.

"It's ok. I don't have much time."

That snaps me out of it. "Where are you? Did he hurt you?" The hand that is not holding the phone balls into a fist.

"I'm fine. That's why I'm calling. I...I just wanted to let you know that I'm safe. I'm fine."

*She's safe?*

"What do you mean? Is he threatening you? Where are you? The house was taken over by the FBI; they will find you."

"No, they won't. They can't trace the call." She exhales, resigned. "I...I had to hear your voice. And tell you that I'm okay. I'll explain everything to you when I see you."

*Explain? See? Wha—?*

"What are you talking about? Babe, where are you? See me when?" I'm shouting now, and I don't doubt that my father will burst through that door in the next few seconds.

"I have to go," she rushes out. "I'll call again. Please tell them to stop looking for me. They won't find me."

*Is she fucking brainwashed?*

"Please don't hang up," I go from shouting to begging.

"I have to go." There is a pause as if she wants to say something else, but then all she says is, "I'll see you soon."

"Calla?"

Nothing. She hung up.

. . .

Legs giving out, I sink to the floor, and my dad chooses that moment to throw the door to my bedroom open. I'm in front of my desk, staring up at him taking over the doorframe. His eyes are wide, and he's surveying the room as if I have Lilly stashed in the closet. And is that—yup, he's holding his forty-five in one hand.

"What happened?"

I stare.

"RHYS!"

My mom's smaller frame is mostly hidden behind my father, and I see more feet in the hallway.

"TALK!" my father roars.

My mom pushes past him. "Tristen, STOP!"

She squats beside me and takes my free hand. The other one still holds my phone in a death grip. "Honey?"

"She's fine," is all I rasp out.

My mom's hands fly to her mouth, followed by her wrapping herself around me and starting to sob. I can't hold back any longer and join her. I don't care that my father and several agents are hovering in my room; it's just mom and me. Mourning Lilly.

# CHAPTER FORTY-TWO

### LILLY

His tone is all casual. "Hello, Lilly."

I stare. No matter how hard I try, no coherent sentence will form. How did I miss this?

"You."

*Right, I already said that.*

My breathing has slowed down. I should've known.

The corners of his mouth quirk up, and he shrugs lightly. "Me."

His nonchalant attitude sparks something deep in my core, and instead of being terrified, like someone kidnapped—for the second time—would be, I bare my teeth at him. "You're psycho." It also helps that the gut feeling that I'm in no physical danger is even stronger now that we are face to face.

He shifts, crosses his arms over his chest, and leans against the doorframe. His posture emanates confidence, not predator. "I've been called that before—and worse."

*What the ever-loving—*

There is a familiarity between us that I can't shake, something beyond my kidnapping past with him, something beyond our first in-person interaction ten years later.

"Nate." My voice holds a warning note.

. . .

Nate Hamlin. Tall, blond, hazel eyes, and a genuine smile. That's who's standing across from me. I talked to him—even shook his hand. And I...I had no clue. He played me, another person that purposefully manipulated me. I steel my jaw.

"We should probably talk." Nate straightens from the doorframe.

His words bring me back to the present, and I focus on my captor.

*No shit.*

I keep quiet but tip my chin up. I'm snubbing my kidnapper; I'm not sure if that's brave or utterly stupid.

"May I come in?"

Is he serious? I scowl. "You kidnapped me; please come in." I wave him inside with my uninjured arm in an exaggerated arm gesture—unable to refrain myself from mocking the man in front of me. Maybe I did lose my mind after all? Or the car accident caused some weird fear-diminishing brain injury?

Nate slowly moves into the room and sits down in the bergère chair I remember from my first *stay* with him.

He rests his arms on his legs and looks me straight in the eyes. "I probably deserve that attitude."

*You think?*

"Why don't you tell me what I'm doing here? Why me?" The number one question that's been on my mind since I found out who I am—or more accurately, who I'm not.

"That requires a longer answer." He looks almost apologetic.

I frown. "I'm going out on a limb that I'm not leaving anytime soon?"

Where does this sass come from? Denielle is the sassy one, not me. But no matter what, he seems amused by it, not angry.

Nate smirks. "You remind me of Audrey."

Audrey. It's the same name he mentioned ten years ago in my memory. Though, back then, he was all emotion, less collected.

Do I want to know? But I ask before I can think about it further. "Who is Audrey?"

He replies without hesitation. "My sister."

*Uh, what?*

He looks at a spot on the wall above my head, and we sit in silence. I wait.

"Audrey died twelve years ago. She was six." His voice is pained.

*Six? Is this why he's been kidnapping all these little girls?*

"I'm...sorry?" My response is more a question.

He continues as if I hadn't spoken. "She died in a car accident together with my mother."

Shit, this time, no words will form. What are you supposed to say to your kidnapper who just spilled his family drama? I just sit there. But instead of saying more, he gets up and walks out, closing the door in the process. I don't hear a click or anything that would suggest I'm locked in, but I know I am. I don't bother checking.

I HAVE no clue how long I've been in this room. It seems like days, but it's probably just a few hours at most. Eventually, I can't sit still anymore, and I ease off the bed. A sharp pain shoots through my shoulder, and I wince. Not moving for so long, I forgot about the injury. It's not dislocated—been there, done that. But something is wrong with it. I cradle my arm to my chest. A few years ago, Rhys and I sparred; Rhys attacked, I didn't pay attention, and hit the ground the wrong way. Tristen was not happy with him. The memory brings the first smile to my face since waking up. Rhys. My chest constricts. I was furious with him when I left school, but now...all I want is to wrap my arms around him and let him hold me. What is he doing? Are they looking for me? He's probably out of his mind. Moisture starts building up in my eyes, and I swallow several times over the lump in my throat before I'm able to focus on my surroundings again. I refuse to show weakness.

Slowly, I start moving around. I'm pretty sure it's a different room from my first time with Nate.

*God, I sound like I'm talking about a past vacation.*

I recognize the white chair and matching dresser, but the bed is different. It's white but doesn't have the same antique style as the rest of the furniture, or a canopy. Also, this one is queen size versus the one back then was for a child, maybe a twin? I have no clue—smaller. The walls are the same pale lavender, but no mirror. I'm standing by the foot of the bed, across the spot Nate occupied not too long ago, when something registers. There is another door to the left and a window to the right on either wall. The old room had neither.

Why didn't I notice that before? Oh, right, because I was focused on the guy who kidnapped me. *Twice.* Looking back and forth between both, I'm rooted in my spot, not sure which one to check out first. What if they are just props and not real? I wouldn't put it past someone who takes little girls.

Three deep breaths later, I'm able to make my feet move toward the door. The doorknob turns without issue, and I'm facing—oh, wow. One of the most stunning bathrooms I've ever seen, a perfect blend between old and new, appears in front of me like an oasis in the desert. I could fall to my knees and kiss the floor because I don't realize how badly I have to pee until I see it. Everything is black and white. The room is rectangular, with the door on the narrow side and a white clawfoot tub with black feet across on the other. There are white subway tiles to the ceiling, the black grout creating a steep contrast, and the floor has an almost ornate pattern of black-and-white mosaic tiles. A square, white sink sits on top of a black table to the left. The toilet is located between the sink and the bathtub. On the other wall are two black metal towel racks with fluffy white towels draped over them. And are those—the initials L.A.H. jump out at me. What. The. Fuck? I ignore the disturbing discovery for now, because nature calls. Closing the door behind me, I triple-check the lock before I take care of the most pressing issue. When I wash my hands, I come face to face with someone in the mirror I barely recognize. My hair is plastered to the side of my head, caked with dried blood. There is an inch-long gash on my forehead that has been cleaned and stitched up, but the rest of me is still covered in grime. Dirt covers my hair, and looking down on myself for the first time since waking up, I can see it's not just in my hair. My clothes are filthy, and I have a sudden urge to clean myself thoroughly.

I mean, who wouldn't want to take a shower in this situation? It's the most normal thing in the world to find out you were kidnapped after you drove your car into a ditch, and instead of trying to escape, you'd rather take a shower. Makes sense, right? I cover my face with my hands.

*Maybe I'm the crazy one, after all?*

Screw it. I turn on the shower and watch the steam rise. After confirming once more that the door is indeed locked, I peel off my clothes, taking it easy on my shoulder, and step under the hot spray. The temperature borders on the edge of burning, but instead of turning down the temperature, I let the scorching water wash away all the emotions crashing over me like waves breaking against the edge of a cliff, trying to overtake my mind and body but unable to grab hold. I shut my brain off, refusing to deal with any of it. If I let it in, I lose control.

A seemingly endless amount of time later, I'm sitting on the edge of the tub, wrapped in one of the large L.A.H. towels—nope, no...still not acknowledging the letters. Looking down at my exposed arms and legs, all four limbs are bright red from the heat of the water.

I debate my next move; I don't want to put my old clothes back on, but I have nothing else. Ten years ago, Nate had clothes for me. I take the gamble and ease open the door. Making sure he is not camped out in my room, I step out of the steam-filled bathroom.

*My room? Good Lord, what's wrong with me?*

With the towel securely fastened and no Nate in sight, I walk over to the dresser and open the top drawers. Bingo! Beyond creepy, but bingo nonetheless. There, neatly folded, are a bunch of dark-colored tank tops and long sleeve shirts. One drawer down, I find a large selection of sweats and leggings, everything close to my size. I grab a tank top, a loose black long-sleeve shirt, and a pair of gray sweats and move back to the bathroom to get dressed.

In the little basket under the sink-table is a brush, and I gingerly disentangle my wet and knotted hair, careful not to come near the stitches. Maybe I should've covered them somehow before the shower. The last thing I need is an infected head wound.

Sitting on the bed a little later, I feel like the shower not only washed away the dirt, but also my last bit of strength. I'm exhausted to the point of barely keeping my eyes open. I push the grime-stained pillows to the floor and lean back onto the remaining ones.

.   .   .

My eyes slowly ease open. The room is dark, and there is a blanket draped over the lower part of my body. Nate was in here. My stomach rolls, and I swallow several times. Yesterday's adrenaline rush is officially gone, and the severity of the situation sinks in. I'm kidnapped. Again. I rub my trembling hands over my face, and pulling them back, I realize the room is not fully dark. In my exhaustion, I forgot about the window. It's covered in white drapes, but given the amount of actual light coming in, they must be heavy blackout curtains. Slowly sitting up, I slide one foot off the bed and then the other, taking stock again. My shoulder still hurts, but the pain is not as sharp as yesterday; it's manageable. On the nightstand, I find a bottle of Advil and a glass of water. Greedily, I drink the water, but I leave the pills. Not that he couldn't have put something in the water, but taking the pills is pushing my comfort level.

My heart beats double time but curiosity wins out, and I close the distance to the window. Easing one panel back, I don't know what I'm expecting, but definitely not...this. The sun is still low, but the rolling hills covered in grapevines are already bathed in sunlight. The scene is surreal.

*Who is Nate Hamlin?*

As if on cue, there is a knock, and before I can say something, the door swings inward. Nate is dressed similar to me in gray sweats, and the long-sleeve black shirt emphasizes his broad shoulders. Well, this is a bit awkward.

*In addition to the whole kidnapping thing, of course.*

We stare at each other. Refusing to talk first, I raise my eyebrows, and his mouth quirks up.

"Good morning, Lilly."

I mimic his casual tone, "Good morning, Nate." Aaaand the sass is back in full force—no more shaking hands.

His eyes crinkle. "Would you like some breakfast? It's time we talk. This conversation is long overdue."

He's offering answers; my pulse instantly speeds up. I jerk my head in a quick nod, unable to hide my eagerness.

"A few ground rules, though."

*This was too good to be true.*

I tilt my head to the side, waiting.

"I don't want to treat you like a prisoner."

I snort, but he holds out a hand to stop me from commenting. "It will all make sense soon enough, but you need to understand that there is no way for you to leave. You are free to walk around, but the property is locked down."

*What the hell is that supposed to mean?*

He steps back, gesturing for me to walk past him out of my prison cell. Okay, cell is an exaggeration given the luxury it holds, but still.

In the hallway, he passes me, and I follow him through seemingly endless white corridors with espresso-stained wooden floors, lined with large windows facing more of the sunny hills. We go down a set of narrow stairs that leads into a massive kitchen, and I can't help taking it all in with wide eyes. Everything is pristine and looks like how you imagine a hotel's kitchen, but it's also...homey. The appliances are all state of the art; the white cabinets have dark-centered cup pulls and give the room a country-like feel. Who needs a kitchen like this?

He sees my awed expression and explains, "This used to be a vineyard that allowed for guests to stay."

Gesturing for me to sit at the long oak table, which can easily hold twenty people, he gets to work on breakfast. I scan the kitchen, and my eyes fall on an enormous knife block with more knives than I can count. Glancing back at Nate, he is watching me with raised eyebrows. "You can't leave, even if you overpower me."

But instead of feeling intimidated, I shrug sheepishly. "A girl has to try."

Shaking his head, he turns back to the fridge and mumbles something along the lines of "So much like your sister."

"What did you just say?"

But he ignores me.

"Nate!"

Nothing. Ugh.

# CHAPTER FORTY-THREE

## LILLY

Nate prepares a feast; there is no other word for it. Pancakes, eggs, bacon, muffins—reheated, not fresh, but still—and toast with the largest selection of jams I have ever seen outside of a hotel buffet. I wonder if they are still housing guests? It seems like way too much food for one—currently, two people—living here. Living here? I mentally slap myself.

"I never expected a kidnapping victim to be treated like this," I quip, gesturing to the amount of food displayed in front of me.

"You are not a victim, Lilly." His tone is calm, but his shoulders are rigid.

"What else would you call my current situation?" Why doesn't he scare me? Despite my training, I'm pretty sure he could easily take me down.

Nate frowns. "I guess you're right." No other comment.

We eat quietly until I can't hold back anymore. "What do you want with me?"

Slowly, he lowers his piece of toast and leans back. He rubs his palms on his sweats under the table. Is he...nervous?

"I've thought all night about how to explain everything to you. I think it makes sense to start with my...story and then come to your part in it."

I wait for him to continue.

Wiping one hand over his mouth, he looks out the window and takes a deep breath. "My birth name is Nate Hamlin, but in public, I go by Altman."

*Altman? He can't be serious.*

"As in *Altman* Hotels?" I interrupt, my voice shrill. I was kidnapped by one of the wealthiest people in the world.

*Well, fuck me.*

"The one and the same." Facing me, he almost looks apologetic. "My father's name was Hamlin, but when I took over the business, I started using my mother's maiden name."

"Was?" *His father is dead, also?*

"He died a year after my mother and sister."

I'm not sure what to say. Is that what made him crazy? I know better than to ask.

"My parents' names were Payton Altman and Brooks Hamlin. My mother was the heiress of the hotel empire. My father was a patent attorney," he explains. "They met while my father was an intern in the Altman legal department. My sister was Audrey Hamlin, but I already told you that. Audrey was born when I was fourteen; she would've been eighteen now."

That makes him, what? Thirty-two?

*Guess I was off with my late-twenties estimate.*

The pain recalling his sister is written all over his features. Nate is staring out the window, and when he doesn't say anything, I prod carefully, "What happened?"

Why do I sympathize with this man? I tell myself that I'm just curious, like when you see an accident. You shouldn't watch, but you do it anyway to see if you can figure out who's at fault.

His gaze snaps back to me as if he completely forgot I was in the room. "Sorry," he mumbles. "I was told my mother found out that my father had an affair a few years prior. She was leaving him. She picked Audrey up from school and was on her way home to pack their belongings when she ran a stop sign. They collided with a truck and died on impact."

"That's...terrible." It truly is, but what does that have to do with me?

His lips press together for a brief moment. "I was away at

school. I left early that year to take summer classes. My father was in a drunken stupor and, apparently, forgot he had another child. I got a call from our family attorney..." He trails off again.

"I'm...sorry." I sound like a broken record.

"I found out what happened when I came home for the funeral. The press ambushed me the minute I stepped out of the terminal at LAX. People at the wake kept giving me *the look*. These *your-father-was-the-reason-you-lost-your-mother-and-little-sister* pity side glances."

Now we're getting somewhere. Nate blames his father for his sister's death.

"I refused to speak to my father during the time I was there. I went back to school the day after they were buried, but I lost focus. I couldn't concentrate, school lost its appeal, and I stopped going to my classes. My therapists later said that I partially blamed myself, because I had promised Audrey to come home the weekend before to take her to the zoo. But I stayed at school to prepare for the fall semester."

*Yup, definitely blames himself, too.*

"About a month into it, my roommate forced me to go out with him and our usual group of friends. But someone brought a couple of guys I'd never met before. Somehow the conversation became about who I was: the *heir* to the Altman Empire. My mom's death had made national news, given the fact who she was. One of the new guys started making comments about how convenient it was for me that my mother *and* sister were dead. Another chimed in that it was her dumb fault, and she should've never been behind the wheel—should've used a driver as all the 'rich bitches' do." He makes air quotes around the two words.

*Whoa—*

"I lost it." Recalling the story, his voice sounded robotic, but this last sentence is spoken in a low growl. The change in his demeanor sends a chill down my spine.

"What did you do?" I whisper. Scenarios run through my head— one worse than the other.

Nate continues in the same detached tone. "I was told that I tackled him and started beating on him—his head, to be precise. Two of my friends had to pull me off. I don't remember any of it. I blacked out."

My eyes bulge as his words sink in. "What...uh, what happened to the guy?"

*Did he kill him?*

"I put him into a coma."

*Ho-ly shit.*

One has to evoke some serious strength to do that with bare hands. I should be scared, but oddly enough, I am still not afraid for my safety. We sit, and I focus on the remnants of my breakfast in front of me. I'm no longer hungry. As captivating and disturbing as this story is, I'm getting more and more confused.

"So, uh—what does that have to do with me?" I ask carefully.

Nate's hazel eyes, which have been vacantly staring at the wall behind me, now glower at me. "I'm getting to that," he barks.

"Okay," is my meek response.

*Maybe I'm a little scared.*

He wipes his hands over his face. "Fuck, I'm sorry. I haven't told anyone the whole story in years."

"It's fine." My voice is still a whisper, definitely no backtalk this time.

"Just, uh... Let me get it all out. You'll understand." His eyes have gentled, and it's evident that his reaction was less geared toward me than caused by the tragedy he is reminded of.

I nod.

"Given who my family is, I had the best defense in court. My attorney was able to negotiate a plea deal that landed me in a medical facility instead of jail. While I was...away, my father took his life."

I press my lips together.

"After my discharge, I returned home—my parents' home in LA," Nate clarifies. "I wasn't going back to school. Not only did I have to figure out my mother's estate, but I also had to sort out my father's affairs. It took weeks to get a handle on things. And then, I found a stack of letters and pictures in his desk at the house."

My heart starts hammering in my chest. This is leading up to the big question.

"The letters were addressed to my father. The pictures were of a little girl, ranging from baby age to about five years old. I didn't have to read the letters to see the resemblance."

Nate fixes his eyes on me, and I hold my breath. Rubbing my hands against the cotton of my sweatpants, I fight the urge to tell him to stop.

"The return address was an Emily Sumner."

This. Is. It. Bile starts to rise in my throat, and I swallow hard. My hands are trembling as I reach for my mug, having to do something to not look at Nate.

He waits for me to collect myself. I drink half of my almost cold tea before I dare look in the hazel eyes that were so familiar from the first day, but yet, I would've never made the connection.

"Emily and your father..." I rasp. There is too much saliva in my mouth. I keep swallowing, but it's not helping.

Nate nods.

"Can I go back to my room?" There is more, his face tells me as much, but the urge to run is too overpowering.

"Do you remember the way?" He's sending me alone. I'm not sure what this means, but I also don't care.

"I think so." I stand up and bolt out of the kitchen the way we came. I don't look back; I don't look around. The thought of trying to escape doesn't cross my mind. I need to be alone.


I WAKE up on top of the comforter in the room Nate has given me —my room, as I've started calling it. (Prison cell didn't seem or feel right no matter what the circumstance.) The sun is high in the sky, and I must've fallen asleep for several hours. I replay Nate's story in my head, and immediately, my pulse is speeding up. This is the third —no, fourth—no, I don't know what number—revelation in the last three months that has made my life a *fucking* lie. And on top of that, I start cursing like Denielle.

I was kidnapped as a child. My memory was erased. My parents are not my real parents. My brother is not my brother, but now my boyfriend. My biological parents are also not my parents—well, half of them anyway. And lastly, I do have a brother—half-brother, but nonetheless a brother—who kidnapped me. *Twice.*

With that last thought, I scramble off the bed and through the door to my left. I make it by a matter of an inch before the remnants of my breakfast make a reappearance. This time, there is no Rhys or Denielle to comfort me, to hold my hair, or to help me clean up. I'm alone in the fancy, black-and-white bathroom attached to my lavender-colored non-prison-cell overlooking a beautiful vineyard I cannot leave. Pulling away from the white porcelain bowl, I lose my last bit of composure, and the tears start flowing. Everything I've bottled up since I left Denielle's house Monday raises to the surface, and the first sob breaks free, followed by full-on body tremors. I wrap my arms around my middle and rock back and forth, crying anything but silently. I miss Rhys, and I no longer care that he kept Katherine's malicious games from me. All I want is to be held in his arms and hear his voice telling me that everything will be okay. But he's not here. No one is here. I'm alone, trapped in God knows where.

I EMERGE a few hours later from my room. After my breakdown, I took another shower and again rinsed all the emotions away. Being numb is the only way to keep my sanity—at least to an extent.

The sun is about to set, and I haven't seen Nate since I left the kitchen this morning. Unsure what to do, I wait in my room until the hunger wins out. For some reason, I am not surprised that my door is unlocked. Yes, he said there is no way for me to leave the property, but I know that his partial confession this morning has changed everything already. I'm no longer confined to my room.

I start my exploration with the kitchen. I find a leftover muffin wrapped up on the counter and instantly devour it. My initial hunger sated, I glance around, and my gaze lingers on the knife block. A voice in my head tells me to grab at least one knife, a small one that I can hide in the pocket of my sweatpants, but if it were that easy to escape, Nate wouldn't let me roam free—sister or not. Interlacing my hands on top of my head, I close my eyes.

*Sister. God, I still am in denial.*

I start moving through the kitchen, my fingers grazing the black-and-gray marble countertop as I walk. Besides the stairwell I've now taken three times, there is a door next to it. It's set back, and from the angle of the table, I didn't notice it earlier.

Should I? Oh, what the hell.

I ease the door open and find another hallway similar to the one upstairs—white walls and espresso-colored floors. This one holds artwork on the side that doesn't contain floor-to-ceiling windows. Slowly inching down the corridor, I take in the paintings. I don't know much about art, but the pictures in combination with the heavy wooden frames make them appear priceless. Knowing that he is an Altman, they probably are.

There are several closed doors between the paintings, but I don't dare try to open any of them. My curiosity only goes so far. An archway opens up into a massive...um, what is this? A living room? A sitting room? Based on my estimate, its vaulted, coffered ceiling is far above the second story I know this house has—maybe even a third? Brown and beige leather couches and armchairs are arranged in various groupings, creating multiple seating areas. One of the most gigantic fireplaces, reaching all the way to the top of the wall facing the vineyard, is framed by more floor-to-ceiling windows. The small fire burning in it looks minuscule compared to the size of that thing.

I stand in front of the fireplace, still trying to gauge the magnitude of it when Nate steps up beside me.

*How the hell does he do that?*

"How are you feeling?" He sounds genuine.

Out of the corner of my eye, I see him staring at the flames as well.

"I'm not sure." Truth. Similar to the day Rhys told me everything, too many emotions assault me. Three months ago, I focused on the rage and anger to stay in control; now, there is so much to process. A voice in my head tells me I haven't heard the half of it yet. Taking a shower has helped me calm down, numb myself, but I can't run to the nearest bathroom whenever I'm getting overwhelmed.

*Though I'd probably be clean at all times with how the revelations keep coming.*

The silence elongates, and I attempt to take stock in my head. There is rage. My hands automatically ball into fists when I think about my parents—birth parents, adopted parents, whoever they are. They all lied to me about something. Did Henry have any idea I'm not his daughter? Did my biological father, Brooks, not want me? There's disappointment in Emily, who cheated on her husband

—the man I believed to be my father for the last three months. Relief, for having some answers. Fear of not seeing Rhys again. Confusion about Nate because, despite seeming completely sane whenever we talk, he is mentally ill. He kidnapped four other children, for Christ's sake. And for what reason? I still don't know the answer to that.

As if sensing my thoughts, he asks, "Do you feel up to talking some more?"

*Do I?*

He sounds hesitant. But instead of answering his question, I counter, "How do you always know when to show up? Do you have a tracker on me?" I'm mostly joking, but still, I hold my breath, waiting for his answer.

He huffs out a laugh. "No."

I finally sneak a peek at his profile, and I see him smirk at my suggestion.

*How can he seem so...normal?*

I shrug. "So? How do you do it?"

Nate turns to face me. After a pause, he points to an upper corner of the room then to another on the opposite wall. "That's how."

I follow his finger and scan the areas he indicated. Squinting, I notice a small black dot on the white wall. Cameras? If one doesn't search for it, it appears merely like a dirt stain. Then it sinks in, and my jaw drops. With a knot in my stomach, I whirl around to my half-brother. "Are there cameras in my room? In the bathroom?" I'm mortified.

He has the decency to look somewhat guilty. "In your room, yes. In your bathroom, no."

*Oh, thank goodness.*

"However, your bathroom has a microphone for safety reasons."

"Safety reasons?" I shriek, aghast.

"I would never spy on you like that with a camera, but my computer is analyzing the sounds and alerts me if it identifies anything that could be considered a threat."

*Oh, so puking my guts out and crying is not considered dangerous by his computer?*

Immediately knowing where my thoughts went, he says, "It did alert me earlier, but after checking the recording, I figured that was not something you would've wanted me to witness."

He is right on that account, which deflates my outrage—a little. However, I can't refrain from demanding, "I want the camera in my room gone. And the mic." Standing there with my hands on my hips, glaring up at my kidnapper-slash-half-brother, must make for an entertaining sight. The ridiculousness of the situation is not lost on me.

Nate's shoulders slump slightly. "I can't do that."

I'm about to protest, but he holds up a hand. "I will switch both to monitoring only."

*What does that even mean?*

My frown triggers him to elaborate. "The computer will analyze the threat level and send an alert. But I won't be able to view the footage or listen to the recording without your permission."

"How do I know that you're telling the truth?"

"You don't. However, my security network is very...proficient. I can put a personal password on every camera on the property. To prove to you that you can trust me, you can put the password for your cameras and mics in yourself. Only you and the system can access them."

I have no idea if he's pulling all that out of his ass, but what else am I supposed to do?

# CHAPTER FORTY-FOUR

### LILLY

I'M STANDING IN NASA'S COMMAND CENTER. AT LEAST THAT'S what it looks like.

I had followed Nate from the sitting room, as he called it, through an arch into the connecting foyer. A vast double staircase leads to the floor above. It comes together in a gallery overlooking the entryway, as well as the various seating areas in front of the massive fireplace on the other side. A set of wrought-iron double doors—the exit, if I were able to leave—takes over half of the wall opposite the arch and is dead center between both sets of stairs. Despite the pristine white walls everywhere—except for my room— the dark wooden floors give this place a feel of...home.

*God, I need my head examined.*

Upstairs, Nate stopped in front of a regular-looking door...until I noticed a large panel set into the wall. I stared wide-eyed as he unlocked the room with his retina scan. His. Freaking. Eye. Oh, and a fingerprint. Don't let me forget the fingerprint. When I thought it couldn't get worse, the panel slid up, and—was that a mic? Yup, it was a mic. He said a random string of words, and something inside the door clicked. I gawked at him incredulously.

When he saw my expression, he deadpanned, "I'm not always alone on the property."

*Of course you're not. How silly of me.*

Now, my brain is trying to comprehend what I'm looking at. There are six, at my guess, 50-inch flat-screen TVs mounted on the wall to the right, all of them off. An antique-looking desk that reminds me of the one from the *National Treasure* movie sits in the middle of the room, in complete contrast to the tech surrounding it. There are more monitors centered on the desk with two keyboards in front of them and two laptops at either end.

I turn in a circle and realize there are no windows. Based on what I've seen from the rest of the house, he must've had them removed. Pictures cover the wall opposite the screens, arranged in no particular order or pattern as it seems. Without waiting for Nate's permission, I step closer. My gaze immediately finds several pictures of a young Nate—probably eighteen or so—with a little girl, which I assume to be Audrey. They have the same light hair color and facial features—the same as me. The realization hits me like a punch in the gut, and I can't stop myself from gasping. It's as evident as the fact that I look nothing like the McGuires—like Rhys. *Don't think of him right now.* My chest constricts, and I start moving along the wall, trying to focus on the photographs instead. I discover about a dozen more of Audrey, ranging from infancy to around five or six years old. In some pictures, she is with a gorgeous woman in her thirties. The woman has flawless, almost ivory skin. Her hair is a shade between red and hazelnut, which, if not natural, would make a person look washed out. On her, however, it has a striking effect. In one of the pictures, she is wearing a red ball gown, which highlights her pale skin, rubicund hair, and slender figure even more. She looks like royalty. This must be Payton Altman.

"My mother."

Despite his voice being low, I jump at his words. I was so absorbed in my half family, he might as well have shouted in my ear. My hand flies over my heart, and I try to get my breathing under control again.

"She was beautiful," I whisper. I can't bring myself to speak at a regular volume.

"Yes, she was." Nate is in his own head and stares toward a section of pictures in the bottom corner of the wall. I follow his gaze and find the only picture containing four individuals. In the background is a Christmas tree; Audrey is on Payton's lap in a tight embrace. Nate sits next to his mother and sister with one arm slung around his mother's shoulders. All three radiate happiness. On the other side of Payton is a blond man with angular features. He is squatting, face angled toward Audrey, but his expression is blank. There is no emotion, a complete contrast to the rest of the photograph, which shouts holiday joy. His skin is sun-kissed, but not too tan, and his light-blond hair is shaggy and curled at the ends. Is this...?

"Yes."

*Did I ask that out loud?*

"You look a lot like him," I tell Nate. I'm not sure what else to say. What is the appropriate reaction here?

"So do you." He's just stating a fact, but the black hole inside of me rips open further.

*Who am I? Where do I belong?*

"It was our last Christmas together as a family," he murmurs.

I'm about to move away from the picture when something unexpected happens. A sharp pain punctures my brain like an ice pick, and I crumble to the floor, holding my head. Squeezing my eyes shut, I see a multitude of colors as if fireworks were set off behind my eyelids. My stomach rolls, and I curl into myself. I don't remember if I cried out loud or not, but the next thing I see is Nate hovering over me with wide eyes.

"Are you okay?" Panic laces his question. He sits on his haunches, waiting for me to straighten up. His hand hovers slightly above my shoulder, as if he wants to help me up but is scared to make that connection.

One of my hands is still at my head, and I have to force myself to lower it to my lap.

"I'm fine, just a memory," I say without thinking.

*Crap!* That's probably not something I should share with him. The line between kidnapper and brother is blurring, and that puts me on edge. Questions my sanity.

"What do you mean?" Confusion replaces the panic in Nate's voice.

When I don't reply, he initiates the first physical contact since the handshake a few weeks ago. Consciously or unconsciously, I don't know, but what I immediately notice...I don't flinch away.

*This is not good.*

Nate leads me to a couch set against the third wall, where the floor-to-ceiling windows should have been. It is mostly hidden behind the massive desk, which explains why I didn't notice it until now. As soon as we reach it, he lets go of my wrist, and I slump down into the plush leather cushion.

"Explain, please." His command is gentle but a command nonetheless. The hair on my neck stands up.

I pull my legs underneath me, and my gaze briefly flickers to his face before settling on my hands resting in my lap. I have the sudden urge to tell him everything. Why? I'm not sure. Maybe because I want to share it with someone else. Perhaps because he is my half-brother. Or perhaps I'm simply on the verge of an emotional breakdown.

"That's how it all started," I whisper and wait for Nate to react, but he just studies me with narrowed eyes.

I continue, "That's how I found out that I am not who I thought I am. I started having migraines. Combined with memories of my past. Of you." This time, I lock eyes with him, and for the first time, Nate is unnerved.

We sit in silence, and he is opening and closing his mouth several times. It seems that he doesn't know how to respond. I assume he isn't aware of what my parents did to me, that I couldn't remember—still can't. Do I want him to?

*Ah, screw it.*

"After you dropped me off at the hospital and threatened Emily, they erased my memory. I was so messed up that they thought I wouldn't be able to have a normal life. And because they were scared of you, they sent me away."

*There, I put it all out there—no sugar coating.*

Nate stares at me, lips pressed in a thin line. Then, with blinding speed, he jumps off the couch and is in reach of the desk within two steps. He grabs one of the laptops and hurls it across the room against the picture wall. Half the pictures shatter to the floor from the force, and the computer joins the chaos in multiple pieces. His entire posture is rigid. His hands grip the back of his neck, and his chest is heaving up and down. For the first time, I'm scared. His outburst is so abrupt and makes me wish I'd phrased it differently.

*I need to stop poking the lion.*

I don't move. I barely breathe. I want to hide in my room, but I don't think I would make it out of here—if the door would even open with the gazillion security measures it takes to get in. Finally, after several minutes, Nate turns toward me, and what I see shocks me to the core. His eyes shine with unshed tears, and his expression is pure anguish.

"I'm so sorry," he rasps out.

It's my turn to open and close my mouth. Nothing. I can't come up with a single word. He's insane. He kidnapped me. He took the other girls. That means he's crazy. *Right?* But what I see is remorse in its rawest form. What am I supposed to do with that?

"Why?" is all I come up with. Why did you kidnap me? Why didn't you just come to me? Why did you threaten Emily? And why the other girls? All those questions are packed into this one word, and he understands. He slumps back down beside me and puts his head in his hands, elbows supported on his thighs.

"I snapped." Nate's voice is hoarse. He talks toward the floor. "Twelve years ago, something broke inside of me. Then the bar incident happened. I found out about you and had a second chance at a family. I was just discharged and still on, like, five different meds. Meds that were supposed to help with my rage and guilt. But they also muddled my rational thinking. I had to have you. My sister. No matter what the cost."

*Okay, sadly, I can see that.*

"But why the other girls?" I probably shouldn't push the issue, but he seems to be willing to give me some answers right now. He's quiet for so long that I think he's going to ignore the question.

"I don't know." His reply is barely audible.

*Well, that confirms that he's crazy.*

I'm not sure what to say. I can understand that, after losing his family, he was...lost? But still, no sane person kidnaps little children for a few weeks to feel less lonely. Before I can prod further, it's Nate's turn to ask questions again.

"So...you remembered the hospital? That's why you came back?"

I stare at the blank monitors on the wall as if they show a rerun of what happened the last few months. The three weeks I thought I'd lost my mind. The night Rhys confronted me. How I ended up in the school parking lot after fleeing the house. The discharge papers and how I decided to go to California. I'm exhausted. I'm tired of the secrets in my life. I don't want to constantly be on guard. It's like something falls into place, and I pivot on the couch, facing my half-brother. He must've sensed the shift in me, because he mirrors my posture, and his entire focus is on me.

"No more secrets." My voice is firm, confident. It's not an act; I'm done with the secrets. Keeping what happened in the last three months to myself won't do any good in this situation. But in return, I want answers from him.

Nate's knitted eyebrows indicate that he doesn't understand the meaning of my words, so I elaborate.

"I'll tell you everything. Everything I remember and figured out about what happened to me. In return, I want answers as well. No more secrets. You say we're family; then we need to deal with this like one." Yep, a cheap shot and slightly manipulative, but it's also the truth. At this point, he is the only blood family I have left, crazy or not. I *need* to know where I come from.

Understanding dawns in his eyes, and he holds out his hand. I stare at it for a moment, hesitant to take it. But my need for answers wins out, and I place my palm in his. It's a brief contact. He squeezes my hand with a quick shake up and down, and it's settled.

I TELL NATE EVERYTHING. From my first migraine to the reason why I left school this week. I've been talking for so long my mouth is parched, and I'm emotionally drained. The clock on the wall shows one a.m., and I realize we've been in here for hours. Nate hasn't spoken once. Every so often, his facial expression changes to something I interpret as surprise, but he never comments.

At some point, he resumes his previous position with his elbows on his thighs, staring down at the floor, though his stiff posture is a dead giveaway of him listening.

When I finally finish, I take a deep breath. Nate doesn't react; his focus remains downward. The first words out of his mouth are, "I caused you a lot of pain."

It's a simple statement, and he doesn't expect a response. He doesn't want me to make him feel less guilty; he knows what he has done. Which, in return, makes me question my earlier assessment of his sanity.

"I guess it's my turn." Our eyes lock for the first time. He is just as exhausted as I am.

I want my answers, but my ability to focus is dwindling fast. "Let's postpone your turn for tomorrow."

"Yeah, that's probably better." The relief in his eyes is palpable.

I still have one request, though, that I didn't dare ask until now. "Nate?"

"Yes?" He tilts his head to the side, wary.

"I want to talk to Rhys." I'm not asking him; I will make this call somehow, but I'd rather have his support. Nate faces forward again but peers at me sideways, and I brace myself to utilize my last bit of energy for a fight.

"Okay."

"Okay?" I ask in disbelief.

He sighs heavily. "Yes, okay. From everything I just heard from you, I am smart enough to know that 'no' is not an option. You are as smart and as stubborn as the rest of your family."

I suck in a breath. My family? Is he referring to him and Audrey? Or Rhys? Or even Emily?

"But I'm asking you for more time. I want you to hear me out before you make the call."

*The condition.*

Rhys is probably going crazy, and so are Heather and Tristen, I'm sure. I don't even want to think about Natty. Closing my eyes, I nod in concession. Arguing will do no good, as much as I hate waiting, or making them wait. It's the only option I have until I get my bearings of this place.

# CHAPTER FORTY-FIVE

**LILLY**

It's mid-morning when I stumble into the kitchen. I still don't have access to a clock, so I go by the sun's trajectory when I finally make my way downstairs.

I woke up earlier to the room flooded with light. In my exhaustion, I forgot to close the drapes last night. Groaning, I flipped over and dragged one of the pillows over my head. It was definitely too early to get up, but I also didn't feel like moving and closing the blinds. The pillow did the trick, and I managed to fall back asleep for a while longer.

After waking up for the second time, I lay in bed, replaying the events of the previous day. This seems to have become a regular occurrence. Something came to the forefront, and my hands flew to my mouth to stifle the gasp that tried to escape me. I didn't want the mic to alert Nate; we didn't change the password yet. Still covering my mouth, I squeezed my eyes shut and remembered last night's *migraine*. With everything that happened, I had pushed it to the back of my mind and completely forgotten about it. Nate was probably too distracted as well to ask what my most recent memory had revealed. But now—in the light of the new day—it was all back. What did this mean? A knot formed in my belly, and I knew I had to tell him. But first, I wanted to hear more of his side before I revealed my trump.

NATE IS SITTING at the massive kitchen table with a mug in front of him, staring out the window. He doesn't react when I drop down across from him in the same chair as yesterday.

"Hi," comes out as a croak, and I clear my throat. I wipe my all-of-a-sudden damp hands against the black yoga pants I pulled out of the drawer today.

His eyes flick to me. "Good morning. Did you sleep okay?" He sounds genuine, like a big brother. I swallow the lump in my throat —*my brother*. My heart starts beating double time. My emotions are contradicting each other again, and I'm more confused than ever. And I thought being in love with your adoptive brother was complicated. Try to enjoy spending time with your half-brother who kidnapped you. I want to bang my head against the tabletop.

*Maybe I have Stockholm Syndrome?*

"Uh, yes. Thank you. You?"

"I didn't sleep much."

He stares at a spot behind me, seeming distracted, and I raise my eyebrows. His gaze swivels back to me. He blinks once, twice, then his focus is entirely on me. "Sorry. I was working most of the night."

*Working?*

"You work?" I ask, baffled, before I can stop myself. Why wouldn't he work? Even rich people work.

Nate chuckles. "Yes, the hotels don't run themselves."

"Oh."

He pushes back from the table. "I had to make sure we're not getting interrupted today, so I was working ahead. How about you eat something and then I'll show you the property? I believe it's my turn to give some answers?"

He phrases it like a question. Does he expect me not to want answers anymore? I fight the urge to roll my eyes. At the precise moment that I'm about to say that I'm ready now, my stomach growls, and I resign myself to nourishment before answers. After all, I haven't eaten much in, what, forty-eight hours? Seventy-two?

"How long have I been here?"

Nate stops his retreat and turns back to me.

"It's Friday. You slept for close to twenty-four hours after the accident." His tone is calm and matter-of-fact, but I see...*something* flash across his face. It's gone as quickly as it appeared. I wonder if he recalls the day I *didn't* wake up.

He turns and leaves the kitchen. I make myself a cup of tea and throw a slice of toast in the toaster oven. After grabbing a banana from the fruit basket, I rifle through the pantry—which could hold our entire kitchen at home—until I find a jar of peanut butter. Sitting back down at the massive table with my PB&B sandwich, I think about Nate's response. Friday. That means I've been gone for three days. Shit. My sense of time is all off. Heather is probably beside herself. I don't even want to think about Rhys. Or Natty. I'd lose my mind. I have to make this call.

THE CLOCK on the stove shows 11:39 when Nate saunters back in. He has my boots in one hand and a long, black, fleece jacket in the other.

"You really planned this out, huh? Buying me all these clothes and whatnot?" I gesture at his arm and then at the clothes I'm wearing, fully aware of how snide I sound.

Mimicking my smart-ass demeanor. "This is Margot's jacket, for when she comes here with me."

*Who the—*

I narrow my eyes at him, and he gives me a smug smile. "My fiancée. We come up here every few months, and she keeps clothes in one of the rooms. Your jacket got ruined in the accident and would be too warm anyway."

*Fiancée? But he's crazy. How can he have a fiancée?*

"Fiancée?" I'm too stunned to ask in a full sentence.

Nate doesn't answer and throws the jacket at me instead. I snatch it out of the air, and I hold it out, eyeing it like it's going to explode. Peeking at the label in the collar, I recognize the brand from Denielle. This thing costs more than all my jackets combined. Before I can say anything else, Nate is back out of the room, and I have to scramble with my boots to follow him. With Margot's fancy jacket in hand, I find him waiting in the foyer, leaning against the rail of one of the staircases.

"Ready?"

*As ready as I'll ever be.*

I nod and follow him out of the massive wrought-iron door, coming to a halt. I'm standing in a ginormous circular driveway. In the center is a Mediterranean-inspired fountain—currently turned off. Behind it is the beginning of a long, winding driveway lined with trees on either side and leading God knows where. I still have no clue where I am. I walk toward the fountain and then spin in a circle. *Holy*— The estate is even grander than I assumed. The outside is the same color scheme as the inside. The walls are a blinding white, as if freshly painted, with dark-brown window trims and shutters creating a dramatic contrast. The roof has a similar shade and stands out against the bright-blue sky. To the left, I can see the beginning of a four- or maybe five-car garage; that part of the building is at an angle, so there could be even more.

A warm breeze caresses my face, and I briefly close my eyes. "Where are we?" I can't hide the awe in my question.

"Northern California. Not far from Santa Rosa, actually."

I'm back where it all started. My eyes pop open. What did I expect? Somehow, I'd thought that he moved somewhere else after what happened ten years ago.

Nate starts walking to the right with his hands clasped behind his back. The narrow cobblestone path seems to go the entire length of that side of the building. When I catch up, he doesn't look my way but keeps a slow and steady pace.

"This estate belonged to my grandfather. He purchased it not long before he passed away, and I don't think either my mother or father knew about it. If they did, they seem not to have cared for it. I came across the title when my mother's attorney handed me the paperwork for the Altman 'Empire'." Nate makes air quotes around empire before he sticks his hands in the pockets of his hoodie instead of interlacing them again. I take in today's attire. Instead of sweats, he's wearing faded jeans that have probably seen better times and a dark-gray hoodie of no apparent brand. Not something I would expect from a billionaire, but so far, everything I've learned about Nate Altman-Hamlin contradicts itself.

He continues, which pulls me out of my fashion observation. "The first time I came here was a few weeks after my discharge. I couldn't stay in LA, deal with all the people. So, I moved up here. My grandfather had already restored the majority of the property, and I finished the rest over the years. Added my touch to it."

*You mean your spyware.*

"I don't know what his intention for the property was, but I decided to keep it. I started growing grapes again about eight years ago but opted against the winery part of it. When the time comes, the grapes go to another vineyard ten miles from here. I have staff that takes care of the property when I'm not in residence. When I'm here, I prefer my privacy. I don't stay long enough these days to require them to be around. I actually prefer to do things myself. I don't know...it helps me relax."

I listen, fascinated. Nate sounds so normal. We reach the edge of the house, and the path branches off in several directions. One follows along the side of the house, one seems to lead toward a small park, complete with stone benches, and the last disappears between the grapevines on the nearest hill. Everything is perfectly landscaped, not one blade of grass longer than the other. We follow along with the house until we reach the backside of the property, and I realize that it's a massive U-shape, which also explains the angle of the garage. Centered between the two arms of the U is a rectangular pool flush with the obscenely perfect manicured green.

"This place is huge."

"It has twelve guest bedrooms, each with a bathroom, not including my rooms, the library, and several sitting rooms. As I said, I have no idea what he intended for it. Most of the rooms are empty; I have no plans to open the property up for guests again."

"Is this where you brought..." *The girls?* I can't stop myself but, at the same time, can't finish the sentence. However, Nate is fully aware of what I'm asking. Hands still in his pockets, his chin dips to his chest, and his shoulders slump forward. His gaze flickers to me before he lowers it to the ground.

"Yes." His tone is eerily quiet, and I can't make out if his crazy side is making an appearance or if he feels...guilty?

"How did you know where to find me this week? Or the day at the gym?" I'm not ready to pursue the other topic. Mentioning the gym, I realize something else. "Wait...one of the pictures—you were in it."

"I have a guy," Nate murmurs.

*A guy?*

He continues before I can voice my confusion. "My security. He worked for my grandfather, and I kept him on the payroll when I took over." His admission that he had someone spy on me makes my blood boil. My entire body goes rigid.

"You paid some creep to spy on me? What the fuck is wrong with you? Did he know your plans for me? You're sick." Every word makes the bile in my throat rise further, and I basically spit the last sentence at him. I'm beyond caring if I make him angry. However, I'm not prepared for his next action. I'm ready to tear past him when Nate places a hand on my forearm and stops me in my tracks. Instead of getting mad for disrespecting and verbally attacking him, he looks at me with understanding.

"George is the best at what he does. He started as a P.I. for my grandfather, investigating people that tried to sabotage the business. Over time, he's become my head of security. I needed help when I was discharged from the hospital, with the press, with the business...with life. In the beginning, he only worked for me when I had a specific, uh... need. Over time, he became more. Yes, he is paid for his *discretion*. Yes, he was following you. No, he wasn't aware of me planning to bring you back with me. He stayed back to deal with the consequences of my decision. George knows *everything* I do or have done." Nate emphasizes the last part, and I grasp the meaning.

*Oh God, the girls.*

I feel sick, but Nate tightens the hold on my arm and keeps talking. "George knows you're my sister. He's known for a long time that I have a half-sister." After a pause, he adds, "He's the one who returns them."

"Why would he let you do it in the first place?" My voice is shrill, bordering on hysterics. Not for me, but for the little girls.

"He doesn't; he travels a lot. But when he finds out—and since he checks in on me regularly, he always finds out—he steps in. I've never harmed any of them, but he also doesn't just let me...continue. If he could be with me 24/7, he would, but his job requires him to be away a lot. Don't ask me why he hasn't handed me over yet. That's something you have to take up with him."

Nate lets go of me and turns away. I can't make out his face, but I see his stiff posture and notice he has his arms wrapped around his midsection. His next words are a raspy whisper. "He is the *only one* I trust to help me make things right. He—" his voice cracks. "He takes care of me."

This grown man in front of me sounds and looks utterly broken. I try to wrap my head around it. When I think he won't say anything else, he turns back to me. "We said no more secrets; that's why I am telling you this. I want you to be the one other person in my life I can trust—with everything. Help me make things right."

My eyes widen at his admission.

"I was doing business in Virginia, and Hank, my business partner, was with me most of the time. There was no way for me to check on you on my own, and I wanted to learn as much about you as possible. I asked George for his help. I couldn't understand how you all of a sudden showed up in California. Why now? Where were you for the past ten years? You had disappeared without a trace, and I'm good at finding things—"

*Things.* Nate focuses on something in the distance. His tone screams sincerity to me. In these short few days, I've seen enough of Nate Hamlin's different *personalities* to know his intention was solely to find out as much as he could about me while staying away. It warms me as much as it causes the hair on my arms to stand up.

I focus on something else from his last statement. "Didn't you say your friend's name is Todd?" I remember clearly that he called the Asian guy at the gym Todd.

"Hank Todd, yes."

*Oh.*

"Why did you have to scare me?" The force behind my voice is gone.

"I didn't see another way to separate you from your friends." He is still looking past me, and the fire ignites again.

"You seem to be a brilliant guy, genius-level smart. Even you should realize that what you did was wrong. You manipulated me. You scared me. YOU TOOK ME AWAY FROM MY FAMILY!"

My voice rises with every word until I am screaming at him at the top of my lungs.

"THEY. ARE. NOT. YOUR. FAMILY!" he roars back, his nostrils flared, eyes blazing.

*There is the monster.*

Any other person seeing this six-foot-three guy would be terrified. He emanates rage. But I am not.

We're facing off in the middle of the lawn behind the estate, surrounded by a breathtaking landscape, both breathing heavy, eyes locked and unable to move. I have no idea how long the standoff lasts before Nate shoves his hands through his hair and does a one-eighty, turning away from me. Stalking off, he doesn't take his hands away from his head until he reaches a set of iron patio furniture on the terrace spanning the entire building's backside. He slumps down in one of the chairs and supports his elbows on his legs, his head still cradled in his hands.

Unsure what to do, I watch Nate for several minutes. When he doesn't move, I slowly walk toward him and lower myself in the chair opposite him.

"Nate?" I prod. There is a possibility my action will backfire on me.

He inhales deeply before lifting his gaze. Raw anguish fills his eyes, and I suck in a breath.

*Who is this man?*

"I know there is something wrong with me; I'm not...normal. I probably should've never been released from the hospital." He sighs, resigned. "Most of the time, I don't remember what I did until it is too late—until George steps in. But the voice in my head tells me that this is the only way to not feel lonely for a little while..." He lets the sentence trail off.

"The voice?"

*Please don't tell me you hear voices.*

He must've seen my bulging eyes, because he huffs out a laugh. "Uh, not the way you're thinking. I meant it in a figure-of-speech kind of way. I don't hear actual voices."

"Oh, thank God." A giggled sigh escapes me, and we both smirk at each other until reality sets back in.

"How do you intend this to go?" I gesture back and forth between us. One breath, two, three.

"I have no fucking clue. I haven't thought that far ahead," he admits.

"Let's keep talking?" The suggestion is out of my mouth before I can second-guess it.

"You still want to?" He sounds hopeful—like a little boy—and I don't have the heart to make a sarcastic remark.

I wait for doubt to set in, but it doesn't come, so I shrug. "I do." And not just because I am stuck here; I want to get to know my half-brother. My chest constricts, unsure how or when that changed.

His head is slightly tilted as if to assess if I'm sincere.

"So...uh, you're engaged?" I have to start somewhere that doesn't revolve around our history, and it's not the time to push the call.

His gaze flickers to the side before it returns to me. "Margot, yes." He has a ghost of a smile on his face.

"Tell me about her," I push further.

"We met about three and a half years ago at a birthday party for Julian's girlfriend, Celeste—now fiancée. Julian has been my best friend forever, and I used to hang out at their house all the time—it was my time to be me. No past, no Altman Hotels, just me. Anyway, Margot was there with a guy who knew Celeste, and it was obvious she was miserable." Nate chuckles at the memory, and I marvel how natural it, all of a sudden, feels to listen to him talk about his life. He has a best friend and a fiancée.

"The guy started flirting with a waitress, and Margot was about to leave when I intercepted her. She was stunningly beautiful, and I knew who she was. Margot comes from family money, and initially, I was mostly attracted to her because of who she was. She wouldn't be with me for my money; she has enough of her own. I didn't have to worry about a secret agenda. And if I'm honest, she made me feel somewhat normal for the first time in years. This was right after—well..."

"Just keep going." I know what he means; I memorized the timeline, but I can't focus on that. This is a topic for another time. And the time will come sooner than I'd probably like.

"We started going out, and I realized there is more to her. She can be vain and eccentric, don't get me wrong; she has never worked a day in her life, and she has quirks everyone rolls their eyes at, but she also has a generous heart. She is involved with several non-profit organizations and, despite her wealth, tries to give back in her own way." I want to ask him why she doesn't make him feel less lonely, but I don't dare.

"When did you decide that she's the one?"

My question gives me another chuckle. "Margot made that decision for me. More or less."

My eyebrows narrow.

"I don't believe in a soulmate; that there is *the one*. Margot and I work well together."

"I don't know about that." My thoughts immediately wander to my soulmate, as Denielle had put it the day I finally admitted my feelings to myself.

"You're thinking about Rhys." He doesn't ask; he has the proof in the form of multiple incriminating photographs to know that Rhys and I are more than adopted siblings.

"Yes," I mumble, heat creeping up my face, and I'm not sure why it all of a sudden embarrasses me.

"I'm sure there are exceptions."

*Is he trying to reassure me?*

And then he adds, "You're definitely a better fit than that Katherine girl."

My breath increases, and I scowl at Nate. "You're the reason for what went down with Katherine at school this week?" I phrase it like a question, though there is no other way for Katherine to have gotten a hold of that photo. I'm sure he hears the warning in my questions.

"Yes." The truth. No matter how awful or painful it has been, he has not lied to me once.

"How?" It comes out as a growl.

He sighs deeply before he reveals that part of the mystery to me. "After you showed up in Santa Rosa, it took me some time to figure out who was with you. If Rhys wouldn't have introduced himself to Margery, there's a chance I still wouldn't know."

"Margery?"

"The nurse who gave you the note."

"Oh—"

*How did he find all that out?*

"How did I find that out?"

*I swear he has a mic implanted in my brain.*

I nod, not trusting my voice.

"I had a program on the hospital server, monitoring your file."

"Are you some kind of hacker?" I squeak.

That makes him grin proudly. "You could say that. Before everything started, I double-majored in business management, which was non-negotiable in my family, and computer science. Computers were, you could say, my thing. And I kept up with it. It's a hobby."

"A hobby?" I scoff. "You don't use a hobby to implant a Trojan horse at a hospital or spy on people by hacking into security cameras." My arms are now crossed tightly over my chest, and Nate narrows his eyebrows.

"How do you know about the security system?"

"You sent a picture from the school's security camera to me." *Duh.*

"I did; you're right." That's all; he says nothing else to that.

We're getting sidetracked from the actual topic. "Back to Katherine and what you did..." I leave the sentence hanging, untangle my arms from my chest, and spread them in a gesture for him to continue. I'm angry, and I'm channeling all of it toward the guy across from me. He has manipulated everyone around me to separate me from Rhys. My heart aches thinking of him.

Nate lifts both hands disarmingly. "Okay, first off, all I did was send one picture to her. Something was going on before my, uh... interference. But I have no detailed knowledge about that. Whatever your *boyfriend* did was not my doing."

I wait for him to elaborate.

"After I found out your new name, I started looking into your friends and family. Heather and Tristen McGuire have done an exhaustive job in hiding you, but some of your friends, especially Katherine—"

"She is not my friend!" I bark.

Nate sighs at my outburst.

"I know she's not. What I was going to say is that some of the people around you have a very public Internet presence, especially

Katherine. It was laughably easy to see what's important to her. What I didn't know was that, until recently, you were completely in the dark about your past. All I found was that Rhys was with Katherine for years until he, suddenly, wasn't. And then George sends me pictures of you and Rhys together, but officially, you are related. My *hobby* allowed me to find out that Katherine suspected something being off with her breakup and your relationship with your brother. It wasn't hard to find some evidence that she was paying close attention and also tried to manipulate her ex-boyfriend. But Rhys kept that from you, which worked in my favor. I admit I got impatient; I didn't plan on being in Virginia that long, and in the end, I decided to fast-track some of the events that probably still would've happened eventually. As callous as this Katherine chick is, she is not dumb."

While he was talking, my body started shaking, and I wouldn't be surprised if steam comes out of my ears. I glower at him until his gaze drops to my hands in my lap. I realize I've been fisting the material of my borrowed jacked to the point of ripping the seam of one of the pockets.

"You're angry."

"You think?" I can't hide my rage any longer. "YOU. OUTED. ME. TO. THE. ENTIRE. SCHOOL! I'm an incestuous slut for everyone now!"

"Yeah, in hindsight, that was maybe a little overboard," Nate mumbles.

Gaaaahhh! I jump out of my seat and stomp away. "I'm done," I bark, walking toward the house.

"Lilly!"

"WHAT?" I whirl around and see him pointing in the opposite direction.

"Your room is in the east wing." He doesn't sound patronizing or condescending at all, but I can't help feeling like an idiot.

"Thanks," I snap and march—now with less dignity—toward the other side of the terrace.

*Great.*

# CHAPTER FORTY-SIX

**NATE**

I'M SITTING IN MY OFFICE, WATCHING LILLY CRY INTO HER pillow. It breaks my heart that I caused my little sister so much pain. The recurring doubt I've suppressed over the years reverberates in my brain since our earlier conversation. Sometimes, I believe that I should've never been discharged—whenever I realize what I've done. *Again*. But I was deemed mentally stable and thrown back into the world. Even after all this time, I see my doctors regularly, which was part of the deal for my discharge/release. They keep changing my meds around every few years to adjust better to my current lifestyle—whatever the fuck that means. If George is not with me, he checks in regularly, and if I don't answer, he shows up at my doorstep within twenty-four hours, no matter where in the world he his. Could I turn myself in? Sure. But until now, I have been too much of a pussy for that.

Having Lilly here makes me want to be a better person—the best possible version of myself. Sitting across from my sister, who has been through so much—most of it being my fault—I genuinely want to do better—*be better*. And I will be. I'll do right by her.

There is still so much I need to tell her, but I understand she needs time, especially after our most recent conversation.

I kill the feed to her room and switch to computer monitoring only. Until she can put her password on the camera, the computer will do its job.

She also hasn't made any attempt to run since she woke up, and if I'm honest, I'm a little confused by that. She did demand to call *the boyfriend*. Thinking about that, the big brother in me comes out. I want to ask her how that came to be. First, the guy dates cheerleader Barbie for years; then, he's with Lilly. I have no right, but I can't help but feel protective of her.

LILLY HAS BEEN in her room for two hours, and I've been procrastinating, looking at the most recent design update for the new Virginia hotel. Hank has sent five text messages in the last thirty minutes, so I switch the camera in her hallway to movement alert and get to work.

An hour later, my phone rings with an incoming video call, and Margot's smiling face in a beach chair greets me.

*Did she tell me she was taking a trip?*

"How are you, sweetheart? I was going to call you later tonight."

"Darling! I'm so glad you answered. Guess where I am?"

*Is that a trick question?*

"I don't know. It looks like somewhere warm."

"We're in San Tropez," she squeals.

*France? What the fuck?*

"Who is 'we'? And how did that happen? I thought you're in LA this week?" I'm slightly confused, which doesn't happen often. I keep tabs on everything and everyone in my life. I don't like surprises.

"I was, but Daddy called that he purchased a new yacht and invited me to come out. And since you're busy and all with your secret project, I figured why not. I brought Celeste with me as a pre-birthday present; it'll be so much fun." She flips the camera to Julian's fiancée, who waves into the camera from a matching beach chair before I see my fiancée's face again.

"Uh, that's great, sweetheart. The two of you will cause havoc with all the French men," I tease. "How long are you gone?"

Meaning, how long do I have until I have to make excuses for not coming back to my house in LA?

"We'll be back for the party next week."

Party? Motherfucker, I forgot about the birthday party. "Uh."

"Darling? Did you forget Celeste's party?" she scolds.

*Maybe? I've had other things on my mind.*

"No, not at all."

We talk for a few more minutes before disconnecting. I lean back in my desk chair, pressing the heels of my hands to my eyes. FUUUCK!

My two worlds have never overlapped before. There has only been *one other* since I started seeing Margot. And that was during a low point in our relationship. I was stressed from work and seeing Doctor Stern twice a week while he switched my meds around once again. Margot was pushing for us to set a wedding date, which was the last thing on my mind, so she disappeared to South America for a month.

I need to figure something out before next week.

## CHAPTER FORTY-SEVEN

### LILLY

I EMERGE AFTER I CAN NO LONGER DENY THE EXISTENCE OF MY growling stomach. The kitchen is empty, and I rifle through the fridge. Pulling out a bunch of random containers, I inspect my haul on the marble counter. The dishes contain cooked pasta, meatballs, sauce, steamed broccoli, more muffins, and some cheese and meats. I also saw eggs and fresh herbs in the fridge. Next, I start my hunt for some cookware and utensils. My eyes briefly stop on the knife block before moving on.

Seeing all the ingredients, the craving for an omelet settles in my mouth. I'll start with that and then maybe make my way to the pasta and meatballs. I briefly wonder where they came from and if Nate made it?

At this point, I no longer fear Nate poisoning me. Plus, since I can't leave the estate, I may as well learn how to survive here, starting with the food. Flipping the omelet, I catch myself humming Linkin' Park's "Good Goodbye" and a knot forms in my throat. *Rhys*. I press my hand to my stomach and take a deep breath. The urge to hear his voice consumes me, and I stifle a sob.

"Lilly?"

I jump at the sound of my name but don't turn around. I don't want Nate to see me vulnerable. I'm still livid with him.

"Lilly, please tell me what's wrong."

*Why can he read me so well?*

I take a deep breath before smoothing my features and face him.

"Did your spy cameras alert you that I'm here?" I focus on my rage instead of the suffocating sense of loss overwhelming me whenever Rhys appears in front of my mind's eye.

"No. I came in for some food." He nods toward the containers that are still sitting on the counter. "I made way too much last night when I got hungry and figured I'd finish it."

*So, he actually did make it himself.*

The silence between us stretches, and he stares at his feet. How can a grown man who is a computer genius and runs a billion-dollar hotel empire all of a sudden look like a five-year-old who got caught stealing his sister's toy? I snort at my pun—not toy, he stole *his sister*. Nate looks up at the sound, but I don't feel like elaborating. Instead, I glare back at him.

He shuffles from one foot to the other. "Uh, I'll just come back later." He turns and walks toward the door with slumped shoulders.

Watching him retreat, my throat thickens, but I can't make myself call out. The door swings shut, and I'm alone with my omelet sizzling in the pan. The smell alerts me to something burning.

"Crap!"

I quickly pull the pan off the stove and inspect my meal. It's burned on one side, but I deem it edible. I don't feel like starting over; my stomach doesn't have the patience for it.

SITTING at the chair that has become *my* spot at the large table, I eat the omelet but don't taste anything. My mind wanders between the two men in my life. Rhys, my boyfriend, who I miss beyond words. I worry about him more than myself since he's completely in the dark as to where I am and with whom. Then, there is Nate, the only living blood relative I have as far as I know. He is a criminal. He is mentally unstable. But he is also wicked smart, kind, and...*my brother*.

I need to find a way to contact Rhys. Let him know that I'm okay. Well, as okay as one can be in my situation. And I still want to know more about Nate and...my father. Something feels off about

Brooks. It's time to share my memory with Nate, and maybe I can use that as leverage to contact Rhys. Decision made.

"NATE!"

I'm pretty sure the spy mics will alert him; I don't feel like hunting down *brother dearest* in this maze. And yup, not three minutes later, he bursts through the kitchen door, looking frantically around for possible danger.

"What happened?" He is out of breath, which makes sense if he sprinted from his NASA command center to the kitchen—or wherever in this palace he was.

My heart rate increases, but I'm not backing out now. "We need to talk."

He appears to be taken aback by the force of my voice. "Uh... sure."

He slowly walks over to his usual chair and lowers himself down. Neither of us speaks. I close my eyes and take a deep breath to prepare myself.

When our gazes lock, it's comforting and unsettling how similar our eyes are. We have the same shade of hazel, a little bit of everything, blue, green, with an outer ring of brown. My eyes are more almond-shaped, but we both have the same long lashes—obviously, courtesy of Brooks.

"I want to know more about our father." Oddly enough, I can call Brooks *my father* when I still have problems referring to Heather, Tristen, or even Emily and Henry as my parents.

"Do you have anything specific in mind?" His head is slightly tilted; he's studying me. It's almost comical how I can read him now. I guess having half of the same genetic makeup helps.

"I do. I have something to tell you as well. And a request."

His eyebrows turn skyward again. "That sounds intriguing. What would you like to begin with?" His tone is businesslike, almost cold.

*How does this intimidate me, but not his outbursts?*

"I want to call Rhys. Today. I can't wait any longer. In return, I think my recent memory revealed something you'd want to know."

We sit in silence while he ponders my words. Finally, he asks, "A deal? What makes you think it's of interest to me?"

"Because I remembered our father."

Nate sucks in a breath. "You what?"

"Do we have a deal?" Folding my hands on top of the table, I mimic his businesslike demeanor. I count seventeen breaths before he answers.

"We have a deal. But..." *I knew this was too good to be true.* "I need some time to set up the call. It can't be traceable, and I don't have it all in place here at the moment."

*Oh.*

"How long?"

"Twenty-four hours. I need to finish some other things first."

Another day? I feel like all of the air has been sucked out of the room, and I push the urge to raise my hand to my chest down.

"Not one minute longer," I say with as much force as I can muster without the appropriate amount of oxygen in my lungs. Not that I could do anything if it takes two minutes longer, but I need him to see that I'm serious.

Nate gives me a tight smile and nods.

"So? Would you care to elaborate on what you meant with your last memory being about our father?"

"I think the picture in your NASA command center triggered something."

"My what?" He looks genuinely confused, and a laugh bubbles up in my throat.

"Your computer room upstairs."

The light bulb turns on, and he grins. "Oh, I guess that's a somewhat accurate description."

And just like that, everything is back at ease between us.

*This is beyond disconcerting.*

"I knew Brooks." I pause for a second before explaining. "I met him—at least once."

Nate goes rigid and sits up straight. "How?"

"My memories are never very long, but I'm a hundred percent sure it was Brooks. It must've been around the same time the picture upstairs was taken. I was at a park with Emily. Brooks was there. Emily introduced him as a friend. He shook my hand, and the way he looked at me...he knew who I was."

"Uh. This is...I...uh, I'm not sure what—" Nate's stammering tells me that this is as much a shock to him as it is to me.

"What does this mean?" It's a whisper because I'm as curious as I am terrified.

Nate's face has turned all shades of red, and his fists ball on top of the table.

"This means our father lied to me."

He pushes the chair back with so much force that it topples over and storms out of the kitchen.

*That went well.*

THE CLOCK in the kitchen tells me it's almost six in the evening. Do I go after Nate, or do I wait for him to come back to me? If I wait, will this impact my timeline to call Rhys?

I clean up everything I used for dinner and head toward the center of the house. Few lamps are on, but between the dwindling light coming through the floor-to-ceiling windows and the illumination along the hallway, I'm able to trace my way through the house. I wonder if there is a way to get to my room from the foyer; it's getting old always having to go through the kitchen.

*Great, now I'm acting like this is my house.*

I smack the palm of my hand against my forehead, and the sound echoes through the quiet entryway.

Climbing the stairs to the second floor, I turn right toward Nate's room. He really could be anywhere, but I'll start my search at his command center.

*I need to come up with a shorter name for that room.*

Slowly approaching the door, I hesitate. Do I knock? What if the door zaps me? I wouldn't put it past him to add something like that to his security measures. Oh, what the hell. I step in front of the door and knock. No zap. I wait. And wait some more. Nothing. Maybe the room is soundproof?

"Nate?" I call hesitantly.

Again nothing. What now? Still contemplating my next plan of action, Nate comes around the corner to the right of me—the west wing of the estate, if my orientation is correct.

"Lilly?" I immediately take note of his state of dishevelment. His sweater is gone, the white t-shirt rumpled, and a fine sheen of sweat covers his forehead.

"Uh, I was looking for you."

"You were?" He stops in front of me, eyebrows squished together.

Looks like his spyware didn't alert him—that's new.

The proximity stirs up polar opposite emotions. After his earlier outburst to my revelation of our father and Emily still being in touch years after their supposed affair, I have the urge to comfort him. I can relate to feeling betrayed by one's parents—more than he already was by Brooks's betrayal. To believe one thing and the truth being something different altogether. But the voice in my head tells me that I cannot feel sympathy for him. He is a criminal. He took children from their parents. He kidnapped me against my will. *But he's also your brother,* the other voice chimes in once more.

"I wanted to make sure you're okay. Are you...okay?"

Nate hangs his head. "My father swore up and down that the affair was over when he confessed everything after the funeral. I assumed he meant back when it first happened. I'm not so sure anymore."

His fists begin to ball again, and I do something that startles us both. I reach out and slide my hand in his. We both stare at our joined hands, and then our eyes lock. My brother's eyes are wide, disbelief written all over his face.

I squeeze his hand. "Do you want to talk about it? That's what helped me...I mean, uh, working through it all."

In one, lightning-fast move, he engulfs me in a bear hug and holds on tight. My body stiffens; that's the last reaction I expected from him. His chin rests on top of my head, and he whispers, "Thank you, Lilly." His voice cracks, and I'm as shocked as he is when I return his hug. His spine goes rigid at first before he relaxes again, and we stand like this for several minutes—brother and sister comforting each other.

We both loosen our hold at the same time and take a step back. Everything has changed. We both can feel it. How we move forward from here will need to be determined.

I follow Nate to the library he mentioned during our brief tour. The room is ginormous. Heather and Tristen's entire first floor could easily fit in here. Floor-to-ceiling bookshelves cover three of the walls, complete with a sliding ladder. The fourth wall is all windows. The combination of espresso-colored wooden shelves and floors, more of the same large leather couches as in the sitting room downstairs, and heavy moss-green curtains is completed with different oriental-looking rugs in the same shades of green, beige, and brown. This room has officially become my new favorite place. It's warm and inviting.

"Can I move in here?" I can't stop myself before the words come out in an awed whisper.

"Sure." Nate is completely genuine, and I stare at him, mouth agape.

"But I'm a prisoner. You can't just let me do whatever I want."

*What the ever-loving—?* It seems my brain-to-mouth connection is currently out of commission, and I peer at him like a deer in the headlights. So much for making progress in the brother-sister relationship department.

Nate goes completely still before he bursts into a fit of laughter. He all but howls until tears run down his cheeks, and he doubles over, holding his belly.

"Ow—tha-t hu-rt-s—"

I just stand there, watching him. Is this part of his less mentally stable side? Eventually, I get slightly annoyed and cross my arms in front of my chest, frowning.

Finally, he regains some composure and faces me straight on. "I'm sorry." Another giggle escapes him. An actual giggle from this grown-ass man. "Okay, sorry. Phew. Man, I haven't laughed like that in years."

I'm still confused about why he deemed this so funny.

"Um...why are you laughing exactly? I'm pretty sure I just insulted you."

He's totally serious now. "You didn't mean it," he deadpans. "That was clear as day written across your face when you realized what you said. Your face is very...expressive, and I think you would've looked less mortified if you'd punched me in the junk."

All the tension leaves me, and my mouth turns into a grin. "You're probably right. So, uh...what are we doing here?"

Nate walks over to one of the shelves on the farthest wall. Following him, I notice a slew of papers on the floor in front of it and between the closest couch. It immediately reminds me of my room when I started my research.

Nate squats down next to it and looks up. "I started going through my father's papers again."

That's when I realize that the bottom two rows on this wall are filing cabinets with several of the drawers pulled out, revealing massive amounts of papers.

Nate points at the pile on the floor. "Those are the letters Emily sent. The ones I know about."

I crouch next to him. "What do you mean 'know about'?"

"After I found the first stack of letters from Emily at my parents' house—the letters that contained the pictures of you—I never looked at any of his shit again. I wanted nothing to do with him. His office at the firm was already packed up in boxes, and I shipped most of it up here. There is still a ton of paperwork at their LA house, but nothing of consequence. I started my research into Emily, and any other important documents came straight from the lawyers. I had no reason to look again—until now. I guess I just assumed that she kept sending him updates, and that's it."

I begin to understand what he means. "You think there has to be more?" This conversation gives me déjà vu. Rhys and I had the same type of exchange just a few months ago.

"I do."

Nate's gaze drops to my stomach, and I realize that my arms are wrapped around my midsection again.

"You do that every time you think of *him*." His tone is subdued, and I'm stunned by his perceptiveness. I can only nod, trying to swallow past the lump in my throat.

I squeeze my eyes shut and feel Nate placing a hand carefully on my shoulder. "Hey."

I peek at him from under my lashes, and he says, "We'll figure this out, okay?"

And with that, I lose it. I crumble to the floor and start sobbing. He has no idea that Rhys said almost the same exact words to me.

*Rhys.* Oh God. How can I sit here and make nice with the guy who kidnapped me?

Despite my inner turmoil, I let Nate pull me close and wrap his arms around me while I cry against his chest. He rocks me back and forth like a little child and mutters something that sounds like, "I'm sorry, I'm so sorry," over and over.

When I finally pull away from him, his eyes shine with unshed tears, and his mouth is in a flat line.

I whisper, "I want to go home."

Nate's gaze drops to his hands. "Okay."

# CHAPTER FORTY-EIGHT

**LILLY**

Nate leads me back to my room.

Even in my post-cry haze, I notice that we are not going through the kitchen. He walks past the double staircase that leads down to the first-floor foyer. I expect to see the same bend in the hallway as in the west wing; instead, we stop at another door. It looks like every other door we just passed, and if I hadn't learned the layout of the building by now, I would expect only to find one more room. Nate steps through, and we're standing in *my* hallway. My room is not two doors down, and I grumble, "You could've shown me this way earlier, instead of making me go through the kitchen every time."

Nate doesn't respond. He simply lets me walk past him. Everything is how I left it, and despite this not being my actual sanctuary, being in these lavender walls calms me instantly.

"I'll see you tomorrow," he says, and before I can respond, the door closes with a soft click.

Exhaustion takes over once more, and I fall face down onto the bed.

· · ·

I WAKE UP WITH A START. The room is pitch black, and it takes a moment for my eyes to adjust. My dream has left me breathless. It was so vivid it almost felt like one of my memories.

*RHYS and I were at Bones, eating dinner, when Brooks and Emily walked in. They sat down at a table nearby, talking animatedly, but I couldn't make out what they were saying. Emily was yelling at Brooks, who tried to calm her down. It was like they were in a soundproof bubble.*

*My focus went back to Rhys, who was scowling at me. "Babe, what's wrong?"*

*"I'm not sure. I think I know those people over there." I pointed to Brooks and Emily only to realize they were replaced with Nate and Katherine having a romantic candlelight dinner, holding hands.*

*What the hell?*

*"You should be happy that your psycho brother is finally out of your life." Rhys scoffed.*

*I turned to him and saw disgust written all over his face.*

*I was confused. "Nate is engaged to Margot. What is he doing here with Katherine?"*

*"Nate and Kat are married. You gave him an ultimatum—you or Kat. He chose Kat."*

*"He would never choose her over me. I'm his SISTER." My voice turned panicked.*

*"Then you and I can't be together. You made your choice." Contempt dripped off his voice.*

NOW, sitting in my bed, panting, I massage my temple. That was— Shit, what was that? Leaning back into the pillow, I replay the words in my head. *I'm his sister.* I don't have to be a therapist to understand that, subconsciously, I've made my choice. I've accepted the fact that Nate is my brother. He would put me first, no matter what. I'm certain of that. Of course, there is still the issue of him being a criminal, and he has to pay for it, but first, he is my brother. Hands in front of my eyes, I exhale a shuttering breath.

*All of this because I picked the wrong topic for my journalism paper. Or was it the right one?*

. . .

Throwing back the comforter, I get up and dress in yesterday's clothes, adding a thick black hoodie due to the chilly temperature at night. There is no way I'll fall back asleep. Barefoot, I pad back to the library. Thankfully, a dim hallway illumination remains on at night, or Nate did this for my benefit. Either way, it helps to find the library. Everything is as we left it.

I settle in the middle of the pile of papers and start pulling individual pieces out. They're all handwritten letters from Emily to Brooks, dating back over several years. I briefly wonder why she would write by hand instead of emailing him but then dismiss the thought. It's not really important. I start putting them in order until I have a neat pile in front of me. Then, I begin to read.

The very first one is dated eight months before I was born. Emily tells Brooks how glad she is that she visited Heather during her conference, and she never thought she'd meet someone like him, how much she misses him, etcetera. At the mention of Heather's name, my heart rate doubles. Did she know? Emily was Heather's best friend. According to Rhys's recollection, Emily and Henry were already married at the time, which means she cheated on her husband. What kind of woman was Emily? Rage surges up inside of me, and I fight the urge to rip the piece of paper to shreds. I read each letter in detail and, based on the way Emily phrased things, it's clear they contained pictures. I wonder if seeing them would trigger more memories. Emily mentions how tall I've grown and the uncanny resemblance to "my father." She means Brooks, not Henry—*her husband*. The dates are pretty spaced out, and I'm starting to understand where Nate was coming from. They are superficial; if someone—Payton, for example—would find them, it just seems that Emily kept Brooks up to date on his illegitimate daughter. But nothing points toward the affair still being ongoing.

When I'm through all of them, I sit back and lean against the back of the couch. I've learned more about myself, but nothing of consequence about Emily and Brooks's relationship. I know that I had a teddy named Bobo that came from Brooks and that I never let it out of my sight. I have to ask Rhys if he remembers that teddy. Apparently, I also got my peach allergy from Brooks. Interesting. In one letter, Emily describes that I'm getting more and more daring, playing with Heather's son, climbing trees, balancing on the top of the swing set, and that she thinks she should enroll me in gymnastics. That makes me smile because it relates to two of my favorites —Rhys and gymnastics.

It's the type of information I've been hoping to learn about myself, but the fact that I find it here, in the house my half-brother brought me to against my will, is almost comical.

My stomach starts growling, and I look over the back of the couch. The clock on one of the shelves shows it's almost five in the morning. I decide to take a break to get some caffeine and food. At home, it's already past my usual breakfast time.

*Home. Rhys. God, I hope Nate comes through with the call today.*

Twenty minutes later, I'm back in my spot; next to me is a steaming mug of tea and a plate with yet another muffin. I've consumed more carbs in the last three months than in the past few years.

Pulling open the drawer to the left to see what kind of files this one hides, I start taking out stacks of yellow manila folders. The first few are annual tax returns, nothing of interest to me.

The fifth folder, however, draws my attention. The first page is a bank statement, Brooks's name on the top, and initially, I don't think anything of it. My eyes scan over it, and most transactions are your usual day-to-day expenses—gas station charges, little amounts for something that looks like a coffee house. Nothing out of the ordinary until my gaze stops at a number with way too many zeros. This can't be a regular expense. Brooks transferred fifteen thousand dollars to an account that's only listed with an account number. No merchant or accountholder name. Every other transaction is meticulously labeled with some information on what the charge is for. I flip to the next statement, and there it is—same date of the month, same amount. Brooks transfers the same amount every month for two years from what looks like his personal bank account. Every so often, there is an even more significant number coming in. I make a note to ask Nate about that later. After the two years, the amount increased to twenty-five thousand dollars.

*Where does he get that kind of money as a patent attorney?*

I set the bank statements aside to not mix them up with the rest of the pile and focus on the next yellow folder. I find the closing documents for a house in Los Angeles dated around the time Nate was born. Not relevant. Moving on.

I pull several financial documents and legal papers from the next folder. Audrey's name is on the top of the first stack neatly stapled at the corner, and further reading reveals that it's a trust fund Payton and Brooks set up for her. I flip to the following one, and my hands freeze. There, in black and white, is my name. Not my current name but my birth name: Lilly Ann Sumner.

*What. The. Fuck?*

My hands shake while I turn the pages. When I come to the page that contains the amount of the trust fund, I drop the entire stack. My hands fly to my mouth, and I'm sure my eyes are about to pop out of their sockets. This can't be real.

"Holy shit!" I whisper against my hands.

Gingerly picking the pages back up, I sit there staring at it. My brain has stopped processing information; all I can do is count the black digits over and over.

I must've stayed like this for quite some time because, all of a sudden, I hear the door open, and Nate stumbles around the couch.

"There you are." The last word is drawn out as he yawns. I can't peel my eyes away from the paper. My hands are clasped around it so tightly that it's starting to wrinkle.

"Lilly? What is it?" He squats down next to me and tries to catch my eye. But I can't look away. Ten million dollars. TEN. MILLION. DOLLARS. There must be a mistake. Where did Brooks get that kind of money?

Finally, I'm able to turn my head; my eyes remain glued to the number until I can't see it anymore, and then my gaze meets Nate's. Eyes narrowed, he's trying to figure out what's wrong with me.

Carefully, like handing him a bomb, I start extending my arms. Both hands remain wrapped around the pile until Nate pries it from my grasp. He scans the first page, and his eyebrows shoot up to his hairline. Seems he wasn't aware of it either. He flips the first page, second page, third page—bingo. His wide eyes snap to mine and ping-pong between my face and the paper several times before he ungracefully plumps on his butt.

"Ho-ly shit!"

A giggle bubbles up in my throat, and his focus is back on me, narrowing his eyes as if to assess if I've finally lost it.

"We"—more giggles—"we tru-ly are re-la-ted." My hands are covering my mouth to hide my idiotic expression.

"Yes?" His head slants to the side.

The giggles subside and I explain, "I had the exact same reaction. It's pretty funny, given the circumstances." I shrug one shoulder and smirk.

Nate's mouth tilts up in the corner. "I guess so."

"What does this mean?" I nod toward the papers in his hands. I feel like I am back in control of my thoughts.

"This"—he waves the document in front of me—"means that *you*, little sister, are rich!"

*Why? How?*

Nate keeps scanning the pages, and his eyes widen several times before his gaze settles back on me.

"I stand corrected. You are *more* than rich."

"WHAT!" I tear the pages from his hand and flip through it. I have no clue what I'm looking for, though. My gaze swivels back to him. "What does it say?"

"We need to find my father's will. But if this document is accurate, your trust fund has been accumulating for the last fifteen years, plus there is one passage that refers to his wealth if something would happen to him."

"But—" Words leave me. I'm back in shock mode.

Nate rubs his face. "Here is what we're going to do. First, I need to prepare your call; give me a few hours to set everything up. Then, we will *tear* this fucking library apart and find out what was really going on ten years ago." The anger in his voice sends a shiver down my spine.

"You'll still let me call Rhys?" I sound hesitant, almost timid.

"I told you I would, didn't I?" He looks genuinely offended.

"You did...but I figured..." I trail off.

Nate places his hand under my chin and makes sure I look straight at him. "Lilly, *you* are *my* sister. My *only* living relative, and when I tell you I will do something for you, I will do it, no matter what. Okay?"

The seriousness in his tone causes my pulse to increase.

## CHAPTER FORTY-NINE

### LILLY

NATE LEAVES ME ALONE IN THE LIBRARY WITH THE PROMISE TO get the call ready as quickly as possible. I keep sifting through two more drawers before I give up and trudge back to my room to shower and change.

All clean, I want to lie down for a minute to rest my eyes, but I must've been more tired than I thought because I wake up with the sun high in the sky.

*That's what you get for waking up in the middle of the night.*

I MAKE my way across the second floor—not the kitchen—to Nate's spy center.

Knocking once, I don't have to wait long. I look him up and down and burst out laughing. *What the—?* He is still wearing the pajama pants he slumped into the library with, but up top, he wears a crisp white cufflink shirt with a navy-blue tie, his blond hair styled impeccably.

He scowls at me. "I had to take a call from the board of directors."

That immediately dampens my amusement. If Nate was working, he wasn't setting up my call. He picks up on the shift of my mood and opens the door wider for me to step in.

Every single monitor is lit up. The top three show a dozen different security-camera feeds from all across the estate. Looking closer, I can see the pictures change every so often to a news feed.

*How many cameras are on this property?*

The bottom three show different news channels, as well as something—I'm guessing, the stock exchange? But to be honest, I have no idea. Lots of numbers and graphs, totally over my head.

My gaze swings to the desk, and the remaining laptop—the one that didn't end up against the wall—has some sort of documents displayed. The two other monitors have...what is that? Command line windows? I turn to Nate, who watches me take everything in. He doesn't hide anything this time; he lets me see it all.

"I'm sorry I'm not done. Hank called with an urgent issue that couldn't wait. But I should be done soon."

"How long have you known Hank?"

"He's been with me since the day I took over. He was an intern at the time and worked his way up. His grandfather was a friend of mine. He can be a pain in the ass, but he's been a good friend. All the senior guys still see me as the..." He leaves the sentence hanging. He's referring to his stay at the mental hospital.

*Maybe they're not so far off, given the fact that...*

"Does Hank know?"

Nate blinks at me. "About...? Oh. No. He has no idea about you or..." *The girls.*

I take a deep breath. "Eventually, we have to talk about that."
Silence.

"Yes, we do." Nate looks at his feet. "But let's get your call done first, okay?"

*If we start on the other topic now and you hear what I have to say, I'm not sure I'll get my call.*

"Okay." I try to give him something resembling an encouraging smile, but I'm not sure I succeed.

Settling back behind the desk, Nate's fingers start flying across the keyboard, and I can see him work in both command line windows simultaneously. The programming courses in school have always come easy to me, and I guess I know now from which side I inherited that trade. I'm not computer illiterate by any means, but seeing Nate at work makes me feel like Grandma Ruth when she decided to use the self-checkout line to save time. None of the produce had a bar code, and, in the end, the poor employee manning the self-scanners ended up being the object of Grandma Ruth's target practice when she whipped celery and carrots at his face, followed by her dropping several F-bombs and leaving without her groceries. To this day, she refuses to set foot into that store again. Chuckling, I shake myself out of the memory and watch Nate, fascinated. I have no clue what he's doing.

All of a sudden, a phone starts ringing, and I jump. I haven't heard that sound in so long, and I frantically look for the device. Zeroing in on the desk, I realize it's not mine, but nonetheless, my heart stops a beat. Taking a step closer, I take in the picture on the screen. A stunningly beautiful woman with an elegant hairdo and evening gown smiles back with brilliant white teeth.

Nate catches me staring and answers my unspoken question. "Margot."

"She's gorgeous."

He smiles. "She is."

"Don't you want to get that?"

He hesitates. "Uh, not right now. She probably wants to tell me about all the trouble she and Ce-Ce are causing in the south of France."

"Oh, wow. That uh...that sounds fun. *Who* is Ce-Ce?" I don't want to be nosy, but I am. He's talking openly with me about everything, and I'm soaking it in like a sponge.

"Julian's fiancée. Celeste. He calls her Ce-Ce, and every so often, I slip and use the nickname. J is the only one getting away with it, though. She hates it." Nate chuckles.

Why does the thought of him having a best friend surprise me? He does have a life despite his, uh...other side. The topic keeps creeping up, and we will cover it in the near future, if I want to or not.

The ringing stops, and Nate clears the screen and starts typing again. A few minutes later, he looks over his shoulder. "I should be done in an hour or two."

*Two hours?*

I get to talk to Rhys in two hours. My pulse speeds up, and the insides of my palms dampen in anticipation.

When I don't move, Nate says, "I'll come find you. You should go eat something; you haven't had anything since early this morning." And as if on cue, my stomach rumbles.

*I guess I could use some nourishment.*

THAT'S where Nate finds me two hours later, as promised. Although, I didn't eat. I made food, but it's still sitting untouched in front of me. Before I could take my first bite, I thought about hearing Rhys's voice, my mouth went dry, and my hands were shaking so bad that I couldn't bring the fork to my mouth without losing everything on it in the process.

*What am I going to say to him? He's probably worried out of his mind.*

"You didn't eat."

Looking up, Nate drops into his usual chair.

"No."

"Talk to me." Eyebrows knit together, concern is written all over his face.

"I'm scared." It's a whisper.

"About?"

"What am I going to tell him?"

Nate draws in a breath and exhales slowly while looking out the window. "You're going to tell him that you will explain everything to him and that you will call him again soon."

"Am I?" I'm too scared to hope.

My brother stretches across the table as if to take my hand, but with the table being the size of a one-bedroom apartment, he can't reach me and places his hands, palm down, on the table.

"Yes, you will. As for the actual explaining, keep it to a minimum for now."

I contemplate his words. I will talk to Rhys again. I have no reason to doubt Nate's words.

"Ready?" He looks at me expectantly.

Pushing back from the table, I exhale. "Ready."

. . .

I'M SITTING on the leather couch with the headset Nate handed me a minute ago.

"You'll have two minutes."

I raise my eyebrows. "Not thirty seconds?" I'm joking—mostly.

Nate snorts. "I'm better than that. I could give you ten, and they wouldn't trace the call. But you and I need to work out some things before you have a longer chat with your boyfriend." He says the last part so seriously that I feel slapped in the face.

*Has my desire to have a brother clouded my judgment too much?*

"Okay, here we go. Stick to what we said earlier."

I nod and put the headset on. My heart is in my throat, and I wipe my palms on my pants. The phone starts ringing in my ear, and my breath hitches. Come on, come on, come on—nothing. Rhys's voicemail picks up, but before I can even listen to his recording, Nate hangs up and dials again. This repeats two more times, and I can't hide my panic.

"He's not answering. What if something happened to him?"

"Nothing happened to him." Nate speaks with such conviction that I wonder what he's done to be so sure.

He dials again, and this time, it only rings four times before someone accepts the call. When I don't hear anything, I look up at Nate, who motions for me to talk with his hand.

"Rhys?"

*Please don't have anyone else pick up his phone.*

A strangled sob travels through the earpiece, and my heart breaks into a million shards of glass. What have I done, playing family while my love thinks the worst?

"Are you there?"

*Please say something.*

"Yes." His response is barely audible, but no matter how low, I would recognize his voice anywhere.

An instant calm settles over me. My anchor. I smile. "Hey."

"Cal, I'm so sor—" I avoid looking at Nate; I'm sure he's listening in anyway.

"It's okay. I don't have much time."

That seems to get Rhys's attention. "Where are you? Did he hurt you?"

*Shit.*

Out of the corner of my eye, I note Nate is making a motion to move on. He *is* listening in.

"I'm fine. That's why I'm calling. I...I just wanted to let you know that I'm safe. I'm fine." What am I saying? I sound insane.

"What do you mean? Is he threatening you? Where are you? The house was taken over by the FBI; they will find you." He's getting louder, and I look with wide eyes at Nate.

*FBI?*

My half-brother gives a casual shrug as if that's the most normal thing in the world. He knows, and I understand that they have nothing on him. The call is untraceable.

*I wonder if they even know that I'm not a McGuire?*

"No, they won't. This call can't be traced." I exhale slowly. "I...I just wanted to hear your voice. And tell you that I'm okay. I'll explain everything to you when I see you." I avert my eyes from Nate. He had said *call him again*, not *see*.

"What are you talking about? Babe, where are you? See me when?" He is full-on shouting, and the panic laced with anger is clearly noticeable.

Nate snaps his fingers to get my attention and makes a "wrap it up" motion. No! It's not been two minutes. I send him a pleading look, but he shakes his head. "I have to go. I'll call again. Please tell them to stop looking for me. They won't find me." I rush everything out as fast as I can.

"Please don't hang up."

Tears start welling up in my eyes, hearing his desperation, and I whisper, "I have to go." Swallowing a sob, I add, "I'll see you soon."

*Click.*

"Rhys?" I yell into the headpiece, even though I know he's no longer there.

"I'm sorry, Lilly."

"THAT WAS LESS THAN TWO MINUTES!" I roar with tears running down my face.

"His phone is bugged," Nate says calmly.

"Bugged?" I echo, incredulous, all fury gone. "Can they trace it?"

"No." He doesn't elaborate. Simply no.

"What's the problem then?" I don't understand.

Nate leans back in his chair, crossing his arms over his chest.

"The problem is that someone was listening. You just told him you're fine—that you're *safe*. They will hear that and start asking questions. How can you be fine if you are held against your will?"

*Oh.*

"What are we going to do now? I told him I would call him again." Panic starts building up, and my nails dig into the leather of the couch.

"You will talk to him again, but we need to get the story straight. And we need a different way to contact him."

I cover my face with my hands and let my entire upper body rest on my thighs. I'm not going to lose it; I'm not going to lose it; fuck, I am going to lose it. I jump up and start pacing with my hands interlaced behind my neck. This cannot be happening.

"We can contact him through Wes...or Den. They can get him out of the house."

Nate watches me. "Okay."

"We need to figure out what the deal with Emily and Brooks was; something is off."

"I agree." There is no emotion in his response.

I fully face him and swallow several times before I get the next words out. "And we need to talk about what you did and how you are going to make it right." I almost said *pay for it,* but the phrase feels wrong. He has done terrible things; there is no excuse for taking a girl from her home, no matter what the motivation was. But I also learned a lot of good about him in the last few days, and deep down, I believe he will listen to me.

"We will, and I will make it right."

# CHAPTER FIFTY

## HER



*I dial Gray's number for the third time—no answer. How dare he ignore my calls; he knows better. Especially after the news he broke to me the day before.*

*The sound of the infinity pool's water is like a rushing river. I massage my temples, but it's not helping. Neither the cloudless sky nor the azure-colored water of the ocean I can see in the distance calms my nerves today.*

*I adore this house, which was why I refused to move after our time in this location was up. People sooner or later ask questions, but this property reminds me of the only person I ever loved. Instead, I replaced the staff and ensured none of the old would be able to talk.*

*Last night still has me on edge. That irritating tremor in my right arm hasn't stopped, and my head is throbbing. When that idiot doctor is done upstairs, we're going to have a friendly little chat. He assured me this would stop after the new injections. I tip my chin with my index finger—it might be time to replace the medical staff as well.*

*I use my left hand to reach over to the small square wooden table and pick up the glass with the 2002 Chateau Lafite Rothschild I had Elise pull from the wine cellar. She gave me her usual disapproving look when she brought it out but knows better than to voice her opinions. She is not being paid to think. Plus, she heard what I did to the last maid that refused my request.*

*It's only nine, but since I haven't slept since the alarm went off at one a.m., it might as well be afternoon. My gaze lands on the monitor sitting on the table. The screen is linked to the camera in his bedroom—he's sleeping. Good, the new sedative seems to be working. That's at least something the staff managed to do right in the last twenty-four hours. I watch our personal physician move around the room and check all the vitals. If he would've gotten to the house phone in the hallway, all hell would've broken loose.*

*I grab my cell phone next to the monitor and send a voice message to my head of maintenance to remove that phone. I dislike voice messages, but my right hand won't obey to type, and my left is holding the wine.*

*It's the first time he got that far. I may have to add the restraints back to his bed. I'm not going to risk him ruining everything. Not now. Not ever.*

*THE COINCIDENCE of that happening the same night I get the call about Lilly's disappearance is not lost on me. I've had my eyes on her for years, but when Gray called to tell me that he hasn't been able to locate her in several days, it was clear the only other person interested in Lilly found her again.*

*AND SO IT BEGINS.*

# CHAPTER FIFTY-ONE

### RHYS

I'M FINALLY ALONE.

In the kitchen, Dad and our *houseguests* kept going over the conversation so many times that, eventually, I tuned them out. One guy kept looking between me and his laptop as if he was comparing something. I replayed Lilly's words over and over in my head—the way she sounded, what she said. She wasn't scared. Then, the agent in charge focused on my father and made a comment that caused me to snap back to attention.

"Miss McGuire said she is safe. What do you think she meant by that?"

I sure as shit hadn't mentioned that particular phrase. Something is off. My father eyed me, assessing if I was listening. I averted my gaze and looked back down at my hands.

"I'm not sure. Let's go over the other case files again." I wonder if he tried to divert the conversation while I was in the room or if there was something in the other files that would help.

Up until then, Mom had been sitting silently next to me at the table. "Excuse me. I'm going to lie down."

She stood up and left the room without waiting for anyone's response or a backward glance. I took that as my opportunity to flee as well.

I caught up to her on the second floor. "Mom?"

She turned, her eyes red-rimmed and her usually perfect eye makeup smeared. I'd never seen her that exhausted. She loves Lilly like a daughter, and where Dad is *unusually* calm, she is the opposite. I haven't seen either of my parents like that. I can only explain it that Dad is in full-on military mode, and Mom is—well, she is the mother whose daughter disappeared.

"Yes, honey?"

We've never been super affectionate, besides with Natty. I think forcing me to keep Lilly's secret drove a wedge between us years ago. "Uh, do you need anything?"

She gave me a tight smile and took a step closer, touching her hand to the side of my face.

"No, honey. I just need to lie down for a bit. The call was a good sign; it was just...it was a lot. For both of us."

Her comment startled me.

*Does she know?*

I nodded, and she released my cheek, disappearing to the third floor.

CLOSING the door behind me in my room now, I immediately zero in on my phone. I want to call Wes or Denielle and tell them about Lilly, but I can't shake the feeling that something is off. The agent knew what she said without me telling them. There is only one explanation, and my father allowing this to happen makes my hackles rise.

I glance at the spot on the floor I occupied not too long ago after Lilly hung up on me. The walls start to close in, and I can't breathe. I need to get out. Pulling my boots on, I slip a hoodie over my head, not bothering with a jacket. I grab my keys and barrel down the stairs. I can hear my father call after me as I sprint to my car in the driveway. Pulling out, the silhouettes of two men appear in the doorway, but I back out of the driveway without slowing down. I'm glad Wes left the Defender in the driveway when he drove us home. If I would've had to go through the kitchen to get to my car, I wouldn't have been able to leave that easily.

. . .

Several hours later, I let myself in, unannounced, to Wes's house through the side door. It's the middle of the night, but having had a key for years, no one in the Sheats's household bats an eye anymore when I walk in at all hours. However, this time, when I round the corner to the kitchen, I find Wes and Denielle huddled at the table. Wes's parents are on the opposite side, mugs in front of them. Four exhausted sets of eyes swivel to me, and I stop in my tracks. Denielle's usually impeccably applied mascara is smudged, and even Wes's eyes show red rims.

*What the fuck is going on?*

Before I can say anything, Denielle launches herself out of the chair, fresh tears running down her face, and I can barely brace myself for the impact before she tackles me. Denielle is taller than Lilly, and with her wearing her usual heels—even in the middle of the night—she is almost my height. Her arms wind around my midsection and squeeze so tightly I have trouble breathing.

"We didn't know where you were," she hiccups into my neck.

I return her embrace and blink rapidly. I want to be strong for my friends who have been my support for the last few days. I mumble, "She's fine," into Denielle's hair, which makes Wes look up from his place at the table. He's been my best friend for ten years, but I've never seen him anything but joking or with a tough exterior. Wes is like me; we don't show vulnerability. But looking at him now, it sinks in how the last few days have impacted him as well. His eyes are bloodshot and have dark circles. Like me, he hasn't shaved since Tuesday morning.

I untangle one arm from Den and hold it out to Wes, who doesn't hesitate and stands up from his chair. Wrapping his arms around both of us, I feel him shudder, and my control snaps, tears streaking my cheeks and soaking Denielle's hair. At school, all three of us are *the tough ones*. We're at the top. We don't show weakness. But right now, we stand in a tangle of arms and hold onto each other. Supporting each other.

I hear footsteps leave the room and turn my head to see Mr. and Mrs. Sheats's retreating forms. My guess is they want to give us space.

Wes steps back first and rubs his eyes with the heel of his hands. "Let's go to my room. We have something for you."

*Huh?*

Denielle mirrors Wes's motion, but it only results in her creating more black streaks under her eyes. She has taken Lilly's disappearance just as hard and keeps holding onto my arm as we follow Wes. I'm still confused why she is at Wes's house in the middle of the night, but I figure with Charlie at school, Wes is the only other person for her to lean on. It's not like I'm very useful these days.

Once inside, I drop into my usual spot on his couch, and Denielle sits close beside me. Wes walks over to his desk, grabbing his laptop. While he walks back over to me, he types in something, and I raise my eyebrows.

"Since when do you have a password?"

"Since two hours ago," Wes deadpans. He holds the computer out to me, and I scan the screen. HOLY FUCK! I tear the device out of his hands and place it onto my thighs. Denielle leans in but doesn't say anything.

*Sender: UNKNOWN*

> *Subject: Rhys McGuire*
>
> *Message:*
>
> *Weston,*
>
> *Or should I call you Wes? I'm contacting you despite my better judgment. Lilly believes that you are trustworthy and that you can reach Rhys without the FBI or his father knowing.*
>
> *Before I get to the reason for this message, let me begin with, you prefer hot cocoa over coffee but pretend with your "buddies" that you drink your coffee black. Let me ask you, do the cool kids drink their coffee black these days? When did that become a thing?*
>
> *Your history shows that every night before you go to bed, you check the local and world news, followed by the stock market. You are not the dumb jock you want your peers to think you are. Which brings me to the following question: why? But this is a topic for a later, in-person discussion.*
>
> *As for this message, I promised Lilly two minutes, but her phone call to Rhys was cut short due to an unfortunate bug infestation on the other end. Not that this would've made the call more traceable. So far, no one has been able to trace me. But Lilly revealed information that was solely meant for her boyfriend's ears, and I had to step in. She was not happy when I*

*disconnected the call, and despite my assurance of her speaking with him again soon, I realize soon is not fast enough. I do not like to see her unhappy.*

*You will receive a delivery that needs to be handed over to Rhys. Lilly will call him tomorrow at 6:30 p.m. to finish their conversation.*

*Here are the rules:*

*1. No one besides the people currently in your room is to know about this message, or there will be no call.*

*2. At the time of the call, Rhys is to be in the same spot where Lilly's favorite picture of them was taken, or there will be no call.*

*3. If anyone—and I mean ANYONE—is in the vicinity of Rhys at the time of the call, there will be no call.*

*I apologize for involving you and Denielle in this exchange, but Lilly's well-being is of utmost importance, and it seems her talking to Rhys is an integral part of it.*

*Rhys and I will have a separate conversation as to how he believes he is good enough for her after spending two years with Cheerleader Barbie.*

*This email is untraceable, but for Lilly and Rhys's ability to talk, I must advise you again: DO NOT share this message with anyone besides the three people involved in this exchange.*

*I. WILL. KNOW.*

*P.S.: Please tell Denielle that she should get the bird excrement on her Audi's hood taken care of. Unless she doesn't plan to trade it in again next year. I did prefer her last model, though—much more her style.*

I STARE at the words on the screen, trying to comprehend what I've just read. I mean, I do understand the words, but...how? I glance up and find both Wes and Denielle watching me. Then something clicks—*involving you and Denielle.* I zero in on the girl next to me. She must've sensed that I caught on, because she reaches behind her, pulling out a cell phone from the back pocket of her jeans.

*What. The. Fuck?*

"This is for you." Her tone is flat as she holds it out. I can't tell if she's upset that she got dragged into this—more than she already was—or what? My hands won't obey and take the small gadget from her. My gaze ping-pongs between the phone, Denielle, and my best friend.

"How?" is all I can muster before my voice cracks.

Wes plops down at the foot of his bed and faces the couch.

"The email came a few hours ago. Your father had just called, telling me that you took off and asked if you were here. You left your phone?" He scowls at me. "I tried to reach you."

I don't respond; I just hold his gaze, and Wes nods. The bug infestation.

"They called me, too, but I just told your dad that I hadn't seen you since I left your house. I was about to go to bed when I got this." Denielle wiggles the phone in her hand.

"How?" My entire vocabulary is reduced to one word.

Wes leans forward and rests his interlaced hands on his thighs, looking at me.

"After I read the email, I puked in my fucking trash can." Shaking his head, he nods toward the now empty and clean basket next to his desk. "How does he know these things about me?"

*I would like to know the same thing.*

I know about the cocoa-coffee deception, but only because we ride to school enough that he can't hide the smell from me. He's never admitted it, though, always pretending it was black coffee—extra strong. However, I didn't know about his news obsession. My stomach clenches. I don't care that he's interested in the world's affairs, but I thought I knew everything about my best friend. And the knowledge that the psycho stalker knows more than me about Wes rubs me the wrong way.

Before I can question him further, Denielle speaks up. "I got a text message to check the door around ten, and I found this on the doormat with a note to go to Wes's." She holds the flat phone in the palm of her hand. "Guess he knew you'd be turning up here at one point or another."

"Why are you so calm?" I narrow my eyes at her. Where Wes is freaked out, she is entirely composed. It's unnerving.

Denielle snorts. "Oh, I'm not calm. I dropped the thing like it was on fire and hid in my closet for a good thirty minutes, hyperventilating. How Lilly can function at all is beyond me," she says, sarcasm dripping off her voice.

"She was still in the closet when I called her," Wes chuckles.

Denielle glares at him. "Fuck you, asshat; at least I didn't hurl."

Wes flips her off, and I can't hold back. "Why did you never tell me about the news?"

"That's what you care about?" Wes stares at me incredulously.

"I thought I was your best friend?" I'm acting like a ten-year-old but can't stop myself.

"Oh, you thought I was your best friend. What about you? Why didn't you tell me that you're in love with your sister—who is not your sister? You've been hiding at my house for years, and I just took your dumbass excuses." Wes sneers at me.

"Are you fucking kidding me? I couldn't tell Lilly, but I should've told you?" He can't be serious. I rake my hands through my hair and grab a fistful, pulling on it.

"WHO. THE. FUCK. CARES!" Denielle barks. "Get it together, BOTH OF YOU! You act like fucking imbeciles." Then, she turns to me. "And stop always raking your hands through your freaking hair; it'll decrease your hairline."

*What?*

"Fuck." My hands let go of my hair, and I rub them over my face then focus on the only two people I can trust these days. "You're right; I'm sorry. The psycho has Lilly, who acts like she's on vacation, my phone is bugged, and that freak knows more about us than we know about each other."

"What do you mean she acts like she's on vacation?" Denielle whispers, squinting at me.

I exhale to the count of five before I recap the phone call to them, followed by what I picked up from the agent in the kitchen. My suspicion was confirmed by the email; my father allowed them to bug my phone. Or was it always bugged? Is that why they never cared where I was? They already knew. My hands curl into fists and squeeze so tight that my nails leave crescent indentations on my palms.

"Do you think the dude brainwashed Lilly somehow?" Wes asks hesitantly.

"I don't know," I sigh.

We sit in silence, all in our heads for what seems like forever, when the phone that now lies between Denielle and me lights up with an incoming text message. As in the past, it merely shows UNKNOWN.

I peer at the little square next to me and can feel two sets of eyes focused on me.

"Rhys?" Denielle prods.

I carefully pick up the phone and stare a moment longer before swiping right to open the message.

**Rhys,**

**I see you got my message and package.**

**I want to remind you again to adhere to the rules if you want to talk to your girlfriend tomorrow.**

**She is fine and wishes all three of you a good night.**

I think I'm going to be sick. I definitely can't fault Wes for puking. This. Is. Fucked. Up. Instinctively, I glance around as if to find a camera attached to a drone hovering outside the window.

"What does it say?" Wes's tone is hesitant but curious.

I hold the phone out to him, but he doesn't take it, just reads the screen. I get it; I wouldn't touch this thing either if I had a choice.

"I feel watched." Denielle shudders beside me.

"No shit." Wes rolls his eyes.

I don't like how this psycho is playing with us. I doubt there is a camera in here, but he knows we're together. This only leaves two alternatives: he is either out there right now or has someone watching us, which means there is more than one.

Logic should tell me to contact the authorities stationed at my house immediately, but the urge to hear Lilly's voice leaves no room, even remotely, to consider that.

"Can I stay here until tomorrow?" I ask Wes. Not that he has ever said no, but the circumstances have changed. I'd understand if he wants this phone and me out of his house.

"Sure, man. It's probably best if neither of us is alone." He turns to Denielle. "You need to call home?"

"No, my parents know I'm here. I called them before I came over. I had no intention of going back tonight."

"They're still gone?"

*When are her parents ever home?*

"Again. They were home for two days, but Mom left with Dad for his conference in San Fran. Agnes is at the house, but it's not like I need supervision anymore."

Agnes is the Kellers' live-in housekeeper slash Denielle's nanny growing up. She's worked for them for as long as we've known Den. One would think her mom would stay behind, given the fact her daughter's best friend disappeared and all, but I guess everyone handles things differently. Plus, knowing Denielle, she also puts up a strong front for her parents. This week was the first time she has allowed me to see her as anything but stone-cold and confident. She's Lilly's rock where I'm her anchor, as Lilly said to me one night when we were lying in her bed.

"Let's try to get some rest. Den, you take the bed. Rhys, you know the drill. I'll go get more blankets."

Wes leaves the room, and I head into his closet to grab my pillow and blanket that took permanent residence there years ago. I send my mom a quick text from Wes's phone, and despite the early-morning hour, she responds immediately, letting me know to be safe.

Sleep does not come that night. Instead, I'm hiding under the blanket, staring at the phone's screen. **She is fine and wishes all three of you a good night**.

I start typing several times and erase it again.

*Fuck, what am I doing?*

The little clock at the top of the screen shows it's 3:12 a.m., and despite my physical exhaustion, I'm unable to sleep. After one last deliberation, I cave. What's he gonna do? Stalk me some more? Or maybe he'll kidnap me and I'd be back with Lilly. My thoughts are in a state between sleep deprivation and borderline crazy.

I type: **Please tell Lilly good night. And I love her.**

I'm about to turn the device off when the bubble with the three little dots appears. Sucking in a breath, my heart beats so fast I have trouble catching my breath. The blanket is suffocating me, but I don't dare take it off and alert Den or Wes to what I'm doing. The bubble disappears, and internally I start panicking. No, no, no—

Then the message appears: **ILY2. It's late. Please get some rest. We'll talk tomorrow. ~Calla**

My eyes sting, and I blink. It's her. Sure, he could know my nickname for her—he knows everything as it seems—but somehow, there's no question in my mind.

Another one pops up: **You need to delete my texts. Wes and Den cannot know. Please trust me.**

I stare at the words for several hours before I finally delete both right before sleep overtakes me. I trust Lilly with my life.

# CHAPTER FIFTY-TWO

**LILLY**

I'm too wired; there is no way I will sleep anytime soon tonight. The sound of fear and desperation in Rhys's voice plays on repeat in my head. Guilt is choking me. I'm playing family with my criminal half-brother, while the family who raised me is going out of its mind. I couldn't even tell Rhys how much I love him.

I beg Nate to let me call him back, but his answer remains a firm *no*. He's right, because me being safe either means I'm brainwashed, or I'm collaborating with a criminal—which, I guess, I am.

*Oh God, what am I doing?*


Nate says he needs to get work done and kicks me out with the vague assurance that we will figure out the next steps tomorrow.

Not hungry and unsure what else to do, I head back to the library. I wonder if this place has a gym. I'm in desperate need of a distraction. My gaze falls onto the financial statements I put on one of the upper shelves to not lose track of them. I forgot to tell Nate about them earlier—being distracted with the whole call situation and all. Something else I have to do later. I can't shake the feeling that these transactions mean something.

I've made my way through two more drawers, which as far as I can see only contain Brooks's old case files, when Nate saunters in with an open laptop in hand. He plops down on the couch I'm sitting behind and leans over the back of it.

"Anything interesting?" He has a suspicious gleam in his eyes, which I choose to ignore.

"As a matter of fact, yes."

His eyebrows shoot up, and I stand to retrieve the bank statements, handing them over.

"Look toward the bottom of the page." I point at the amount. "He transfers that amount every month for years before it increases from fifteen to twenty-five thousand dollars. All the accounts and transactions are meticulously labeled, except this one."

Nate flips through a few pages before he looks up. "It's the same account number every time?"

I nod.

"I'll look into it. Shouldn't take too long." He grins up at me. "Good work, sis." His praise, coupled with the endearment, makes my cheeks heat.

I can no longer ignore the mischievous look he gives me. He looks like a little kid who's done something naughty.

Narrowing my eyes, I peer over to the laptop screen. I freeze, instantly recognizing the location of the photo that's taking up most of the screen. Something like an email is partially hidden behind it.

"Nate," I start cautiously, "what did you do?" I can't pry my eyes from the house and three cars displayed on the screen. I would recognize Wes's house anywhere, but the red 4Runner, Denielle's Audi, and Rhys's Defender are a dead giveaway.

"I made sure you get to talk to your boyfriend sooner rather than later," my half-brother says with a smug face.

*Oh. No.*

I'm scared to ask. "How exactly did you do that?"

"I had an untraceable phone delivered to your friend, Denielle, and the instructions for the call to Wes," he says as if he's simply telling me it rained earlier today.

"YOU DID WHAT?" I shriek and dive for the laptop. He relinquishes it without a fight, and I click on the email in the background. My eyes grow wider with every line I read until I feel like they're about to pop out of their sockets.

I re-read the message twice before I close my eyes and take a moment to not go ballistic on my half-brother. Opening them again, I face the man in front of me and level him with what I hope is a death glare.

"Why on earth did you have to sound like a psychopath?" I tilt my head and pause. *Wait a minute.* "And how do you know any of that information? And why do you have a picture of Wes's house? From when is that picture?"

Nate takes the computer back and sets it on the low coffee table across the couch. He motions for me to take a seat, and I make my way around the sofa.

"Any particular order you want those questions answered?" Again, he's devoid of emotion.

I look at him—like, really look at him—and he holds my gaze. He has no remorse for what he's done. Another epiphany about my brother hits me. He shows no emotion because this is equivalent to business for him. He removes any feelings and deals with the problem at hand. I wonder if this is part of his level of genius or a result of his mental instability?

*I probably shouldn't ask him about that.*

I blink once, twice, and peek over at the screen. Taking in a deep breath, I ask, "When was this picture taken?"

"About an hour ago."

Zeroing in on the clock on the bookshelf, I internally add three hours to it. "That was one in the morning."

"That would be correct." Nate smirks as if to amuse a small child who just said something idiotic.

"Stop being such an ass," I snap.

"Ass?" His mouth morphs into a thin line.

"Yes, ASS. Do you get off on these mind games? Why do you have to scare the only people who mean something to me shitless?"

Nate's eyebrows draw dangerously close together.

I wince as it sinks in what I said, and I mumble, "You know what I mean."

"No, little sister, I don't. Why don't you enlighten me?" It's clear I've pushed it too far. My initial reaction is to flee and hide in my room—preferably inside the clawfoot tub behind the curtain.

*I have to save this somehow.*

"Shit. Nate, I'm sorry." I am. Despite everything, we have formed a bond over the last few days. No matter how much I deny it or avoid thinking about it, it's as certain as the fact that Nate has committed several crimes he needs to be held accountable for. "I... uh..." After a deep breath, I go for the truth. "I feel guilty as hell. I'm playing house with my brother while my adopted family, my boyfriend, and my two best friends are going out of their minds. And then you are scaring them half to death. I mean, think about it. How would you feel if someone did that to *me*?" I'm pretty sure that's a cheap shot, but he needs to understand.

I'm rambling without making eye contact. When he doesn't respond, I chance a glance and am stunned by the change in demeanor. Nate's entire expression has softened, and he looks at me with pure affection—not creepy, but brotherly love.

"You just called me your brother," he states with awe.

"I guess I did," I reply with a small smile.

"Thank you." Just like that, all the anger and fight has left both of us. I remember the times when I got into arguments with my *adopted* siblings. You fight; you make up.

"Can we talk about this? I promise I won't attack you anymore." I nod toward the computer.

Nate glances at the screen and back at me. "I may have gone a bit psycho on them." He looks slightly guilty. "Old habits?" He shrugs, and one side of his mouth pulls up.

I only roll my eyes. "Explain. How do you know all of this?"

He settles into the corner of the couch and faces me. "I told you George is still in Westbridge."

"Your bodyguard?" I want to clarify that there are not any more players in this I don't know about.

Nate nods once. "Head of security, but yes. He delivered the phone to Denielle, and he also took the picture earlier."

I narrow my eyes at him. "And why does George think he is spying on my friends and delivering phones?"

"As I mentioned before..." He huffs, exasperated. "He's dealing with the consequences of me bringing you here. Your family thinks you've gone missing, and I want to know what's transpiring on that end. As long as I don't request him to do something illegal, he doesn't ask questions—this time."

"But you did kidnap me. Twice." I cross my arms over my chest and give him a pointed look.

"You're right; I did. But I also said you could go home, so technically, the situation doesn't apply anymore." He grins like he just negotiated his way in or out of a business deal.

"How did you know that it would be the three of them there and not just two when you sent the email?" What if someone else would've been there? Not that I could think of anyone really, but Rhys could've stayed home, or Denielle could've not gone until tomorrow.

"I've watched all of you long enough; I'd say the chances were pretty good. Plus, if one of them wouldn't have shown up, I could've always given that person a little push in the right direction."

*I'm not going to ask what said push would've been.*

"So, what now?" I have to pass the time until tomorrow somehow.

Nate grabs the laptop and clicks a few times. "They're all still at Wes's. Your friend really should get curtains or at least close the blinds."

My eyebrows narrow. He states that so casually that I pull the laptop over to get a better view of the screen again. Sure enough, there is a zoomed-in picture of Wes's room. Rhys and Denielle are sitting on the couch, and Wes is across from them on the bed. Wes's parents' house is a split-level with Wes's room on the first floor, which made taking the picture through the open blinds probably laughably easy. I see another picture behind this one and click on it without asking for permission. It just shows that the room is dark now, and there is a soft glow of...a phone screen under something. A blanket?

"What is this?"

Nate leans over. "The latest picture. George made sure to stay until we knew if one of them left again."

"I get that. But what is *this*?" I point at the glow.

"Probably your boyfriend staring at the text I sent him?"

"WHAT TEXT? You didn't say anything about a text." My voice immediately goes Minnie Mouse on helium.

A rueful Nate looks everywhere but at me.

"Nate." The warning is clear in my tone.

"Chill. Here." He grabs the laptop and pulls another window to the forefront that I didn't notice. He turns the computer toward me, and reading it, my blood starts boiling once more.

"This sounds completely psycho. AGAIN! *If you want to talk to your girlfriend tomorrow*," I purposefully imitate his tone.

Nate looks at me steadily before he places the laptop back on the table. "I am looking out for us. For you! We are not scheduling a lunch date with your BFF. Do you understand the severity of the situation?" I know he doesn't mean to sound condescending, but I can't help but feel talked down to.

"No shit," I snap. "But if you hadn't kidnapped me in the first place, we wouldn't be in this situation."

How ludicrous is this conversation? I'm talking about my kidnapping but refer to it as our situation. I smack my palm against my forehead, and Nate arches one eyebrow.

Shaking my head, I say, "This situation is beyond insane. Just listen to us."

Nate chuckles. "Yeah, I guess you could say that."

At that moment, a ping comes from the laptop, and both of us turn simultaneously.

"What was that?" A chill runs down my spine, and I can't help but glance over to Nate suspiciously.

He grabs the computer and smirks at me. "Loverboy says good-night and that he loves you."

It takes a few seconds for his words to sink in. Loverboy? Who is he talking—Rhys! I rip the device from Nate's hands and stare at the words in front of me. Tears well up immediately.

"Can I reply to him?" My voice is just a whisper.

I can't avert my gaze from the screen. Rhys loves me. He sent the message, not knowing who would read it or if I would ever get it. My heart aches. I miss him so much.

I hear Nate inhale deeply, deliberating. "Yes."

The magnitude of this is not lost on me—what it means for Nate to let me respond. The logical side of my brain tells me to give

Rhys my location; there can't be that many massive vineyards up here. My heart, however, swells at the knowledge of how much my brother trusts me to not expose him, and I can't abuse that—I just can't.

My hands hover over the keyboard...what should I type? I glance sideways. "Can this be traced?"

I'm met with a look that means *You did not just ask me that.*

Turning back, I look at the clock in the corner of the screen. It's so late; Rhys should be sleeping. As much as I want to tell him how sorry I am for running off or that I am not upset anymore about him keeping the Katherine stuff from me, I decide to keep it short.

**ILY2. It's late. Please get some rest. We'll talk tomorrow. ~Calla**

I sign the message with Rhys's name for me. I need him to know it's me. Though, I have no clue if Nate knows about the nickname.

"Remind him to delete the message." Nate's voice brings me back to the present. I quickly type the request and hand the laptop back before I'm tempted to write more. Or completely break down.

"Are you tired?" Nate looks at me with concerned eyes.

"Not really. You?" I slept too long earlier.

"Not really. I never sleep more than a couple of hours."

"Do you have a gym in this palace?"

*I'm mostly joking, but I could use a good workout right about now.*

"How is your shoulder?"

My shoulder? Oh wow, I totally forgot about that. I slowly rotate my shoulder, move my arm up and down. It's still a little sore, but nothing like it was just a few days ago. It feels more like a faint bruise now. I should probably take it easy, but the need to work myself to utter exhaustion is too overpowering.

"It's fine."

WITHOUT ANOTHER WORD, Nate stands up, and I trail after him. He leads me through the foyer and down the hall of the west wing. I haven't been down this way yet.

*Maybe I should ask him for a map.*

At the end of the corridor, Nate opens a set of double doors, and I follow him down another set of stairs. The staircase is double-wide, wider than I would have expected it to be. This was probably another one of his additions. The color scheme of espresso floors and white walls extends to the lower level as well. Stopping on the last step, Nate flips a switch and—whoa.

"What the—?"

Standing on the step next to him, I take it all in. In front of me is a gym that puts the one at school to shame. Any equipment one could ever use is set up in neat clusters.

Nate walks farther into the room and starts pointing at the different groupings. "Free weights, cardio, sandbag, weight machines." He turns to the far wall with two sets of double doors. "The showers are over there." He points at the left set, followed by the right. "And the pool is through there." Before I can say anything, he continues, "The running track is over there."

"Pool? Running track? What the fuck, Nate?" I don't know why I sound so angry; I'm more stunned than anything else. Maybe it's that he has surprised me once again? I'm tired of getting blindsided. Nate stares at me as if to assess the reason for my outburst. I rub my hands over my face. "Shit, I'm sorry. I don't know why I just went off on you."

The corner of Nate's mouth pulls up into a smirk. "You had an eventful day. And night." He leaves it at that.

"I guess," I concede.

"Well,"—he puts one hand on my shoulder—"knock yourself out. I'm heading back up; I need to go through some paperwork before the morning." And with that, he turns and walks up the stairs.

I spin in a circle and grin. The area must span most of the estate's footprint above, if not more.

## CHAPTER FIFTY-THREE

### LILLY

It's past four in the morning when I finally get back to my room.

After I scrutinized the entire gym—everything was high-end, of course—I decided to hit the running track. In the locker room, I found shelves stocked with workout clothes—male and female. I briefly wondered if the female clothes were *mine* or Margot's. In the end, it didn't matter.

*Note to self: ask Nate what to do with the dirty laundry.*

Indoors, I usually stick to the treadmill for my cardio, but running "free" was just too tempting. Despite Nate letting me move around on my own, I didn't realize how caged I felt until it was treadmill versus track. I have no clue how far I ran; the distance seemed longer than the average running track, but it also could've been an illusion since it's all underground. The first few rounds, I marveled how Nate, or maybe his grandfather, had pulled that off— the construction must've been extensive. After that, I turned my brain off and just ran...and ran...until my legs gave out. I'm no long-distance runner by any means; however, when I finally stopped, the clock on the wall showed that it was an hour and a half later. Not to mention that I couldn't even see through the sweat dripping down my forehead. Looking in the mirror, I might as well have jumped into the pool with my clothes on.

Post shower, I found myself sitting by the pool on one of the lounge chairs, staring at the almost sapphire-looking water.

I replayed the phone call with Rhys in my head; he was so broken. Seeing the pictures from Wes's house didn't help ease my guilt either. My friends are worried sick. They're probably scared out of their minds, and I'm playing house in this mansion. I had just worked out for Christ's sake while my family and friends probably haven't slept in days.

*What the fuck is wrong with me?*

My breathing increased, and I put my head between my legs.

I'm not sure how long I tried to get it back under control before the door behind me opened. A moment later, the lounge chair next to me dipped, and I felt a hand between my shoulder blades.

"Talk to me." Nate's voice was low and hesitant.

"Were you spying on me again?" Still being bent over, the question came out muffled.

"I was worried. You're still injured. I didn't want anything happening to you."

*That would be a yes.*

At his admission, my throat tightened, and a whimper escaped me. I tried to keep it all in, but my body had a mind of its own. The tears started flowing. Despite my attempt to keep the sobs to myself, Nate felt the tremors going through my body. Carefully, he grabbed me by the shoulders and turned me toward him. I didn't want to look at his face; if I saw his worry and love for me, I wouldn't be able to focus on my guilt. I shouldn't feel happy about Nate's affection for me. I shouldn't enjoy spending time with a criminal. He took me against my will. He took me from Rhys.

I tried to push him away, but his hold just tightened.

"Let me go!" There was no force behind the words, and we both knew it.

I didn't even attempt to struggle. Instead, I slumped against my big brother and let him hold me. He didn't say anything; he just held me until I had no more tears left.

"You need to get some rest."

Not responding, I just nodded, stood up, and left him sitting there.

OPENING the door to my room, I get yet another surprise. There, on my nightstand, lays a phone. My heart rate increases, and I dive at the small device. As soon as I pick it up, I realize it's not *my* phone. It's a newer model. My gaze falls on a short, handwritten note on the nightstand.

*LILLY,*

*This is your new phone. Your old one was damaged in the accident. With everything that's going on, it took me some time to download your personal data and transfer it over. This is a secure device, but until we can get all the details straight, I won't connect the phone to the network. However, I thought you might want to have your pictures. I also took the liberty of adding some new ones.*

*N.*

SECURE DEVICE? Not connected? What does that even mean? Tapping the screen, the phone lights up, and I stare at the *Enter Passcode* screen. Is this a joke? He's giving me a locked phone. No, he isn't. Nate would find a way to reprogram this phone with *my* passcode.

Slowly, I press my thumb on the four digits, and sure enough, I'm met with my background screen—a picture of Denielle and me from last summer. Sloane took the photo when we all were at the lake together.

Hesitantly, I click on the rainbow-colored flower. At the top is an additional folder labeled "Lilly." I tap the album, and my breath hitches. The first picture is the one of Rhys and me at Bones. The one in which I had leaned into him, eyes closed, looking so...happy.

I keep scrolling and find the picture that made it to the Internet, thanks to brother dearest. As much as I would love this photo for reminding me of the moment Rhys kissed me on the steps of Denielle's house, the negative association of everyone staring at me with judgment and contempt has ruined the picture for me. My thumb briefly hovers over the little trash can icon, but I decide against it. I want—no, I *need* every picture of Rhys I can get at the moment.

Next is a picture of me at Magnolia's. It's the day I met with Denielle and told her everything. Denielle is walking away from the counter, and I'm looking at her retreating form—probably trying to figure out what my best friend is wearing. I smile to myself, remembering the moment I took in her unusual attire, when something else catches my eye. I zoom in with my thumb and middle finger. A few steps beside me is the creepy guy who talked to me that day. He is slightly blurry as the camera's focus is on me, but you can make out how he's staring at me. Leering. A shudder runs down my spine.

Following are random shots of me with Denielle. From the gymnastics meet and us walking to or from school. I don't look closer and keep scrolling.

The surprises keep coming as I stare at the photo now displayed on the small screen. We were so careful. We waited over ten minutes to even get out of the car, but there it is, clear as day—or night, for that matter. Rhys and I are sitting at the small corner table in the café several towns over the night Nate sent his first message. Rhys is holding my hand, and we are looking at each other.

I'm sure that no one entered the café after us that evening.

The last photo makes my breath hitch. It's not a photo at all; it's the still of a surveillance or security camera. In. My. Living room. Rhys and I are cuddled up on the couch under my favorite throw blanket. He's placing a kiss on my temple, both of us holding a mug in our hands. What is this? I'm going to be sick. I jump off the bed and race out of my room.

"NATE!" *Where the fuck is this piece-of-shit brother? He went too far!* I roar his name as I run past the staircase coming up from the foyer. I pound at his office slash NASA control center but don't get an answer.

"NAAAATE!" I'm shaking from rage.

My brother comes tearing out of the last room before the hallway turns; he is still trying to pull his shirt over his head when I attack. I hit him full force across the jaw, and he stumbles back—stunned.

"What the—?" He's holding his jaw, and I'm panting, trying to catch my breath.

"You sick asshole! How could you?" I clench and unclench my hands. I'm ready to strike again, but I'm sure he'll block me now that I got one hit in.

"What the fuck are you talking about?" Now Nate is fuming, but at the same time, he looks at me with wary eyes.

"This!" I shove the screen in his face. "Wasn't it enough for you to spy on me from afar? You had to break into my home?"

Nate glances at the screen then back to me. "That wasn't me."

With those three words, my rage deflates. "What do you mean?" I rasp.

All of a sudden, Nate looks...nervous? Apprehensive?

"Come with me."

As soon as Nate sits down in his desk chair, all the screens come to life. It's as creepy as it is fascinating. The wall monitors currently show the surveillance cameras of the property—some inside the house, some outside with what looks like night vision.

I stand behind him as he starts typing in a command line window on his laptop. He types something and flips everything to the monitors on his desk. Then, he opens a second window and starts typing there—then a third and a fourth. Both monitors on his desk display black windows with green lines of code. It looks like he's running some kind of program, but what do I know?

"This may take a moment. Tristen changed the passwords," he murmurs.

*Tris—what?*

All I can do is stare at the screens. Every so often, Nate types something in, and then lines of code start scrolling over the screen again. According to the clock on one of the wall monitors, it's 4:30 a.m., and by the time all six screens on the walls go dark, the little numbers on one of the desk monitors show 5:12. The entire time, I stand there watching, neither of us talking.

"Here we go." Nate's finger hovers across the enter key. "I want you to know that I had nothing to do with this. I didn't know about it until the week I decided to speed up the timeline. George came across it while doing recon, and I later went back through the feeds as far as I could. *That's* how I got the picture. I honestly just thought that you would like that picture of you and...your boyfriend. I'm sorry. I'm an idiot." The last few words are spoken so low they're barely audible.

Nate turns for the first time since we came in here, and our gazes lock. He scrubs a hand over his mouth.

"Okay," I rasp out.

He hits the key, and all six wall screens come back to life. This can't be. I try to draw in a breath. I can't breathe. I clutch my hands to my chest and stare. In my kitchen are several strangers. Tristen sits at the head of the table, half-hidden behind his laptop. I focus on the other pictures in front of me: the living room, the entryway, the garage, Heather and Tristen's bedroom. I squint, and sure enough, Heather is curled up in the bed. My eyes take in every small rectangle displayed on the wall right now. There must be at least two dozen cameras in the house, including—FUCK.

"This is my room..." I'm going to be sick. I force myself to look at Nate. "Did you go through the feeds?" What I'm asking is *Are there videos of Rhys and me?*

"I have." Nate's face gives me the answer without having to voice the question. My knees buckle.

THE FIRST THING I hear is the clicking of keys. My cheek sticks to the material I'm lying on—what the heck? I slowly start moving, and when I attempt to turn over, a wall stops me. Oh, I'm on the leather couch in Nate's office, a blanket draped across my legs. My face was stuck to the seat cushion, and now I am plastered against the back of the sofa.

*How did I get here? What time is it?*

"It's almost noon," my brother's voice informs me.

*Did I ask that out loud?*

I drape one arm over my eyes, debating if I should go back to sleep. If I'm asleep, there can't be any more surprises. No more lies that make my life an even bigger farce.

"I'm sorry you had to find out like this." The sorrow in his statement is palpable and makes me want to curl up in a ball.

"Why are there so many cameras in my house?"

"I don't know, little sister. I'm trying to find that out."

That gets my attention, and I sit up. "What do you mean?"

"I mean, it doesn't make sense that the house is wired like it's for an episode of *Big Brother*. That your and Rhys's phones were tracked; this all seems to be overkill. If it were just about me"—Nate pauses and looks at me with his mouth pressed in a thin line before continuing—"it would be sufficient to cover the entrances, maybe the phones." He trails off again.

"You think there is more behind it?"

"I do. Until last night, I only went in once—right after George informed me of the *'internal surveillance within Miss Lilly's residence,'* as he called it." Nate chuckles, and I cock my head.

"George can be very...formal," he explains and, after a breath, amends, "when he wants to be. He switches from cussing me out to talking like an old English lord within the blink of an eye."

"Um...is he...?" I make a swirly motion with my forefinger next to my head. It wouldn't be surprising if one crazy dude employs another, right?

Nate barks out a laugh. "No, he's as sane as they get. He is more levelheaded than anyone I've ever met."

"Sooo...?" I let the sentence hang, hoping Nate will continue without me having to probe.

"He was raised very...traditionally. His parents were part of New York's high society. He had a personal tutor and all the shit that comes with it. George rebelled, left school, and joined the military. He left his life behind and didn't look back. But after he got injured —he never told me exactly what happened—he needed to start over. That's when he came back to New York and became a P.I. He refused his family's fortune. He ran into my mother one day, and she remembered him, even though he was several years older. They used to run in the same circles. Somehow, the connection to my grandfather was made. He's been working for us since, in one way or another."

*Or another.*

"Couldn't you find out what happened to him?" My curiosity is piqued.

My brother looks thoughtful for a moment. "I could. I checked him out on the surface, but whatever he did in his past is well hidden. He is very good at disappearing. Unless you know where to look, you won't find anything about George Weiler. He had already worked for my grandfather for years. I've seen him around for just as long growing up. I trust the man, and it seems wrong to invade his privacy more than necessary."

I almost laugh out loud. Nate, who has no qualms about hacking into a school surveillance system or implanting a program on a hospital server, doesn't want to spy on his bodyguard—or whatever the man is. However, the sincerity in Nate's voice makes me refrain from making a snarky remark. Instead, I change the topic. "So, what are we doing about the cameras in my house?"

"Nothing."

"Nothing?!" I want to demand answers as to why the hell there is so much surveillance in my home. I'm about to say so when Nate's raised hand stops me. Apparently, he recognizes the signs of an oncoming rant by now.

"It's not important at the moment. They've been there for a long time from what I've seen. For now, we have to focus on the tasks at hand."

"Which are?" I finally round the desk, looking at the monitors. One is covered with surveillance pictures and one with—I have no clue. It seems like some interface, but I have no idea for what.

Nate holds up one finger. "Getting your story straight. Our story." Finger number two joins the first. "Making sure you get to talk to Rhys and"—he adds a third finger—"figuring out our next steps."

I blankly stare at him for several moments before conceding. "Okay"

SUDDENLY, Nate stands up and walks out of the room. Over his shoulder, he calls, "Hold on one sec."

At first, I am shocked that he leaves me here alone, all the computers unlocked, but before I can even debate using this to my advantage, the door clicks open again. Nate rolls another desk chair through the opening and positions it next to his. "Sit."

I follow his command and wait, unsure of what's happening.

"Before we do anything else, we are changing the security in your room, and I am going to show you how to navigate the system. I want you to learn your way around."

*Wait. What?*

I can't believe my ears. He's giving me access? To the *whole* system? I must have misunderstood. Nate starts hitting some keys, and in addition to both monitors now showing the same interface, the wall screens are lighting up with the usual surveillance footage of the property. A few more keystrokes and I am looking at the rumpled sheets of my bed on full display on the bottom middle screen.

My stomach clenches at the thought of Nate watching me sleep like that. But before I go down the rabbit hole too far, he starts pointing at the screens on his desk and explains, "This is the interface to the security system for the property. You can also control everything via command line, but until I can properly teach you, this will be easier." He points to a drop-down field. "This lets you select the main area you want to look at: 'East Wing – Second Floor.' Then, you click here and choose which camera you want to review." He points at another drop-down. "Your room is labeled 'Bedroom: Lilly.' Most rooms have just numbers unless it's something obvious, like the library or an assigned room. See..." Nate changes the first selection to "West Wing," and in the next window, I see an option for "Bedroom: Margot."

Confused, I ask, "Why does Margot have a bedroom?"

My brother grimaces. "Umm..."

My eyebrows draw together.

He finally sighs and confesses, "Margot doesn't sleep in my bedroom."

"Huh?" They don't sleep in the same bedroom?

"I don't let anyone stay in my private bedroom on this property. It's my, uh...*space* if you want to call it that. The first place I felt safe again after I left the hospital. Margot thinks that the bedroom we share here is where I always sleep. She doesn't come here that often and usually just for a weekend, so she's never questioned it."

What do you respond to that? As excited as I feel about him sharing more information with me, I'm just as weirded out. I can't fathom not wanting to share my bedroom with Rhys. But then, Nate has a whole other set of issues.

After an awkward moment of silence, he clears his throat and begins to explain more of the interface, neither of us wanting to talk further about the topic. Nate even shows me how to navigate it via command line, though he might as well have spoken Urdu at that point. Eventually, he changes it back to my bedroom and shows me how to pull up the password console with a combination of keys. There is no menu option to change the password, just a key combination.

*I should probably take notes.*

"Here." Nate pushes the keyboard to me. "Change the password to whatever you like, but nothing too easy. It was laughable how quickly I got into your phone and email. I didn't even need an algorithm."

*My email?*

I hit him over the back of the head. He looks at me sheepishly, knowing exactly why I did it.

"No more hacking into your emails; got it." That gives him another smack, and Nate laughs. "And the phone."

I glare at him. Pulling the keyboard over, I try to think of a password. Hitting the enter key after confirming my password three times—not twice—I mumble, "This is the weirdest program I have ever seen."

"I designed it."

My head jerks around, and I search his face to see if he is messing with me. He designed it? *The entire system?*

"I knew what I wanted, and it wasn't available on the market...so I built it myself."

My brother is a freaking genius. If I had any doubt before, I am sure now.

"Can you teach me?" I'm in awe. I always knew I wanted to do something with math or computers, but seeing this...I *need* to learn how.

A broad grin spreads over Nate's face. "Of course."

# CHAPTER FIFTY-FOUR

## LILLY

NATE TELLS ME TO GO SHOWER AND EAT SOMETHING. HE ate earlier while I slept and needs to talk to George about the call. George has been keeping an eye on Rhys and my friends all morning. Nate promises to bring me up to speed when I'm back but emphasizes that I should take my time. Translation: go away; you're slowing me down.

STANDING in the shower after scarfing down yet another round of carbs, my adrenaline spikes as I think about him leaving me alone with his computers. I could've woken up at any point, used the opportunity to try and contact someone. The trust he has in me after these short few days is humbling. If I thought the line between brother and criminal-slash-kidnapper was blurred before, the boundaries of acceptance of my current situation have shifted to the point of no return. I won't be able to label him a criminal, turn him over, and move on when this is over. My stance on him paying for what he's done hasn't changed; he needs to take responsibility. But I know that I will be by his side through all of it.

. . .

I'M BACK in front of the NCC—the now official callsign for Nate's NASA command center—at precisely 2:13 p.m. One hour and seventeen minutes to go. I took as much time as my nerves allowed me, which was fifty-two minutes after Nate closed the door in my face.

I knock, and I give Nate a shoulder shrug with my best *hi-I'm-back* grin when he looks me up and down. My brother's shoulders slump when he sees I am here to stay.

He swings the door open and moves out of the way. Walking in, I come face to face with—holy shit. I stumble backward and bump into my brother's tall frame. His arms shoot out to steady me, and he whispers into my ear, "Lilly, meet George."

On one of the two monitors on Nate's desk is the face of a man —a man that could haunt nightmares. All I see is the massive scar. It runs from the left side of his forehead, down across his cheekbone, over his nose, and down to the right side of his neck. His skin is weathered, and his pronounced cheekbones and small eyes remind me of the picture of a mummy I saw in history class last year.

HIS DEMEANOR SOFTENS when he spots me, and his entire face turns...friendly? "Hello, Miss Lilly. It's nice to finally meet you." George's voice is gentle and in such a stark contrast to his... appearance.

"You just cursed me out, and 'Miss Lilly' gets a full-on smile. I didn't even know your mouth could turn that way." Nate scoffs and steps around me, walking back to his desk.

George follows Nate's movement with narrowed eyes. "That's because you either act like a spoiled, entitled brat, or I have to clean up your mess. You don't give me a reason to be friendly with you." The words are harsh, but his mouth twitches ever so slightly in one corner. He cares for my brother.

"Let's get back to the task at hand. Lilly, sit! We only have one hour until call time; let's not waste it more."

I follow his command, unsure of how to take the sudden tension. Sitting down in the chair Nate brought in earlier, George's gaze meets mine before he looks back at my brother.

"Denielle Keller left the Sheats's residence a few hours ago. She is back at her house. Weston and Rhys are still at Weston's house. I scoped out the location earlier, and everything is secure. I installed the wireless cameras you requested, so we have eyes from every angle. I also added one at the entrance for early warning."

Nate nods at George's recap. "The trackers are in place?"

My head snaps up. "What trackers?"

My brother briefly glances sideways. My gaze swivels between the two men; their silent communication makes me clench my jaw. I don't like being out of the loop.

"Nate..." I growl.

Instead of Nate, George speaks up. "I advised your brother to track everyone's movement today. Not just Rhys's. I understand that your relationship with your brother has...evolved." He gives Nate a pointed look. "We can't be too careful at this point. Even though the situation has changed on your end, there are a lot of unknown factors here. With the FBI at the McGuire residence, I am making sure that Nate and you are protected."

I'm speechless. This man just met me, and yet he acts like I'm—what?

When I don't say anything, Nate addresses George. "Thanks, man. Is everything plugged into the network yet?"

"The trackers, yes. The cameras, shortly. I just finished the placement before you called. I'll message you once it's done. Shouldn't take more than twenty minutes."

"Sounds good. Establish connection in an hour."

He disconnects the video-chat without saying goodbye.


WE SIT IN SILENCE, and I replay George's words in my head.

"Should I be worried?" My voice is timid.

My question is vague, but Nate understands what I'm asking him. "Your story needs to be ironclad. And even then, I don't think I can protect you from everything. People will ask questions; some won't believe you. You'll be under surveillance."

My heart is already beating double-time, but I catch on to Nate's words. "You have a plan." It's not a question; I know he does.

"I do, but it will require you to stay, um...a little longer."

"How long?" I peer at him carefully.

"Ten days."

"WHAT? WHY?" My entire body begins to shake. Ten days? That'll make it two weeks. *No.* "NO!" I jump up and start pacing. "You said I could go home," I cry.

"Sit down, please." Nate's gaze follows my every step.

I don't want to sit. The sensation of being trapped builds inside my core and starts spreading. I can feel it all the way to my fingertips. I need to get off the property. I have access to the system. I can find my way out.

On my eighth lap, two strong arms circle my upper body, pinning mine to my side. "Lilly! Listen to me."

I begin to struggle against his hold.

"Please, little sister." Nate is pleading with me, and I stop my fight. He immediately loosens his hold, and I turn. He points at the chairs. "Sit. Please?"

Facing me in the chair, he draws in a deep breath. "I understand you want to go home. And you will; I promise you." His tone is sincere. "But..." *Here we go.* "I need to make sure my alibi is also in place, and for that, I need more time. Plus, none of the others have ever, uh...reappeared after just a few days. All these things would raise more questions—questions I can't help you with once you leave here."

I sigh, covering my face with my hands. He's right; the others were all gone between two and three weeks. Looking back at him, I ask, dejected, "What's the plan?"

"I have to go back to LA next week. It's just three days, but I can't get out of it, which in the end, will work in our favor. I'm well-known and will be recognized in public. If there's a suspicion linking me to your case, this will solidify my alibi."

At his last sentence, my eyes snap to his. The way he says it, it would sound casual to an outsider, but I notice the slight drop in his voice. Talking about it makes him uncomfortable. *As it should*, the voice in my head chimes up for the first time in a while.

"I see," is all I come up with.

"As soon as I'm back, we'll start the process of getting you home. But since you can't just get on a plane, we have to find another way. I have some ideas but need to run them by George first."

*Why does he need an alibi if he's going to pay for his actions?*

The voice inside of me is on a rampage.

"Nate?"

"Mhmm?" He has started typing in one of the command line windows again.

"Why do you need an alibi if you are going to take responsibility for what you've done?" Despite focusing on my hands in my lap, I notice immediately that the typing has stopped. Sweat starts building inside my clasped palms—I'm risking my phone call by confronting him.

Suddenly, my head is tilted upward with a gentle hand, and my eyes hesitantly meet my brother's. The anger I expected is not there.

"Because I have to make sure that you are safe and settled before I go away. I don't want to be rushed and risk your life in any way."

Understanding hits, and I squash the voice that is telling me that he's just making excuses to not go to jail. Deep down, I believe him. The same way I have the urge to take care of him, he wants to take care of me before he faces the consequences. I nod and turn to the monitor. No idea what he's doing, I watch, fascinated, as his fingers start flying over the keyboard again.

Fifteen minutes later, according to the clock on the screen, a message window pops open and reads: **All set**.

"Finally," Nate grumbles to himself.

Another five agonizing minutes go by before the wall monitors flicker to life. Holding my breath, I take in the scene in front of me. Woodland Park. I haven't been there in a while, but I'd recognize it anywhere. Nate adjusts certain angles, and eventually, all cameras point to the same spot. The spot our picture was taken so many years ago. My eyes sting, and I realize that tears are running down my face.

"Thirty minutes to go. George will call in shortly." Nate squeezes my leg.

. . .

NATE IS in the process of setting up the headset as an incoming video call pops up on the screen. Without pausing what he's doing, Nate says, "Accept," and George's scarred face fills the screen.

"WHAT THE HELL?" I shriek.

Nate smirks without looking up, and George assesses my probably bulging eyes with a raised eyebrow.

"How the fuck did you do that?" I address my brother, who is still ignoring me.

"Language, Miss Lilly," I'm chastised by Nate's bodyguard—how wonderful.

"Sorry," I say like a five-year-old caught repeating a curse word she heard from her big brother. Nate snorts. He seriously snorts, and I smack him over the head. Again. This seems to have become my go-to reaction.

"What? I told you I designed the system," he responds, exasperated.

I'm amazed by how much we behave like siblings. He teases me; I retaliate in juvenile, little-sister fashion. Something else occurs to me: Rhys and I never acted like this. We bantered, we teased, but in a completely different way. For as long as I remember, I had this underlying feeling that I used to chalk up to him being my best friend. But having my real brother next to me, I realize there has always been more. Den's words come back to me. "Whatever that memory doctor did to you, he wasn't able to fully erase what you and Rhys already had..."

Before I can say anything else, George begins with his updates. "Weston has left his house and is on his way to Miss Keller's residence. Two minutes out. Agent Camden left the McGuire residence and went home; no one else has come or gone. Rhys left Weston's house about four minutes ago and should be at the location in seven."

By the time he finishes, I feel like I have a unibrow. "Uh..." I hold up a finger, and two sets of eyes first look at my finger then at my face.

"Yes, Miss Lilly?"

Since George is the one giving me his attention, I face him. "How do you know all that?"

George, in return, dips his head at my brother. "Show her."

Something is sucking all the air out of my lungs. *Show me what?*

Nate remains mute and starts typing.

*Does he ever use a freaking mouse?*

One of the six mounted monitors changes, and it takes me a moment to grasp what I see—a map of Westbridge. There are different colored dots—red and blue. Each dot has a small rectangle next to it, showing initials. I stand up and get as close as possible. D.K., W.S., T.Mc. I scan the map, and there he is, still moving and getting closer. R.Mc. Then I notice that there are duplicates. There are two D.K.s and two W.S.s. Focusing back on the only dot I care about at the moment, I see only one R.Mc.

"What are the dots? Why are there two for some?"

Nate finally joins the conversation. "Some are trackers; some are cell phones." His tone is conversational, as if he just informed me we'd be having two different kinds of pizza for dinner.

"You hacked into my friends' phones?" I ask him incredulously.

"No, I used their Friend Finder app. It's not my fault none of them have any sense of privacy and have their location service permanently enabled. Tristen, well...yeah, he's a bit more cautious." That's where he leaves it.

I focus back on the map; Rhys has arrived at Woodland Park. I turn to the other monitors and see the Defender parked in the small lot by the picnic area.

"What time is it?" I whisper. It feels wrong to speak at a normal volume.

"3:20 Pacific Standard Time, 6:20 Eastern Standard Time," I faintly notice George answering.

"Are you in place?" Nate's question startles me, and I swivel around to see his face.

"I am."

"In place where? Where are you?" This is the second time I directly address the man with the massive scar. The bone-jarring fear his appearance initially instilled in me is gone.

George seems to notice as well; his eyes widen for a fraction of a second before he smoothes his features. "I've parked 1.3 miles away from the call location. We have eyes on everyone; there was no need for me to be on site." He sounds like he's talking about a military mission.

In my peripheral vision, something moves on the upper right wall monitor. Rhys has gotten out of the car and is making his way across the grassy field. The instant sensation in my abdomen causes me to smile. There he is. My gorgeous boyfriend. I missed him, but I didn't realize how much I missed this feeling—my hornets on steroids. Before I ended up here, I was so furious about him hiding something from me that I withdrew myself out of self-preservation, suppressed all my emotions to not risk getting hurt.

I feel a hand on my arm, and I peer at my brother over my shoulder.

"It's time." He holds out the headset.

I want to take it, but my hands start shaking, and I can only stare at the outstretched device.

"Look at me." His soft command makes my eyes travel upward to meet his. "It'll be ok. We have all the security measures in place. Talk to him." He puts the headphone on my head, making sure it sits properly, a gesture so familiar, like he's taken care of me his whole life. My lips press together in a tight smile, and I blink rapidly.

"Let's get going." Nate directs his attention back to George and the screens on the desk.

My focus is on Rhys. He is jumping in place and keeps tapping the phone in his hand. He is as nervous as I am. It's like looking into a mirror. I zone everything else out and watch. Nate and George are running through...I have no clue and, to be honest, also don't care. All I want is to hear Rhys's voice again.

"Little sis?"

"Mhmm?" The typing and chatter have stopped.

"I asked if you're ready?"

*Oh!*

Nate sounds hesitant, probably confused as to why I didn't respond. Watching Rhys made everything fade into the background.

"Yes," I breathe, still staring at the screen.

"Let's do this." Two more clicks and I hear the dial tone in my ears. I focus on the beeping as if I could miss Rhys picking up.

"Lilly?"

*God, how I have missed his voice.*

Just hearing my name from him makes everything fall into place, and I can't stop the broad grin spreading across my face.

"It's me," is all I can think of saying. I mean, duh.

George's voice penetrates my happy haze. "Car approaching!"

"FROM WHERE?" Nate is shouting. I've never heard anything even remotely close to panic in his tone—until now.

"Main gate. CUT THE LINE!" The last three words are an order. George has taken charge.

I flip around. "WHAT? NO! NATE! YOU CAN'T!" But the line is already dead. "RHYS!" I cry, gripping the headset, spinning back to the monitor, but of course, there is no answer.

I feverishly gaze between the screen and my brother. "Nate? What is happening? Who is this?" Tears are streaming down my cheeks as I witness the scene unfold in front of me.

*How is this even possible?*

"NATE, DO SOMETHING!" This can't be happening. My entire body is shaking. But there is nothing anyone *can* do.

I faintly register my brother questioning how George could've missed this. He is furious with his head of security. I can't watch any longer. They are still arguing when I turn and address the men in the room and on the monitor. "FIX THIS!"

"Lilly."

"Miss Lilly."

They both start at the same time, but my adrenaline is so high that I lose all control over the little rational thinking I seemed to have left in this situation.

"I DON'T GIVE A FUCK HOW YOU DO IT. FIX IT!"

I zero in on Nate and force myself to lower my tone to a less hysterical volume. "You promised me I'd get to talk to him. Fix it. YOU. PROMISED. ME!" I jab my finger at the space between his eyes.

I need to get out of here. Before either of them can respond, I charge toward the door and tear it open.

"FIX! IT!" I scream again before I let the security door slam shut.

## CHAPTER FIFTY-FIVE

**RHYS**

I thought six-thirty would never come. From the moment I opened my eyes—which, thankfully, was mid-morning due to my late night—I felt this constant current running through my body. A perpetual need to move.

Around two, Den announced that if she saw me pace the room one more time while raking my hands through my—in her words —"*already receding hairline*," she'd kick me in the balls, followed by tying my hands behind my back and stuffing me in the closet. Those were her parting words as she stormed out of the room.

*Dramatic much?*

I was about to yell after her where she could stick her bitch attitude when Wes put a hand on my shoulder. One head shake was all it took to deflate the anger toward Lilly's best friend. For a brief moment, my rational thinking was back. I got it. I would drive myself fucking bat-shit crazy if I had to sit there and watch.

Wes received a text from her when she got home, but she didn't come back for the rest of the day. We attempted to distract ourselves with video games, but that only lasted for so long. I would continually stare at the phone laying on my thigh and fuck up. Eventually, I told Wes to get out. It was almost six, and I'd be leaving anyway. I wouldn't need any more babysitting. My best friend didn't look convinced until I pulled out my phone and dialed Den's number.

"Everything okay?" Her answering tone was panicked, all the earlier annoyance gone.

"Yeah. All good." I had called her on speakerphone and looked directly at Wes when I continued. "Listen...uh, I'm about to head out. Wes is coming over to your place."

Wes narrowed his eyes at me while the other end of the phone remained quiet. My friends are no idiots; they knew what I was doing. I didn't want all of us to be separated. I needed the assurance that they were together. Safe.

"I'll be over in ten," he addressed Den while giving me a curt nod.

"'Kay. You got the code for the gate. I'll open the garage for you to pull in." Den was all business. Her guard-dog persona that always watched over Lilly had extended to Wes and me over the last few days.

I hung up before either of them could add anything else.

"You sure you're okay?" My friend's concern was laced through the question.

My hands halfway to my head, I paused mid-action and huffed out a laugh. My arms fell to my sides, and I stared at the ceiling for several heartbeats.

"No. But you read the email." That was all that needed to be said.

Grabbing his jacket from the back of his desk chair, Wes left the room without another word. I was alone for the first time since getting the email and phone. The urge to send another text message overwhelmed me, but I couldn't. For one, I had deleted the incoming texts. And two, I couldn't risk not hearing her voice tonight. Tapping the screen, I saw it was 5:53. It was a ten-minute drive at this time of day.

At one point before she left, after I had paced probably a mile and a half through Wes's room, Den asked cautiously if I even knew where I was supposed to go.

"Yes," was all I said. Neither asked for more detail—not that I would've given it. The location was a no-brainer after reading the email. Woodland Park. Lilly kept the picture on her desk for ten years. It was the first picture we took together after she moved in with us. Even after I froze her out, it remained on her desk. I used to stare at it from the hallway whenever her door was open and she wasn't home—fuck, I don't think I could've been more pathetic.

Grabbing the phone and my coat, I made my way to the Defender. The current had transformed into a raging river of adrenaline coursing through my veins.

*Thirty more minutes. You gotta keep it together for thirty more minutes.*

THE PARK IS EERILY DARK. I don't think I've ever been here at night. Whenever someone had suggested hanging out here, I came up with a better suggestion—a suggestion that usually got one of us in trouble. But this was a place I would never tarnish with my drunk friends or Kat. This was our place: Lilly's and mine. Even when there was no us during those two years.

I drive to the parking lot closest to the picnic area. From there, it's only a couple hundred feet to the spot where I grinned into the camera while Lilly looked up at me. The picnic area, which consists of about a dozen rectangular wooden tables with attached benches, is surrounded by trees, thicker on one side with a small stream running through. The perfect place for kids to run, climb, and play, which is exactly what Lilly and I used to do whenever we came here on the weekends. God, how I loved coming here. It was almost like before. Just the two of us playing. No pretending. No hiding. Even at eight years old, the secret was suffocating me.

The screen on the phone displays 6:20. It's time. Opening the door of the Defender, my breath immediately becomes visible in the illuminated dome light. The nights are still freezing even though we're approaching spring. I shut the door and use the flashlight of the phone to make my way over to the spot. With every step, my heartbeat quickens more and my legs become unsteady. When I think I've reached the place—I sure hope the psycho doesn't expect me to stand in my ten-year-old footprints—I turn in a circle. It's pitch black on three sides. The only illumination comes from the few streetlamps along the paved road leading to the parking lot. I wonder if the lack of light was intentional by the city to avoid people loitering here at night.

Three minutes to go. I rub my hands over my arms and jump in place on the balls of my feet—the urge to move is back. I can't stand still, no matter how hard I try. Touching the screen over and over, I will the numbers to change to six-three-zero.

I tap again and see how the six, two, and nine turn into a six, followed by a three and a zero. If someone connected me to a blood pressure cuff right now, they'd call an ambulance. My pulse feels like I just did ten 50 40s in a row. My breath is so ragged that I close my eyes and start counting backward from thirteen, hoping to slow my breathing down enough to not pass out from hyperventilating.

That would be my luck, passing out right before the phone call. I make sure not to let the display go dark again the entire time when the last digit jumps to one.

*Why isn't she calling?*

What if everything she said was a lie, and she is not safe at all?

The phone starts vibrating in my hand, and I almost drop it.

UNKNOWN.

I stare for a second then swipe and lift it to my ear.

"Lilly?" I can barely get her name out; my voice is just a rasped whisper.

"It's me." The pitch in her tone makes it clear that she's smiling, and calm washes over me.

Before I can say anything else, I hear a male voice in the background. "FROM WHERE?" It's evident that he is yelling, or I wouldn't have heard him. This is bad. Really. Bad.

"WHAT? NO! NA—" are Lilly's last words before the phone call disconnects.

"LILLY!" My voice is back, and a guttural scream finds its way out of my previously constricted lungs.

That's when I see them. Headlights. They're slowly coming up the paved road and stop right next to my car.

WHAT. THE. FUCK? No, no, no...

*This can't be real.*

The beams are on me, and I'm completely blind. I shield my eyes with the hand that is not holding the phone and can make out that the driver's side door opens.

If Wes or Den followed me here, I will kill them.

"Rhys?"

Oh, you've got to be fucking kidding me. This has to be a joke. I bend over and crouch down, head in my hands, gripping my hair. I pull as hard as I can, hoping to get the utter rage under control, which has replaced the previous *nervous* current. I probably pull several chunks out, but the red haze doesn't go away. Footsteps approach on the frozen grass, and I force myself to stand up. My fists are clenched so tightly they're shaking. It's a miracle the phone casing doesn't crack.

"Rhys?" There it is again. My name. The name she only ever used when she was not happy with my performance as the perfect boyfriend.

I face the last person I expected to see tonight.

"Kat." My tone is detached. I want to wrap my hands around her throat and squeeze. I tighten my fist even more to not follow through. She is the reason the psycho disconnected the phone call. She is the reason I don't get to talk to Lilly. If I remain here, I don't think I can control myself. I want to hurt her, and I've never wanted to harm a female in my life. Ever.

I slip the phone in the back pocket of my jeans and brush past her without a word. I need to put distance between us. She tries to reach for my arm, and I round on her, getting straight in her face. "If you touch me, I can't guarantee anything. If anything happens to Lilly because of you, I will kill—"

*Fuck, what am I doing?*

I spin on my heels and walk away as fast as I can without breaking into a full-on sprint.

Thankfully, I didn't lock my car. I'm in the driver's seat and have the car in reverse by the time my ex reaches my window. I can hear her muffled voice calling my name again, but I don't stop. I reverse out of the spot and speed down the narrow pathway faster than I probably should.

FUCK. FUCK. FUCK.

I hit the steering wheel several times before I let go of the feral scream that has been building up all day until my throat hurts so badly I can't even swallow. What am I supposed to do now? I can't go home. The fact that my father has been spying on me still has me reeling. He betrayed me. Without thinking, I find myself keying in the code to Denielle's parents' mansion not fifteen minutes later. As

I pull up to the garages, one gate is already open, and I see Wes standing at the end of the spot against the wall. His hands are clasped on top of his head, and he stares at me with worry in his eyes. I pull in and sit there, not breaking eye contact with my best friend. I hear the gate close behind me; a glance into the rearview mirror confirms the sound.

Denielle's form joins Wes's. Scanning my face, her hands fly to her mouth, and tears immediately begin running down her cheeks. I take one more deep breath before I open the door and step out. I can't even begin to process what just happened. I had Lilly on the phone. I heard her voice, and then Kat showed up. He was there in the background. He cut her off. I have no idea if I will ever get another chance to talk to her. My legs give out, and I crumble to the floor.

I'm faintly aware that two arms are wrapped around me, preventing me from face-planting onto the way too polished cement floor while gut-wrenching sobs make my entire body shake.

They lead me into the house. Wes has my arm strapped over his shoulder to keep me from tripping over my own feet. I can't see a thing with my blurred vision, and I press my free hand over my mouth in an attempt to restrain some of the whimpers escaping my hoarse throat. I'm past caring how I look.

Somehow, we end up on the back patio. It's fucking freezing outside. What the hell are we doing out here? But realization seeps into my muddled brain, and I notice the flames crackling in the massive build-in fire pit. Sitting in one of the four chairs surrounding the blaze, one of my friends drapes a blanket around my shoulders, and I slump forward. My face in my hands, I bend forward, resting my entire upper body on my thighs. This is a nightmare. No, this is worse than a nightmare.

"What happened?" I don't know how long we've been here when Wes's wary question pulls me out of my semi-catatonic state, and I untangle myself. I must've been in this position longer than I thought. My back is stiff, and my neck hurts like a mother when I look up at him.

"Kat."

"Come again?" Den's mouth hangs open.

"Kat happened." I tell my friends everything, including how I fled so I wouldn't physically assault her in my rage. With a ragged breath, I conclude, "I don't know what to do."

"Maybe I can help with that."

The deep voice is coming from outside of the illuminated circle around the fire. The three of us spin around at the same time, and I squint, trying to make out the speaker. When a man steps into the light, I grab onto the armrest of my chair to not fall off.

"HOLY FUCK!" Wes shouts. He does fall off.

Denielle screams.

# CHAPTER FIFTY-SIX

**RHYS**

I stare. Wes makes a noise somewhere between wheezing and gagging while gawking up at the intruder, and Denielle continues to scream. Every time she stops to take a breath, I relish the sudden quiet—until she starts back up. If she keeps going like this, her voice is going to sound like the time Oliver, Denielle's brother, took her and Lilly to a Bieber concert. Neither of them could get out more than a pathetic croak for days. Eventually, her cries turn into a muffled whimper.

*Thank you, Jesus.*

During the entire time, my eyes don't leave him, and his focus is solely on me. My first thought is he is going to kill us. We're as good as dead. I mean, what other purpose could a man looking like that have? I don't think he's much older than Dad, but whatever happened to him made him age triple-time. His skin is leathery, and in combination with the ginormous scar running over his entire face, he must've been through hell—and survived. I can't look away from that jagged white line. My second, more rational thought is: why he would offer his help if he's here to kill us?

"Where is Lilly?" Nothing else matters at the moment.

"Miss Lilly is safe."

*Miss?*

"Are you him?" I chalk my conversational tone up to shock. In truth, I should be shitting my pants. But weirdly enough, I'm not.

"No. *He* is with Miss Lilly."

*There are two? Well, fuck me.*

I glance sideways. Wes is still on the floor, staring at the intruder. Even in the darkness, I can see that he is white as a ghost, but the wheezing has stopped. I sure hope he doesn't puke again. Denielle has her hands over her mouth, trying to control her sobs. Instinct takes over; I stand up and walk over to her chair. Pulling her to her feet, I wrap my arm around her shoulder. She immediately latches on to my midsection and squeezes until I can barely take in a breath. I don't tell her to stop, though. With Denielle tucked to my side, I lean over and extend my free hand to Wes. He slowly grabs it, pulling himself up, not looking away from the guy.

Fully upright, I let go of Wes, and with Den in the middle, we face *Not Him* as a united front.

When we don't talk, he says, "I am here to rectify my mistake."

I raise my eyebrows, but Wes voices my question. "Mistake?" Some of his color has come back—potential puke crisis averted.

"We don't know how Miss Rosenfield found you. She was not on my radar during all of this. An error on my part. I apologize."

"Apologize? Who. The. Fuck. Are. You?" Denielle has recovered as well, and her resting bitch face is in place. And thank fuck, I can breathe again. I suck in the much-needed oxygen.

"I am..."—he pauses—"the head of security."

*Security for what?*

"You obviously suck at your job," Wes mumbles, and *Not Him*, aka the head of security, trains his narrow, rodent-like eyes on my best friend, who immediately turns chalk-white again.

I can't help but snort.

"Miss Lilly is furious. And he is not happy either. We are in the process of tracing back Miss Rosenfield's steps to figure out what happened. In the meantime, Miss Lilly demanded that I fix this. So here I am."

I raise my hand to the base of my neck. She demanded? From him? Who would have the guts to demand anything from this guy? How can she make *any* demands?

As if sensing my thoughts, he amends, looking straight at me, "You will understand soon. But you have to come with me."

"WHAT?"

"HUH?"

"NO WAY! You're not taking him anywhere." Denielle is the most articulate of us.

Scarface continues, "I am here to ensure you get your answers and talk to Miss Lilly. But only you, Mr. McGuire." His formal talking stands in complete contrast to his appearance. The scar has held my attention on his face until now. For the first time, I take in his entire person. He is decked out in full paramilitary gear of dark-gray cargo pants, tight black shirt with the matching gray cargo jacket over it, and black combat boots. I recognize the bulge on the side of his hip immediately for what it is. Growing up with my Dad, I've seen the getup many times.

"Why would I go with you anywhere? You kidnapped Lilly." I'm proud of how badass I sound.

"I did not kidnap her. Watch your mouth, *boy*!" he snaps, and all badassness leaves me. The possibility of shitting my pants crosses my mind again, and I avert my eyes.

*Not Him* calms his tone. "The only way I can allow you to establish a connection to Miss Lilly is in a secure location. This house"—he gestures around himself—"is not secure."

"This is a gated community. We have a second gate!" Denielle exclaims like he's personally insulted her.

"That is correct, Miss Keller. However, the guard at the front gate is fast asleep, despite the two energy drinks he consumed, and your second gate only helps if the code is not a combination of your and your brother's birthdays."

"Oh." Den has joined the club of one-word answers.

I don't care about anything that was said after "establish a connection." I'm going to talk to her. "When do we leave?"

"RHYS!"

"Dude, have you lost your fucking mind?"

I face my friends. "He's giving me another shot at talking to her. There is no way I'm passing that up."

"What if this is all a game and he's going to kill you? I mean, look at him!" Denielle whisper-shouts at me, and all three of us turn to look at the head of security who, in return, arches one eyebrow.

"If he were here to kill me, I'm sure he wouldn't have had to show his face. To any of us. And I'd probably be dead already."

"That is correct," a voice lacking any emotion comes from behind us.

*Well, that's reassuring.*

"I have to go." I focus on Denielle and Wes. The guy is scary as fuck, but the way he talks about Lilly, I just know that his end goal is not to slit my throat—or make use of whatever he's got strapped on under that jacket.

Neither of my friends look convinced. When a shadow appears next to us, all of us jump. I guess I'm not the only one who didn't notice him moving.

I'm back to staring at the *face divider*.

"Mr. McGuire will return here tomorrow evening. Until then, no one must know that he is not here. He will contact you to let you know that he is safe. Understood?" The underlying message is clear as hell.

Denielle's eyes flick between mine and Wes's, and Wes's shoulders slump in defeat. They know I won't change my mind.

Without another word, Scarface turns around and disappears between the bushes surrounding the fire pit.

I rub my hands on my jeans, and after one more glance at the two people who are now in as deep as I am, I track past the head of security.

IT IS PITCH BLACK. I have no clue how this dude navigates his way through the property. The sky is cloudy, and there are no lights back here. Maybe he has built-in night vision, and that's how he got his scar. Surgery gone bad. Okay, probably not. This reminds me of when Wes and I were sixteen, raided his parents' liquor cabinet, and had the grandiose idea to hit the skate park in the middle of the night. Let's just say my face got very well acquainted with the concrete. Very. Well.

I stumble for the fifth time and barely catch myself on a branch while Scarface doesn't make a sound moving through the shrubbery.

A curse escapes me. Finally, he takes pity on me and directs a small flashlight to the ground. Thank you very much.

When we emerge right next to Denielle's front gate, I can't keep quiet anymore. "Dude, you just led me ten minutes through the bushes when we could've just walked out the front door?"

He stops and stares at me for a long moment. I must've said something idiotic, because my mom's favorite quote comes to mind: *He couldn't pour water out of a boot with instructions on the heel.*

"What?" I ask, exasperated.

"Mr. and Mrs. Keller have security cameras around the premises. Why do you think *Miss* Keller is allowed to remain here unsupervised all the time? The east corner of the gate is not on any camera, and for forty-two seconds, every thirteen minutes, the entire gate isn't either. Unless you want to be on tape and your parents being alerted as soon as Mr. Keller reviews the online feed before he goes to bed tonight, I suggest you trust me on this."

Wow, that's the first time he's said more than one sentence. Also, I'm not going to ask how he knows any of this.

"Sorry," I mumble, eyes trained on my boots.

We wait until something starts beeping—I assume it's his watch—and then we simply stroll out the front gate and to a black SUV parked across the street. Approaching the vehicle, I notice that there is no license plate, just a blank—is that a screen?

*Who are these people?*

Opening the trunk, he looks at me expectantly.

"Oh, fuck no!" I take a step back.

"You have exactly twenty-one seconds, or I will be leaving without you." His tone is devoid of emotion.

*FUCK. SHIT.*

"FUCK!"

Knowing that he will leave without me, I sit down and swing my legs inside. When I think it can't get worse, he holds out a black cloth.

"Oh, come on, man!" He can't be serious. I feel like Sandra Bullock in that *Bird Box* movie—minus the whole mysterious creature stuff. Well, looking back at the man in front of me...I take that back.

"I have my orders. And my orders are to get you to a secure

location so Miss Lilly can talk to you." For the first time since he stepped into the light by the fire pit, the corner of his mouth twitches ever so slightly. Lilly means something to him and not in a creepy way.

I sigh, grab the cloth, and pull it over my head. Getting comfortable on my back, I cross my arms over my chest and bend my knees. The hatch closes. And to think that a week ago, my worst fear was Lilly finding out about Kat's mind games.

The car dips as my driver climbs into the front, and off we go.

"I should probably know your name now that we are basically BFFs," I tell him like it's the most normal thing in the world to be lying in the trunk of an unmarked car with a black cloth bag over my head.

I make out a chuckle and am quite proud of myself for getting a reaction out of the guy.

"My name is George."

"It's nice to meet you, George," I say with semi-false cheeriness. I can't figure out why, but I'm not afraid of Scarface anymore.

He doesn't talk for what seems like hours. I must've dozed off—the trunk actually turned out to be fairly comfortable—when he announces that we are almost there.

# CHAPTER FIFTY-SEVEN

### RHYS

THE CAR COMES TO A HALT, AND ALL OF A SUDDEN, THE CLOTH seems to tighten around my face. My breath becomes ragged. Any attempt to suck in air fails. Faintly aware of the trunk opening, I am pulled out by the arms. My feet land on the ground, and *Not Him*—no, wait...George pushes my upper body forward so my head is almost between my knees.

"Breathe, Rhys!"

*Not Mr. McGuire—I guess we really are on the next level of our friendship.*

I draw in short, shallow breaths until they become manageable again, and I'm able to inhale all the way. George pulls me upright by the back of my jacket, and I'm about to pull the cloth from my head when he stops me.

"Not yet."

*Fuck.*

I want this thing off my face. I no longer feel like I'm being choked out during a sparring session—yes, that happens when you train with Spence—but I want to know where we are. For a split second, I wonder if Lilly will be here.

George leads me by the arm across something that sounds like gravel, up two steps, and inside a structure. Through the fabric, I can smell the rancid air—scratch that, I no longer want to know where we are. Maybe he's going to off me after all? That would definitely explain the stench—his previous BFFs. George lets go of my arm, and I hear beeping sounds. A keypad? Something clicks, and a gust of fresh-er air pushes my new favorite accessory flush against my face.

*I hope George washed this thing before he forced it on me.*

He latches onto my bicep once more, and we head down two flights of stairs. More beeping, something that sounds like metal grinding against metal, and another click.

*What is this? Federal prison?*

Not yet finished with the thought, the cloth disappears, and I squint against the blinding light. It takes an eternity for my eyes to adjust. Finally used to the harsh glare, I realize the room is lit up by dozens of fluorescent lights hanging from the ceiling. I spin in a circle. No windows, which is not really a surprise given the fact we climbed down.

On my next turn, I focus on the rest. We're in a massive rectangular room—by my guess, about a thousand plus square feet. The walls are a bright white, and the floor is polished concrete. Two green, military-style cots are set on the wall to my left, several green trunks—the same type that occupy part of our basement at home— are stacked on top of each other between the makeshift beds. The wall opposite the door has four fireproof filing cabinets lined up— also something we have in our basement. I'm starting to think the guy has some military affiliation. The far wall to my right is one massive screen with an industrial metal table a few feet in front. A single laptop sits in the center.

"Umm..." is the only thing that comes to mind when I've completed the second scan.

"You can wait over there." George points to the cots. "It'll take me a moment before I can establish the call."

I follow his instructions and lower myself onto one of the cots. Although I am ninety-nine percent certain that he didn't bring me here to dismember my body, I don't dare to mouth off. I also won't risk my chance to talk to Lilly. So, I sit and wait.

George opens one of the filing cabinets, and even from my angle, I can see that he converted the thing to a gun safe. My eyes widen when I watch him remove a Kimber .380 from a holster under his pant leg, followed by a Glock 19, which was the bulge I noticed earlier inside his jacket. Leaning further to the side, I spot several AR-15s inside the cabinet and can't stop myself from inhaling sharply.

*Yup, definitely no mouthing off happening.*

His eyes flick to me, but his expression is blank. It's like the man has no mannerisms except for the one time he talked about Lilly. This is so disconcerting; the term fucked-up may also come to mind.

I follow George's every move. After unloading his small arsenal and locking the cabinet, he walks over to his desk. He puts a headset on and starts typing. Part of the monitor wall lights up with individual pictures. Squinting, I make out the black SUV on one of the rectangles and deduct that this is his security system. This whole setup reminds me of a futuristic movie—it's creepy. Distracted with the wall images, I didn't notice that he's typing again. I'm so far away that there is no chance in hell to make out what he's doing. Resigned, I settle against the wall, ankles crossed, and my arms resting over my chest. My eyelids start to droop. What time is it anyway?

"HE'S WITH ME."

I jump at George's voice, and my eyes pop open.

"Yes, everything is secure." Pause. "How is she?" I hold my breath. "I guess that's understandable. Have you told her yet how Miss Rosenfield located him?"

What. The. Actual. Fuck? I sit up straight and try to peer around him on the monitor without getting up, which results in me falling off my temporary bed with a thud.

"You might as well come over." George's casual tone makes heat shoot to my face.

*Busted.*

I slowly push myself off the floor and approach the desk. Before he takes his headset off, and my new *bestie* says, "Yes, we'll establish connection in a few minutes. And Miss Lilly?" Pause. Is she on the other end? A knot forms in my stomach. "I am sorry for not considering Miss Rosenfield a possible interference."

The headset lays on the tabletop when I finally step next to George, and he turns to look at me.

"Was she on the other end?" My voice is no more than a rasp.

"She was."

George stands up and motions for me to sit down. I stare at the sleek black-and-silver office chair. It looks like something you'd see in a fancy high-end office, not an underground lair. I wonder how much this thing costs.

*What the hell am I thinking?*

Shaking my head, I slowly lower myself down and face the laptop. The background picture of the New York City skyline distracts me for a second. I didn't take good ol' George for a city guy.

He leans over my shoulder, opens a black window, and types a few quick commands. I try to follow what he's doing, but let's face it, Lilly is the computer geek in the family, not me.

Three dots appear in the bottom line. They disappear and reappear every few seconds one after another. It reminds me of a ringing phone. I'm not sure what to expect. When my lungs start to burn, I realize I've been holding my breath.

Suddenly, the screen goes black and is quickly replaced by Lilly's face. My hand flies up, covering my mouth, and I suck in a sharp breath as I stare at her. I don't know what to do...or say. I gawk at her like an idiot. She has a healing cut on her forehead, and I feel the bile rise in my throat. Did he hurt her? I scan every inch of her face—she looks fine otherwise. Her hair is straight, and she's not wearing any makeup, but she is still the most beautiful girl I've ever seen—*my* girl.

Something wet hits the hand that's still covering my mouth. I should probably feel embarrassed, but I'm not. After nearly six days of agonizing hell, I am face to face with her.

Lilly's eyes flicker to the side and back to me. Her eyes draw together. "Rhys?" She sounds confused and...scared.

*Of me?*

"Is he hurt?" Lilly's question draws my attention back to the screen.

"No, Miss Lilly. I believe Rhys is trying to process," comes from behind me.

She nods, and her eyes move to something outside of the frame again. My hand finally drops from my face and joins the other on my thighs.

"Is he there?" My tone is harsh, and I did not plan for them to be the first words out of my mouth.

Lilly's eyes bulge at my outburst before her shoulder's slump. "He is." Her response is just a whisper.

"If you touched her—"

"I would never harm her," my threat gets cut off, and I am stunned to silence. He is right there. Next to her. But what did I expect? Of course he wouldn't let his captive out of sight.

I immediately notice the glare Lilly throws in the direction she's been glancing at, and I frown. It's her shut-the-fuck-up look. I was on the receiving end of it for years.

*What the hell is happening?*

"Lilly?"

Her eyes snap back to mine. "Yes?" She looks hopeful. This is not how I envisioned seeing her again.

"Please tell me what's going on." I sigh.

This time, she doesn't look at him but closes her eyes briefly. Her shoulders rise and fall; she's collecting her thoughts. I know this girl better than myself.

Her hazel eyes open, and she looks straight at me but speaks to him. "I have to tell him."

"Lilly..." It's a one-word warning, and I hold my breath.

She turns away from the screen and addresses the voice. "Listen, N—" She stops herself and glances over for a fraction of a second. "I need to tell him. He's been through hell for almost a week. It's cruel to leave him in the dark for another."

"Another?" I sit up straight.

"The risk is too high. If he doesn't keep his mouth shut, the entire plan goes down the drain."

"He won't say anything."

*Plan? Could this exchange get any more disturbing?*

"Rhys?" the voice addresses me, and despite seeing how comfortable Lilly is with him, my adrenaline spikes.

"Yes?" I try not to let my wariness bleed into my response.

"If you repeat anything back to anyone—and I mean anyone—not your little friends, and most certainly not the *people* in your house..." He leaves the sentence hanging.

"Stop going all psycho again. I told you he wouldn't say anything. He didn't tell me about anything for ten years, for fuck's sake," Lilly snaps. Turning back to me, she says, "Sorry, babe. I didn't mean to say that."

"Uh, it's ok?" My response sounds more like a question.

I'm in an alternate dimension or some shit; that's the only explanation. Lilly rarely curses; she looks confident and fierce, not like someone who's held captive.

Lilly's invisible friend is still not convinced. "I have no problem ordering George to bring him back here if I find out he talked."

Lilly seems to ponder his threat but then shoots back, "Like that'll do any good. How would we explain that to anyone?"

"We?" I didn't mean to say that out loud, and Lilly's gaze swivels back to me. I can feel George's stare on the back of my head.

She sighs. "When I told you that I'm safe, it was the truth. Not something he"—she cocks her head to the side—"told me to say." She knows that I would assume she was forced.

My brow pulls together. "So, he is not the one that kidnapped all those girls?"

*Logical conclusion, right?*

"No, he is the one." Lilly presses her lips together and waits for me to process the information.

He is the one that kidnapped those girls. He is the one that kidnapped her ten years ago. He is the one that kidnapped her again. She. Is. Safe.

"WHAT THE ACTUAL FUCK, CALLA!" I can't stop my outburst. "WHAT THE FUCK IS GOING ON?" And then another thought hits me. I immediately realize how irrational it is, but my mouth speaks before my brain can interject. "Are you sleeping with him?"

"WHAT?" Lilly shrieks. "EWW, NO!"

"Watch your mouth!" *he* snaps in the background.

I believe her—both of them. Both reactions were too genuine, but the possessive asshole in me still won't let it go.

"Then why the hell are you staying there if you're not—" It's a sneer, and I wouldn't be surprised if she hangs up on me any second.

"BECAUSE HE IS MY BROTHER!" Lilly shouts, and I feel like she kicked me in the balls.

*Brother?*

# CHAPTER FIFTY-EIGHT

## LILLY

FUCK, SHIT. I PROMISED MYSELF I WOULD EXPLAIN EVERYTHING to Rhys calmly and rationally. So much for that. Why did he have to go down that road?

Tears well up in my eyes, and I blink several times. This is not how this was supposed to go.

"He is my brother, Rhys," I whisper, pleading for him to hear me out.

Rhys stares back at me, dumbfounded. He opens and closes his mouth several times, and eventually turns to George. "Brother?"

I can't see George's face as he is still standing. He must have nodded or something, because Rhys slowly turns back to me.

"How?" His anger is completely gone. Instead, I see several other emotions flitter across his face. Surprise, confusion, sadness, relief...more confusion.

I'm not sure where to begin, so I start with the most obvious. "Henry wasn't my father."

Rhys's eyes widen for a second, then he bursts out laughing like a hysterical clown. I look over to Nate, who shrugs and crosses his arms over his chest. With a smug grin on his face, his entire demeanor shouts *You wanted this; now figure out how to deal with it.*

I sit on my hands so I don't slap him over the head again.

It takes Rhys several minutes to calm down. As the laughter slowly subsides, he starts shaking his head. He looks everywhere but the screen, and I'm starting to worry. I'm not sure if I should say something, leave him be, or what?

Finally, after what feels like hours, Rhys looks back at me with a somber expression. "Of course he wasn't."

I tilt my head to the side.

He must see my confusion and elaborates. "I mean, think about it. Given the shit we had already found out before you, uh...*left*, it's not really a surprise to hear that there were more secrets."

*Oh.*

"Oh."

Rhys takes a deep breath. "I'm sorry, Cal. I have a hard time wrapping my head around any of this."

"Me too. This is not how I wanted to tell you about..." I trail off.

"Him?" Rhys completes my sentence, lips pursed.

"Yes," I mumble, and Nate scoffs next to me.

I narrow my eyes at him, and he makes a zip motion across his mouth, chuckling. God, this is so—I can't even think of a word to appropriately describe the absurdity of the situation. I look down at my now clasped hands in my lap. I've come to terms with my relationship with my half-brother—that there will be a relationship no matter what the outcome is after I leave here. But this is the first time my old and new lives are overlapping, and I have no idea how to handle it. I want Rhys to tell me that everything will be ok, that we will figure this out together. I want him to hold me while I tell him everything. I don't want to talk to him through a computer, almost three thousand miles between us. I most definitely don't want Nate and George to listen to every word.

My dream from a few days ago comes back to mind, and a knot the size of a soccer ball starts forming in my stomach. How can I ask Rhys to accept my relationship with Nate? Tristen and Heather work for the law. Nate has broken said law—several times over. I love Rhys more than anything, but I can't expect him to take my side. If he doesn't want to be with me because of this, I can't go home. Everything I ever knew and loved would be gone. Rhys would be gone.

My breath increases, but at the same time, it feels like all the air is being expelled from my lungs. I push the chair back so I can put my head between my legs—a motion I've been getting way too familiar with lately. In the distance, I hear Rhys call my name, but I can't be sure over the ringing in my ears. My entire focus is on drawing in slow breaths.

A hand is placed on my back and starts rubbing back and forth. All of a sudden, I'm enveloped in my brother's arms. Nate murmurs in my ear to inhale and exhale.

"YOU!" This time I'm sure it's Rhys. "GET YOUR FUCKING HANDS OFF HER!"

*Why is he so angry?*

"Would you shut up for a minute? Don't you see that she needs a moment," Nate snarls. Who is he talking to? Oh. My. God! The realization that Nate has just revealed himself to Rhys—to help me through my panic attack—slams into me. I sit up abruptly, and my brother jumps back before I head-butt him in the chin.

With wide eyes, I glance between my brother and Rhys, who are locked in a stare-down.

*SHIT! No, no, no.*

I need to do something or this will turn bad quickly. I have no idea what instructions Nate gave George regarding Rhys. Now that the airflow to my lungs is reestablished, I take a deep breath and plaster the fakest smile on my face. One could say I'm channeling my inner Katherine Rosenfield—artificial as the blonde in her always perfectly curled hair.

"Rhys, this is Nate, my brother. Nate, say hi to Rhys."

My heart is still racing from concluding what just happened, but on the outside, I sound creepily cheery. Nothing like introducing the boy, who I *thought* to be my brother then adopted brother and is now my boyfriend, to the man who I thought was a nice guy at the gym, who turned out to have kidnapped me—twice—and revealed himself as my *real* half-brother. Nope, nothing unusual about this situation. As totally normal as seeing a sparkly pink unicorn walking down the street in a tutu, drinking a macchiato while smoking a cigar.

A high-pitched titter bursts out. My life has become a terrible reality TV show.

Both guys' eyes swivel to me, and I slap my hand in front of my mouth, trying to hold in the giggles. I can see Nate glancing back and forth between Rhys and me before he fully turns to the screen.

"Rhys, man. I'm Nate, your future brother-in-law and the guy who kidnapped your girlfriend. Twice." He even adds a slow-motion, rainbow-shaped wave.

I jerk my head toward Nate, but all he does is grin at me and shrugs. "The cat is out of the bag. Now we have to figure out a way to deal with it."

*Well, shit. I did not expect that.*

I peer at Rhys, whose narrowed eyes are fixed on the guy beside me. Rhys's gaze flickers to me and back several times before it settles on Nate again. "Good to meet you. To be clear, you will not stand up in our wedding. Now, how about some privacy so I can talk to Lilly?"

*Brother-in-law? Wedding? Wha—*

I blink several times. Rhys's face is dead serious and doesn't show any signs of fear or anger. Or disgust. He's clearly in shock; that's the only explanation.

Nate huffs out a laugh. "The boy has guts. I like it." He leans forward so his face is in the middle of the screen. "G?"

"Yes?"

"Is your place secure?" In Nate terms, can Rhys contact anyone or escape?

"It is."

"Let's give them some privacy." With that, he pushes his chair back and stands up. "If you need me, I'll be in the library."

All I can do is nod before I'm alone in the NCC. Nate left me alone with all his computers. On the other end, George murmurs something to Rhys, who dips his head and then turns back to me.

We sit in silence, and I am finally able to look at him. A lone tear escapes my eye, and I stifle a whimper. I've missed him so much.

NATE INITIATED the call from one of the laptops, so I unplug the device and make my way over to the couch. It's almost midnight, and I'm exhausted. Today's rollercoaster of events has left me completely drained, but the need to talk to Rhys is more powerful than my physical requirement for sleep.

With the computer settled on my lap, I stifle a yawn. I'm trying to figure out where to start when Rhys whispers, "I love you so much, Calla."

The affection reflected in his eyes is my undoing. A sob escapes, and the floodgates open. I cover my face with my hands.

"It's ok, babe. I'm here," Rhys's voice comes through the speaker.

*This is all too much.*

"Calla, please don't cry. It'll be ok…"

I pry my hands away from my face and look at the boy on the screen. "You think?" I hiccup.

"I know." Rhys's confidence is contagious, but how could he possibly know that?

"How?" I whisper.

His face gentles, and the corner of his mouth quirks up. "Because we'll get through it together."

I want to believe him. I do. But I can't shake the small doubt remaining in the back of my head. "How can you still want to be with me?"

Rhys's eyebrows furrow. "Why wouldn't I?"

I'm scared to speak the words out loud, the thoughts that have been occupying my mind for the last few days. I close my eyes, and without looking at him, I say, "Because I am related to a criminal." I draw in a deep breath. "And because I will stand by my brother's side."

When I don't get a response for several moments, I slowly open my eyes, prepared for Rhys to have disconnected or walked away from the computer. He is still there, but his face is unreadable.

"Please say something." My heart is beating in my throat.

"You're only saying this because you are still angry with Mom and Dad. And with me, for keeping the whole Kat thing from you." His voice is cold and detached.

It would be easier to deal with him being upset.

"No, I'm saying this because I know Nate—"

"IT'S BEEN A FUCKING WEEK. ONE. WEEK," Rhys bursts out.

*He is angry.*

"How can you possibly know this guy? He's a fucking psycho!" Rhys is trying to rein in his temper, and I'm waiting for George to show up in the background after Rhys called Nate "a fucking psycho." George remains absent.

"Please let me explain?" I rasp out.

If he'd hear me out, maybe I can make him understand? Heck, I don't even comprehend what's going on inside of my head; how can I expect him to? That realization makes a wave of panic surge through me like a tidal wave, and the thought of not being able to return home threatens to choke me again. I put the laptop next to me on the couch and bend forward to concentrate on breathing. This is the second time in one night. Ugh.

"Calla?"

When I don't react, Rhys gentles his tone. "Babe, look at me. Please."

It's still hard to breathe, but I force myself to face the boy who essentially will decide for me if I'm going home or not. Without him accepting my relationship with my half-brother, I don't have a home to go back to.

"Listen, Cal. I, uh...I'm trying. I am, but I know I will fuck this up. This past week has been a nightmare. Mom is a mess; Natty is with Olivia; Den and Wes are a shit-show. We had no idea where you were—if you were alive. I can't put into words how relieved I am that you are...safe. But how you can be ok with what this guy has done..." Rhys trails off, sadness in his eyes. Hearing him say out loud what I feared my friends and family were going through while I played family is devastating.

"I'm not ok with it. Nate will take responsibility. For everything," I tell him cautiously. Perceptive as he is, he picks up on what I'm not saying.

"But?"

"There is more. More than any of us thought. Until Nate and I can sort through that, he won't come forward." I neglect the part of Nate also wanting to make sure that my finances are sorted before he goes away. My new money situation is a conversation for another day. Somehow, I don't want Rhys to know—yet. After a pause, I add, "I won't make him. Not yet. We both need answers," I beg Rhys to understand.

The boy on the screen shakes his head, and my heart sinks. We don't speak for a long time. Rhys stares at something in the distance, and I can't look away from his distraught face. I'm hurting him with my decision, and it kills me, but I also can't turn my back on Nate.

My gaze keeps moving to the clock on the top of the screen. We sit there for almost twenty minutes before Rhys's eyes find mine again.

"Tell me," is all he says to me, and I do.

Over the next two hours, I try to summarize everything that has happened from the moment I walked out of school on Tuesday. Apparently, no one could figure out why I crashed my Jeep and assumed I was run off the road by my captor. I confess how angry I was at Rhys for keeping Kat's games from me but that I don't care about that anymore. He wanted to protect me, and the relief in his face is palpable. For the most part, Rhys lets me talk. I explain how Nate found me after our visit to Santa Rosa, and Rhys curses under his breath. We led him straight to us. When I mention my most recent migraine, his eyes widen, but he remains mute. Though, when I get to the financial statements, Rhys starts asking questions.

"You think Emily and...uh, Brooks had an affair all those years?" Tone skeptical, Rhys still assumes this is all part of an elaborate scheme Nate came up with.

"I don't know. Between my memories and the letters, it makes sense. And then there is the money Brooks transferred every month. But some things don't add up. I have this gut feeling..." I try to put it in words as well as I can. "It's like when I started researching for my paper. The more articles I read, the more I was drawn to it. It's the same with this." Deep down, I'm convinced everything we've discovered so far is still just the tip of the iceberg.

"Since your brother is such an awesome hacker, can't he just track the money?" Sarcasm drips from Rhys's tone.

"He's working on it." I don't want to start fighting again, so I leave it at that.

We sit in silence until Rhys points out, "None of this explains why he kidnapped you in the first place—or the other girls."

Up until now, I haven't mentioned much about Nate's past, so I backtrack and tell Rhys about Payton and Audrey, what happened to Nate after their accident, and how he later found out about me.

"Well, fuck. That'd make anyone crazy."

"I don't think it was just that. At least not the only reason..." I mumble. I've kept my suspicion to myself ever since Nate told me about his mental health.

"What do you mean?" Rhys is squinting at me, probably questioning if I've also lost my mind.

I glance at the door as if Nate may barrel through it at any moment, subconsciously knowing that I'm revealing personal information about him.

"I think it's his meds..." I leave the sentence hanging.

"His meds?" Clearly, Rhys doesn't buy it.

"Nate and I talked a lot, and something he said stuck with me. I want to do more research on it, but I haven't had access to a computer until today." I pause, and Rhys lets me collect my thoughts. "He mentioned that every time he, uh...needed company..."—I can't bring myself to say *kidnapped a girl*—"it's right after his shrink switches his meds around. So...uh, remember when Heather and Tristen talked about that guy who used to be in Tristen's unit? The guy who, after his discharge, always went off the rails when his counselor put him on new antidepressants?" I'm referring to a conversation Rhys and I had eavesdropped on years ago and were not supposed to hear. We got caught lurking on the stairs while Heather and Tristen were in the living room and got a massive tongue lashing never to repeat a word about that to anyone. I see a flicker of recognition in Rhys's eyes—he remembers—so I continue, "That's what I think happens to Nate whenever he gets new meds."

Rhys purses his mouth in a slash of disbelief. "Don't you think that's a little farfetched? That you're looking for an excuse?"

I understand where he's coming from but can't suppress the anger that his statement sparks inside of me. "He's going to pay no matter what, Rhys," I snap. "But there is a difference between intentionally committing a crime and being helpless to meds fucking with the chemicals in your brain."

Rhys winces at my outburst. Up until now, I've taken the brunt of his anger and suspicion. I feel like I deserve it after hanging out with my brother while my loved ones were worried out of their minds. But I'm tired, and my patience—even for the boy that I would do almost anything for—wears thin. It's past two in the morning, which makes it after five for Rhys, and as if on cue, Rhys starts yawning.

"Can we talk about something else for a bit? I don't want to fight anymore," I murmur.

Rhys's face immediately softens, and he smiles. "Of course, babe."

With that small gesture, my chaotic world falls into place, and for this brief moment, we're just us again. We're in the little bubble we created every time Rhys snuck into my room at night. I settle deeper into the couch and lean my head against the back of it. Rhys rests his chin on his stacked fists on the tabletop and softly smiles at me. At that moment, everything else is forgotten, and my heart is full. We talk about frivolous things. Magnolia's took Wes's favorite drink off the menu—some Christmas-y hot cocoa concoction with a bunch of seasonal flavors—and he's outraged. He threatened the owner to start a petition, who just responded that it'd be back next Christmas. I laugh out loud because that's typical Wes; the poor guy does not like change. At. All. Rhys is looking forward to a new video game that's coming out in a few weeks. It's "the shit," and all the guys from school are taking bets against each other on who will get the higher score. Boys. But that's what I needed to hear—something that has absolutely nothing to do with our situation.

# CHAPTER FIFTY-NINE

## LILLY

I wake up with a start and grab the computer right before it completely slides off my lap toward the floor.

*Where is my bed?*

Rhys! The video-chat. We were talking and must've fallen asleep? I hit the space bar on the laptop—nothing. I press the power button—again nothing. The laptop is dead. No, no, no. I didn't say goodbye.

I jump up without thinking, and this time, the laptop does hit the ground. Shit. I pause for a second and then dismiss the device, charging out of the room.

"NATE!" I stop outside the door in the hallway. Silence. I run to the library, but there is no sign of him. The clock on the shelf shows 10:37. Oh God, I slept for-like-ever. Fuck, what if George took Rhys back already?

Racing downstairs to the kitchen, I keep calling my brother, but he is nowhere to be found. He always comes to me when I'm looking for him. Where is he? Finding the kitchen empty as well, I spin in a circle. My entire body is vibrating from the inside out. Back in the hallway, I start flinging open doors along the way, but all I find are either empty rooms or bare-looking guest rooms.

On the second floor, I find Margot's bedroom—the room she

believes is hers and Nate's. I recognize it from the brief view on the security feed. It's the only room I've found so far that looks somewhat lived in with a white, fluffy duvet draped over the four-poster bed and about a hundred throw pillows accurately positioned. Three picture frames are on the dresser across from the bed. I take a step closer; all the pictures display Nate and Margot. In the one closest to me, both are wearing formal wear. Nate wears a sleek, black tux with a crisp, white cufflink shirt, while Margot looks stunning in a strapless, floor-length, blood-red sheath dress that clings to her every curve. The second picture was taken at a—is that a racetrack? Margot is dressed to the nines in skinny jeans, knee-high stiletto boots, and a cropped leather jacket—everything black. She looks like a fashionable assassin. Nate, however, is wearing a black-and-gray racesuit, standing next to a dangerous-looking motorcycle. He races? Squinting, I can make out the letters MV and, further up, F4, but because of the angle, the rest is unreadable. Let's be honest; even if I could read it, I know as much about motorcycles as a third-grader does about the stock market. The last picture was taken at a New Year's party. A ginormous "Happy New Year" banner is in the background, and they're kissing. But something stands out to me; besides the kiss in the third photograph, they all look staged. Nate's words echo inside my head: *I don't believe in a soul mate, that there is the one. Margot and I work well together.* My mind completes the unspoken part of the statement; they don't love each other. Knowing how I feel about Rhys, that realization makes me sad for my brother.

The room has completely distracted me; I'm wasting time. Spinning around, I finish my search on the second floor. I even walk into Nate's actual bedroom—knocking first, of course—and take in the stark contrast to his fake bedroom. This one is masculine and sparse. Dark-navy sheets, no throw pillows, and no pictures.

Closing the door behind me, I'm running out of options. Fuck. What if he left the property? Then it hits me: the gym.

HE IS SWIMMING LAPS. I'm standing at the edge of the pool and watching Nate swim one lane after the other. He's in the zone, and I have never seen him not on guard. It's fascinating. Glancing around,

I see his phone and tablet on one of the lounge chairs, and the small voice inside my head perks up, telling me to grab both and make a run for it. My gaze shifts between the devices and my brother a few times before I sit down on the other chair. I'm past running.

I'll give him a few more minutes before I make myself known and walk back to the edge of the pool. He is about to turn for another lap when he notices me and pauses.

"You're awake."

Attempting to stifle my giggle, I look him up and down. He looks ridiculous with only his head sticking out of the water, goggles over his eyes, and his hair dripping in his face. It's a whole new side of my brother.

"You left me," I say accusingly after my initial amusement has worn off.

Nate pulls himself out of the pool and walks over to the shelf containing a stack of towels. Dropping into the lounge chair I previously occupied, he drawls, "Little sister, you were out of it. I came in several times, even called your name. You were out like a light."

*Oh.*

"Is Rhys home?" I'm scared to hear his answer.

"No, but he has to leave soon. He has to be back before anyone starts asking questions—more questions, I should say."

I put my hands on my hips and tilt my head toward the ceiling, calculating how long he's been with George. Would Heather and Tristen be looking for him? They never have before.

As if guessing my train of thought, Nate says, "Rhys has been in touch with his parents through Wes. Since he left his phone at home when he ran out Saturday, Wes has been sending messages for your boyfriend from his phone."

I furrow my eyebrows.

*I guess with me missing, they care where he is?*

"Tristen had been checking up on him through Wes's parents. Now that neither of them is at Wes's house, Tristen called Denielle's father, who gave him access to the security system. I'm telling you, your adopted father has quite the cards up his sleeve. I'm no longer surprised I couldn't find you until..."

*I made myself known*, I finish the sentence in my head. Then,

Nate's words register, and my heart rate increases. "If he has access to the security feed, wouldn't he know that Rhys is not there?"

A smug smile appears on my brother's face. "George is the best at his job. There is no trace of Rhys leaving on any of the footage, and the cameras inside the house are only in very specific locations. Wes got detailed instructions on what to communicate. As far as Tristen is concerned, Rhys has locked himself in one of the guest rooms on the top floor and will only open the door when Wes brings him food."

"But..." I pause; I'm still confused. "Heather and Tristen have never checked up on Rhys before. They just let him leave two years ago. Is it because I'm, uh...gone?"

Nate glances to the side before his eyes lock on mine. He looks almost pained. "My guess? They never had to check up on Rhys because they always tracked him through his phone."

*What?*

"Why? Why didn't they just make him stay home?" My voice is just slightly above a whisper.

"I wish I could answer you that. But I'm suspecting it has something to do with the reason they wired the entire house with cameras like a high-security prison."

*More secrets.*


BEFORE HEADING BACK to the NCC, we take a detour through the kitchen. Nate assures me we can spare ten minutes to eat. He's been in touch with George and Rhys, and they're just hanging out. When I inquire what that means, he switches the topic and tells me about what he is planning on putting in his post-workout protein shake.

*Yup, my brother is insane.*

I'm leaning against the cabinets next to the fridge while Nate has his butt parked on the edge of the massive kitchen table across from me. He is sucking away on a shake that looks like something between throw-up and swamp water. I'm wolfing down another round of carbs, followed by some fruit, as Nate informs me that George procured a secure device for Rhys. I almost choke on a grape as he says the words.

"You're letting me talk to him? Any time I want?" My mouth hangs open.

"I am. But only if you and Loverboy follow my instructions. If anyone finds out about the phone, I will remote wipe it and cut the connection immediately."

I'm too stunned by Nate's show of good faith that I just mumble something resembling, "I promise," crumbs of breakfast falling out of my mouth.

My brother chuckles at my dumbfounded expression. "I can't cut you two off for another week, can I? George and I had an extensive conversation this morning while the two of you were getting your beauty rest. I already spoke with Rhys a little bit ago to get a better feel for my future brother-in-law," Nate says nonchalantly.

I gape at him for a long moment before I push off the counter and tackle-hug him around his midsection. He reached out to Rhys. He is letting me talk to him. My voice is choked up as I whisper, "Thank you."

Nate's arms wrap automatically around my shoulders as if we've always been brother and sister—ordinary siblings, without the whole kidnapping history. Hugging him starts to feel natural.


With the laptop still charging, Nate establishes the connection from one of the desktops. He doesn't have to wait for the other end to pick up or anything; it connects straight to George's place.

*Note to self: Ask where that is.*

What I see on the screen makes me spray my tea all over Nate's keyboards, and he curses, diving for a box of tissues. He allowed me to bring my caffeine in a secure travel mug. What he didn't take into account was that there would be another way for me to ruin his tech with my tea.

"Uh, George? I thought we concluded that the boyfriend is not a threat?" Nate seems as shocked as I am.

In front of us, several feet away from the computer on George's end, are both men in a standoff. George has an AR-15 trained at Rhys—thanks to Tristen, I knew the difference between an AR and an MP5 before I turned thirteen. Instead of looking alarmed, Rhys is standing across from him with his hands on his hips and head cocked to the side.

At Nate's question, the guys turn to the monitor.

"Hey, babe." Rhys grins at me.

"Good morning, Miss Lilly." George nods in the same direction and lowers the rifle.

Nate and I look at each other and then back at the screen.

*What the hell is going on?*

Rhys takes quick strides toward the desk and plops down in the chair like it's the most natural thing in the world. "Babe, did you know George was a Marine back in the day? His stories make Dad look like a boy scout. And how he got the scar...holy fuck. I can't believe he survived that..." He trails off.

I open and close my mouth several times but can't come up with an adequate response. I glance over at my brother, and his confused expression confirms that he is out of the loop as well.

"How come the boy knows how you got your scar, and I don't?" Nate growls.

George slowly walks over and chuckles. That's the most emotion I have seen on his face to date. "That's because you never asked. I don't run around advertising my past."

*Okay, then.*

"George was just showing me the silencer he got for his AR-15. This thing is so badass; Wes would shit his pants." Rhys literally jumps in the seat. I'm not sure if that is cute or disturbing.

"What happened since I last spoke to you two hours ago? You barely looked at each other," Nate inquires with narrowed eyes.

"We bonded. Your head of security is not so scary once you get to know him." When neither Nate nor I say anything, Rhys looks straight at my brother and smirks. "What? Are you jealous he likes me better?"

"Since I fund his little operation, he doesn't have to like me," Nate snaps, and George's eyebrows lift in the background. He concluded the same as me at this point. My brother is, in fact, jealous. I press my lips together to stop myself from laughing out loud. This is just absurd.

I clear my throat. "So, uh, George. Where exactly are you right now?" I'm not sure if he'll tell me, but I need to change the topic somehow.

"We're near Morristown, New Jersey," George immediately responds.

"Really? You made me lie in that fucking trunk for over four hours?" Rhys looks up.

"You fell asleep for three and a half of that; stop complaining," he shoots back.

*They are seriously bantering with each other. What the ever-loving—*

"Okay, let's get back to business. My sister needs to talk to her boyfriend before he has to head back. We still have to go over some of the logistics for the next week. Let's postpone this little bonding thing you two have going on until your road trip." Nate's tone sends a cold shiver down my spine, and I wonder if he is truly mad at George or Rhys.

George nods. "I will get the car ready. We'll be leaving in thirty minutes."

Nate turns to me. "I'm going to shower and be back before that."

"Okay." Before I can say anything else, he is out of his chair and out the door.

I turn back to the monitor, and Rhys grins at me. "He is so jealous."

This time, I allow myself to laugh and shake my head.

## CHAPTER SIXTY

### RHYS

Lilly fell asleep at some point, and I watched her until I couldn't keep my eyes open anymore, which was somewhere around six a.m., I think. I wake up with a start, trying to figure out where I am.

"Good morning, Rhys," a deep voice comes from behind me, and my head whips around.

George is standing in the middle of the room with a compound bow in his hand.

"Uh...good morning?"

*What the fuck is he doing with that? In here!*

Without elaborating, he opens one of the fireproof cabinets and puts his archery equipment away. "I spoke to Nate while you were napping."

"O-kay?"

"We have concluded that you are not a threat to Miss Lilly."

"No shit, dude!" Great, my brain still seems to be napping as my mouth talks without considering the consequences. The guy has enough firepower for a small town during the zombie apocalypse in this room, and I have to run my stupid trap.

This time, George turns to me and chuckles.

"Whoa, man. You have actual facial expressions!"

*Shut up, shut up, shut up.*

But instead of choking or shooting me, he barks out a genuine laugh. "Rhys McGuire, I like you."

"You do?" I can feel my eyebrows rise.

"Yes. You have guts. Miss Lilly means more to you than your own safety, and now that you are aware of her brother, we will see a lot of each other," George deadpans.

"We will?"

A stoic nod.

*And there go the facial expressions.*

The man with the huge scar walks over to me and leans against the table. "Nate wants to talk to you when you're awake. Let's get that over with so the man can say his piece."

"Where is Lilly?"

"Miss Lilly is still asleep. Nate assured me that he'd wake her up before we have to leave."

"What's with the *Miss* Lilly thing?"

"It's a way to show respect; you may try it sometime," he says with a not-stoic face; unfortunately, the facial expression he does display is not a friendly one either.

*Okay, officially shutting my piehole now.*

George leans over me to reach the laptop and establishes the connection to Nate, aka Psycho.

His face appears on the screen, and before I can say anything, I'm greeted with, "If that's not my future brother-in-law," sarcasm dripping from his words.

*He would get along perfectly with Denielle.*

He seems to be sitting in a kitchen, based on the white cabinets in the background. I stay quiet. I'm not sure how smart it is to provoke the guy who holds Lilly captive—well, not captive, but you know what I mean.

Nate looks at George. "Have you filled him in yet? How his ex-girlfriend ruined the call to his *new* girlfriend?"

The mention of Kat perks my attention.

"I have not. I was leaving that up to you. He just woke up."

"Awesome." Nate rubs his hands together like a loon. I'm starting to question Lilly's assessment of his sanity—more than I already was.

I swallow over the lump in my throat and try to sound like he doesn't intimidate the shit out of me—now that his sister is not sitting next to him. I channel my school persona and drawl, "So? How did she find me?"

Nate chuckles, entertaining my charade, but I don't give him the satisfaction of showing him any other emotion besides indifference.

He looks down, and I see the top of some type of tablet at the bottom of the screen. "I've spent quite some time tracing back Barbie's steps." I snort at Nate's accurate assessment of Kat, and he looks up.

"Sorry, just a perfect description for her," I explain myself.

Nate nods, and a smirk appears at the corner of his mouth. If I didn't know better, I'd say we're bonding—a little.

"As I said, I retraced her steps. What I was able to find is that when neither Lilly nor you showed up in school, she started asking questions. As of now, there are no news reports about Lilly's, uh... disappearance, and all I could find is that your parents excused both of you from school. The same goes for your two friends. I assume your father kept everything—including the people camping out at your house—under wraps. My question for him would be why, but we're getting off topic.

"I checked Barbie's phone activity. You never disabled your Friend Finder for her. She had access to your location, as well as your friend Wes's at all times." Nate looks up and gives me a disapproving glare before he continues. "As her location service is permanently enabled as well, I was able to retrace her steps laughably easy. She regularly drove by your house and Wes's. My guess is she noticed your car was gone, but your phone was still at home, so she checked the next best option. While doing that, she kept texting half your class, asking if they had seen Lilly, but no one could give her any answers. The only responses she got were that no one had seen Lilly, your friends, or you since the incident last week. Some speculated that you were all hiding out somewhere together." His face grimaces in disgust, and I'm betting it's about the shit my so-called friend said.

"Saturday, she was staked out at the coffee shop near Wes's house all afternoon. She must've seen Wes's location changing and decided to drive by and check on you." Nate's eyes meet mine. "By the way, suggest to your friend to get some curtains." His eyes drop back to the tablet. "She followed you from Wes's house to the park. I'm not sure why she didn't drive up immediately since you were there for over ten minutes. Since then, she's been driving by Wes's and Denielle's house several times. I have advised both of your friends to turn off their location services and disable the numerous Friend Finder apps you kids all have."

Nate seems to be done with his report and faces me now straight on.

"Advised?" I can't help myself.

"I've been in touch with both of them to make sure they relay the correct information to their and your parents."

"And they're doing it?" I'm a bit stunned by Denielle and Wes cooperating so easily—mostly Den.

George chuckles, and Nate throws him a death glare. When neither of them answers my question, I turn to the man behind me. George looks down, and for the third time since waking up with my face stuck to the metal desk, I see real emotion on the man's face. Amusement. "Miss Lilly previously ensured that her brother would not sound like a '*complete psycho*' anymore."

I bark out a laugh. That's my girl.

"Well, now that this is clarified," Nate's voice pulls my attention back to the screen, "let's talk about your part in this."

Nate fills me in on the plan, as much as it already exists, and when he says that he would provide a phone for me, my eyes nearly bulge out of their sockets. Maybe he's not so bad after all—besides the kidnapping issue, of course. He reiterates what I am to tell everyone, and after the fourth time of him explaining in detail what would happen if I don't comply, my brain goes into nap mode again.

A sleek new cell phone is placed in front of me on the desk, and Nate explains that I can reach Lilly, George, and him with it—no one else. The phone will only connect to the numbers he makes me repeat several times. I'm to memorize them before George deposits me back at Denielle's. If I don't know them by then, I have to wait until one of them contacts me. Biting my tongue, I swallow the retort I want to spout off out of fear he'll take the phone back.

After we disconnect, George has me learn the phone numbers backward and forward. When he's satisfied that I finally have them etched into my brain, he provides me with coffee and granola bars. That he doesn't bust out MREs from one of his green trunks surprises me a bit. We have several storage bins in the basement that contain *Meals Ready-to-Eat*. As Dad always says, "You never know when you can use them." So far, we haven't needed them, and I'm sure some date back to a Pre-Rhys or Lilly time.

The wait for Lilly to wake up is excruciating. I need to find something to pass the time.

"So..." I tentatively probe, "were you in the military or what?"

George, who is head deep in one of the fireproof cabinets yet again, turns to me. "I was."

"Is that where you got that, uh...scar?" I don't know if I'm brave or utterly stupid.

"Yes."

I shouldn't, but I ask anyway. "What happened?"

Staring past me, he remains quiet for several moments, and I assume that means he won't tell me shit. His eyes swivel back to me. "I haven't spoken about that in over twenty-five years."

"Why?"

"Most people are not as intrusive as you, Rhys." He might as well have said *suicidal*.

"Most people are scared shitless by you."

*Fuck my stupid mouth.*

"And you are not?" Eyebrows raised, he means to look intimidating, but he can't hide the smirk.

No one probably ever challenges him, looking like the child of Kylo Ren and Matt Addison before he fully turned Nemesis. As obsessed as Lilly is about all the *Blade* movies, I'm the same way with the *Star Wars* and *Resident Evil* franchises—movies, video games, you name it.

George seems to enjoy me having no control over my trap. I'm also pretty good at reading people, and he has shown, on many occasions since yesterday, that he cares about Lilly, and even her psycho brother. He won't hurt me—*much*.

"Not really. Not anymore, at least," I admit. "You care about Lilly in a way I don't fully get yet, but you do care. You protect her, and that tells me you're not all that bad." I shrug and grin at the man.

"I was on a mission—the details of what or where are not important. I was distracted, and the enemy used that to their advantage. They overpowered me—six to one." I lean forward in my seat as George keeps talking in a detached voice. "I was able to incapacitate three, but my strength was dwindling fast. I had been on recon all night. One was able to get close and sliced a knife across my stomach, stabbed my right kidney." He lifts his shirt and reveals a just as gruesome scar as on his face. Before I can exclaim how fucked up that is, he continues. "His mistake was coming close, and I returned the favor." The diabolical grin spreading across his face makes my blood run cold. Maybe I should be scared for myself. "I was losing blood fast, and the last two managed to pin me down. They told me they would use me to set an example; they planned to cut my face off, return me to my unit, and use it as a warning." Bile starts to rise in my throat, but George is oblivious. "One was sitting on my legs, the other on the chest. He had just started cutting when a bomb somewhere nearby went off. That was my chance. They jumped from the explosion and gave me the leverage on my body to kick them off. Unfortunately, the knife was still close to my face." He traces his scare almost subconsciously. "I was told that I overpowered both and stabbed them a combined eighty-three times. The next thing I remember is waking up in the hospital."

"HO-LY FUCK!" My mouth hangs open, and I'm not sure what the appropriate response here is.

I squeeze as much information out of George as I can—once you get past the scary exterior, the guy is like a wet dream for badass war stories. Don't ask me why, but he answers every question I throw at him. We already established that I'm nosy as fuck, so I guess he has resigned himself to my *intrusive* personality. Most of his replies are completely expressionless, though, as if he detaches himself from recalling the memories. He's just shown me the new scope he got for the AR-15 at this location—he wouldn't divulge how many others he has—when we are interrupted by Nate's voice.

It probably wasn't the most genius idea to provoke Psycho with my bonding with his head of security, but I couldn't stop myself. It made me feel like shoving both middle fingers in his face and doing a whole na-na, na-na, na dance. He deserves so much more after what he has put my family and me through.

. . .

GEORGE LEAVES my favorite accessory in his secret lair. I look at him curiously as he drops the black cloth on one of the cots on the way out, but he ignores me. When he leads me to the backseat, he says I need to lie down until we're out of city limits. I stare at him, and he deadpans, "Traffic cameras." The duh afterward was not spoken out loud but written all over his face. That makes four facial expressions total, and I want to pat my own back. We've totally bonded over the last twenty-four hours.

Occasionally, he quizzes me on the phone numbers; I'm proud to say that I can rattle them off like they've been part of me for years.

I replay the conversation I had with Lilly before it was time to leave. She told me that Nate has to go to LA for the weekend, and that's one of the reasons it'll be another week before she can come home. The alarm bells in my head immediately start to shrill when she mentions the word *alibi*. Yes, her reason makes sense, but I can't shake the feeling that she's hiding something from me. Of course, my brain goes to the worst-case scenarios, like she's not coming home, or he won't take responsibility after all. What happened to these poor girls will never be rectified. Lastly, even though I know deep down it's bullshit, my mind goes down the rabbit hole of Nate not being her biological brother, and this is all a big fat lie. She is *with* him and will never come home. I keep shaking my head several times at that thought. I. Trust. Lilly.

Eventually, George asks me if I'm having some sort of seizure. I guess I'm still shaking my head, and after a deep breath, I ask flat out, "Is Nate really Lilly's brother?"

George's eyebrows knit together as he looks at me, puzzled, through the rearview mirror. I push further. "I mean, how do we know? After all, he kidnaps little girls for fun."

With squealing tires, George brings the car to a standstill on the side of the deserted road. We're in the middle of nowhere in the state of New Jersey. I curse myself once again for my stupid mouth. He may be my new BFF, but I'm pretty sure his loyalty lies with Nate first.

George turns in his seat and pins me down with a glare. "I want you to listen to me very carefully, Rhys. Nate has his faults, but he is Miss Lilly's biological brother. I made sure of that as soon as Nate informed me that he had found her. I have known of Miss Lilly for years, but neither of us was able to locate her. Once I had the DNA proof, I did most of the work. I followed Miss Lilly, not Nate. You can say what you want about him and his past, but he loves his sister. He would do anything for her. If she'd ask him to turn himself over tomorrow, he would. However, both of them need closure. There are a lot more questions to be answered. And Nate needs to make sure Miss Lilly is taken care of. I worked for Mr. Altman for years before his death. I kept in the background after that, but when Miss Payton died, I made myself available to Nate. Someone had to look after him. His mother and sister's death broke him. After everything Mr. Altman had done for me, that was the least I could do. You need to trust your girlfriend to do the right thing. This past week has not been easy for her, either. If she keeps something from you, she has her reasons."

My mouth hangs open, and I stare at George wide-eyed. This is the first time he has spoken like this about Nate, and it makes it clear that he cares about him in a way that goes beyond employer and head of security. I simply jerk my head up and down.

We're quiet for the rest of the drive, and eventually, I lie back down in the seat, not even caring to see the route.

# CHAPTER SIXTY-ONE

**RHYS**

IT'S PAST SEVEN IN THE EVENING WHEN WE ARRIVE BACK IN Westbridge. When the car comes to a halt, I don't bother getting up. I know the drill and wait for George to bark the next order at me.

Through the gap between the front seats, I see him typing on his phone before he lifts it to his ear. "We're here." Pause. "Nine minutes. Send the message. I will text you when it's time." Another pause. "Yes, understood."

When he places the phone on the armrest in the middle, I can't contain my curiosity. "Time for what?"

George turns around for the first time since giving me the lecture about Nate and trusting Lilly. "To cut the power."

That does make me sit up. "What?"

"I have to get you back in the house unseen. Furthermore, into the guest room that everyone believes you've been in for the past twenty-four hours."

*Oh.*

"What's the plan?" I'm genuinely curious.

"We can't cut the security feed unnoticed; therefore, your friend will flip the breakers from inside the house. The only cameras with night-vision capability are the ones outside and at the main entrances."

"Uh, and how do we get in if they will still see us?"

George flashes me a wide, toothy grin that makes alarm bells shrill in my ears fire-engine-siren style.

I. AM. SO. FUCKED.


YUP, fucked indeed. After, once again, stomping through the shrubbery of Denielle's parents' backyard property for God knows how long, we emerge at the southeast end of the house near the kitchen. I can see the freaking SUV on the other side of the fence from where we're sitting ducked between two massive planters. George pulls out his phone, set to the dimmest brightness; I have no idea what he is doing even though I am right next to him. He types several words and pockets the device again. I try to catch his eye, but he stares at something along the wall I can't identify.

Suddenly, the entire house goes dark, and a few seconds later, something hits me on the head from above.

*Mother—*

I look up and wait for my eyes to adjust to the complete darkness. The "something" is a free-climbing rope Oliver must've left behind when he went to college. I remember this was one of his hobbies growing up. It's hanging down from the third story window, and a head peeks out from above. I glance over, and George's Pennywise grin is back.

*Just. Great.*

He gestures at me, then at the window, and I mouth, "What?"

He points again, and I get what he expects me to do. "You're not fucking serious?" I keep my voice low, but I might as well have shouted; it's that silent.

Pennywise turns his usual self again. "Get your ass up that rope and into the house. You have three minutes before the backup generator kicks in, and then you can kiss the phone in your pocket goodbye. Nate was very clear about what to do when you don't follow the plan. And this is the plan."

My inner five-year-old comes out, and I mumble, "Nate can kiss my ass!"

George starts reaching for the pocket I stashed the phone in, and I jump backward. "Jeez, dude. Chill out. I'm going!" He seriously would've taken the phone back. Fucker.

The grin is back on George's face. He is enjoying himself immensely, and for the first time, I have the urge to clock my new friend. Scary or not.

I wrap the rope around my calf and ankle and grasp it with both hands. One more look to the side and I'm off. Thankfully, this is something we do regularly during practice, and I reach the window's ledge in no time. Wes grabs me by the belt loop and hauls me into the room. We land ungracefully on the floor, and before I can say anything, Wes has the rest of the rope pulled into the house, the window shut, and is dragging me across the hallway into another room. The door closes behind us, and when I turn, I see Denielle leaning against it. She scans every inch of me—probably for injuries—while both her hands cover her mouth.

"You're back," she breathes out.

Without another word, she launches herself at me. My arms instinctively wrap around her. Wes's hand lands on my shoulder, and I glance over at my best friend of ten years. Standing here, the last day seems unreal.

I'm sitting at the foot of the bed in the guest room I supposedly have occupied since arriving here last night. Denielle and Wes take the floor, sitting oddly close together—shoulders, hips, and knees touching. I cock my head and examine them closer. There is nothing romantic going on, but everyone's relationships are shifting. Denielle and Wes are growing closer while I'm drifting apart from my friends—and girlfriend. A sharp pain shoots through my jaw, and I realize I've been grinding my teeth.

"So...?" Denielle looks at me expectantly.

Guilt travels upward, coating my throat. I want to tell them that Lilly will be home soon, but I am not allowed to reveal anything but the agreed-upon story. All I can do is channel my mask—the façade I've perfected over the years. Don't show your true feelings and most importantly, lie your ass off. I pray my friends will forgive me.

"This cannot leave this room. This has to stay between the three of us." I level both with the George-face—stoic and serious. "I am telling you as much as I can—am allowed to."

Before I can continue, Wes interjects, "Allowed to? What the fuck is that supposed to mean?"

*And it's already starting.*

I have difficulty swallowing. I want to blurt everything out, but one, it wouldn't be fair to Lilly—it's her life, past, and future. And two, if I'm honest, Nate still scares the crap out of me, despite what I said to George earlier. He's a genius with the computer, and I'm a little worried about what he could do to me on a cyber level.

I sigh. "Please just let me get it all out."

Wes opens his mouth again, but Denielle places a hand on his knee, and some silent communication passes between them.

*Fucking perfect.*

I lean forward with my elbows on my thighs, hands clasped, and start talking toward the floor, making sure I stick to the script. "As I said, I am telling you everything I'm allowed to. In the end, this is Lilly's story; she needs to tell it to you, not me." I lift my head and make sure both my friends see how serious I am. "She is safe. She is not harmed in any way—besides the injuries she sustained from the car accident. She is healthy." Denielle's eyebrows rise, and I amend, "Lilly crashed the Jeep because she was avoiding a fox that ran across the road. He did not run her off as the feds suspected. She has a cut on her forehead, and her shoulder was injured. But both are healing."

"Did she tell you who the psycho is when you talked to her?" I don't think I have ever seen Wes this angry. Unsettled. He is the goofy one, always a joke or sarcastic remark ready.

Here comes lie number one. "No." I pause to collect my thoughts. "I video-chatted with her—saw her. She is telling the truth. Her..."—I can't bring myself to use the word kidnapping anymore—"disappearance, then and now, has something to do with her past. With her...family. She is trying to get the answers she needs to be able to move on. She wants to come home, but other things have to fall into place first."

*I don't think I could be more vague if I tried.*

"Do you know when she's coming home?" Denielle asks fervently.

Lie number two. "No. She didn't say, and I'm not sure she knows."

"Where is she? Why can't she figure all this stuff out from here? Why would she stay with this...*person*? WHO. IS. THIS. GUY?" Denielle is starting to work herself up. She's worried about her best friend, and I can't fault her.

"I didn't get to talk to her for long." Lie number three.

"THIS IS FUCKING BULLSHIT!" Wes jumps up and storms out of the room, slamming the door so hard that the picture on the wall crashes to the floor.

My head swivels from the door to Denielle, who is slowly getting up. I have to peer up at her from my position.

Lilly's best friend inhales deeply before she opens her mouth. "Wes is... He's been fighting with his parents to cover for you, lying to your parents. That psycho has been blowing up our phones with instructions. Wes hasn't slept. He was worried sick that crazy-scar-dude was going to kill you. And you just lied to our faces like it's nothing. I hope you have some pretty good reasons for that, because I'm not sure Wes will forgive you otherwise."

With those parting words, she turns and follows my best friend.

# CHAPTER SIXTY-TWO

### LILLY

**I don't know if I can do this.**

I stare at Rhys's text. Nate and I are sitting at the kitchen table, ready to eat dinner, when my phone lights up. I haven't let it out of my sight since my brother informed me that they're on their way to Westbridge. I've forced myself not to message Rhys, even though that's all I want to do. He seemed as okay as he could be when we disconnected, but I can only assume what's going on in his head. He's forced to lie to everyone. Again. The more I think about it, the less appealing the homemade pizza in front of me looks.

George dropped him off about an hour ago and has stayed in the vicinity of Den's house in case he's needed. I could tell he was worried about Rhys when he called in for the status update. Nate made a scoffing sound at George's suggestion to stick around, and I elbowed him in the ribs. As weird as it is that he and George *connected*, it's a huge relief for me. It was no surprise that Rhys has issues with my brother—who wouldn't?

"What does Loverboy have to say?" Nate mumbles while shoving almost an entire slice into his mouth.

"Has no one ever taught you to not speak with a full mouth?" It was meant as a joke but came out much harsher as I glance at the screen again. My chest tightens, and I force myself to inhale and exhale to the count of five.

Nate looks at me for an indefinable amount of time. "He can't handle it, can he?"

I flip the phone over so my brother sees the text.

"Fucking great. I knew it," he curses under his breath.

"Stop it! Let me talk to him and see what's going on before you jump to conclusions."

I pull the device back and type: **What happened?**

The little bubble with the three dots appears, and it seems like an eternity until the reply pops up. I put the phone on the tabletop and rub my palms against the cotton of my gray sweats.

**D knows I'm lying my ass off. She made that uber-clear before she stormed out. Wes is pissed that I have no fucking answers for them. He's been lying to his parents and Mom and Dad for me. 4 US. And to top that, the 2 of them are now BFFs or some shit. And I'm stuck in this damn room by myself while you hang out with brother dearest.**

*Shit.*

I glance up at Nate, who, in return, raises his eyebrows.

What do I say to that? I'm stunned by Rhys's angry reply. I don't remember him ever talking to me like this. I push the phone back over to Nate so he can read it himself.

I wait for my brother to make more snide comments, but instead, he looks back at me, forehead wrinkled and mouth in a thin line. "Do you think he can stick to the plan?"

*Do I?*

"I don't know," I admit with a sigh.

*What's the alternative? Kidnap him as well?*

"That's a problem, Lilly." Nate is calm; he doesn't have the *I-told-you-so* voice I expected.

Hands clasped next to the phone, I stare at the untouched slice of pizza on my plate.

We sit in silence when my screen lights up again: **Can we talk?**

With the device in hand, I push back from the table and tap the video icon while walking out of the kitchen. Rhys's face fills the screen immediately. He's sitting with his back to a tiled wall, water running in the background, and I assume he's in the guest bathroom. His mouth moves, but I don't understand a word over the background noise. I point to my ear and shake my head. He nods in understanding and disappears, the phone facing the ceiling. A moment later, he's back with headphones in his ears.

When he doesn't speak, I attempt a reassuring smile, which probably makes me look more constipated than anything, and say, "I'm so sorry." I blink several times as my eyes start watering.

"I'm sorry, too." Rhys looks past the screen with his lips pressed together.

I stop in the large sitting room and plop down on one of the couches close to the fireplace and pull my legs underneath me.

I stare off into the small fire when Rhys's voice brings me out of my guilty thoughts.

"How big is this place you're at?"

I glance at the small picture of myself and see why he would ask that. He can see the rest of the room and part of the foyer in the background.

"Big," is all I can come up with. I want to tell him about the estate and how beautiful it is, the vineyard and the underground gym—he'd love the gym. However, this is not the time.

Rhys nods.

"Talk to me."

He sighs. "It's just all crashing down on me. Wes is so fucking angry. I've never seen him this way. And when Den called me out on my lies..." He trails off, and my chest constricts. I want to help him, but I don't know how.

"I'm so sorry." I sound like a broken record.

"I gotta go." Before I can say anything else, Rhys disconnects.

*What the—*

My heart starts racing a million miles a minute as I try to make sense of what just happened. Why did he hang up like that? Was someone in his room? Is he that mad at me that he can't even bear talking to me? Am I losing him?

I'm paralyzed.

I don't know how long I sit there when my phone starts ringing. I pick up before even looking at the caller ID and am startled when George's face appears on the screen.

"Miss Lilly," he greets me.

"Is he safe?" The call has to do with Rhys, no question.

"He is."

The unspoken is hanging between us and I whisper, "What's going on?"

"I just got off the phone with him." Rhys called George. My eyes widen, and he continues, "I believe I was able to get through to him. He's going to stick to the script, but I'm not sure what this will do to his friendship with Miss Keller and Weston."

Tears are running down my face. What have I done? "This is all my fault."

"It is not, Miss Lilly. If someone is at fault, it is Nate. But even he can't be blamed for all of it."

I nod. Could Nate have handled everything differently when he first found out about me? Probably. But I don't blame him anymore either.

"Give him time. It's been only twenty-four hours. He has a lot on his shoulders for the next seven days. But I am confident that he will be able to handle it. I will remain close by until Friday morning."

"Why Friday?" But before George can answer, it clicks. "The party. You're coming here while Nate is gone?"

"Yes."

"It's not that I don't trust you. But I'll feel better if you are not all alone on the property," Nate's voice interrupts from the doorway to the kitchen hallway. He's leaning against the doorframe, and I assume he's been eavesdropping for a while.

Suddenly, I'm completely drained. I look back at the screen. "Thank you for being there for Rhys, George."

"It is my pleasure, Miss Lilly."

*Is that a smile on his face?*

We disconnect, and I slowly stand up.

Nate walks toward me, stopping a couple of feet away. He seems unsure of what to do.

I step forward and wrap my arms around his midsection. He's not Rhys, but the next best thing. He's family. Nate returns the embrace, seemingly knowing what I need. No words are spoken.

Eventually, I step back, my brother's arms fall to his sides, and I walk away.

. . .

I SPEND the next several hours in the library. I intended to look through more files; there are still half a dozen drawers unopened. But instead, I curl up on one of the couches, clutching my phone and just staring at the bookshelves on the opposite wall. I feel like this heavy blanket has settled over me, and it takes too much effort to move.

The antique table clock on one of the shelves shows 10:23 when my phone vibrates in my hand.

**ILY.**

Tears start immediately flowing. It's a miracle I am not completely dehydrated the way things are going.

I sit up and cross my legs. Holding my phone in both hands, I start typing.

**I love you more than I can ever put in words. I can't imagine what you must be going through, and I am so so sorry. I promise I will make everything right. Please forgive me.**

The bubble appears immediately, then disappear. I stare at the screen, but nothing happens. Rhys is not responding. Did I make a mistake in choosing to stand by Nate? Have I lost him already?

When the little digital clock in the top right corner of my screen switches to 10:30, and there still is no reply, I press the button on the side. The screen goes dark, and something inside of me breaks into a thousand pieces.

EARLIER TODAY, Nate gave me my access code for the NCC. I'm one hundred percent in. I have access to his computers and the security system—though I don't fully understand how that works yet. But any way you look at it. I. Am. In.

Still, the thought of betraying my brother's trust doesn't cross my mind. Instead of snooping or trying to figure out how to work my way out of here, I simply sit down at the massive desk and pull one of the keyboards toward me. I need a distraction, or I'll break down.

The left monitor on the desk lights up when I hit the space bar.

I pull up a search engine and start researching my suspicion of Nate's mental state. I don't know how smart I am for doing this on his computer, but I'm beyond caring. Let him get mad. He's invaded my privacy more than enough.

Around four in the morning, my eyes are burning, but I'm ninety-five percent sure that my hunch is correct. I found several studies, articles, and even personal blogs. People recount their experiences of how certain drugs impacted their ability for rational thinking, their feelings, and what they did while taking said medications. Some of it is more than scary, and to think of losing control over your mind like this makes my chest ache. Next, I plan on finding out what medications Nate is currently on and digging further into cases with the same ones.

I'M on my way back to my room, eyes barely open, when I smack into a hard body coming up the stairs from the first floor. I yelp in surprise, and two arms shoot out to steady me.

"It's me," Nate's voice penetrates the sleepy fog.

"God, you scared the crap out of me. Turn on some lights next time," I mumble while rubbing both eyes with the heel of my palms.

The irony of me walking in the dark is not lost on me. But rather than pointing that out, he asks, "Are you still or already up?"

I'm more alert now that the adrenaline rush from the impact is subsiding. "I was researching something on the computer." I won't elaborate; he can look up the browser history anyway. "Why are you awake?" I finally get a closer look, and my brother is a sweaty mess. I raise my eyebrows and take a whiff. "Ewww...you smell."

Nate snorts. "That's what tends to happen when one exercises."

My eyes narrow. "It's not even five in the morning."

"Your point?" he drawls. "Between you and my job, I have to fit it in my schedule somehow." The response is a big, fat *duh!*

Usually, I'd enjoy the easy banter, but fatigue takes over again. I've lost track of how long I've been awake, and my brain and body are screaming for a break. In the dorkiest way possible, I bump my right fist against Nate's left shoulder as I start moving again. "Cool. See you tomorrow."

Before I make it through the door that leads to my *wing*, Nate calls, "It is tomorrow, little sister."

Instead of dignifying his statement with a response, I just hold up my middle finger. Right before the door closes, I hear him bark out a laugh.

The last thing I remember is falling face-first into my pillow.

## CHAPTER SIXTY-THREE

### HER

IT'S BEEN EIGHT DAYS SINCE LILLY WAS LAST SEEN. NO MISSING *person's report was filed, yet there are unmarked black SUVs parked in front of the house. It doesn't take a genius to know what Tristen is doing. He is pulling strings. Calling in favors, yet again. I'm growing very tired of this— of him.*

*Usually, Gray returns to me right after he has checked on Lilly. His visits have increased over the last few months now that the date gets closer. Not that he complains; it gives him an excuse to check on* her. *However, when I order him to remain in Westbridge, Gray is not happy with me. He has already been there for a week, and he doesn't want to risk detection. Plus, he now has to change his usual detour.*

*But until I can set everything in motion, I need to know what's happening locally. Moving up the timetable was not something I foresaw. I scheduled the plane for three weeks from now. If things progress this way, I may have to leave my "pawn" behind and return sooner.*

IT'S LATE AFTERNOON, *and I'm standing at the foot of his bed. He's been in and out for the past five days. Every time he comes out of the sedation, I order the nurse to administer more—until today. She thought I didn't notice the relief in her eyes when I agreed to her continuous pleas to reduce the dosage. As if I don't know what the long-term effects are—I simply don't care. He is nothing to me, but I'll need him to get to Lilly. Maybe.*

*It's time he hears about what happened. Again. Not that he can do anything about it, but it still brings me great pleasure to witness his torment when it comes to his little girl.*

*When I see movement under his closed eyelids, I know I don't have to wait much longer.*

*Ten minutes later, we are locked in a stare-down. I haven't visited him in two years—while he was awake. He knows something is up. Lips pressed in a thin line, he refuses to speak first.*

*This is going to be so much fun.*

*"How are you, my love?" I smile sweetly at the man lying motionless in front of me. I made sure the idiotic nurse did not reduce the paralytic drugs along with the sedative.*

*"What do you want?" His voice is raspy from years of barely using it.*

*I tilt my head. His courage is entertaining. "Now, now. If I were you, I'd watch my tone."*

*"What are you going to do? Drug me some more?"*

*Is he challenging me?*

*"Well, if you put it like that, we can always change the approach to keep you from running." I arch my eyebrows, pointedly glancing at his legs.*

*Turning chalk white, he understands my insinuation, knowing I won't hesitate to follow through with my threat. Usually, Gray does the dirty work for me, but it might be a nice change to assist in a procedure.*

*Realizing that my thoughts have wandered off topic, I focus back on his face. "Lilly is missing. Again."*

*That gets a reaction, and his head jerks, no doubt trying to push himself up, but his muscles won't obey.*

*"What do you mean?" he whispers, wide-eyed.*

*I make sure my tone is low and void of any emotion. Not that this is a challenge, I haven't felt anything in a decade. "He found her. He took her again."*

*"How?"*

*I would like to know the same thing, but I won't admit that. Tristen has kept Lilly under lock and key for so long; if he knew where she was, he would have collected her sooner.*

*"If she hasn't returned within the next forty-eight hours, I will take the necessary steps."*

*I turn and am halfway to the door when his voice stops me. "You know who has her?"*

*Without turning, I say, "I do."*

*But he is of no consequence to me—never has been.*

*I'm about to close the door to the bedroom when he whispers, "You have always known."*

*"Of course I have."*

# CHAPTER SIXTY-FOUR

### LILLY

I don't get up until Nate barges into my bedroom. I've been awake on and off, but every time I tap the screen of my phone, it basically screams at me: *NO NEW MESSAGES*. So, what does a girl do? Go back to sleep. Which is not a hard task, given the fact that my body demands more rest.

"I've waited long enough. GET. UP!" Nate pulls on the comforter until it hits the floor.

I sit up. "What the fuck? I could've been naked."

"You've been wearing the same shirt for the past two days. The likelihood of you also wearing the same pants was high enough to risk it," my brother deadpans. "Now get your ass in the shower and then come to my office. It's time to start."

"Start what?" I curl into a fetal position, phone clutched in my hand.

All of a sudden, my phone is gone, and I'm pulled up by the hands. "You wanted to learn how to get information."

*I want to get my phone back.*

My damn brother is holding it over his head and even jumping; I can't reach it. Heat floods my veins, and I'm tempted to kick him in the junk. "Give. Me. My. Phone," I growl.

"No." He takes a step back. "Loverboy is in his room. He's fine.

He will contact you when he pulls the stick out of his ass." And with that, he turns and walks out *with* my phone.

Balling my fists, I let out a blood-curdling scream and stomp my foot. Yes, I'm throwing a total temper tantrum. Rhys ignores me. Nate treats me like a little child. I'm stuck in this mansion for seven more days with nothing to do but wait. I grab the comforter from the floor and haul it onto the mattress. Staring at the rumpled sheets, my shoulders slump. Resigned, I make my way to the bathroom with *no* intention of rushing through my shower.

*Take that, brother.*

IT'S past three in the afternoon when I walk through the door to the office. Nate turns briefly before he starts typing again. The top three wall monitors show the usual surveillance footage of the property. The bottom three have the news, stock market, and—what the hell?

"Are you watching *The Bachelor*?" I look between my brother and the screen.

A sheepish grin appears on his face. "I missed the last two episodes and figured I'd catch up on it while I prepare your homework."

"Why on earth would you watch—wait, what? Homework?" My head is spinning.

"The current Bachelor is Julian's little brother, and I can't miss a chance to bust his balls over it this weekend. Plus, it's pretty entertaining. All the drama. Almost makes me miss the LA scene."

*He has lost his mind.*

I let his TV choice go. "What homework?"

"You said you want me to teach you how to hack. That's what we're going to do for the next few days. Maybe then you will also stop moping." Nate shrugs.

"I'm not moping," I mumble while I push the spare chair closer to the desk.

Nate is typing again and doesn't turn when he says, "I'm not going to dignify that with an answer."

His condescending tone makes the blood pound in my ears. "Well, not everyone can have a surface-level relationship like you. I love Rhys, and he's going through all of this BECAUSE OF ME." My voice raises at the end.

Instead of snapping an angry retort at me, my brother turns, and his eyes gentle. "Rhys will come around. I may not be able to relate to what the two of you have, but I do know that it is special. If you could forgive him for all the secrets he kept from you, he will get over this as well. And if not, we can always have George torture him a little." Nate winks at me.

That makes me smile for the first time since yesterday, and I try to push everything else out of my mind.

I will give Rhys space to deal.

I wish I could talk to Den and Wes and tell them everything, but I can't. At least not until I am back home.

IT'S FRIDAY MORNING. Nate is getting ready to leave for LA, George is on his way, and I've spent the last two days *studying* under my brother's watchful eyes. I still haven't heard from Rhys, and the only thing that keeps me from blowing up his phone is George's assurance that he's fine.

George relayed that he spoke to Rhys and that he moved back to Wes's house Wednesday afternoon. I tell myself that he probably isn't alone and can't contact me, but a voice inside my mind keeps whispering, *If he was not alone, how could George talk to him? What if he won't come around after all? Nate is a criminal.*

"Are you done?" Nate's question penetrates the cloud of doubt that's been overshadowing my mind.

Hands hovering over the keyboard, I glance over. "Almost."

THE FIRST DAY, we went over what I know about coding, which is what school taught me. Nothing out of the ordinary—basics. Once Nate was satisfied, he started giving me little tasks: write a program that does XYZ. Simple things. Then he started timing me. I thought he was messing with me, but he just stared at me blankly and pressed the start button on his phone's stopwatch.

Later that evening, he handed me several textbooks to go over. He'd be quizzing me in the morning. He wasn't joking about that either. I got to see a whole other side of my brother. He was in his element, and his genius was apparent. Instead of going to my room that night, I napped for a few hours on the leather couch in the NCC—books all around me. I didn't anticipate that an eight-hundred-page textbook could make such a comfortable headrest.

After I passed his pop quiz, he pulled up several scripts written in what I had to study up on, and said, "Tell me what that does." He started the timer again. Oddly enough, I scanned the lines on the screen and was able to give him the correct answer. It just made sense as soon as I read over it. There were still several commands I didn't know, but something clicked into place in my brain. I've always known that computer science comes easily to me, but by Thursday afternoon, my brother declared that I'm a natural.

After dinner, for which we had to go to the kitchen—no food in the computer room after my tea incident—he showed me how to execute the scripts he uses to get into *places*, what he needs to modify every time, and how he obtains said information. As an example, he used my high school's security feed. A shiver ran down my spine as I scanned the empty hallways of Westbridge High. I immediately recognized the frame where Rhys and Katherine's encounter had taken place a few weeks earlier.

"And they don't know that we're watching?" That was mind-boggling to me.

"No. As long as you don't forget to run the first three commands that execute the subroutines, you're invisible to the system," Nate reiterated. He'd shown me everything in detail, answered all my questions, and explained why he designed it the way he did.

"How did you learn all this?" I asked him at almost two in the morning on Friday.

A small smile appeared on his face. "I told you that anything computer-related always came easily to me." I nodded, and he continued, "My high school teacher had me do college-level course work freshman year. Eventually, he called one of his old friends at MIT, who let me attend his online lectures. I started designing my own stuff sophomore year and had a full ride to several of the best colleges in the country. But I wanted to stay close to Audrey and chose Caltech instead of going to the East Coast. While I was, uh...away, I read. A lot. Every textbook I could get my hands on since I didn't have access to an actual computer."

We talked more about how he designed the estate's security system, and I started studying the code for that until I literally passed out on the keyboard.

BEFORE NATE GOES to pack his bag mid-morning on Friday, (he doesn't need much since he has everything at his house in LA) he tasks me to write a subroutine for my security camera and mics. He wants the system to send an alert if the mic detects a specific phrase. Essentially, it's nothing useful, only good exercise. Nate leaves the details to me, and my pulse speeds up as I grin to myself and finish the final lines of code.

"So, what did you decide?" My brother tries to look over my shoulder, but I quickly minimize the window.

"You'll have to wait and see." His narrowed eyes tell me he doesn't like that one bit, which gives me even greater satisfaction.

Nate lets the topic go. Instead, he says, "George will be here soon, and I'll head out around one. You have the plans for the weekend on your phone. I'll be back Sunday night."

I nod, trying not to roll my eyes. That he didn't plan out his potty breaks and put them on my calendar is a surprise. He even put in when he plans to go to bed, and at what time he'll be with whom. I have all of Margot's information, including the IMEI to her phone. Nate installed a GPS tracking program on his phone and modified it so it is only visible to George and me. A simple Friend Finder app wouldn't do—not secure enough. Hence, why my friends had to remove those from their phones.

Sitting next to me in his desk chair, my brother is playing with his phone. I look at him for a long moment before I voice my thought. I haven't spoken to Nate about Rhys in two days, mainly because my brother has kept me busy the entire time, but that doesn't mean I didn't think about it.

"Nate?"

"Hmmm..." He doesn't look up, typing away on what looks like an email.

"What if Rhys won't forgive me? He still hasn't texted or called," I whisper.

My brother's eyes meet mine, lips pressed in a thin line. "I don't know, little sis. He'd be a fool. His problem is with me, not you."

"Has George mentioned anything to you?" I haven't spoken to George either since his last status update on Wednesday out of fear of what he might tell me.

Nate sighs, and I don't know how to take that reaction. "George says Rhys has texted him a few times, mainly to check how you are. He's been playing a lot of video games since Wes went back to school. Denielle has been by in the evenings—she went back to school as well. Also, Heather came by earlier today to bring Rhys his phone. She stayed for about an hour."

*And that's why I didn't ask.*

My mind starts reeling. Den and Wes are back in school. Has anyone said anything to them? Or, more importantly, how did they explain where they were? Heather went to see Rhys. Why now? If he's been alone all this time, why hasn't he contacted me?

I bite my lip and swallow over the lump in my throat. Whenever my thoughts have gone there, I've forced myself to block everything out not to fall apart, but the mention of my adoptive mother makes a wave of emotion crash down on me that I can barely control. We haven't discussed yet what I will tell them when I'm back home. It's only five days away, but it seems like a lifetime.

"We need to talk about what I will say to everyone when I go home," I start hesitantly, not sure if this is a good time to bring that up.

Before Nate can respond, a beeping sound comes out of a speaker I didn't know existed in this room. The top right wall monitor, as well as one of the screens on the desk, switch to full-screen, showing the circular driveway in front of the main door. A blacked-out Explorer is pulling into the drive, and I glance at my brother. Nate doesn't seem alarmed at all, which can only mean that our head of security has arrived.

*Our? When did his change to our head of security?*

. . .

I STAND at the top of the stairs while Nate is halfway down when the front door swings open. I've seen George on the screen several times; I've spoken to him just as many. However, seeing the man in person is a whole different story. The heavy wrought-iron door slams shut, and the noise makes me jump. The flutter in my stomach is swallowed up by a pit the size of the Grand Canyon as I watch the scene below unfold.

Nate greets the other man with a handshake and one of those half *guy*-hugs.

"It's good to see you, George. Any trouble coming in?"

"Nate," he greets my brother. "No, Joel had a new co-pilot that almost shit his pants when I got on board, but otherwise, no issues." The corner of George's mouth twitches ever so slightly.

My brother takes a step back, and both men turn to look up the stairs at me.

"Miss Lilly. It's a pleasure to meet you in person."

# CHAPTER SIXTY-FIVE

## NATE

SPEEDING DOWN THE DRIVEWAY, I WATCH MY LITTLE SISTER IN the rearview mirror. She stands in front of the main door with her arms wrapped around her midsection. Behind her, George's gaze follows my car until I'm out of sight. I shift down and push the gas pedal of my silver Ferrari 812 to the floor. If I don't get out of here, I'll turn around and stay—consequences be damned.

I don't think Lilly is aware of how well I can read her—the small tic she has, snapping her thumb against the rest of her fingers when she's nervous or, like now, hugging herself when she thinks about her boyfriend.

*Rhys McGuire, what am I going to do with you?*


WHILE I LOADED my bag in the passenger seat, Lilly was admiring the other vehicles I keep here at the estate. I keep several model cars on all my properties—anything from my toys, aka fast but impractical, to big-ass SUVs, like the Escalade two spots down.

I don't think she realized it herself when she mumbled, "Rhys would love this one." All the while, she walked the length of my matte-black Audi R8. I bought it on a whim when Julian and I decided to race on one of our boys' weekends, and neither of us had a bike available. We had driven his Viper to the place we stayed at, so what does a person with an unlimited amount of money do? They walk into the next luxury dealership and buy the fastest car on the floor. Which was a showroom model to demonstrate the custom options they offered. I've barely driven it since because, with the 5 % tint, you can't see shit—the things I did in my twenties. I shake my head at my younger self.

Lilly had stared off into the distance, hand still on the roof of the R8, as George met my eyes in understanding. She's not taking Rhys's silence well—one of the reasons I pushed her to the brink of mental exhaustion for the last two days. All so she would not think about him.

George has kept me updated on Rhys's whereabouts, which aren't a whole lot. He hasn't left Wes's house at all, and according to George, all he's been doing is playing video games and sleeping. I guess the boy also needs a distraction.

I twist my arm and glance at the Richard Mille 031 watch my fiancée gave me for Christmas last year. I made sure to put it on before I left. Going back to LA means ensuring I look the part. Joel sent a text right before I left that we're delayed for two hours due to weather along the route. I have three hours until takeoff. I pull over to the side of the road and take my laptop out of the canvas messenger bag I've had since college. One of the last few memories I made with Audrey—she picked out the patches that are sewn all over it. This bag goes everywhere with me, despite Margot's objections.

I push the driver's seat back as far as possible, which makes typing on the laptop propped up in the middle a tad bit easier. I installed all the necessary programs on this computer before I packed it up. The set-up only takes a few minutes, and I hit dial. I can't stop the smirk on my face, thinking about the name that's about to pop up on the screen on the other end.

Knowing that it may take a moment for him to answer, I try to be patient. But when I listen to it ring for the seventeenth time, I grow frustrated. Just as I'm about to stop the call program on my laptop, he picks up.

"Hello?" He sounds cautious.

"Soon-to-be brother-in-law!" I greet him with exaggerated cheer.

"Really? What if someone would've seen the screen?" he hisses. Aww, I detect annoyance, which makes me grin even more.

"It was worth it. We need to talk."

"Is that so, PSY-CHO?" Rhys repeats the ID I programmed in for this call. I know what he's been calling me behind my back, but it doesn't bother me. He's a kid in love, and even my baby sister has called me that a few times over this past week. Neither of them is that far off—sadly. But things will change soon enough.

"It is. Our girl is upset, and I don't like her upset," I explain my call.

"She's not your girl! Stay out of our business," he seethes into the phone.

"She is my sister. Everything involving her is my business." I consciously make my tone go cold.

*After all, I am a psycho, right?*

That shuts him up, and I continue. "I understand that you have a problem with me. That's fine. But none of this is Lilly's fault. You are making her believe her loyalty to me—her *real* brother—is something she needs to regret. I never asked her to choose me over you, and that's not what she did. You need to get your head out of your ass and try to see her side. She is my only family, and I am hers—as far as we know. But she also needs you. You ignoring her makes her question everything you promised her."

There is more silence on the other end, and I gaze at the dash to make sure I'm not running out of time. I hear Rhys inhale deeply before he says, "I need time. I'm tired of lying. I don't want to lie to her and tell her everything is fine when it's not."

"Of course nothing is fine. I fucked up. You fucked up. But she still forgave both of us. *Our* girl has more heart than you and I combined. She doesn't deserve this. Even if you need time... Talk. To. Her! Tell her that."

I don't wait for a response. I've said my peace and will know soon enough if he listens or not.


Thanks to LA traffic, I pull up to my house as the sun starts setting. I notice several rooms on the top floor are lit up.

*FUCK!*

I take my time parking my Aston Martin One-77 in its usual spot next to the white G-Wagon in the motor pool. I texted Hank earlier to leave it at the company's private hanger. I had no desire to deal with a car service today, and he stopped asking questions about my random requests a long time ago—rich people's eccentrics, as you could call it. I basically turned him into my P.A. years ago.

Glancing over, my first thought is that Lilly would probably enjoy the Mercedes since she totaled her Jeep. "Maybe someday I'll be able to give it to her."

Mentally preparing myself, I slowly make my way inside. I stop in the kitchen for a glass of water before heading upstairs. Margot stands in the middle of my bedroom with several garment bags draped over the king-size bed, both armchairs that sit in front of the floor-to-ceiling window overlooking the pool, and even hanging from the doorframes leading to the master bath and closet.

*You've got to be fucking kidding me.*

She hasn't noticed me yet, digging through one of her three Louis Vuitton Courriers—also occupying my bedroom.

"Sweetheart?" I keep my voice low and force my hands to unclench. I hadn't expected to see my fiancée tonight. It's almost nine, and I want to check in with Lilly. George has sent me several texts, and I know everything that's happened since I left, but I want to talk to my sister. Seeing her face, even if it's on a screen, would help release the tightness in my chest.

Margot whirls around. "DARLING!" Her face lights up with a smile, but she doesn't move away from the trunk. For the first time since we've been together, I notice how *atypical* our relationship is. Any normal couple that hasn't seen each other in weeks would at least embrace, if not rip each other's clothes off. But neither of us makes any indication to do any of that.

I try not to sound like an ass, but the urge to just kick her out is taking root and spreading through my entire body. "Why are you here, sweetheart?"

She has her own seven-bedroom house on the other side of town.

*Why is she in my house?*

She finally straightens and comes over to me. Placing her hand on my chest, she raises to her tiptoes and places a kiss on my cheek.

"Your house is closer to the airport. We just landed from France, and I didn't want to drive all the way home if I have to be back here tomorrow for the party."

"What do you mean *here?*" I hope she is just using here as the figurative way of describing this part of the greater Los Angeles area.

"Darling, don't you remember? Celeste's party is here. Julian is renovating the pool, and their house is a disaster."

*Fucking Julian.*

I swallow my curse. He did that on purpose so that he doesn't have to deal with this ridiculous party.

"No, I don't remember. When exactly did we decide on that?" There is no point in arguing now. I'm sure everything is already planned, ordered, and paid for.

Margot puts her finger on her chin, looking away—a gesture that is endearing on my sister but makes me want to rip my hair out looking at the woman in front of me.

"I think we talked about that while I was in France."

*We most certainly did not.*

"I want everything back in order by the time I leave Sunday afternoon." I can no longer hide my annoyance and stalk out of my bedroom before I say something I'll regret.

*I should've stayed home.*

Home? This is the first time I've referred to the vineyard as home. It's always been my "sanctuary," but home? Though, it's not actually the vineyard that prompted the thought.

Margot doesn't know about my NCC—as Lilly has started calling my office—here in LA. It's in the basement, behind the gym, and my fiancée rarely ventures down here—sweat stench and all. It has the same security measures and the same security system I have at all my properties. I don't hide my office from my fiancée, but it has also never come up. Here. At the vineyard, it's in plain sight, and she accepted that my office is for business only. I could hide a dozen clowns on unicycles in there, and she wouldn't know—or care.

*Again, what does that say about our relationship?*

I start up the cameras for this property, make sure Margot

remains on the second floor, and set the motion sensors for the stairs on alert before booting up the other computer to log into the feed of the vineyard.

The one room I have no cameras in, on any property, is my office. I find Lilly running on the track. Based on the appearance of her hair and clothes, she must've been at it for a while. When I don't see George on any of the cameras, I dial his phone.

"Nate," George greets me as usual. He has never wasted time with formalities, though my sister at least gets *Miss* Lilly.

"How is she?" The tightness in my chest turned into a vice when I discovered the state my little sister is in.

"He called," is all George has to say.

Glancing back at the monitor, Lilly is just starting another round of the quarter-mile track.

*This is not good.*


AFTER HAVING TURNED my bedroom into the showroom of *La Déesse*, one of the most overpriced boutiques I've ever had to set foot in and lose three hours of my life, Margot eventually ventured downstairs. I abandon my post watching my sister run for dear life in order to avoid my fiancée coming down to find me.

Margot wants to order in Chinese, something we used to do all the time, and I used to enjoy with her. However, right at this moment, I don't want to eat or have meaningless chitchat. I want to banter with my little sister, push her buttons to get a rise out of her. I need to know she is okay. I never expected our relationship to develop the way it did when I brought her back. I don't know what I expected at all, to be honest.

"Did you hear what I just said?" Margot's sharp tone snaps me out of my thoughts.

"I'm sorry, what?"

She huffs and pushes her chair back. Both hands on the table, she leans over. "What is going on with you? I've basically been talking to myself for the last forty-five minutes. You could at least pretend to care about Celeste's birthday."

*But I don't.*

At that precise moment, my phone vibrates in my pocket, and I fumble to get it out as fast as possible.

**She is back in the office.**

I push my chair back and walk out without a second glance.

"NATE!" Margot yells after me, exasperated.

*This will most likely bite me in the ass very soon.*

"CALL LILLY," I bark out as soon as the door of my office closes behind me.

The monitor on my desk comes to life, and before I can sit down, my sister fills the screen. Her face is still red from the run, and I immediately notice the puffy eyes.

*I'm going to kill this boy—figuratively speaking, of course.*

I have tunnel vision, and the urge to throw another monitor across the room overcomes me, but instead, I try to steady my voice. "Little sis. Talk to me."

The dam immediately breaks, and I curse under my breath. All the different ways how I can make Rhys's life hell—or worse than it already is—assault my brain at lightning speed.

"What happened?" I try to control my accelerated breathing.

Between hiccupping sobs, I understand something along the lines of, "Rhys called," "Heather," and "my fault." The rest is drowned out by her crying. While Lilly is still trying to get herself under control, I text George.

**WHAT THE FUCK HAPPENED?**

His response is immediate: **I don't know. She was in the gym when he called, and he won't answer my texts or calls.**

That little shit. He's lucky I'm stuck here for another thirty-six hours, or I would go to Virginia myself.

Since Lilly is in my office and we are still on the phone-slash-video call, I can't pull up the historical feed of the gym—yet.

Another message from George lights up my phone: **Do you want me to check on her?**

I see him pacing the entire length of the kitchen on one of the little rectangles.

**Not yet. Still have her on the screen.**

I focus back on my sister who is slowly starting to calm down.

"Baby sis?" I try again.

Her eyes find mine, and she whispers, "This is all my fault."

My eyebrows draw together. "What is?"

Lilly takes a deep breath. "Rhys called earlier." I gathered that, but I swallow my sarcastic remark and let her get it out at her own pace. "We didn't talk long. I asked why he hasn't called." The moisture wells up again, but this time she stays in control. "He said because he doesn't want to hear anything else he has to lie about."

I nod. "I see. What else did he say?" I hope he at least gave her some assurances.

"He said Mom came by earlier to bring him his phone." Mom, not Heather. She continues, "He said she's lost weight, she's not sleeping, and Natty keeps asking when she can come home. He's been avoiding Dad's attempts to talk to him. He can't face anyone, knowing what he does."

We're quiet for some time, and an idea starts forming. "What if we let them?"

Confusion clouds her features. "Huh?"

"Let them know," I clarify.

My sister's eyes widen. "How?"

I press my lips together. I don't like it, and, in the end, it will be her choice, but the option is there. "Give me a minute. I want George to be in the room with you."

I shoot a message to the man pacing a hole into my kitchen floor to get his ass to the NCC. When he sends me a question mark back, I have to chuckle. Lilly's nickname has already taken root in my brain.

**The office,** I reply.

Not a minute later, I see the door in the background opening, and our head of security takes the seat next to my sister. He is her bodyguard now as he is mine.

She props up her phone against one of the monitors on the desk, and two sets of eyes look back at me. One with hope, the other with wariness. George suspects that whatever I'm going to say will be a "security risk."

I lay out my plan, and Lilly immediately shouts, "I'll do it," while George barks, "Absolutely not!"

*Yup, I knew that would go over well.*

Lilly turns to the man next to her. "Why not? They need to know!"

"Miss Lilly. Please think about it. It will cause more questions. Especially when you return and all of a sudden have no recollection. You need to lie to everyone to protect your brother's identity." Quietly, he amends, "If that is what you still want."

My sister looks appalled, and I have to chuckle.

"Of course I do. He is my brother!"

Hearing her say that makes my heart beat faster. I'm her brother.

George tries to reason with her again. "We don't know what chain reaction this will set off. It could cause more problems than it solves. The authorities won't believe you."

"I can do it! They need to know," she says with such conviction that I almost believe her. But to be honest, I am terrified of the outcome. I won't be able to protect her, and even if I send George with her, he won't be able to interfere. All he can do is stand by in the shadows.

The man that has protected me for the past ten years turns to me. "I don't like this, Nate. You are both risking too much. If this goes sideways, you may have to take responsibility sooner than either of you wants."

I know he is right, but there is only one answer. "Lilly comes first."

"Very well. I'll make the necessary arrangements and will contact you when we're ready."

## CHAPTER SIXTY-SIX

**RHYS**

I DIDN'T THINK MY DAY COULD GET ANY WORSE.

After Mom's visit to bring me my phone—per Dad's order—and Wes recounting the newest rumors about Lilly when he got home from school, the last thing I expected was to receive a call from *him*. Thank fuck my best friend was in the bathroom, taking a shower, when the phone in the front pocket of my hoodie started vibrating.

It was the same hoodie that hasn't fit me since freshman year. I probably looked like Wes's dad in his high school yearbook—he swore up and down that crop tops on men used to be in, but whatever. I couldn't have cared less at that point. When Mom called Wes's cell at seven a.m. to inform me she'd be coming by, I asked her to bring the sweatshirt with her. She didn't question why, and I'm beginning to suspect she knows.

Wes and Den have been back to school for the last few days, and from what they've been telling me, it's not pretty. Wes even skips practice because of the shit our teammates spewed out the first day. Wes got into a massive blowout with Jager and had to be pulled apart by Coach and several of the guys. He hasn't been back since.

*Jager was lucky it was Wes and not me.*

I let the phone ring until I was certain Wes wouldn't suddenly come out. Unfortunately, that involved sneaking in and making sure he was indeed in the shower. What I witnessed can never be unseen but will make for excellent blackmailing material. Humming Carrie Underwood's "Blown Away," my best friend was rubbing one out—God, I wish I had taken a video.

Door securely closed, I answered the phone and had one of the most bizarre conversations of my life. Getting patronized by Lilly's kidnapper-slash-psychotic-brother was the last thing I'd expected. But his words had hit home.

*"Of course nothing is fine. I fucked up. You fucked up. But she still forgave both of us."*

The words kept reverberating through my mind for several hours. Wes no longer questions my behavior. I've walked out on him multiple times to message George when I was about to lose it. He is the only person I don't have to pretend with, one way or another.

*How ironic is that?*

So, when I left my roommate this time, he didn't even look up. I wanted to be as far away as possible from potential listeners when I made the call. I ventured down to the family room's adjacent bathroom and turned on all the water sources at my disposal. This time, I also came prepared with headphones.

I typed the number to Lilly's cell phone several times before I could get myself to press the green button. It rang three times before I heard the one voice I'd missed and dreaded hearing so much the last few days come through the earpiece.

"Rhys?"

We were both quiet after that. She knew it was me but didn't seem to know what to say. Or she was giving me time until I was ready. I didn't know.

"Hey," I finally whispered after several minutes of silence.

"Hey." The relief in her tone was palpable.

The knots in my stomach started loosening. If I could just hold her right now...the need to feel her was consuming me.

"I'm sorry I haven't called." The words had been on my mind for days, yet I couldn't bring myself to call her until he put me in my place.

She sniffled but didn't say anything, and all I heard was her slowly inhaling and exhaling. I counted to five for each; she was trying to gain control. The loosened knot tightened back up. I'd been selfish; I'd distanced myself from everyone, including Lilly, so that I wouldn't have to lie. I didn't want to pretend I was fine, having to reassure her. But hearing her like this...

Before I could say anything to explain myself, she whispered, "Why haven't you called?"

The tightness from my stomach spread to my chest. As much as I didn't want to admit it, I told her the truth. "I didn't want to hear anything else I have to lie about."

"Oh," she breathed.

I could only imagine what admitting this did to her. I tried to lighten the mood and changed the topic. "What have you been up to the last few days?"

When she was quiet again, unease spread through me, and I probed. "Babe?"

"I, um...Nate has been teaching me some computer stuff."

*What the—?*

It didn't take a genius to read between the lines. Her psycho of a brother had been teaching her to hack! To become a criminal—like him.

Something inside of me snapped, and before I could stop myself, the words just flew out. "So, while I had to face my mother who, by the way, looks like she's lost twenty pounds, listen to her tell me how all Dad does is try to find you, and my little sister is not allowed to come home, your psychotic child-kidnapping brother is teaching you how to hack? You've got to be FUCKING KIDDING ME!" My tone rose with every word until I was shouting. Panting, I clutched the phone in my hand so tightly that it was a miracle that it was still fully intact.

Lilly's sobs came through the phone. "I'm so sorry, Rhys. Please, you have to believe me. I'm sorry. Please. I love you."

*I love you, too. More than anything. That's why this is so hard.*

But once again, instead of saying the right thing—the one thing that would help both of us and most likely save our relationship—I couldn't get the words out.

All of a sudden, a banging at the door startled me.

"Dude! What the hell are you doing in there?"

*Wes! Shit!*

I hung up in a panic and shoved the phone back into the hoodie.

Not only did I yell at the love of my life, but now I also hung up on her after she told me she loved me.

FUCK, FUCK, FUCK!!!

Face flushed, I swung the bathroom door open. "WHAT?"

The urge to sucker punch my best friend was so strong I tightened my grip on the door and shoved the other hand into the pocket of my sweats, hiding my balled fist.

Wes looked me up and down, and his face contorted into what probably was meant to be a knowing grin.

"Ahhh, I get it, man. You needed some 'alone time.'" He made air quotes around "alone time."

*He's got to be fucking kidding me.*

"Get what?" I ground out between clenched teeth, still gripping the doorframe.

His face fell a bit, and he stammered, "Uh, you know...uh."

Too far gone, I blurted out the first thing that came to mind. "Oh, you mean whacking it while singing a fucking country song? No, I didn't need alone time for *that*."

Wes's face turned a shade of burgundy. I finally stopped my attempt to permanently imprint my hand into Mr. and Mrs. Sheats's family bathroom door and pushed past my best friend.

Halfway across the room, I turned and walked backward. "And by the way, I would've chosen Taylor Swift's 'Shake it Off.'"

Wes's mouth fell open, and as I was almost out the door, I heard him burst out laughing, which put a small grin on my face as well.

Until I remembered what he interrupted.

*I needed to fix this.*

I DIDN'T GET to fix it. I couldn't find any alone time to contact Lilly or George. After the call, I felt the phone vibrate several times inside my hoodie, but I couldn't check who it was. Wes had been glued to my side since the moment I got back to his room, and an hour later, Denielle joined us. If I had disappeared again for more than taking a piss, he would've started asking questions, especially after blowing up in his face.

I did get to check some of the texts during my 1.5 minute bathroom break, but I hadn't even read half of George's messages when Wes hollered, "If you are not *whacking* it, what's taking so long?"

*Motherfu—*

The only thing that kept me semi-distracted was Denielle's odd behavior. She wasn't her usual self—no snarky remarks about my second-skin-looking crop top, as I would've expected. She plopped herself next to me on the couch while Wes and I engaged in another video game. The entire time, she didn't say a word.

Eventually, Wes coaxed it out of her in his usual sledgehammer, charming way. "Why are you acting so fucking weird, D? There were no new rumors at school today, so what's crawled up your hot ass?"

As it turned out, Denielle and Charlie got into a fight, which explains a lot; they never fight. They don't even argue; Charlie is too much of a pussy to ever stand up to his strong-willed girl-friend. Den asked him if he would visit for the weekend. With everything going on, Wes and I were always together, and she wanted him home. Her admission stunned and humbled me at the same time. Denielle never lets her guard down, and her telling us that meant she trusted us. Anyway, Charlie made some excuse about a party he had already RSVP'd to and couldn't get out of. Even to me, that sounded like utter bull, but seeing Den's face, I bit my tongue.

We played until three in the morning, and by the time Wes turned the TV off, Denielle was fast asleep on Wes's bed. Wes looked at me questioningly, and I shrugged, so he simply scooted in beside her, and I took my place on the couch.

I REREAD George's texts several times.

**Rhys, what happened?**

**Rhys, I know you contacted Miss Lilly. What happened? She is upset.**

**Rhys, if you have any sense of self-preservation, you will answer me. I like you, boy, but I work for Nate. When Nate sees the state his sister is currently in, I cannot guarantee your safety.**

His last text came almost two hours ago, and despite being suffocated under my covers to hide the glow of the phone, a shudder runs down my spine. I don't doubt the damage this man could do to me. His loyalty is to Nate and Lilly first.

I waited until almost four before sending a message to Lilly.

**I got cut off earlier. Wes came in. I didn't mean to hang up. I love you.**

I wait several minutes, and when she doesn't respond, I text George.

**I texted Lilly. She's not responding. Wes caught me on the phone earlier, and I haven't been alone since. Is she ok?**

The bubble pops up almost immediately, and I sigh in relief... until I read the message.

**Things have been set in motion, despite my advice against it.**

*What the fuck does that mean?*

**What things???**

I wait, but my BFF ghosts me. I'm as confused as I am worried. Sleep doesn't come that night.


It's Saturday—again, and we have nowhere else to be. The only way I know this is because my friends don't have school. I stopped actively keeping track of the day of the week when I found Lilly's Jeep flipped on the side of the road. Mr. and Mrs. Sheats left earlier, and who knows where in the world Denielle's parents are.

The three of us sit in the kitchen, eating a late breakfast. And by eating, I mean Wes is using his fork like a conveyor belt. He probably should've made the entire carton of eggs, instead of only six. Denielle nibbles on some plain whole-grain toast, and I'm sipping black coffee. My barely existent appetite had officially said goodbye at four a.m. last night.

As if on command, all our phones—my personal one, not the phone I got from George that is stashed in my pocket—start vibrating on the table. I ignore mine since no one besides my parents have contacted me in over a week. Wes and Denielle both pick up their phones. Denielle's eyes turn to saucers, and my best friend spits an orange mass across the table.

Neither of them says anything and just stare at their screens. I tap my phone and nearly choke on the sip of coffee that I held in my mouth. There, in all caps, is the last name I expected to see on my phone: LILLY.

When I glance back up, two sets of eyes are on me, and Wes mumbles, still with some remaining food in his mouth, "Uh, dude?"

Both hold their phones out to me and show the exact same.

I'm at a loss. What is this? Without a word, I open the message.

"It's a video," I tell my friends.

Almost synchronized, they click on their messages.

"Same."

"I got one, too."

After a moment of silence, I say, "Let's do this together."

Den and Wes move their chairs closer to look at my screen. My heart rate is out of control, and my hands shake so hard that I can barely press play. I place the device on the table since there is no way my hands can hold it steady enough to watch. Lilly fills the screen, and I hold my breath. I can't look away from her beautiful face; the cut on her forehead is almost healed. She sits cross-legged on the leather couch in Nate's office, the bare wall behind her gives no indication where she could be if I hadn't spent hours talking to her in the same spot.

"Hey, guys," her hesitant voice comes through the speaker. "God, this is weird." She chuckles to herself, wringing her hands. "Um...I know you are worried about me, and I'm so so sorry that I haven't been able to contact you sooner. I, uh... I just wanted you guys to see that I'm fine." She points at her head. "This is from the accident. A fox ran across the road when I left school after the whole Kat *thing*, and I crashed my Jeep. We all learned you're not supposed to swerve the wheel to avoid an animal, but as you can see, I did it anyway." She shrugs sheepishly, and I feel the all too familiar flutter in my belly when I look at her. "I promise it was an accident." She takes a deep breath, and her eyes flicker briefly to the side. "Which I told Rhys during my brief call with him. I can't tell you where I am or with whom, but I want you to know that I'm ok and that I'll be back soon. I will make everything right. For everyone. I promise." Lilly's eyes start glossing over, and she wipes them—it is clear what she is thinking, or more likely of whom. "All of you are receiving the same video, but I wanted to say something to each of you individually." She pauses and glances to the side as if waiting for a signal. "Wes." The boy next to me makes a choked sound while she continues. "I want to thank you for being there for Rhys and for letting him crash on your couch. Being there with you gives him a lot of, uh, comfort. Den...hey, babe. I'm pretty sure you're at Wes's right now, and that also means the world to me, knowing the three of you are together and there for each other." Den's hands are covering her mouth, and tears are running down her face. I wrap my arm around her shoulder, and she leans into me. "Rhys. None of this is your fault. I'm fine, and everything will be ok." I read between the lines; she means us and our relationship. George told her that I got cut off yesterday. "I need you to do me a favor. Please show this video to Mom and Dad, but no one else. I need them to know that I'm fine and that I'm coming home soon. You cannot tell anyone about this message, and I apologize in advance about what I have to do to make sure unwanted eyes won't see it. Den and Wes, I really hope you backed up your phones." *What the—?* While Wes dives for his phone, Lilly continues, "Rhys, once you play this video again, your phone will wipe itself. I'm sorry."

*Man, Nate is good. Or is it Lilly who's doing all this?*

"One last thing." She doesn't attempt to hide the tears now. "Mom, Dad, Rhys, Natty, Den, Wes, I love you. Please trust me. I'll see you soon."

The video goes blank, and I hear Wes cursing under his breath.

"What the fuck. My phone is reset to factory setting." He looks at me incredulously.

Den is not moving away from me. Instead, she turns into my embrace and faces me. "You are not surprised."

I narrow my eyes at her. "What do you mean?"

"The way she worded everything. The way you acted when you got back. You've been in touch with her since..." Den states it so matter-of-factly that I'm at a loss for words.

My eyes hold hers, and I'm pleading with her to stop asking questions.

"I don't want to lie to you," I whisper so low that only she can hear it. Still engrossed in his phone, I doubt Wes is even paying attention.

Lilly's best friend stares at me for several moments before she disentangles herself from my arm. The unspoken message is clear, though; she will get her answers sooner or later. Denielle doesn't concede that readily; however, she trusts her best friend. She reaches for her phone and is not even phased when it's reset as well.

"Thank goodness I have it set to back up every night." She shrugs and winks at Wes with a smug smile. That's the Denielle I know. She swipes a few times, types something in, and puts it back down. Glancing over, I see the small bar that indicates she's restoring her backup.

Wes is not that lucky and spends the next few hours copying over phone numbers from Den's and my phones.

It's been a week since I've last been home. The closer I get, the more my heart rate accelerates. Only one black SUV is parked in front of the house, and I pull straight into the garage into my spot. Agent Lanning and Agent Camden are in their usual places at the kitchen table.

*Do they ever go home?*

"Where is my father?" I address no one in particular.

Camden, the only female agent assigned to Lilly's case, looks up. "He is upstairs with your mother."

If she's surprised to see me, she doesn't let it show.

Climbing the stairs, my phone feels like it's burning a hole into the back pocket of my jeans.

I knock on the door before turning the knob and let myself into my parents' room on the third floor. Mom is sitting on the bed, legs covered with a throw blanket, book on her lap, while Dad is in one of the chairs in the small sitting area, typing on his phone.

Mom straightens. "Honey!" The surprise in her voice is audible.

I'm frozen inside the doorframe. I force myself to unclench my jaw. " Can I come in?" I don't think I've ever asked to enter my parents' bedroom, but at this moment...

"Of course." Mom pats the spot next to her. Slowly, I make my way across the room, inhaling and exhaling through my nose. Dad tracks my every move.

I lower myself down next to my mother, and she wraps her arm around me. Leaning into her, my pulse calms a little. Mom has always had that ability.

I allow myself to relish in the sensation for a few heartbeats before turning toward Dad. "I need to show you something."

Bile rises in my throat, and I swallow several times.

Mom places a hand on my forehead. "Honey, you are covered in sweat. What's wrong?"

Dad's eyes haven't left mine, and I can see the wheels turning in his head. I shift so I can pull my phone from my jeans.

"Dad, you want to come over for this."

Eyebrows raised, my father pushes himself out of the chair and makes his way over to the bed. He sits on Mom's other side.

I place my phone in my mother's hand; the video is already pulled up. She glances down and notices Lilly's frozen face immediately. "Oh, my God!" She grips the phone, glancing between my face and the screen.

Dad leans in and draws in a sharp breath. "Rhys?" His tone is almost detached, yet he is asking a million questions at once with just my name.

I press play for them, and my parents watch Lilly's video with wide eyes. Tears are streaming down Mom's cheeks, and even Dad is stunned. It's the first time since this all started that I'm seeing him with unfiltered emotion.

When the video finishes, my phone immediately goes dark.

Mom keeps pressing on the screen, but besides the little bar indicating that the phone is being reset, nothing else is happening.

Her gaze flicks between her husband and me. "What does this mean? She is ok? When is she coming home? I don't understand. Where is she? Why can't she tell us?"

I gently pry my phone from my mother's hands, and she turns to Dad as if he has the answers. "Tristen?"

My father stares at me like he knows that there is a lot more I'm not revealing—the same way he's been keeping secrets from us. I hold his gaze, waiting for him to yell or interrogate me. Instead, my father stands up and storms out of the room.

*Well, that's not what I expected.*

## CHAPTER SIXTY-SEVEN

### LILLY

I'M GLUED TO THE SCREENS. ALL SIX WALL MONITORS IN THE NCC show the security feed, and I follow Rhys's every move. When the tracker on his phone alerted us about movement fifteen minutes ago, my heart rate immediately doubled. By the time he pulls into the driveway, my hands are clammy, and I keep counting my breaths.

WITH NATE BEING COERCED to host Celeste's birthday party, we knew he wouldn't be able to help today. Instead, he walked me through the necessary steps ahead of time. Before he went offline, I probed if my brother wasn't happy to see his fiancée this weekend, but he just grumbled something about "fucking Couriers everywhere" and "no privacy."

*O-kay, then.*

George chuckled but remained otherwise mute. He'd been planted on the leather couch in the NCC all day, reading a weathered-looking paperback. At one point, I asked flat out if he is supposed to shadow me the entire weekend Nate is gone, to which he simply ignored me.

The feed doesn't have sound, but nonetheless, I haven't looked away since the first picture appeared on the top left wall monitor hours ago. At one point, I maximized the kitchen to get a better look at the two strangers in the house. When Nate revealed the cameras to me a few days ago, a lot more agents were sitting at the table. I wondered why the number changed but then got distracted by movement in the master bedroom. I switched to that camera and watched Tristen place a throw on Heather's legs on the bed. Heat crept up my cheeks; I was invading their privacy.

*But they have invaded your privacy for years*, the voice piped up inside my head.

A beeping sound brought my attention to the screen on the desk. George got up and walked around to stand beside me.

"He's on the move."

*It's time.*

"WHAT JUST HAPPENED?" I ask George with eyes that must resemble saucers.

Rhys sits with Heather on their bed, arm wrapped around his mother, while Tristen rushes out of the room. They watched my video, and the wipe routine activated as soon as the signal came through. I can't focus on the satisfaction that I was able to run all the commands and steps without Nate's guidance, because Tristen's reaction has completely thrown me off. I was prepared to see him be angry, question Rhys, maybe get upset like Heather, but as soon as the video finished, he jumped up and left.

George looks just as confused as I am. "I don't know."

I focus on the other cameras in the house and find Tristen in his office, typing away on his laptop.

*What the—?*

An hour later, Heather looks like she is taking a nap, and Rhys makes his way to his room. The urge to talk to him is all-consuming. I want to know if Heather is okay, if he has any idea why Tristen has locked himself in his office, but I can't risk it. Rhys needs to initiate contact when it's safe.

My stomach rumbles, and George scowls. "When was the last time you've eaten?"

"Umm..." I rack my brain but come up blank.

"Let's go," the man next to me commands and leaves the room without a second glance.

I look at the wall monitors one more time and decide to leave the feed up—no one is going to come in here.

I SPEND the rest of the afternoon between watching the camera feed of my house and working on a small project to keep myself busy. I'm not sure if Nate will be proud or upset if I manage to pull off what I set my mind to.

I'm updating another line of code when a video call pops up on the second screen on the desk. I glance over, expecting it to be my brother, but instead, I see Rhys's name on the caller ID. Welcoming the familiar hornets in my belly, I answer the call, and Rhys's face fills the screen.

A smile tugs on his mouth. "Hey, babe."

*God, I've missed him looking at me like that.*

"Hi," I sigh. Warmth is radiating through my body, our last conversation forgotten. I do a double-take. "Where are you?" It's dark around him, and his face is illuminated only by the phone's screen.

"In the car. Dad wants me home from now on, and the only way to call was telling him that I'm going to get my stuff from Wes's."

"Oh." I'm biting my lip. "What happened? I don't have any sound on this end."

Rhys snorts out a laugh. "Of course you were watching. Why am I not surprised?"

I grin sheepishly. "I was worried."

"Riiiight." He winks at me. "So, what did you see?"

*That's a good question.*

"I saw you showing Heather and Tristen the video, Tristen running out and locking himself in his office, you in your room, and, uh, Heather taking a nap..." I trail off.

"You didn't see Dad giving me the third degree?" Rhys asks surprised.

"No. When was that?"

He shrugs one shoulder. "As soon as I went to my room."

*Crap.*

"That must've been while I was in the kitchen."

A quizzical expression flits over Rhys's face, but he doesn't say anything.

"How is Heather? Please tell me I didn't make it worse. I was just trying to help." I wrap my arms around myself, wishing it could be Rhys holding me.

He exhales slowly. "Mom was upset. She doesn't understand. She kept asking how I got the video, when you would be home. But I think seeing you, seeing that you are not injured and stuff, helped her."

Still hugging myself, my hands fist into the fabric of my shirt. "What did you tell her?"

Rhys stares off into the distance for several moments before he speaks. "I avoided answering her for the most part. I said, 'Lilly wouldn't send us this message unless it was the truth. No one would be able to manipulate her to lie to the people she loves. We have to believe that she is okay and will be able to give us answers when she is back.'"

My mouth hangs open, and I'm not sure what to reply. Pride and dread equally build inside of me. Rhys found a way to give Heather what I intended with the video, but at the same time, he also had to bend the truth again.

"Thank you," I whisper.

Rhys's eyes are gentle. "You did the right thing. Though, I never would've expected you to send us a video," he chuckles. "You should've seen Wes's face when his phone reset. I thought he was gonna cry like the time he ran over Riddell."

I bark out a laugh. Riddell was the football Wes got for his seventh birthday. It became the fourth member of the Sheats's family, and we used to make fun of Wes whenever he brought it along—which was all. The. Time. He treated Riddell like a little brother—until the day Wes got his license. The second he got home with his license in hand, Wes wanted to take his brand-new 4Runner for a ride. He backed out of the driveway, running over poor Riddell in the process. The whole scene was like a bad horror movie. You'd have thought someone had chopped off Wes's arms for how he was wailing.

"You need to tell me how you did that. It was sick." Rhys shakes me out of the memory, and the proud undertone in his voice makes my cheeks heat.

"I will, but first, I want to know what Tristen said to you. Was he pissed?"

He leans his head against the headrest and stares at the roof of the car. "Confused would be a better description." Rhys looks back at the phone in his hand.

"Confused?" My brows draw together.

"The first thing he asked was what phone that is. When I told him it's mine, he wanted to see it. He inspected it as if you were gonna climb out of the screen like the creepy girl from *The Ring*. I wouldn't have been surprised if he'd busted out a screwdriver to take it apart."

Something clicks, and I smack my hand against my forehead. "He checked because the bug didn't alert him or record anything."

"WHAT?" Rhys's voice goes an octave higher.

"You know your phone was bugged." Rhys nods. "It was a pretty sophisticated program, according to Nate. He wrote a subroutine that executed when you opened the text and deactivated the tracker," I explain proudly. Mainly because Nate made me write the execution part, and it actually worked.

*Surprise, surprise.*

"That's fucking insane. This sounds like a bad sci-fi movie." Rhys rubs his free hand across his face.

"What else did Tristen say?" That cannot have been all.

"He asked if this is the first time you contacted me. I told him yes. He kept staring at me forever and then walked out with my phone. I yelled after him, asking what he intended to do with it, but he didn't answer. You know how he gets." Rhys huffs a non-comical laugh. "He brought it back an hour later, saying I'm staying home from now on. I told him, 'Fuck that. I'm going back to Wes's.' That's when it got interesting..."

I inhale sharply. Rhys's expression speaks volumes. "What happened?"

"He went big bad Marine on my poor door. Slammed his palm against it, yelling I will remain at home, and that it is not up for discussion. All he has ever done was to keep us safe. Not you; he said *us*. He was dead serious. It was the first time he's showed some type of reaction since you...uh, left."

Tristen is a professional. He doesn't let emotions get the best of him. Ever. We're missing something here.

"He is hiding something."

Rhys nods in agreement. "There is more than just him getting surprised by the video."

We sit in silence for several minutes before Rhys asks, "Now tell me, how did you pull that off?"

I open and close my mouth. My pulse accelerates. The last time I told him Nate had been teaching me, Rhys flipped his lid. "Do you really want to know?" My voice is low.

He picks up on my hesitation. "I'm not gonna go apeshit on you again, Cal. I promise."

I press my lips together, still not convinced.

"You surprised me last time," Rhys adds.

I take a deep breath. Here goes nothing. "It wasn't that difficult. Nate is a genius; he can type out the most complex code in a matter of minutes. And he's a good teacher. He says I'm a natural." I pause, assessing Rhys's face. He seems relaxed and listening, so I continue. "Den's and Wes's videos had a subroutine with a counter and a timer. As soon as they opened their texts, the timer activated. The video is less than three minutes, so I implemented it for the wipe to execute five minutes after the message was opened. If they had played it, the counter would've started the wipe as soon as it switched to 'played once'."

"You?" Rhys interrupts.

"Um, yes. Nate helped with the main part, though." My cheeks heat.

"What about my video?" Rhys's tone is now emotionless, and I don't want to continue.

"Calla?" he pushes.

"Are you mad?" I can't help but ask.

"Uh, not mad. I don't know. I guess it's a bit weird that you are so into it." He sucks in his lower lip and looks off to the side. When I think he won't say anything else, he adds with a wink, "But I also think it's pretty hot that you can do this."

"Hot?"

*I must've heard him wrong.*

Rhys grins sheepishly and shrugs. "My girlfriend, the badass hacker. We need to give you one of those hacker names."

There is a flutter in my belly; I don't know what to say.

"So, explain my video. Obviously, you couldn't put a timer on that one since it had to play twice, and you didn't know when I'd be home." Rhys seems genuinely curious, and my adrenaline level spikes. I didn't realize how much this new skill excites me until I tell him about it.

"Yours had a timer as well, but I set it to twelve hours—I was guessing there. The counter on yours was set to execute the wipe once it hits two or if the time ran out."

"Why not leave it just with the counters?" His eyebrows draw together.

"Well, uh..." I feel a little bad saying it out loud. "There was always a chance one of you wouldn't watch it since you guys were most likely together, and George didn't want to leave it to chance that the video could end up in the wrong hands. Even though Den or Wes would never do that intentionally." I add the last part quickly because I do trust my friends completely. "We were sure that they would at least open the text."

Rhys seems to think that over. "I guess that makes sense."

I let out a huge breath.

We sit in comfortable silence for a while, and I glance at the clock. "When do you have to be back home?"

"Soon. But grabbing my stuff doesn't take long. I'd rather talk to you as long as possible." The affection in his eyes makes tears prick in mine.

My paranoia takes over. "What if Tristen checks your tracker? He'll think you're hiding something from him."

"It's fine. I'm parked on the street in front of Wes's house. If Dad wants to get into it, I'll just tell him I left my phone in the car, which I had planned anyway. He can start following me in person for all I care." Contempt is dripping from every syllable.

"I miss you so much." I sniff.

Rhys sits up straighter. "Babe, why are you crying?"

The tears flow faster, and all the suppressed emotions from the last few days seem to rise to the surface.

"I...this...I...a-all...s-s-so...m-much..." is all I get out between sobs.

"Calla, look at me." Rhys's gentle voice penetrates my violent cries.

When my full attention is on him, he continues, "Babe, this is a clusterfuck of epic proportions. You feel guilty for spending time with your brother while we've all been worried out of our minds. Mom still is. There are more secrets than answers. And I can't even begin to comprehend how confusing this all is for you. You will be home soon. We will figure this out." He pauses for a second. "And when all of this is behind us, we will go on a proper date."

*How does this boy always know what I need to hear to feel better?*

The moisture on my face has dried. Remembering something he said to me not too long ago, I try to make light of this messed-up situation. "You just want to take me on a date so you can finally get into my pants."

Rhys snorts out a laugh. "You caught me, babe. Though I've already been in your pants, just not that...deep." He winks, and heat fills my body, remembering the night in my room he is referring to.

"Remember when I had to press my hand over your mouth because you were about to wake Natty up?" he teases, and every cell of my body is officially on fire.

It's at that moment that the door behind me clicks, and George walks in. I turn, and he pauses, his gaze swiveling between Rhys and me.

"Uh, Miss Lilly. Rhys."

*Oh my God, he so knows what he just interrupted.*

I fight the urge to cover my face.

"GEORGE, MY FRIEND!" Rhys's shout redirects my attention back to the screen.

It is my turn to chuckle. Both men's faces show genuine happiness to see each other. Who would've thought?

"Did you need something?" I ask him.

Still standing, he looks down at me. "No, Miss Lilly. Nate just asked me to check on you since you didn't answer his message."

Sure enough, I didn't notice Nate's text come in on my cell.

"I was distracted," I admit.

"I gathered that."

*Is that a smirk on George's face?*

"I probably should get going anyway," Rhys interjects. I'm not sure if he needs to go or if he wants to ease the embarrassment factor the three of us are experiencing.

I don't want to hang up, but I understand that he has to get home. "Okay. Will you text me if you can?" I know that calling will be out of the question from now on.

"I promise, babe." His smile tells me everything I want to hear but he doesn't want to say in front of the man next to me. And with that, he is gone. Instantly, a part of me is missing.

I must've been staring at the dark screen for quite some time when a hand gently touches my shoulder. "Why don't you respond to Nate and then take a break? You've been in this room all day."

My gaze meets George's, and I marvel how this man scared the bejesus out of me just a few days ago.

# CHAPTER SIXTY-EIGHT

**NATE**

MY PHONE KEEPS BUZZING IN THE POCKET OF MY FADED JEANS. Whereas Margot is dressed like we're attending a dinner at the White House, I could blend in with the crowd at skid row—except for my watch. My jeans are most likely ten plus years old, have several holes, and I've paired them with a faded black T. This is my way of expressing my displeasure for being ambushed with this party.

*Buzz, buzz, buzz.*

*What. The. Fuck?*

Except for my sister and George, everyone who'd contact me is right in front of me. George knows to only call me if there's a real emergency.

I glance around. My backyard is decked out with two dozen cocktail tables. Each is draped in white and gold chiffon with an ostentatious bow on the table's leg and topped with flower bouquets the size of a hot air balloon. Fairy lights hang from every tree on the property, and candles float on little white plastic swans in the pool. I turn to head inside and—what the fuck is that? Oh, for Christ's sake, she didn't. Next to the pool house, two swans waddle between the guests—actual fucking birds. There is no way in hell this shit will be cleaned up by the time I leave tomorrow.

Margot is in deep conversation with Celeste and one of their friends. Despite having grown up in these circles, attending galas and fancy events regularly, I am like a fish out of water. This. Is. My. Home. Pulse pounding in my ears, I'm completely on edge. I don't want any of these people here. My nostrils flare, and I try to rein in the urge to physically kick every single one of these pretentious assholes out—including the swans. Margot and I will have a serious conversation when this is over.

*Buzz, buzz, buzz.*

Oh, for fuck's sake.

I tear my gaze off my fiancée, turn, and stalk into the house. I pass Julian without sparing him a second glance and ignore him calling out my name. Taking two steps at a time, I aim for my bedroom. Disappearing downstairs would be too suspicious at the moment.

I'm almost at the double doors when I pull out my phone and halt—fifteen text messages from UNKNOWN.

*What the—?*

I enter my room and close the doors behind me, locking them for good measure.

Clicking on the texts, I begin reading.

**Margot looks pretty tonight.**

**The red dress suits her.**

**Is the dude with the pink shirt Julian? I saw you talking to him when he first arrived.**

**Which one is the birthday girl?**

**Is this the only pool you have? How do you swim your laps in that tiny thing?**

**Are those actual swans in your yard? Holy shit!**

**Oh...I finally get your Courrier comment, what's in those things?**

I stop reading and turn to the corner above the door, staring straight at the spot on the ceiling.

*Buzz, buzz, buzz.*

I look down and scan the newest text message.

**Hi. :)**

A flush of adrenaline hits me. I don't believe this.

Pulling up the number pad, I key in the digits I never saved to my contacts. She picks up on the first ring but doesn't say anything.

"Little sister, did you hack into my security feed?" I inquire with a purposefully icy tone. I turn away from the camera.

"Maybe?" she answers meekly.

*Holy fucking shit. She's probably smarter than me.*

A broad grin spreads across my face, but I keep my back to her.

"And you thought that was a good idea, why?"

*Do. Not. Laugh.*

"Um..." Lilly seems worried, and I can no longer pretend.

I turn and look up at the camera. She inhales sharply when she sees my expression.

"You're not angry with me?" she inquires, still hesitantly.

I laugh. "Fuck no. That's genius! How did you get past the second firewall?"

The excitement in her voice is contagious when she explains to me how she altered the script I showed her when I walked her through getting into the feed at her house in Westbridge. I'm floored.

"That is some serious coding, sis. I don't know if I should leave you unattended with a computer anymore."

She laughs, but I'm serious. Not that I don't trust her, but hell.

We talk a moment longer, and I confirm that the guy in the pink shirt is, in fact, Julian. She tells me he looks nice, and she's happy I have my best friend there. Such a simple statement. Her sentiment makes warmth spread in my chest. When was the last time I felt anything like that? The last time someone was genuinely happy for me and it had nothing to do with business or my fortune?

AFTER I HANG up the phone, I remain in the bedroom for a few more minutes, collecting my thoughts. With a little more training and proper education, my sister will surpass my abilities without much effort. I make a mental note to look into the best schooling for her—if she wants to go down that road. She said as much, but I would never force her.

Julian meets me at the bottom of the stairs. "Dude, where did you disappear to?"

"Had to take a call." I'm still pissed at him for allowing this party to happen at my house.

He raises an eyebrow with the unspoken question.

"None of your business," I tell him flat out. Let him come to his own conclusions.

He blocks my attempt to walk around him. "I'm sorry, man. I know how you hate people in your space."

"I do." I cross my arms over my chest.

"I figured it'd be fine. Margot will soften you up. You always end up giving her what she wants." He must've seen the ghost of something on my face. "Nate? What's going on?"

I want to tell my best friend about Lilly. He knows what Audrey's death did to me. He was there. Instead, I say, "I'm not so sure Margot is right for me anymore."

Julian's eyes nearly bulge out. "Where is that coming from?"

He's known me most of my life and thought Margot filled the void Audrey and Mom's death left behind. For a while, I thought the same. However, spending time with my sister, seeing the effect she has on George—a man who I've seen smile more in the last week than in the previous decade—and seeing her relationship with Rhys and her friends...it's made me realize everything I've been missing and want to have—one day.

"I can't talk about it yet. But I will. Soon."

Looking at me sideways and then glancing through the French doors out at the patio where both our fiancées are standing and laughing with the other guests, he nods.

"Okay. But you call me as soon as you are ready." Worry is laced in his tone.

"I will." I give him a stern nod then plaster a broad grin on my face. "Now, let's go give your brother shit for his latest episode. What the fuck was he thinking, giving that hot blonde the boot off the show?"

Julian snorts. "Man, you don't know the half of it. That chick was nuts. She snuck into his hotel room after they wrapped the day before and laid on his bed covered in whipped cream with cherries on her tits and pussy."

I squint at my friend. "And that's bad how?"

"Her fucktard boyfriend was there as well—in the same getup."

I stare, unblinking, as a mental image forms in my head, and I can no longer stop myself from cracking up.

I slap Julian on the shoulder and smirk. "Dude, you just made my night. Let's go find baby bro."

# CHAPTER SIXTY-NINE

### LILLY

I SPIED ON THE PARTY A LITTLE LONGER. I FELT LIKE I WAS watching one of those *The Real Whoever of Wherever* shows—just, you know...*real*. It was equally addicting and disturbing; I swear I saw several people snort white powder off the pretty cocktail tables. I wondered if I should send Nate another text, but George assured me that Nate was aware of what was going on at his property and would intervene if he deemed it necessary.

HAVING SPENT my entire Saturday sedentary, I start the next day off at the gym. Well, technically, it's already noon when I emerge from my room, but it's still Sunday—just not that early on Sunday.

Rhys had messaged me after Heather and Tristen went to bed, and we continued texting until the early morning hours. He refused to get off the phone until someone started to move around in the house. We had already exchanged "Good Nights" when a video call popped up on my screen. However, my initial panic immediately subsided when I saw Rhys's smirking face. I grinned like a loon as he held his finger against his lips, mouthed "I love you," and hung back up.

Seventy-two more hours.

.  .  .

I DON'T EXPECT to hear from Rhys for a while, and Nate messaged last night that he is going to meet up with Julian before heading back to the vineyard. I find George in the sitting room with another book. This guy reads faster than Natty. He looks content, and I smile to myself. It's probably the least he's done in months—stalking me and all. I'm about to walk toward the door leading to the gym when I stop in my tracks.

I must've stood there for a while, because all of a sudden, I hear George's voice. "Miss Lilly? Is everything okay?"

Glancing around the sitting room and foyer, I take it all in before settling back on him and smile. "Yes, everything is good."

I turn on my heel and head to the gym. For once, I'm not driven by anger, fear, or guilt. Something has shifted, but instead of trying to analyze it, I've decided to leave it be. Just for a few hours, I want to feel okay.

I GOT three hours before everything came crumbling down. Three. Hours.

Emerging from the bathroom, I find a message from Nate on my screen: **NCC. NOW!**

*Shit.*

I glance at the clock in the top corner. It's four p.m. I spent over an hour in the bath, indulging in all the fancy toiletries my little spa contains—a decision I regret now. Nate wasn't supposed to be back until late tonight. Something happened. Unease immediately builds in my core.

I dress quickly, not bothering to blow-dry my hair, and speed-walk across the second floor to the office. As soon as the door opens, I am bombarded with a cacophony. Every monitor has a different news channel running.

*I didn't even realize the monitors had sound.*

George and Nate hover over the desk; my brother is ferociously typing. Neither man has noticed me over all the noise.

"What's going on?" I try to take it all in, but I don't know where to begin.

Two sets of eyes jerk in my direction, and I stumble back like being pushed. George is trained to keep his cool—at all times. Taking in the man in front of me, a pit opens up in my stomach. His forehead is scrunched, and his mouth is pressed so tightly that almost the entire pink is invisible. The only thing missing is a flashing neon sign with the words "WE'RE FUCKED" above his head. One of those that illuminate one letter at a time, then all the letters start blinking, followed by a border of multicolored light-bulbs. My brother, however, radiates white-hot rage. His nostrils are flared, and the only thing missing is steam coming out of his ears.

I swallow a few times. My attention snaps to the wall monitors when two words jump out from the multitude of voices.

"Lilly McGuire."

I try to figure out which monitor spit out my name when every-thing goes quiet.

"Someone released to the media that you are victim number one and have gone missing again." Nate's voice is like a bucket of ice.

*NO!*

I can't turn my head away from the bottom left screen. My face just popped up, a picture from our last gymnastics meet with a caption that reads: "Lilly McGuire, the alleged first victim of The Babysitter has gone missing again."

"The Babysitter?" I croak.

*What is going on?*

A hand settles on my shoulder and slowly forces me to turn away from my picture. Angling my head up, hazel eyes meet mine, and the anger is replaced with fear. My brother's mouth is in a thin line, and I glance over to our head of security.

*Our.* Because that's what George is. He protects both of us.

"How?" I whisper.

Nate doesn't look away from me, but George answers, "We don't know. The news broke shortly after you went to the gym."

"I had already seen the first report when George called. I was on my way to the airport. If your name pops up anywhere on the Inter-net, I'll know about it." My brother's tone is fierce.

"What about Rhys?"

*Does he know?*

"I haven't been able to reach him," George answers.

I turn back to the six wall screens. "Can we see if he's okay?" Meaning, I want to see the security feed. At this point, I could do it myself, but Nate is still faster.

I see him sit down out of the corner of my eye, and not long after, the feed in front of me switches.

I inhale sharply. Heather and Rhys are sitting in the living room in front of the TV. His arm is wrapped around his mother, and she is wiping her eyes with a tissue. Tristen is pacing his office, talking—no, yelling into a phone. The two agents that previously occupied the kitchen table have multiplied as well and are talking animatedly.

"We need to get ahold of Rhys. We need to know what happened on that end," Nate announces with an icy tone. He can't possibly think Rhys or someone there leaked the info?

"They don't seem to know what's going on either. Look at them." I gesture at the monitor displaying the kitchen. The authorities don't look very authoritarian. The scene is almost too painful to watch. They seem as lost—no, confused as I was after my first migraine.

"Rhys is not going to answer his phone for a while," George interjects, watching the living room feed closely.

An idea starts forming, and I turn to my brother. "My phone is untraceable, correct?"

He squints at me. "Yes, what do you—" He's unable to finish his question.

I've already hit dial and pressed the speaker button. Three sets of eyes are glued to the device in my hand.

*Come on, come on, come on.*

"Hello?" a hesitant voice comes through the phone.

"WES!"

*Oh, thank God.*

"Lilly?" Rhys's best friend squeaks.

Nate slaps his forehead and gives me a what-the-fuck look, and I avert my eyes, focusing on the conversation.

"Hey, um...I need you to do something for me."

"Wha—?" Poor Wes has never handled surprises well, and I don't have time to explain either.

"Listen, I'm sorry I'm calling like this. I need you to go to my house and get Rhys to answer his phone. Don't call him. You need to go over in person."

"Bu—?"

*Oh, for Christ's sake.*

"WES!"

"Lilly?"

"Yes," I sigh. "Tell Rhys I called you. But only when you two are alone. My parents can't know."

When he doesn't say anything, I add, "Please, Wes!"

"Okay." His response is only a whisper.

I hang up.

"WHAT THE FUCK WERE YOU THINKING?" Nate roars at me.

"Miss Lilly, that was not wise," George adds, calmer, but his anger with my rash decision is clear.

"We need to figure out what happened, and we can't just call the house phone and ask for Rhys," I defend myself.

My brother throws his arms up. I brace myself for more shouting, but instead, he storms out of the room.

I chance a glance at George, who remains mute. He must see something on my face, because his expression gentles. "Give your brother time to calm down. He is worried about you. This took us all by surprise."

I'm not sure if by "this" he means the news or my call, so I stay quiet. I hope I didn't make a mistake. Sitting down, I watch the security feed on the wall monitors. I should probably Google myself to find out what is being reported, but I'm not ready yet.

Ten minutes later, Nate walks back in and plants himself in the chair next to mine. George has moved to the couch and is looking at something on his phone.

None of us talk until George announces, "Weston is on the move, heading toward the McGuire residence."

*So that's what he's been doing.*

Sure enough, not long after, Wes's red 4Runner pulls up and parks behind the black SUVs in the driveway. I hold my breath as I watch Rhys's best friend make his way into the house—walking straight in. All eyes are on him, and Rhys and Heather jump up from the couch, Heather's hand on Rhys's forearm as they face the newcomer.

Wes says something. I can't see Rhys's expression, but I notice Heather nod at him. Both boys make their way upstairs.

Nate enlarges the camera in Rhys's room to full screen, but when neither of them shows up, I frantically search the remaining feed. Rhys and Wes are in my bedroom, and a blush creeps up my cheeks.

*What are they doing?*

Not that I have anything to hide in there, but seeing the two boys in my private space...my face, neck, and ears feel like I just opened the door to an oven.

We switch to that frame, and I recognize my name on Wes's lips. Rhys darts into my closet and emerges with—what the hell? He has my purple satin grip bag in one hand, and he latches onto Wes's arm in passing, dragging him into my bathroom.

"Uh, little sister, why is your boyfriend and his best friend going into your bathroom with sex toys?"

My head whips to my brother. "WHAT?" I shriek, then it clicks, and I smack him across the head. "That's my grip bag." When he just raises an eyebrow, I slap him again. "For gymnastics, you moron."

"Ohhh." He grins. "Not my fault that it looks like the, uh...gift I gave Margot for our second anniversary."

I cover my face. "Oh my God, just shut up. Rhys probably used it to hide the phone." I keep the *duh* to myself.

I hear a snort from the couch, and even George can't keep it together. Thankfully, that's the moment my phone starts vibrating on the desk.

Before I can answer, Nate snatches it and swipes, pressing the device to his ear. "This better not have been you or your little friends!" His tone is calculated, and I recognize how my brother is running through several scenarios in his head. He listens and nods to himself. "How do you know?" Pause. Another nod. "Okay, keep me posted. Here." Nate hands me the phone, and I give him the evil eye.

"Rhys?"

"Hey, babe! Sounds like he is not too happy right now." Rhys's tone is subdued, and I hear water running in the background.

"This, yeah...this was quite a shock."

"No, shit!" I hear Wes's muffled voice.

"Am I on speakerphone?" My heart rate picks up.

"No! Do you think I'm an idiot?" Rhys huffs. "Wes has one of my headphones."

Wes heard Nate talking. Oh my gosh, this is getting worse by the minute.

"Did he hear..." I trail off.

Instead of Rhys, Wes answers coolly, "I did. You have a helluva lot to explain."

*SHIT!*

"I will," I mumble. Glancing over at Nate, he's glaring, and I shrink in my seat. "Rhys?"

"Yeah, babe?"

"Tell Wes."

There is silence on the other end.

"Maybe Den as well, while you're at it. But only if there is no chance of anyone overhearing you."

George jumps up from the couch, staring at me. He shows no expression whatsoever, which is worse than the way Nate glowers at me. He is close to blowing a gasket. Holding George's gaze, a cold shiver runs down my spine.

"Uh, are you sure?" Rhys also seems to think I've lost my mind.

"Wes?" I address him directly.

"Here."

"Can we trust you?"

"You kidding me?"

*Why is everyone so angry with me? I'm the one who got freaking kidnapped.*

A red haze starts forming in front of my eyes. "No, I am not kidding. This. Is. *My*. Life."

"Of course you can trust me, Lil." Wes is himself again.

"Thank you." I exhale slowly. "Then yes, Rhys, I am sure."

"Okay."

"He's going to catch you up. You guys need to get out of my bathroom before someone comes looking."

Rhys chuckles, but Wes's reaction is less amusing.

"How does she—?"

"Don't ask, man." Then Rhys addresses me one more time. "I'll be in touch later. Love you."

"Love you more."

Wes and Nate simultaneously make a gagging sound, and I hang up.

FOR THE NEXT COUPLE HOURS, we try to make sense of what happened. Rhys told Nate that they were just as surprised as we were. One of the agents got a call, followed by several more suits showing up at the house with screeching tires. Tristen had been on the phone with the different news channels for hours, dodging questions and, at the same time, trying to figure out how they got their information. I'm not surprised that he won't let the FBI handle it. One fact that no one has caught on to yet: I am not a McGuire. And I wonder how long that will take, given the fact that the whole incest thing is all over social media.

Nate can identify the first report, and almost all the news channels followed suit, reporting mostly the same. Some used my most recent yearbook photo, others one from a gymnastics meet that is posted on Butler's website. The news started calling Nate "The Babysitter," as he treated all the girls like he was just *watching* them for a while. The nickname seems to be what gets to him the most. At one point, he excuses himself without an explanation and leaves. We're in the middle of another news video, and I pause it, watching the door close behind my brother.

Unsure what to do, I look at George, who nods at me. I push myself out of the chair and go after my brother. I find him two floors down, swimming laps. Looking at the pile of clothes on the floor, I squint at my brother, butterflying his way through the pool with violent strokes. He didn't even take his jeans off.

*This could take a while.*

EVENTUALLY, Nate changes to freestyle but doesn't slow down for a good twenty minutes. When he pulls himself out of the water, his chest is heaving, and he leaves a trail of water on the floor, walking to the lounger next to mine. He lowers himself down, facing my chair, and I mimic his position, our knees almost touching. Head in his hands, he's leaning on his thighs, and neither of us speaks.

"I'm sorry."

Nate's pained voice startles me. We've sat in silence for so long that his whisper sounds like yelled words inside an echo chamber.

I reach over and pry one of his hands away from his head, trying to catch his eyes.

"What for?" I ask carefully.

My brother looks up, holding my gaze. "If I weren't so fucked up in the head, none of this would've ever happened."

I think that over and choose to give him the truth. "That's true. But we can't change the past. All we can do is deal with it and move forward. As a family."

# CHAPTER SEVENTY

## HER

*For the last forty-eight hours, Gray has been following every lead I've thrown at him. Especially when I stumbled across the social media accounts for one Kat Rosenfield. The rest of the McGuires have never been of interest to me, as long as they kept Lilly alive and away from him. What I didn't take into account was the possibility that they would allow their children to enter into a relationship. It seems to be a relatively recent development, so I consider the possibility of them not being aware of it yet. Though, knowing Tristen, there is no way the kids could've kept this from him. There is nothing the man doesn't find out. All they had to do was keep Lilly in the dark until the date. What set all these events in motion?*

*I'm sitting in my office, staring at the white walls. There are no pictures—anywhere. I like my house clean. Art is distracting; it evokes feelings—a characteristic I no longer value having.*

*My hand swipes over the top of my glass desk and stops at the keyboard to my silver laptop. Silver, gray, and white—the only shades I tolerate in my space.*

*Gray's room is full of color, blues and greens with mismatched furniture. I refuse to set foot in it. He can come to me whenever he desires, but I will not engage in any physical contact in that dreadful bedevilment. It's appalling.*

*I open my untraceable email account, the one I use to contact my source of information that has kept me up to date on him. It's pathetic how easy one can get people to talk if you throw enough money at them. If it's not cash, it's something else. Everyone can be bought.*

*Gray doesn't know about my informant or him. He is useful on different levels, my tool for many tasks—sex, murder, he makes the most delicious Russian cheesecake—but confiding in him? No. No one is worth my trust. I lost that ability years ago.*

I*T'S time to change the story.*

M*Y DEAREST FRIEND,*

*We have a problem, and I am incredibly disappointed. You know what happens when I am not satisfied with your performance.*

*You are being compensated very generously in the currency of your choosing. May I remind you that I can change this instantly by sending an anonymous message to our mutual acquaintance?*

*It is in your best interest to execute this next task precisely as I will outline in the attached file. I want the information to be broadcasted by every news station by the end of the day tomorrow.*

*Failure to complete the request will end our very lucrative arrangement, effective immediately, and I will have my associate pay you a visit to collect.*

# CHAPTER SEVENTY-ONE

## LILLY

**DAD ISSUED A PRESS RELEASE.**

The chime of the incoming text wakes me, and I squint at the clock in the corner of the screen, trying to clear the fog in my brain. 5:37. Rubbing my eyes, I read the words over and over. Press release. Press...release. I drop the device onto the comforter and sit up in a jerked motion. Tristen issued a press release. I throw the covers back and dash out of my bedroom and across the second floor.

Placing my index and middle finger on the small glass panel, I immediately raise myself on my tiptoes to reach the retina scanner —this was not designed for short people.

*Come on, come on, come on.*

I rattle off my string of words as soon as the mic is exposed and push the door open. The NCC is empty, and I stand in the middle of the room, unsure of what to do. Goosebumps appear on my bare legs and arms. Looking down, realization sets in that I'm just wearing a pair of sleep shorts and a tank top.

Finding more clothes or my brother? Another full-on body shiver decides for me—clothes first. I race back to my room and grab a pair of gray sweats and a white hoodie from the dresser. Pants on, I start speed-walking out of my room, sweatshirt halfway over my head, and slam into something solid. Owww.

Pushing my head through the opening, I look around, disoriented. I ran straight into the door frame. Rubbing the bump on my forehead, I wince and look at my hand; red stains my fingertips. Beautiful. I managed to aim perfectly at my almost healed cut.

*It's too early for any of this.*

DRESSED and with a wad of paper towel pressed against my forehead, I set off to find my brother. After checking the gym, library, and even the kitchen, I make my way back to the office—nothing. He is usually long awake at this time. The possibility of him sleeping didn't even occur to me until I stare at the empty desk chair.

Knocking gently, I push the door to Nate's bedroom open. A gap between the curtains lets enough moonlight in for me to identify his sprawled-out form in the king-size bed. I watch him from the door. One arm is draped over his head; the other rests on top of the navy comforter over his chest. His features are relaxed for the first time in days, and I don't have the heart to wake him.

We didn't leave the pool area until George came for us, and then we finished going over the news reports for the rest of the night. The entire time, Nate was withdrawn, no snarky remarks—very unlike the big brother I've gotten to know.

Closing the door, I make my way back to the computer room.

*WE RECEIVED an exclusive statement from the agent in charge assigned to Lilly McGuire's second disappearance. Miss McGuire has been missing for the past ten days after her totaled Jeep Wrangler was discovered on the side of the road between Westbridge, Virginia and the neighboring town of Fallsbrook. It is confirmed that Lilly McGuire was indeed the first victim of The Babysitter, a perpetrator who has kidnapped five girls between the ages of five and seven in the last ten years. Miss McGuire was abducted at age six, during a field trip to the San Diego Zoo, and reappeared at a hospital in Santa Rosa, California several days later. Miss McGuire had no recollection of the time she had been held captive and was released into the custody of Col. Tristen McGuire, USMC, and his wife, corporate attorney at Webb, Sinclair, and Sinclair, Heather McGuire, who later adopted the girl. The statement did not reveal why there was never a missing person's report filed for either kidnapping or where Miss McGuire's birth parents are. We will keep you updated on the case as the authorities release more information.*

OR YOU START DIGGING *into my personal life.*

I pause the video and sit back, exhaling slowly. It's just a matter of time before someone figures out my birth name and who my biological parents are—well, mother, since I doubt they'd be able to track down Brooks.

I pull out my phone and send Rhys a text.

**Why did T issue the statement now? They already reported yesterday that I was the first.**

As expected, there is no reply. The door behind me opens, and George walks in with a travel mug. Handing it over, he sits down in Nate's chair.

"He's still sleeping?"

I nod and raise my eyebrow, glancing at the mug in my hand.

"I assumed you wanted your morning tea."

I smirk. "How did you know I didn't already have it?"

He looks at me in true George-fashion and deadpans, "I know everything."

I must've resembled a telescope eye, because he winks. "You've been using the same thermos every day, and it was still sitting in the kitchen."

*Oh.*

Instead of continuing this trivial conversation, I move on to the more pressing topic at hand. "Did you see the news?"

"I have."

"Why now?" I whisper.

George thinks that over before responding. "If it were me, I would want to get ahead of the press—before they start digging into your personal life."

I bark out a laugh. "They'll still dig. I mean, the statement basically told them that something happened to or with my birth parents. They never reported me missing."

"That is true. However, I believe the press release was not meant to deal with that part of your past. If your brother couldn't find that information, the press definitely won't." He pauses for a breath. "I've been following Miss Rosenfield's online activities since last week. She's been busy. She's asked around if anyone has heard from Rhys, putting out speculations as to why neither you nor your boyfriend have been to school. And my favorite, why Weston is, all of a sudden, acting as if his dick is permanently shoved down Miss Keller's STD-infested mouth."

Offended on my friends' behalf, my nose scrunches. "That. Is. Disgusting." Tilting my head to the side, I add, "And it doesn't even make sense!"

"Miss Rosenfield's words, not mine." George's disdain is as visible as the white line across his face. Not making eye contact, he continues, "The social media posts with the photograph have increased as well."

*That damn picture.*

"Do I want to know what's being said about me?" I have a pretty good guess. Having gone to school with Katherine for the past three years, I've witnessed how she operates. It never ends well for the target of her obsession.

"You have to face the consequences of Miss Rosenfield's virtual rampage eventually, but while you are here, I would advise concentrating on the task at hand. There is nothing any of us can do about the girl at the moment."

*Or to the girl.*

My fists ball, and I visualize using Rhys's ex as a Sparring Bob. Executing every single offensive move Spence has taught me over the years on her in my head, a diabolical grin spreads across my face.

"Miss Lilly?"

Hearing my name, the red haze clears, and I blink a few times. "Uh, yes?"

"Dare I ask what just went on in that head of yours?"

No doubt I looked like a rabid animal poised to strike. "Um, probably not."

Suddenly, a thought hits me as if George has slapped me across the face. "Do you think Katherine leaked the information about me to the press? I mean, she saw Rhys in the park."

"No."

"How can you be so sure?"

"Miss Rosenfield is fixated on the relationship with Rhys. I would know if she had anything leading toward Nate or what actually is happening." His response is matter-of-fact.

"Nate did something to her phone," I state, not ask.

"I underestimated the girl once. I will not make the same mistake again." His sneer makes the scar around his mouth contort, and he looks downright terrifying. Thank goodness his contempt is not directed toward me, or I'd pee my pants.

Trying to make light of the situation and distract both of us, I quip, "Why George, that's, like, the fifth time this morning you've shown some emotion."

The man in front of me lifts a hand to his chest and grins—a full-on toothy grin from ear to ear.

"Don't tell your brother. You have that effect on people." He winks.

Feeling all warm and fuzzy, it sinks in. I was so focused on the secrets that are piling up higher than Natty's collection of classic novels and my guilt of putting my adoptive family and Rhys in the middle of me figuring out the relationship with my criminal brother that I ignored what I did find. Amid this pandemonium, I have gained a new family. A slightly—scratch that, a dysfunctional family, but both men, Nate and George, care deeply about me. And I'm pretty sure George's affection extends to Rhys as well.

Taking a sip of my tea, I voice the question. "So, who?"

"Leave that up to me," Nate's voice interrupts from the door, and I take in his disheveled appearance of a rumpled gray t-shirt and low-hanging blue-and-green plaid pajama pants. I was so concentrated on George that I didn't hear the usual buzzing sound of the door opening. He slouches in, and when George makes a move to get out of the second chair, my brother waves him off and, instead, makes his way to the leather couch, grabbing the laptop off the desk in passing.

George focuses back on me and amends our previous conversation. "I believe the statement was to clarify your blood relations with the McGuires."

*Oh.*

"Oh!"

Settling into the couch, Nate opens the computer and starts

typing. Not stopping at all, he informs us casually, "Lilly, we will have to start medicating you, effective immediately."

*Wait, what?*

"Excuse me?" Oh, goody. Minnie Mouse is back. I must've heard him wrong.

Nate completely ignores me and addresses George. "I need you to call your guy and get everything we need. Come Wednesday, her bloodstream needs to match the story."

*Oh, hell no!*

My body tenses.

George nods and is about to get up when I latch onto his wrist. The guy who could haunt the nightmares of grown men raises an eyebrow, but I don't care if no one ever touches him. "You're not leaving until one of you explains to me What. The. Hell. Is. Going. On." They can't just dump this shit on me and move on, like, "Oh, let's go grab some donuts for Lilly before we send her off."

*What. The. F?*

George lowers himself back down while I intensify my grasp on his wrist.

I steady my tone and turn to my brother. "Explain!"

Nate closes the laptop and pinches the bridge of his nose. "This is the only way I can protect you."

"By drugging me?" I shriek. *So much for keeping it together.*

Nate's voice is eerily calm, almost detached. Over the last week, I've suppressed this side of my brother—the scary, calculated part of his genius personality. "We have two separate situations to deal with. I told you sending the video would have consequences. Your friends and parents know that you are not a typical kidnapping victim. Even if you manage to keep the truth from Heather and Tristen for a while longer, the media will tear you apart. You are not a scared child anymore; you should remember what happened to you, especially if nothing *traumatizing* happened to you." He makes air quotes around traumatizing. "You don't have a mark on you. I didn't beat or rape you." I flinch, but Nate continues with brutal honesty. "The other issue is the fucking press release and all the shit Barbie has put online the last few days. Your relationship with your brother will be another focus. How long have you been together? Have your parents known and condoned the relationship?"

My heart beats so fast I have trouble catching my breath.

For the first time since starting his speech, my brother looks me straight in the eye. "The only way we can take some of the pressure off of you is by letting the public believe that you don't remember a thing from the last two weeks. I can't help you with the other problem. I can try to block and take down some of the posts, but I won't be able to get them all. Someone will question who is doing it." With a sigh, he finishes, "I'm sorry, little sis."

Nodding, I shove my shaking hands in the pocket of my white hoodie.

I'M SITTING in the kitchen when George returns with a large black duffel bag slung over his shoulder. I nearly choke on a cracker when he drops it on the table with a thud. How many drugs do they need? My entire body would fit in that thing.

I still haven't been able to reach Rhys; all I know is that he's at home and that Wes and Den are there as well. Nate wouldn't let me hack into the feed; he said it would only make it harder for me to see them. There was some yelling and throwing of a wireless mouse involved—he never used that damn thing anyway—and in the end, he kicked me out.

George settles across from me. "Talk to me, Miss Lilly."

"Can you drop the Miss? I think we're way past that." I try to sound annoyed but can't stop the smile forming on my lips.

"As you wish, my lady."

I roll my eyes.

At that moment, my phone starts ringing, and my breath hitches. My hands start shaking so violently that the device slips though my hands twice.

"Shit!" I hiss.

George reaches over and picks it up, pressing the speakerphone button. "Rhys." His tone is stoic, but he winks at me.

"Uh."

"How can I help you, Rhys?" George sounds murderous but cracks a smile.

*Good Lord, he's enjoying this.*

"Um."

"Oh, for fuck's sake, George. Give the kid a break," Nate snaps, coming from the hallway, and I jump. I snatch my phone, turn the speaker off, and press it to my ear.

"I'm here. Sorry."

Nate saunters over to the fridge, George still grins to himself, and I turn around to leave the room when my brother calls after me, "Tell the boyfriend that you will be out of touch the next two days."

*Wha—?*

I face Nate again and raise my eyebrows.

"Lilly?" Rhys's voice echoes in my ear, but I can't form a reply.

He points his head toward the duffel on the table, and it clicks. I won't be able to contact him. Oh God, my memory. My brother is going to mess with my mind. My chest tightens and everything starts to spin. I race up the stairs. I need to be alone.

Somehow, I make it to my room. Leaning against the back of the door, my legs give out, and I slide down in slow motion. Every breath feels like it stops in the back of my throat, the oxygen not making it to my lungs.

Between the blackspots, the face of a man flashes in front of my eyes. The memory is accompanied by the sharp pain I almost forgot about—*almost*. A moan escapes me, and I press the heel of my free hand against my forehead. He has thinning brown hair, beady eyes, and an oval face, but the lower half is covered with one of those surgical masks. The memory doctor.

Bile rises in my throat. The stabbing sensation won't go away.

*Why won't it go away?*

"Babe, are you there? What's going on?"

*Why does his voice sound so far away?*

Leaning forward, I put my head between my legs and mumble something along the lines of, "I'm here. Need...a...moment."

"Lilly, what is going on? Put George back on. You're freaking me—"

That's the last I hear before the phone slips out of my hand.


"—DEHYDRATED—"

"—fucking panic attack—"

"What the fuck are—"

"Calm the fuck—"

"Stop saying fuck!" I rasp out, and everyone goes quiet.

"Babe?" Rhys's voice is close to my ear. He's here? No, he can't be.

I blink my eyes open, and my brother's face slowly comes into focus, hovering above me.

"What happened?" My words are slurred.

"Rhys called me when you didn't answer. We came to check on you." I turn my head and see George squatting beside me, phone in hand and lit up with a call.

I pat next to my body.

*Where is my phone?*

"Are you looking for this?" Nate holds something out. "You dropped it when you passed out."

I push myself into a sitting position and take my phone, cradling it to my chest like it's my actual boyfriend. He's not even on that line.

"I felt dizzy. I couldn't breathe..." I trail off, neglecting to mention the migraine.

"I had to push the door open because you were blocking it. Never knew your tiny body could be that heavy." My brother winks.

"You had another panic attack. Not surprising, considering what's about to happen," George says matter-of-factly.

"Dude, what is he talking about?"

*Wes?*

"Oh great, the whole *Scooby gang* is on the phone," Nate snarls.

"Rhys, Lilly will call you back in a few minutes." Before anyone on the other end can respond, George ends the call.


ABOUT TEN MINUTES LATER, I'm alone in my room. Two glasses of water downed and propped against a mountain of pillows—not sure where they all came from—I dial Rhys's number.

"Oh, thank fuck!" are the first words through the earpiece.

"Hey." I still sound raspy.

"Babe, what the hell happened? Why did you have a panic attack? George wouldn't tell me shit. I was about to drive to the fucking airport." He speaks so fast it takes me a moment to comprehend it all. I don't want to talk about it.

"I'm sorry. It's been a...long day." I exhale slowly. "Is Wes with you?"

"No, I am," my best friend's voice startles me, and my pulse accelerates instantly.

"Oh."

"Yeah. Oh. What the fuck, babe?" Denielle whisper-shouts.

"Where is Wes?" I mumble.

"He's on watch duty—not that it is any less suspicious that Den and I are in the bathroom together," Rhys huffs out with a laugh.

"D?" I ask meekly.

"Yes." Her tone is clipped.

"I'm so sorry." Moisture building in my eyes, I sniff loudly.

"Babe. All I care about is that you are okay. The rest is fucked up, and I'm sure there is a shit-ton Rhys hasn't told us yet, but seriously? Your brother? And what's up with the scary scar dude? I'm just glad he's not going to kill us; Wes can finally stop pissing himself."

A sound between a sniffle, a hiccup, and a laugh comes out of my throat. "I swear I will tell you guys everything soon."

"I'm going to hold you to it." Den sounds more like herself again.

"Can I talk to Rhys for a moment?" I feel bad asking her to leave, but it's bad enough having to tell him about the upcoming days.

After a prolonged pause, she says, "Sure, babe. I'll see you soon?"

"See you soon." I force some enthusiasm into the three words.

A minute or two go by without anyone speaking; then, I hear the voice my body has been craving all day.

"Okay, I'm alone. Now tell me what's really going on, Cal!"

He knows me well. A sob bubbles up. "I love you!"

"I love you, too. What. Is. Going. On? Why are you freaking out, babe?"

I inhale and exhale several times before I lay out Nate's plan.

"ARE YOU FUCKING SHITTING ME? NO! NOT HAPPENING!" Rhys didn't take the medication part well.

"It's our only option." No matter how much it scares me that someone will mess with my memory again, it's necessary.

"There has to be another way!" He sounds desperate.

"Nate would never harm me." Am I reassuring Rhys or myself?

"FUCK! Babe, I don't like this." In front of my mind's eye, I see Rhys pacing the small bathroom, tugging on his hair. "I want George to keep me updated if you can't. But if you can, you have to call or text. Give me some type of sign. I need to know you're okay." I'm pretty sure I can hear Rhys choke up.

"I promise." Not that I can enforce the promise, but I believe that my brother and George will follow through.

We talk for a few more minutes, about nothing in particular; I'm simply not ready to get off the phone.

After we hang up, I swing my legs off the bed and make my way to the NCC. Both George and Nate sit in front of the desk. Newsfeeds are still playing on half the wall monitors; the other half is our local security feed.

They turn, and I ask, "Anything new I need to know?"

Nate shakes his head. "No, same stuff."

I inhale deeply then look at the bag that's now sitting next to George's chair. "Okay, how are we going to do this?"

---

# CHAPTER SEVENTY-TWO

---

**RHYS**

I'VE BARELY SLEPT IN OVER 48 HOURS, AND EVEN CAFFEINE doesn't help anymore. I feel like I'm in a constant state of being buzzed with a side of jitters. In short, I'm a mess. George followed through and sent regular texts. I even got two messages from Lilly, but all they said were, "I'm fine. Don't worry. See you soon." Nate could've sent those for all I know. The only reason I believed Lilly herself sent the texts was that "worry" was spelled with three Rs and "soon" with four Ns. What the fuck were they pumping into her bloodstream?

I've successfully dodged spending more than five minutes with either of my parents. Avoiding Mom makes me feel like a piece of shit. The only reprieve is that she's barely left the third floor, which has reduced the likelihood of me randomly blurting out that her daughter would be coming home in a few days. Also, the increased testosterone presence in the kitchen was making my dick itch. But it served as the perfect excuse when Dad cornered me yesterday as to why I'm holed up in my room. Wes and Denielle are an additional buffer toward my father, taking turns babysitting me since he's ordered me home.

By day two, I've caught my friends up on everything I know, including the constant surveillance by my own family. That tidbit freaked Den out more than Lilly being kidnapped by her biological brother or said brother's mental issues. We talked in the confinement of my bathroom—shower and faucet running—which would raise questions in itself if my father checked his feed. He's not stupid; he could put two and two together. Why he hasn't confronted me yet is a mystery.

One would think that a tragedy like this would bring a family together—not mine. Everyone is on their own, hiding more secrets than Area 51.

Lilly has been officially missing for fifteen days, and George filled me in on the plan last night. Nate already left for LA and is meeting with his business partner to solidify his alibi—part of me still believes that this is all just a ruse not to have to get locked up. Before reaching the drop-off point, Lilly would get another dose of God-knows-what. George refused to reveal their destination, probably assuming I'd be on my way immediately.

*He knows me well.*

A BUZZING UNDER MY PILLOW, which is where I keep my second phone at night, made me jerk to a sitting position around five this morning. I couldn't have slept more than an hour and a half, because the last time I rolled over to stare at the alarm clock on my nightstand was 3:32. I stumbled out of bed and beelined for the bathroom, having to get away from the prying eyes of our home surveillance. Denielle and Wes both slept over, but in my groggy haze, I forgot about Wes's sprawled-out form in front of my bed. Denielle took the recliner while Wes ended up on the floor. Neither wanted to co-sleep—more space for me. Fumbling my way across the floor, eyes mostly closed, I stepped on Wes in the process, who, in return, started bitching like a little girl. Ignoring the whining, I locked myself in the bathroom—the only room where I'm not being watched these days.

NOW, several hours later, I'm again sitting on the closed toilet seat, re-reading the text messages for the hundredth time. They were the first coherent messages from Lilly since Monday.

**We're about to leave. I'm scared.**

Letting her words sink in, nausea made me swallow several times before I was able to respond.

**I know, babe. I will be there as soon as I can. We'll get through this. ILY.**

I didn't expect her to reply again, so when I saw the bubble pop up immediately, I held my breath. Her next words calmed my churning stomach but caused an entirely different reaction in another body part.

**I love u so much. I can't wait to be able to touch u again. You have no idea how badly I want to kiss u.**

No matter how many times I read the message, my brain is unable to tell my groin area how inappropriate its reaction in the current situation is. My dick will never be mine again when it comes to Lilly.

I just put the phone back in its current hiding spot and am about done readjusting my jeans once more when my father's shouts fill the house.

"RHYS! HEATHER! COME DOWN HERE!"

*Showtime.*

We arrive in Podunk, Nebraska a little after nine p.m. local time. I don't bother remembering the town's actual name. Nate chose this place for two reasons: the security is minimal, and George would be able to get in and out undetected. Nate can monitor everything through the hospital's security system which hasn't been updated in over a decade.

The hospital entrance is a madhouse. I count seven news vans. As soon as we pull up, we're swarmed from all sides. It reminds me of the day the cheerleaders noticed a cafeteria attendant add fat-free yogurt to the lunch line. The poor woman couldn't get out of the way fast enough.

Dad leads Mom and me through without acknowledging the press, and even Mom looks like she's on her way to court. Both my parents have their professional fronts up. I channel the quarterback and follow their lead, ignoring the microphones that are shoved in my face.

A local FBI agent greets us and the two suits that accompanied us from Virginia as we pass the double doors.

"Where is she?" My mom drops her calm facade as soon as we're in the privacy of the elevator and reaches for my hand, eyes glistening over.

I squeeze her fingers in return, needing the physical contact just as much. Dad, standing behind us, places both hands on Mom's shoulders, and all of us wait for the local dude to answer.

"She's in a private room on the third floor. We have security staff posted in front of her door because a member of the press was able to sneak in about an hour ago and tried to corner Miss McGuire."

Mom's other hand flies to her mouth, and I swallow a curse. We knew this could happen, but I assured George that I would be with her to face the media. I hope Lilly has been able to stick to the plan. I have no clue how out of it she is.

We exit the elevator, and I immediately spot the two wannabe cops down the hallway. Without thinking, I take off. Dad shouts after me, but I don't stop. The two guards close ranks when I reach the door, but before I can say anything, someone behind me calls, "Let him through."

I shoulder past them and burst through the door. As soon as I'm past the threshold, every muscle in my body locks. I skid to a halt in the middle of the room, unable to move. Heart beating in my throat —if from the sprint or nervousness, I don't know—my eyes zero in on Lilly. I suddenly have a hard time comprehending that she's here, in front of me. It's like I'm watching the scene from the outside. It doesn't feel real.

Lilly sits cross-legged on top of the covers in the bed. She's wearing a green hospital gown up top and blue scrubs at the bottom. Her head snaps up at the sound of my entrance, and her eyes widen. Her lips part, and she blinks a couple of times as if to ensure that I'm really here.

Our eyes lock, and everything snaps into place. It's been *only* two weeks, but it feels like I haven't seen her in years. My need to touch her, to feel her, propels me forward. I'm at her side in two strides, yet not fast enough. Moving up to a kneeling position, Lilly wraps her arms around my neck and buries her face in the crook right underneath my ear. Her shuddered exhale sends goosebumps down my spine, and my arms encircle her midsection. I hold on as tight as I can without causing her physical pain—I hope. My fingers want to dig into her skin, make contact in every way possible. I can't get close enough. The whole thing is somewhat awkward as she has multiple drips going into both arms, but my girl doesn't seem to care. She clings to me as if her life depends on it—in a way, it does.

"I missed you so much," I whisper, letting my lips graze the top of her ear.

Knowing Mom and Dad will walk through the door any second, it's the only slip I allow myself from the script the four of us agreed upon.

I pull back to get a better look at Lilly's face, and my heart skips a beat. The corners of my mouth turn down as I study her. The cut on her forehead looks like it reopened recently. What happened? Apart from the head wound and being paler than her already fair complexion, she looks fine. Her eyes, however, convey her actual state of mind. She's as scared as I am. Lilly is torn between two worlds and has to navigate them alone, for the most part. I will do my damndest to protect her, but even I know a time will come when I can't be there.

By their own volition, my hands move to either side of her face. My thumb moves along her cheekbone, and she turns into the caress. Finally close to her again, being able to touch her, instinct takes over. I lean in and press my mouth to hers. Lilly immediately opens up for me like I'm the oxygen she needs to survive. God, how I have missed these lips, not to mention the feel of her tongue tangling with mine. It's like I've touched a live wire; every nerve ending in my body buzzes with the need to feel her.

The clearing of a throat makes us break apart. I reluctantly pull away, but instead of letting go, I interlace my left hand with her right.

*So much for the script.*

My parents and three agents stand in the doorway with various expressions. The agents look stunned, Dad's face is expressionless, and Mom has a smug smile on her face. At that moment, I'm sure she's been aware of us the entire time; I'm just not sure how she figured it out—home security feed or, well, our inability to hide our feelings.

A tear slowly runs down Lilly's cheek, and she reaches her other hand out. "Mom?"

With that one word, Mom bursts into violent sobs and launches herself at her daughter. Lilly lets go of my hand and wraps herself around our mother.

I glance at Dad, trying to gauge his level of anger about our show of affection, but instead of the expected disapproval, I see my father tear up. Not once, in eighteen years, have I seen the man cry, and it shocks me to the core.

His gaze meets mine, and he gives me a small nod. I have no clue what it means—for us, or Lilly and me.

Time will tell.

THE ATTENDING physician comes in and gives my parents a thorough rundown of Lilly's bloodwork and physical well-being. The agents moved toward the corner of the room but keep taking notes on their tablets and phones. It's a lot of medical blah blah, but my parents both keep nodding in understanding. Mom hasn't left Lilly's side, her right hand in her daughter's left and the other permanently attached to a spot right under her throat, while she listens intently. Lilly's free hand finds mine again, and I squeeze it. We don't make eye contact.

When the doctor concludes his report, everyone turns to Lilly as if they expect her to say something. Her eyes widen, and her hand becomes a vice around mine.

*Fuuuck, that hurts.*

One of the agents is about to say something, but Dad holds up a hand.

"When can we take her home?" My father wants to know. His entire person emanates *I'm in charge*, and the other man snaps his mouth closed.

The local agent, however, has no clue who my father is. "We need to finish questioning Miss McGuire before, uh..." He trails off when he looks up from his tablet and meets Dad's glare. There is a reason my father is one of the best in his profession. No one tells him what to do, and I hide a snicker by coughing into my fist. Mom gives me a disapproving look, and I mouth, "Sorry."

For the first time since Lilly's attending physician entered the room, our eyes meet, and I can see the slight tuck at the corner of her mouth. This ghost of a smile results in a flutter within my chest equal to a level seven earthquake. Still standing next to her bed, I smirk down at her before letting go of her hand and lowering myself to sit on the edge of the bed. I drape my arm around her shoulder, and she stiffens for a fraction of a second but then melts into my side. Neither Mom nor Dad give any indication that our behavior is unusual.

*Our family is damn good at pretending.*

"As I was saying," my father begins again, "when can we take her home?" Turning to the authorities, who hold zero authority, he adds, "You can ask all your questions when my daughter is' back in her regular environment."

The doctor clears his throat. "The repeat tox screen shows that her body is responding to the treatment, and the drugs she had in her system will have cleared in about twenty-four to forty-eight hours. I want to repeat the test in twelve hours. If Miss McGuire keeps improving at the same rate she has since she was brought in, I am willing to release her into your custody by the end of the day tomorrow." He pauses. "However, I will advise you to keep her under observation by your family doctor to make sure there are no permanent side effects of the sedative."

*Permanent side effects? What the fuck—*

George didn't say anything about this shit causing long-term damage. As if she is reading my mind, Lilly places her palm on my thigh—her way of reassuring me that she's okay. I need to get her alone—and soon. I have way too many questions I want answers to.

A NURSE BRINGS in a second recliner and two more chairs, though the agents excuse themselves to the hallway once they realize they won't be questioning Lilly—not here. Mom keeps fussing over her, constantly asking if she needs something, fluffing her pillows, and patting her hair—reassuring herself that her daughter is really in front of her. Reading Lilly like an open book, I see how exhausted she is, but she takes it in stride. She won't tell Mom to stop.

After the agents leave, Dad makes his way over. I slide off the bed and take a step back, giving him space. His eyes briefly flick to mine then down to our once again joined hands before he places his hand on Lilly's leg.

"How are you, sweetheart?" It's the first time he's addressed her directly. His tone is gentle.

Lilly smiles weakly. "I'm fine, Dad. Just really tired."

My father's throat bobs. She hasn't called him "Dad" in forever. He peers down at his phone and nods. "It's late. Why don't we all get some rest?"

When he's seated in one of the chairs, his legs propped up on another, he tries to get Mom's attention, but she doesn't look away from Lilly. "Heather? Why don't you take the recliner?" He nods to the one positioned next to his.

Mom glances back and forth between her husband and her daughter until Lilly touches her arm and smiles. "I'm okay." Mom nods hesitantly before she slowly makes her way to the other side of the room.

I pull the second recliner closer, so it's lined up with Lilly's bed, and make myself comfortable. There is no fucking way I am leaving her side. Suddenly, *the phone* vibrates in the inside pocket of my jacket, and my body involuntarily stiffens. Lilly's head snaps up, sensing the change in my posture. I watch her for several heartbeats before she dips her chin ever so slightly, and I make my way to the private bath attached to her room.

*So much for not leaving her side.*

Both my parents turn, and I stammer, "Uh... gotta take a piss."

"Language, sweetheart," Mom admonishes, and I hear a chuckle behind me.

With the door securely closed, I pull out the phone.

**How is she?**

Nate. I want to ask why Lilly, according to the attending physician, could have permanent side effects, but if I start this now, I have no clue how long I will be in this bathroom. One can only pee for so long—even if I'd say I took a dump.

**Ok. Tired. Doc said she'll prob be released tmrw.**

**Good. Thanks, FBIL. G is close by if you need him.**

*FBIL? Oh, future brother-in-law.*

Ha, this is the *friendliest* message I've gotten from him, and I can't keep from replying.

**NP, PBIL. I'll take over from here.**

**Btw you have a stain on the right sleeve of your fancy leather jacket.**

Fuck, this guy really is everywhere. Heat creeps up my face, and my eyes dart around in the bathroom before shaking my head. There are no cameras inside the rooms; he saw us walking in earlier.

A knock on the door makes me shove the phone back into my jacket pocket, and I crack the door open. Outside, Mom has an arm wrapped around Lilly while Lilly holds onto the IV pole.

"Lilly needs to use the bathroom as well. Are you done?" Mom asks with raised eyebrows.

"Uh, yeah, sure."

I'm about to squeeze past them when Dad's voice comes from across the room. "Flush?"

*Shit!*

I backtrack, flush, and then head back to my recliner without making eye contact with anyone. In my peripheral vision, I see my father staring at me, but I eagerly inspect the stain on my leather jacket.

*Thank you, Nate, for giving me a distraction.*

## CHAPTER SEVENTY-THREE

### LILLY

I'M SLOWLY EMERGING FROM THE BLACK VOID THAT PULLED ME under as soon as Heather turned off the overhead light last night. The blinds are lowered, and the room is dark except for the faint glow coming in through the glass window in the door.

I lie still, trying to figure out why I'm awake, when the soft murmurs of Heather and Tristen register in my mind. Heather sounds upset. Quickly closing my eyes again, I don't dare move and alert them to me eavesdropping.

"I'm sorry, honey. I didn't want you to worry about anything else right now."

"Are you sure?" Heather whisper-shouts, confusion and agitation equally present in her tone.

Tristen draws in a deep breath. "There are some things I haven't told you. And right now is not the right time to talk about this."

"Since when have you known?" The question sounds more like an accusation.

"A while." I don't think I've ever heard Tristen sound so... uncomfortable?

"What is that supposed to mean? How. Long?" Heather's voice rises, and her husband shushes her.

I hear rustling, followed by footsteps and the door softly opening and closing.

*What the—?*

Rhys's hand is still securely in mine. Turning my head, I blink slowly. Instead of his sleeping body, I find green eyes staring back at me.

"You heard that, too, huh?" he whispers with raised eyebrows.

"Yeah, what was that about?" My throat feels like sandpaper, and I add, "Water."

Rhys turns in the recliner, reaching behind him and grabbing a plastic straw cup with water from the nightstand. I take gentle sips. The nurse told me that the stuff they're pumping into me could make me nauseous. As if on cue, my stomach revolts, and I swallow multiple times.

Too much saliva. I cover my mouth with my free hand, closing my eyes again.

*I hate you, Nate. No, I don't, but you will pay for this—somehow.*

"Babe? What's wrong?" Rhys sounds panicked, and his grip intensifies. I hold up my pointer finger without removing the other hand from my mouth.

Inhale. Three, two, one. Exhale. Three, two, one. Repeat.

When I'm sure I don't have to make a beeline to the bathroom, I face him. "Sorry...I'm fine. Just got nauseated. They told me that could happen."

"They?" Rhys narrows his eyes at me.

I smile weakly. "The nurse."

He blows out a long breath. I know when he's trying to rein in his temper. My thumb moves back and forth over his hand, a gesture I know soothes him. "I'm okay," I assure.

Rhys glances toward the door and lowers his tone even more. "What the fuck did George give you?" His nostrils flare. "Why would the doctor assume there could be permanent damage?"

I shrug, trying to play it down. "Any drug could cause long-term effects."

*Just take my brother, for example.*

Not satisfied with my explanation, his mouth is in a thin line.

I add, "They think I've been getting it for the past two weeks, so that's what they treated me for. I. Am. Fine. Nate's plan worked, and that's all that counts."

"I'm going to have a nice chat with my BFF when we get outta here," Rhys growls, and I have to chuckle. Their relationship is so bizarre, even to me who shouldn't say anything given my *family* situation.

"What time is it?" Subject change.

Rhys glances over to the small alarm clock situated behind us. "Almost six."

I scoot over as far as my IVs allow it. "Come here."

There is no point in keeping up the pretense. Heather and Tristen obviously know about us and, so far, haven't commented one way or another. And I want to be close to Rhys. No, *I need* to be close to him. Is that appropriate for our current situation or location? Probably not. Okay, *definitely not.* But from the moment he burst into this room, a low current has been buzzing through my body like an itch I'm unable to scratch. *I want him.*

His eyebrows almost touch his hairline, and he looks back and forth between me and the door. "I don't know if that's a good idea. We're in a—" Rhys's eyes widen, and he trails off when I lift the covers.

All I'm wearing is the hospital gown; I rid myself of the scrubs at some point last night when I got too hot—apparently, another side effect from detoxing.

"Fuuuuuck," he groans and rubs both hands over his face. Glancing at me between his fingers, he mumbles, "Why are you doing this to me?" His chest is rising faster than just a few seconds ago, and I can't deny that I take great pleasure in the effect I have on him.

Inhibition and fear of getting caught have officially exited. "Because I want to feel you. That's all I could think about for the last two weeks. I need you to hold me."

Rhys blows out a sharp breath and *readjusts* in his seat. I chuckle, raising my eyebrows.

Clearing his throat, he pushes off the recliner and climbs onto the bed next to me. I drape the covers over his lap, and he motions for me to lift my head so he can place his arm around me. He gently untangles my IVs, making sure he's not cutting off any tubes going into my arms. I curl myself into his side, one leg over his, and nuzzle my face in the crook of his neck.

*Home.*

A gentle hand tilts my head up, the sensation of his touch sending tingles through my body, and I gaze into the eyes that will always be my undoing.

"I love you so much, Cal. Don't ever do this to me again." His tone is soft, but I can read him like an open book. The concern for my safety and the rage over what Nate has put us through is as visible as his love for me. A vulnerable boy replaces the always strong and confident guy everyone else gets to see. This side of him is usually as sealed as a vault, but I know the combination.

Instead of answering, I reach up and trace the contour of Rhys's strong, angular jaw, zeroing in on his mouth. My heart rate picks up, and I move my finger over his upper lip, lingering ever so slightly. A sly grin spreads across his face, and he softly bites down on the pad of my thumb. I suck in air between my teeth and let my lids flutter closed. Oh, my God. Heat pools in my core, and in an attempt to press my thighs together—still having his leg between both of mine —I create more friction. My eyes spring open, and a whimper escapes my throat. My hazels find his greens—gone is the little boy. Nostrils flared, it only takes the shortest of moments before he crashes his mouth to mine. There is nothing gentle about this kiss. Rhys invades my mouth with expert movement, forcing me to open up. His tongue frantically stroking against mine, I nip at his bottom lip.

*I need more.*

With a groan, his free hand tangles in my hair, tugging on it as he angles my face to gain better access. My entire body is on fire, and I grasp for the hem of his sweater. Slipping my hand under the fabric, I trace the contours of his taut abs. Rhys tenses under my touch, and his thigh pushes against my most sensitive spot. *More.* His reaction and the feel of his skin under my fingertips ignites something feral inside of me. The IV in my arm constricts my movement; I've stretched the tubing to its max, but I can't bring myself to care. The room fades into the background as I give in to the desperate need to mold myself to him. Hiking up my leg, the thin hospital gown shifts and exposes my light-gray boy shorts and lower abdomen. With a moan, I grind against Rhys's body, and he utters a string of incoherent words that resemble something like, "Oh God" and "Feels so fucking good."

Mimicking my movements, I feel his hard length straining against his jeans. The room is suddenly way too hot, and I fight the urge to rip the constricting material off my body. I shift to move on top of him. Need. To. Get. Closer. A loud crash and stinging pain in my arm brings everything to a halt. We spring apart and stare at each other, panting. Rhys's cheeks are flushed, eyes hooded, and we both look down at my arm. The IV pole didn't withstand my urge to climb the boy in my bed. It toppled to the floor and, in the process, dislodged the IV in my arm. Wide eyes, we face each other, and I can't stop the giggle that bubbles up in my throat. Rhys places his forehead to mine and chuckles, "Only you can make me dry hump you in a hospital bed with my parents and FBI outside."

"Sorry?" I grin.

"You. Are. Not. And neither am I. I needed this." He gives me a peck on the nose before pulling back and glancing down at my arm. Following his line of sight, I scrunch my nose. It doesn't hurt anymore, but there is a little blood where the IV should be.

"I should probably call a nurse to fix this mess I made." I smirk.

Shaking his head, Rhys gets up. "I'll go get one."

When he's gone, I sink into the pillow and pull the covers back over my legs. This is the first time I've been alone since my family arrived last night. Even when I went to the bathroom, Heather was with me. A shiver runs down my spine. I wrap my arms around myself and glance at the door out of the corner of my eye. I know there is at least one security guard outside, but nonetheless, I wait for another reporter to ambush me. I was still slightly out of it when a guy, disguised as a male nurse, cornered me yesterday. I just stared, wide-eyed, while he threw question after question at me, shoving his phone in my face. Thank goodness my real nurse walked in and started screaming for security. Who knows what would've come out of my mouth in the state of mind I was in? It's a miracle I didn't reveal anything at all in the hours between George pulling up around the corner of the emergency entrance and Rhys walking in.

Looking over to the recliner next to my bed, I notice a phone laying there. *The phone*. Shit! It must've slipped out of Rhys's pocket.

I quickly stretch over to grab it when the door opens, and I almost topple out, catching myself on the rail before making a head dive. My adrenaline level skyrockets, and the voice in my head screams, *they're back!* They as in the press. I clutch cue rail, pushing myself upright, and hold my breath.

When I hear Heather's voice, my body relaxes. "Sweetie, why is Rhys looking for a—oh my gosh, what happened?" She rushes over and starts inspecting my arm.

My face heats. "It's fine. I tried to reach something and didn't pay attention."

*I wanted to reach something alright.*

My adopted mother's expression calls *bullshit*. We stare at each other, neither of us saying what we want to say.

I'm the first one to look away. Biting my lip, I inspect my nails like I just got the most gorgeous manicure.

Hands unexpectedly cover mine. "Sweetie?"

I don't want to look up, but in the end, I force myself to face the woman who has raised me most of my life. She is about to say something when I blurt out, "I know!"

Heather's mouth snaps shut, and she eyes me for one, two, three, four, five, six, seven—

"I know you do."

Her tone is so gentle, so understanding that floodgates open up again.

I blink several times, but it's no use. "Mo-om?" I sniff, and she places a hand on my cheek.

"My sweet Lilly, no matter what you know or *think* you know, you *are* my little girl." There is a pause before she lowers her voice even more. "We will talk about everything when we're at home. Not here."

My eyes widen.

*Should I be relieved or worried?*

It's that moment when Rhys returns with a nurse following close behind. He halts abruptly when he spots me crying, and the short woman plows straight into his broad back. Narrowing his eyes, his gaze flicks between his mother and me before he peers over his shoulder. The nurse seems to take that as a cue to walk around him and get to work.

"Oh my, how did that happen?" I cringe. She must be the new day nurse as I haven't had *the pleasure* yet. She sounds like the weird-ass clown Heather and Tristen hired for Natty's fourth birthday after he sucked in helium from a balloon. He scared the crap out of all the toddlers, and Tristen had to make him leave.

While the woman works on my arm, I hold Rhys's gaze. His lips are pressed in a thin line, questions written all over his face.

As soon as Heather engages the nurse in a conversation about my repeat tox screen, when it's scheduled, and when she can expect for me to be released, Rhys makes his way over. I incline my head toward the chair, and his eyes turn to saucers as he catches on and basically throws himself at the recliner. He lands with a thud on the dark-red vinyl, and I have to smother a laugh.

*Smooth, babe.*

Heather turns to her son with raised brows, and he grins innocently.

Five minutes later, the nurse is gone, my IV is back in place, and we know my tests are scheduled for ten. We have two hours. Suddenly drained, I unsuccessfully stifle a yawn.

Heather places a hand on my thigh. "Why don't you rest some more, and we'll be back in a bit." Rhys makes no move to get up, and Mom rounds my bed, leaning down to whisper something in his ear. He stiffens, and Heather straightens, winks at me, and leaves the room.

"Uh, what was that?"

Rhys clears his throat. "She, um...she said to make sure your IV stays in this time."

"Oh, God." I cover my face, and the boy next to me cracks up in hysterical laughter. "This is not funny," I mumble through my hands.

"It is a little," he cackles.

I level him with what is meant to be a death glare, but he shrugs. "Hey, at least we know one of them is on our side."

I guess he's right on that account. But we still don't know what measures Tristen will take, even if the fact that I'm adopted is out.

Rhys takes my hand and squeezes. "Let's rest. I'm beat."

I start scooting over, but he stops my movement by tugging me back to the middle. "Babe, if I climb into that bed again, there is no way we will get any rest."

Rhys's tone is low, and my entire body heats at his insinuation. I would love nothing more than to pick up where we left off; I crave this boy more than finding the truth at this point, which feels *so* right and *so* wrong at the same time.

Exaggeratedly, I let myself fall back into the pillow. "Fine."

He places a lingering kiss on my knuckles and winks. "Soon, babe."

I MUST'VE DRIFTED off to sleep because, the next thing I know, the nurse is back and taking my vitals. She draws more blood for the next round of tests, and when I sweep the room, Heather and Tristen are both back in their seats. Tristen is murmuring intently into his phone, but I can't understand a word. Heather looks stiff while she stares at her husband. Turning, I see Rhys softly snoring in the recliner. His hand is still in mine, headphones in place. He hasn't noticed the commotion in the room.

A few hours later, the test results come back as expected, and I am being released into my parents' care by eight p.m. Rhys excused himself to the bathroom at one point and gave me an imperceptible nod when he returned to his place by my side. He was able to give my other family an update.

Tristen or the agents—though my money is on my adopted father—somehow arranged for us to leave the hospital through a side door. We avoid the media vans that are still camped out front and drive straight to a small airport. When I spot the private plane we are aiming toward, I pull on Rhys's arm. His hand has not left mine since we entered the car, and neither Heather nor Tristen seem to care anymore. Though, I've noticed the female agent that came with my family from Virginia sneaking glances when she thinks no one sees.

Rhys's focus is on me, and I nod toward the plane's direction, mouthing, "What the hell?"

He leans over and murmurs, "No clue who scored that little toy, but that's how we came here."

*What. The. Heck!*

---

# CHAPTER SEVENTY-FOUR

---

## LILLY

*Umpf.*

Turning toward the door just in time, Denielle tackles me, and I catch us at the last moment before we would've gone down in a tangle of arms and legs. My best friend is sobbing into my hair, her arms around my neck like a chokehold. I cling to her midsection and squeeze just as hard. It feels like a lifetime since I've seen her. In a way, it has been. My life, more accurately. *I am not the same girl I was a little over two weeks ago.*

A sniffle makes me glance over Den's shoulder. Wes is standing in the doorway, hands shoved into the pockets of his dark-gray hoodie. His favorite blue beanie is covering most of his shaggy, sandy-blond hair and matches his school-issued sweatpants the boys always wear before and after wrestling matches. Scruff on his jaw, he looks exhausted, and my chest tightens at the sight of Rhys's best friend. His eyes glisten as he watches us, and I smile. The corners of his mouth tilt upward, but it doesn't reach his eyes. Behind him, I can make out the form of Rhys, who had gone downstairs to open the door for them. It's almost one in the morning, but my friends refused to wait to come over. Rhys texted them updates throughout our travel, and they arrived not fifteen minutes after we got home.

*Home.*

Walking into the house, I felt like an intruder—a stranger that doesn't belong. Since waking up in the hospital, the doubt about how we would look for answers when I'd be in Westbridge and Nate in California has steadily grown. Lord knows where George is. Probably somewhere close by, but I mean, he wouldn't be able to do anything without revealing himself. Before leaving California, I was convinced I could do this. I was not prepared for the increasing havoc inside my mind as the hours tick by and I face my old life.

I promised Rhys that Nate would take responsibility, but the condition is that we learn the truth first. I may not be in the dark anymore, but I'm also not out of it. I'm rooted to a spot between light and dark. Rhys had years of perfecting his façade; he convinced everyone that he couldn't stand me. I, on the other hand... I can't act for shit. No matter how many times I told people I didn't care about Rhys's actions, everyone knew that I did. As Nate put it one night, *Your face is very expressive.*

Now, facing my two closest friends, a sheen of sweat starts building on my skin, and my mouth feels like it's full of cotton. I swallow several times—it's no use. All the air is getting sucked out of my lungs, and I can't get any oxygen in.

Rhys must see what is about to happen, because he's at my side in milliseconds. He pries me out of Denielle's hug, and his strong arms envelop me.

"Breathe, babe," his voice filters through the cotton that has also taken root in my ears.

As he counts for me, I draw in slow breaths, and the nausea subsides. Tears streaming down my face, I cling to the front of his shirt, pressing my forehead against his chest.

"I'm so sorry," I mumble, avoiding eye contact with the other two people in the room.

A hand carefully touches my shoulder, and I turn slightly.

"You have nothing to be sorry for, Lil." Wes's tone is gentle, understanding.

The guilt that has been festering for so long finally destroys the fragile dam that has kept my emotions in check, and I crumble to the floor. Rocking back and forth with my arms around my bent legs, I can't keep it together. Somewhere in the distance, I hear a buzzing, and instead of Rhys, I am suddenly sandwiched between Denielle and Wes. I'm half in Wes's lap, and Denielle has her arms around me, stroking my hair.

Neither of them speaks. However, I hear Rhys's muffled voice from my bathroom. Water is running, and I know who he's talking to. I jump up like from a four-point start, knocking my two friends backward in the process, and burst into my bathroom. Startled by my entrance, Rhys jumps back and hits the shower door, which slams into the tiled wall.

"Hold on," he interrupts the person on the other end.

I stare at him, and he nods, holding the phone out.

Similar to when you watch someone in a movie having an out-of-body experience, I watch my hand reach out in slow motion and take the device.

Holding it to my ear, I whisper, "Nate?"

"Yes."

I never anticipated these two men, who couldn't be more opposite, would end up having the same calming effect on me. They dislodged the life I had become content with in the most unexpected ways, making me question who I am over and over, evoking different emotions I didn't know I was capable of and pushing me to my limits at the same time. I need them to make it through this. Both have become my home in their own ways: my family and my love.

"How are you?" I don't know if he has ever spoken to me with such uncertainty.

I confess, "I can't do this."

Rhys has made his way over and wraps his arms around me. Leaning my back into his front, I listen to my brother.

"Yes, you can. We knew this wouldn't be easy, but you're a fighter."

He sounds so convinced that I blurt out my biggest fear. "What if I slip and give you up before we find all the answers?"

"Then you will find the truth on your own," he replies without hesitation. "You are smart—probably smarter than me." My brother chuckles. "And George will be at your side." There is no trace of anger in his tone; he truly means it. He would go away without a second thought if it meant keeping me safe.

The words slip out of their own volition. "I love you, big brother."

I stiffen. I never thought about it before, but even in these short few weeks, Nate has become family. I hold my breath, knowing Rhys heard my surprising admission, but he doesn't give any indication one way or another.

Through the phone, I hear Nate choke up before he replies, "I love you, too, little sis."

"Are you watching?" I assume that's why he called.

"I was, but I'm going to exit out now. I had to make sure you got back okay." He doesn't use the word *home*. Does he know that I'm no longer sure where my home is? That it's no longer tied to a place.

"Will you call again?" I press my hand against my chest—a similar gesture to what I used to do when I thought of Rhys while being separated from him.

"No. George is going to check in with you. I'm still working on the other...thing." After a pause, Nate adds, "The one tied to your birthday."

*Oh!*

Rhys goes rigid, and I know for sure that he's been listening to both sides of this conversation. I still haven't divulged the extent of my inheritance to him.

My brother continues, "Stick to the story, and we'll figure out the rest soon enough." He blows out a long breath. "After that, I will do what's right...like I promised."

I nod, more to myself than anyone else. A lump forms in my throat.

"Okay."

"We'll talk soon." Before I can reply, my brother hangs up.

Rhys and I stand in the bathroom, back to front.

"I'm going to take a shower." The sudden urge to scrub the last few days off of my body is overpowering me.

"Do you want me to wait?"

I turn in his arms and raise my eyebrows.

Rhys smirks. "I won't peek."

I try to smile at him but fail miserably. So instead, I raise on my tiptoes, planting a brief kiss on his lips, and tell him the truth. "I want to be alone for a little while."

"Whatever you need." He kisses me on the forehead. "I'll be outside."

I DON'T KNOW how long I stand under the hot spray. I go through my *ritual* of letting the scorching water wash away the turmoil inside of me.

I'm back in Westbridge. My brother is across the country. We are no closer to finding answers. I have to lie about what happened to me—about who I am—and I still have to face my adopted parents. Thanks to Rhys not leaving my side, I haven't had to deal with them alone—yet. I have no clue how much to reveal to them or what they will think of me.

When exhaustion overcomes me, I turn off the water and wrap myself in the towel that hangs on the hook outside the glass door. I search for the monogram I've gotten so used to, but of course, it's not there. My throat thickens. Swiping over the mirror above my sink, I take in the features of the girl staring back at me.

*Who are you?*

Arms around my midsection, I close my eyes. Before I can go down the rabbit hole of conflicting emotions any further, I grab Rhys's old hoodie and a pair of gray-and-pink plaid pajama pants from the hook behind the door. He must've snuck them in while I was in the shower.

Stepping out, I blink. My bedroom is almost dark; the only light comes from the small lamp on the nightstand.

Rhys's large frame is sprawled across my comforter, one arm draped across his eyes, the other resting on his belly. There's a gap between his hem and waistband, and I instantly zero in on his smooth skin. My feet start moving of their own volition. He changed out of his travel clothes as well and is wearing his own school hoodie and gray sweatpants. Despite the dark loungewear being loose, the outfit emphasizes his physique, and my tongue sweeps over my bottom lip. I glance around, but Den and Wes are nowhere in sight.

Almost to the bed, I peek into the hallway. I have a direct line of sight to Rhys's room and can make out the shape of a body in his bed—that's where the others are.

Climbing on the mattress, I pull on the covers. Rhys startles awake, his eyes frantically searching the room for a potential threat. I place my hand on his arm, and as soon as he finds me beside him, all the tension leaves his body.

"You were in there for a while." He yawns and sits up so his head is leaned against my headboard. Holding out an arm for me to come closer, my heart skips a beat, and I glance at the door before looking back at him.

Reading my mind, Rhys says, "It's okay. The 'rents gave their approval. Den and Wes took my room."

I choke on my saliva and start coughing. It takes several moments to regain control and to be able to voice my question. "You asked their permission to sleep in my bed?"

He chuckles. "No, I simply declared I'd be in your room if they needed me. We already knew they—"

I interrupt him in typical Minnie Mouse fashion. "And they were fine with that? Tristen okay'ed it? Just like that?" Something isn't right here.

Sighing, he pulls me across the bed and tucks me under his arm, like I weigh nothing. Wrapped in his embrace, Rhys continues, "They agreed to let us *sleep* together, under the condition the door stays open. Mom added that we would all have a long conversation tomorrow."

"And Tristen?"

He hugs me closer and, with his arm around my shoulders, starts tracing small circles. "He was his usual unreadable self. Didn't say a word."

His caress causes shivers to run down my spine.

"I don't know if that is comforting or not," I admit, mimicking Rhys's movement with my fingers on the blue material that clings to his chest.

The circles stop, and I'm about to protest, when he tightens his hold. His other hand lifts and pushes a strand of hair from my forehead. His fingers linger near the cut, before moving down and resting on my neck.

He needs the physical contact as much as me, and I'm sure he's fully aware of my rapid pulse under his palm.

"Let's deal with that tomorrow. All I care about is that you're here, and we'll get some rest."

"Rest?" I tilt my head upward and meet Rhys's gaze, my hand flattened against his pecs, heat igniting in my core, and I move my hand slowly down his abs.

With hooded lids, he smirks at me. "Rest. As much as I want a repeat of the hospital—sans the blood and gore you caused—I need to get some sleep. We both do."

Face ablaze, I swat his arm.

"You act like I had blood spewing out of several open wounds."

"Well, not spewing, but..." He trails off, and a devilish grin crosses his face. "I wouldn't mind a little tongue action, though."

*He did not just say that.*

I pull back, and Rhys bursts out laughing. "Shit, babe. I'm sorry. I couldn't resist."

"That's something I would've expected to come out of Wes's mouth." I huff.

"Forgive me?" Rhys pulls me back into his arms and places a tender kiss on my forehead. "I'm sorry. I was just trying to distract you from whatever was going on inside that head of yours."

Snuggling closer, I smile. "Mission accomplished."

Reaching over me, Rhys switches off the bedside lamp, and I wrap my arms around him as soon as he is back in place.

"I'm glad you're back, babe," he murmurs into my hair.

"Me, too," I reply automatically.


AT SOME POINT, I managed to shift both of us under the covers. Rhys is snoring softly, but I can't calm my mind. The last two days are a blur, and being at the vineyard seems like a lifetime ago. Instead, I keep rewinding our trip home in my head. Tristen's behavior is getting weirder by the day, and I wonder if he knows more about my past than he is letting on.

Getting discharged took forever. I'm still baffled by our mode of transportation—a freaking private jet. How did Tristen organize that thing? The two agents ushered us on board, and I curled up in one of the oversized, buttery-soft leather seats. Rhys settled in next to me, and Heather across from us. After takeoff, Tristen brought all of us blankets and took the seat next to his wife. It was the first time he had addressed me in hours.

"Are you comfortable, sweetheart?"

I forced a smile on my face. "I'm fine, Dad."

Rhys automatically reached over and grabbed my hand, knowing that I was far from fine. Physically, I was, but mentally, I was slowly losing the battle against blocking out the ginormous elephants in the room: my kidnapping and the social media incest posts about Rhys and me. I'd have to address both sooner or later.

I shook myself out of the thoughts and faced my adopted father, who was eyeing my hand in Rhys's. My insides constricted, and I instinctively pulled away. Rhys glared at his father, who, in return, watched me more closely. I've known this man my entire life, and he's been the only father I remember, but that was the first time I was afraid. Not for my safety, but if he would take Rhys away from me again.

Tristen looked away first and pulled out his phone—something he has always done to shut everyone out. I flicked my gaze to Heather, who was in a stare-down with her son. She gave him the briefest of nods, and my hand was back in his. I curiously turned to Rhys, but he avoided making eye contact by pulling his phone out as well. Resigned, I leaned my head back against the seat.

*What has happened to all of us?*

I WAKE UP WITH A START, my heart hammering in my chest. I'm alone in bed, and there's honking and shouting outside. What the— then it clicks. The reporters have arrived. I have no clue how we've managed to avoid them this long, but I'm sure it—again—has something to do with Tristen's connections.

I listen to the muffled yelling, unable to make out what's being said. Swallowing several times, I try to calm my breathing. Thank goodness my room is facing the back of the house. The urge to know that George is close by overcomes me, and I jump out of bed. Unsure where the phone is, I stop in the middle of my room, arms hanging at my sides. I don't remember what happened to it after the call. Rhys must've hidden it somewhere.

*Shit.*

Still rooted to the spot, a soft knock comes from the open door. Spinning around, I am face to face with my best friend. She looks disheveled—so unlike the Denielle I'm used to. Even when she just wakes up, she usually looks all put together and presentable—not like me, who sports a bird's nest of epic proportions every morning.

"Hey." My tone is subdued.

"Hey, yourself." Den attempts a smile. Aside from her not being a morning person, there is a lot of damage repair to be done to our friendship.

A hollow feeling settles in my stomach. We stare at each other for a long time before she crosses to my bed and plops down at the foot. "Where are the guys?"

I follow her movement and sit down next to her. "Not sure, I just woke up."

She wrings her hands in her lap. "So, uh...how are you doing?" She won't look at me.

"I have no clue." Heart pounding in my throat, I whisper, "I'm scared everyone will find out the truth and he has to leave before we get answers."

Denielle remains quiet for several breaths. My palms start sweating profusely, and I swipe them on my pajama pants. Den's fingers close on mine, and she finally faces me. "Babe, I have no idea what you're dealing with. Rhys has told us some, but I'm sure there is a lot more. I have no clue what to think or how to deal with this. I don't think anyone would, given the circumstances. I mean, babe... he's a..." She trails off, and my heart sinks. "But..." she adds after an indefinable amount of time, "I know you. There is no one out there that's more levelheaded. You would never allow anything to happen to your family or friends."

"Of course not!" I squeeze her hand. "D, I swear to you, there is so much I never expected to find when I woke up after the accident."

I'm about to confess how smart and funny Nate is, how peaceful the vineyard is, and the way George looks out for my brother, when we get interrupted. The yelling outside gets louder, and I cock my head, still unable to make out actual words. My fingers tighten around my friend's, and I slowly stand up, pulling her with me. Walking across the hall to Rhys's room, my steps falter for a second before I reach the window. It has a direct line of sight to the driveway and street. Denielle follows close behind, and I step up to the wooden blinds but remain far enough in the shadows that my silhouette is hidden from view. I see three news vans and four unmarked cars—not counting the black SUV and Wes's red 4Runner. Some of our neighbors are lingering on their front lawns, and I rub my upper arms with my hands. This was expected, but at the same time, I'm unprepared. A middle-aged man in jeans and a gray bomber jacket argues with a dark-haired woman dressed in a cream pantsuit. I do a double take and recognition hits. I've seen him in several videos. It's Lancaster, the reporter who's obsessed with the missing girls' cases. I don't recognize the woman and assume she's from another media outlet. Suddenly, a muffled, "Upper left window," makes every single head snap up, and three cameras focus instantly on the house. Denielle pulls on my arm, and we both drop to the floor.

"This is fucking nuts!" my friend hisses as I try to figure out why my lungs start burning.

*Oh God, I can't do this.*

Arms wrap around my stomach from behind and force me out of the crouched position, dragging me into the hallway. Fingers still clasped around my best friend's hand, she follows close behind.

"Breathe, babe." Rhys's voice reaches my ears, but it's like I'm underwater. "Cal. I. Need. You. To. Inhale."

*I can't. Why can't I breathe?*

I open my mouth to do as he ordered, but the air doesn't reach my lungs. It's like someone has me in a choke hold, and my vision turns blurry.

"Calla, look at me!"

I want to, but everything is out of focus. A wheezing sound reaches my ears, and I realize it's coming from me.

"What's wrong with her?"

"Sweetheart?"

*So many voices. I can't do this.*

My legs leave the ground. I'm tucked against a chest. The faint scent of a familiar shower gel mixed with laundry detergent and coffee penetrates my nose—Rhys. I want to tell him that I'm okay, but I can't make the words come out. I'm not okay.

Back on my feet, I sway when something cold and wet hits me in the face. A scream rips from my throat. Stumbling, I try to get away. Arms wrap back around me.

"I told you to breathe, babe. You should've listened," he growls, but there is no anger behind his words.

"Oh, thank fuck." Wes.

"Wes!" Another male voice barks. Tristen.

"Sorry, sir."

My breathing is regulating itself again, and I blink against the water, drops clinging to my lashes.

"EVERYONE OUT!" This time Rhys does sound murderous.

"Rhys," a calm and collected Tristen addresses his son.

"Not now, Dad! We'll be downstairs in a few. She needs a fucking minute; not everyone is a robot like you." I've never heard him talk to his father like this. No one challenges Tristen—except maybe Heather.

After a pause, there is shuffling, murmurs, and a door is closing.

A towel wraps around my shoulders, and Rhys's forehead touches mine. "Babe, you need to stop scaring the shit out of me. I've aged ten years in the last two weeks. I'm not ready to turn thirty," he softly chuckles.

## CHAPTER SEVENTY-FIVE

### RHYS

*I don't know how long I can keep this up.*

With a clenched jaw, I help Lilly change out of her drenched clothes, and for once, my dick has zero reaction to seeing her naked. Pulling the soaked hoodie off her body, I wrap a fresh towel around her shoulders. I'm not even tempted to take a peek. Lilly shimmies out of her PJ pants while I return to her room to find something dry to wear.

Her panic attacks are becoming more frequent, and it's starting to freak me out. I mean, sure, who wouldn't lose their shit in her situation? It's a miracle that she still functions the way she is, but how long is this supposed to go on? The press just arrived; she hasn't even faced the vultures yet. Not to mention everything that's been going on at school. She has to go back eventually, and from what Wes and Den have been reporting, Kat has basically resurrected the Salem witch hunt with Lilly as the main target. I fight the urge to embed an imprint of my fist in the drywall of her closet.

*Fuck, I'm exhausted.*

"Rhys?" Lilly's tentative voice drifts to where I still stand, staring at her neatly hung shirts. I grab the first thing off a hanger and make my way back to the bathroom.

Sitting on the closed toilet, she peers up at me. "Do you hate me?"

I kneel in front of her, and she scans my face, tears pooling in her beautiful eyes. My chest constricts, seeing her like this.

I gently place my hand on the side of her face and wipe away a tear with my thumb. "Why on earth would you think that?"

Lilly leans into my touch, closing her eyes. "Because all I've done is make a mess out of your life."

Unable to respond right away, I mull that over for a moment. "Babe, I'm not going to lie to you that all of this doesn't affect me. The last few weeks have been hell. I'm so fucking tired, and not knowing what the future will bring freaks me out, but what's worse is seeing you like this. I don't agree on much—or really anything—with your brother, but Nate was right on one account. You are a fighter." I place a kiss on her nose.

She smiles sadly. "I don't feel like one right now."

I stand up, pulling her with me, and wrap my arms around her shoulders. Lilly clings to my midsection, burying her nose in my damp sweater. I should probably change as well. Inhaling her signature coconut shampoo, I silently swear to myself that I will find a way to help her through this, even if I have to involve her brother and George.


LILLY'S HAND securely in mine, we make our way downstairs. The first thing I notice is that all the blinds are closed, and the curtains in the living room are drawn. Agent Lanning and Agent Camden are in their usual spots in the kitchen, and both glance up from their laptops as I lead Lilly through the kitchen to the living room. The other suits haven't returned since we got back with Lilly.

Mom and Dad are quietly talking to each other. Wes and Den are opposite my parents on the U-shaped couch. Wes is scrolling with his thumb over something on his phone; Den has her arms crossed, head leaned back, and eyes closed. This is the first time since last night I take in Den's appearance; she's a mess. She's wearing an oversized green hoodie that I'm pretty sure is Wes's, black leggings, and her hair is up in a loose bun.

I purposefully ignore Dad as he tracks our movements. We sit down on the middle section of the couch, and I wrap my arm around Lilly's shoulders.

Out of the corner of my eye, I see two figures hovering in the doorway. Lanning and Camden have abandoned their chairs at the kitchen table.

"Not yet." Dad's barked command makes everyone jolt to attention, and the two agents retreat without a word.

"How are you, sweetheart?" Mom addresses Lilly with a genuine smile.

Lilly leans closer to me and stares at her hands in her lap. "I'm fine, Mom."

*Her go-to response to that question.*

"Uh, do you guys want us to leave?" Wes hesitantly asks no one in particular.

Lilly's eyes snap to his. "No! Stay. Please." The last word is almost spoken like a plea.

Dad clears his throat. "Lilly, we need to talk about what happened."

I peer down and find her already looking at me. I have no clue how my parents will react; my mouth has gone dry, and I force myself to put on a façade. I don't like pretending in front of Lilly, but it's as much for her as it is for me. I give her a nod, relaying everything I can't put into words in front of the people in the room or the listening agents in the kitchen in this one movement.

Lilly presses her lips into a thin line and inhales deeply through her nose before letting the air back out. She talks to the room but doesn't avert her eyes from mine.

"I was working on a journalism assignment when I came across an article about a missing girl. After reading the first one, I knew there was something...I had to find out more. The longer I looked into the case..." She pauses, a slight quiver in her voice. "I got this feeling. Then I started seeing these flashes. Memories that were not mine—or at least I didn't think they were at first."

"Oh God." Mom's hands fly to her mouth. I take in my father's face, and even he looks surprised. Not much can rattle Tristen McGuire.

Lilly doesn't go into details about her migraines; she leaves out the ones about Nate and, instead, recaps her memories about Emily and Henry. She tells them how I confronted her and how she talked me into going to California. My dry mouth has extended down my throat, and I would kill for some water right about now. My insides are one giant knot.

"I am sorry I lied to you." She finally turns toward Mom and Dad. Mom is so shocked that all she does is stare at her daughter, wide-eyed.

It's Dad that surprises all of us. "I knew where you were."

My eyes snap to him. *Motherfucker!* I had my suspicions when I found out that he tracked our phones, but I wasn't positive until now.

"You did?" Lilly squeaks.

My father scans the room. Both Wes and Den shrink into the couch under his scrutiny, aware they got caught as accomplices to our deception, but when he lands on his wife, he says, "I'm sorry, honey."

*She didn't know.*

Mom straightens, slowly removes her hands from her mouth, and places them folded in her lap. "You knew, and you didn't tell me?"

When she is not in the courtroom, my mother is the kindest and most nurturing woman I've ever known. Looking at her right now, though, she scares the shit out of me—she's seething.

Dad opens his mouth, but she holds up a palm. "We've kept Lilly safe for ten years. She is my daughter, even if not by blood. I stood by your decision when you forced Rhys out of the house because he fell in love with her—something we knew would happen—but I trusted your judgment on the situation."

My cheeks are burning. Can we please move on from my relationship?

Mom continues, oblivious that the four of us are staring at her like she's grown a second head. "I've given you free rein on how to protect us, but you promised me you would never keep anything from me anymore after Hannah. It's not bad enough that you kept *the other thing* from me, but now I have to find out that you knew Lilly was putting herself back onto his radar. What else is there?"

*The other thing? And who the fuck is Hannah?*

My leg won't stop bouncing. As fascinated as I am by this

exchange, I'm fighting the urge to bolt from the room. Lilly's hand lands on my leg, and the contact calms me instantly.

Mom turns away from her husband, and Dad's face reminds me of the time they caught me driving the Defender down the street at age fourteen. I thought Mom would never forgive me. No one puts Tristen McGuire in his place.

Back in control and eerily calm, she says, "I'm sorry you had to witness this. Your father and I will talk about that later." She meets Lilly's gaze, and her hand clenches down on my leg.

*Fuuuck, that hurts.*

I try not to wince or make a sound, but her hand is like a claw digging into my muscle.

"Sweetheart, what happened after California?"

All eyes are back on Lilly. I pry her hand from my thigh, interlacing our fingers and squeezing them gently.

"I started getting text messages, with pictures of myself. Later, some of me with Den and Rhys."

"Why didn't you tell us?" Mom's tone is quiet. Careful.

Lilly turns to me, and I dip my head, urging her to tell them.

She whispers, "You betrayed me."

Dad rubs his hands over his face, and Mom swipes a tear away that has escaped her glistening eyes.

Suddenly, Lilly's head snaps up, and I pull my hand away, startled by the sudden movement. She glances at me sideways, and I take her hand back, shrugging a shoulder. We're all jumpy.

She pins Dad down with a glare that would make George proud. "So, if you bugged our phones, how didn't you know about the texts?"

Dad's eyebrows shoot up. "I didn't bug your phone."

My vision instantly clouds, and I'm interjecting myself into the conversation. "Yes, you did. Or how did that suit know what Lilly said when she called the first time?"

I mean, we know he did because of Nate, the genius hacker, but I can't say that.

Dad clears his throat and won't look in Mom's direction. "I only tracked your phones. I didn't install the listeners until Lilly went missing."

Wes eyes his phone, and Denielle snorts, "Not yours, dumbass." Then she peers to my father. "Uh, right?"

"Correct," Dad deadpans, and Lilly stifles a laugh next to me.

Mom collects herself and moves the conversation back on track. "Okay, so you got text messages. What then?"

Lilly swallows hard. The closer we get to Nate, the more she struggles.

I decide to take over and give her a break. "Lilly wanted to know what he wanted before she told anyone else. Kat tried to blackmail me into getting back with her. She figured out that something was going on but couldn't put her finger on it until she got a hold of the picture." I don't have to tell them which picture; everyone has seen it by now. "She posted it on her social media and cornered Lilly in front of the entire school. Lilly didn't take her bullshit and left."

"What happened after you left the school grounds?" The voice behind us startles everyone, and Agent Camden steps forward.

Lilly's eyes widen, and she quietly seeks my encouragement. I squeeze her hand and nod.

"I wanted to be alone. I was going to drive home but needed a moment. I was on the back road when I noticed another car behind me. It didn't come close, so I couldn't make out who was in it. A fox ran across the street, and I jerked the steering wheel to avoid hitting it. I missed the fox but lost control of the Jeep instead." She takes a long pause, and my heart is hammering in my throat while I wait.

*Here it comes. Let the acting begin.*

"I don't remember anything else until I woke up in the hospital three days ago."

No one speaks for several minutes.

Agent Lanning breaks the silence. "Tristen, can we speak in private?"

Dad gets up without a word and leads the agent to his office, Agent Camden following on their heels. I glance around the room, and everyone seems unsure what to do next.

*Are we done with the interrogation?*

Mom pushes off the couch. "Let's all get some breakfast. We'll continue when your father is back."

And with that, it's like the last weeks haven't happened. What the fuck? I exchange a confused look with Lilly and our friends. That's it? That can't be it.

Mom gets busy in the kitchen, and Denielle helps her make pancakes while Wes sets to the task of brewing enough coffee to keep us all awake for a week. Narrowing my eyes at the scene in front of me, I take a seat next to Lilly on the barstools. Pressing my thigh against hers, I get her attention and mouth, "Are you okay?"

She gives me a jerked nod, and my stomach sinks. No.

WHEN DAD DOESN'T COME out of his office even after our house guests take their seats at the kitchen table again, the four of us go upstairs to my room. Inside, I flip the lock, and we pile into my bathroom. At this point, I don't give a flying fuck what Dad thinks if he checks the security feed. Looks like his pile of secrets grows by the day, and Mom doesn't know the half of it.

I sit with my back against the bathtub, Lilly between my legs, Den on the closed toilet seat to the left, and Wes across, leaning against the door. Six months ago, I would've laughed my ass off if someone would've told me I'd be *hanging out* in my bathroom with my best friend, *sister*, and Denielle 'The Bulldog' Keller—in Wes's hoodie, nonetheless.

"How are you doing, babe?" Denielle looks at Lilly with her head cocked to the side.

Lilly is nestled against my chest sideways with her legs pulled up and her head tucked under my chin. She turns to get a better look at her friend and shrugs a shoulder. "I feel like a prisoner."

Not surprising with the media camped out on the front lawn.

Mom informed us earlier that she's going to pick Natty up from Olivia's tomorrow but is worried what this chaos outside the house will do to her. We've tried to keep her routine as normal as possible under the circumstances, and so far, it has worked. Mom would spend time with her at Olivia's house, but we've kept her away from the FBI in our home. With the press now trying to track down information on Lilly, Dad wants everyone under the same roof. He doesn't want to risk someone cornering my little sister at her ballet lesson or school.

"Were you not held prisoner by your brother?" Wes voices the question that I had bounced around in my head for a while in his usual sledgehammer way. The few times we FaceTime'd, I got a small glimpse of the place. I know it was not a one-bedroom apartment, but Lilly had been mum about more details.

She doesn't answer right away, and I lean forward to assess her face better. She chews on her lower lip, flicking her thumb against her fingers.

*Why is she nervous?*

I exchange a look with the other two in the room, and both mirror my confused expression. When I think she won't answer at all, she whispers, "I wasn't. I couldn't leave the estate, but I never felt like a prisoner."

*Estate?*

"Estate?" Denielle hesitantly asks.

Lilly inhales and holds her breath for several beats. "I haven't told any of you where I was for several reasons. For one, no one can know about the location. Not because I...*we* have to hide anything there, but because it's Nate's home. The only place he feels at peace, and I would never take that from him."

*She is protecting her brother.*

"Two, I didn't know how you would react or look at me if you knew the truth. But there is no point in keeping this fact from you now since you know everything else."

Lilly turns to me and places a hand on the side of my face. "I didn't want you to feel differently about me."

Alarm bells instantly start to shrill in my head. What the hell is she talking about? I narrow my eyes. "Why would I do that?"

As she continues, Denielle and Wes hang on her every word. The longer she talks, the lower their jaws drop.

"I was at the family vineyard. It belonged to Payton's father, and Nate restored most of it over the years. He grows grapes there but doesn't allow the processing on the property. He has a ten-foot wall around the whole place and a huge wrought-iron gate, which is the only way in or out. An electric current secures everything, and the only way on or off the property is with a code. If you try to get in, or out, you get shocked—not terribly, but enough to knock you on your ass and fry any electronic you may carry with you. There's no cell service unless you're hooked into the network. I have no clue how he did all this, but he designed his security system, so it wasn't a surprise. The house is a massive Mediterranean-style building with two separate wings. It has an outdoor pool in the back, and the indoor pool is underground next to the gym. He built an indoor track under the house and a motor pool that can hold twelve plus cars. He has an R8 there that you guys would lose your shit over." She stops and presses her lips together, realizing how she got carried away. It's obvious now that she loves the place.

The three of us must have similar expressions: gaping at Lilly.

"Uh...why would you leave there?" Wes attempts to break the tension, and Denielle whacks him over the head. But the goal is accomplished. Lilly smiles.

"Babe, did you think I'd be upset about where he took you? That you liked it there?" I'm still confused as to why she was so scared to tell me. She must've been worried about what I would think of her, knowing that she was content where she was. It sounds like she was living the dream—minus the kidnapping and secrets.

She looks everywhere but my face. "The estate is one thing. There is something else I haven't told you yet."

*What now?*

My pulse picks up, and everything from Nate not taking responsibility to her choosing to leave me and stay with her real family crosses my mind.

"Brooks left me money."

Okay, so she got a small inheritance. What's the big deal?

"That's, uh...great. I mean, that means he cared about you, right? You can buy yourself something and know it's from your biological father." I try to make sense of why she looks like she's about to throw up the half pancake she forced herself to eat earlier.

"It's ten million dollars." Her voice is so low I'm sure I misheard.

"Come again?" Denielle's shrill voice echoes like a bullhorn through my small bathroom.

Wes chokes and goes into a coughing fit.

*I guess I did hear her right.*

"Plus interest for fifteen years."

*Fuck. Me.*

# CHAPTER SEVENTY-SIX

## LILLY

I TOLD THEM. IN TWELVE DAYS, ON MY EIGHTEENTH BIRTHDAY, I will have more money than every single person I know combined—not counting brother dearest. Before I left the vineyard, Nate spent several hours dissecting the trust Brooks set up. It took us hours and emptying every single file cabinet drawer in the library, but we found a copy of my biological father's testament. Just weeks before his death, he revised his will. Besides half of his fortune, my trust, I was to inherit every last penny that was meant for Audrey. Nate is set through Payton and the Altman Empire; I got the rest. It's been accumulating interest over the last ten plus years since Nate never considered there being additional funds to what his mother's attorneys handed him. When Nate gave me his final estimate, I crushed the plastic water bottle in my hand. Unfortunately, said bottle was open, and the water splashed all over the desk. Again.

After that, my brother was close to frisking me whenever I entered the NCC. He even sent George out with his covered mug because there was a chance I could spill it. I had a few choice words for him on that.

I still haven't admitted the full extent of my future fortune to Rhys or my friends; the amount of the trust alone was enough to put them into a state of shock. The tension finally left my body when neither of them made any comments one way or another or looked differently at me once the surprise wore off. I scolded myself for not confiding in them sooner.

WE'RE in Rhys's room when Heather knocks. The boys are playing a video game, sitting at the foot of the bed, and Denielle and I are lounging against the headboard. Up until that moment, I was as content as one in my situation could be. For a few hours, I pretended to be a normal girl—no secret past, no unknown future. I blocked out everything as I listened to my boyfriend and his best friend bicker over who has the better aim shooting the zombies in their various body parts. Facing my adopted mother, my stomach drops like I'm sitting in the first car of a rollercoaster and we're pushing over the edge.

"Lilly, can you come down for a few minutes?" Her face is her usual, gentle self whenever she talks to one of her kids, but deep down, I sense that something is about to happen—again. I want to say no, hide behind my friends, maybe even call George to come to pick me up...but none of that is an option. Whatever they're going to tell me, I have to face it.

Rhys pauses the game and is about to stand up when his mother holds up her hand. "Just Lilly."

"Not happening!" Rhys is on his feet in the blink of an eye and puts himself in front of me.

I place my palm between his shoulder blades. "It's okay."

Pulse rushing through my body double time, I want him with me, but Heather and Tristen would never *harm* me.

"Are you sure?" Rhys turns, and his eyes switch back and forth between mine.

"Yes." I try to smile reassuringly at him as I follow Heather out of the room.

In the hallway, she laces her arm through mine and leads me down the stairs into Tristen's office. "Sweetheart, Dad and I want to talk with you about a few things."

The reassurance I plastered on my face falls off like the sheet mask during Denielle's beauty salon sleepover party freshman year. That darn thing would not stay on—at all.

As we enter, Tristen rises from behind his desk to meet us. My heart stutters a beat as I take him in. I've never been able to read him; the man invented the poker face. However, looking at him now...I want to turn and run back upstairs.

He gestures toward the sitting area in the corner of the room—a gray twill loveseat and matching armchair with a round end table in between.

My mouth has gone dry, and I tuck my thumbs inside my fists so I don't start flicking my fingers. I take the seat next to Heather while Tristen lowers his large frame into the armchair.

Hands folded, he leans forward with his arms on his thighs. "I wanted to speak to you without Rhys in the room. He is very... protective of you, and I want to make sure you get the answers you need—without interruptions. There are many unanswered questions, and I will answer them to the best of my ability. What you want to share with him is up to you."

"Okay?" I reply warily. I barely get the word out over the sandpapery feeling in my throat. Where is this going?

Heather places her palm on my thigh, and I jump, jerking my head in her direction. "Dad and I had a long conversation, and though I'm still very upset with him for keeping certain facts from me, I understand his reasoning. We're sure there is a lot you want to know, and I wish you would've come to us before driving to California."

I furrow my brow and study her for a long moment. "Would you have told me the truth?" I challenge her.

She exchanges a look with her husband, and it's Tristen that answers. "Not if I would have seen another way."

I appreciate his honesty, yet it's like a slap in the face. I can feel the invisible handprint on my cheek.

"We cannot change the current situation. You are young, and you felt we did wrong by you. I'm trying to put myself in your shoes. As an adult, it is hard for me to relate to your decisions, but people make mistakes when they're young." Heather leaves the last sentence hanging.

I simply nod and glance between them. Waiting.

My adopted father's next sentence makes the pulse in my veins go into overdrive. "Your video was a surprise."

*Do. Not. React.*

"Wh-what video?" I attempt to keep my voice steady. With my eyes locked on Tristen, I clench my balled hands even harder, making my hidden thumbs crack. The compulsion to flick the rest of my fingers is like a mosquito bite you're trying not to scratch.

I told them I don't remember anything from the past two weeks, which would include the video, but if he keeps pushing...

Neither of them speaks. Tristen peers at his wife and, after another beat of silence, clears his throat. "First, I want to tell you how very sorry I am for the way you had to find out about all of this. I never expected this to happen. I was assured it wouldn't."

My breath hitches. He's letting the video go. Why? Then his words register. "Assured by whom?"

The face from my migraine appears in front of my mind's eye: *The memory doctor.*

Heather lets go of my thigh and takes my hand between hers, forcing me to open my palm to hers. "You have to understand that when you were in the hospital in California, you were in a very fragile state. We were not there yet and only knew what Emily had relayed to us. She wouldn't let me talk to Henry or a nurse to get a better picture. You have always been like a daughter to me. You and Rhys have been inseparable from the day you were born." She smiles to herself. "When you cried, I would put him in your crib, and you instantly calmed down. There were many times you would be at our house for a whole day or two. Emily was my best friend since childhood, but..." She trails off, and the hair at the nape of my neck stands. What the hell is she trying to say? Or rather, not say?

"We flew out to California as soon as we could after getting the news." Tristen directs my attention to himself. "As Mom said, you have always been like a daughter to us, and this hit us as hard as it did Henry."

*Henry? Not Emily.*

My heart beats so fast against my ribcage it physically hurts. But I can't voice my question before Tristen continues, "When we arrived, everything happened very fast. Henry showed us the messages Emily had received and caught us up on the medical diagnoses. You immediately asked for Rhys." The corners of his mouth tilt up. It's the first time he shows an actual reaction to *Rhys and me*, which in return makes my face heat. "Your primary nurse, uh..."

"Madeline Cross," I finish for him. No point in pretending I don't know about her.

"Yes, Madeline. She spoke to all of us at length and recommended for you to get therapy to deal with the trauma. We had already discussed this during the flight and suggested to your parents for you to stay with us for the time being. They knew I had access to the best specialists in their field. It was never meant to be forever."

Specialists? That's one way to sugarcoat it. I'm torn between fear of what else they have to say, rage for what happened to me, and curiosity. The number of questions assaulting my brain make my head hurt. "Why didn't they just go to the authorities?"

Heather looks upset. "To this day, we have asked ourselves that many times. Henry wanted to report you missing, but Emily wouldn't let him. He attempted it without her knowing, and when she found out, she threatened to take you away from him—when you came back."

I'm so confused. I knew Emily didn't want to report me missing because Nate threatened my safety, but threatening to take me away? Something isn't adding up. Pulling my hand away from Heather's, I place it in my lap and decide to change the direction of this conversation. "So, they just handed me over, and then what?"

Tristen blows out a long breath. "They did not just hand you over. We discussed this for hours. Henry refused at first; he wanted to run with you."

*Alone?*

Heather takes my hand back, and I have to force myself to not rip it out of her grasp. I didn't notice that I'd been flicking my thumb against my fingers until she constricts the movement. "Sweetheart, you have to believe us when we say that all we wanted was to keep you safe."

"What did you do to my mind? Why can I remember certain things and not others?"

Heather sucks in a sharp breath, and Tristen closes his eyes briefly before leveling me with a gaze devoid of emotion. The only other person I have ever seen with this expression—or lack thereof —is George. A cold shiver runs down my spine.

"I called in a favor with an associate of mine. We had worked together before, and I recently had consulted with him on another issue. He was—is—specialized in certain techniques." My adopted father seems to be struggling for the right words.

"What. Techniques?" My mouth feels like it's full of cotton.

"It's called coercive persuasion. Though he also uses a unique type of hypnosis. It's a rather delicate subject. Very controversial."

*Excuse me, what?* A shrill voice screams at me in my head, and I flinch to myself. I must've misheard him. This cannot be happening. How is this happening to me over and over. Why me?

Oblivious to the havoc his admission has stirred up inside of me, Tristen continues with his gaze trained at the floor. "He has the ability to arrange memories in an individual's mind. While under hypnosis, the individual is made to believe that certain events happened or didn't happen. With the help of persuasion, new memories are created. Those get connected by moving the memories around until they make sense again. There are several different techniques of persuasion, a lot of them not...*pleasant*. We consult him during operations when our regular tactics don't work; he deals with the special cases. However, he never used those types on you." He amends the last sentence so quickly that it takes me a moment to process it.

*Well, if that isn't reassuring*, the same voice now snarls. But the sarcasm of the internal speaker has no effect on the overwhelming panic gripping every fiber of my body. The term coercive speaks for itself—it's forced. There is nothing voluntary about altering someone's mind, and the first picture in my mind's eye is my kid-self being tied to a chair while someone messes with my head. I close my eyes and draw in slow breaths, exhaling at the same count. I need to calm down.

A hand gently touches my knee. "Lilly, please look at me."

Instinctively, my knee jerks away from the contact. I force myself to open my eyes and look at the man in front of me.

"He was able to help you forget by moving your memories around while under hypnosis. He made you believe things to be the truth, while other memories got locked away."

He tries to reassure me, but I can no longer listen to this. They violated my mind. I can barely contain the urge to jump up and run. George has to be somewhere close by; he would find me if I made it out of the house. But so would Lancaster, who is still camping out on the front lawn. I'm trapped.

I stare past Tristen, not looking at anything specific, while I attempt to calm my thrashing pulse.

"Where are my parents?" I need to change the topic. I can feel the bile rising in my throat and a fine sheen of sweat coating my skin. If he keeps talking about what happened to me, there is a good chance of me having a panic attack, and I can't let that happen. Not in front of them. I can't.

Tristen peers at Heather, and an entire, yet silent, conversation takes place in front of me. Without looking at me, he says, "We don't know."

Something is off. *Something else.*

A new kind of agitation rises to the surface. "And you never attempted to contact them? I don't believe that they would just abandon me—their only child."

My adopted mother starts tearing up. I'm so freaking tired of these riddles, never getting the full truth. I clench my jaw in an attempt not to say something I may regret. Or give something away that I shouldn't. I fail miserably on both accounts.

"So, you decided to brainwash me instead of finding real help? My mother handed me over without a second thought and took off? You make it sound like I was nothing to her. You say that Henry was upset. Henry wanted to call the cops. Not Emily. The man who wasn't even my father seemed to be the only one who actually cared. You guys tell me that you wanted to protect me. Well, fuck that. You manipulated me, lied to me, AND TOOK MY BEST FRIEND AWAY." My tone gets louder with every word until I'm full-on screaming. Heather mirrors my distraught expression, and Tristen's mouth hangs open.

Instantly, Rhys bursts into the room, eyes wild. "What the fuck is going on?" I'm not surprised he was camped out right in front of the office. He's at my side in three strides, and his arms circle me protectively. My fists clench the front of his sweater, and I bury my face in his chest. I can't face my adopted parents; I completely lost it.

Tristen is the first to collect himself. His tone is a low growl. "What do you mean by 'Henry was not your father'?"

*Shit! Fuck! Shit!*

Instead of waiting for me to answer, Rhys moves one arm around my waist and leads me out of the room.

"This conversation is over." He doesn't leave room for discussion.

"WHERE IS THE PHONE?" My heart still beats out of control, and my eyes are pleading for Rhys to hand it over.

"Why? What's going on?" His hands grasp my upper arms.

Rhys led me to my room. Den and Wes were about to get up from his bed across the hall to follow us when he shook his head and closed the door.

I don't want to tell him what his parents allowed to be done to me; the relationship with his father is already damaged. If he finds out the truth about my memory loss, there is no way to repair it. Hell, I don't know if I can forgive them—again. Not anytime soon. But the need to protect Rhys from the knowledge is as prominent as the fact that I will never be able to get my old life back.

"Please just give me the phone. I have to talk to him," I whisper. I need to tell someone what happened to me.

Rhys scans my face, his internal conflict playing across his features like a movie on a theater screen. Eventually, he nods and points for me to sit down on the bed. I follow suit, and he walks back out. I don't look up and only assume he goes to his room. I stare at the floor beneath my feet, focusing on my breath.

The phone appears in my vision, and I glance up at the somber face of my boyfriend—my *home*. Right now, though, I need the other home—my family. Two halves that make a whole.

"Do you want me to leave?"

I don't answer, and Rhys's face falls ever so slightly before he smoothes his features. He turns on his heel and leaves me alone in what used to be my sanctuary. The door closes a little too forcefully, and my shoulders scrunch up at the sound.

Almost robotic, I make my way to the bathroom, turn on the faucet and shower, plug in the headphones I grabbed from my desk in passing, and slide down the tiled wall. As opposed to the other times I had found out about a new lie in my life, I don't cry. Ever since entering my room, I'm numb. I don't know if that's good or bad. Dialing Nate's number, I wait.

"Lilly? What happened?" The panicked voice of my brother fills my ears after the fourth ring. We had agreed not to contact each other. If I need something, I'm supposed to call George.

I try to tell him what I just found out, but I can't get the right words to form. So, I simply say, "They used persuasion." My voice sounds detached to my own ears, like listening to someone else.

"Lilly, you're not making sense. Where is Rhys?"

"You can't tell him."

"Tell him what?" My brother's worry morphs into anger. "What did he do this time?"

"Not him." I draw in several breaths and force the words out through my clenched teeth. "Heather and Tristen wanted to talk to me alone. Tristen told me how they made me forget. They let someone brainwash me with hypnosis and coercive persuasion."

"THEY DID WHAT?" The roar forces me to pull the phone away from my ear. I hear a door slamming in the background and a faint clicking of keys.

"They said they wanted to help me. But I don't understand why they couldn't just send me to a therapist."

"There is more. It makes no sense. They were not just protecting you from me."

It's disconcerting how casual we can talk about my kidnapping these days. After everything that has come to light, it almost feels like the most trivial event of my life.

*How disturbing is that?*

"I know," I admit.

"I'm going to put George on it. Tell me word for word what they said."

Over the next twenty minutes, I do exactly that. I hear Nate type in the background, not sure if he's taking notes, but also not caring.

After he ensures that our head of security will be in touch, we hang up. I turn all the water sources off and make my way back to my room. Logic tells me that I should feel something—the emotional onslaught of betrayal, rage, and disappointment. However, standing at the foot of the bed, my gaze wanders over to my desk and laptop on top. All I want is to tune out the world. Forget. Everything here reminds me of my life being built on lies. I left my new phone, the replica of my old one, including my music, at the vineyard. There was no way to explain the device to anyone once I returned. With the headphones still in hand, I grab my computer. It's connected to my *Spotify* account, and I scroll through the songs until one jumps out at me, and I press play. Closing my eyes, I listen to "Castle of Glass" by Linkin Park blare into my ears.

---

# CHAPTER SEVENTY-SEVEN

---

### LILLY

I wake up to "Master of the Pendulum" by Avantasia. It's my go-to song to get into running mode, and for a brief moment, I smile, thinking of the underground track at the vineyard. Then, the tidal wave of reality comes crashing back in. I blink my eyes open; my room is dark. Turning, I notice the curtains are not drawn. All I wanted was to block everything out for a few minutes, but I must've fallen asleep.

I shut off the music and pull the headphones out.

"Hey."

Rhys's voice comes from across the room, and I sit up with a start. Holy shit. Pressing my palm against my chest, I glance into the darkness. He's sitting with his back against the door to the hallway.

"Jesus. You almost gave me a heart attack." My tone is harsher than I mean it to sound, and I wince.

His legs are bent with his arms resting on his knees, hands dangling down. He doesn't look at me. "Sorry."

I scoot to the edge of the bed. "How long have you been sitting there?"

The silence between us stretches, and I narrow my eyes at him.

"A couple of hours?" He won't meet my gaze.

"Rhys?" I push. What's wrong with him?

He finally lifts his head, and I suck in a breath. His eyes are puffy; even in this light, I can see it clear as day.

My chest constricts as if someone has sent me to the ground with a push kick to the sternum, and I have the urge to rub the spot in the middle of my chest. "Come here." I hold out my hand.

He stares at it for a whole minute before slowly pushing himself up and walking over to the bed. I clasp his hand and pull him down next to me. We sit side by side, my fingers around his, our legs pressed together, yet there are miles between us.

"I feel like I'm losing you," Rhys confides with a raspy voice.

Another kick. My eyes sting. "I'm so sorry."

His next question shocks me. "Is it because of what they did to you? Because I'm related to them?"

My heart breaks at the sound of disdain when mentioning his parents. I allow myself time to collect my thoughts, risking him taking my hesitation as a confirmation. But I don't want to lie to him.

"I would never hold their actions against you. You've proven time and time again that I can trust you. From the day you told me the truth, you've put me first, and I know that it wasn't easy."

"What did they do to you?" Rhys speaks the words so low, so careful. He won't look at me. I should reach up and make him face me—make him see that I mean my words—but at the same time, I can't do it.

I inhale slowly and hold the air to the count of three before letting it back out. "They told me why I couldn't remember. How it happened." I can't bring myself to go into more detail. I can't bear to burden Rhys with the knowledge. "Please don't ask for more. I...I don't want to lie to you."

Finally, he turns to me, searching my eyes. "Why would you lie to me?"

"Please trust me?" I whisper. Maybe I'll tell him one day when his relationship with Tristen is not on cracked ice anymore.

His gaze moves back and forth between my eyes before he nods. He accepts my reply. Thoughts of *I don't deserve him*, and *he's too good for me* reverberate through my mind.

"Did they say anything to you?" I swallow over the lump in my throat.

"I talked to Mom for a while," Rhys answers quietly.

"About?" I know it wasn't the brainwashing, or he wouldn't be sitting here like this.

"Us."

"Us?" My voice is three octaves higher.

His eyes crinkle, and the shift in his expression makes my stomach summersault. "She asked me if we were serious."

"Oh God. And what did you say?" The mortification is clearly written all over my features.

"The truth. That there is nothing I'm more serious about. If Dad has a problem with it, it's his deal. You're eighteen in a week."

My pulse quickens, and I know what he's insinuating. Would Tristen do anything about it? The only thing he could do, at this point, is make one of us leave. But let's face it, I have the financial means to support both of us easily. I don't know how Rhys would feel about that, but money for food and a place to live is at least something I don't have to worry about. My nerves calm a little at the realization that I am not dependent on anyone—unless I want to be.

"Did she give you the sex talk?" I smirk, changing course inside my head.

He huffs out a laugh. "It's a little late for that. Thankfully, she knows I'm not a walking hard-on. When it comes down to it, I am responsible. Mom's cool; she's not oblivious to what's going on." He rakes his hand through his hair and looks at the ceiling. "Did I really just say that about my mother and sex?"

I giggle. "Yes, you did."

Rhys's face turns somber again. "She did say, though, to not make any more rash decisions. We can come to her for anything." He shrugs one shoulder. "Essentially, Mom said she is happy for us. She's known it would happen since we were little; we never had a typical sibling relationship. They would've told you the truth eventually—or part of it."

"Meaning that I'm not their daughter, but not the rest." I grind my teeth.

"Yes." He doesn't sugarcoat it.

Rhys touches his hand to the side of my face, his callused fingers caressing my cheek. The feel of his rough skin against my smooth skin makes shivers rock through my body in waves. His eyes roam my face, and he murmurs, "We can be together."

The words echo in my mind, and everything else fades into the background. We can be together. The press release announced that I'm not a McGuire. Heather said she's okay with it—us. I don't give a flying fuck what Tristen thinks, adopted father or not. I can't even look at the man after what he revealed earlier.

Leaning into his touch, I block out everything that came to light just mere hours ago—everything that has come out of the dark.

Butterflies erupt in my belly, and my body vibrates with excitement. Licking my bottom lip, his eyes track the movement, reminding me of an animal tracking its prey. It's in that moment that I decide I want this, no matter how screwed up my life is or how many secrets are still being uncovered.

Right now, I am a normal girl in a normal relationship, doing what a boy and girl in love probably would've done weeks ago.

Before reality can take this away from me, I rub my trembling palms against my thighs and stand. Stepping between Rhys's legs, I remain far enough away to take in his expression as my thumbs hook into the waistband of my black leggings. Despite the darkness in my bedroom, I can see how his breath hitches as I slowly push my pants down. I bite the inside of my cheek, not averting my gaze from the boy in front of me as he follows my movement with wide eyes.

"Calla?" His tone is full of awe.

Leggings kicked off to the side, I clasp the bottom of my shirt and pull it over my head. I am so far out of my element and am solely acting on instinct. I never put on a new bra after this morning's shower incident, and I am in front of him in nothing but a pair of white lace shorts.

Chest heaving visibly, Rhys takes in my body. He has seen pretty much all of me before, but suddenly, I fight the urge to cover myself. It felt like a good idea a minute ago, but now I wonder if I've made a mistake. What if he doesn't think I'm pretty? He's been with Katherine, and she is in a league of her own. Her body is perfect, and mine... I start to cross my arms when he stops me.

"Don't."

Rhys's hands hover at the sides of my hips before he touches them to my skin, tracing my hip bones with his thumbs. Oh, God. I'm on fire, and my breath becomes labored as his eyes slowly travel up my torso. He stops at my breasts, *inspecting* them in meticulous detail before lifting his greens to my hazels. His hands have not moved an inch, and yet, every cell in my body has come to life by him merely looking at me. My nipples harden under his lingering gaze, and Rhys's nostrils flare when he sees my body's reaction. I can feel the wetness in my shorts and press my thighs together.

"What are you doing to me, babe?" His tone is laced with the same desire that's building inside of me.

I bite my bottom lip and reach for the hem of Rhys's sweater. I want him naked, to see his mouthwatering body. He lifts his arms compliantly, and I slowly pull the fabric upward. My hands graze his ribcage, goosebumps appearing where my fingertips make contact. His physical response makes my last bit of hesitation—my insecurity over my inexperience—disappear. I throw it on the pile with my clothes and push with both hands at Rhys's shoulders, forcing him to lie back.

"Cal, you don't have to do—" He cuts off as soon as my fingers curl into the elastic of his sweatpants.

"Fuuuuuck." He rubs his hands over his face before pushing himself up on his elbows, watching me through hooded lids. He lifts his butt far enough off of the mattress, and his pants land next to my leggings. My mouth waters at the sight of him.

Only separated by my panties and his boxer briefs, I straddle his lap, leaning forward until our bodies are flush together. We've made out before, but this is different—maybe because we both know what's about to happen. The heat of his defined torso against the flesh of my sensitive breasts causes my entire body to tingle, and a soft moan escapes my mouth. This is almost too much, and we haven't even started yet.

I'm ready for the next step. *So ready.* But this whole time, my inexperienced side avoided looking directly at Rhys's lower half as I undressed him. Now, having only two very thin pieces of fabric between us, I have no doubt that he wants me. His erection is pressing against my core, and I automatically rock against him.

Groaning, his hands glide down my back until he reaches my ass, squeezing it hard and forcing my already throbbing clit further against him. My eyes roll back inside my head at the sensation, and I stifle a curse.

"You are so fucking beautiful." His voice is hoarse, as if he's been screaming all day.

Holding myself up far enough, I place chaste kisses along his jaw until my lips line up with his ear, and I whisper, "Make me forget."

I yelp when Rhys flips us over with lightning speed and hovers above me. "Are you sure?"

Searching my gaze, he waits. I read him like an open book—*my* open book. He doesn't mask his worry of me changing my mind or *not* changing my mind. This gorgeous boy in my bed, who has way more experience than me, is as nervous as I am.

I reach up and trace his cheekbone with the tip of my index finger. "There is nothing I want more," I reassure him.

That's all he needs. Rhys's lips descend on mine in a heated kiss, his tongue immediately seeking entrance. He invades my mouth, and I match every stroke with one of my own. Feels. So. Good. Suddenly, his mouth leaves mine. Nooo, a voice shouts inside my head. I want to protest, but then his lips are back on me. Good Lord. I whimper, fisting my hands into the duvet underneath me, and I feel him chuckle against my skin. He trails kisses down my neck, and as he nips at my flesh, I turn my head to give him better access. I'm about to combust, and we aren't fully naked yet.

His tongue explores every inch of my body until he reaches the top of my panties. I let go of the comforter and stretch my arms over my head, holding my breath as he slowly pulls the lacey material down to my ankles. Rhys's body is completely off of mine, and I don't dare look at him. Squeezing my eyes shut, I concentrate on breathing, which has become more strained the lower his mouth travels. When I feel his warm exhale against my opening, I can no longer suppress the moan I've been holding in.

A soft growl reaches my ears, and I involuntarily open my eyes, inhaling sharply. While I tried to calm my body, Rhys rid himself of his boxer briefs and is now standing fully naked in front of my bed. *Everything* is standing. I stare at him. It. His dick. Whatever you call it. My brain has officially short-circuited.

"Last chance, babe." He smirks at me.

I lick my lips, my eyes meeting his. "Nightstand," is all I say, and his cocky smile vanishes.

I give him a devilish grin of my own.

Way too slowly, Rhys walks around the bed. I clamp my mouth shut to not order him to hurry the fuck up. It's like my body has been taken over by a stranger. Pushing myself up until my head is on my pillows, I readjust the comforter until I can slip in between the duvet and the mattress.

Reaching inside the top drawer, he pulls out a condom. I follow his every move as Rhys rips open the foil packet and rolls it down his length. Heat pools in my core, and my mouth goes dry. He is huge, and I'm starting to worry about how he'll fit inside of me.

Sliding between the sheets next to me, Rhys remains propped up on his elbow. As he lifts the covers, the motion lets much needed cool air hit my overheated body. His free arm moves up the side of my body until he reaches my face. He tenderly forces me to look at him. He's all serious. "I'll be as gentle as possible."

I nod, my whole body shaking in nervous anticipation. His hand leaves my cheek and glides down my side to my center. When he reaches his destination, Rhys circles my clit with his thumb twice before slipping a finger inside of me.

*Oh God.*

"So wet," he groans against the skin under my ear, and I moan loudly, quickly pressing my lips together to not make the entire house aware of what's going on in my room. I grip his shoulder with my hand, digging my nails into the muscle as he moves in and out. "Rhys, I...this..." What was I going to say?

I hike my thigh up his side to give him better access. He inserts another finger, and my hips buck.

"Ahh," I'm going to wake up the entire neighborhood if he keeps that up. I'm losing control over my body's reactions, but at the same time, I don't care.

"Fuck, you are so sexy writhing underneath me with my fingers buried deep inside of you," Rhys pants, and I haven't touched him at all.

Den and I had talked in vivid detail about her first time with

Charlie, and I know it'll hurt, but she also assured me that I would know when I am ready.

My gaze roams the face of the boy hovering half above me while his talented fingers drive me to the brink of madness. I love him with all my heart, and after everything we've been through and still have ahead of us, I need this. I need him.

I signal him that I want more than just his fingers by pulling him over my body. He removes his hand and settles between my legs. Taking charge, I reach down to position him at my entrance. As I wrap my hand around his dick, a guttural sound escapes Rhys, and he touches his forehead to mine.

"Babe, I'm about to blow if you don't take your hand away right now."

A giggle erupts in my throat. After one more torturing stroke and him making a sound between a groan and a growl, I move both my palms to his shoulders. His body trembles as he slowly pushes forward, and I don't take my eyes from his. Just feeling his tip at my opening could send me over the edge, but I force myself to take a steadying breath.

"Tell me to stop if it gets to be too much."

I nod, and he enters me. The slickness makes him sink in easily, and I try to relax. I fail. Every muscle in my body tenses. I didn't think it would be that bad, that everyone always just exaggerates, but nothing, not all the girl-talks with my best friend, prepared me for this. A sharp sting makes me squeeze my eyes shut, and I dig my nails into Rhys's shoulder blades. He instantly stops moving. "Look at me, Cal."

I can't, not right away. I breathe through my nose before I follow his command, locking eyes with Rhys.

"You're doing great. I'm sorry, babe." After a pause, he adds, "Fuck. You feel so good I got carried away. Just keep breathing; I promise I'll go slow."

But instead of letting him remain in the lead, I place my hands on his butt to urge him forward. Something tells me that slow will not make the pain go away faster. At first, I regret my rash decision; maybe I should've let him ease in. But then my body adjusts to his size, and the uncomfortable feeling morphs into something...*holy shit.* I did not anticipate that. Every nerve ending is buzzing with pleasure, and pure ecstasy takes over my body. Rhys and I are connected in a way—not just physical—that can never be undone. He's my endgame.

I start matching his every move, and soon we're both covered in a sheen of sweat. I'm pretty sure I left marks on his back.

"Babe, I...I don't think I can last much longer."

I grasp his head and pull him down to me. The ache is building deep in my core, and I begin to kiss him frantically. In my eagerness, I accidentally bite his lower lip, but instead of stopping, it only turns Rhys on more. His movement speeds up as he literally pounds into me. I never thought I would enjoy it like *that*, but I do. *Holy shit, I do.* The contact and friction on my sensitive spot whenever he buries himself to the hilt is too much. Stars explode behind my closed eyelids. I moan loudly, and Rhys muffles my sounds by tangling his tongue with mine. This is not helping; all it does is send another wave of pleasure through me. His entire body goes tense as he thrusts forward one last time and then uses my mouth to swallow the growl leaving him as he releases himself inside of me.

Rhys collapses over me but holds himself up enough to not crush me under his weight.

"What. The. Fuck?"

I raise my eyebrows, and he huffs out a laugh.

"Babe, this was...holy fuck. I...fuck, I don't have words." His expression sobers. "Did I hurt you?"

I don't have to think about my answer. "No."

Rhys was the right guy, and as much as the discomfort was part of it, I don't consider the experience *painful.*

He rolls off of me and heads to the bathroom to discard the condom. When he's back, he holds a washcloth in one hand and moves the covers out of the way with the other. As he cleans me up, our eyes meet, and the entire gesture is just as intimate as what happened minutes before. My heart skips a beat as I watch him care for me.

Back in my bed, he lies on his back and holds out his arm in an invitation to come closer. I snuggle into his side, my cheek against the side of his neck and my palm flat on his pecs.

For the first time in forever, my mind is filled with nothing but bliss. I know it can't last, but I'll take it for as long as I can.

Right before I drift off to sleep, Rhys's low voice makes its way through the fog rising in my brain. "Please don't shut me out again."

# CHAPTER SEVENTY-EIGHT

**NATE**

I STARE AT THE REMNANTS OF YET ANOTHER LAPTOP ON THE floor.

*Fuck, I need to stop doing that.*

When the number of Lilly and Rhys's burner flashed across my screen, I instantly knew something was *very* wrong. We agreed to communicate through George, *and only* in an emergency.

It made my skin crawl as Lilly recalled what she learned from her adopted parents. I typed as fast as I could to not miss anything she was saying.

Coercive persuasion? You've got to be kidding me. Having spent a year in a fucking mental hospital, I'm well aware of what that is. Thanks to my attorneys, I ended up in one of those places the rich and famous check themselves into for all their first-world problems. The only difference was, I wasn't allowed to check myself out until a new court order was issued.

They practiced all kinds of shit in that fancy-ass place—anything to make the client function in society again. So yes, we had specialists for all of it. One of the guys got hypno-treatments for his coke addiction. Regular detox was too simple; it would've taken effort on his part. So why not pay ten grand a day for someone to do the work for you?

But someone who can perform all of these methods is news to me. My left hand is still clenched in a tight fist as I dial George's number with my right.

"Nate?" His voice is tired.

He had been setting up perimeter surveillance around Lilly's neighborhood to keep track of all the comings and goings. Thank fuck the McGuires bought their house on a street ending in a cul-de-sac; that makes it a little easier. For the first time, I wonder if that was on purpose; Tristen McGuire doesn't leave anything to chance.

"Lilly called." My words instantly put George on edge.

"What happened?" I hear rustling on the other end, and knowing the man, he is getting ready to strike down anyone that's wronged my little sister. In the short time he's been around Lilly, he's gotten as attached as I have. Her kind heart and witty personality suck you in until you cannot *not* love her.

When I'm done repeating everything Lilly told me, my adrenaline level is once again through the roof. My fingers itch to throw something else to join the laptop.

"Motherfucker!" George shouts, and a loud crash on the other end comes through the line.

*I'm not the only one losing his temper over this.*

I don't think, in all the years I've known him, he has ever cursed. He doesn't even say "shit." Not until recently. Hearing him use the F-bomb in any type of combination with another word instantly triggers an alarm in my head.

"What is it?" Given his reaction, he knows something.

"Hector Lakatos." It's more a growl than words.

"Who?" I ask, confused.

"Goddamn it. I didn't know he was even on U.S. soil. Last I heard, he was still somewhere in the Middle East." More commotion on the other end.

"George! Who. The. Fuck. Is. Hector. Lakatos?"

After several beats of silence, he answers my question, and every hair on my body stands.

"Hector Lakatos is Lilly's memory doctor."

*Fuck!*

"You know him?"

"I know *of* him. He's an independent contractor. His services are for hire to whoever pays the price."

"Illegal?"

George scoffs. "What's not illegal when you mess around in someone's brain?"

*True.*

"What are we going to do about it?"

I'm leaning on him for advice because my rational thinking exited as soon as Lilly told me what happened.

"I will contact an associate who most likely would know where to find someone who can contact Hector."

As George speaks, I've already typed the name into one of my search programs. I will find out what size underwear the fucker wears, and then I will set them on fire—with him in them. Okay, most likely not, but I will make his digital presence a living hell. He won't be able to take a piss in a public bathroom without my knowledge.

I take several calming breaths, before saying, "you do that. I'll see what I can find on my end. I want to know everything he remembers about Lilly. And if he can reverse what he did to my sister. I don't believe that her memory was only fucked with because of me." My fists ball again, and I force myself not to throw more technology across the room.

"I'll be in touch," George replies before hanging up.

# CHAPTER SEVENTY-NINE

**LILLY**

I HIDE IN MY BEDROOM FOR THE REMAINDER OF THE WEEKEND.

Den and Wes left Saturday morning to give Rhys and me alone time—as my best friend informed me with a wink.

*Oh God, did they hear us?*

She'd be staying at Wes's until school on Monday. When I asked her about Charlie, she ignored my question, kissed me on the cheek, and dragged Rhys's best friend out of the room. Seeing the two this...close is still weird, but I guess I shouldn't say anything, having formed a connection with a former Marine who serves as personal security to my criminal brother. When we Face-Time'd that evening, Den finally confessed the suspicion of Charlie cheating on her. We spent two hours dissecting his actions and words while Rhys and Wes threw in random comments from the background, giving a *male* perspective on the situation.

Heather came in to check on us a few times, but she remained standing in the doorway, and I didn't invite her in. I'm back to not wanting to be around either of my adoptive parents, but this time, I don't have to put on a show. My contempt is as visible as the sorrow on Heather's face. Rhys only left my side when he ventured down to get us something to eat. The few times Tristen tried to talk to me,

Rhys slammed the door in his face. Rhys doesn't know the truth—yet, but he knows me, and that's good enough for him.

Sunday afternoon, the door to my room bursts open, and a small, dark-haired figure launches herself at me. Natty is sobbing in my arms, and my throat thickens.

*God, I missed her.*

"Shhh." I hold her close with one arm, stroking her hair with my other hand as tears are running down my face. "I'm here, baby girl. Everything is okay. Shhh."

I catch Rhys's eyes over the top of Natty's head, and he blinks rapidly, trying to make the moisture disappear.

It feels like hours before the little girl in my arms starts calming down. We're still in the middle of my bed, while Rhys moved to lean against the headboard some time ago, watching us.

He mouths, "I love you," and I smile at him in return, a swarm of butterflies instantly causing havoc in my stomach.

Eventually, Natty moves away from me and scans my face, settling on the scar from my car accident. "Did he hurt you?"

My pulse increases, and I take a deep breath. "No, he didn't hurt me." I touch my forehead. "Please don't worry about that. I hit my head when I crashed the Jeep. It was an accident."

She stares at me for a moment longer. Knowing her, she's trying to figure out if I'm keeping something from her. I pull her back into a hug and whisper in her ear, "I'm fine. He didn't hurt me, I promise. You will understand very soon."

One day, the entire truth will come out. I wonder if Natty will forgive me, if she'll end up having some type of relationship with Nate. He would love having another little sister, even if they're not related by blood. I smile to myself at the thought when Natty pulls back and studies my face once again with her head cocked to the side. Her gaze flicks to her brother and back to me. "You both look happy."

It's an odd statement from an almost eleven-year-old girl, but Natty has always been mature and more intuitive than most of *my* friends. "Well, I am happy. I'm home with you." I smile at her.

Her eyes narrow, and she glances at Rhys, who straightens his shoulders under the scrutiny of this little human in front of us. "So, you and Rhys can be together now?"

"Wha—?" Rhys's eyes bulge out, and a choking sound comes from the doorway. Being so wrapped up in Natty, I didn't notice Heather and Tristen standing there. My mouth hangs open; all the words have left me. We all stare at the girl in front of us.

Heather makes the first move, stepping farther into the room. "What do you mean by that, love?"

Natty turns to her mother. "Well, Rhys loves Lilly, and the news said that Lilly is adopted. I heard Olivia's mom talk about it on the phone. You don't have to keep it a secret anymore." She turns back to me. "You love him, too, right? That's why you were always so sad when he wasn't home."

"I, uh..." I have no clue how to respond, and, in my confusion, I even make eye contact with Tristen, who's slack-jawed.

Rhys clears his throat. "Nat, um, how do you know all this?"

She looks innocently at all of us one after another. "I heard Mom and Dad talk about it."

Heather turns pale, and Tristen rubs his hands over his face before addressing his youngest. "Nat, when exactly did you hear us?"

She shrugs, eyeing her father. "I don't know—last year or so. I heard Mom crying in the living room when I came down to get more water after bedtime. She was upset that Rhys hadn't been home in a few days. You had another fight with Rhys about how he looked at Lilly. You told Mom that it was the only way to keep the secret." Natty looks between her parents before continuing, "Mom asked why you couldn't tell Lilly that she's adopted, that she is old enough to understand, and then Rhys could come home because he wouldn't have to lie about his feelings anymore. You told her it wasn't safe."

"Oh God," Heather whispers, covering her mouth with one hand.

My lungs start burning, and I realize I'd held my breath as she was talking.

*Safe for us?*

Rhys gently touches Natty's arm to get her attention to him. "Why haven't you said anything?"

"Because it was a secret, duh. And I wasn't supposed to be out of bed."

I can't help but snort a laugh at that. Of course my ten-year-old sister knew about my adoption before I did.

LATER, Tristen calls Rhys downstairs. I'm still digesting that Natty had picked up on all of it. We thought we were so good at pretending. But what has me more on edge is that she hasn't asked anything else about my time with Nate—I refuse to call it kidnapping anymore. Was my reassurance that she would soon understand enough? Does she know more than she told us?

I sit on the edge of my bed, flicking my thumb against the rest of my fingers. It's been twenty-one minutes since Rhys left to talk to his father. I have a sinking feeling in my stomach. Another ten or so minutes later, my bedroom door opens, and Rhys halts at the sight of me. Our eyes lock, and I know: something is wrong. He fails to put the mask in place in time.

"Tell me." My tone is flat.

Rhys sighs, crossing the distance between us, and squats down in front of me. Taking my hands in his, his thumb moves across my knuckles several times before he looks up at me through his lashes.

"I'm going back to school tomorrow."

My heart rate accelerates. "What about me?"

I forced myself earlier to look up the social media posts Katherine and her minions have been spreading on several different platforms. I don't know if I have the energy to deal with *Psycho Barbie* yet.

"He said you could take as long as you want, but..." Rhys averts his eyes again.

"What?" I can barely hear his words over my pulse rushing in my ears.

"Camden—the FBI chick—wants to give an official statement. With you. The press is getting restless."

"NO!" The word comes out as a croak.

Rhys stands up and positions himself against the pillows, pulling me with him. I end up sideways between his legs, my shoulder against his chest, while my legs are draped over one of his. His arms wrap around my waist, and I nuzzle my head in the crook of his neck.

"Babe, the longer you hide, the more shit the idiots camping out on our front lawn pull out of their asses. The articles are getting more fucked up by the day—and I mean more-than-the-truth fucked up."

His hand has started moving up and down my spine in an attempt to calm my erratic breathing.

*It's not working.*

I know he's right, but at the same time, I'm terrified I'm going to let something slip like with Heather and Tristen. It's a miracle they haven't followed up on what I meant by Henry not being my birth father.

*Did they already know?*

I press myself closer to Rhys and inhale deeply. His familiar scent in combination with the soothing movements on my back slowly calm my nerves.

"When?" I whisper as I fist his white t-shirt with my hand.

"Tomorrow morning. Before I leave for school." The worry in his tone is audible.

"Okay."


I DON'T GET any rest that night. Rhys fell asleep sometime after two in the morning.

We never had the long conversation with Heather about our relationship, and neither Rhys, nor I care. Especially not after they revealed how I lost my memory. Rhys has been sharing my bed since I got home, and I don't even bother keeping the door open.

Once I'm sure that he's out, I sneak into the bathroom and open the cabinet under the sink. I don't turn on the light to avoid alerting the boy in my bed. The faint glow coming through the narrow window that's set high into the wall by the shower is all I need. Staring at the box of tampons for a minute, I contemplate what to do. I shouldn't.

*Screw it.*

I reach into the carton and pull out the burner phone that's hidden under several layers of feminine products.

The phone lights up, and I navigate until I have a new text message pulled up on the screen.

**They're going to give a press conference tomorrow.**

Adding the number on the top of the screen, I hit send.

The response comes almost immediately: **We knew that this would happen. You know what to do.**

I inhale deeply.

**I know. But what if they don't believe me?**

**They can't prove otherwise. Addressing the media is the appropriate step.**

Ugh, he's right.

**Will you come?**

The three dots appear and disappear several times, and I brace myself for a rejection. It's too dangerous.

Then the reply pops up: **I will be there.**

All the tension leaves me, and my body suddenly feels like rubber. I sit in the dark bathroom for another fifteen minutes before I tuck the phone back into its hiding spot and slide back into bed next to Rhys.

He rolls over, wraps his arm around my waist, and pulls my back to his front.

"You talk to George?" he murmurs, his voice raspy from sleep.

"I did." I move his hand from my stomach and place a kiss on the inside of his palm.

THE KNOCK STARTLES me so much that I shriek. The door to my bedroom flies open, revealing a wide-eyed Heather, searching for the potential threat, while Rhys bursts into the bedroom from my bathroom—only wrapped in a towel.

Understanding settles in her eyes, probably assuming I'm on edge because of what's about to happen.

"I'm so sorry, sweetheart. I didn't mean to scare you." Heather remains inside the doorframe.

"It's okay. I didn't expect anyone." I look everywhere but at her.

Rhys and I lock gazes; he silently checks if I want him to stay. I shake my head, and he turns, disappearing back into a cloud of steam.

The little clock in the top corner of my laptop screen shows that it's six a.m. I'm showered and fully dressed since I gave up on sleep around 4:30. A long, hot, and numbing shower later, my hair is blow-dried, and I've applied a little makeup—just some foundation and mascara to make me feel presentable. I won't be able to relax until I face the vultures—as Rhys calls them.

"Did you need something?" My tone is harsher than I mean it to be.

My adoptive mother flinches. "No, I just wanted to let you know that Agent Camden notified the media that we would give the statement at seven-thirty, and she wants to talk to you ahead of time."

"I'll be down in a few." I force myself to gentle my tone. I'm still angry with both of them, but it's Tristen that makes my blood pressure rise.

Heather doesn't say anything else and just nods before closing the door again.

Turning back to the screen, I focus on what had me so distracted when the knock came.

*KAT ROSENFIELD:*

*Our little quarterback-stealing skank has "reappeared." Wonder if the kidnapping was even real. It prob took the thirsty bitch this long to learn what to do with her mouth.*

*COMMENTS:*

*Meghan LG: Haha! She's never had a bf, 2 weeks are not enough for that.*

*Nora Ross: LMAO. If she even figured out how to open his pants.*

*Kellan J: Meow! Kitty Kat has her claws out.*

*Kat Rosenfield: Fuck off, Jager.*

*Kat Rosenfield: Meghan:: Right? She couldn't learn how to give a BJ if she had a whole YouTube library of tutorials giving her step-by-step instructions.*

*Lisa Bennett: Unicorn?*

*Nora Ross: LOL. Duh!*

*Owen J: Nora—articulate as always. You should give L a tutorial since I know you def know what to do with ur mouth.*

*Kellan J: ROFLMAO*

*Meghan LG: Don't be such a fucking asshole, O!*

*Nora Ross: You haven't complained yet, Owen. ;)*

*Lisa Bennett: Kellan, why don't you call Rhys and ask what his whore of a little sister still needs pointers on?*

*Owen J: I volunteer as tribute!*

*Nora Ross: OWEN!*

*Kat Rosenfield: You don't know what diseases you'll get touching that slut!*

*Owen J: I'll take my chances. Have you seen that tight ass?*

*Kellan J: I second that. I'd tap that.*

*Meghan LG: GAG!*

CLOSING MY LAPTOP, I squeeze my eyes shut. I wonder if Rhys has seen how his *friends* talk about me. The bathroom door opens, and he emerges dressed in faded, light-blue jeans, a gray-and-white plaid button-down with a white t-shirt underneath, and the football team's baseball cap on backward.

My mouth waters at the sight, and I shake my head.

*Not appropriate right now.*

"See something you like?" Rhys smirks at me, and I forget all about the shit I just read.

I stand up and cross the distance to him. Wrapping my arms around his midsection, I lean my head on his chest. The steady thump of his heart increases, and I squeeze. "Always."

We pull apart, and Rhys's smile drops. "Ready?"

I answer honestly. "No."

DOWNSTAIRS, we find Agent Camden and Lanning in their usual spots. Heather is standing at the island with a cup of coffee in her hand, and Tristen sits on the other side on one of the barstools, typing on his laptop.

"Where is Natty?" I scan the room and look over into the living room as well.

"She is still upstairs; I told her she could play until it's time," Heather answers my question.

"You mean read," Rhys's voice comes from behind me.

"True," his mother smiles, but it doesn't reach her eyes.

Rhys and I are not touching, but he stands close enough for me to feel his body heat radiating off of him.

"Lilly?" Agent Camden brings my attention to her. "Why don't you take a seat? We need to go over what we will tell the media."

My body goes rigid. "Do I have to talk to them?"

The two FBI agents exchange a look before they both make eye contact with Tristen. Tristen gets off his seat and walks over. "Let's sit, and we'll discuss what options we have."

I glance behind me at Rhys, who, in return, gently touches my lower back, signaling for me to sit down. We take the bench seat on the opposite side of Tristen and Agent Lanning, with Camden at the head of the table. Rhys folds his hands on top of the table, leaning forward. His entire posture screams *Let's hear it*. Under the table, his thigh is tightly pressed against mine in support.

I cross my arms in front of my chest. I'm sure whoever looks at me will assume it's to shield myself from what's about to come. They're probably not too far off.

Thirty minutes later, I'm aware of everything that's about to happen, and we have another twenty to go. My stomach feels like it's about to expel the tea I sipped on while Camden filled me in. Her male counterpart only spoke up when she specifically asked him to clarify something. After handing me my mug with tea and Rhys his coffee, Heather stood behind her husband, hands on the back of his chair, while Tristen's focus jumped between the talking agents and me.

Camden looks between Rhys and me. "I am aware that this is a rather unique situation, and given the fact that we want this to focus on Lilly and her kidnapping, I would advise that you two do not touch while we are outside."

Rhys snorts, and my cheeks flush.

*Could this get any more embarrassing?*

"Rhys," Tristen warns.

"Jeez. Chill, Dad. I'm not gonna stick my tongue down *Lilly's* throat while we're facing the cameras."

I suck in a breath at Rhys's tone. He's been showing less and less respect toward his father.

"Rhys, that's enough," Heather says calmly but with authority behind it.

He pushes up, hands flat on the tabletop. "Sure, Mom. He can treat all of us as puppets in his little military games and do God knows what to Lilly—which by the way, she won't tell me out of fear I'll blow a gasket. That alone tells me that it has to be pretty fucked up, and for some unknown reason, she's still protecting him."

How did this situation escalate so quickly? I place my hand on Rhys's, whose knuckles have turned white from the pressure by now. "Rhys?"

His eyes flick to me, and he pulls his hand out. "I'll be back in fifteen." With that, he stalks out and up the stairs, leaving all of us stunned in the kitchen.

## CHAPTER EIGHTY

**RHYS**

I PACE THE LENGTH OF MY ROOM.

"Fuck! Fuck! Fuck!"

Stopping near the window, I glance through the half-open blinds. Three news vans are parked on the curb, and the vultures are already waiting. I pull on my hair and crouch down. I need to calm my nerves before we go out there.

I had no intention to go off on Dad, but the longer I avoided him, the more wound up I got. Camden's comment was just the final straw. I need to know What. The. Fuck happened for Lilly not to be able to look at my parents anymore—again. They finally had gotten back to a point where everything seemed normal. Why can she confide in her brother but not me? I bet even George knows, and I'm the only one left in the dark.

I'm her freaking boyfriend! I chuck the first thing I can reach across the room—the controller for my video console. It shatters into pieces against the wall, and I take in the scene of black plastic shards everywhere.

*Fucking great.*

Then there's the minor issue of my psychotic ex. Lilly thinks I didn't see what was pulled up on her screen earlier—well, I did. I've made it my mission to be up to date on Kat's malicious games.

What pisses me off more are the comments of my so-called friends and teammates. Wes already got into it with some of them, but it seems I have to rearrange some faces today to put them back in their place. The day will probably end with my suspension.

*At least then I can stay home with Lilly.*

I go into the bathroom and stare at the guy in the mirror. I barely recognize myself anymore. My hands grip the edge of the sink until my knuckles turn white. Closing my eyes, I focus on breathing. Eventually, I'm calm enough to put on my poker face to make it through the freak-show of a press conference. Let's hope Lilly will be able to lie her ass off, or I'll have other things to worry about than pounding Jager's face as soon as he crosses my path.

LILLY IS STANDING in the foyer next to Natty. Her arm is around our little sister's shoulder. Blood relation or not, Natty will always be her sister.

I scan Lilly up and down; she is wearing black skinny jeans that look looser than I remember. Despite the chilly temperature this morning, she put on her white Adidas Superstars—no socks—paired with a white V-neck t-shirt and her dark-blue denim jacket over it. The warmest item is the oversized brown Burberry scarf Den gave her two Christmases ago. I love the outfit; it makes her look *I-don't-give-a-fuck* casual, but at the same time, she's put together and, to me, sexy as hell.

*Mine,* my inner caveman growls.

I grab my varsity jacket from the hook next to the stairs and make my way over, draping my arm around Lilly's waist. I pull her into me and bury my nose in her hair. Inhaling the scent of her shampoo, my nerves calm some more.

*I can do this.*

Lilly, who still has Natty in her embrace, pulls back and searches my eyes.

"You okay?" Her tone is so low that only our little sister can hear us.

I force a reassuring smile on my face. "I'm fine. I just needed a moment."

Lilly's eyes narrow; she knows there is more to it, but she doesn't push the issue with Natty next to us.

Natty looks up, "Are you still angry with Dad?"

*Why does she have to be so smart?*

I pull her into a hug with my other arm and decide to give her the half-truth. "I am, but I mostly don't want to leave Lilly alone today."

Truth.

Omission: I am going to rearrange my friends' faces, give Kat a piece of my mind, and hopefully not lose my shit in front of the media in a few minutes. Who knows what the fuck they'll throw at us?

"It's time," Agent Camden announces, and Lilly's arm around my waist tenses. I tighten my grip on her and lean down to her ear. "Everything will be okay. I'm right here. I don't give a fuck about her no-touching rule."

Lilly chuckles and kisses me on the cheek.

"Eww. Gross!" Natty screeches and darts over to Mom, whose eyes crinkle in response to her youngest's outburst.

The FBI agents position themselves at the door, followed by Mom and Natty. Lilly and I are next with Dad in the rear.

As soon as the door is open, the flashes start, and people haul questions at our group. Lilly takes a step back and bumps into me. My hands automatically clasp around her upper arms to steady her, but I let go quickly and move sideways. Dad steps past me to her other side, and her five-foot-four figure is now framed between two six-foot-plus walls.

We're on the patio, with ten or more people on the lawn. I see several neighbors peek out their windows, if not even openly gawking from their properties' yards. The two agents close ranks in front, Mom has Natty wrapped in her arms to the left behind Lanning, and the three of us are to the right behind Camden. The female agent takes charge and holds up one hand. It's fascinating how the quiet woman all of a sudden commands the group in front of us. While she waits for them to settle down, I scan our surroundings. Lancaster, the dude who's been obsessed with the case for a decade now, is front and center. There are several unmarked cars in addition to the news vans which, I assume, belong to the reporters or whoever the people shoving their recording phones at us are. My gaze settles on a tall figure leaning against the rear end of the farthest van, and my eyes widen. He's dressed casually in dark jeans with a black hoodie under a black leather jacket. The hoodie is pulled up, and the brim of a baseball cap covers most of his face, including *the scar*. Arms crossed over his broad chest, I can see a phone sticking out in one of his hands, camera pointed toward us.

*They're both here for her.*

I make eye contact with my BFF, but George's expression doesn't change a millimeter. Since we're partially hidden behind the two agents, I touch Lilly's arm to get her attention. She looks up, and I lean down to her ear, whispering as low as possible. "He's here. They're *both* watching." I don't dare say more. So far, no one has paid us any attention.

Lilly's eyes close briefly, understanding the meaning of my words. Then she turns back forward and faces the vultures, not looking around at all.

The knowledge of their presence is enough to calm her nerves, and something clicks into place for me. She's told me many times how I'm her home. We've talked about it a lot, especially during the first few weeks when we analyzed why she had always felt a certain way for me, despite not knowing. Things had shifted once Nate came into the picture, and I thought I was losing her. I was dead wrong. Nate—and with extension, George—have become an equally important part of her life. She needs all of us in different ways to make it through this.

"Ladies and gentlemen, thank you for coming." Camden's voice snaps me out of my revelation. "I am Agent Vivienne Camden and the lead agent in Miss McGuire's case. We have asked you here to give you the exclusive statement to this investigation. Miss McGuire and her family are in attendance; however, we ask you not to address them directly. Agent Lanning and I will answer your questions to the best of our ability and what we are able to disclose at this point."

Murmurs go around the group, and—surprise, surprise—Lancaster asks the first question.

"Miss McGuire was the first victim of The Babysitter. Since

then, he abducted four other girls before he captured Miss McGuire again. What's his motive?"

"That is still open to investigation. Due to the perpetrator never harming any of the victims, we suspect that he has an underlying mental condition that drives him to take the girls."

"He drugs them. How can you say that he doesn't harm the little girls?" a woman holding her phone toward us snaps.

"That is correct. Let me rephrase my statement. Since Miss McGuire's first disappearance, the perpetrator has used a mild sedative to calm his victims. The girls are not being drugged to render them unconscious; he keeps them alert but calm. They receive food, have access to a bathroom, and are being entertained. He has not physically harmed any of them."

I can feel Lilly getting more agitated, and I involuntarily make eye contact with my father over her head. He's noticed as well. My heartrate picks up, and I fight the urge to grab her hand and drag her back inside.

"Agent Camden." A woman from a local news station steps forward, her cameraman right behind. "What does Miss McGuire have to say about her kidnappings? We understand that, the first time, she was severely sedated and, according to previous reports, traumatized. Why was there never a report filed or an active search for the kidnapper? If this would've been handled appropriately, the following kidnappings could've possibly been prevented."

"This is part of the investigation we cannot disclose at this point."

*Yeah, because you have no clue.*

I'm pretty sure my father has kept ninety percent of the facts from the suits.

"Lilly, what does The Babysitter want from you? You're the one he wants. The parents of these little girls deserve to know why their kids were taken." Lancaster steps in front of the other chick. Dad squares his shoulders, which puts me on high alert. My fingers begin to twitch, and I curl them into a fist to avoid drawing attention.

"Mister Lancaster, please take a step back," Lanning warns, looking straight at the guy.

Lancaster doesn't comply right away. Instead, he stares at Lilly, who—holy shit, she holds his gaze without so much as blinking.

Finally, Lancaster mumbles something under his breath and moves back in line.

Camden takes over again. "Miss McGuire has no recollection of what happened during either kidnapping."

Shouts erupt all around us.

"How is this possible?"

"That's bullshit."

"She's lying."

"She is not a child anymore; she has to know something."

"What are you keeping from the public?" Lancaster again.

*Fuck, this dude is gonna be a problem.*

Out of the corner of my eye, I notice George straightening up. He's zeroed in on Lancaster. This guy better shut up, or George might snap his neck in front of everyone.

This time, Lanning holds up a hand. It takes several minutes until everyone stops yelling, and he speaks up.

"Miss McGuire was severely sedated when she was admitted to Hill Crest Medical Center. She was found on a bench outside the facility by a staff member. Miss McGuire remained under close observation for twenty-four hours while the necessary medication to counteract the drugs were administered. The combination found in her bloodstream has the known side effect of short-term memory loss. She will continue regular visits to local specialists to ensure that there is no permanent damage to her well-being."

What the—? I fight the urge to storm over to George. He left Lilly on a fucking park bench? No one cared to tell me that tidbit—probably because I would've flipped a lid.

"Why would The Babysitter drug Miss McGuire that way if she's the one he wants?" a new voice asks, and I take in the reporter that has stepped forward. Beside me, Lilly goes rigid, and I look down. She's gone pale.

*What the—?*

I glance back. The dude is tall and well-built; he's got me beat by an inch or two. He has black curly hair that's thinning at the hairline, a goatee, and his nose looks like it was broken one too many times. But his most prominent facial feature is his ice-blue eyes; they're so light they appear almost white. The hairs at the nape of my neck stand in all directions. Even when George had stepped out of the dark in Denielle's backyard, I didn't have that reaction. And my BFF is scary as fuck.

Reporter guy wears a tan trench coat over a light-blue button-down and brown khakis—the outfit screams *costume* to me.

I avert my eyes and focus on Lilly. Her thumb is flicking against the rest of her fingers. She's about to bolt.

*Fuck it.*

I wrap my arm around her lower waist, and she immediately leans into the touch. I don't pay attention if anyone notices, mainly because I couldn't care less.

As if from a distance, Camden's voice drifts into my brain. "What's your name, sir?"

"Francis Turner," Trench Coat Guy replies without hesitation.

"Mr. Turner, at this point, we believe Miss McGuire was drugged so she couldn't fight back. As you stated, she is older, and the perpetrator could not have foreseen how she would react to him."

"So, essentially, you have no fucking clue what happened to any of the girls or who The Babysitter is!"

Ah, Lancaster is back in play.

"Mr. Lancaster, this is an ongoing investigation. We are unable to release all the information at this point, not to compromise the case."

*As he said, you have no fucking clue.*

THE PRESS CONFERENCE, aka joke of the year, goes on for another ten minutes, but no real information is being released. Oddly enough, none of the vultures brought up our relationship, despite it being splashed over several social media sites.

Lilly is as white as a ghost and shaking like a leaf by the time we get back inside. As soon as the front door closes, she charges upstairs, taking two steps at a time.

Mom calls after her, but Lilly doesn't respond. Dad gives me a look that I would interpret as worry if I didn't know that the man has no feelings. Okay, maybe he does, but it's easier to be pissed at him if I pretend he's the robot he always acts like.

Following Lilly to her room, I find it empty. Knowing where she is, I flip the lock and make my way to the bathroom. Water is already running, and when I step inside, I'm met by a cloud of steam. Lilly sits in front of the running shower, arms wrapped around her bent legs and forehead resting on her knees. In her one hand, she's clutching the phone, and I notice the box we stashed it in on the floor, contents spilled everywhere.

The little alarm clock she keeps above her sink shows that it's well after eight, and I should be on my way to school. I sink down next to Lilly and place my hand between her shoulder blades.

"Talk to me, babe." I lean over and place a kiss on her hair right above her temple.

"Something isn't right," she mumbles into her legs.

I squint at her, moving my hand up and down her spine. "What do you mean?"

"He was there. What was he doing here?"

I'm not sure I understand her correctly. "He, who?"

Lilly finally lifts her head, and my chest constricts. I haven't seen that expression since the text messages.

"The guy from Magnolia's," she whispers.

*I'm lost.*

"Babe, what are you talking about?"

As she recalls the day she met Den at Magnolia's and, later, when she saw him again right before Nate got to her, I try to make sense of it. Nothing that has happened in the last five months has been by chance—apart from Lilly stumbling over the article that started it all. My heart feels like it's about to explode out of my chest.

"Does Nate know?" I force myself to steady my tone and not follow my instinct of ripping the phone out of her hand to call her brother myself.

"No. I forgot about him. Until today." Her gaze jumps between my eyes. "Do you think it's a coincidence?"

*Truth?*

"No."

# EPILOGUE

## HER

*She has grown up. I've seen the occasional pictures Gray has taken over the years, but looking at the young woman in front of me, I'm reminded more than ever who her father is. She looks so much like him—and her brother.*

*I'm partially hidden behind a fence, two houses down. I sent Gray to stand between the reporters and told him to make himself known. I want to see her reaction. She's smart; she'll put two and two together.*

*Gray revealing himself to her back in January was not part of the plan —but neither was her disappearance. I didn't account for Nate to be in the picture before I could get to her. Something happened while she was gone; otherwise, his bloodhound wouldn't be standing a hundred yards from me, watching Lilly like a hawk.*

*Why couldn't she have just let it go for a few more months?*

*Now, I have to improvise.*

# OF LIGHT AND AND DARK

*book 3*

# PROLOGUE

## HER

Six days ago

*I'm the last to climb the steps and enter the private jet.*

*My little lap dog followed through. By mid-Sunday, the news of Lilly McGuire being victim number one had broken everywhere. They even gave Nate a cute serial offender name: The Babysitter. How very fitting.*

*I can imagine how he reacted when he got the alert. I hope he lost his temper in front of his dimwitted fiancée; he has never been able to handle it when someone bad-mouths his family.*

*As soon as I tasked my informant, I set everything else in motion. It was not easy to organize transportation for my pawn and the medical staff I require to keep him in check, let alone a place for all of us to stay. It needs to be secure and large enough so I don't have to listen to him yell at the nurse every time she administers the paralytic drugs. I thought, after years of not using his legs, he would be too weak. Obviously, I was wrong. Last week's escape attempt was proof of that. A mistake I will not make twice.*

. . .

*GRAY ASSURED me the house he procured is far away from any other residence in the area, close enough to drive to Westbridge on short notice, and still meets my aesthetic requirements. This is going to be interesting, knowing Gray's taste in interior design.*

*EVERYONE IS ON BOARD, and he is secured in the back of the plane. As far as the pilots and flight attendant are concerned, the unconscious man is my terribly ill husband that will be receiving medical treatment in the United States.*

*Standing in the door, I take in the interior of the jet. This will do for the next ten hours.*

# CHAPTER EIGHTY-ONE

## RHYS

*MOTHERFUCKER, THAT HURTS!*

I shake my hand, looking down at Jager's busted face. My *friend's* eyes are wide, and blood is gushing out of his nose like a freaking waterfall.

"What the fuck, McGuire?" He tries to push himself off the ground, but I plant my boot in the middle of his chest, holding him down.

Thanks to the farce of a press conference, followed by Lilly's revelation about trench-coat creep, and an endlessly long call with Nate and George, I was two hours late for school. I arrived just as the bell announced the end of second period. With one objective in mind, I made my way through the crowded corridors, ignoring the conversations that halted mid-sentence and the fact that everyone, except the freshmen who are too chickenshit, openly gawked at me. Entering the senior hallway, I spotted Jager coming out of his classroom.

*Perfect timing.*

As I let my tunnel vision take over, I picked up my pace and reached his side precisely as we were in front of the guys' bathroom. My hand shot out, gripped his neck—probably tighter than necessary—and steered him through the door.

"LEAVE!" I barked at the two juniors taking a leak. Both whirled toward my voice and immediately scrambled to get out—one of them still having his dick in his hand as he headed for the exit.

I pushed Jager against the closest stall and let my fist fly—a well-aimed cross punch straight at the nose. Dude went down like a ragdoll.

*Pussy.*

WITH MY FOOT now on his chest, I contemplate what to aim for next. As much as I want to let all my pent-up frustration out on the fucker, Spence's number one rule won't allow for it. Unless it's a life-or-death situation—*for you*—you never use your feet on someone that's already down.

*That would make hands acceptable, right?*

I shift so my knee replaces the shoe on Jager's sternum and am about to strike again as something wraps around my wrist.

"What the fuck are you doing?" my best friend's voice penetrates the pounding in my ears.

Still in a full-on rage, I whirl on Wes, and he takes a step back, holding his hands up. "Dude, you gotta snap out of it. They called Harvey."

I want to laugh. Wes is fully aware that my baby sister would have a better chance holding me back than Harvey. He's the school's forty-some-year-old security guard. Five-foot-six and two hundred-plus pounds—he's a joke. He's also a huge wrestling and football fan and kisses my ass whenever he sees me.

"Let him come," I scoff, turning back to Jager who is halfway to his feet. "Did I tell you to get up?"

Hand in front of his face, which is completely stained crimson, my teammate lets himself drop back to the tiled floor.

The door flies open, and Harvey walks in, in all his non-threatening glory. "What's going on here?" he booms then does a double-take between the guy on the floor and me. "Rhys, my man. You're back!" His face lights up like a Christmas tree.

"Sure am, Harvey, my friend." I slap his palm as if my classmate is not lying at my feet behind me.

Wes rolls his eyes behind the security guard's back.

"Uh, is everything okay in here?" Harvey glances around me.

"Ab-so-lute-ly." I plaster a fake grin on my face and point my thumb behind me. "Jager here slipped and hit his pretty nose on the edge of the sink. Isn't that right, Kellan?"

I don't bother turning around to make sure he'll confirm my explanation. My superfan bobs his head slowly. I didn't take him for being that dense, but whatever.

"Well"—Harvey clears his throat—"if that's all, I'm not needed here."

"Yup, it's all good," Wes chimes in, plants his hands on Harvey's shoulders, and steers him out the door. He then moves in front of it so no one can come back in.

I lock eyes with my best friend and rub my hands together, slowly turning. "Let's continue our chat."

Jager's eyes widen. I'm channeling my inner George and must have succeeded, because the boy on the floor looks like he's about to shit himself.

"Rhys, bro, we're c-cool. N-no hard feelings," he stammers.

"No hard feelings? I thought you were hard for *my* girlfriend. Didn't you want to tap that?" I force my tone to remain eerily calm. If I learned one thing from George, it was the calmer you act, the scarier you are.

"Fuck!" Jager hisses. "Man, that was just a joke. You know I would never..." I cock my head to the side, and he trails off.

"I know, huh? Wes, did you know when you came back to school last week, and Lilly was still kidnapped? From what you overheard, the entire team—*my team*—ran their mouths." I don't take my gaze off of the shaking boy in front of me.

"Nope, he seemed pretty set on making a move." It's audible in his reply that Wes has his trademark smirk on full display.

"That's what I thought." I slowly sink to a crouch until I'm at eye-level with Jager. He shrinks even lower, and I get in his face. "So, what are we going to do about that?"

"I...I swear, I was joking. I would've never touched Lilly. She's always been off-limits—for all of us. We were just talking shit. Kat started it!" His voice pitches at the end of his speech, and I bite at the inside of my cheek to not burst out laughing. What a fucking loser.

"Oh, now you're blaming it on my ex. That's rich."

Behind me, Wes can't keep his composure and snorts loudly.

I pat Kellan's cheek. "I would advise you to watch your trap going forward. I may not always be around, but I *will* know."

"Uh, dude?" Wes's tone makes me shift my focus.

*No fucking way.*

"Did you seriously just piss yourself?" My eyebrows shoot up as I take in Kellan's ashen skin.

He closes his eyes briefly but remains mute.

My best friend cackles behind me. "I don't think we have to worry about him." A flash lights up the bathroom, and I can't contain myself anymore. Laughing, I stand up and walk out. Wes took a picture of a bloody and pee-stained Jager.

A slight sense of satisfaction settles in my chest. I'm done with him. On to the next one.

As I walk through the door this afternoon, I am proud to say I didn't get suspended. It was a close call when I finally caught up with Owen in the locker room after last period, but Coach let me off with a warning.

*Note to self: Be more careful next time.*

Oddly enough, I didn't run into Kat the entire day. We have three classes together, and I saw her car when I pulled into the lot. The only explanation was that she heard I'm back and made a run for it.

I stop abruptly in the empty kitchen. Camden and Lanning are nowhere in sight, making the room look weird after their asses have been basically superglued to the chairs for weeks. Natty enters the room as I'm heading for the stairs.

"Where are the suits?"

My little sister shrugs then looks me up and down. "Were you in a fight?"

I squint at her. "Are you psychic now?"

The tiny human in front of me rolls her eyes. "Your knuckles are all busted up."

Instinctively, I shove my hands into the pockets of my jeans. "Just had a minor disagreement with someone."

"Uh-huh." With a scowl that tells me she doesn't buy my lame excuse one bit, she moves past me.

Shaking my head with a grin, I make my way upstairs two steps at a time.

I knock once and push the door open. Lilly sits at her desk and closes the laptop quickly as she turns. My chest tightens, and my grin falls.

*What now?*

I cross the room, pull her up, and wrap my arms around her slender waist. She's getting too thin. Burying my nose in her hair, I whisper, "I missed you." Her signature scent of coconut and vanilla instantly calms my nerves.

Her arms wind around my midsection, and she squeezes tightly. "How bad was it?"

"Not bad at all." I'm not lying, but I'm also not telling the truth.

By the time lunch had rolled around, word had gotten out about what happened to Jager and Maxwell. Tyler Maxwell didn't participate in the online smear campaign, but I overheard him telling someone that I wouldn't have been able to jump him like that. He'd still plan on going after Lilly; if she were so eager to fuck her brother, she'd be more than satisfied with what he had in mind. I contemplated letting Lilly's real brother handle it but decided against it. The damage Nate could inflict on Maxwell would most likely result in consequences for years to come, but planting my foot in the back of his knee and sending him to the floor was much more satisfying.

*He was upright, so I didn't break any rules.*

After that, the stares and whispers stopped. When I entered the cafeteria, the conversations halted, but no one looked my way. Suddenly, the floor seemed to be tremendously interesting for the entire student population. My teammates, sitting at the table I used to occupy, scrambled, assuming I would want my old seat back. Wrong. Yet, the gratification of their reaction made me grin inwardly. With Wes on my heels, I carried my tray to Lilly's table. Den was already there, nibbling on some carrot sticks and ignoring her surroundings. Sloane and Emma, next to her, looked around frantically as I approached.

"Ladies. And Den." I greeted, winking at her as I dropped into Lilly's usual chair.

Denielle flipped me off but smirked. The shift in the social hierarchy over the last few weeks had our classmates unsettled. It was never a secret that *The Bulldog* and I didn't see eye to eye. Den was Lilly's guard dog, shielding her from me, and now we acted like best friends. Correction, we don't have to act. I consider her one of my closest friends.

After I made my stance clear throughout the day, no one would dare come after me, but I had my doubts about Lilly—especially once Kat emerges from wherever she had hid today.

"I know what you did to Kellan and Tyler," Lilly announces against my sweater.

I assumed she'd find out, but that was quick. "How?"

She pulls back and looks me straight in the eyes. "Someone filmed you; it's all over social media. You could've seriously injured him with that push kick to the knee."

*Shit, I didn't notice someone taking a video.*

"He deserved it," I defend myself.

Lilly sighs. "So, it's bad."

With a bitter taste on my tongue, I admit, "Yes."

She turns and walks to her bed. Sitting down on the edge, elbows on her knees, she covers her face with her hands. "I should've stayed in California."

# CHAPTER EIGHTY-TWO

### LILLY

"What the fuck are you talking about?" Rhys is at my side in an instant. Squatting down, he pulls my hands away. I was mostly talking to myself, but he's searching my eyes for any hint of seriousness.

"I'm sorry. I didn't mean that," I mumble, swallowing over the sudden lump in my throat.

*Did I, though?*

I stare at our interlaced fingers.

Rhys rolls back on his heels, not letting go of me. "Babe, talk to me." His tone is wary.

I'm a coward. I didn't think twice about chasing my past, despite being fully aware of my kidnapper being out there. But the mere thought of walking back into Westbridge High makes me want to run. Add Francis Turner into the mix, and I'm more scared than when I woke up at the vineyard.

I force myself to make eye contact. "Nate doesn't think it's safe here."

"What do you mean?" Rhys cocks his head, watching me closely.

I feel sick just thinking about what my brother found out today. "Francis Garrison Turner died thirteen years ago."

His face drains of color, and I continue, "Turner was a former

Army Ranger. He was dishonorably discharged for attacking a superior officer under the influence of narcotics. He died not long after. His car went over a cliff on the Pacific Coast Highway."

"California?" Several emotions flash across Rhys's face at once.

I nod. *This is not a coincidence.*

"Are we sure it's the same guy?"

Standing up, I pull Rhys with me into the bathroom. I motion for him to take a seat on the closed toilet while I dig through my feminine products. With the burner phone in hand, I move in front of him and hold it out. "Check the texts."

Rhys does as he's told. I don't have to ask if he found the evidence my brother sent over; his grip on the phone intensifies to the point of his knuckles turning white.

Nate discovered the proof that we're dealing with the same guy after doing some *digging*. Don't ask me how he did it, but he got a hold of Francis Garrison Turner's old driver's license picture, as well as the police accident report and death certificate.

Rhys looks up. "The report says the body was unidentifiable."

"Keep reading."

I memorized it hours ago. The accident happened in the middle of the night; the crash site wasn't discovered until mid-morning. Turner's SUV went through a barrier and crashed onto the rocks. The car caught fire on impact, just to later be submerged by the tide. The first responders were able to secure the vehicle enough to pull the body out. The DNA evidence indicated that the remains were Turner's, who owned the SUV.

"What are we gonna do now?" Rhys's question snaps me out of recapping the gory details in my head.

*He is* so *not going to like the answer to that.*

I pry the phone out of his hands out of fear he'll send it flying. "Nate wants me to come to LA, and George wants me to stay put and act as bait to figure out what Turner wants."

*Crash.*

And there goes my toothbrush holder. Damn it!

"ARE THEY FUCKING INSANE?" he yells.

"Lower your voice! Tristen is home," I whisper-shout.

Rhys stands, jamming his hands in his hair and tugging on the strands. With his back to me, he exhales, "I can't take this shit anymore!"

Those are his parting words before I'm alone in my bathroom.

Unsure what to do, I stare at my bed through the now open bathroom door. I'm about to return the burner to its hiding spot to follow Rhys when it starts vibrating in my hand. Quickly, I close the door again and answer the call.

"He didn't take it well, did he?" my brother's voice greets me.

"What did you expect?"

"Not that he would storm out of the house like a little toddler throwing a tantrum," Nate sneers.

"He did what?" I jump up from my crouch in front of the vanity. Even before racing into the hallway, I know I'll find Rhys's room empty.

Not paying attention, I slam straight into a body coming down from the third floor: Tristen. Stumbling back, we stare at each other. His eyes dart to the device plastered against my ear before he scans my face.

"Lilly? You there?" Nate's voice filters through the speaker.

Tristen's gaze snaps back toward my lifted hand. "Whose phone is that?"

Heather hasn't gotten around to getting me a new one since the accident, and I haven't pushed the issue. I'm with the people I'd contact anyway. One of them always has a phone I could use—not that I need to.

My mouth opens and closes several times. I glance toward the stairs. If Rhys left the house, he's already gone. My mind begins to race. If I stay here, there is a likely chance of my adopted father cross-examining me. I do the only thing I can think of. I dart around Tristen and break into a sprint, taking two steps at a time to the first floor.

"Lilly."

I pretend not to hear him calling after me. Standing in the doorway to the garage, I realize my mistake. I don't have a car.

*Shit, shit, shit!*

Footsteps on the stairs make me react on instinct. I grab the keys to Tristen's Raptor from the hook and make a run for it, slapping the garage door opener on the wall in passing. Thankfully, no one in this family ever locks their cars inside the garage, and I climb in.

Starting the truck, "Hail to the King" by Avenged Sevenfold blares out of the speakers, and I jump. Jeez. Twisting the volume button down all the way, I hear my brother's voice.

"Lilly Ann, if you don't tell me, right this fucking second, what the fuck is going on, I'm going to send George to pick you up. I don't give a fuck what he wants to do; I'm the one writing his fucking paychecks!"

Lifting the phone back to my ear, I scoff, "You realize that you just used the word fuck four times."

"I don't give a flying fuck!" Nate barks.

A knock on the driver's side window makes my head snap around. Heart beating in my throat, I lock eyes with Tristen. I hold his stare for several breaths before putting the Raptor in reverse and pulling out of the garage. My adopted father stands, hands on his hips, in the spot his car occupied a few seconds ago. His face is expressionless—as usual—and I push the garage door button on the visor. I'll deal with the consequences later.

Lancaster's car is still parked on the street. Thankfully, the windows to Tristen's black monstrosity are so tinted that the guy doesn't recognize me, and I hit the gas as soon as I have the massive truck in the middle of the road.

I PUT the phone on speaker and place it on the center console. "Sorry, I'm back. Tristen caught me with the burner, and I kind of just stole his truck." Heat creeps up my neck.

That makes my brother burst out laughing. "Now I want to hack into the feed to see his face."

"How did you know that Rhys left if you weren't already watching?" I assumed he was when he called.

"His tracker started moving again. Fast. I know he just came home, so I figured you told him, and it didn't go well."

Of course they're following everyone's movements like a hawk after what we found this morning.

Nate stays on the phone but doesn't say anything else. I drive by Wes's but don't see the Defender anywhere. "Where is he?"

*I should've asked that first.*

"Almost at Woodland Park." I hear the clicking of keys in the background, and I wonder what Nate's doing.

Focusing back on the road, I turn right at the next intersection. Wes's house is not far from the park, but I was heading in the wrong direction, and the following streets are all one-ways or cul-de-sacs. I come to a halt at the light in front of Café Chai. It's similar to Magnolia's, but the cheerleaders had declared it their spot years ago, so I never ventured into the enemy's territory. The light turns green, and I take my foot off the brake when someone darts across. Pushing the pedal back down, I roll my eyes at the idiot. Why can't people wait the extra minute until it's their turn again? Suddenly, *the idiot* pivots back. That's when it registers who is standing in front of me: Katherine Rosenfield.

This is the first time I've seen her since I had let my rage take over and planted my fist in her face. A red haze forms in front of my vision, remembering the confrontation. How was that less than three weeks ago?

Neither of us breaks eye contact, and my surroundings fade into the background as I tighten my hands on the steering wheel. It's just her and me. Everything I've read over the last few days about myself floods my brain at once. *She* started it all.

Head tilted, Katherine pulls something out of her purse. Her arm lifts, and with a mixture of a sneer and a smug smile, she takes a picture of me.

I press the gas pedal down, not paying attention that my signal has switched to red again. I go around her but cut off another car that was in the process of turning. The driver beeps at me, and I swerve just in time. Looking in the side mirror, I have a clear view of Rhys's ex. She moved all the way into the street—filming me.

"FUCK!" I hit the steering wheel. The burst of adrenaline is now accompanied by pounding in my ears.

"Did you just say the *F-word*, little sister?" my brother chuckles.

I totally forgot that he's on the line.

Forcing myself to calm my voice, I joke, "Can George make someone disappear for me?" Okay, maybe I'm a little serious.

"Why?" The humor is gone from his tone.

"I ran a red light, trying to get away from Katherine, and the bitch just took a video of me."

"You really know how to keep a low profile." Nate attempts to lighten the mood but achieves the opposite.

"Shut up." My eyes start to sting, and I blink.

"Want me to send her a virus?"

That makes me laugh, and my chest feels a little lighter. As much as I want to say yes, I reply, "She'll find a way to blame that on me as well."

"It's your call. Though, you could probably do it yourself with as good as you already are." Nate's praise distracts me from the Wicked Bitch, and the corners of my mouth turn up.

"I miss you, big brother." The words are out before I can think about it.

"I miss you, too, little sister." I can hear him smile as he returns the sentiment.

"I'm almost at the park. I'll call you later, 'kay?"

"Be careful. George is working on tracking down Turner. We need to figure out what he wants."

"I will."

Nate disconnects as I pull into the lot by the picnic area. I park next to the Defender and let the car idle as I watch Rhys sitting on one of the tables. He's facing away with his feet planted on the bench below and his elbows resting on his thighs.

Getting out, I shove the phone into the back pocket of my black jeans. With everything going on today, I'm still wearing the clothes I had picked out for the press conference. A shiver runs through my body. It's definitely too cold for what I'm wearing: a denim jacket over a thin tee.

Wrapping my arms around myself, I try to keep warm.

Rhys's back is to me as I approach, and his voice startles me. "How did you find me?"

Climbing the picnic table, I take a seat next to him. "Nate."

I want to scoot close enough for our thighs to touch, but an invisible force won't let me. It's as if we're two like poles of a set of magnets, repelling each other.

He huffs. "Of course." A little quieter, he adds, "And here I thought we still had the bond that always led us to one another."

*What?*

"What do you mean?" I ask, puzzled.

Rhys turns toward me. I can't read his expression, and my chest tightens.

"When we were little, I used to take off a lot. You would always find me. It became like a challenge. In the beginning, I would leave small clues for you to follow. Eventually, I stopped. No matter how far I ran or where I hid, you would come for me. It was like we were connected somehow."

I draw in a deep breath, but my chest only constricts further. "I don't remember that." A lone tear runs down my cheek, and I close my eyes.

The sensation of his thumb swiping away the wetness on my skin makes me face him. His eyes are filled with sorrow.

"I know." His sadness opens up the floodgate, and my tears are flowing. I'm not sure if I'm crying for him or me. How can I mourn something that is no longer there, something I have no recollection of? But Rhys...he remembers it all. I may have lost parts of my memory, but he lost us. What we had from the day I was born.

He bridges the distance between us, wraps his arm around my shoulder, and pulls me into his side. I latch onto his jacket, burying my nose in the crook of his neck.

*Home.*

We sit like this until the urge to scream overtakes every cell in my body. I'm sick of being in the dark, then finding answers— finding the light—just to be thrown back into the black void. I know life consists of light and dark; one cannot exist without the other. Yet, mine seems to be lacking the gray that should connect the two. I'm tired of being someone's chess piece—a game that has been going on for years and has used me as its pawn.

My breath quickens, and I jump off the bench, taking several steps until I'm in the middle of the clearing. My fingers curl into fists, nails digging into my palms as I give in. I'm sure I resemble a crazed banshee, but I don't care. Let them hear me.

Arms encircle me from behind, and Rhys draws me against his chest. "It's okay. Let it all out."

And I do.

When my throat feels like sandpaper, I turn in his embrace and hold on for dear life. "Please tell me you forgive me." His clothes muffle my words.

"There is nothing to forgive, Cal. None of this is your fault. I'm sorry I flipped my lid earlier."

At his warm breath against my ear, butterflies erupt in my stomach. It's always him reassuring me. I pull back, and Rhys studies my face. I place my hands on either side of his neck, right underneath his ears, the spot that drives him crazy when I kiss it. He lowers his forehead to mine, and I inhale his exhale, tasting the mint from his gum on my tongue.

"There are no words that can express how sorry I am for what you had to go through because of me, because of what happened and is still happening. You've been by my side, even when I thought you weren't. You watched over me time and time again." A brief chuckle escapes me. "You let George, every grown man's nightmare, drive you to God knows where for a chance to talk to me."

Rhys smirks. "He's not so scary once you get to know him."

A smile tugs at the corner of my mouth, but I continue. I'm not done. "I need you to know that no matter what happens, no matter where we are or how long we're apart, I'm yours. I'll always find my way back to you. You are my home. I love you."

Rhys's gaze jumps back and forth between my eyes before he lowers his mouth to mine. The kiss starts as a featherlight caress, but it's not enough. The fluttering sensation in my belly spreads to my chest. I want more. Need more. I raise to my toes, and his arms around me tighten. Arching my back to get even closer, my lips part, and I nip on his bottom lip. Rhys groans and immediately follows suit. His tongue invades my mouth with tender strokes, and the initial peck turns into a frenzy of mind-numbing kisses. Heat builds in my core, and I don't want this to end. By the time we break apart, my body is on fire, and I no longer feel the chill from the cool March temperatures. Rhys watches me closely through hooded lids before he pulls me into a tight embrace, resting his chin on the crown of my head.

We remain like this until, suddenly, another hand lands on my shoulder, and I squeal in surprise.

"Miss Lilly." George's soft tone breaks the little composure I had gathered just moments ago by distracting myself with Rhys's expert tongue.

I let go of Rhys and fling myself at my bodyguard, head of security, friend—whoever this man has become to me. George goes rigid at my assault but then relaxes and hugs me back. I wonder when he was hugged last.

"Did you find anything?" Rhys asks him.

"I have. But it's not safe to talk here."

George disentangles himself from me and gently pushes me toward Rhys, who interlaces his fingers with mine. I sweep the park. We are the only ones here, but I understand what he is saying. After this morning, we have no clue who is watching. And here we assumed Nate is the one who has eyes on everyone—aside from Tristen, that is.

I guess there is a third party that no one knew about until today.

# CHAPTER EIGHTY-THREE

**HER**

*"YOU TOLD THEM YOUR NAME! YOUR REAL NAME, YOU IDIOT!" It takes every ounce of self-control not to wrap my hands around Gray's throat as he drives us back to the property. I told him to reveal himself to her, not to lay himself—and, by extension, me—out on a silver platter.*

*I know what Nate is capable of. He'll find out everything there is to know about Francis Garrison Turner by the end of the day. More accurately, that there has been no Francis Turner in thirteen years. Not since I helped him disappear. It was the one time I ever did the dirty work myself. To this day, I can smell the decaying body as we maneuvered it into the SUV. The only reprieve was that the rigor mortis had already lessened. But it was necessary for Gray to become invisible. To put the plan in motion. Getting my revenge was the added bonus. Back then, I didn't intend to keep him around for over a decade, but he has served his purpose over the years.*

*As soon as Gray parks the car in the garage, I make my way into our new —and definitely temporary—home. The place is filthy, and even after two days of Elise cleaning it from top to bottom, I can barely stand setting foot in it.*

*Just a few more days.*

*There is one thing I know will lift my spirits. Since my personal physician is adamant that I cannot increase my dosage, I need to find other ways to numb the violent urge to punish someone for Gray's irresponsible actions. Opening the door to his new bedroom, I take in the dark space. It's a joke compared to our previous houses—not that I care where he is* stored. *I'm only keeping him around until I have what I want and he's no longer needed as potential leverage.*

*His eyes find mine. He's awake. Perfect.*

*"How do you like your new accommodations?" I haven't spoken to him since we left South America.*

*"Are you fucking serious?" he snarls at me. "I wake up in this shithole, and Elise refuses to talk to me. Where the fuck are we?"*

*He is almost cute when he tries to appear threatening. If it weren't for the restraints on his hands and feet, I might even buy it. Why couldn't he have shown this type of backbone when we met?*

*I move until I am right beside his bed and pull out my phone. While hiding in the shadows, I made sure to take a picture of his precious Lilly. I hold the screen in front of his face.*

*"We are home, my dear."*

---

# CHAPTER EIGHTY-FOUR

---

**LILLY**

"Dad gave you the Raptor?" Rhys peers at me suspiciously.

We're approaching the cars. Another black SUV is on the other side of the Defender—George's mode of transportation. I avoid direct eye contact when I mumble, "Not necessarily."

I feel myself blush and speed up my pace as George rats me out. "Your father caught her with the burner. She *took* the truck as she made a run for it."

Maybe I should just broadcast my every action since I have zero privacy as it is.

Spinning on my heels, I'm about to snap a retort when Rhys snorts. "You're giving me a run for my money in pissing Dad off."

He's referring to the fact that the Raptor has replaced the Defender on the *do-not-touch* list. No one but Tristen drives it. He loves his black monstrosity, but the real reason is that he has an AR stashed in a locked box under the backseat, and when Heather found out, she laid down the law. Her kids would not drive an assault rifle through town—loaded or not.

I don't have any desire to continue this conversation, plus I want to know what George found out. "Where are we going?"

"You are both going home. I will be in touch later. We can't risk being seen together, and as soon as your mother is home, Tristen will be on his way here," George explains and then levels Rhys with a glare. "You didn't leave your phone."

"Fuck! I forgot."

*He couldn't get away from me fast enough.*

Rhys reaches inside his jacket and pulls out his cell. Three sets of eyes take in the device. The movement makes the screen light up with several social media notifications, and when I lean closer, I read the one name I didn't expect to see: Kat Rosenfield.

Narrowing my eyes at him, he lifts both hands in a surrendering gesture, his phone between his thumb, index, and middle fingers. "I'm getting push notifications whenever she posts. I want to know what she's up to and who I have to deck next."

I rub my hands over my face. I have a good idea what she's posting about this time. I let my arms drop to my sides and gaze past the two men into the distance.

"Calla?" Rhys says my name carefully.

"I ran into Katherine on my way here," I admit.

Rhys swipes over the notification and starts reading with George hovering behind him, focused on the screen as well. Rhys's nostrils flare, and a knot starts forming in my stomach.

"What?"

When neither of them responds, and George's mouth turns his usually stoic features into a slash of disapproval, I tear the phone out of Rhys's hand and scan the newest rumor.


*K*AT *R*OSENFIELD:

*If banging her brother isn't enough, now she's trying to run me over. Check out that bitch's deranged face when I tried to cross the street to Café Chai earlier. Psycho much?*


*C*OMMENTS:

*Meghan LG: OMG, she's insane!*

*Nora Ross: R u ok? What's wrong with her? First she steals ur bf, then she tries to kill u? Someone do something!!!!!!!!!*

*Owen J: Don't u think ur exaggerating a bit? What's with all the !!!, Nora?*

*Kellan J: I'm with O*

*Lisa Bennett: U guys r just pissing ur pants that Rhys finds out.*

*Kat Rosenfield: If you don't believe me, here is the proof. She almost crashed into poor Mrs. Heatherway.*

IN THE COMMENTS, Katherine posted the video of me cutting off the other car in the intersection, followed by speeding down the road. Sure enough, it's Mrs. Heatherway's ancient Honda I almost slammed into. I didn't recognize her in my haste to get away. She's the sixty-plus-year-old woman who owns the tailor shop next to Café Chai and does all the alterations for the school's cheer uniforms. She took in my homecoming dress last year and is the sweetest lady. Kat using her to make me look certifiable ignites a rage I haven't felt in a while. I skim over more comments.

*Nora Ross: They better not let that crazy slut come back to school. None of us are going to be safe. We all know what T. McGuire drives around in that truck.*

*Kellan J: Oh, come on, N.*

*Kat Rosenfield: Nora is right. What if the #boyfriendstealingbrotherfuckingwhore walks into school with a gun?*

*Meghan LG: What if the whole kidnapping is just made up and her parents actually sent her away for seducing their son?*

*Kat Rosenfield: Megan:: OMG, you're right. She probably was in some military mental place.*

*Meghan LG: Psych ward for incestuous sluts.*

*Kellan J: M is using big words. Did you Google that one?*

*Meghan LG: Fuck you, KELLAN. Start using our full names, or do you need help with spelling like a big boy?*

*Lisa Bennett: That would definitely make sense. I mean, who would want to kidnap her? She has nothing anyone could ever want. #skinnybitch*

*Kellan J: Meghan, I'd fuck you any day. Name the time and place.*

*Meghan LG: OMFG, someone block this asshole!*

*Emma: I told Sloane we should no longer sit at that table, even with her not being there, but she's too scared of D.*

*Nora Ross: Fuck Denielle, she's probably cheating on Charlie with Wes. We all saw how those two all of a sudden stick together. #theyaresodoingit*

I STOP READING. Emma, *my friend*, sided with Katherine. Denielle has a target on her back because of me. My throat starts aching, and I close my eyes for a second to collect myself. None of them would've dared to badmouth my best friend before...*I need to get out of here*. I thrust the phone at Rhys, who barely catches it, and turn on my heels.

"Calla!"

I don't make eye contact as I climb into the Raptor, put the truck into reverse, and leave him and George standing in Woodland Park.

PULLING INTO THE GARAGE, I expect Tristen to be hovering in the door to the kitchen. I stole his truck, after all.

I gently close the driver's side door, minimizing any sound—not that the roar of the engine isn't enough to announce my arrival—and hesitantly approach the entrance leading into the house. Voices are audible inside, but I can't make out what's being said. Heather is talking, Tristen is responding, and Natty is laughing. Suddenly, the door swings open, and Tristen halts abruptly. Our eyes meet, and we're locked in a stand-off. When black spots start appearing in my vision, I suck in the breath I was unconsciously holding.

My adopted father lifts something, and I lower my gaze. Oh, he was taking out the trash. Sidestepping, I let him through, and he dumps the white plastic bag into the bin by the roll gate.

On his way back, he pauses and leans in. "Mom doesn't know. I told her you needed to get out for a bit, and I let you take the truck. Don't do it again."

My eyes widen, and I jerk my head up and down.

"Oh, and sweetheart?"

"Yes?" I squeak.

"We are going to talk about that phone."

My pulse is thrashing in my ears, and I murmur, "Okay."

I follow him into the kitchen, and Heather's face lights up. "You're back! How was the drive?"

My cheeks are aflame, and I'm about to reply when Rhys enters through the front door. He must have left the Defender in the driveway. Another quick escape?

*I'm not bitter at all.* Lie.

All eyes swivel to him, and Heather's expression falls. "I got a call from your coach earlier." She doesn't elaborate, but we all understand the meaning.

Rhys smoothes his features, not letting what went down at the park show. "They deserved it." No excuses.

"I agree with you, son. But next time, don't do it on school property." I whirl around to confirm I'm not hallucinating. Tristen stands slightly behind me, arms on his hips, and levels his son with a gaze I can't decipher. It's something between pride, disapproval, and a smug grin.

"Tristen!" Heather admonishes.

I turn back toward the rest of the family. Heather's lips are pursed, Rhys's eyes nearly bulge out of their sockets, and Natty tries to cover her snicker behind cupped hands.

Tristen steps forward and shrugs. "You know what these little shits said about our daughter. They deserve much more than what Rhys did to them."

Heather throws her hands up and turns toward the stove. Rhys seems to be in the same state of shock as me because we just stare at his father, slack-jawed. Tristen walks over to his son, places a hand on his shoulder, and squeezes before leaving the room.

I haven't seen that type of affection from him in years.


LATER, after Heather and Tristen retire to the third floor and Natty is sound asleep, Rhys and I sit in my bathroom in front of the open vanity cabinet, each having one headphone in our ear.

I haven't been able to concentrate on anything all evening. My nerves have been in a state of permanent buzzing since Tristen's proclamation that we will *talk* about the phone.

"George. Let's recap what you could find out from your guy." My brother's voice brings me back to the present.

"Unfortunately, not much." George's frustration is clear. When no one speaks, he continues, "I reached out to some old contacts. Francis Turner was a loner. He didn't socialize."

"Sounds familiar," Rhys mumbles, and I elbow him in the side.

George chooses to ignore the comment. "Turner had a drug problem that, in the end, got him dishonorably discharged. He was not married, but there was a rumor of him having a child. Supposedly, he got some eighteen-year-old girl pregnant and moved her close by, but no one ever saw her. He kept an apartment on base as well. The speculation was he only used that to meet with his girlfriends. He was never caught with the actual drugs."

"Girlfriends? Plural?" I ask incredulously. I stop listening after that. The guy is so...eww. I shudder and Rhys side-eyes me.

"That's what was said," George confirms, oblivious to my thoughts.

"Do we know when that was? The year or base?" Nate is typing in the background.

"Georgia. He wasn't clear about the timeframe. I will get back to you on that."

"Sounds good," my brother replies absently. We can still hear the faint clicking of keys.

"Do you think his girlfriend or kid are involved in this?" Rhys's question makes the hair on the back of my neck stand up.

*Who are these people?*

"I'm still saying Lilly should come to LA. At least we know she's safe here." Nate has stopped typing.

At that, Rhys barks out a non-comical laugh. "And do what? Hide in one of your mansions and hope it all disappears?"

"Nate, I strongly advise against pulling Lilly out of her current environment. It would raise too many questions and would make any future reintegration extremely difficult. You don't want her to be on the run her entire life, do you?" George attempts to reason with my brother.

"What life is that? Did you see what her so-called friends have been plastering all over the Internet? I want to send all of them a nice virus or, even better, put some unpaid parking tickets into the database, or give them a fun STD on their school medical records and leak them all over the Internet."

Oh boy, one really doesn't want to get on his bad side. He's hella inventive—and vindictive—which, embarrassingly, I quite enjoy at the moment.

Nate needs to show me how to do all these things—only theoretically, of course. Maybe. One practical execution test on the Wicked Bitch won't hurt, right?

In the end, we settle on me staying in Westbridge, but George will be keeping me under 24/7 surveillance. Nate doesn't want to miss anything on the Turner front. George has not been able to locate him since the press conference, which I sense neither of the men in my immediate life like very much. They're not used to being in the dark.

*Who is Turner, and what does he want with me?*

"Have you made any progress on Brooks's transactions?" I'm desperate to change the topic.

Hearing Nate type again, I assume he's pulling something up on his computer. "Some. I was able to trace it through four shell corporations down to South America, but I'm hitting a roadblock. The last one was owned by someone who died around the same time the transfers started in the U.S. Whoever set this up knew what they were doing, how to create false trails, use deceased individuals as a decoy, etcetera. Since there is no information exchange between these countries and the U.S., no one questioned it."

The frustration in his voice is palpable. Nate is one of the best, and yet he's unable to find who's behind this or who Brooks transferred money to all these years.

"Do we really care who he paid off? Maybe he had a gambling problem? Plus, it's not like he didn't have the money for it." Rhys remains unconvinced.

"It's all connected. I know it," I say to no one in particular. My gut feeling has not been wrong over the last five months.

RHYS SKIPPED HIS MORNING PRACTICE. He said if he sees Kellan or any of the guys, he'd probably end up pounding their faces for no reason other than breathing.

Entering the kitchen, I stop in my tracks. Camden, Lanning, and both of my adopted parents sit at the table, talking in hushed tones. Rhys is still upstairs, getting dressed, and I intended to make my tea while waiting for him. Taking in the scene in front of me, I get the feeling I should've stayed in my room and let him bring me my tea. Lanning clears his throat, and four sets of eyes instantly are trained on me.

*Well, if that isn't uncomfortable.*

"Lilly, you may want to sit down." Heather's voice forces my focus on her. I don't like where this is going.

Slowly, I approach the empty chair at the end of the table and lower myself down. Heart pounding in my chest, I scan the faces of all four adults. Agent Camden returns my gaze with a wary expression. Lanning radiates pity, and where Heather has concern written on her forehead, Tristen is once again indecipherable.

I swallow hard. "What's going on?"

Camden exchanges a look with Heather, both women seemingly debating how to breach the news to me, when Lanning slides his tablet over to me.

"Connor!" Camden barks at her partner.

"What? She has to deal with it one way or another. There is no way to sugarcoat this," he defends himself as I draw the device closer.

I lower my eyes to the screen. A news article with today's date shines back at me from the display. It's not one of the big, reputable papers, but it's still a well-known source for entertainment news. The headline alone makes me want to throw up.

*KIDNAPPING VICTIM #1, Lilly McGuire, in a Secret Relationship with Her Adopted Brother*

UNDERNEATH IS the famous picture of me wrapped around Rhys, tongue down his throat, and his hands on my ass in front of Denielle's house. I force myself to read one line after another until I can't stomach it anymore.

. . .

*THE ABOVE PHOTOGRAPH has been circulating on dozens of social media accounts linked to Westbridge High, the school Lilly and Rhys McGuire are currently attending. A reliable source revealed to us in an exclusive interview that the illicit affair between the adopted siblings seemingly has been ongoing while Mr. McGuire was still in a relationship with his longtime girlfriend and head cheerleader, Katherine Rosenfield.*

*Shortly after the relationship news broke, Miss Rosenfield attempted to confront Miss McGuire to clear up the rumor, which resulted in Miss McGuire attacking her peer violently in front of the entire junior and senior class, followed by her fleeing the scene of the physical altercation.*

*That was the last time she was seen until her reappearance, six days ago, at Hill Crest Medical Center in Nebraska. An independent media source was able to get a visual of Miss McGuire after her admittance and told us that she appeared to be heavily medicated but was unable to determine if said medication was self-administered or by the hospital. The question that arises now is, was she really a victim of The Babysitter? Could this all be an elaborate scheme to redirect from the lack of adult supervision in the McGuire household? Or is this something Miss McGuire did to herself because of the guilt of seducing her adopted brother?*

MY PULSE INCREASES with every word until my hands are trembling so badly that I let the device drop back onto the table. I'm going to be sick. Pushing the chair back with too much force, it topples over. I'm unable to look at the four people in the room. The chance of them, the public, not believing my memory loss was a possibility, but this?

Mortified, I spin and slam straight into Rhys's chest. His hands shoot out to steady me, and our eyes lock. His jaw tenses, but he doesn't ask what's wrong. He wraps his arm around me and leads me upstairs to his room.

# CHAPTER EIGHTY-FIVE

## RHYS

Lilly has completely withdrawn.

I brought her to my room, despite it facing the front of the house and our reporter stalker, Lancaster, being camped out underneath my window. The dude has not left his post in days. At this point, I'm convinced he has a *Luggable Loo* in the back of his tinted SUV. He is careful not to set foot on our property, but his fucking camera is permanently angled toward my window. It's beyond me what he expects to record.

She curled up on her side on top of my comforter before I fully closed the blinds, saluting Bomber Jacket in the process. I lower myself to the edge of the bed and carefully place my hand on her hip. "Babe?"

Staring blankly ahead, she doesn't respond. A dull pain forms in my chest. This is worse than when she found out whatever my father did to her—*let happen* to her.

She almost appears catatonic, and I have no clue what to do. I rub my free hand against my jeans. "Babe, what happened? Please talk to me."

Still, no answer. I'm this close to getting on my hands and knees and start begging.

*Fuck.*

Do I call Nate? He'll immediately dispatch George to *extract* his sister. His stance on all of this is clear. George wants Lilly to stay, but in the end, he works for Nate. He'll do whatever his orders are.

What the hell could've happened in the eight minutes it took me to get dressed? The tablet! Lilly read something on the federal douche's iPad. With one more glance at her, I place a gentle kiss on her temple and whisper, "Be right back."

*Nothing.*

Unsure what I'm going to find but determined to get answers, I take the stairs three steps at a time. I'm in the kitchen and grab the device that's still where Lilly left it. My parents and the federal wastes of oxygen are where they were a few minutes ago, talking in hushed voices. As I reach for the iPad, Mom's gaze jerks to me. "Rhys!"

I have no idea if she's admonishing me for taking the guy's property without saying *pretty please* or if she doesn't want me to see what's on there. It's a news article. I'm able to read the headline before it disappears from my grasp. I level my father, who is now holding the device in his hand.

"What the fuck is this?" I attempt to take it back, but Dad just throws it at its owner, who catches it with an oof sound. "Dad?" I growl. My fists curl into themselves, and my nails dig into my palms. I've shown less and less respect toward my father, and I wouldn't be surprised if he snapped soon.

"Let him read it, Tristen," Agent Camden speaks up, and I peer at her.

"Vivian!" My mother tries to insert herself.

"She's right. This impacts all of us, Rhys just as much as Lilly, even though they try to put the spotlight on my daughter." I don't miss how Dad claims Lilly as his, and a rush of adrenaline bursts through my body.

*Is it possible our family is not as broken as I thought it was?*

"Sit," my father orders, and I reluctantly comply. I need to know what is on that screen. His head swivels to Agent Mouthbreather. "Give it to him."

Lanning stares incredulously, like he wants to say, "You just threw the damn thing at me," but he doesn't have the balls to use his actual voice to follow through.

Dad cocks an eyebrow at the clearly inferior man, and the iPad is back in my hand before I can suppress the snort building in my throat. Could this guy be a bigger joke?

I scan the article in front of me, but it's like my brain has shut down. I don't comprehend the words and have to read it twice before it sinks in. There is only one person who could be the *reliable source*. Right about now, she can thank the Lord that she has a fucking pussy, or she would be in the hospital, eating through a straw, by the end of the day. My grip is so tense that the plastic case around the device crackles.

Dad pries Lanning's tablet from my fingers, and my hands instantly curl back into tight fists. My entire body is shaking, and I can't make out my mother's words through the pounding in my ears. Jumping up from my chair, I kick the one beside mine across the kitchen, where it crashes into the island.

"RHYS!" My father's commanding tone finally penetrates the red haze. I clasp my hands on the top of my head and turn away from the audience. I need to get a grip. The urge to punch the drywall across from me is taking over my senses. I'm ready to take the three steps it would require to turn the kitchen and living room divider into my next victim when a band of steel wraps itself around my upper body. Dad immobilizes me with his arms.

*The man is strong for his age.*

"You need to calm down, son!"

I struggle against his hold until my father says the three words that can deflate my rage. "Lilly needs you!"

Stopping my fight, I sag against his chest, giving him all the power. He instantly releases me, and I crouch down, trying to get my labored breathing under control.

A hand lands on my shoulder. "Go upstairs and take care of her. We'll talk later." These last few days, my father has shown more emotion than in the previous years—hell, the last decade. I follow his order without a second glance back.

*Was his behavior also connected to all of this?*


I DIDN'T GO to school. Instead, I lay in bed, wrapped around Lilly—not in a sexual way. She didn't speak one word. Mid-day, she got up to use the bathroom, but as soon as she was done, she aimed for the bed, curled into a tight ball again, and that was it. I returned to my big spoon position, one arm under my head and the other tightly around her belly. The first sign of life was when Lilly took my hand, which was splayed on her flat stomach, between hers and placed a kiss on the inside of my palm. In response, I pressed my body even closer. The weight in my chest had gotten heavier as I watched the minutes tick by on the alarm clock. The feeling of losing her had been growing all day.

I've ignored the buzzing coming from my desk. I have a decent idea who is blowing up my phone and what it's about, but I refuse to let go of Lilly. Something deep down tells me that I may not have many more chances.

It's dark when someone knocks. After the last bathroom break, I moved us out of the dual fetal position—my back couldn't take it anymore. I'm sitting against the headboard, and Lilly is tucked under my arm, with her head on my chest. Our fingers are intertwined on my lower abdomen, and I'm playing with the strands of her hair with my free hand.

"Come in."

The door slowly swings inward, and Mom's face appears in the gap. She zeros in on her daughter immediately but doesn't enter. "Sweetheart?"

When Lilly doesn't react, her eyes shift to me, asking a million questions without uttering a single word. Drawing in a deep breath, I flex my fingers around Lilly's. "Babe?"

"Hmm?" Her eyes still don't focus, but this is the first sound all day.

I tilt my head down. "Cal? Mom is here." I squeeze her hand again and rub my other up and down her back, mentally preparing myself to have to shake her out of this lifeless state.

Lilly's head slowly turns toward the other side of the room.

*Thank fuck, she's back. I think.*

"Hi, sweetheart." Mom's tone is wary.

"Hi," Lilly croaks. Why am I surprised at the rasp in her voice? She hasn't had a drop of water all day.

My mother's eyes flick to mine before she addresses the girl in my arms again. "Dad and I were wondering if we could talk to you."

My mouth is already open to protest when she amends, "Both of you."

I shift away from Lilly to see her entire face and for her to see me as well. When I'm sure I have her attention, I speak. "It's up to you, babe. Your decision."

Out of the corner of my eye, it's apparent that Mom is about to argue, but I throw her a glare. She pinches her lips together.

Lilly searches my face, and I smooth my features in an attempt to appear confident and strong—two of the last emotions I feel at the moment.

"Okay." It's just a whisper, but Mom hears it and expels a long breath.

"We'll wait for you in Dad's office. Whenever you're ready."

I give my mother a curt nod in acknowledgment without averting my eyes from Lilly.

TEN MINUTES LATER, we find Dad behind his desk and Mom in the single chair in his office, leaving the sofa for us. I expect to see my father's usual stone-cold demeanor. What I find, instead, makes a pit the size of the Grand Canyon form in my stomach. His hands are clasped tightly on top of the desk—to the point of the skin being stretched over his knuckles. His shoulders are stiff, and under the desk, I can see his leg bouncing. A small but—for my father, the man without emotion—clear sign that something is very wrong.

Leading Lilly to the two-seater, I pull her down next to me. I'm in the same position as the day we met with Madeline, my ankle crossed over my knee and my arm stretched over the backrest. Yet, I don't feel the confidence I'm attempting to portray. My insides churn in anticipation of whatever my parents are about to drop on us. It can't be good if they asked both of us down here.

Dad clears his throat and makes quick eye contact with Mom. I follow his gaze and see her nodding at him. Lilly misses the exchange, being focused on her hands in her lap. I pull her into the crook of my arm, needing the contact more than her at the moment. Once she is settled, I hold my other hand out, palm up, and she automatically interlaces her opposite hand with mine. Both my parents follow our movement but remain mute.

The silence stretches, and I stroke my thumb over our intertwined fingers. It's as much to calm my thrashing pulse as it is to reassure her.

"You have both seen the article that was published this morning," Dad begins.

A low growl builds in my throat.

"Other news outlets have already followed suit. We have received multiple requests to comment throughout the day." Lilly's eyes fly to my Dad's as he speaks, but he continues, "After long deliberation with Agents Lanning and Camden, we have issued a statement this afternoon."

"Why would you give them the fucking satisfaction to react? This has Kat written all over it," I burst out, barely able to contain the pent-up rage that has surged back to the surface.

Lilly's head jerks to face me. "How do you know? Why would she do that?"

Instead of making me answer, Mom leans forward and places a hand on Lilly's knee. "It was easy to force the paper to give up her name. All I had to do was threaten them with defamation and other legal actions. You are the victim of a crime, and this has nothing to do with it." Lilly's eyes flicker to me as Mom mentions her being a victim.

"But with that being said," Dad amends, "we had to react to the accusation of turning a blind eye to your relationship. The last thing we need is the state trying to take Lilly away and bringing charges against all of us—including you, Rhys."

My eyes bulge, and Lilly's hands fly to her mouth.

*What the fuck?*

"Can they do that?" A hollow vacuum builds in my chest.

"I haven't looked into all the legalities yet, but Lilly is underage, even if just for another week. And no matter how you turn it, once the suit is out, it will follow us forever. Not only would you"—she levels me with her courtroom face—"be *labeled*, but Dad and I would be charged with neglect. I'm confident we could fight it, but it will ruin everyone's reputation, even if we'd win."

"So, what did you do?" Lilly's whispered question drags me out of the rabbit hole I was already halfway down. They could charge me with rape because of my ex talking to the media.

*How did this happen?*

"Agent Camden released a statement that Mom and I were fully aware of your relationship. Lilly has known of her adoption for some time, but we decided, as a family, to keep it on the down low until she was ready to talk about it. Your emotional relationship evolved over the years. We didn't encourage it but also didn't permit it, knowing this would only push you more toward each other. We kept open communication with both of you, and once it became clear that you two had developed feelings for each other, we set clear rules for both of you. We have raised all our children to be responsible and honest. You are mature for your age, and along with the rules, we trusted you to make the right decisions." Dad concludes his recap by pushing himself off of the desk chair.

"So, you lied your ass off," I deadpan.

"We did." There is no remorse in my father's tone.

I begin to question my judgment on his motives all those years. Maybe he is not the emotionally compromised robot I made him out to be? Along with a sense of gratitude, the gut feeling that his actions are linked to everything that has happened to this family is growing.

"What happens next?" Hearing Lilly speak after a day of silence still startles me.

"We expect there to be more reports about the kidnapping. So far, the clusterfuck your ex has caused has distracted everyone from that," Mom sneers, and I stare at her with wide eyes.

"Mom! Did you just drop the F-bomb?"

My mother smirks at me sheepishly. "I do curse when it's warranted, honey." Then she turns to Lilly. "As for what happens next, this is what we wanted to discuss with you."

*I'm so not gonna like this.*

Dad rounds his desk and leans against the front of it with his arms crossed over his chest. A silent communication passes between him and Mom, and the vacuum in my chest expands.

He nods at her, and she inhales deeply before speaking. "We would like for Lilly to return to school tomorrow."

A whimper escapes the girl in my arm, and I tighten my hold on her.

"Are you crazy? Have you not seen what everyone's been saying about her?" There is zero point in trying to rein in my temper.

Both of my parents remain calm. "Hear us out, son," Dad begs. He actually pleads with me. This man never so much as asks; he demands. And people follow. That's who Colonel Tristen McGuire is.

I press my lips together, waiting for the second *Danner*—not any regular shoe—to drop.

"The longer Lilly stays in hiding, the worse the rumors get. Camden got a hold of another article that is set to print tomorrow, questioning Lilly's memory loss."

Dad cocks his head, scanning both of us intently. I'm ninety percent sure he questions it himself.

*If the FBI chick found that article, why hasn't Nate?*

The prolonged silence is beginning to choke me. I don't want Lilly to face WH. I can only do so much in school—meaning I can only rearrange the faces of the male student population. Kat has the female one cowering at her feet, and I don't think even Den has the power to prevent the things that will happen. My ex is their *Queen Bitch*.

"Okay."

All eyes in the room swivel to Lilly. I lean forward to get a better look at her face, and what I see there is such a surprise it makes my brows furrow. Her eyes are hard and determined, but her flipping of her thumb against the rest of her fingers tells me the opposite.

Reaching up, I turn her face toward me. "Are you sure?"

Lilly bobs her head, and I peer at my mother. Her narrowed eyes show that she's not buying it either.

Lilly excludes herself from the remaining conversation where we discuss that she will drive with me, but we will keep our distance. We are making a statement by going together, but we don't need to fuel the fire.

Back upstairs, while Lilly is taking a shower, I check my phone for the first time since this morning. I missed several texts from Wes and Den. Both have read the article, and with me not being in school, they want to know what's going on. I'm surprised they haven't shown up at the house.

A message from Jager says: **It wasn't me. I SWEAR !!!!!!!!!!!**

*I really did a number on that asshole. Good!*

Several more texts from my former friends, similar to Jager's.

*Pussies.*

And one from UNKNOWN: **Answer the fucking phone, or I will come to pick her up personally.**

I probably should call him back before he jumps on his fancy jet and reveals himself.

WE HAD SPENT ALMOST an hour on the phone with Nate last night, who, needless to say, was pissed with a capital P—scratch that, make all the letters caps. When we didn't respond to his twenty-three missed calls and forty-four messages, he hacked into the security feed to check on his sister. After that, he sent the text to my personal cell and waited for us to reach out. Asking why he didn't check the cameras right away was on the tip of my tongue, but I swallowed the question not to push him further.

By the time we finally called him back, George was camped out one street over, waiting for his boss's orders. George agreed with my parents' plan of offense, versus Nate, who still insisted she should not be here. He's grown extremely protective of his little sister.

The first genuine reaction Lilly showed all day was when her brother admitted that he sent a couple of viruses to Kat. She activated one of them on her phone, and every single photo she had was copied to Nate's cloud, followed by the device being wiped. Nate then went through the pictures and videos and extracted the ones that would serve as future blackmail material. According to him, there is a lot to choose from. Lilly barked out a laugh, and the sound made the hollow vacuum finally shrink to a manageable size.

NOW, on the drive to school, Lilly is sitting next to me in the passenger seat of the Defender, flicking her thumb against her remaining four fingers. I fight the urge to grab her hand; the movement is starting to make me twitchy.

When we pull into the parking lot, I drive past my usual spot and pull in next to Denielle's Q3. She's already leaning against the driver's side next to Wes's 4Runner, but my best friend is nowhere in sight. That's odd.

At the sight of my car, students stop walking mid-step. I notice Lilly stiffen out of the corner of my eye, and my breathing speeds up. I have no fucking clue how this day is going to go.

I reach over and touch Lilly's leg lightly. Her nervous tick stops immediately, and her head jerks toward me before facing forward again. She scans the front of the school with wide eyes.

I don't give a fuck if anyone sees me touching her, but I retract my hand nonetheless. "Cal?"

She slowly turns back, but her eyes don't follow until she has to focus them on me.

I hold out my hand, palm up, and she glances down.

"What is this?"

"The spare key for the Defender. If you want to leave, leave." I need to know she can get away if she has to.

Lilly slowly reaches out and takes the key from me, tucking it into the front pocket of her faded blue jeans. I take in her outfit, and besides her skinny jeans, she is wearing my old hoodie—definitely a statement—black John Fluevog boots, and her black leather jacket. Her hair is up in a messy bun, and she neglected her usual minimal makeup. I don't think she's ever gone to school like this. The boots were from last Halloween when she dressed up as Abigail Whistler, and she refused to buy any boot but the exact same. I just hope she never added the blade modification as she originally intended. That could end disastrously today.

"Ready?" I ask her after she makes no move to leave the car. Den has already planted herself in front of the Defender's hood, arms crossed and ready to bite anyone's face off who comes too close.

Without another word, Lilly opens the door and joins her best friend outside. In an attempt to calm my nerves, I expel one last breath and follow suit.

*May we all survive this day without suspension—or a murder charge.*

Denielle and I flank Lilly on either side, and together, we walk toward the main entrance. It's fair to say every single head is tracking us. Conversations halt, cameras point, and the hushed whispers cannot hide the exclamations of *slut, she fucked her brother, it's all a lie, psych ward,* and *does Kat know* assaulting us from all sides.

Lilly holds her head high, and her gaze is straight ahead. We don't touch, and neither do Denielle and her, who used to link arms all the time.

As we near Lilly's locker, my best friend comes into view. I narrow my eyes, and my heart rate doubles. Wes is scrubbing ferociously on the door. As we get closer, I can make out the words written neatly across Lilly's and the *surrounding* lockers in various types of paint and markers, all probably requiring a different method of removal.

*"Lilly McGuire is an incestuous slut who fucks her brother and lies about losing her memory. We don't want you here!"*

We're not going to make it through this day. If Lilly doesn't lose it, I will. Or Nate will send George to torture half the student population if he finds out.

*Either way, we're fucked.*

# CHAPTER EIGHTY-SIX

**LILLY**

I spent yesterday going down one rabbit hole after another, trying to figure out how to feel or react. The shock of the article and my impending return to school had eventually worn off, but I was still no further than before. My fight-or-flight instincts were in a battle of tug of war. One moment, I was ready to take the entire Westbridge High population with its *Queen Bitch* at the top head on—who are they to pass judgment over me? A minute and four seconds later, I was close to dialing George's number to pick me up—because why would I do that to myself? Or my family and friends, for that matter? I expected a lot, but statutory rape? This was spiraling out of control at an inconceivable rate, and I felt more helpless than when I was trapped in my crashed Jeep.

Nate's small act of revenge gave me some satisfaction, though Katherine deserved a lot worse after this article.

Rhys fell asleep around one in the morning, but no matter what I tried to relax, it didn't work. Finally, I gave up and snuck out of bed.

Sitting in front of the vanity, I typed in Nate's number: **Hi.**

The bubble immediately popped up: **What's wrong? It's one in the morning in VA.**

**I can read the clock. Thank you very much, dear brother.**

In response to my sassy reply, he sent me the emoji with the straight mouth and raised eyebrow. Who knew that bantering with my big brother would give me the type of normalcy—the distraction—I needed?

**I can't sleep**, I admitted.

**Talk?**

I thought that over. **Can't. I don't want to wake Rhys up.**

We ended up texting for over an hour, and I confessed how my conflicting emotions confused the hell out of me. Shouldn't I be one or the other? Nervous/worried *or* don't care.

We talked through my different trains of thought, and in the end, Nate helped me realize that both extremes are a reasonable reaction to my current situation.

My (at times) unstable brother made a pretty decent therapist.

Now, standing in the school's hallway, a semi-circle of probably more than fifty juniors and seniors forms around me. I stare at the words on my locker. And stare some more.

Wes has taken a step back, sponge in one hand and what looks like a Clorox wipe in the other. He won't look at me. "Dude, I tried. I have no fucking clue what they used to write this shit." Contempt drips from every word.

Rhys and Denielle have gone rigid on either side of me. Where Rhys is shaking with rage, Den is eerily still, eyes narrowed on the words.

Out of the corners of my eyes, I notice the number of students surrounding us increases. Everyone wants to have a front-row seat to the show.

Nate's last message before saying goodnight reverberates through my head: **Remember what's important. You've done nothing wrong. Your boyfriend and adopted family love you and would do anything to protect you. And so do I. Nothing they do will change that. You're in charge. Don't let your emotions overpower your intelligence. That's what they want. George will be outside the school if you need him.**

*I'm in charge.*

I pull my shoulders back, take two steps away from Denielle and Rhys, and unlock the door to the little space of privacy I have at Westbridge High. My books are where I had left them over three weeks ago. Grabbing what I need for my morning classes, I turn, look at Denielle, and plaster a smile on my face that makes my cheeks hurt. "Ready?" I chirp, ignoring my audience and envisioning blinders around my face like at a horse race. I will not give them the satisfaction of acknowledging them—or worse, cowering.

Den narrows her eyes at me, peers at Rhys sideways, but plays along. "Sure thing, babe."

We fall into step beside each other, and the mass of students shrinks away as we make our way down the hall. Rhys and Wes follow close behind. There is no way he'd let me walk alone, so I don't even attempt to leave without them.

After we say our goodbyes, and I promise to stay put until one of them is back to walk me to my next class, I swivel on my heels. Having to spend my first three classes without my best friend, my senses go on alert as soon as I enter the classroom. All conversations stop, and the air is instantly charged like lightning is about to strike. Just as I sink into my chair, Bria and Hailee, two girls who were always friendly with me and occupied the desks surrounding mine, get up and move to the back of the room. My body tenses, and I concentrate on keeping my breath steady. I zero in on a spot in the front and put on my best George expression—none.

*Don't let your emotions overpower your intelligence.*

The only person not abandoning his seat is Lucas, a boy from the chess club. He meets my eyes when he approaches his desk in front of mine but turns his focus quickly to his shoes. Miss Foy, our American History teacher, furrows her brows at the new seating arrangement until her gaze lands on me. Her eyes widen for a microsecond before she composes herself. This is only her second year of teaching, and she probably has no idea how to handle the situation. Hence, she ignores it.

Class itself passes quietly, and when the bell rings, I take my time gathering my things. I can't leave anyway until one of my bodyguards arrives. I'm bent sideways, dropping my notepad into my messenger bag, when my textbook shoots off the table and lands under the chair next to me. I inhale to the count of four before slowly turning in the direction my book got launched from.

"Oops." Bria shrugs, a sweet smile turning her mouth into the perfect target for my fist. Instead, I do nothing. When she doesn't get a reaction from me, she walks away with a huff.

I exhale slowly through my nose and lean down to reach for my book when something slams into my head, and I can barely catch myself before face-planting onto the linoleum floor.

"Slut," the owner of the bag—the weapon of choice—whisper-coughs.

Blood starts pounding in my ears. Balling my fists, I take a deep breath, uncurl my fingers, and grab my book.

*Do. Not. Engage.*


THE NEXT TWO periods go similar, and it's getting increasingly more difficult to keep my cool.

Instead of my classmates moving away, my lab partner in AP Chemistry, Arianna (Ari), *stumbles* and spills the nitric acid we're using for our experiment. It ends up all over my chem book and splashes on my lab coat. After ripping the white fabric off and making sure it didn't hit anywhere else, I stare at her incredulously.

"Oops." She smirks and begins cleaning up, acting as if nothing happened.

*Is that all these girls can say?*

Of course, she timed it perfectly with our teacher rummaging around in the back of the room. By the time he pulls his head out of the supply cabinet, everything appears as before—minus my lab coat.

I've never talked to this girl outside of class, and I didn't think she was associated with Katherine. I'm starting to wonder if the Wicked Bitch has put a hit out on me.

In third period, Algebra II, I find a big fat "WHORE" carved into my desk. My pulse quickens, but I keep repeating my new mantra in my head. My pointer finger traces the indentation. It's a good quarter of an inch deep. How the hell did they manage that without Mr. Mann noticing?

Cocking my eyebrow theatrically, I place my textbook over the word. I count back from thirteen, unclenching my jaw before I do permanent damage to my teeth. It won't do any good using them as my personal punching bags. Though, I'd probably feel a lot better.

Fourth period, I get my first reprieve. Denielle and I share P.E., and as soon as she is at my side, no one glances at me twice. Lunch passes similarly. People stare at the four of us sharing the table, but no one dares to speak up or fake cough an insult in my direction. I don't keep what happened in periods one through three from my friends; there is no point. One of them would find out eventually. I've been *the talk* all morning. So far, I was kidnapped, followed by my kidnapper kicking me out when I sucked in bed. (The thought of Nate and any intimacy triggers my gag reflex.) The next rumor was that I was pregnant and faked my kidnapping while I was getting an abortion. Some guy even suggested I delivered the baby and gave it up, to which I made the first eye contact. The speaker was some dude from the soccer team. He's probably middle class in the school's social hierarchy and therefore seemed to have missed what happened to Rhys's *friends* who ran their mouths. I bit my tongue. Asking him if he had paid attention in sex ed would've been a waste of oxygen—I had a flat stomach three weeks ago.

My last class of the day is French, a subject I always looked forward to. However, after the previous six periods, pretending not to hear any of the whispers—some not so quiet—I'm mentally drained. Rhys will pick me up from here, as he's right above me on the senior floor, and then we can finally go home. Thinking about getting out of here, I miss the noise level in the class rising. When the mumbles and gasps register in my brain, it's too late. Something wet hits me from behind, and I instinctively duck. Not fast enough, though.

*What the fuck?*

My shoulders scrunched up to my ears, hair dripping into my face, I take inventory. I'm not hurting, so it's not chemicals this time—or at least nothing that could burn my flesh off. Then, I take a whiff and gag. The stench of algae and...fish penetrates my nostrils. I don't want to touch whatever is at the back of my head, but I have no choice. With a trembling hand, I slowly reach back and disentangle the object from my bun. Holding it between thumb and forefinger, I force myself to look at it—*it* being a half-dissected fish from, I'm guessing, the biology lab. The liquid still dripping down my face is probably water from the numerous tanks the school has for said fish. I swallow the pool of saliva in my mouth but end up choking in the process. The stench and visual make my stomach revolt. I let the dead animal fall to the floor, and after briefly closing my eyes to collect myself, I turn in my seat. The row behind me is occupied by several cheerleaders, including Emma and Sloane. I scan both of them with narrowed eyes, and where Sloane looks shocked, Emma is radiating glee.

*Did she throw this thing at me?*

Madame Morel chooses that moment to enter the room and stops in her tracks. "Mon dieu, ce qui s'est passé ici?" *What happened here?* Whenever she gets upset or flustered, she falls back into French, even though she's lived in the U.S. since she was a child. I face my teacher, and when no one answers her question, I speak up for the first time all day.

"It seems this fish ended up in the wrong classroom. May I please go clean up?"

There are a few snickers around me, and I hear a huffing sound from the cheerleader's row, probably pissed that I don't burst into tears or lose my shit. But I swore to myself that I wouldn't do that, no matter what happens today. They will not see me bow down. Between Turner and all the other secrets Nate and I still need to get to the bottom of, I refuse to let a bunch of girls in too-short skirts and over-curled hair break me.

"Absolument. Vite. Go get cleaned up."

As I exit the room—with my bag, since I have no intention to return—I hear my teacher demanding who's responsible for the mess. Of course, she doesn't get a response.

After a quick detour to the bathroom, where I hold my entire head under the faucet followed by wringing my hair out and putting it back into a bun on top of my head, I strip out of my hoodie. It caught the brunt of the attack, and for that alone, I want to sic my big brother on them. This is my favorite piece of clothing these days. I stop at my locker, grab my jacket I had stashed there earlier, and head to the Defender.

Sitting in the security of Rhys's car, I pull out the new phone Heather handed me before school this morning and send him a message: **Waiting in the car for you.**

I follow that with a text to Den and Wes, in case they had planned to come to pick me up as well: **Left early. Waiting in the Defender for Rhys.**

When none of them respond, I double-check that the bubbles have the small "delivered" underneath.

*Did I put their numbers in wrong?*

I haven't finished that thought when the front door of the south wing bursts open, and I see Rhys and Wes rush toward the parking lot. A few seconds later, the side door of the west wing opens and reveals my best friend, turning in the same direction.

*Uh oh.*

All three stop in front of the Defender, and we stare at each other through the windshield. Rhys takes three more steps and tears the passenger door open.

"What happened?" Then, he inhales and holds his hand over his nose. "Jesus Christ, Cal, what the fuck is that smell?"

"Dead fish." The adrenaline spike from the incident has worn off, and I'm too exhausted to even be upset at this point. All I want is to go home and take a shower.

Denielle comes to the side of the car and scowls. "Why is your hair drenched?" Then she takes a whiff and mimics Rhys's reaction. "Oh, my God."

I really don't want to rehash this now, but I am fully aware that neither Den nor Rhys will let it go until they know what happened. I recap the fish incident, and Denielle immediately does a one-eighty on her heels to head back into the building. Wes grabs her around the waist and holds her in place.

"LET ME GO! I will show that little skank what it means to smell like fish. Wait until I get my hands on that bitch!" My best friend is kicking, and with every word, her voice gets louder, but Wes keeps a firm grip on her. He murmurs something in her ear, and she goes limp.

*Since when does he have that power over her?*

I watch the scene with my head cocked to the side. Den and I need to have some girl time. I seem to have missed a lot over the last few weeks.

Rhys rounds the Defender and plants himself behind the wheel. "Let's get out of here."

I sigh. "Best words I've heard all day."

# CHAPTER EIGHTY-SEVEN

### LILLY

Neither Heather nor Tristen are home when we pull into the garage. Spotting Lancaster aim his damn camera at the Defender as soon as we come into view, I sink lower in my seat, shielding my face. Who knows what headline my wet-dog appearance will cause?

With the garage door securely lowered, I straighten up and reach for the door handle.

"I want to kill these motherfuckers." Rhys's tone is low and menacing. Those are his first words since reversing out of the parking spot at school. As much as I relished the silent drive after this day of insults, my sweaty palms were a clear indicator that I was just waiting for Rhys to lose it. Not that it was my fault, or he'd blame me, but he's already been through enough in the last few weeks. I don't want to see him make the entire school his enemy.

I turn my head and see emotions ranging from rage to utter helplessness play across his face. It kills him that he can't be with me during class.

"Did anyone say anything to you?" We only talked about what happened to me, not if he experienced similar treatment.

Rhys's nostrils flare, and his hands grip the steering wheel tighter. "Yes and no."

I narrow my eyes, waiting.

"The guys learned their lesson. Jager won't make eye contact, and Owen even ran the other way and ditched class, but Kat...she's challenging me." Rhys is referring to their position at the top of the school's food chain. "She knows I can't do anything to her...physically."

He's holding back.

"What did she do?" After what I experienced first-hand in the past few hours, it can't be good.

"She's been telling everyone and their mother how you threw yourself at me when she and I were together. That she's suspected for *years* that something was wrong with you. The first kidnapping fucked you up to the point of your parents not being able to handle it anymore, and the second was all just a ploy to divert from our relationship."

I let it all sink in, and besides my parents not wanting me, it's similar to what I've already heard. *My parents didn't want me because I was too fucked up.* My heart rate seems to slow. Is that the real reason, after all? Is that what Heather and Tristen are keeping from me?

Without another word, I exit the Defender and head upstairs. As soon as I'm over the threshold of my room, I begin to strip, leaving pieces of clothing on the floor on my way to the shower.

By the time Rhys enters the bathroom, it's full of steam from my scorching shower. I haven't gone through my purging ritual in a while. Today, though, I need it. I didn't give them the satisfaction of breaking me, but I can't deny that it's been challenging. I trace the small crescent-shaped indentations on the heels of my hands with the tips of my fingers. The dozens of times I balled them into fists throughout the day have left permanent marks.

The glass door opens, and Rhys steps in. It took every ounce of energy to keep my façade in place throughout the day, but I can finally let it slip off. Standing directly under the spray, the water pelts on my skin, and my hair is plastered against the sides of my head. I stare up at him through my wet lashes, and he reaches for me, pulling my body against his. My arms circle his waist, and I press my cheek against his chest.

Rhys tightens his hold. "You did good today."

His praise is my undoing. All the comments and humiliations—

some whispered, some not—come back and assault me from all angles: Slut. She's crazy. Whore. Brother-fucker. Lying skank. Bitch. The first tear starts flowing, followed by a second and a third until my body is shaking with gut-wrenching sobs, the running water muffling my cries.

*What have I ever done to any of them?*

Rhys hugs me tighter and places a kiss on the top of my head, but he doesn't speak. There are no words that can make it better. We remain like this until I run out of tears and the shower starts to cool. He hasn't moved the entire time, and as my body calms, I listen to the low thud of his heartbeat against my ear. The sound stirs a new emotion inside of me, and I loosen my grip. I turn my face to place a chaste kiss on his chest, right above his left pec. It was meant as gratitude for him being there for me once again, but when my lips connect with his skin, he jolts ever so slightly. He didn't expect me to do that. His embrace loosens, and his hands slowly glide down my back until they rest on my hips. My eyes flutter closed as the tips of his fingers press into my flesh, and his thumbs start circling my hip bones. Heat surges to my core, and I feel myself become wet. *More,* a voice inside my head all but shouts at me.

Where his hands traveled down, I let mine move up his torso, trailing each muscle of his ripped abdomen, over his pecs, until my arms intertwine behind his neck. My hands bury in the wet strands of his hair, and I tug ever so slightly. A low rumble of approval erupts in his throat, and my need to touch him—*let him touch me*—overwhelms all rational thought.

His breath quickens, and I know if I were to press my ear against his chest right now, his heart would beat anything but steady. I tilt my head up, blinking my eyes open. Rhys's chin is dipped down, and his lids are hooded. He's hardening against my belly, and I lick my lips. I'd be lying if I say his arousal doesn't please me.

When he stepped into the shower with me, neither of us intended for this to become anything other than the means of me working through my emotions. Rhys knows of my little ritual. But as we stand in front of each other, the air around us shifts to something else entirely. I raise myself on my tiptoes and press my lips lightly against his jawline, teasing him with the tip of my tongue. He hasn't shaved, and the scruff on his chin gives him an edge that makes me clench my legs together. Looking at him like this, water dripping down his taut body, chest heaving with desire...*I want him.*

Noticing my—no doubt, heated—gaze, Rhys inhales sharply, and the gleam in his eyes reminds me of the night of our first kiss right before he flipped me over on the couch and took charge. As if on cue, he shifts and grabs me at the back of my thighs. His hold pinches my skin, and a soft moan escapes me. Instead of it registering in my brain as painful, I react instinctively and wrap my legs around his back, right above his ass. He stares down at me, scanning every inch of my face, while my painfully hard nipples are pressed against him. What the hell is he waiting for? I rock myself against him, and he arches an eyebrow at my impatience, the corner of his very kissable mouth quirking in a cocky smirk. But despite his attempt at acting nonchalant, the rapid rise and fall of his chest is a dead giveaway to how much he wants this as well. Everything else, the reason we ended up in here, becomes unimportant.

*I need this. No, I crave this. Him.*

I stretch up, but before my lips reach his, Rhys's mouth is on mine, tongue inside. Finally. With a whimper, I clasp the back of his neck, pressing myself further into him. He groans into my mouth as he grinds himself against me, creating friction against my most sensitive spot that makes me roll my eyes back inside of my head. I stop holding back. My hips begin to move up and down, coating his length with my wetness. Rhys's hold on my thighs tightens to the point of me being convinced that he's leaving marks. I can't bring myself to care, though. My body vibrates with need, and I try to shift in his grasp so he's aligned with my entrance.

He suddenly pulls back, and I whine in protest. No, no, no!

*What is he doing?*

"Cal, wait." Rhys gently pushes me back as I try again. He holds my confused gaze. "Condom," he clarifies almost scoldingly.

*Oh.*

"Oh!" My face flushes. I briefly debate pushing the topic. I've been on the pill since I was fifteen—irregular cycles and all—and he knows it, but he wants to be responsible.

"Whoops." I shrug sheepishly and untangle my legs, albeit a

little reluctantly. Rhys places me on the tiled floor of the shower. I don't want this to be over.

He shoves the door open. "Stay here," he orders, but before I can say anything, he disappears, dripping wet, into my bedroom, leaving footprints on the carpet.

*I guess we're done?*

The water has turned almost cold, and I quickly turn the spray off. Stepping out, I reach for the towel on the rack to dry off when a low growl makes me halt. "What do you think you're doing?"

I turn and watch this sexy-as-hell guy stalk toward me. My eyes widen at the determination written across his features. Aiming straight for me, he finishes rolling on a condom, and I take him in in all his glory. Dear Lord. Another wave of heat hits me straight to the core.

A wicked grin spreads across his face, and as soon as he reaches me, I'm back in his arms. I yelp at the sudden loss of contact with the floor and cling to his broad shoulders.

Nose to nose, Rhys's tongue darts out, tracing the corner of my mouth. "Where were we?"

I moan at the sensation, all coherent thought escaping me. "I'm, um...not sure." My response is no more than a breathy whisper. Closing my eyes, I nip at his bottom lip, which makes him hum in approval.

Without another word, he attacks my mouth with his, moving hard against mine, forcing his way in. Despite the initial force, his tongue does the opposite. He caresses me with soft strokes until I lose all self-restraint. The pulse between my legs throbs, and I want him inside of me. Now.

I'm on fire, my heart beating so fast I can barely catch my breath. Still moving my lips in sync with his, I flex my arms and pull up enough to align myself with him. Before he can stop me this time, I let myself sink down on his dick, and a guttural groan comes from Rhys. "Shiiit. Cal..."

I have no idea what he was attempting to say, but I don't really care, either. I deepen the kiss as I move up and down his length, letting him stretch me from a whole different angle than the first time.

Rhys adjusts his grip, and his hands move to my ass. He pushes farther into me, and I cry into his mouth. "Oh, God. Yesss."

He is so deep, the ecstasy steadily building as he keeps driving into me. I let my lips trail down his neck, kissing and nipping along the way. As one thrust hits my cervix, I instinctively moan and bite down on his shoulder.

With a growl, Rhys flips us around so my back is against the cold, glass wall of the shower, and I cross my ankles behind his back, not wanting to fall.

"I got you, babe." His fingers knead my butt, and the friction against my clit makes every nerve ending inside of me come to life.

My breasts bounce with every thrust, and when Rhys tilts his head and captures my nipple with his mouth, I'm done for.

"Rhys...shit..." My orgasm is beginning to crest, and he pumps into me harder.

"Let go, babe. Come for me." His voice is muffled as he moves to my other breast.

I don't want it to end, but as Rhys gently tugs with his teeth on my pebbled nipple, I go over the edge. My vision clouds, and I clench around him. After only two more thrusts, I feel him shudder against me. "Fuuuck."

His mouth is back against my neck, and his incoherent mumbling makes me smile as I come down from a high I've never experienced before.

We stay like this until our breathing has returned to a normal pace. He blinks down at me with a lazy grin on his lips. "You are so fucking beautiful when you come."

I swat his arm, blushing, and slowly unwind my legs from behind his back. Rhys pulls out and lowers me down until my feet touch the ground. I'm glad I'm still leaning against the glass, because my legs barely support my weight. He cups the sides of my face, bending down. His warm breath is like a caress to my skin. "I love you, Cal."

I gaze up at his green eyes. "I love you, too."

He places a gentle kiss on my mouth. "We can do this. Together."

I don't respond.

. . .

LATER, in my room, Rhys sits against the headboard of my bed, playing with the strands of my hair while I'm nestled into the crook of his arm. My arm and leg are draped over his body, and I relish the goosebumps his twirling of my hair causes. My new phone begins to vibrate on the nightstand, and a shot of adrenaline puts me on instant alert. I disentangle myself from him to check the caller ID, and when Den's picture on the screen registers, my rapid pulse begins to calm.

I swipe to answer the call. "Hey, babe."

"Hi," she says hesitantly. "I just wanted to check in on you." Her tone is less than cheerful.

"I'm...okay." It's not a complete lie. I do feel better. Letting everything out in the shower has helped. Then, a mental image forms of what happened after, and my face heats. My thigh automatically pushes against Rhys's leg, and he chuckles, knowing exactly what just went on inside of my head. Yup, that definitely distracted me from the shit show at school today.

When my best friend remains silent, my momentary happiness disintegrates like a dried flower petal. I prepare myself for the worst. Finally, she expels a long breath. "I got a call from Rhys's BFF."

Rhys is close enough to hear Denielle's statement, and his eyebrows knit together. "Why wouldn't Wes just—oh..." He leaps off the bed and charges into my bathroom. It takes me longer to comprehend the meaning of Den's words. When I hear Rhys rummaging through the vanity, it clicks.

*His BFF. George.*

I follow with my cell phone still pressed to my ear and find Rhys sitting on the floor, scrolling through something on the phone.

"That little cunt. If I get my hands on her tomorrow." His body is shaking with rage.

"Call me back later?" Denielle's voice filters through to my brain as I'm staring at Rhys white-knuckling the device in his hands.

"Hm-hmm." I lower my phone without hanging up. Crouching in front of him, I try to get his attention, but he is focused on whatever he's looking at.

"What is it?" I whisper.

His eyes snap up as if he just now realizes I'm in the room. He draws in a slow breath and expels it at the same pace, which makes his nostrils flare. "Nate messaged."

"Okay?"

*What has him bent so out of shape?*

"He stopped the article that was supposed to print today. I forgot about it with the shit show in school."

Tristen mentioned another press release yesterday, but like Rhys, I didn't remember it until now. His face, however, tells me that this is not all. I wait.

"Your brother figured out who tagged your locker. Seems like he's been *following* you all day. And he wants to know why you left French class early with wet hair."

There are no cameras in the classrooms, just the hallways, cafeteria, auditorium, and gym, etc.—all the places big groups of students congregate. It makes sense that he didn't see the actual incident but was able to find out who wrote *the lovely message* on my locker.

"What did he do?"

*Please tell me you didn't do anything stupid, Nate.*

He made it clear that he will do anything to protect me.

Rhys hands me the phone, and I start scrolling. The first message contains a video and several stills from the security footage. Even from the frozen picture, I instantly recognize who vandalized my locker: Emma.

Something breaks inside of me. Emma. Why? We've been friends for years. Maybe not *best* friends, but friends, nonetheless. I ungracefully fall out of my crouch onto my butt. My gaze meets Rhys's, and the betrayal he feels for me is written all over his face. I take in the pictures that follow the video and see Kat huddled with Emma in a corner. According to the timestamp, their meeting was shortly before Emma tagged the school property.

My brother's next message is about the article.

**Below is the article that was supposed to print today. I was able to "remove" it from the paper's server and sent the fucker who wrote it a little present, but that won't stop it from being published. We just delayed it. He's already in the process of rewriting it.**

It still baffles me how Nate does all this without being traced. I move on to the message that contains the actual article.

*Lilly McGuire—Is Her Memory Loss Real or Is It All Just a Ploy?*

My breath hitches at the picture underneath the headline. I'm staring at myself sitting on my hospital bed at Hill Crest Medical Center. My eyes are bloodshot and wide with shock from the reporter invading my hospital room. I'm in the clothes George dropped me off in—the clothes I wore the day I crashed the Jeep. This was all part of the plan, but seeing myself like this makes my throat close up. My hair is wild, unkempt. I look crazed.

Parts of the timeline fall back into place. I didn't remember much from when the guy snuck into my room to when the nurse helped me change out of my filthy clothes, but things are starting to come back. My breath is getting labored, and I faintly register Rhys's hand on my leg. He's saying something, but the memories flash in front of my eyes. The nurse and doctors had just placed the IVs to counteract whatever was still in my bloodstream. It was like I'd had one too many drinks. Everything was fuzzy, and concentrating was impossible. I was waiting for the nurse to come back with a change of clothes—the only reason they discovered the intruder so quickly.

*We got a first-hand glimpse at Miss McGuire right after her discovery at Hill Crest Medical Center. Miss McGuire is the alleged first victim of The Babysitter, who was taken a second time by the perpetrator on March 2nd and reappeared on March 21st. When we spoke to Miss McGuire, she kept asking where "he" was. A fair question of a real victim if she hadn't followed with the statement of "I can't go home. We need to figure out what happened."*

Oh, no. What did I do? I don't remember this at all.

· · ·

*THE MEDICAL STAFF of Hill Crest Medical Center refused to let us continue the interview, and we, therefore, have to speculate what Miss McGuire meant with her words. Who was she referring to? Is she somehow involved with The Babysitter? And what does she need to figure out? Is her memory loss real, or is she playing all of us? Is she lying to the families of the other victims to protect herself or, worse, the perpetrator himself? We tried to get a statement from the McGuire family, who refused to comment at this point on anything other than their children's relationship.*

THERE IS MORE, but I stop reading. This is so much worse than anyone could've anticipated.

I skip to the following message.

**Call me as soon as you get this. We need to talk about what happens next.**

WITH TREMBLING FINGERS, I switch to the Phone screen. It takes me three tries to type in Nate's number, and when Rhys attempts to help me, I snap at him in return.

"I can do it!" Closing my eyes briefly, I follow my outburst with, "I'm so sorry."

Rhys nods, but his features turn to stone. I know he's not angry with me, but I can't help the need to keep apologizing.

It only rings twice before Nate answers. "Hold on a sec."

The line goes quiet as if he muted me. I stare at the little clock over my sink, and it takes three minutes until my brother's voice comes through the earpiece again. During the entire time, Rhys's hand rests on my leg, but neither of us speaks. I can't look at him. This is all my fault. Maybe I shouldn't have come back.

"Sorry, I was just leaving the office. Hank was with me."

Nate answering my call while he is in public—with his business partner, nonetheless—tells me how serious the situation is.

"Is it safe?" Still paralyzed from what I just read, I'm not sure what else to say.

"Yes, I'm in the car, heading home."

The typical tick-tocking of a turn signal is in the background, along with the sound of what I assume is LA traffic. Exhaling, I voice the question I'm afraid to hear the answer to. "What are we doing now?"

I listen to more traffic noise until Nate replies, "You know my stance on it, but removing you from the situation will make everything worse. I spoke to George earlier, and he will be shadowing you more than he already is. You'll stick to the story of memory loss; you don't remember ever saying what the reporter claims. I was unable to locate the original footage on his computer before sending the second virus. My guess is he's storing it somewhere else. I'm still looking for it."

"Second virus?" Rhys interrupts my brother. I didn't put Nate on speaker, but since we neglected to turn on the water, he can easily follow the conversation in the small space.

"The first one was to access his laptop. The dumbfuck fell for the *get-one-month-free-porn* trap. Why is humanity so predictable?" Sarcasm drips from his words. "The second one wiped his hard drive, but I made sure a watcher remains in place for the future—even when he reinstalls the OS." This time, you can hear the grin in his voice.

"But that is only one out of who knows how many trailing Lilly. I mean, look at the piece of shit that is camped out under my window."

"Leave Lancaster up to me."

Of course he knows who we're talking about. I meet Rhys's gaze, neither of us asking for the meaning behind my brother's words. Better not to know.

I decide to change gears. "What did you do about what happened in school?"

"Which incident are you referring to?"

*Shit, crap, shit!*

I play dumb. "How many are there?"

"Do you take me for an idiot, little sister?" Nate sneers.

"No?" I answer meekly, but it sounds more like a question than a convincing response.

Rhys stifles a laugh, and I narrow my eyes at him. I'm glad he thinks this is funny.

"Well, then let me enlighten you." My brother deadpans. "I took the liberty to send the footage of the locker incident to another news outlet with the comment that Westbridge High seems to ignore vandalism of school property, as well as students getting ostracized by their peers for being a victim of a traumatic experience. Said news outlet might have received a small contribution to publish an article with the footage by morning."

Where I suck in a breath in shock, Rhys cackles, "Dude, that's fucking awesome! I'm starting to like you more and more."

"What is wrong with you guys?" I burst out. "You just made it ten times worse for me tomorrow. Now I really have a target on my back."

Nate's voice comes through the phone. "Lilly, you already had a target on your back. The size of that hasn't changed. And I'll be damned if I stand by and let them terrorize you."

His protectiveness makes the empty cold in my stomach shrink the tiniest bit, but I can't help the fear of what they will come up with tomorrow. More graffiti, more physical assaults with random objects... The possibilities are endless.

I press my lips together. It doesn't matter. They can't break me.

# CHAPTER EIGHTY-EIGHT

**LILLY**

LAST NIGHT'S DINNER WAS THE FIRST TIME WE HAD EATEN AS A family since before I...*left*. Our federal guests are no longer camped out in the kitchen 24/7. Camden and Lanning only swing by to bring Heather and Tristen up to speed or to form a new plan of attack.

Tristen brought pizza home. While we were eating, Heather attempted to get information about school, but I made Rhys swear that we wouldn't involve them in my war at WH. It's bad enough that Nate inserted himself into the mess. Thinking of Heather taking legal actions or Tristen pulling *strings* to deal with the issue...no, thank you. I gave them the toned-down version of being called names, and tomorrow, by this time, they'll have heard about the locker incident, but until then, I don't need anyone else tangled up in that mess.

WALKING down the hall toward my locker on day two of being back, I hold my breath—prepared for anything. I'm flanked again by Rhys and Denielle, with Wes in the rear. Instead of being stared at, though, most are averting their eyes as soon as they spot the four of us—everyone except the cheerleaders, who continue to openly glare.

When we arrive at my locker, I'm surprised to see that *the message* is almost gone. You can still see the faint outline that something was there, but not what it said.

I place a change of clothes—just in case—in my locker, and my friends walk me to American History. I keep my head down, Miss Foy still ignores the new seating arrangement, and besides some whisper-coughed *slut* and *whore* insults, class runs smoothly. I don't get attacked by objects, and none of my books end up on the floor —or worse.

Entering the AP Chemistry lab, I find a new partner standing at my table. Approaching the station, I make eye contact with the boy I have certainly seen around but never exchanged a word with. Theo transferred in earlier this semester from somewhere in the south. But that's where my knowledge of him ends. He keeps to himself—not sure why, though. He has the whole bad-boy vibe going. He wears faded, distressed jeans with Frye boots—the purposefully aged kind—and a matching leather jacket. His tight, black, long-sleeve shirt clings to his bulging biceps and broad shoulders, showing off his athletic body. I briefly wonder what he does to be this...ripped. His ebony hair is tousled with a little gel in the perfect messy style, and his blue eyes and sharp features give him an edge that screams danger. Add to the whole package that he seems uber smart whenever he does speak up in class. You'd think the female student body would form a line for him. They don't, though. Everyone gives him a wide berth. My curiosity is piqued as to why *he* is here at my table, and I quickly scan the room, finding Ari at Theo's old table.

*Deep breath. Here we go.*

"Hi," I greet him as I place my bag under the table. I try not to stare, but he is freaking gorgeous, after all.

*If I had any interest in anyone other than Rhys, of course.*

We'll see what his strategy is: ignoring, attacking, or indifference.

He glances over while arranging some of the materials for today's class. "Hey."

He speaks; that's something.

We listen to our teacher explain the assignment, and once

everyone is busy, I address the elephant in the room. "Why are you here? At this station, I mean."

There is a beat of silence while he keeps messing with the beaker, and I assume he has switched to ignoring, but then Theo replies in a low tone, "Arianna requested a transfer. Better not ask what her reasoning was."

I snort. "Oh, I can guess. So, you got the short straw?"

This time, my new partner faces me head-on, and the corner of his mouth quirks up. "Nah, I volunteered."

His smirk would melt the panties off any other girl, but I'm instantly suspicious. I scrunch my eyebrows. "Why?"

He shrugs a shoulder and turns back toward the experiment. "I have no issue with you. From what I heard, you've done nothing wrong." With a sidelong grin, he adds, "Maybe a bit kinky, with the adopted brother and all, but I'm not judging."

"Um..." My mouth hangs open. What do I reply to that?

"Don't read anything into it. Take it as one hour of not being harassed. I'm in your French class, remember?"

He has a point. I don't realize how tense my body had gone until it all melts away. We settle into a comfortable silence and finish the assignment just as the bell rings.


WES IS on babysitting duty and walks me to Algebra II. We haven't talked much since I've been back. He is either with Den, or the four of us are all together.

I bump his elbow with mine. "So...how are you doing?"

Rhys's best friend glances at me out of the corner of his eye. "Fine."

Neither Rhys nor Wes have been back to practice, and I heard from Rhys that Coach is starting to get frustrated with them. So far, he's given them slack—probably because he also wants to avoid further injuries not caused by practice—but that won't last forever. Especially because Wes got scouted for a scholarship to his dream school, and it'll look bad not finishing his athletic activities, even though we're past football season.

We're approaching my classroom, and I mumble, "I never meant for you and Den to get pulled in like this." The guilt has been steadily building, but so far, I've been too scared to voice my thoughts, not wanting to hear what my friends would potentially have to say.

Wes pulls me into a side hug. "You and Rhys have been my best friends forever. Did you honestly think I wouldn't stay by your side, Lil?"

This is one of the most serious conversations I've had with him in the ten years we've known each other, and I give him a tight smile.

"Plus, I'm finally on the bulldog's good side. I never would've anticipated that happening in this lifetime." He grins down at me.

I huff out a laugh. "Don't let D hear that."

Wes gives me one more squeeze before we say our goodbyes, and I enter the room. Bria and two cheerleaders are in this class with me, and I get greeted with, "Oh look, she not only fucks her brother but also the best friend. QB. Tight end. Who's next? Wide receiver? Safety?"

My adrenaline level instantly spikes as she addresses not just me but everyone else who's already here. Kellan and Owen are in said positions. The thought of them coming anywhere near me...no thank you. I've never had an issue with either; they've been Rhys's teammates and friends for years. They used to greet me in the halls, but since I read what they had to say about me on social media, just looking at the guys makes my skin crawl. I hear some guy bark out a laugh and mutter something inaudible, but I force myself not to look around.

I want to tell Bria where she can shove her petty remarks, but instead of sinking to her level, I hold her gaze until I reach my table. I keep my expression blank, which causes the reaction I was looking for. Bria scowls and then looks at her friend for support. I sit down at my desk, placing my bag over the carving with a loud thud, and allow the satisfying smirk to appear on my face.

*They won't break me.*


EMMA'S SUSPENSION is all over school. The rumor that she might get expelled was *the topic* over lunch. As promised by my brother, the article hit the paper this morning, and several screenshots appeared all over social media by the end of first period.

With this being the second time Westbridge High has been mixed up in a bullying scandal, the school's board is already involved, and I am supposed to meet with the school's guidance counselor tomorrow afternoon. Today, it seems, they're trying to do damage control.

When I muse why Kat's name is not mentioned anywhere, despite the footage Nate pulled from the school's server, Rhys smirks. "Probably because he has a special plan for her."

"Where is the Wicked Bitch, anyway?" Denielle looks around the cafeteria.

Rhys's smile falls, and the guys glance at each other.

"Rhys?" I slant my head at him.

His lips are in a thin line, and he holds my gaze.

"Kat has been extra lovely this morning. Your man got into it with his psycho ex," Wes clarifies.

My eyes widen, but before I can recover, Denielle asks, "Is there anything worse she can say or do at this point?"

My best friend is referring to the possible statutory rape charge that's still hanging over our heads.

Wes picks up on the meaning. "Well, maybe not jail-time bad, but definitely ruin-your-school's-rep bad."

Rhys takes a sip from his water bottle, not making eye contact and speaking toward the table. "She cornered me in class and demanded to know how we got the footage of Emma. With her minion gone, Kat lost one of her best cheerleaders. It was also clear that she was fishing to find out if we saw their conversation. She didn't make a secret out of her involvement. She's getting bold."

My chest tightens. "Why does she think it was us?" I mean, it was us—Nate, technically—but how could she know?

Rhys finally looks up, pinning me down as he explains, "I guess she's starting to put two and two together. That there is a third player. Otherwise, how would she have gotten the picture of you and me that started it all."

Denielle huffs. "Fuck, when did she grow brain cells."

"You need to be careful," Rhys says in a low tone, which makes the hair on my nape stand up.

"Why do you say that?"

"She insinuated that no one takes what's *hers*. And now you've taken her boyfriend and cheerleader." He pauses for a breath. "She's planning something, and it won't be pretty."

I pull my sleeves over my hands and hide my trembling hands by sitting on them. We all know Katherine; she is ruthless when her position is threatened, which makes her feared by almost all the girls in school.

*So much for 'the size of the target hasn't changed.'*

After Rhys's revelation during lunch, I contemplate skipping French. But with Emma not there, the remaining members of the bitch squad suddenly are rendered mute. Surprise, surprise. Sloane shrinks so far down in her chair that her butt hovers in the air in front of the seat, and I'd be lying if I don't admit to the gratification I feel seeing my former friend like this. Theo notices as well and winks before focusing on something on his notepad.

ARRIVING HOME, we're greeted by Heather and Tristen, waiting for us sitting in the kitchen. Startled, I come to an abrupt halt, and Rhys bumps into me. Stumbling forward, I catch myself before tripping over my own feet.

*Why are they home?*

Taking in his parents' grim expressions, Rhys narrows his eyes. "What's going on?"

Tristen leans back in his seat and crosses his arms over his chest. "It's time we talk."

Heather glances sideways at her husband before straightening her back and interlacing her fingers on top of the table. Her attorney pose.

I slowly approach the closest chair and pull it out, my heart hammering in my chest as I lower myself down. I peer at Heather but am forced to focus on my adopted father when he begins to speak. "We would like to know how the article Agent Camden informed us of *disappeared*, and instead, Mom and I get phone calls to comment about our daughter getting bullied in school."

Rhys mimics his father's posture. "What makes you think we have the answers to that?"

"Do. Not. Treat me like an idiot, son," Tristen barks, and I jump in my seat. He levels me with a glare that could make grown men pee their pants. "Whose phone was that the other day? And who did you talk to?"

*Crap, crap, crap.*

"What phone?" Heather interjects, confused.

Speaking to his wife but not taking his eyes off me, Tristen explains, "The day Lilly *took* the truck, I caught her with a phone that we didn't give her."

My adopted mother opens her mouth, but Rhys beats her to it. "I gave her the phone. I wanted to be able to reach her. It was just a prepaid one."

Following the exchange, I try to appear unaffected, but let's be honest, I might as well have a billboard with "She's hiding something" hovering over my head. Between my rapid pulse and sweat pouring out of every pore, I look either guilty as hell or like I just sprinted a mile at full speed.

Where Heather purses her lips, Tristen's cocked eyebrow screams *bullshit.*

"Who was on the phone then? I know it wasn't you." He levels his son.

*Because your tracker would've recorded a call coming from Rhys's phone.*

"Wes!" I blurt out without thinking.

Two sets of eyes focus on me, and the needle in their built-in lie detectors goes haywire. Both remain mute, and I'm ready to confess when Rhys deadpans, "After all the secrets you've been keeping from her—from us. What makes you think we'd tell you anything?"

Tristen slams both fists on the table, and I yelp in shock. "Because this is not a fucking game, Rhys! This is all for Lilly's safety. And yours."

*Wha—?*

Rhys narrows his eyes at his father. "What is that supposed to mean?"

Heather places a hand on Tristen's forearm. "We wish you would tell us what's going on so Dad can protect you."

Rhys barks out a laugh. "Could you be more cryptic? Protect us from who?"

When neither of them speaks, Rhys pulls me up by the hand. "And *that's* why we don't tell you jack shit!"

I let him lead me from the kitchen. Not good.

We spend the remainder of the day upstairs in my room, without dinner.


REPLAYING Heather's and Tristen's words in my head over and over, I barely slept that night. In the morning, I waited until I heard the Raptor pulling out of the garage and Natty was downstairs eating breakfast before leaving the safety of my room. Using my little sister as a buffer to not deal with Heather is cowardly, but it's all I can think of not to get confronted again.

I'm starting to believe that there is something other than just the threat of my kidnapper—which is not a threat at all, but they don't know that.


As I use one of the bathrooms between second and third period the next day, I discover some new *love notes* inside the bathroom stalls.


*LILLY MCGUIRE IS A BROTHER-FUCKING SLUT.*


CLASSY.


*IF YOU WANT A CHEAP LAY, call the QB's little sister. She spreads her legs for everyone!*


NOT SURE WHY this is in the girls' bathroom, but okay. The tags go on, and eventually, I stop reading.

I manage to get through my first three classes with minimal insults and am glad the next few periods are with Denielle. I stayed true to my mantra and didn't let my emotions overpower my intelligence, but I'm drained. The lack of sleep and the energy of keeping my guard up at all times are taking their toll. I'm going to need this weekend to recharge and prepare for the last five days before spring break.

Friday is track day in P.E.—unless it's pouring rain or a blizzard outside—something I used to enjoy but now have to mentally prepare myself for. The idea of showering with the enemy has my mind coming up with all kinds of mean-girl scenarios. I've seen too many movies where clothes get stolen and whatnot.

I've successfully avoided it for the last two days since we played badminton and I was able to keep the sweating to a minimum, but I know I won't be that lucky today.

I take solace that my best friend will be with me and nothing would happen with her around.

## CHAPTER EIGHTY-NINE

**RHYS**

I'm sitting in U.S. Government, bored out of my skull, when I hear the sirens. Everyone's heads start turning questioningly, and the ones with a window seat peer outside. I glance over at Wes, who is shrugging a shoulder dismissively. It's not the first time someone has hurt themself in Chem. Usually, once a year, some dumbass whose IQ never developed past the single digits has to *test* if acids really hurt when you pour them on your hand or other body parts.

Then, my gaze lands on my ex-girlfriend. She's already zeroed in on me, waiting for me to look at her.

I study her expectant expression. Something isn't right. At that moment, my phone starts vibrating in the back pocket of my jeans, and I know. I'm out of my seat and in the hallway before I have the device pressed to my ear.

My teacher yells after me, but I don't stop.

"WHERE IS SHE?" I bark into the phone.

"Locker room. Hurry!" Denielle's hysterical sobs assault my ear, and my legs threaten to buckle as several scenarios flash through my mind. Denielle is never hysterical.

With Wes on my heels—apparently, he came to the same conclusion—I take three steps at a time down to the first floor and push through the double doors with so much force they slam into the brick wall, bounce back, and almost hit my best friend in the face. Thank fuck the guy has good reflexes. Without checking that he's okay, I break into a run and aim for the gym.

As I'm turning the corner from the east wing, an ambulance pulls into the small parking lot next to the fieldhouse. The paramedics jump out and rush inside with multiple bags strapped to their bodies. The sight makes me pick up my pace to almost tripping over my feet—my athleticism has officially exited.

Wide-eyed juniors file out of the doors of the gym as I approach and force myself to slow my pace. The whispers and murmurs stop instantly, and one guy flattens himself against the wall. I faintly register a random voice saying, "He's going to lose it."

The closer I get to the girls' locker room, the slower my legs move. My feet feel like I'm dragging them through knee-deep mud. Commotion from inside filters into the hallway, and— Lilly yells out. Not in an *I'm-having-an-argument-with-someone* way, a full-on scream of pain. My throat closes up, and my hands shake violently as I push through the last barrier separating me from her. I have no idea what to expect.

The girls' locker room is a mirror image of the guys'. The paramedics crouch on the floor near the entrance to the showers. One is rummaging through his bag while the other is examining someone —*please no*. Not someone. Lilly.

I can't move.

Her P.E. teacher and my coach stand off to the side, hands deep inside their pants pockets, and watch with a mix of worried and horrified expressions.

Another scream fills the room, and between the legs of the paramedic who's prodding on Lilly's back, I see her hand curl into a fist.

"Rhys." My head swivels to the side, and I take in Denielle's tear-streaked face. She's clutching her cell phone to her chest. Her eyes are wide, and she is anything but *The Bulldog* right now. She reminds me of a helpless child.

Lilly's whimpers get louder, and my head whips toward the sound so fast my neck cracks. Fuck, that hurt. My gaze turns to tunnel vision. I dart toward the group on the ground, getting my first direct glimpse of her, the sour taste of bile immediately coating my tongue.

*What the fuck!*

Lilly is on her stomach, one arm goal-posted, the other alongside her body. A bunch of school-issued towels are padding the tiled floor underneath her with more draped over her lower half, covering her legs and butt. Her back is fire-red with blisters ranging from marble size to golf-ball size across her shoulder blades to her lower back. I lift the back of my hand to my mouth.

*Don't throw up.*

"Rhys, you can't be—" my coach starts but clamps his lips shut as I glower at him, daring him to continue.

I circle Lilly's body to not interfere with whatever the EMT is doing to her back. My mind has gone blank, but somehow, I can think logically enough to understand that pushing the medic away from her would be counterproductive.

Dropping to my knees next to her, my shaking hands hover in the air, not knowing where to place them.

"Cal?" I rasp over the razor blades in my throat.

"Rhys?" Lilly attempts to lift her head and groans. I bend my upper body down farther to meet her eyes without her having to move. Her eyes are red and puffy, and despite lying on the cold floor —pretty much naked—she's covered in sweat. Her fingers inch toward me, and after a moment of hesitation, I gently place mine over hers. I'm scared to touch her. Her arms are as red as her back but show no blisters—at least from what is visible.

"I'm here, baby." I'm not sure who needs to hear the words more, Lilly or me. A sob escapes her, and my lungs close up.

*I'm going to kill whomever is responsible for this.*

"What happened?" My best friend's question registers in my brain, but I can't focus on the reply. All I see is my injured girlfriend. I don't avert my eyes from hers and carefully interlace our fingers.

The paramedics treat Lilly's back, and words like "hot water," "burns," and "hospital" filter through the pounding in my ears. Whenever they come near one of the blisters, Lilly's hand in mine turns into a vise, and I clench my teeth to not make a sound. My emotions are all over the place. I border between numb—most likely shock—and losing my shit, wanting to trash the room and clock the damn guy causing Lilly pain—more pain, that is.

I have no clue how long they work on her until she is ready to be moved onto the stretcher that seems to have appeared out of thin air. After her lower half is covered with an emergency blanket, they place a light cloth on her upper body. Her long, wet hair is falling off to the side, and I briefly wonder if it should get tied up to not tangle in the stretcher's legs.

What the hell am I thinking? Lilly just got her back almost scorched off. Her hair is the least of our problems. I mentally slap myself out of my stupor.

*Get your fucking brain to work, dickhead.*

The wait, while two guys secure the straps around her without touching the burned areas, makes me want to pull my hair out. It can't be more than a few minutes, but it sure as fuck seems like hours.

I stand with the stretcher, not letting go of her hand. Exiting the locker room, we pass Wes and Denielle. With Wes's arm draped around her shoulder, Den is still strangling her cell phone, fresh tears creating black trails down her cheeks.

They fall into step behind us with the teachers pulling up the rear.

I ignore the murmurs that get louder the closer we get to the doors leading to the parking lot. We're instantly surrounded by half of WH's student population. Since it's still the middle of fourth period, some fucktard must've wanted his or her five seconds of fame and sent a blast out. I better not find any pictures of Lilly's injured body on social media.

Gasps run through the crowd as we emerge, the murmurs and questions getting louder, but my focus is on Lilly's closed eyes as she's wheeled along the side of the building.

The paramedics are about to lift the stretcher into the ambulance's back, and I reluctantly let go of her. Peering to the side, my gaze lands on my ex-girlfriend. Her arms are crossed over her chest, and instead of shock or compassion, she radiates pure gloating. My heartbeat stutters.

*She did this!*

Wes and Den follow my line of sight. The EMTs are busy

getting Lilly settled, and a red haze settles over my vision. At their own volition, my feet start moving slowly toward the person responsible. Wes grabs Denielle around the waist as she must've come to the same verdict. No one stops me, though. The sea of students parts as I zero in on my target. A growl builds in my throat, and my hands curl into fists. All bets are off.

*I'm going to jail for this.*

I'm just a couple of feet away from Kat when two arms wrap themselves around my upper body.

I fight against the hold of whomever is stupid enough to interfere. "LET ME GO! I'm going to kill this fucking bitch! It was her. SHE DID THIS!" I'm going ballistic in front of everyone.

Kat's expression turns from smug to wary to panic, and her eyes flick left to right.

*Oh yeah, you better run, you cunt.*

"Not here, Rhys!" The low tone of the last person I ever expected snaps me out of the rage, and I go limp.

"George?" My voice is shaking.

"Let's go. Miss Lilly needs you." He lifts me and turns me the other way like I'm my ten-year-old sister, not six-one and two hundred pounds. His grip loosens slightly, but he doesn't let go until he deposits me into the back of the ambulance.

Once I sit next to the paramedic, George takes charge. "He is her boyfriend; he's going with you." The man's eyes turn to saucers as he takes in my BFF and jerks his head up and down.

"Rhys?"

"Yes?" I force myself to look away from Lilly's body in front of me.

"You will not let her out of your sight until I get to the hospital."

I nod, too stunned to comprehend what just happened.

George turns and looks at Wes and Den, who are off to the side of the ambulance. "You two are coming with me." Both are visibly pale but trail after the man without a word.

THE DRIVE to the hospital is a blur. The raging river of adrenaline that kept me going since Denielle's call has turned into a dried-up stream. The EMT removes the cloth they placed over Lilly during the transfer from the locker room to the ambulance. He asks her questions about her pain level while making sure nothing touches the burns, to which she replies with a grimace.

Kat's satisfied bitch face flashes in front of my eyes, and my fists keep clenching of their own volition. She is responsible for this. If George hadn't shown up, I'm not sure what I would've done. I remain mute despite the million questions I have. I need to get my temper under control before we reach the hospital.

The paramedic glances over several times, opening and closing his mouth. I cock an eyebrow at him.

*Spit it out.*

"Who was the guy with the scar?"

The corner of my mouth pulls up to a one-sided, most likely lunatic smirk. "Someone you never want to see again."

That was the only time he talked to me.

We arrive at the emergency room entrance, and I follow the two EMTs, never letting go of Lilly—my hand placed either on her leg or foot. Her eyes are closed, but she's awake. The thin line of her lips is as much a giveaway as her thumb flipping against the remaining four fingers of her hand.

After she's transferred off the stretcher onto a bed, the two guys leave us just as a nurse enters the small room and stops in her tracks when she spots me. "You need to wait outside."

"He is not leaving." George's voice comes from behind the woman, and she jumps in surprise. However, that is nothing compared to the reaction when she *sees* him. She yelps and bumps into the small table next to Lilly's bed, various items clattering to the ground.

"O—oh goodness, I—I'm s—sorry," the poor nurse stammers.

"George?" Lilly's rasped voice makes all eyes snap to her. It's the first time she's said anything since the locker room.

*I'm fucking sick of seeing her in a hospital bed.*

One side of her face is pressed into the mattress. The EMTs removed the pillow to accommodate her prone position, and she lifts her head slightly.

"Yes, Miss Lilly?"

"Don't scare the nurse." Even in her battered state, she ridicules this bad-ass former Marine, and a snort escapes me.

*I love this girl.*

George moves closer to make eye contact. "My apologies, Miss Lilly. I am simply ensuring you are not alone until Heather and Tristen arrive."

My parents! "Did someone call Mom and Dad?" I ask no one in particular.

George turns to me while his hand rests next to Lilly's head on the bed. "Yes. Weston called your father, who informed your mother. Your mother was in the city and should be here within the hour. Your father is"—he pulls out his phone and glances at the screen—"about eight minutes out."

The flustered nurse's jaw hits the floor.

George addresses the woman. "I didn't mean to startle you. I'm Miss McGuire's..."

There is a beat of awkward silence.

"Uncle," Lilly supplies.

"Uncle," George and I parrot simultaneously, though our response sounds more like a question.

The woman peers at the dangerous-looking man out of the corner of her eye but knows better than to question Lilly. I clamp my mouth shut. I'm not getting into this.

She turns to her patient. "Miss McGuire, how is your pain level? The doctor will be with you shortly; he's finishing up with another patient. Once he assesses the wounds, I will clean them up."

"Whatever the guy in the ambulance gave me is working," Lilly declares groggily. At least she is not in pain anymore—or at the level she was at when I first saw her on the floor.

"I'm glad to hear that. I will be back shortly. If you need something in the meantime, please press this button over here." She places a small remote on the mattress next to Lilly's hand. "Or one of your, uh...family members can come to get me from the nurses' station."

"Thank you," Lilly whispers, and it's apparent how exhausted she is.

As soon as the nurse leaves the room, I square my shoulders and round on George, who is staring at his phone.

"Dude, where the fuck were you when this went down? I thought you're supposed to 'shadow'"—I make air quotes— "Lilly?"

Logically, I know he didn't have eyes in the locker room, but my irrational side needs to blame someone.

"Your father just pulled up. I will be waiting outside. Weston knows where to find me." And with that, he's gone. The only thing missing is George dropping a black curtain like a magician and purple smoke remaining in his place.

*Motherf*—

I slowly walk to the other side of the bed and lower myself onto the rolling chair probably meant for the medical staff. I wrap my fingers around Lilly's, and she blinks at me.

"What happened?" My voice breaks, and I avert my gaze from her exposed back.

She draws in a shuddering breath. "We were running track today. We were on our way to the showers when a sophomore showed up with a slip for Den to come to the office. She said she'd go after she showered, but Mr. Landon told her to go immediately. The other girls were already done and almost out the door, so I figured it wasn't a big deal. Den would be back in a few." Lilly pauses, and I swipe away the lone tear running down her face with my thumb. I wait for her to collect herself.

"I even brought my clothes with me out of fear they would take them." Lilly breathes out a non-comical laugh. "I was rinsing the shampoo out when the water turned scorching hot." She squeezes her eyes together but keeps talking. "I tried to turn it off but couldn't get to the lever fast enough. The water burned me. When I tried to get out of the stall, someone pushed me back in." Lilly's breathing picks up. "I...I couldn't see. My wet hair was in my face, and I tried to get my head away from the water. Someone held my hands and shoulders, and the water hit my back." Another tear escapes. "Rhys, it hurt so bad."

I gently place my palm on her cheek. "I'm so sorry, babe."

I feel sick and have to fight the urge to haul the tray with medical supplies across the room.

"I heard Den scream. That was when they finally let go." Lilly's lids spring open. "They're going to pay!"

A cold shiver runs down my spine. In all these years, I have never seen the girl in front of me anything but kind and compassionate—even with what I put her through for two years. She is one of the most empathetic human beings I know. But at this moment, her eyes are wild, almost...deranged. Everyone has their limits, and Lilly has reached hers.

I make sure our eyes are locked when I speak. "They will, babe. I promise you." She will get revenge. The question is only when, how, and who gets to execute it. The list of people who would do anything for my girl is long. Anything from torture to erasing the target from existence—in a cyber sense—is possible between George and Nate alone.

Just as I'm about to place a kiss on her forehead, Dad storms through the door. He stops abruptly and zeros in on Lilly's exposed back. His eyes turn wide, and he presses the back of his hand against his mouth, mimicking my own reaction earlier.

His gaze jumps to me. "Who did this?"

"Still working on it, Dad." He will find out soon enough.

My father jerks his head in a nod. He has seen some of the worst shit a human can be forced to endure during his time in the Marine Corps. He hasn't talked openly to us kids about it, but I've heard bits and pieces over the years. He has never so much as shown concern or remorse about it, but the emotions playing on his face now tell me that this will end badly for everyone involved. Maybe not in a physical way—unless one of my *former* friends had anything to do with it—but between Nate and my parents...they messed with the wrong family.

Mom arrives as the nurse has finished cleaning Lilly's skin with saline and is putting aloe on her back. Nurse Julie, as I find out when I finally take the time to read her name tag, explains the process as she goes along, and Dad and I are standing in the corner, letting her do her job. Every time Lilly winces, I'm about to punch Julie's lights out. Not that it's her fault, but I can't take much more of seeing her in pain. Dad eventually has his hand firmly planted onto my shoulder, aware that I'm holding on by a thread and may lose it at any point.

Mom's eyes water immediately at the sight of Lilly, and her eyes fly to Dad. He holds out his other hand, and she launches herself at him, unable to hug the person she wants to embrace.

The doctor, who assessed Lilly's burns earlier and declared them to be second degree, enters the room again, and it's getting crowded. He seems to come to the same conclusion. "We only allow two visitors at a time. May I ask one of you to wait in the waiting room while we finish up with Miss McGuire?"

"Rhys." Dad looks at me, and I want to protest.

The thought of letting Lilly out of my sight causes my chest to constrict. I try to inhale, supply my lungs with the oxygen they demand, but it's like I'm breathing through a pillow.

However, seeing my mother about to fall apart, I can't do that to her.

"Okay," I concede. Before leaving, though, I take the two steps to Lilly's bed and squat down so she doesn't have to raise her head.

"I'll be outside with Den and Wes." *And probably George,* which I don't say aloud.

She smiles at me tightly. "Okay."

"I love you." I place a kiss on her nose, not giving a fuck about who's watching.

"Love you, too," she whispers.

As I straighten, the doctor says, "We will discharge Miss McGuire shortly. I don't see a reason to keep her overnight. You want to watch the burns, keep them clean, and when the blisters burst, do not pick at them. They will heal in seven to fourteen days. No lotions or creams and loose clothing. She can take Motrin for the pain and sleep on her stomach..." He keeps going on, but I exit the room in search of Lilly's head of *failed* security.

## CHAPTER NINETY

**RHYS**

I FIND WES AND DENIELLE HUDDLED IN THE FAR CORNER OF THE ER's waiting area. The large, rectangular room is packed to max capacity between people who need to be here and students who want to get their hands on the newest WH gossip. Lilly's *former* friend Sloane sits next to Jager, her hand between both of his. That's a surprising development, but I can't bring myself to care at the moment. My coach and two of Lilly's teachers are in another section. I ignore them, not willing to answer potential questions. Jager notices me first, and his lips part. Sloane follows his gaze, and her eyes turn wary. I probably look unhinged. If I find out any of them had something to do with what happened to Lilly, pissing his pants will be the highlight of Jager's week. I pass them, not taking my eyes off him, and he gets the meaning. He inclines his head, and with an unspoken message, I know he wasn't part of this. My former friend is a cocky fucktard who thinks with his dick most of the time, but he would never physically harm someone on purpose, let alone a female.

Wes stands as I approach, and Denielle follows suit, her hand gripping his bicep. Without a word, he makes his way toward one of the many doors leading from the room. I trail after them, my fists deep in my jeans pockets so I don't accidentally clock someone who looks at me the wrong way. A new wave of anger hits me when I see all the assholes camped out in the waiting area. I'd bet George's fancy AR on the fact that half of them don't even know Lilly personally.

We're in a hallway we have no business being in as my best friend stops in his tracks, pulls out his phone, and types something. A few seconds later, he starts moving again, and after two more turns, we're in a staircase that's definitely not open to the public. Heading down two flights, we find George standing on the landing between the floors.

He has his phone pressed to his ear, listening intently before he replies. "I have to advise against that." Pause. "No, you cannot force her." Deep breath. "You and Miss Lilly are my first priority." Pause. The person on the other end is getting louder, yet I cannot make out the words. "I am fully aware that this was possibly our only shot, Nate, but —" George clamps his mouth shut, and it's clear that he is struggling to keep his cool. "I understand. Keep me posted on what else you find."

He extends the hand with his phone toward me, and I lift the device to my ear.

"Yes?"

I expect Nate to go apeshit on me, but instead, a shuddered breath comes through the earpiece. "How is she?"

My inner asshole wants to blame him. If he hadn't come back, stalked and kidnapped Lilly, none of this would've happened, but even I know that that's not true. He had nothing to do with my psycho ex's plan of revenge.

"She's in pain, but whatever the doc gave her is helping. They're releasing her later."

"Thank you, Rhys. I..." He hesitates for a moment. "George will fill you in on everything else."

The line goes dead, and I pull the device away from my ear, frowning at it. Fill us in on what? I don't like the sound of that.

George plucks his phone out of my hand and pockets it. "We need to talk."

I'm used to zero-expression George. I've even seen amused George—not much, but I was privy to get a glimpse of him. Yet, what currently shows on his face makes the blood in my veins turn to ice. Denielle seems to come to the same conclusion, because she shuffles closer to Wes.

Nate and Lilly's head of security leans against the wall across from the stairs and motions for us with a jerked chin-dip to sit. The last thing I want is to plant my ass on these damn stairs, but I follow his silent order, knowing he probably will make me sit if he wants to.

"The reason I wasn't there to 'shadow' Miss Lilly"—he makes air quotes around shadow, referring to my earlier yelled accusation —"was that I was following a...lead."

"What lead?" Denielle frowns at George. She's no longer scared of him.

"I was parked in my usual spot off of Baxter Drive when I noticed an SUV idling not far from the main entrance." Baxter and 11th make up the T-intersection the school is located at. I want to question why that would be suspicious; students often have to park off-campus when they're late and the parking lot is full. Or someone gets picked up outside the gate. But George keeps going. "Something was off. I had Nate run the plate, and it came back registered to a recently deceased veterinarian."

"Fuck." Wes curses under his breath.

I have an idea where this is going. "Turner?"

George levels me with a look that I've only ever seen from one other person: my father. "I couldn't confirm one hundred percent that it was Turner, but from the brief glimpse I got of the driver, it was likely. I informed Nate and decided to follow the car."

"Did you lose him?" Denielle inserts herself into the report. I throw her a glare that hopefully tells her to shut up and let the man talk.

"No. I followed him to a warehouse outside of Alexandria. Nate tracked my location from his end." George halts, and I scan his face. What is he not saying? This man never needs time to collect his thoughts, and the waiting makes the hair stand up on the back of my neck. He stares at me. "I need you to stay calm."

*What the—?*

I narrow my eyes, and he expels a long breath. "Once he arrived at his destination, I confirmed that the driver was, indeed, Francis

Turner. He walked into the warehouse and returned later with a large duffel bag."

My heart rate increases. Before I can ask what that means, though, Wes inserts himself into George's report.

"Okay, the guy went shopping. What's the big deal?" He tries to play it off—for whose benefit, I don't know. He's not *that* brainless.

"The big deal is that this particular row of warehouses belongs to someone under investigation for running a sophisticated network of illegal substances. Specifically, medical-grade sedatives and paralytic drugs you cannot get from your local drug dealer at the street corner."

George waits for us to put two and two together.

When it clicks, I jump up and punch the nearest concrete wall. "FUCK!" *Punch*. "FUCK!" *Punch*. "FUUUUCK!" *Punch, punch*. I shake my hand, followed by flexing and unflexing my fingers to see what damage I did. While doing so, I let out another string of very explicit and beyond X-rated phrases. My pulse is pounding in my ears. Can this day get any worse?

Denielle flinches at my outburst, and I round on the former Marine. "He's coming after Lilly."

Stoic George is back. "That's a likely conclusion."

"How do you know about the drugs?" Denielle voices the question I ignored.

I'm still in the process of assessing if I broke anything but turn my attention back to the conversation.

"Nate traced the owner through a couple of shell corporations after I gave him the address. Once he had the name, it didn't take long to find what we know now. I was following Turner back toward Westbridge when I got your call." George looks at Denielle. "I was another twenty-five minutes out."

This time, it's my eyes that nearly bulge out of their sockets. I stare at her. "*You* called him?"

Denielle looks something between guilty and proud. "I had to. I mean, Lilly was injured."

My gaze swivels between the three people in front of me, and I stop at Wes. "You also have his number?"

Wes's tone is almost apologetic. "I do."

I scowl at George who remains mute.

*What the fuck? He might as well give it to my parents.*

AFTER GEORGE all but took a blood oath that he would not abandon his post again, we made our way back upstairs, waiting for Lilly to get discharged.

Neither of us move to enter the ER's waiting area, and my father finds us in the hallway outside of Lilly's room.

"We're ready to leave. Mom is with Lilly, but I want you in there while I'm pulling the car around." Dad doesn't allow for any questions or negotiation. The man who could give George a run for his money when it comes to emotional paralysis looks like he had about one too many coffees. I don't think I have ever seen my father this jumpy. Tristen McGuire is a professional. The man in front of me...is not.

I give him a curt nod and walk toward Lilly's door. I'm about to enter when I hear my father address our friends. "I spoke to your parents. You two take Heather's car back to our house." I glance over my shoulder and meet Wes's confused gaze.

*Does Dad know that they don't have any mode of transportation here?*

As he steers my two friends toward the exit, probably telling them where Mom parked, I enter Lilly's room. She sits at the edge of the bed, a hospital gown covering her front and the back loosely tied, most likely so that the one size fits all—or not—won't randomly open and fall off of her tiny frame.

Our eyes immediately lock, and relief is written all over Lilly's face. "Hey," she breathes.

"Hey, babe." I force my voice to remain steady and calm, even though my pulse has been somewhere above the 150 range since George confirmed my conclusion that Turner is after her. It'll be a miracle if Lilly is allowed to pee in peace going forward. Nate is probably going to implant a tracker in her arm or neck.

Lilly frowns. Of course she reads me like an open book—I can't keep anything from her. I imperceptibly shake my head. *Not here.* Instead of nodding, she slowly blinks in affirmation. I want to pat my back. We totally have this silent communication thing down.

I continue my way to her and interlace our fingers, placing a kiss on her forehead. "How are you feeling?"

She smiles weakly. "I just want to go home." My breath hitches, and I study her face.

*Which home is she referring to?*

Mom remains mute. I glance over and see her watching us intently. Her face is closed off, and it's almost as if my parents have changed roles. She takes a step forward and addresses her daughter. "Let's get you ready. Dad is going to pull the car around any minute."

Lilly eases herself off the bed, and I grasp her elbow as her feet hit the floor, and her legs wobble. "Easy, Cal."

Leaving the room, Mom walks ahead of us alongside Julie, who leads us through back corridors to a set of elevators not accessible for someone who is not staff. Lilly's nurse takes us down to an underground bay meant for the ambulances to deliver their patients. Dad's Raptor is idling as close as possible to the elevators without blocking any emergency vehicles.

I climb in the backseat ahead of her, and once she is inside, Lilly lies down in my lap, making sure her back doesn't touch anything.

Mom and Dad take the front without a word, and we're off. As we come out of the delivery bay and around the side, I understand why we chose this route. Once again, the hospital entrance is lined with news vans.

*Fuck.*

AT HOME, only our friend Lancaster awaits us. The rest of the vultures are likely camped out in front of the hospital. I already see tomorrow's headlines:

*First victim of The Babysitter attacked in school's locker room shower stall. Did she try to boil herself to distract from the incest with her step-brother or her suspected illicit relationship with her kidnapper?*

AT THIS POINT, nothing will be a surprise.

DAD PULLS STRAIGHT into the garage, where we find Mom's GLS 580 in its spot. Den and Wes are already waiting in the kitchen, and

Lilly's best friend is by her side as soon as she follows me through the garage door.

Reluctantly, I let go of Lilly's hand as Denielle leads her upstairs without a word, which leaves me with Wes and my parents in uncomfortable silence.

"Where is Nat?" Now that we're home and the tension leaves me like air out of an untied balloon, I realize that my little sister is nowhere in sight. I grimace. I was so preoccupied with Lilly that Natty's absence completely escaped me. I'm a shit brother.

"She went home with Olivia after school," Mom explains. "I'm going to pick her up in a few minutes. We didn't want her to have to sit in the hospital."

I nod at no one in particular and silently promise to make more of an effort with my little sister. I need to be there for her as well.

Dad walks over to the fridge and pulls out a bottle of water. "Camden arranged for Lilly to give her statement tomorrow morning." He takes a sip. "A police officer will be here at eight o'clock. I want all of you to be there."

"All?" Wes's croaked question makes it clear that he did not anticipate that.

"Yes. You are all witnesses," my mother clarifies in her attorney voice then amends more emotionally, "Whoever did this to my daughter will be charged with the max penalty we can demand." Her stern gaze lands on me, and I have a hunch she suspects my ex to be involved somehow.

"I'll make sure she's ready," is all I say before walking past them and up the stairs. I hear Dad tell Wes that their parents are aware of him and Denielle spending the night. Mom says something I don't understand, and Wes mumbles a response. By the time I step on the landing on the second floor, he's beside me.

"Dude, I thought your dad was scary, but your mom almost made me piss myself just now. She makes the chick from *The Ring* look like your girl next door. Kat will regret fucking with your family."

I snort a laugh. "Tell me about it."

Entering Lilly's bedroom with Wes on my heels, we find Lilly sitting on the edge of her bed with Denielle squatting in front of her, holding each other's hands. Both girls have tears running down their cheeks, and an instant knot forms in my stomach.

Den turns and launches herself at me. "I'm so sorry!"

I'm shocked by her sudden attack, we stumble backward, and Wes puts his hand in the middle of my back to stop us from falling over. My eyebrows knit together as I try to comprehend what she's apologizing for. Lilly meets my gaze, but I'm no closer to understanding.

"D, let the man go to his woman." Wes carefully pries her away from me and envelops her in a tight hug, where she completely breaks down, holding onto him like a lifeline. Denielle sobs into his shoulder. I've never seen her this way.

I slowly make my way over to the bed and sit down, taking Lilly's hand in mine. I was about to drape my arm over her shoulder as usual but caught myself at the last moment.

We watch our friends, and Lilly whispers, "She blames herself for leaving me."

My head jerks to her. "That's ridiculous. If someone is to blame, it's Kat and whomever she got to do it." My tone is way harsher than I intended. I glance at Denielle to make sure she knows my rage is not directed at her.

She has calmed down some and turned in Wes's embrace to face us. "I'm sorry, Rhys. I shouldn't have left."

I grind my teeth, hating that she thinks she is to blame in any way. I stretch my hand out, and Wes nudges her toward me. When she's within reach, I grasp her hand. "D, no one blames you for any of this. And if anyone *ever* so much as suggests that, you tell me, and I'll sic good ol' George on them for some fun torture time. He'll have a blast." I wink at her, and a half laugh, half sob bubbles up in her throat.

Wes steps beside her. "Did you see who did..."—he hesitates mid-sentence—"it?"

Denielle levels each of us before speaking. "There were four. I recognized three. The fourth bolted as soon as I came in. Only one was a cheerleader. Two juniors. The third was a sophomore. I've seen all of them suck up to the Wicked Bitch before."

Where Wes exclaims a string of curse words, Lilly and I remain quiet. I don't have it in me to get the names of everyone involved right now, and it seems neither does Lilly.

She sighs. "I'm exhausted."

I take that as her cue that she wants to get some rest, and I scoot back until my head hits the pillows on her bed. Lilly follows me and drapes herself over my chest, tucking her fingers between me and the mattress. Having her this close, an instant sense of peace settles in my chest. Her head is nestled under my chin, and I try to figure out where to place my hands when the hospital gown she's still wearing falls open. Wes flinches, and Den's eyes widen, but neither of them say anything.

After a beat of silence, it's clear that Lilly is done for the day. Our friends slowly turn and head to my room, leaving both doors ajar.

# CHAPTER NINETY-ONE

**LILLY**

I turn to my side and stifle a groan. Waking up on top of Rhys's chest, my neck is stiff, and all I want is to turn on my back. The urge to change position and alleviate the stabbing sensation overcomes me. However, it takes about .3 seconds after starting to roll over for yesterday's events to come back alongside the feeling of someone peeling the worst sunburn off my back—with a blunt knife. During the blissfully numb hours of sleep—courtesy of pills the nurse made me take before we left—I suppressed what had happened.

*Where are the pain meds they handed me last night?*

Rhys begins to shift underneath me at my sudden movement.

"Babe? Everything okay?" His voice is raspy from sleep, and it stirs something inside of me that makes me momentarily forget everything else. Instead of responding, I press myself closer to him, nuzzle my nose in the crook between his ear and collar bone as he lifts a hand, gently pushing the strands of hair from my face.

"Cal, talk to me."

I angle my head upward to meet his gaze. "I'm fine," I lie. Of course I'm not fine, and he knows it. His narrowed eyes say as much.

"Try again, babe." A smug smile tugs on the side of his lips. He can read me as well as I can read him. Why I try to pretend is beyond me.

"I'm angry." I pause. "No, scratch that. I'm fucking pissed!" My tone is hard, and Rhys cocks an eyebrow.

"You have every right to be upset—" he begins, but I interrupt him by jerking into a sitting position.

"I'm not *up-set*," I enunciate the two syllables. Upset doesn't come close to covering the turmoil inside of me. "I'm pissed. Furious. Livid. All of it. Those bitches attacked me like cowards in the shower. Naked. Four against one. Who does that?" By the time I finish, I'm breathing heavy, and I'm fisting the duvet, one of the pin-tucks having ripped.

*Just awesome.*

Gaping with an open mouth, Rhys clearly didn't expect this outburst from me upon waking up.

I inhale and exhale slowly. "I'm sorry. It's just... I'm sick of being a target."

He dips his head in a small nod before asking warily. "What do you want to do?"

I sigh. "I have no idea. Yesterday changed things."

Once again, my emotions are all over the place, and I need time to sort through them. The anger clouding my vision when I think of what happened in the locker room makes the fear of the unknown —my past and future—shrink to a barely noticeable tickle in the back of my mind. But it's there. The question of what Turner wants with me hangs over my head. Between the kidnapping and incest scandal, the media follows my every step. The desperate need to hide is at war with my instinct to fight back. To get revenge. I'm not a naturally violent person, but I refuse to cower to Katherine Rosenfield with her psychotic delusions.

"I'm gonna take a shower," I announce. That wasn't the response Rhys was looking for, but that's all I can give him at the moment.

"Do you think that's, uh...okay? With your injuries, I mean?" His forehead wrinkles. He doesn't press me for more answers, and the ache in my heart lessens, knowing Rhys is on my side.

Sliding off the bed, I turn. "They said as long as the water doesn't hit the burns, I can shower. It just has to be quick."

How fast is up for debate. I'm in desperate need of my purging ritual.


IN THE END, reason wins out. I keep the shower short, not to worsen my condition. The skin on my back feels like it's stretched to the max, and every movement hurts. After letting the hospital gown drop to the floor, I chance a glance in the mirror. I wish I hadn't. I heard the nurse and doctor talk about the blisters, but seeing them is a whole different thing. I'm not super squeamish, though taking in the extent of the burns makes my stomach churn.

Sitting in front of the vanity, I have a towel wrapped around my lower half and one on my front side, tucked under my armpits. The cool air feels good on my back, and I need to ask someone to help put more aloe on.

Slowly, I lean forward and pull the cabinet door under the sink open. I study the pink box with its writing for a moment before digging out the burner and headphones I left there.

Without thinking, I initiate a video call. The phone rings five times before his face appears on the screen.

"Lilly." My brother is breathless. In the background, a door closes behind him before he lowers himself into a desk chair similar to the one he has at the vineyard. His face is red, his blond hair plastered to the sides of his forehead, and sweat drips from his chin.

"Are you okay?" I tilt my head to the side.

"Shouldn't I be asking you that?"

If the dark circles under his eyes weren't a dead giveaway, him rubbing his hand over his face for the third time since picking up the phone would be. His demeanor mirrors his behavior from when the first article about my kidnapping was released.

"Talk to me, big brother," I prod gently.

He stares at something past the camera. When his focus is back on me, he confesses, "I was on my way to the jet yesterday when I got the call about...what happened. I lost my shit. Ran out of a business meeting. George was still on his way back from Alexandria, your friends didn't pick up their phones, and there are no cameras in the locker rooms. I couldn't check on you."

*George was in Alexandria?*

I drop the question of why George abandoned his post—for now. It must have been something important. Or why neither of my friends mentioned that they had a missed call from my brother. They either didn't notice or didn't want to put anything else on me.

"Please don't expose yourself," I whisper. *Not yet.*

Nate's eyes gentle. "You come first, little sister."

A sad smile makes the corners of my mouth turn up. "I know. But I need you...*out*. There are too many unanswered questions." The selfish side of me is not ready for him to go away.

He nods his head in understanding.

"What were you just doing?" I force a change in topic.

"Running. I needed to move after..." Nate trails off. I pinch my brows, and he elaborates, "I've been...busy. It was that or coming to Westbridge. George threatened to call my pilot if I so much as breathed in the direction of the airfield again." He rolls his eyes.

"He wants you safe as well," I say softly.

Nate inhales slowly. "I needed to distract myself, and I'm still at a dead-end with the money our father transferred. Whoever owned the account withdrew all the money. I need to try a different approach on that front." He pauses, and I wait.

I can read between the lines, though, and my pulse speeds up.

"I found Hector Lakatos."

"Who?"

"Your memory doctor."

I blink. My memory... My hand tightens around the phone, and a wave of dizziness hits me. "How?" The question is barely audible.

My brother explains, in the detached business-like tone I had become used to at the vineyard (whenever his genius mind switches to task orientation only), how he informed George about Tristen's revelation. And how our head of security put two and two together. Through George's connections, they were able to track Hector Lakatos to the continental U.S., and Nate took it from there. My brother had to keep himself distracted after the attack, and this was his contribution—he found the person who messed with my mind. According to Nate, Lakatos seems to have mostly retired from his *profession* and only in rare cases still makes an appearance in public. However, my brother found him—in rural Oregon, of all places.

"He set up a specific protocol of how to contact him. Even I couldn't narrow down his location further than a post office box in the middle of nowhere. He has nothing in his name," Nate concludes.

"Sounds like his choices caught up with him. Why else would he try to disappear this way?" I scoff. I mean, seriously, this guy fucked with brains for a living; I'd be surprised if more people don't want to get their hands on him.

That makes him chuckle. "When did you become so ruthlessly sarcastic? But yes, I agree with you. He probably made quite a few enemies with his *services*."

"What's next?" I hold my breath as I wait for his answer. What are we going to do about the man who rearranged my memories?

"George will set up a meet. It'll take some time since he won't leave your side for the foreseeable future."

"Why don't you contact him?" I don't want to wait.

"George is the better choice. His name is well known in his, uh, line of work," Nate explains then switches gears. "How do you feel?"

Is he asking physically or mentally? "It hurts." Describing the actual sensation of razorblades shaving the skin off my back whenever I move won't do any good, so I add, "I want revenge. They went too far."

A joker-like grin spreads over Nate's face, but before he can respond, the door creaks open, and Rhys's head appears in the gap.

"Hey." His tone is hesitant.

"Hi." I turn away from the small screen.

His sleepy appearance makes me smile.

"The cop taking our statements will be here in a few minutes. I just wanted to see if you need anything." His gaze flicks to my exposed back.

"Um..." I glance at the phone and back at Rhys. "Yeah, can you help me with the aloe? And I'll need one of your shirts. The doctor said to wear only loose clothes for now."

Nate's voice filters through the headphones. "I'll let you go. We'll finish our conversation later."

I'd rather talk revenge plans with him than deal with another cop, but I don't have a choice.

We say our goodbyes while Rhys goes to get something for me to wear, and I get ready to give my statement.

. . .

To my surprise, the police officer had the names of all five girls when she walked in. Five, not four, which made everyone's jaws drop. The female cop, who introduced herself as Officer Martinez, was accompanied by Agent Camden. She informed us that the school handed over the security footage. The attackers were traced back by who entered and didn't leave the locker room after P.E. The girls—one senior, two juniors, and a sophomore—gave their statements last night and ratted out the fifth member of my attack squad —another junior. Number five was the one who manipulated the shower by shutting off the cold water in the maintenance room. How the girl knew where to go and what to do remains under investigation, but in the end, they got released into their parents' custody. All of them have been suspended, effective immediately, and Camden commented that they most likely will be expelled.

No one asks me if I want to press charges, which I do, but apparently, it was already done. The girls admitted to the attack. Their reason: I seduced the school's QB, aka my adopted brother, and ruined his *and* the school's reputation.

*What the fuck?*

As soon as Officer Martinez concludes her report, shouts erupt around me.

"Are you fucking kidding me?"

"That's complete BS!"

"That fucking cunt!" Which comes from Rhys and earns him a good tongue lashing from Heather. She does not want to hear the C-word in this house. Tristen remains quiet, as usual.

I watch the scene like a passive observer. Everyone is basically foaming at the mouth, but the small crescent-shaped indentations on the insides of my palms are the only visible sign of how I feel about this.

"Are you saying someone else is behind the attack?" Camden inserts herself.

Rhys balls his fists on top of the kitchen table and growls between clenched teeth, "This was all Kat. She's a fucking psycho. Her mindless bitch followers did what she would never attempt herself."

"That's why there were four in the locker room! Everyone knows Lilly can put any guy at WH on their ass in less than a minute," Wes adds. The last part is spoken with a proud undertone, and I can't suppress a tiny smile.

I'm lucky to have friends like them in my life.

"Do you have proof for your accusation?" Officer Martinez tilts her head.

"We don't need proof. The Wicked Bitch has had it out for Lilly since Rhys broke up with her," Denielle snarls.

Heather purses her lips but doesn't chastise Den for her choice of words—probably because she thinks the same.

Camden glances at Heather and Tristen before her gaze settles on my best friend. "Without evidence, Officer Martinez cannot bring Miss Rosenfield in."

She believes my friends, but she's right. They can't touch Katherine unless one of her minions comes clean. Rhys's ex may be an evil, manipulative—not using the C-word despite it being an accurate description—but unfortunately, she's also smart. That's how she got where she is in the WH hierarchy.

When I don't jump on the blame-the-ex train, all eyes land on me.

Chewing on the inside of my lip, I remain quiet. Heather scans me with concern. My friends look at me in disbelief, most likely wondering why I don't back them up.

Martinez reads my silence as me being upset. "Miss McGuire, I ensure the responsible parties will be held accountable."

*Yes, they will.*

Rhys and Den both snort sarcastically, and Wes mumbles something along the lines of, "Yeah, right!"

Only Tristen sees through me. I swear this man knows more than he lets on. Way more! And in this case, he is right. Katherine Rosenfield will pay, and I'll get my revenge. Though, I won't admit that here. She talked five students into attacking me. Of course, they could've said no, but their actions of taking the blame speak for the fear Katherine Rosenfield has instilled in the female population of Westbridge High. They ruined their futures for the approval of *one* girl.

We finish our statements, Denielle's taking the longest since she was the one that saw the most. The entire time, Tristen's gaze doesn't leave me.

When we're done, Officer Martinez takes more pictures, in addition to the ones the hospital took yesterday, followed by Camden walking her out. I guess since the female agent basically lived here for weeks on end, I shouldn't be surprised how casually she moves around the house.

Heather gives me a careful hug. Our relationship is still on thin ice, but I let her. She busies herself with an early lunch, roping Denielle into cutting the onion for her, and Rhys and Wes are deep in conversation with Tristen when I head upstairs.

I stop at my little sister's door. Natty has remained in her room, and besides a short glimpse on my way down, I haven't seen her since before school on Friday.

We sit on her bed while she scans me up and down. All my injuries are covered, but it's as if she can see right through Rhys's t-shirt.

"Are you okay?" my observant little sister inquires. I'm growing tired of the question, but she's not the one I'd let my frustration out on. They are all worried, but I'm over talking about it.

"I am. It's not that bad." I smile at her.

"You're not supposed to lie," Natty scolds.

*What is it with the McGuires and their built-in lie detectors?*

I try a different approach. "I know, baby girl. I just don't think I need to unload my, uh...*stuff* on you."

"You could, though. I'm your sister."

Needles prick at the back of my throat. Her words bring the first tears since the attack to my eyes. "Yes, you are."

I swipe with my index finger under my eye and motion for Natty to lie down on my lap. Her face lights up, and genuine happiness settles in my chest. We used to do this when she was a little girl. Natty would lie down in my lap, and I would comb her hair with my fingers. We haven't spent time together like this since it all started, and I swallow hard over the guilt.

"Tell me about your newest book," I say after she gets comfortable on my thighs. I don't have to ask if there is a new book. Natty always reads.

That's where Rhys finds me twenty minutes later. He leans

against the doorframe, watching us with his arms crossed over his chest as Natty talks about a new series she discovered. The books play out in Virginia and follow two brothers solving mysteries.

Rhys locks eyes with me and mouths, "I'll wait in your room."

I nod my head in confirmation and focus back on the girl on my lap.

---

# CHAPTER NINETY-TWO

---

**LILLY**

The rest of the weekend flies by.

Tristen takes Wes and Denielle home after lunch on Saturday, and both return Sunday afternoon. We hang out in Rhys's room. The boys sit at the foot of the mattress, playing video games, and Den and I are just...us. We lounge on the bed—me mostly on my stomach—when she announces that she is thinking about surprising Charlie during spring break. He's been distant, missing their usual video chats, and she hopes that some quality time together will help. Rhys and Wes exchange a glance I can't interpret, but neither comments on Den's plans. I'm not used to seeing my best friend anything but confident. She's the one with the I-don't-give-a-fuck attitude. Something is up with her, but I also don't want to put her on the spot in front of the guys.

I avoid every phone and computer in the house—except the burner—needing a break from the social media drama and news articles. Rhys confirms that there are a handful of news reports covering the attack at school. Surprisingly, though, most of them are factual. They describe how four female students attacked me, and a fifth was charged as an accomplice. Since no one (officially) knows about Katherine's involvement, the conclusion is that the girls wanted revenge for their own personal gain—the same B.S. they served the cops.

Rhys barely leaves my side. He makes sure I have everything I need, including letting me sleep on top of him, as that's the only bearable position. The dark circles under his eyes are proof of him forfeiting his rest for mine, and a pang of guilt hits me.

Monday morning, I wake up before the alarm goes off. Rhys is going back to school today; I'm excused until after spring break. Though, I've been playing with the idea of online classes and the possibility of graduating early. I have the credits due to the summer classes I took over the last few years, and after this coming Thursday—my eighteenth birthday—I'll have the financial means to support myself if Heather and Tristen had any issues with that plan.

The sensation of getting the skin shaved off my back at every move has also lessened. It still hurts—a lot—but it's manageable. I prop myself on my elbows, taking in the sleeping boy next to me. His long lashes fan over his cheekbones, and his hair has grown out over the last few weeks, the slight waves standing up all over his head. His eyes flicker under his closed lids, and his mouth presses into a thin line. He's dreaming, and from the looks of it, it's not a good one. The need to stop whatever is going on in his brain makes me lean in. With a flutter in my chest, a sensation I experience every time we touch *anywhere*, I gently press my mouth to his. *Home.* Rhys's tense features soften, and I sweep my tongue over his bottom lip ever so slightly.

A hum rumbles in his chest, and my butterflies morph into their hornet form. Eyes still closed, Rhys's hands slide up my arms, and he caresses my biceps with his thumbs as he returns the kiss. He doesn't wrap his arms around my back like he usually would, which tells me he is awake and aware of his actions. I part my lips, and his warm tongue instantly invades my mouth. I can't stop the moan escaping my throat, nor do I want to.

*Thank goodness the door is closed.*

I move until I'm completely on top of him, and he grinds his hips against me in response, never breaking the contact to my mouth. Feeling his hard length against my core makes heat shoot through my body, and I inwardly curse my injuries. I want him so bad, his hands all over me, him inside of me. But my limited movements make it impossible. Not impossible, but it definitely wouldn't be the most enjoyable *experience* for either of us. Despite not breaking the kiss, Rhys isn't oblivious to my inner battle of desire, anger, and frustration.

"Stop thinking, babe," he murmurs against my mouth.

I grin against his lips; he always knows. "I want you so bad." To drive my point home, I push my hips forward and create more torturous friction for both of us.

*Moooore,* my insides whine.

He pulls back, and our gazes meet. "Trust me?"

There is a gleam in his eyes that instantly put me on guard. What's he planning? He'd never do anything to cause me (more) pain, so my answer is the only obvious one. "I do."

Rhys shifts until we're both on our sides, facing each other. He scans me carefully, and I smile. "I'm okay."

Slowly, never looking away, he leans back in and starts a gentle assault of my mouth with his. I love the feel of his tongue against mine, and a tingling sensation spreads through my entire body. Why can't it always be like this?

Suddenly, the waistband of my sleep shorts is pulled away, and Rhys's hand dives under the fabric. I jerk at the unexpected contact and latch onto his arm with my hand to not fall backward. The heel of his palm presses against my sensitive spot, and he enters me with one finger.

*Yesss.*

My eyes flutter closed, and a whimper escapes me. I part my thighs, draping one leg over his, to give him better access. I deepen the kiss and press my throbbing clit against him.

"Already so wet, Cal?" He smirks against my mouth.

"More." The word comes out in a breathy moan, and Rhys chuckles. I'm so turned on that I can't bring myself to care if he laughs at or *with* me.

"You know I never say no to you." And with that, another finger joins the first.

*Fuck me—literally.*

I nip on his bottom lip and most definitely leave claw marks on his arms, but I can't stop myself. Rhys changes his angle, and now his two fingers pump in and out as his thumb circles my clit.

"Ahhh. Rhys, I..." I want to tell him that I'm about to come, but he speeds up his movement, and I lose all train of thought.

"Shhh...just let go."

And that's what I do. I completely fall apart. I clench around his fingers deep inside of me, Rhys not stopping until the last shiver has wracked through my body.

I slowly peel my eyelids back and gaze at him in my post-orgasm fog. He pulls his hand out of my shorts and does the last thing I'd ever expect. He licks his fingers with a devilish grin on his face. "Mhmmm."

My eyes nearly bulge out of their sockets, and I cover my face with my hand that had been holding onto him.

"You did not just do that," I exclaim, peering at him between my fingers.

"If that wasn't a wake-up call—" He winks.

At that precise moment, the alarm goes off, and both of us burst out laughing.

*God, I love this boy so much.*

EVERYONE IS at school or work. I try to pass the time, but I can't concentrate on anything for more than a few minutes, and by lunchtime, I am so bored that I cave. Typing my name into the search bar, I expect all kinds of results, but not this. With Rhys and me not giving them more ammunition in the kidnapping or incest category, the attack already being covered, and the FBI not releasing any leads toward the capture of The Babysitter, the media begins to grasp at straws. And said straw is my little sister.

*Is Natty McGuire a Victim of Parental Neglect?*

READING THE HEADLINE, my pulse skyrockets, and my fingers clench around the edges of my laptop.

. . .

*A SOURCE BROUGHT to our attention their suspicion of Natty McGuire, the younger adopted sister of The Babysitter's first victim, Lilly McGuire, being neglected by her parents.*

*Tristen and Heather McGuire have previously been under crossfire for condoning the relationship of their son, Rhys McGuire (18), and their under-age, adopted daughter, Lilly McGuire (17). The secret affair was exposed by very incriminating photographs leaked by Westbridge High's students via various social media accounts.*

*Since then, Tristen and Heather McGuire have issued a statement regarding the accusation of turning a blind eye to the relationship, which resulted in the case being dropped.*

*How the McGuire family was able to evade legal actions, despite the evidence presented by an undisclosed source, is currently being questioned by several enraged Westbridge residents, as well as other members of the press.*

*This morning, our office received reliable evidence that during all this, the youngest member of the McGuire family, Natty McGuire, is being neglected by her family. Not only was she deposited at a family friend's house the entire time her older sister was held captive by The Babysitter, but she also has been banished to her room whenever she is home.*

*WHAT THE FUCK?*

I stop reading and take in the picture below. Natty sits in her window on the second floor, reading a book. She is content. I know my little sister; this is where she spends most of her time. Her room faces the backyard, which is enclosed by a tall privacy fence and several trees lining the edges of the adjoining properties.

*Did someone sneak onto our property to take that photo?*

I scramble to my bathroom, digging under the sink for the phone.

The line rings twice before George picks up. "Miss Lilly?"

Adrenaline level through the roof, I stammer, "I saw...Natty...backyard...photo..."

"Miss Lilly, please calm down." His voice is quiet. Professional.

I inhale slowly and exhale at the same count before asking, "Did you see the article about Natty?"

The sharp intake of breath tells me he hasn't. "No. I was busy with a different matter, and Nate is in meetings all morning. I assume he hasn't been able to read or act on it yet. I would be aware of it if he had."

*Shit, shit, shit.*

"I need to talk to him." I don't remember if there are cameras in the yard, and even if George knew, he can't pull up the footage.

"Let me see what I can do." George disconnects without a goodbye.

I remain sitting on the bathroom floor, chewing on my thumbnail. I don't have to wait more than five minutes before the burner begins to vibrate in my hand.

Knowing my brother will drop everything when necessary, I don't check the screen for his number before answering. "Someone was in the backyard!" My voice borders on hysterical. Thank goodness I'm alone in the house.

"What do you mean?" Nate's confused question is accompanied by footfalls.

"Th—there is an article about Natty. That Heather and Tristen are neglecting her. Someone took a picture of her sitting in her window." I rush everything out. Nate is familiar with the property's layout.

"Fuck!" He doesn't say anything for several moments until a car door slams in the background. "Okay...I'm going home. Tristen doesn't have cameras besides the entrances and inside the house, nothing pointing at the house or far enough away from it, but George put up surveillance all over the neighborhood. I'll go over those.

"Can I help somehow?" The thought of sitting here useless makes me want to scream. Even in my sitting position on the bathroom floor, my knees won't stop bouncing.

"I'm sorry, little sister. I wish I could give you access." *But it's not secure*, I complete my brother's sentence.

I stay on the line until Nate pulls into his garage, promising to call as soon as he finds something. He has a similar setup in his LA house as at the vineyard and can search several cameras simultaneously. He assures me that he should have something in a couple of hours.

It's 1:30 when we hang up. Another hour and a half until Rhys gets home. I have the urge to pick Natty up from school, but replacing my totaled Jeep was low on everyone's priority list. I'm stuck here. Restless, I walk down the hall to my sister's bedroom and step up to the window. After glancing down at the photo on the laptop in my hands, I scan the outside. It's not hard to narrow down the spot. Someone could've taken the picture across the fence from Mr. Hollencomp's backyard. Mr. Hollencomp is a consultant for some big firm and never home, so no one would've noticed a stranger marching across his lawn.

I've just placed the laptop back on my desk when I hear the humming sound of the garage's roll gate. My gaze flicks to the clock at the top of the screen. This is not good.

Running through all the options of who could be home this early, every possibility results in the same conclusion. Something happened. *Again.*

I take two steps at a time and round the entrance to the kitchen when my little sister bursts through the door from the garage. Tears are streaming down her face.

"Natty, what—" But she hurries past me and up the stairs before I can finish the question.

Heather appears in the kitchen with a somber expression, and our eyes lock.

"What happened?" I whisper, palms pressed against my chest.

She sighs, setting her purse on the kitchen island. "Some girls got a hold of the article that was published today." She scans my face to see if I know what she's talking about. I nod, and she continues, "They cornered her in the bathroom and must've said some awful things. I got a call from the counselor that Natty got into an *altercation* with a girl named Victoria Rosenfield. Natty refused to go into details."

*No way!*

"Rosenfield?" I choke out in disbelief.

Heather turns to face me head-on. "Did you know Katherine's little sister goes to school with Natty?"

My hand fists my shirt near the neckline. "No! I didn't even know Katherine had a sister."

*When did the Wicked Bitch get a sister?*

"Rhys has mentioned her once or twice. But last I heard, she was at a boarding school in Maine." She lets herself drop onto the barstool. "Lilly, this is getting out of hand. What is happening?" Heather's eyes gloss over, and I swallow over the lump in my throat. By forming a relationship with my biological brother, I've turned my entire family into targets.

*This is all my fault.*

I ATTEMPT to check on Natty, but she refuses to open the door. I could easily pick her lock, but the coward in me chickens out. Instead, I sit in the middle of my bed, clutching a throw pillow until screeching tires announce Rhys's arrival at home.

Natty is getting targeted because of me. Because I chose to protect the man who kidnapped not just me, but four other girls. Because I fell in love with her big brother. It's all on me.

Rhys storms into the house and up the stairs with Wes on his heels, heading straight for his little sister's room. I stand in my doorway, and as soon as Rhys hammers against her door, she opens up, flinging herself into his arms. I cover my mouth with my hands.

Wes's gaze swivels to me, and as Rhys disappears with Natty into her room, his best friend slowly moves toward me.

I stare up at the blond boy who's been part of my life for so long. He has always been the one with a joke on his lips, the one with the ability to dissolve any tension and make you feel better. But at this moment, none of that is present. Hurt, anger, and sorrow flicker in equally quick succession across his face. Wes and I are toe to toe, neither of us speaking, and my heart beats a million miles a minute.

*Does he blame me as well?*

I shuffle backward, ready to hide in my room, when his arms shoot out, and he pulls me into a tight hug, interlocking them behind my neck, careful not to touch the injured skin below. The motion is so sudden that my body stiffens. Wes places a kiss on my hair, and I melt into the embrace. I swallow hard.

"It'll be okay," my friend murmurs.

This brings back the memory he and I share from over two and a half years ago. Rhys had made his first public appearance with Katherine in school. I was hiding near the side entrance of the east wing, wiping away tears, when Wes found me. Back then, he did the exact same thing. He hugged me and told me it would be okay. In the end, it was, but what did we have to go through to get to that point?

WES and I sit in silence on my bed when the burner phone I kept in the pocket of my sweatpants starts to vibrate. I jump off the mattress as fast as my raw back allows and speed-walk into the bathroom. Wes follows at a slower pace, and I've already accepted the call by the time he closes the door behind us.

George's face fills the screen, and I suck in a sharp breath. George, the man who could be the poster guy for Botox—with the lack of facial expressions and all—looks back at me with a scrunched forehead and unsmiling mouth—not that he smiles a lot. His scar is stretched around his eye and chin, which makes him appear more menacing than usual.

"This is not good." Wes glances over my shoulder and comes to the same conclusion.

"Miss Lilly," George greets me. His gaze flicks behind me. "Weston."

"What did he find?" I peer over at Wes, whose narrowed brows express his confusion.

"I'm going to send you two photographs Nate was able to pull off our surveillance cameras. You will notice on the timestamp that they are from Saturday morning—around the time you met with Officer Martinez."

*Natty was alone upstairs.*

"Nate will explain everything to you later. He had to go back to the office since he left a meeting with two board members this morning."

I'm about to question why George can't give us the details when he adds, "I need to make a phone call in twelve minutes and still have to set up a secure line."

He is more cryptic than usual, but I let it slide—for now.

"Is he getting in trouble?" It's the second time my brother ran out of work for me.

"The alarm at his home was triggered, and he went to check on it."

I have to smile. I'm sure Nate actually triggered the alarm somehow to back up his story. Nonetheless, we are getting careless.

It takes less than ten seconds after George disconnects before a text message alert pops up. I click on the first picture and stare.

"MOTHERFUCKER." Wes's shout echoes through the bathroom.

# CHAPTER NINETY-THREE

**LILLY**

"Francis-fucking-Turner. Who is this fucking cocksucker?" I snatch the burner out of Rhys's grasp before he can launch it like my poor toothbrush holder—which I haven't replaced yet. Wes and I were still in my bathroom when he walked in. He had spent the past hour talking to Natty and, therefore, was already high strung.

The first picture Nate found was of Turner walking down Chester Drive—the cul de sac parallel to ours. Why George installed cameras there is beyond me, but right about now, I'm just grateful. The second one is of him driving down Grand Avenue, which is the one our street breaks off of. There is no question in my mind; Turner is behind the photo of Natty. But is he also the source of the article? What the hell is his endgame? It makes no freaking sense.

Rhys rubs his hands over his face. "Babe, Nat was a mess. No one has ever treated her like this. She didn't know how to respond to being bullied. You know her, she's the sweetest kid. Everyone likes her." His fists ball at his side, and he growls, "I want to fucking strangle Vic."

"Why did you never mention Katherine's sister before? Let alone that she goes to school with Natty?" My question comes out like an accusation, and I quickly take his hands. "I'm sorry, I didn't mean it the way it sounded." I sigh. "I hate hearing how upset she was. She wouldn't talk to me."

Rhys huffs. "Because Kat's sister has never been of any concern to me. She's two years older than Nat and attended some fancy boarding school up north for as long as I've known Kat. I've seen her once or twice during breaks. The Rosenfields always travel over the holidays, so our paths haven't crossed. I had no clue she was back. Nat's school is a K through eight, which is the only reason Vic has access to her. Otherwise, they would've never met."

"She sounds like a mini version of your psycho ex." Wes's tone is equally as harsh as mine was a minute ago. Not what I'm used to from him.

"Which is why she was sent away," Rhys deadpans.

Glancing sideways at Wes, he also waits for Rhys to elaborate, but he remains mute. I'm sick of Kat, and now her sister, messing with our lives. We have enough going on as it is.

*All because of you*, a voice echoes in my mind.

I shake my head, willing the thought to go away, which makes both boys scowl at me.

"Will this turn into another Kat *situation*?" Translation: Will Victoria Rosenfield physically attack our little sister?

Rhys glares at the wall behind me, not making eye contact and deliberating. "I don't think so. Kat probably sicced Vic on Natty, but people would put two and two together if anything happened to her—with your attack and all."

It's some consolation, but I'm still worried about what nonviolent bullying will do to Natty.

W ES LEAVES AROUND FIVE. Natty refuses to come down for dinner and won't talk to me either. Guilt gnaws at my insides as I lie in bed that night. Rhys is the only one Natty lets into her room, and that's where he's been since dinner. All I can do is sit in my room and wait.

I spot him heading into his bedroom around 9:30, and a couple of minutes later, he walks across the hall in sweats and a clean t-shirt. He takes his place on my bed, and we stare at each other, tears pricking in my eyes.

Rhys leans forward, swiping under my eye. "Don't cry, babe. Nat's fine. We talked. I gave her some big brotherly advice on how to handle it when she gets cornered again. Everything will be okay." His tone is soothing, and my nerves calm a little.

"I hope you didn't tell her to sucker punch the mini witch." I smirk, blinking against the moisture in my eyes.

"I might have." He grins but then sobers. "No, I told her that the only reason these girls are doing this is to hurt her. They can't touch her, and spewing lies is their way of trying to get to Nat." His tone is gentle, and I'm grateful that he was able to talk her down. Nonetheless, I can't help the hollow sensation that has settled in my stomach and has been growing since this afternoon. The feeling of being responsible for all of it.

As we move into our new sleep position, "Lover. Fighter." by SVRCINA comes through the speaker next to my bed. How fitting. I forgot I added the song to my playlist a while ago. Rhys pushes a strand of hair from my face and places a soft kiss on my forehead. "Get some rest, babe."

THE LAST TIME I had glanced at the clock on my nightstand was around two a.m. My mind kept running through all the consequences my adopted family has had to deal with because of my selfish need to hold onto my brother a little longer—to find the answers to my past.

I wake up with the alarm and watch Rhys from the bed as he gets ready in my bathroom. While he brushes his teeth, I take the opportunity and walk down the hall to Natty's room. Her door is ajar, and I knock against the doorframe with a trembling hand. My pulse accelerates with every step that brings me closer to her. She sits in her window nook with a book—even this early in the day— and her head whips around.

"Hey, baby girl." I chew on my thumbnail, waiting for her response. I've never bitten my nails until the last few months. Now they're basically nonexistent.

"Hi." She smiles genuinely, and relief crashes through me.

I cross the room and lower myself down next to her. "I just wanted to see how you're doing and tell you how sorry I am."

"What for?" Natty's brows knit together.

"For what happened in school. If Kat didn't have it out for me, her sister wouldn't have come after you. I—" my voice cracks. I shouldn't have to have this conversation with my little sister.

"Are you kidding me?" Her incredulous expression makes me freeze. When I don't speak, she leans forward. "Vic thinks she is *someone* because of who her sister is. She can say whatever she wants about you, me, or our family. I know the truth. She is just a bully hiding behind a mask of insecurity."

*Excuse me, what?*

It takes me a good minute to form a coherent sentence in my head. "Uh, how old are you again?"

*And why don't I have this confidence?*

Natty giggles. "I heard Mom say that a while ago when she talked to Grandma about Kat and thought it sounded cool. And it fits in this situation, right? Vic *is* Kat's sister."

Unsure of what to reply, I agree with her. "Uh, yeah. Right." Still skeptical if she's truly okay, I force myself to dig deeper. "So, you're not upset? You were crying yesterday, and Rhys told me these girls said some awful things to you."

The ten-year-old—going on thirty—girl in front of me sighs. "Sure, I'm upset. They talk about you and Rhys, people look funny at Mom when she drops me off, and all my teachers watch me like a hawk, but none of this is your fault."

My eyes begin to gloss over. *But it is*, I want to yell. If I had handed Nate over, none of this would've happened. Probably. Maybe. Not to this extent, at least, I tell myself.

"Cal?" Rhys stands in the doorway, and we both turn at my name. "Hey, Nat. How're you doing?" he greets his little sister.

"I'm good," she chirps.

He arches an eyebrow, peering at me, and I shrug. It looks like his advice took root.

"Well, okay. I'm giving you a ride to school today."

"Sweet!" Natty jumps up, grabs her backpack, and waves before disappearing into the hallway. "Bye, Lilly. Don't worry so much."

*Uh, that went...well?*

.   .   .

THE DAY GOES BY QUICKLY. After my *talk* with Natty, I can relax enough to get lost in a romance novel by this fairly new indie author, S.J. Sylvis. I started the book weeks ago and never finished it with my life turning into a roller coaster of disastrous proportions. The main character, Ivy, falls in love with this boy, Dawson, in seventh grade, but of course, it's not that easy. *It never is.* I sure hope they end up together. I heard that the beginning of the book is based on how the author met her husband, which sucked me in instantly. Plus, her husband is a Marine like Tristen. That makes it a must-read, right? I just got to the part where the main characters meet again after years apart when Rhys walks in, and I place my e-reader down on the comforter.

He plops down next to me on the bed. "You're reading." His eyes light up.

I haven't touched a book in what feels like months. "I am." I smile back. "How bad was it today?"

"The usual." Rhys shrugs it off, and I take it as: *don't ask.* "D said she'd call you in a bit and that she'll swing by tomorrow after Oliver heads back to school."

"Sounds good." Lying on my stomach, I cross my arms underneath my head, resting my cheek on my forearms to face Rhys. Den texted yesterday that her brother, Oli, showed up unannounced this weekend, introducing his new girlfriend, Elena, to the family. Everyone was shocked. Oliver Keller has never had a serious relationship in his life. I think he's been the role model for many of Westbridge High's male student body over the years with his talent of picking up girls using ten words or less. And for Den to also instantly approve of Elena means this girl is something special. I can't wait to hear all about her.

"Have you talked to Mom?" Rhys's question catches me off guard.

"No. Why?" I lift my head to get a better view of him.

"I don't know. She's been acting weird since last week," he contemplates.

I mull that over for a moment. Rhys is right. Heather has been withdrawn. After the attack, I would've expected her to be a helicopter parent, no matter how we left it after their revelation about how I lost my memory. But she hasn't. "Do you think it has to do with what they won't tell us?"

"Who the fuck knows? There are too many damn secrets in this family," Rhys grumbles, and it feels like a punch to the gut.

I'm the one keeping the biggest secret from everyone and, in the process, forcing him to do the same.

I drop the topic, and we spend the rest of the afternoon in more or less comfortable silence—him on his phone and me reading. It almost feels...normal. Almost.

"DINNER!" Tristen's voice travels through the house, and I glance at Rhys.

*Family dinner?*

He shrugs, climbs off the bed, and reaches his hand out toward me. When I don't immediately move, he sighs, pulls me up, and wraps his arm around my shoulder. I'd rather be hiding in my room without food, and he knows it.

As we enter the kitchen, we look more like Rhys having me in a chokehold than a loving embrace. I pretend it's because my back is off-limits to touch and not that he had to literally *force-lead* me downstairs. Facing the people in this house has become increasingly more difficult over the past week and a half.

Lord, was it just a little over ten days ago that I found out how my memory got erased, Francis Turner came into my life (officially), Rhys almost got charged with statutory rape, Heather and Tristen faced accusations of negligence, I got attacked in the school's showers, went to the hospital *again,* and Natty became a target to a bunch of hateful middle schoolers?

Silently listing off everything that has happened has me so distracted that I jump at Rhys's euphoric shout.

"OHHHH...spinach lasagna!" He lets go of me and shoots over to his mother, who is pulling two baking dishes out of the oven.

She smiles up at her son. "One spinach and one meat. You know your father."

"That's right. Real men eat meat." Tristen winks at Natty, who's already in her usual seat.

I'm rooted in the entryway. *Am I in the freaking Twilight Zone?*

This whole scene reminds me of a family dinner that would've happened three years ago, but not in the recent past. Rhys seems to read my mind and makes his way over, leaning down to whisper in my ear, "Don't question it. Let's just enjoy it for as long as it lasts."

It lasted all of twenty minutes. Twenty minutes of us being a *regular* family.

"Nat, how did it go today? Did the Rosenfield girl give you any more trouble?" Tristen asks flat out after swallowing a mouthful of his *manly* meat lasagna.

I hold my breath as we wait for her to answer.

Natty looks up from her plate. "It was fine."

Both her parents narrow their eyes at their youngest.

"Love?" Heather pushes. That's all she needs to say. It's her special mom-power. She can make her kids spill their guts by simply addressing us with her nickname for us. Rhys calls it her attorney hypnosis.

"Fiiine." She sighs dramatically. "In homeroom, some girls talked about how you and Dad are going to go to jail for letting Rhys and Lilly have sex."

Some of the water I was in the middle of drinking goes down the wrong pipe, and I begin to cough violently. Rhys makes a choking sound himself, but Heather and Tristen remain stoic.

I gape at her while Rhys is strangling his fork and knife. Yet, Natty continues as if nothing happened. "Some girls called me names, but I ignored that."

Something tells me this wasn't all, and Tristen seems to come to the same conclusion. "Is there more, Nat?"

She remains mute until her father puts his utensils down at either side of his plate, palms flat next to them, and levels her with a *start talking* glare.

Rhys lets go of his knife and places a hand on my bouncing thigh.

"Vic came up to me after lunch. I ate outside on the front lawn with Olivia, and she kept going on and on about how Lilly faked her kidnapping to distract from what's really been going on. I told her she should go tell her lies somewhere else. That's when she got into my face and pushed me against the shoulder."

Heather's eyes go wide as her daughter recalls the event.

"I dropped the rest of my lunch, but when a teacher came over, Vic took off."

Everyone at the table exhales a sigh of relief until she finishes her recollection.

"My apple rolled down the pathway toward the gate. This reporter guy picked it up for me and gave it back."

My heart stops a beat. Reporter? Since when does the media hang out at Natty's school?

"What reporter, love? You know you're not supposed to talk to the press without Dad or me present." Heather slants her head. Her tone is sincere, but the lawyer in her rises to the surface.

"That was the first time. Swear!" Natty rushes out. "I know I'm not supposed to talk to them." She rolls her eyes as if to say, *I'm not stupid.* "All I said to him was thank you."

"He? Have you seen the guy before?" Rhys inserts himself into the conversation with a hesitant tone, his fingers starting to clench down on my leg. I place my hand over his and pry it off, interlacing our fingers instead.

"Oh yeah, the guy was at the press conference last week. The one in the front with the trench coat. Frank or Francis or something. His name sounded like two first names."

I grip Rhys's hand until I sense one of his fingers crack. He doesn't show any sign of feeling it, though. His jaw is locked as he stares at his little sister.

"Francis Turner?" Tristen asks in confirmation.

*No!*

"Yes! That was it. Like I said, two first names." Natty grins proudly.

I drop Rhys's hand and clamp both of mine over my mouth. Pushing the chair back, I sprint up the stairs and make it to my bathroom just in time before my dinner comes back up.

The man who is after me was at my sister's school. He spoke to her. He took pictures of her. I'm putting her at risk—my entire family. Tears are streaming down my cheeks as I grasp the toilet bowl, retching.

. . .

LATER THAT NIGHT, after I assured my adopted parents that the pain meds must've messed with my stomach, I lie next to Rhys, listening to his even breathing. Instead of lying on his chest, as I have the past four nights, I'm on my stomach beside him. He is facing me on his side, holding my hand between both of his.

Once Heather and Tristen were satisfied that I didn't need medical attention, Rhys helped me change into a fresh t-shirt. I washed my face, and we ended up sitting in the bathroom in front of the vanity.

"Turner did this to scare you. From everything we know, he has no interest in Nat." I'm not sure if he was saying that for his or my benefit.

"I know." I did. But that didn't change the fact that this man had stalked her. And based on him taking the photo of her, it's likely he was the source for the article accusing Heather and Tristen of neglect. Is this all part of his plan? To achieve what? Isolate me from my family. Forcefully removing them from my life by having them accused of a crime they didn't commit.

I can't let this continue.

"Do you want to talk to George? As long as you're at home, he can follow Nat," Rhys suggested. He was right. That *would* be an option.

But that wouldn't keep them safe. "No." I didn't explain myself, and apart from scowling, Rhys didn't press the issue.

Eventually, we settled back in my bed, and long after Rhys fell asleep, I was still watching him.


TAKING in his stunningly gorgeous face in the dim light, my breath hitches. This boy is mine. Knowing what I have to do next makes me want to cling to him, but I'm too scared of waking him up.

As I recall what I said to him not two weeks ago, tears begin to pool. *No matter what happens, no matter where we are or how long we are apart at times, I'm yours. I will always find my way back to you. You are my home.*

When I uttered those words, I didn't expect them to become a reality so soon. I knew we'd be apart eventually, but I thought it would be because of something *trivial* like college.

*I hope he will forgive me—one day.*

Gingerly, I push myself up on all fours and crawl off the bed, careful not to make any sudden movements.

With the burner in hand, I head across the hall to Rhys's bathroom. I can't risk him overhearing this conversation. Sitting on the closed toilet seat, silent tears run down my face. I type in my brother's number but then hesitate.

*No, I don't have a choice.*

Hitting the dial button, it only rings twice before Nate's anxious voice comes through the phone. "What's wrong?"

We haven't spoken since he called about the surveillance camera stills of Turner that George had texted me.

After dropping everything twice for me, George insisted that Nate focus on his life in LA before someone—namely, Hank or Margot—starts asking questions. George has kept me up to date with the progress on the Hector Lakatos front—the call he had to make yesterday—and the lack of progress on the Turner front. Little did we know, he was following Natty.

It's almost midnight in LA. Thanks to my brother's fiancée being a social media serial poster, I know he was at some charity event with her, Celeste, and Julian that ended at eleven.

"I need you to do me a favor." My heart is pounding in my ears, and it takes every ounce of strength to steady my voice. My body wants to break out in violent sobs, but I don't allow myself to lose it.

"Anything. You know that."

"I do."

I haven't told either of them about Turner showing up at Natty's school yet, and I'm going to wait until I see my brother.

"What do you need?" Nate presses carefully.

I take one more breath before speaking the words I have thought but have torn me apart inside since the first article was issued and dragged my family into my mess. "I need to leave."

Nate is quiet for so long that I'm not sure he's still there. "Nate?"

"George will be outside in twenty minutes. Pack only essentials and bring the burner. We'll set you up with everything once you get to your destination."

Relief floods through me, and I whisper, "Thank you."

After a moment, Nate asks, "Does he know?"

*He. Rhys.*

"No."

"I see." His disapproving tone surprises me.

"Can you do one more thing for me?"

He seems to understand the seriousness of the second request and simply replies with, "Yes."

"I need to be able to get a message to Rhys and my family."

"Okay." He doesn't ask why or what. He simply says, "Send me what you want to say from the burner."

Then the line goes dead.

I wrap my arms around my stomach and bend forward. Biting the inside of my cheek, I rock back and forth, letting the tears stream down my face but refusing to make a sound. A metallic taste fills my mouth, and I swallow several times, forcing the coppery taste down my throat. I count to 193 before my body stops shaking and I trust my legs to carry my weight.

Heading back to my room and into the walk-in closet, I move slowly, not to make any sound. I pull out the small duffel bag I stashed in the back of it on the second day after coming home. For some reason, I had a feeling this day would come.

Dropping the bag again, I cover my face with my hands and breathe in slowly. I can still back out. Tell George that I changed my mind.

No. Before I can talk myself out of it, I drop my hands from my face, pick up the bag, and walk back into my bedroom.

The duffel contains everything I need, which is not much. The only thing I add on top of the pile of clothes is the ten-year-old framed photo of Rhys and me from my desk. I can't bear to leave it behind.

I gingerly pull Rhys's old hoodie over my head, wincing as the movement makes the healing skin on my back stretch. I slip into my Adidas Superstars and tighten my hand around the handle of the bag. My vision turns blurry once again as I take one last look at the sleeping boy in my bed.

## CHAPTER NINETY-FOUR

**RHYS**

BLINKING, I REALIZE IT'S STILL DARK OUT—TOO FUCKING EARLY. My body and brain are beat from the last few days. I haven't had a decent night of sleep since Thursday. Though, knowing Lilly gets the rest she needs is all I care about.

*God, I'm tired.*

My eyelids sag again. Turning over, I expect to find Lilly's sleeping body, but instead, my hands touch only the cold, empty sheets. I shove my face into the pillow she slept on not too long ago and inhale deeply. Her scent of vanilla and coconut lingers in the fabric. A picture of her lying on her side, one hand tucked under her cheek, smiling back at me, forms in my mind. I can't wait until I can let my hands roam again, hug her sexy body to mine without the fear of causing her pain. Every time I see the healing burns on her back, the adrenaline coursing through me makes me all twitchy. I have to fight the urge to punch someone—or something, since the person responsible is unavailable.

I lift my head and glance over my shoulder. The bathroom door is open, and the light is off.

After shifting around to push myself up and lean against the headboard, I dig the heels of my hands into my eyes. Waaake uuup.

A buzzing sound comes from the nightstand, and I pull my

hands away from my face. A text message lights up my phone. I glance at the alarm clock. It's not even six.

*No one texts me that early unless*— My heart stutters a beat, and I stare at the device.

When it lights up again with the repeat notification, it's like it's taunting me. I can't move. Lilly is not in bed with me. It's too early for anyone but two people to message. Lilly is not here.

Two minutes later, the third alert makes my phone move across the wooden surface once more. Why the hell did I set the damn thing to three alerts? Oh right, because pussy-whipped me doesn't want to miss a text from his girlfriend.

The illumination of the screen appears like stadium lighting to my heightened senses.

My heart rate has already doubled, but I can't stall any longer. Seeing my hand tremble in the dim light, I reach over, pick up my phone, and tap the screen with my thumb. UNKNOWN.

*Fuck! Fuck! Fuck!*

I want to chuck the device but, instead, clench my fingers around it.

I don't understand. He hasn't used this caller ID since...*before.* Whenever he had contacted me directly, he'd make sure to be extra obnoxious and use "PSYCHO."

I slide my legs off the side of the bed and sit with both hands now clutching the phone. My stomach churns as I tap the screen once more—yup, still there. UNKNOWN. I swallow over the lump in my throat and swipe the message open.

*My Rhys. My best friend. My love.*

*By the time you read this, I'll be on my way. There are no words to describe how sorry and heartbroken I am.*

*I thought I was doing the right thing by coming back. That I could find the answers to my questions while being in Westbridge—while being with you—and move on at the same time. And in the end, once everything is over, for him to be able to take responsibility. But all I have done is bring misery and pain to you, our family, and it is only a matter of time before Wes and Denielle will be part of the crossfire.*

*None of you should have to go through this because of my lie. I asked too much of you by keeping my secret and protecting him for me.*

*I promise you, I tried to stay. I really did. But between the media camping out in front of the house, the potential lawsuits against you and our parents, Katherine targeting me, Natty being bullied in school, and now Turner following her, I couldn't risk it any longer. There are too many odds against us, and I would never forgive myself if something happened to any of you.*

*None of this changes my feelings for you. You are and will always be the love of my life, and I hope with time, you will understand and forgive me. I want nothing more than to build a future with you, but for that, I have to say goodbye to the past and make sure the demons hiding in the dark are no longer following me to find my starlight.*

*I'm getting poetic, and you can probably guess what's been on repeat on my playlist as I'm writing this.*

*I'm sending messages to Heather and Tristen, as well as Den and Wes. Please don't worry about me. I'm going to make sure you have a way of getting in touch with me—if you want to. He promised he would set everything up, and I will contact you as soon as I can. I'm safe with both of them.*

*I LOVE you more than life.*
*Calla*

READING the message two more times, it finally sinks in. She went back to Nate. George picked her up. He fucking picked her up in the dead of night. *Motherfucker!*

I glance around.

Lilly is gone. *Again.*

I'M NUMB.

At first, I was pissed. How could she fucking leave me? *Leave us!* Then I bawled like my mom when she watches those shitty, made-for-TV movies. Why is Lilly giving up on us? After that, I started planning my revenge on everyone who caused her to run—until logic set in. I couldn't do shit about the media or Turner. I was useless. Cue the self-pity. I grabbed one of the pillows off the bed, lifted it to my face, and bit down, letting out the scream that had been building up in my chest since the moment my phone lit up. I screamed until my throat felt like sandpaper, then I sent the pillow flying. It hit something across the room on Lilly's desk, and as I looked over, I noticed the empty spot next to her laptop. Her glass cup with pencils was toppled and broken, its content scattered all over the tabletop. But that was not what changed everything. I didn't give a flying fuck about the damage or glass shards everywhere. She took our picture. She's not coming back. Suddenly, there was nothing. No anger. No sense of loss. No more resentment. Just...numbness. She left me.

Still sitting in the same position as when I read the message, I stare where our picture used to be for years. Light has begun to come through the window when my phone vibrates, this time with an incoming call. It's too soon for it to be Lilly. Wherever Nate sends her, there is no way she's already at her destination. So, I let it go to voicemail. It only takes a couple of seconds before it starts right back up. Resigned, I lift the screen to meet my line of vision: Wes.

*Guess he received his message.*

I accept the call. "Yes?"

"YES? What the fuck is this, dude? Where is she?"

"I don't know." My voice sounds computer-generated. Emotionless.

"You don't know? He fucking doesn't know. HOW THE HELL CAN YOU NOT KNOW?"

"What do you mean he doesn't know?" Denielle's pissed-off bark is audible in the background.

My eyebrows draw together. "Why is D with you at"—I peer over to the nightstand—"6:52 in the morning?"

"I woke him up, asswipe!" Lilly's and, as it seems, now also Wes's best friend sneers. Looks like I'm on speaker.

"Who're you calling an asswipe, *Bulldog*?" My nails dig into the palm that's not holding the phone. Why am I lashing out at her?

None of this is Den's fault. But I am no longer numb. I feel again. Rage. And I want to let it out. She simply gave me an opening.

"Man, I have no idea what's going on with you guys, but—" Wes tries to reason with me, but he gets interrupted by the door to Lilly's room crashing inward with so much force the door handle makes an indentation on the wall.

*Fucking great. Couldn't she have spaced the messages out a bit?*

I spin slowly so one leg is angled on the mattress while the other foot remains on the ground, and I lock eyes with my father—my extremely red-faced, nostril-flared father who, with his wide stance and balled-fists, takes over the entire doorway.

"Where. Is. She?"

I snort and shake my head at the mindfuck I woke up to. Did Lilly really think a simple message saying *I'm fine* would satisfy these people?

"I'm gonna have to call you back," I say into the phone. Not waiting for a response, I press the red button.

"Who was that?" My mother's question comes muffled from behind Dad.

"Wes," I reply in a flat tone. "If you want to be precise, Wes and Denielle, asking the same question."

Mom pushes past my father and slowly walks into the room, scanning it like Lilly is going to pop out from the closet or some shit.

"She's gone, Mom," I snap.

My mother's eyes fly to mine and instantly begin to water.

*Aw, crap.*

I stand up and walk over, wrapping my arms around her. "I'm sorry. I'm just..." I trail off. Maybe remaining numb would've been better after all.

I need to get out of this damn room. The urge to trash every piece of furniture in here is too overpowering. I shift so my arm is around my mom's shoulders and lead her past my father. Thankfully, he lets us by without the third degree.

WE'RE SITTING in the kitchen, Dad in his usual chair at the head of the table. Mom is next to him, both hands strangling the coffee mug in front of her, and Natty is next to our mother, glancing warily between the three of us.

After I led Mom downstairs, I busied myself making coffee. I had to do something to delay the inevitable conversation. Once I placed cups in front of my parents, I leaned against the wall next to the garage door. Arms crossed in front of my chest, I refused to make eye contact. I couldn't. I had no clue what their message from Lilly said, so I wasn't going to make the first move. Resentment was fully present since the numbness had left, but despite her running away, I wasn't going to throw her under the bus.

Just as my father opened his mouth to start what most likely would've been a military-style interrogation, Natty walked in. All eyes turned to her, and my little sister stopped in her tracks, staring like a deer caught in the headlights.

"Uh, what's going on?" Her tone was hesitant.

Without a word, I pushed away from the wall and made my way over. Placing my hand between her shoulder blades, I gently guided her toward the chair next to Mom, followed by planting my ass in the seat at the other end of the table, the space between my family and me serving as a barrier.

Now, I glance at the clock on the microwave. We've been sitting here for seventeen minutes. Someone needs to speak up.

"Where is Lilly?"

*Aw, fuck. Not her.*

My father's eyes swing from Nat, to Mom, to me, and he raises his eyebrows expectantly. Slowly, Mom's gaze follows until three sets are trained on me.

I clear my throat. What the fuck am I supposed to say? Opening my mouth, nothing comes out, so I snap it back shut.

"Is she with him?" My father's question hits me like a push-kick to the balls.

"Uh, what?" is my very profound response.

"Him who?" My mother wrinkles her forehead, her gaze ping-ponging between both ends of the table.

Without taking his eyes off me, Dad answers, "Whoever was on the phone the day I caught her with a burner Rhys did not give her. Whoever was not Wes." His tone is eerily quiet.

*Fuck me.*

My lips part. "Uh..."

My father slams his flattened palms onto the tabletop, and everyone jumps. "DAMN IT, RHYS! Start fucking talking. I'm sick of your secrets."

My secrets? Is he for real? I bare my teeth at him. He wants to play this game? Bring it on! I mimic the position of his hands, but instead of remaining in my chair, I shove myself up and look down at Colonel Tristen McGuire. "My secrets?" I seethe. "*You're* one to talk."

My father scowls at me, and I cock my head in a challenge, daring him to push me. I'm ninety-nine percent certain Mom has no clue about the surveillance features in her home.

The wheels in his brain are turning. He can't figure out how much I know. Past caring, I raise one eyebrow and peer toward the corner where one of the cameras is located. Looking back, I smirk, and my father's face pales.

*Who is keeping secrets now?*

"Rhys?" My mother inserts herself into the standoff, and I glance to the side. "She says she has to leave for us to be safe. What does she mean by that? Where is my daughter?" The floodgates open, and tears are streaming down her face again. Natty wipes under her nose to stifle her sniffling, and Dad reaches over and takes one of Mom's hands.

He exhales a long breath, and calmer than before, he pleads with me, "Please tell us where she is. All we ever wanted was to keep her safe."

His change in demeanor momentarily throws me off. I can handle angry, pissed-off Tristen McGuire. Even scary, Marine Corps Tristen McGuire. But the desperate father...

My anger disintegrates. How much does she want me to reveal? I rub my palms over my face.

"Fuck," I mumble into my cupped hands. Pulling my hands away, I lock eyes with my father. "Lilly is with her family."

"Oh, my God!" Mom's eyes widen in shock.

"Excuse me?"

I think, for the first time in my life, I've truly stunned him.

"What family?" My mother's voice is shaking.

I have to give them something, but telling them who Nate is... I refuse to betray Lilly in that way, even though she *left* me. Instead, I stall. "What did her message say?"

My father's mouth flattens. He doesn't like to be the one who's not in charge. After a moment, he concedes, "She said she had to go away to keep us safe. That the reporter that showed up at Natty's school is not who he says he is and that she is afraid that if she stays, she puts us in danger." Natty stiffens next to our mother, and Mom wraps her arm around her. Dad continues mercilessly. "I'm asking you again, son. Who is Lilly with?"

Still standing, I finally lower myself back into the chair and cross my arms over my chest. "Her brother."

What I see next on my parents' faces confuses the shit out of me. Relief. Both school their features quickly, but I know what I saw.

*What the hell?*

"I don't understand. What brother?" Mom is the first to speak up.

Time to lie my ass off. Again. One would think this is second nature for me by now. "After she came back, her biological brother got in touch with her."

"How does she know this person is who he says he is?" My mother has gone into lawyer mode, and Dad lets her take the lead.

"Henry was not her father." I give them a pointed look. Lilly had blurted that out the day in my father's office, so from a timeline perspective, I'm telling the truth. Though, I am also convinced they knew that already. "They did a sibling DNA test," I continue, pulling shit out of my ass.

I want to smack my forehead and pat my back at the same time.

"Why does she believe she is safer with this...person? Who is he?"

I have to be careful about my next words. "I've never spoken with him in person." Not a lie. Face to face, yes. In person, no. "He has the means to keep her safe. She said she'd be in touch once she gets there. You can ask her yourself when she calls." The ice is getting thinner, and I'm sick of the lies. The part of me that resents Lilly for leaving me wants her to sweat as she comes up with an explanation for our parents.

Dad is about to speak when the front door opens, and Wes,

followed by Denielle, stalks in. Seems like Wes still has the spare key I gave him years ago. My two friends take in the scene in the kitchen, and my father sighs. The conversation is over. He's not going to push the topic with them around, no matter how much they already know. He slowly raises himself out of the chair. "I'll be in my office." Before he rounds the corner to the hallway, his eyes meet mine. "We're not done."

Of course we're not. He'll probably boot up all the cameras in the house, hoping to catch something between Denielle, Wes, and me.

Mom shuffles Natty to the stove, ordering her gently to help with breakfast. It seems to have become Mom's go-to way of distraction. I doubt anyone wants food at this point, but I don't give a fuck.

With my friends on my heels, I make my way upstairs.

# CHAPTER NINETY-FIVE

## HER

*"WHAT DO YOU MEAN SHE IS ON HER WAY TO CALIFORNIA?" I shriek into the phone. Deep breaths. I need to control my temper.*

*I don't like talking to this imbecile directly. Informant or not, I avoid speaking to him when possible. That's what the encrypted emails are for. But when I received his message five minutes ago, I immediately dialed his cell phone.*

*"I notified you as soon as possible," he defends himself. "He sent the jet to Westbridge in the middle of the night. I wasn't able to message until now. I didn't have my laptop, and you said not to call you directly."*

*Dear Lord, his high-pitched lamenting makes me want to stab the wine opener I'm still holding in my hand into his jugular and watch him bleed all over himself. I smile at the visual forming in my head. That would be the highlight of my week.*

*Glancing at my white knuckles wrapped around the Code38—a gift from my sweet girl—I force myself to unclench my hand and slowly place the tool on the table in front of me. Focus.*

*Why is Nate bringing Lilly to California? How could that happen? That doesn't make sense. Something must have triggered the move.*

*"Where is he?" I growl into the phone. What do I pay this idiot for? I'm losing patience with him.*

*"I haven't been able to reach him since he woke me up. My best guess? He is on the plane."*

*What? Why would he risk getting seen together with her?*

*The closing of a door alerts me that I'm no longer alone. I turn to see Gray making his way to the cream-and-white barrel accent chair I had him pick up the day we moved into this dump. He lets himself fall into the cushion, his unkempt exterior in contrast with my clean décor. Per usual, he displays no manners and just barged in without knocking.*

*I hold his gaze as I speak into the phone. How do you know that the jet is not picking up Weiler?"*

*Gray frowns when understanding sets in. His eyes bulge for a fraction of a second before he averts them, and he begins to fidget with his black KA-BAR. It's a habit I don't believe he's aware of. He never leaves the knife out of his sight. For as long as I've known this man, he's always had a blade with him. This particular knife is a remnant from his active military days. Maybe it makes him feel less of a failure than he is. And whenever he is nervous or on edge, he pulls it out.*

*I narrow my eyes at Gray. Without a word, I disconnect the call and slowly make my way across the room until I stand between his legs. When he just stares ahead, I place my pointer finger under his chin and forcefully tilt it up. He doesn't put up a fight, but the little nudge that is needed confirms my suspicion.*

*"Do you have anything to tell me?" I keep my tone calm, but my other hand automatically clenches at my side.*

*When the man I've known most of my life finally locks eyes with me, I know he is to blame for Lilly's sudden departure. I bend down and pry the knife out of his hand, slowly moving the sharp tip down his leg.*

*"Gray," I warn.*

*He draws in a breath. "I went to the little McGuire's school. She saw me." His admission is no more than a whisper.*

*Without hesitation, I raise the hand holding his prized possession and bring it down on his thigh. The blade slides in without resistance, and it reminds me of that day thirteen years ago. The day I got my revenge. He also saw the knife coming, just like Gray today. But he never expected me to have the guts to pull through with my threat. My threat of cutting his eye out if he so much as looked at me again.*

*Gray's spasming in front of me rips me out of the memory. He's gripping the armrests of the chair but not making a sound. He knows better.*

*I let go of the hilt and straighten. Looking down, I see a speck of blood on the linen covering my legs. Just wonderful. I just bought these. I open the drawstring that holds the pants up and let them fall. Stepping out, I leave them in front of the chair and head toward the door. "Get everything ready. We're going to California."*

*I pull the door shut behind me and leave him to clean up the mess in my office.*

# CHAPTER NINETY-SIX

**LILLY**

It's pitch black. Dark clouds cover the night sky. It's as if the impending storm is a reflection of the havoc my life has become.

Through sheer luck, Lancaster was passed out—asleep, not literally—in his car. George was prepared to distract him somehow, but for once, something worked in our favor.

I stumbled twice due to my trembling legs as I crept along the fence to meet George two properties down the road. The second time, I remained on my hands and knees for several minutes, trying to get my breathing under control. I didn't bother wiping the tears away anymore. The moment I stepped out the back door, I let them fall freely.

We've been driving for forty-five minutes, and neither of us has said a word. Even when I opened the passenger door and climbed into the Navigator—which I finally identified today—George just gave me a solemn look. He disapproves of my decision. I almost wish he'd say something, yell at me, tell me I'm making a mistake. The silence is worse. It leaves me alone with my thoughts, regrets, doubt...guilt.

His phone has lit up a few times, but he would just check it and then place it back in the cup holder without responding.

I shift restlessly, trying to keep my healing back away from the seat. But no matter how I position myself, eventually the muscles in my back (upper and lower), my neck, even my butt start cramping. Driving anywhere for longer than five minutes in my current physical state is as pleasant as running a marathon wrapped in barbed wire.

Eventually, I can't take the quiet anymore and whisper, "Please say something."

George takes a deep breath, and I prepare myself for a scolding, but instead, he reaches over and gives my knee a gentle pat. I don't think George has ever initiated physical contact with anyone in the few weeks I've known him.

"I will do whatever it takes to keep you, your brother, and your family safe. Rhys will not take it well; you have to prepare yourself for the consequences. But I'm sure you've thought long and hard about it."

His insinuation is clear: I haven't thought this through.

That's where he's wrong. I've been thinking of nothing else since Turner revealed himself at the press conference. It's all connected; I can feel it. Despite it being the opposite of support for my decision, his words bring the reason "why" back to the forefront of my mind, pushing the guilt and doubt further back. The longer I stayed, the more I put my family in danger.

*I'm doing the right thing.*

We're parked inside a hangar of a small private airfield in God knows where.

After our brief conversation, we drove for another twenty minutes. George pulled up to a gate, exchanged a few hushed words with the security guard stationed there, and then pulled in. Through all of it, I averted my face out of the window. Keeping a low profile has become my number one priority.

Whenever doubt and guilt tried to take hold again, I kept repeating *'You're doing the right thing'* silently in my head. I know this will be a continuous battle until I can speak to Rhys and explain myself. *Rhys.* My throat closes up, and I squeeze my eyes shut.

*I'm doing the right thing. I'm protecting the people I love.*

Once George stops the Navigator in the back of the structure, near a small office space, he gets out and walks around the SUV. He opens the passenger door, staring at me expectantly.

"It's warmer in the office, Miss Lilly. There is a heater in there. It'll be a while." His tone is low yet commanding.

I unbuckle myself, swing my legs out, and let my feet hit the ground. The slap of my soles echoes through the massive hangar as I trail behind my bodyguard. Inside the square room is a metal desk, a few metal chairs, and a military-style cot.

"What is this place?" I scowl.

"The best I could come up with on such short notice. We can't fly commercial now, can we?" George deadpans, walking past me and depositing my duffel bag on the table with a thud.

I slowly follow him. "So, how are we getting...wherever we're going."

He swivels around and leans against the desk, leveling me with a glare that gives me the chills. He is truly disappointed in me for *running*. "Nate is sending the jet. But since we have to stay under the radar—the Altman jet does not necessarily blend in—I had to find a private airport that will keep this under wraps."

*Meaning, my brother had to drop a good chunk of change.*

Guilt charges to the front like a 5.56 leaving the barrel of an M-4, and I swallow hard.

"We have approximately another three hours; you might as well get some rest." He nods toward the cot.

I blow out a non-comical breath. Is he joking? There's no way in hell I'll be able to sleep. Nonetheless, I sink onto the makeshift bed and pull out my phone, aka the burner. Plugging in headphones, I click on the notes app and start typing. "Good Goodbye" by Linkin' Park and "Under Your Scars" by Godsmack are blaring on constant repeat through the small speakers into my ears. As soon as I type the first word, my vision blurs, and by the third line, I can barely make out the screen. A George-like shape, distorted by my tears, is watching me closely, but he remains mute.

The tightness in my chest constricts my airflow, and I have to stop multiple times to put my head between my legs.

*I'm doing the right thing. Please forgive me.*

Signing Rhys's message with his nickname for me feels like the end. I refuse to believe that it's the end for us. It can't be. But the mere thought of him not forgiving me... My fingers are shaking so badly I drop the phone. George is at my side in two strides and clasps my hands between his.

"Please, look at me."

*I can't.*

"Miss Lilly. Look at me!" My body automatically obeys at his order.

He levels me with a look that is equally stern as it is...empathetic? My eyebrows draw together, and I study him. Emotions I have never seen flicker across his face. It's like he's lost in his own memory for a second.

"I'm not going to lie to you. I don't agree with your decision." I open my mouth, but he cuts me off. "However, I understand it." *He does?* "I had to make a similar decision once...leave someone behind that I cared about. The difference between you and me is, though, I believe you and Rhys will have a happy ending. He will be angry with you, but he loves you. You will find a way to work it out."

I'm not sure what to say. He left someone? Is that why he is so distant? Instead of responding, I wrap my arms around him and hold on tight. After a moment, he places his hands on either side of my head and pulls back gently. He forces me to make eye contact, and then...he smiles at me—a genuine, heartwarming smile.

"It will be okay."

And I believe him. Next are Den's and Wes's messages, saving the one for Heather and Tristen for last. Those ones are easier. Maybe because I'm all cried out. Maybe because I do trust George's words.

I decide to give my friends a watered-down version of Rhys's, that with Turner showing up at Natty's school and her being targeted by Katherine's sister, I can't risk anyone coming after them as well. When I get to Heather and Tristen's, I stare at the screen for a long time. I have no clue how much to reveal to them, so I settle on the half-truth. Turner is not who he pretends to be, and I'm scared for their safety if I stay. I start typing that I am with family but then erase the words and end the message with *Please know that I'm safe and that I will call as soon as I can. Love, Lilly.*

After reading over everything one more time, I send each

message to Nate. My brother responds within minutes that he will make sure my family and friends will receive my notes. Glancing at the little clock in the corner, I'm surprised to see that it's not even six. We've only been here for about an hour and a half—over two more to go. I lie down on my side, clutching the burner in both hands. "Unstoppable" by Red starts playing, and I want to laugh at the irony. I don't turn it off, though. Instead, I scroll through the pictures that somehow made it onto the device. It's the same folder that I found on my phone at the vineyard, and I suspect Nate transferred them on somehow before George gave it to Rhys.

"MISS LILLY." Someone gently touches my arm. My eyes spring open, and I jackknife up.

*Shit, my back does not take the abrupt motion lightly.*

"Oww," I moan and try to focus my eyes. "Did I fall asleep?"

George stands above me, and the answer is kind of obvious, but he indulges me. "You did. The jet just landed and will be here in a few minutes. It's time to go."

My pulse picks up. It's time to go. Last chance to back out. But even as the thought crosses my mind, I know returning to Westbridge is not an option until Turner is out of the picture.

At that moment, the noise level rises to the point of having to cover my ears, the metal structure amplifying the sound of the jet's engines as it rolls in.

I step beside George right outside the office, and we wait for the aircraft to come to a halt. Men who I hadn't noticed before and, I assume, belong to the small airstrip jog over and start working on the plane. They put the chocks in, and one heads to a fuel truck parked right outside the hangar doors.

My heart is beating in my throat as I watch the door lower. A flight attendant—no, one of the pilots appears in the opening and descends the steps. He gives George a curt nod and makes his way to the airport employee.

"That is Joel. He is Nate's personal..." He trails off, and I follow his gaze to see what has him distracted.

My hands fly to my mouth, and my feet take off of their own volition until I am full-on sprinting. I reach him at the same time he steps onto the concrete floor and jump, wrapping my legs and arms around him like a monkey.

Sobs wrack through my body as his hands try to hold onto me without touching my injuries.

"Hey, sis. Shhh, it's all good," my brother coos, and it instantly calms the turmoil inside of me.

I pull back, and he lets me sink to my feet.

"What are you doing here?" My fingers keep clutching Nate's sleeves, afraid he'll vanish into thin air if I let go.

"I would like to know the same thing. What were you thinking?" George's voice comes from behind me.

"I was thinking that my sister needs me," Nate snaps in a tone I have never heard him use toward George.

I nervously glance around, expecting the workers and pilot to watch the exchange, but no one pays us any attention.

George steps closer to my brother. His next words are a low growl that would make most grown men pee their pants. "Get. On. That. Fucking. Jet. Nathan Edward Denton Hamlin. Or I will *put* you on it." He jabs his index finger at Nate's chest.

Oh crap, George using the F-bomb is not a good sign.

*Wait... Edward Denton?*

I peer at my brother out of the corner of my eye, not turning my back on George. I know he would never do anything to hurt me, but his current demeanor—despite no longer being scared of him—makes the blood in my veins run cold.

Nate rolls his eyes and grabs my hand, pulling me behind him onto the plane. "George will get your stuff. Won't you?" he remarks with a smirk.

I don't dare make eye contact with the man behind me.

The door is located at the rear, and my eyes bulge as I follow Nate on board. The inside is everything you imagine a private jet to be—and more. A door to the right is ajar and leads into a bathroom —an actual bathroom, not just one of those airplane lavatories you have to be anorexic to fit in and still can't turn around. The color scheme is light yet sophisticated. Each of the cream-colored leather seats could easily fit two people. There are eight in total, two opposite each other with a small table between them. Toward the front of the plane is a couch on one side with a bar across from it. A small kitchen area, a seat for a flight attendant, and the door to the cockpit could be closed off by a curtain, which is currently held back by a hook that looks like it's made of gold. *It probably is*. An almost-white carpet covers the floor, and a matching runner lays in the middle row.

Keeping everything this pristine must be challenging.


THE JET TAKES off an hour later.

As we gain speed on the runway, my heart is hammering out of my chest, not because I'm scared of flying, but because of the unknown. I feel like I'm in the dark again—this time because of the future, not the past.

I curl up in one of the buttery-soft leather seats in the back. George stretched out on the couch, one arm over his eyes, after he had placed my bag on an empty spot across the aisle as soon as he boarded the plane. The next few hours are probably the only rest he'll get.

Nate sits across from me, his laptop in front of him on the table. He's been typing away since he made himself comfortable there—right after he showed me around the aircraft.

"I forwarded your messages as soon as you sent them."

My eyes snap to his. I hadn't even considered that he could send them while he was on his way here. He must've sensed my confusion, because he elaborates, "The jet has Wi-Fi. I wouldn't be able to work otherwise. I've spent a lot of time in the air over the years." The corner of his mouth quirks up.

*Oh.*

"Do we know if they got them?" My whispered question is barely audible over the pounding in my ears.

He clenches his mouth before speaking. "No. They were delivered and received by the devices, but I didn't have time to write a routine to check if they read them. I would assume they did, based on the time." He tilts his wrist, and I notice the fancy-looking watch on his arm for the first time. He follows my gaze and mumbles, "A gift. I was still wearing it when I left the house."

I smile at him. He always appears so...embarrassed?...uncomfortable?...when he has to showcase his money.

"You still haven't told me what happened," my brother prods carefully.

I draw in a shaky breath and expel it at the same rate. "Turner was at Natty's school."

Nate's eyes widen, and George sits up instantly.

*I guess he wasn't sleeping after all.*

I tell them about Natty being targeted by the kids at school, specifically Katherine's little sister, and conclude how she recalled Turner showing up during her lunch break.

"We need to figure out what he wants. His endgame." George has switched to security mode.

"I'll start digging more into his past. There has to be something, and I haven't gone back far enough." Nate immediately starts typing on his laptop.

"Can you do that from here?" I don't even attempt my surprise.

He glances up between his fingers flying over the keyboard. "Don't be silly, sis. I would never do that on such a minimally secured network. I'm letting Hank know that I am taking tomorrow off as well."

Nate just snubbed me. What the—?

THE REMAINDER of the flight is uneventful. Unable to do anything until we land, George resumes his pose on the couch, and eventually, he does fall asleep—soft snoring being the dead giveaway. Nate works on his laptop, and I listen to my playlist on repeat, letting the tears fall as they come. He looks up every so often but then leaves me to deal with it. If I want to talk about it, I will, and he knows that.

As we descend, the pilot's voice comes over the intercom. "We are approaching LA and will be landing shortly. Nate, I confirmed that your car is waiting for you in the hangar and that George's truck was also brought in."

Nate presses a button. "Thank you, Joel."

"Won't he wonder who I am? To you?" I assume everyone has seen my name plastered in the media by now.

"He won't."

That's all my brother gives me, and his expression tells me not to ask any further questions.

After touchdown, the jet taxis directly into a similar structure as we departed from. However, this one screams private airport, not dingy drug-smuggling airfield. As I peer out the window, I see a massive sign on the wall reading *Altman*, and my eyes widen.

Nate gets up and digs through a bag, pulling out a plain hoodie and a baseball cap. "Put this on."

I look down at myself. "I'm already wearing a hoodie."

Before he can respond, George steps up to us. "Yes, but yours has your school's logo on it. If anyone would take a picture right now, they could easily trace it back." After a pause, he adds, "Leave your hair inside the hood, pull the hat down low, and put these on." He grabs something from Nate's hand and presses a pair of black Wayfarers into mine.

I argue that I'll stick out like a sore thumb like this, but Nate assures me that Californians dress like Eskimos in seventy-degree weather, and no one will look twice.

*Well, okay then.*

HE WAS RIGHT. I don't get a second glance as I follow Nate to a fancy-looking car, which he identifies as an Aston Martin One-77. The first image in my head is how Rhys and Wes would drool over this *vehicle*. I shut down that train of thought as fast as it came—I can't go there. I can't break down in public.

George will follow us in his truck, a matte-gray monstrosity with blacked-out windows that would make Tristen proud. As we pass him leaving the airport, I'm able to recognize it as a RAM 3500.

We drive for almost two hours. LA traffic is something one has to experience to understand. Holy crap, what a cluster. Where are all these people coming from—or going to—in the middle of the day?

When we enter a neighborhood like ones I have only ever seen on TV, I crane my neck to take it all in. One wrought-iron gate after the next. Behind some, you can see mansions that make the vineyard look like a mobile home. Others have an endless driveway with no house in sight.

"Nate?" The awe in my voice is apparent.

"Hmm?" His shoulders are tense, and he doesn't look away from the road.

"Where are you taking me?" I don't think he would bring me to his house.

"My parents'," he replies absently.

It takes me a moment to grasp the meaning. He's letting me stay at his childhood home. The home he has barely set foot in in over ten years. My father's house.

"Nate," I choke out his name. "You don't have to. I can stay at a hotel or..."

"This is your house as much as it is mine," he cuts me off. "And this way...maybe I can associate that place with something good again."

Tears prick at my eyes. "Thank you," I whisper.

This time he turns to me. "For what?"

"For being here."

---

# CHAPTER NINETY-SEVEN

---

### LILLY

I DIDN'T THINK I WOULD BE ABLE TO FALL ASLEEP LAST NIGHT, but I was out as soon as my head hit the pillow. That's what staying up for almost two days will do—and still recovering from getting attacked by delusional high school girls with no backbones.

After we arrived, everything was a blur. Nate showed me around the mansion—there was no way to call this place a house. The bottom floor alone could fit Heather and Tristen's entire square footage twice, if not more. And did I mention that it had three stories with a full finished basement? Talk about ostentatious. This was *worse* than the vineyard.

The kitchen was fully stocked, and when I raised my eyebrows to my brother, he explained he had the house readied for me. No one had lived here since Brooks, so it had to be cleaned top to bottom and the pantry filled.

Still staring at the packets of instant oats and pasta in front of me, reality crashed in. This was where my father took his life, where Nate found the letters—the reason his mother and sister were dead. I shouldn't have been here. A simple motel would do just fine. As I expressed my concern, Nate pretended like I hadn't spoken at all and continued the tour. Acting oblivious was his way of coping, but it didn't stop the voices in my head.

The first floor consisted of several living spaces. Why would one need two dining and four living rooms? There wasn't even a TV—apparently, that was what the theater room was for. The second floor had several guest rooms, Brooks's home office, a library, an art studio—Payton loved to paint, as Nate informed me with a sad smile on his face—and Audrey's playroom. Nothing had been touched since the last resident of the home...*left*. The more I saw, the more I felt like an intruder.

We stood in the library, overlooking the back of the property, when thoughts of Rhys crept into my mind. I'd refused to go there since we spoke about the messages and Turner on the plane. Allowing my brain to even think his name brought me too close to my breaking point. I instinctively wrapped my arms around myself as if the gesture would make the ache disappear.

My brother glanced down at me. "Do you want to call him?" His tone was careful.

A pit opened up in my stomach. I wanted to talk to him more than anything, but at the same time, I was terrified of him not wanting to speak to me.

My inner conflict must've been apparent because he answered his own question for me. "I'll let him know that you are safe and that you'll call him tomorrow. I'll bring a computer over from my place in the morning and teach you how to initiate encrypted video chats. The burner is still just set up to call George's and my numbers." After a pause, he added, "If that is okay with you?"

All I could do was nod, my voice not working as I tried to keep the sob steadily building in my throat locked in.

"'Kay." He gave my shoulder a squeeze. "Let's find you a place to sleep."

Nate turned and led the way toward the staircase leading to the third floor where the family's bedrooms were. As we ascended, he informed me that there were two more guest rooms upstairs, besides his parents', Audrey's, and his old bedroom. He'd be staying in the other one, whichever one I didn't pick, and George would be on the second floor. I could choose between any of the spare rooms, but he'd prefer me to be on the top floor. I dipped my head in confirmation and then picked the first room he showed me. Funny enough, it was very similar to my room at the vineyard *and* in Westbridge. The nightstand and dresser were white with black hardware, the king-size bed had a gray, upholstered wingback headboard, though way fancier than the one I had gotten from our local furniture store in Virginia, and a matching bench sat at the foot of it. The bedding was a white pin-tuck duvet; however, the accents were cream and gold instead of lavender. If that also would've been the same, I would've walked right back out.

George was busy for the rest of the day, setting up a security perimeter since nothing besides an alarm system had ever been installed. Nate admitted that—in the past—he didn't *give two shits* if someone broke in, so he never bothered putting in one of his designs. By the end of the day, wireless cameras were set up outside on the property and at the entrances to the house. That would have to do for now.

Around 6:30, the three of us ate in silence, but I excused myself immediately after. Before we sat down, Nate had disappeared for about an hour and later assured me Rhys knew I was safe. He wouldn't elaborate on how he had communicated with him, and I was too scared to ask. What if he had spoken to him personally? What if Rhys had told him he wouldn't forgive me for leaving? I forced the dinner down simply because I hadn't eaten all day, but I didn't remember what we had.

I EMERGE from my room sometime after eight in the morning. I had slept for almost thirteen hours, and despite the multitude of conflicting emotions that have been wreaking havoc in my body and mind, I am semi-rested—at least physically.

George sits in the breakfast nook—nook being used loosely, as it could easily fit an entire football team—and is reading one of his weathered books. Nate is nowhere in sight. Pulling out the chair closest to him, I lower myself down, careful not to let my healing skin make contact with anything.

"Where's Nate?"

Without taking his eyes off his reading material, he replies, "He went to his house to pick up some items."

I stare at him for a long moment. "George?"

"Yes, Miss Lilly?" He won't look at me, and my chest constricts.

"Are you still mad at me?" My question is a barely audible whisper. "For leaving," I add.

This makes him pause, and his fingers tighten around the paperback. He slowly closes his book and places it down before turning toward me. "I am not angry with you, Miss Lilly. Never was. I am..." George lets his gaze wander to the opposite wall, where it lingers for several moments before returning to me. "Concerned."

My eyebrows pull together.

*Concerned?*

He draws in a deep breath. "For you. I have only been concerned for one person for over a decade, and that was your brother." There is a beat of silence before the corners of his mouth pull up, and the sudden boyish smirk shocks me almost as much as when he had reprimanded Nate yesterday. "Your brother was never in physical danger. He could take care of himself—for the most part. I'm not used to being worried like this about someone anymore. Not since —" He cuts himself off, and I want to ask who he's talking about. "If something happened to you—something else"—he is referring to the attack—"it would destroy Nate. He wouldn't come back from that. And he would not be the only one. You have the ability to wrap people around your finger."

My face heats, and I'm speechless. Emotion clogs my throat, but before I can go all mushy on the Altman Head of Security, he gets up and makes his way over to the stove, turning on the kettle.

"Earl Grey, Miss Lilly?"

I smile. It looks like our *moment* is over.

"Yes, please."

I SIT AT THE ISLAND, my hands wrapped around the now empty mug, and let my gaze wander through the three sets of French doors. The property behind the mansion is as grand as the house itself. The bluestone patio is visible as far as the eye can see through the glass. There is an inground lap pool with adjoining hot tub and lush green grass that has been well cared for even if no one lived here.

Around ten, Nate walks in from the hallway leading to the

garage. He balances a large white box in one hand while two black duffel bags are strapped over each shoulder.

"Too lazy to walk twice?" George remarks in a dry tone as he faces my brother.

Nate places the box next to me on the island. "Nope, just left the heavy stuff for you."

Their comfortable banter is new, and I don't know if Nate is this relaxed because I am finally where he has wanted me for the past week or if it's something else. My gaze ping-pongs between the two men, waiting for what happens next. I expect everything from George pulling his Glock—which is strapped to his side at all times—to walking over and smacking my brother over the head. Instead, his stoic face is on full display, and all he does is glower at Nate for several breaths before he walks out, muttering to himself.

I focus back on my brother. "What's all this?" I dip my head toward the items he deposited in front of me.

He unzips the first bag and reveals enough electronic equipment to put one of those Best Buy stores Dad dragged us to as kids out of business.

"What the—?" My eyebrows shoot upward.

"Everything you'll need, little sis." He shoves his hand into his jeans pocket, and something flies toward me. "Oh, and here."

I barely catch the object.

"Happy Birthday." He looks like the Cheshire cat.

*This grin is never good.*

Slowly, I glance down and frown at the item in my palm. Is that —? My eyes shoot back up. "You're giving me a car?"

Nate shrugs nonchalantly. "Well, it's kind of my fault you totaled your Jeep. So, it's appropriate I replace it."

I turn the key fob over and suck in a breath. "A Mercedes?" My voice is shrill, and I'm not sure if it's from shock or excitement. My rapid pulse could be from either.

Misinterpreting my outburst, his face falls. "If you don't like it, you can buy something else."

"Don't like it? ARE YOU NUTS?" I jump off the barstool and tackle my brother. "Thank you, thank you, thank you!"

He chuckles. "You don't even know what model it is."

I squeeze tighter. "I don't care." Peering up at him, I add, "I know you. You would never give me anything less than the best. You don't do *average*."

The corner of his mouth tilts up. "Guess you *do* know me."

Suddenly, I feel like someone has punched me in the stomach, and I jerk back. Nate scowls, about to say something, when my hands fly to my mouth, and I blink against the stinging sensation in my eyes.

*It's my birthday. My eighteenth birthday.*

"What's wrong?" He gently grabs me by the upper arms.

I haven't been away from Rhys on my birthday for as long as I can remember. Even when we didn't speak, he was always there that day—in the background, but he was there. Tears stream down my face, and I press my lips together, not to start sobbing uncontrollably.

"Good Lord, Nate. What did you do now?" George's exasperated tone brings me back to the present.

I wipe under my nose. "I'm sorry. It's just..."

"Rhys?" Nate concludes in a flat tone.

I nod. The waterfall is back in full force. I'm such a mess. I left to keep them safe then break down if someone just mentions his name.

"Let me set up the system, and we can call him?" Nate phrases it more like a question.

I want to hear his voice more than anything, but— I cut my thoughts off.

"What am I supposed to say? He probably hates me." The words barely make it out of my mouth.

"He doesn't hate you."

My head jerks in George's direction, who is depositing several medium-size moving boxes near the door to the foyer. His statement is spoken matter-of-factly.

"You talked to him." I hiccup yet manage to sound accusatory.

"I have."

"How?" My rasped question is followed by a growl from my brother. "Why is this the first time I'm hearing of this?"

*I brought the burner with me.*

"He messaged me last night. He has my number memorized, as you know." The unspoken *duh* is like a slap to the face. George continues without waiting for one of us to answer. "He wanted to know where you are and if I'm with you. I confirmed that I am but didn't tell him the location. He told Heather and Tristen that you are with family—"

"WHAT THE FUCK?" Nate's outburst makes me jump, and he drops his hands from my arms.

*He what?*

I press my hand against my chest, feeling my heartbeat under my palm.

"Rhys had to give Heather and Tristen something. What did you two expect?" George's irritation is apparent. All that's missing is the eye roll.

My chin starts wobbling again, and his eyes soften. "He is not angry with you, Miss Lilly. He is...confused."

"Confused?" Nate scoffs.

George flexes his jaw. "Get everything set up so Miss Lilly can talk to her boyfriend. She doesn't have to give him a location, but she does owe him an explanation face to face."

As much as his words sting, he is right.

"Whatever." My brother grabs one of the bags and marches toward the back staircase. "Bring the rest to the office," he barks at no one in particular, and I scramble for the second bag, even though I'm pretty sure he didn't mean me.

BY THE TIME I reach the top of the landing, Nate is nowhere in sight. He said office, so I assume he meant Brooks's home office. During yesterday's tour, he pointed out the room but only stared at the door. The look on his face as we stood in the hallway for several minutes made it clear that he still has a lot of unresolved issues with our father.

My father's office was the only one I didn't get to see, so my steps are hesitant. Slowly reaching out for the handle, George's voice comes from behind. "He's not in there."

I whip around, scowling at him.

*I'm going to attach a bell to this man.*

"This room hasn't been opened in a decade," George explains in a gentler tone than he used downstairs. "Besides the cleaning personnel, that is."

"Oh."

"He's in here." Turning around, he makes his way three doors down.

Following him at a slower pace, I step over the threshold and come to an abrupt halt. I try to take everything in, but my brain has a hard time catching up. This was one of the guest rooms yesterday, complete with a four-poster bed, dresser, armchair, and stand-up mirror. The low-sitting, cognac armchair is still there, and so is the tall, rustic-looking mirror, but the bed...is gone.

"What happened in here?" I mumble as I make my way farther into the...new office?

Nate straightens from the desk he is leaning over while attaching cables to various monitors. "You needed a place to work." His casualness makes my brows pinch together.

"Where is the bed? And the dresser?" I spin in a circle.

"In the basement," George inserts with a slight grudge. "Your brother decided to change his career to interior designer while you were sleeping."

"Oh, shut up, old man. You were just as excited to pick out the office chair as I was." Nate is now under the table, messing with more cables.

I smirk as their banter distracts me from what we're about to do. *Who* I'm about to talk to.

"What can I help with?" I carry over the bag.

"I'll show you how to set up a secure network so you know for the future. It won't be anything like mine but enough to get you started and call h—uh...Rhys."

It sounded like he was about to say *home*, but I let that go. Instead, I squat down and let my brother give me networking lessons.

## CHAPTER NINETY-EIGHT

**RHYS**

**Lilly is safe. She arrived at her destination and will contact you tomorrow.**

As everyone in the house is most likely fast asleep, I sit at the edge of my bed and stare at the message I received from UNKNOWN earlier this evening. I'm sure Dad's spyware alerted him of the incoming text, but so far, he has not started his interrogation. Why? Who the fuck knows these days?

*Tomorrow*. This one word makes me want to launch the phone across the room. She can't even let me know herself that she's okay. Wherever she is. What the fuck happened to us? Everything was fine—as fine as it could have been.

If someone would've told me, twenty-four hours ago, that Lilly would run away in a cloak-and-dagger operation while I was sleeping in her bed, I would've laughed in the fucker's face.

I focus on breathing through my nose until the red haze in my vision turns to a faint pink. My pulse has calmed enough for rational thoughts to make their way back into my brain. I refuse to accept that I have to wait another day.

Opening up a new message, I enter the number I memorized weeks ago: **I want to know where she is.**

The little bubble with the three dots pops up within seconds. **I cannot tell you that.**

**WTF, G? She left me in HER bed and snuck out. U picked her up. I thought u were against her leaving.**

It takes several minutes until the reply appears. At that point, I already assumed he wouldn't respond at all.

**Rhys, as you know, your phone's activity is being tracked. I can assure you that she is safe, and she will contact you as soon as everything is set up. We are working on it. She didn't make the decision lightly. She is worried for her family and friends. For you.**

Understanding hits that he *can't* tell me shit since my father would instantly know.

"FUCK!" I jump up and reach my desk within two strides, swiping everything on it to the floor in one motion. "AAARRRG." A roar leaves my throat, but I'm past caring who hears me. When no one, aka my father, bursts through the door, gun swinging, I look back at the screen. George needs to give me something. I don't give a flying fuck anymore who finds out.

**Can u give me an idea when she'll call?**

*Great, now I sound like a whiney toddler again.*

This time the answer is instant: **No.**

Motherfucker! My arm lifts to chuck the phone, but I catch myself at the last second.


At 5:47 A.M., my bedroom door flies open. I still haven't gone to bed, and I switch my focus from the video game on my TV screen to the red-faced man taking over my doorframe.

I'm tired, and I'm pissed at pretty much everyone in my life for one reason or another, so I do what every mature male would do. I concentrate back on the game, casually acknowledging his presence. "Dad."

My father stalks into the room until he's in front of my bed, blocking my view of the zombie I was just about to blow up. "Who the fuck did you text last night?" He enunciates every word in a low growl that makes it clear he's a tad salty.

*Well, tough shit.*

"I don't know what you mean." I cock an eyebrow.

After George's last message, I let the confusion of why Lilly would leave without talking to me and the frustration of not being able to do jack shit about any of it turn into rage against my father. I convinced myself that if his fucking tracker weren't on my phone, Lilly's bodyguard would've given me something.

I expect Dad to explode at my defiant reply. Instead, he shocks the hell out of me. My father sinks down on the mattress and puts his head in his hands. All I can do is stare. What the hell?

We sit in silence for what feels like hours but a glance at my alarm clock reveals to be only four minutes.

Dad turns his face toward me, letting his arms drop to his thighs. "I've messed up with you, haven't I?"

"Uh..."

He continues, "All I tried to do was keep you...my family safe."

"Safe from who?" It can't be *just* Nate. He had no clue where Lilly was until we showed up in Cali.

"Did Lilly tell you why she can't remember?"

Of course he doesn't answer my question. "No." The memory of storming into my father's office when I had heard the raised voices and seeing Lilly's distraught face burned itself into my brain. Of-fucking-course I remember.

"I had consulted with a former associate on how we could help her cope. Lilly went through a lot at such an early age, and I didn't think she would make it out of it without long-term consequences, psychologically speaking." A lot? What the hell is he talking about? Dad's eyes are unfocused, and I clamp my mouth shut, afraid if I say anything, he'll stop talking. "She's a special girl, you know that?" The corner of his mouth tilts up, and he briefly catches my gaze before training it back to something on the wall. "She has a kind heart, always has. She spent a lot of time with our family as a little girl, and your mom and I *needed* to help her. I explained to your mother what my associate could do. Initially, she was furious with me for even suggesting such an option."

My stomach churns at his vague descriptions. What could he have suggested that would have made Mom that angry? I swallow hard. "What did you do to her?"

Dad zeros in on my face. He's torn between walking out and

coming clean—a conflict I've never seen on my father's face. He's always confident in everything he does.

"Her memory was manipulated through a form of hypnosis and persuasion."

*Excuse me, what?*

I stare at the man in front of me, refusing to believe what I just heard. I know he's been ruthless when it came to his job, no remorse and shit, but his child—adopted or not. How could he?

"Get. The. Fuck. Out." My body is shaking, and I keep my voice low to not wake up my little sister at the end of the hall. It takes every ounce of willpower not to take a swing at him, my balled fists already twitching with the need to pound something. Someone. Him!

He must realize that it won't do any good to argue, so he draws in a deep breath, stands up, and leaves. As soon as the door clicks shut, I grab the closest pillow, bite down, and let out a guttural scream, followed by taking said pillow and ripping the case into shreds.

I don't leave my room until my stomach growls so loud Lancaster —still camped out in the front yard—can probably hear it. I intend to go straight to the kitchen, grab every granola bar in the pantry, and head back upstairs—water from my bathroom sink would suffice for the foreseeable future. What I don't anticipate are the raised voices from Dad's office.

Heart beating against my ribs, I sneak down the hallway. The door is ajar.

"Honey, I'm sorry. I didn't want to give you another reason to worry. You barely agreed to stay after she was found. I took every precaution I could without packing up and moving us again."

"Three years, Tristen. Three. Years." Mom is crying—and not the pretty kind. The anger in her voice is apparent. "Has anyone had access to this footage? This is a complete invasion of privacy. Did you watch it?"

"I only checked the main living areas. The cameras in the bedrooms were just a precaution."

*Slap.*

Holy shit, did she just smack him?

My mother's voice turns hysterically shrill. "You made it sound like Hannah's death was an accident—a burglary gone wrong. Then I find out the person came back? Now this. Did *she* kill Hannah?"

Again with this Hannah person. Who is this chick? And who the fuck is *she*?

There is a beat of silence before Dad speaks. "I think so."

"Oh, my God!"

Fuck this shit.

I push the door open, finding Mom covering her mouth with her hands, tears streaming down her face and my father's arms wrapped around her.

"Rhys!" Dad's head snaps toward me.

"Who is Hannah?" No point in beating around the bush.

My father briefly closes his eyes in resignation, and Mom uses that opportunity to move away from him. She steps next to me. "Your father has informed me about the extent of the surveillance cameras in the house."

*So, she really didn't know.*

"Who is Hannah?" I repeat myself, enunciating every word. I'm running out of patience.

"Was."

"Huh?"

"Was. Hannah is dead," Dad clarifies in his normal, detached tone. I'm looking at Colonel McGuire, not my father.

"Hannah was our housekeeper. She started working for us when we moved back to Westbridge until she..." Mom won't make eye contact with Dad. "Until she was killed in our house."

"What the fuck?" My gaze jerks back and forth between my parents. So many questions assault my brain at once. How is this possible? "When was this? Why have I never heard of this person, let alone that someone killed her in our house?"

Mom has herself back under control and swipes at her smudged eye makeup. "We didn't want to worry you when it happened. Hannah would always come during the day when you were in school. It was easier for her to get her job done in an empty house. We never thought twice about the arrangement. Dad had her checked out, and we trusted her. We didn't have any reason to be concerned. She knew the alarm code and would arm it once she left." She draws in a shuddering breath and stares at the opposite wall. "One day, three years ago, the security company called us that the alarm was triggered. I was in the city. Dad went home to check on it and..." She trails off, fresh tears running down her face.

"I found her in the hallway," my father continues with a more subdued tone—so he was affected by it, after all. "She must've been able to hit the alarm button on the panel before she died. It happened on a Thursday, and I told Mom to take you straight to Grandma's house for a few days while I took care of everything. We excused the three of you from school, and since you always had clothes at Grandma's, it was easy to manage."

Holy shit, I remember that day. Mom came to pick us up from school and said it was a surprise trip.

"At the time, we were worried that it would trigger something in Lilly's memory, or you would let something slip about her past." He looks at me apologetically.

I narrow my eyes at him. "Oh-kay." Something in his story doesn't add up. Why would that trigger Lilly's memory? Traumatize, maybe, but what was she supposed to remember? "Sooo...someone broke into the house while Hannah was cleaning and off'd her. Why did that make you put in cameras in every single room in the house?"

Mom crosses her arms over her chest, avoiding Dad's gaze.

"The...person came back," my father finally declares.

*The Person.* The Killer. My eyes nearly bug out of their sockets, and I feel like trying to breathe underwater. This is fucking insane.

At his words, my mother's posture stiffens. Did she not know about that? Is that what they were fighting about? Besides the cameras?

"The police had already released the crime scene, and I had a cleaning crew go over the entire house. Mom was supposed to bring the three of you back the next day."

"What happened?" I choke the words out.

Dad exhales slowly. "I got another call from the security company. Someone had entered the house with the old code and triggered the alarm again. I had them disarm it and told them one of the kids must've triggered it by accident since we just changed it.

I was at a meeting nearby, but when I got to the house, it was empty. We had cameras in the entryway and on all doors leading outside—something I've installed in all our houses since Lilly came to live with us. I pulled up the footage and saw the intruder exiting the house. She had several personal items with her, including Bobo."

She. Bobo. My thoughts are a jumbled mess my brain is scrambling to put in order.

"Lilly's bear? Why on earth—"

My father holds up a hand. "That's when I put the system in place. The person came back and stole personal items. I promise, it was a mere precaution, to be able to trace every step of a possible intruder if that would've happened again."

I study his face for several breaths, trying to wrap my head around why someone would kill our housekeeper and steal an old-as-fuck, ugly bear. Or would come back a third time, for that matter. Then something else clicks. "Why didn't you hand the footage over to the police?"

"It wouldn't have been of any use. They wouldn't have found anything."

"But you knew who it was." I'm not asking.

"The video feed never showed the person's full face." My mother, who has remained quiet the entire time, doesn't deny my statement.

"Let me guess, you are not going to tell me who you *think* it was." Sarcasm drips from my voice. Even now, we're keeping up the damn secrets.

When neither of them speaks, it's clear that that is Dad's way of shutting down the conversation.

I turn and leave the office without a backward glance.

*Guess I'm keeping my secrets as well.*


I'VE JUST scarfed down the third protein bar when my phone buzzes twice next to me on the mattress—text message. Tapping the screen, I scan the two words. The fuck?

OPEN ME.

The grudge-holding toddler in me wants to flip the small device the bird and ignore it. I pick up the game controller but then place it back down. Aww...shit, I can't do it. Taking the phone, I swipe the text open and tilt my head. It's empty. Seriously?

I still stare at the screen when an incoming video call pops up: LILLY.

My heart begins to pound in my chest. I briefly close my eyes before accepting the call.

Lilly's face fills the screen, and she smiles hesitantly. "Hi."

That voice. *Her. Voice.* I want to say something, but my mouth won't obey. I take in her surroundings. She sits at some type of desk. Behind her is a cream-colored wall with fancy artwork and crown molding visible at the top of the screen. Her face falls, and I instantly feel like an asshole.

*She left you*, a voice pipes up inside my head.

*She didn't leave* you, *asshole. She left to keep you safe,* reason yells back.

It's like having whiplash. I want to be pissed at her. For leaving. For not talking to me about how she felt. I understand "the why," but it has driven a wedge between us. Yet, I love her more than anything.

"Hey." I force the corners of my mouth upward, but the expression won't take hold. The last thirty-six hours have been too much to keep up any pretense.

"How angry are you with me?" Lilly's voice is below a whisper, and I contemplate how to answer her question without sounding like a resentful prick.

"I..." *Fuck.* "I'm not angry—much." I dig through my muddled brain to find the right words. "I'm disappointed. I guess I would've expected for you to come to me first." Truth.

Her chin dips slightly, and moisture builds in her eyes. I want to be there for her, but at the same time, she ran. I just can't. When she looks back up, there's a beat of silence. "That's fair."

My eyebrows raise. I expected her to defend herself.

Recognizing my confusion, she says, "I had a long conversation with George and Nate. I understand now that I should've filled you in on my plan. I was just..." She blows out a breath. "I was scared you'd talk me out of it. You're the only person who could have."

Somehow, her confession releases most of the tightness in my chest. "I guess that's fair as well."

We have to work through our double truckload of baggage eventually, no question there. We'll probably have a full-on freight train by the time this is over, but we've also already spent years ignoring each other. Well, I stayed away from her. That guilt will haunt me for a long time.

"I also had an interesting conversation today." My rational side wins out, and I shift gears.

"Oh?"

"Where are you?" I'm not ready to rehash my parents' newest revelation yet.

She inhales deeply followed by expelling all the air at the same rate. "Los Angeles."

I knew it! It's what I would've done. *Great, now I'm relating to a criminal billionaire.*

"How is brother-dearest's mansion?" What I can see in the background already looks like the shit.

"I'm..." She pauses, and I tilt my head. "I'm at Brooks's house."

Well, shit. I didn't expect that. I would've assumed he'd lock her into some fancy hotel penthouse if he didn't bring her to his house. "How do you feel about that?"

"Fine?" Lilly shrugs one shoulder. "I don't think I've really made the connection yet."

Instead of responding, I watch her closely, waiting for what comes next. Emotion after emotion flitters across Lilly's face before she speaks.

"How is everyone at home?" She looks everywhere but the camera.

Her question sends my insides into another tailspin. Is that how she's been since finding out the truth about her past? About Nate. This constant back and forth between *resentment/red haze/I want to pound someone's (anyone's) face* and *I understand/I miss her/I'm a fucking pussy for not staying angry* is turning me fucking bipolar.

"Depends. Den and Wes were pissed. I told them about Turner. And even though they want to help, they get it. I guess we all just want to move on."

More accurate words haven't formed in my brain all day.

"Me, too." Her eyes are on her hands, and by the slight twitch in her arm, I'm guessing she is flicking her thumb against the rest of her fingers.

"Dad was a little more pissed than the rest. But that was mainly after his little spy app informed him about my texts with George."

Her eyes jerk to mine.

"In the end, we got sidetracked." I picture my father sitting on the bed, revealing what he let someone do to Lilly. My grip instantly tightens, and the case around my phone crackles.

"What do you mean?"

I attempt to calm my temper by breathing through my nose, and Lilly waits patiently. She can read me better than anyone and knows when I'm about to *flip my lid*, as she calls it. Twenty-three inhales and exhales later, I'm sure I can recall both conversations in a manner that will not end in me destroying any more pillows or electronic devices. I say, "Dad told me what happened to your memory and why there are cameras in the entire house."

Lilly's hands fly to her mouth.

"You might want Nate and George there," I continue.

She stares at me for a long moment, probably trying to figure out why I'd voluntarily suggest speaking to her brother.

"Okay. Uh, give me a minute." She doesn't immediately get up but then shakes her head and disappears from the screen. I take in the framed paintings on the wall behind the desk and finally recognize the object on them as an abstract version of the same black horse, one galloping and one standing. The weird shit rich people hang on their walls.

It takes several minutes before Lilly is back. She lowers herself into the chair, and I hear rummaging in the background. A moment later, two tall figures are carrying more chairs into the picture. When all three are facing the camera, I'm not sure where to begin.

"Rhys," George greets me in his usual, unemotional fashion.

"G." I nod at him, mimicking his detached tone. Oddly enough, I can remain pissed at him for picking Lilly up instead of putting his foot down—not that that really would've been an option.

My gaze swivels to Nate, who sits with his arms crossed slightly behind his sister. "Psycho."

Yup, still resentful for him allowing Lilly to leave.

Where Lilly glowers at me disapprovingly, George's lips twitch at the corner.

Nate simply rolls his eyes. "Why were we summoned, Rhys?"

Well, here we go. "My father explained to me how Lilly lost her memory and—"

"We already know how. George has a meeting with Lakatos set up for next week," he interrupts me.

*Who—*

"You didn't tell me that!" Lilly's head turns to her brother.

"I finalized the details yesterday. I didn't have time to fill you in yet," the other man inserts himself.

"Who. The. Fuck. Is. Lakatos?" the question is more a feral growl than an articulated string of words.

"He's the memory doctor." Lilly glances back at me.

I suck in a lungful of air. *Holy—* "Can he...uh, reverse what he did?" Is there a possibility for Lilly to remember?

"We don't know. I had to follow his extensive contact protocol before I could even set up a secure call with him."

"He's a paranoid motherfucker." Nate blows out a non-comical laugh.

George ignores his employer. "As I was saying, we spoke on the phone, and it took multiple days to agree on the terms to meet in person. The only reason he even considered it was my...reputation. He has heard of me, as I knew of him."

Well, if that isn't wonderful. "Maybe you can form a club." I can't swallow the snide remark that formed on my tongue.

This time, I'm at the receiving end of George's displeasure.

Thankfully, he doesn't evoke a sudden bladder release anymore, so I just shrug. "What?"

"Okay, now that we are all up to speed on that topic." Lilly narrows her eyes at the two men in the room with her before making eye contact with me again. "What else did you find out?"

Oh yeah, the *our-housekeeper-got-murdered-by-a-teddy-thief* news.

"I overheard Mom and Dad arguing in the office. Turns out, Mom had no idea about the cameras. She was li-vid." I want to relay in vivid detail how she slapped Dad but then refrain from that. "Anyway, when they became cryptic, I confronted them directly."

Three sets of eyes look at me expectantly, and I repeat what my parents told me in Dad's office.

"I read about this teddy in the letters." Lilly's eyes light up as some puzzle pieces from her past finally seem to fit back together. Then her brows furrow. "Why would this person take Bobo?" Her excitement turns to confusion.

"They didn't tell you who the intruder was?" George sits up in his chair.

"No, they just said it was a she. But they know. I'd bet the Defender on it."

"Why wouldn't they tell us? Why would Tristen keep it from Heather until now? This makes no sense." Lilly searches my eyes.

I wonder if our family would even function if there were no secrets between us. I'm about to tell her that her guess is as good as mine, but Nate beats me to it.

"You got this teddy from our father? What did it look like?"

Lilly's face falls. "I don't know. I don't remember him. I only read about him in the letters."

"I do," I speak up. "No one could forget this ugly thing. He was ancient. You carried him around everywhere. He was white—well, I assume that was his original color. He was more gray-ish by the time it went AWOL. Very simple, one eye was missing, and he was patched up on the back with some red fabric."

Nate turns chalk-white at the description, but with him sitting slightly behind, the other two haven't noticed.

I lift a finger and point. "Uh, why does he look like he's about to puke?"

Both heads jerk around, and we wait for Nate to elaborate.

He rubs his hands over his face before looking at his sister. "That teddy used to be mine. It was a gift from my grandfather when I was born."

# CHAPTER NINETY-NINE

**LILLY**

I open and close my mouth several times before I can get the words out. "B-Bobo was yours?"

Nate attempts a smile but looks pained instead. "His name wasn't Bobo at the time, but yes, he used to be mine. I named him Sir Denton, after my grandfather."

Something clicks, and my eyes widen. "*You're* named after your grandfather."

"Both, actually." Nate smirks. "Denton was my mother's father: Denton John Altman II," he clarifies, then adds, "Last I remember, the bear was in some keepsake box. Mom would save all the things she was sentimentally attached to. She probably never noticed that it was gone."

He doesn't elaborate on his other middle name, and I decide to ignore it as well. It's not important for the current topic.

"Why would anyone want that stuffed bear?" Rhys's question comes through the speaker, and I turn back to the screen.

I wrack my brain. "There was nothing special about him. Was there?" I peer at Nate, who shrugs in confirmation.

"Not that I remember."

"This shit is getting too fucking weird." Rhys rubs a hand over his mouth.

"Language," George barks from the chair next to me, and I roll my eyes.

"So, we finally understand why Tristen wired the house like a high-security prison. He wanted to be able to trace this person's every move—if *she* ever came back," I summarize.

Whoever this *she* was.

"Yup." Rhys pops the P in a bored manner. He moved to his desk, the phone propped up, and his arms crossed over his chest, leaning back in his chair.

"And they said for sure it was a she? That would mean Turner is out." I tap my index finger against my chin.

"We have not confirmed that he works alone." George stomps on my theory like one would crush a nasty bug under a shoe. "Everything I learned about Francis Turner, and what Nate was able to find, points toward him not having the intellect to mastermind all this."

"Well, who then?" Rhys's frustration is audible.

"I'll start digging more into his past," Nate informs Rhys of what he already told me on the plane. "But at the same time, I'm still trying to trace the money our father paid to that shell account. I'll work as fast as possible, but I have to make an appearance in the office tomorrow and Saturday since I missed two days this week. Hank is up my ass already, and Margot set up a lunch date with Julian and Cece for Sunday."

"You need to keep up with your life, Nate. You've been cutting it too close already. You"—George levels us with a stern face—"are not ready."

Guilt constricts my chest. *Nate has to take responsibility for his actions.* Between Turner and the shower attack, I refuse to go there. My brother will go to prison. Pulling my lips between my teeth, I stare at the desk, unable to make eye contact with any of them.

"You should talk to Mom and Dad." My eyes fly back to the screen.

"What?" I squeak. The tightness in my chest is replaced by an out of control beating heart.

"They deserve to hear from you. Face to face. Not just a text message that says, *I'm fine*." Looking past the camera, Rhys sighs. "I'm not their biggest fan either, and I probably would shut them out. Hell, I did for years. But you're a better person. There are too many fucking secrets."

"I agree with Rhys. Though, you need to keep it brief. Don't give details that could compromise you."

I shift my attention to George. When he doesn't say anything else, I glance at Nate, who just lifts a shoulder.

What am I supposed to say to them? Everything could potentially compromise where I am or who Nate is. I struggle to get my rapid pulse under control; it's of no use. The overflow of saliva combined with nausea steadily building tells me what's about to happen.

"Well, okay then. I take that as my cue to go back to cooking dinner. George, I want you to be in the room in case Lilly needs anything. Just...stay out of the picture, or Heather might have a heart attack, seeing your scary mug and all." My brother stands up, and his words snap me out of the oncoming panic attack.

Latching onto his arm, my nails dig into his flesh. I must've somehow agreed to it. Did I nod my head? Shit, I have no idea. "You want me to talk to them now?" I'm on the verge of being hysterical.

Nate levels me with an unidentifiable look. "Get it over with, little sis. It'll help you as much as it'll help them. Trust me."

*What?*

What is he not saying? Am I supposed to read between the lines? Is there another meaning to his words that I don't understand? Every neuron in my brain fires at the same time. His words don't match his expression. I open my mouth, but before I can form the words, my brother pulls me up and wraps one arm around my shoulders in a careful hug. He places a kiss on the top of my head and leaves the room.

I stare at the empty doorframe. What the hell just happened?

In slow motion, as if this would delay the inevitable, I swivel back to the desk. George has moved the extra chairs out of the picture, and I lower myself back down, closing my eyes.

I count to twenty before making eye contact with Rhys through the camera. He probably expects me to have a panic attack any second—he's seen enough in the last few weeks. Heck, I almost did have one just a few minutes ago.

I fill my lungs with as much air as possible and hold it in, releasing it only once my lungs begin to scream for air. "I'm ready."

"You sure?" His brows furrow.

I bob my head up and down as confidently as I can because—let's be real—I am nowhere near ready to face my adoptive parents.

Rhys regards me warily before he disappears from the screen, and I wipe my damp palms on my leggings.

"It'll be okay, Miss Lilly." I peer around the monitors to see George give me one of his half-smiles.

I'm unable to respond because fast footfalls echo through the speaker, and Heather's face appears in front of me. She merely stares—hands covering her mouth—as she blinks rapidly against a waterfall of tears.

"Hi, Mom," I whisper hesitantly.

A sob escapes her, and Tristen appears in the frame, followed by Rhys, who remains in the background. Tristen sinks in Rhys's desk chair and pulls his wife to his lap. A gesture that was nothing unusual for them before all of this began. It gives me some comfort that, despite all the secrets, the relationship between the two of them seems to be fine—as much as it can be.

"Hello, sweetheart," Tristen speaks first.

"Hi." The other end of the call starts to swim in front of my vision.

Tristen's expression is not what I am used to. The Marine is nowhere in sight. He is just my father. "How is your back?"

My bottom lip trembles, and I bite down on it to make it stop. His concern is worse than if he were to yell at me for again making irresponsible decisions without talking to them first. Eventually, I manage, "It's good. The burns are healing well."

"Rhys told us you are with family. Are you safe?" His tone is sincere, but he's gathering information.

"I am. I...I wanted to tell you, but there is so much I still have to figure out." The words tumble out. Scanning their faces—seeing them in front of me—Heather and Tristen are my parents. The two people who have raised me for as long as I can remember. *The only* parents I remember. All the secrets and lies, everything that has come to light, and everything still in the dark is unimportant. I want them to know I'm safe, and I hope, with time, they will understand and forgive me—when they learn the truth about Nate.

"Where are y-you?" Heather's question ends with a hiccupped sob.

"I'm..." I hesitate, not wanting to make it obvious that I'm seeking George's approval. He must sense my distress and steps toward the desk, dipping his chin in confirmation.

I'm about to respond to Heather when he mouths, "Nothing more."

Not wanting to make it obvious that there is someone in the room with me, I focus on the monitor. "I'm in Los Angeles."

Heather and Tristen's eyes widen. The irony of being so close to where it all started is not lost on me.

"Can we speak to your brother?"

My heart skips a beat, and I pause before coming up with the semi truth. "He's not here right now." Technically, he's downstairs.

"But he is keeping you safe. You left because of Francis Turner. How do you know he won't find you there?" The Colonel is back.

"I have twenty-four-seven security at the house. My brother is...wealthy." Understatement of the year.

They exchange a look I can't decipher.

Heather focuses on me with something like hope in her features. "Do you have more family there?"

Brooks's face flashes in front of my eyes, followed by Audrey's, and I swallow over the lump. "No." I glance down at my hands.

"I see," she replies. "We have a lot to talk about." The sadness in her tone is apparent. If it's for me not having more family or if she's disappointed in me running away, I don't know, and I'm too scared to ask.

After an elongated pause, I peer back up. "We do."

Tristen leans forward. "Thank you for letting us know that you're safe, sweetheart. With everything that has happened in the last few weeks, it means a lot to your mother and me."

The flutter in my chest caused by his words could mean anything from relief, to utter confusion, to guilt. I'm in desperate need of my emotional purging ritual to make sense of today's onslaught of news. Instead of the frown that wants to take over, I force a smile on my face. "Thank you for not being mad."

"Honey, let's give Rhys and Lilly some more time to talk," he addresses his wife, ignoring my statement of them not being angry with me. They probably are. Who am I kidding? They definitely are.

"Wait!" My shout makes three sets of eyes swivel to me. "Where is Natty?" Why is my little sister not there?

"She's downstairs, watching a movie."

*Oh. Does she not want to talk to me?*

"She doesn't know you're on the phone. We wanted to speak to you alone first. We told her it's a special day and to rent whatever she wants since your mother and I also had to discuss a lot," Tristen continues.

"Will you call again?" Heather rushes out. "We'll make sure Natty is here next time."

They're not keeping her from me. Relief washes over me like one of my purging showers. They just want her life to remain as unaffected as possible—less unaffected after what she went through herself this week.

"I will." This time the corners of my mouth pull up on their own. I'll get to speak to Natty soon.

*I sure hope Nate is fine with that.*

"Okay. Good." She's about to stand from Tristen's lap when she turns back, "Oh, and Lilly?"

"Yes?"

"Happy Birthday."


ONCE HEATHER and Tristen leave Rhys's room, George exits as well.

Rhys drops down in his chair, and we stare at each other for six minutes, according to the clock on my screen. For the first time in a long time, I can't read him.

"What are you thinking?" I bite down on my bottom lip until I taste blood. Not being able to decipher the mask that has settled over his face is freaking me out.

He doesn't answer right away. When he finally does, he speaks so quietly that I have to strain my ears. "It's your birthday."

*Oh.*

"I've never not been with you on your birthday." His voice remains low, subdued.

"I know." I understand what he's really saying. Even before I became a McGuire, we would be together on this day. Heather has photographs from my first birthday to my seventeenth. Rhys is in all of them. Not being with me hurts him as much as it hurts me.

Tears representing a mixture of sadness, guilt, and love are slowly running down my face.

"Don't cry, babe." His expression morphs into something worse than the blank mask. Sympathy and understanding.

"I'm so sorry." I blink to clear my vision.

*How do I deserve this boy?*

Rhys's genuine smile calms my nerves. "We're still together. Maybe not physically, but we get to see each other. Talk. That's more than the last few years where I was in the same room, but we wouldn't speak."

He's right. This is more than we did over the last few years on either of our birthdays.

"I love you." The words are out before I can think about my response.

"I love you, too." After a pause he adds softly, "Happy Birthday, Calla."

The corner of my mouth pulls up. "Thank you."

We watch each other in comfortable silence until he suddenly perks up, changing the topic. "Well, Mom and Dad sure as shit didn't react how I thought they would." He rubs his neck with one hand, grinning crookedly.

I smirk at his way of shifting the mood. "Definitely not." Where was the yelling, the gazillion questions, the demands to come back? In the end, all they asked was if I was safe.

Rhys laughs non-humorously. "I gave up on trying to figure out why Dad does anything. They're clearly keeping a shit-ton to themselves. And they know we are too."

"I guess." I replay the entire conversation. "Do you think they know who Nate is?"

"Uh, should we be using his name? I mean..." Rhys glances at the ceiling where his camera is hidden. One would never see it if you didn't know. They blend in even better than what Nate has at the vineyard.

"The cameras don't have mics; there is no sound recorded. I think we're good," I explain.

He tilts his head. "Sooo...if he can't listen, why did we hide in the freaking bathroom all the time?" Sarcasm drips from his question.

Unable to stop myself, I roll my eyes and match his tone. "Because a) he could've seen us hovering over a phone neither of them bought us, and b) they could've heard us talking from the hallway."

I swallow the duh.

Rhys cocks his head then slowly nods in an exaggerated motion. "*That* makes sense."

His expression makes me squint at him. "How long have you been awake?" He's acting...drunk. Loopy.

He turns his head to glance at the alarm clock then shrugs. "Long."

"Okay, why don't you get some sleep and call me tomorrow?" I didn't realize how tense I was until all of it suddenly leaves my body. I sink lower into my chair. I'm not oblivious that I will have a lot to explain and work through with my family and friends when all this is over, but the fact that Rhys hasn't broken up with me gives me the strength to keep going.

His scrunched forehead brings me back to the present. "And how am I supposed to do that? You took the burner."

I explain, "The message you opened before I called disabled Tristen's tracker. As long as you don't restart the phone, he can't follow your calls or texts."

Rhys's brows shoot to the hairline. "Was that you or your brother's handiwork?"

"Kinda both," I admit sheepishly. "He told me what routines to use but made me write the execution myself." It's still a miracle to me when the programs do what I want them to do.

"I'm gonna call you Whistler from now on," he announces proudly.

"Whis— Wha—?"

"I told you before, you need some cool hacker name, and you're obsessed with Abigail Whistler." Rhys grins.

I shake my head but can't suppress a laugh. "You're such a dork."

*I like it, though. Whistler.*

We talk for a few more minutes. He tells me to call Den and Wes. I instruct him to memorize the number I'm going to send him and then delete the text. Even if Tristen can't follow Rhys's phone activity anymore, I don't want to risk it.

For the first time since leaving the house in Westbridge, my heart feels a little lighter.

Nate had to leave after dinner. Margot had been blowing up his phone with calls and texts while we were eating, and he ran out of excuses. Mostly because she figured out that he's not in the office—she checked with Hank and called my brother out on it.

Before he left, Nate hooked the little NCC upstairs into its big brother network and gave me full access. When he told me, I couldn't stop myself from clapping my hands and jumping up and down, which resulted in both men scowling at me.

"What? Can a girl not be excited about her tech?" I frowned right back with my hands on my hips. I could hack into the feed and watch Rhys. That wouldn't be borderline creepy at all.

Nate shook his head and walked toward the garage entrance. "I'll talk to you later."

George settled in one of the living spaces downstairs with another book. I have no clue where he always pulls them from. It's like he has a secret bookstore in one of his many green duffel bags.

I am left wandering the mansion.

Not knowing what else to do, I make my way to the library on the second floor. Why rich people all have these massive accumulations of books is a mystery to me, but I won't complain. I'd rather read than watch TV anyway. Shelves dominate the two walls flanking the door from floor to ceiling with the center wall across being one large window overlooking the back of the property. This room is in complete contrast to the vineyard's decor with white shelves and a cognac-colored leather seating area—two big armchairs and a matching couch divided by a low white coffee table

—on top of a white-and-beige oriental rug. I browse until I find a section with romance novels. Seeing Rhys earlier has made me miss him even more, and reading about someone else's tragic love story sounds better than wallowing in my head for the rest of the night, questioning if I made the right decision. The books were all published prior to the last decade, which I guess makes sense with the house sitting empty for so long. I pull them out one by one, scanning the back until I find a plot that piques my interest.

*Buzz, buzz, buzz.*

My groan at the constant vibration coming from my bedside table is muffled by the comforter over my head. Whyyy won't it stoppp?

The book ended up completely sucking me in, and I finished it at three in the morning. Last thing I remember is plopping face-first into the pillows. Pulling the blanket down, I glance to the side where the alarm clock sits next to my phone, alerting me to yet another message. It's past noon.

*Oh, crap.*

I bolt into a sitting position and reach over, unplugging my phone from its charger. The number of messages on the screen explains why my nightstand sounded like a beehive had taken up residence in the top drawer.

**Nate: Good morning, sis. Heading to the office and will try to swing by after work.**

**Nate: ?**

**Nate: Lilly, where are you?**

**Rhys: Hey babe.**

**Nate: George said you're still in bed. Everything okay?**

**Rhys: Called G since ur not answering. U sick?**

**Nate: Call me!**

Chewing on my bottom lip, I wonder if George came up to check on me. I should've kept the volume up. I reply to Nate and Rhys that everything is fine, and I slept in. Both text back immediately, and I apologize several times for making them worry. I can't fault them; I would be freaking out if they were the ones not responding.

After breakfast, I trail the second floor twice—both times stopping in front of the same door—before finally gathering the courage to step into Payton's studio.

An easel sits near the window with a stool in front, a small roll table next to it with jars of brushes and paint tubes. There is no canvas on the stand, but several large frames are stacked along two walls covered with white tarps. If it weren't for the layer of dust, you'd think Payton would be home any minute to continue her hobby. A sudden wave of sadness crashes down on me. No wonder Nate hasn't set foot into the house in years. The memories are everywhere.

With my emotions somewhat back under control, curiosity wins out, and I slowly pull one cloth off of a stack of three pictures.

*Oh, wow.*

I didn't know what to expect. I couldn't draw a stick figure if my life depended on it and automatically assume most people are as artistically challenged as me. Payton clearly wasn't. In front of me is a stunning mountain range with a vast lake. The detail is breathtaking.

I move from stack to stack and marvel at her talent. Most of them are landscapes, but the last pile of smaller canvases contains portraits. The first one is of Audrey; the original picture is taped to the top corner. Behind that, I find a young Nate with Audrey on his lap, looking back at me. The reference photo she used is attached as well. Based on the backdrop, it seems like a professional photograph. The last one is of a small Nate and makes me suck in a sharp breath. He is around five or six, and the similarity between his and my own features at that age is shocking. But that's not what makes me pause. It's the teddy he is holding in the picture.

"Bobo."

The word hasn't fully left my mouth when my head is assaulted by what feels like several icepicks at once.

*Owwww.*

I grab my temple, and tears pool in my eyes. Why does it hurt so much worse than it used to? A groan breaks free, and I let myself drop to my knees.

*Make it stop.*

I'm at a small, round table at an outdoor café. Emily sits to my right, Brooks to my left, and they are arguing. My mother's expression is furious, and Brooks looks at her with an equally angry expression. Like in the dream I had at the vineyard, I can't hear what they're saying. I'm clutching something to my chest. Bobo? Brooks places a hand on my shoulder, turning to me with an unreadable gaze. His mouth moves. I try to read his lips, but Emily grabs my arm and yanks me away from him. His eyes turn wide, and he's trying to hold onto me, but I'm no longer in his reach.

**LILLY**

"Miss Lilly." Someone is shaking me. "Lilly, answer me!"

I slowly blink, but as soon as the daylight registers, fireworks explode behind my eyes again, and I moan. Why does it still hurt? I squeeze my lids shut and fist the hair around my temple. Maybe if I pull hard enough, it will make the feeling of someone filleting my brain go away.

"Lilly, if you don't tell me this instant what's wrong, I will...." I recognize George's voice, but at the same time, I don't. I've never heard him anything but calm. Angry maybe, but definitely not...panicked.

More awareness starts seeping in. I'm on my side, curled into a fetal position. I slowly open one eye to a tiny slit, letting it adjust to the brightness. The bottom of the canvas comes into view, and the memory floods back.

Emily and Brooks. Together. They sure as hell didn't look like they were still having an affair. The hatred was coming off of my biological mother in waves.

I release the strands of my hair and place my palms flat on the floor to push myself up. When my elbows buckle, hands grab me under my arms and pull me upright like a ragdoll. As soon as I'm on my feet, one eye still slightly open, everything begins to spin, and my stomach churns.

I clamp a hand in front of my mouth. "Oh, God."

Before I know what's happening, I'm airborne, one arm under my legs and one behind my back, pressing against the healing skin. Another wave of agony hits me as the pain receptors in my back join the ones in my head.

Bile rises higher, and it's clear there is no way to stop it. "I...need..." I attempt to communicate the inevitable, but George is already dropping me in front of the toilet in the hall bathroom.

I immediately empty everything in my stomach into the white porcelain. When the retching finally stops, I let myself fall back on my butt.

With my knees bent, I rest my head on top. "Fuuuck," I groan. My clothes stick to my skin, and a shiver runs through my body. I'm freezing, yet I want to curl back into a fetal position and just lie on the cool, tiled floor.

A hand awkwardly pats my head. "Lilly, what happened?"

"Memory," I mumble.

"I'm going to kill Lakatos." Knowing George, he would follow through on his threat, and a smile finds its way onto my lips. His loyalty and protectiveness is like a soothing blanket in my current state.

I slowly turn my head, and his face comes into focus. "It has never been this...bad," I admit.

"Do you want me to call Nate? Or Rhys?"

If I look remotely how I feel, there's no way I can face them. Rhys would instantly be jumping into the Defender and driving to the airport—if not straight to LA. I shake my head, which causes another wave of nausea to hit me. Swallowing, I manage to keep it at bay this time, plus I don't think there's anything left in my stomach.

"I'll tell them myself. Just...give me a few." I close my eyes again.

"Whatever you need, Miss Lilly," my bodyguard, and now nurse, concedes.

. . .

IN THE END, George refused to let me stay on the floor and walked me to my room to take a shower, only leaving after I reassured him that I'd be fine.

My body is covered in the remnants of cold sweat, and not aiming properly as my breakfast made a reappearance has left me with chunks of toast and banana in my hair.

*So gross.*

Emerging an hour later and feeling almost back to normal, I have a foot on the top step of the staircase to the first floor when George's voice drifts up to me.

"I tried. He refuses to come earlier." Pause. "No, there is nothing I can do. If I press any harder, he'll cancel the meet altogether." Pause. "No, there is no point for you to come right now. She is taking a shower."

Listening to his words, my pulse speeds up.

*That traitor. He called Nate after all.*

I make my way downstairs, not hiding my approach. George is standing in the large kitchen, already facing the doorway as I enter.

I cross my arms over my chest, glaring at the man with the large scar. I'm no longer scared of him. Unfortunately, my accusatory glower doesn't do anything to the former Marine. George continues his conversation with my brother without a blink of emotion, making the pounding in my ears become even louder. A sound resembling a growl escapes me, but George is still unaffected.

"She just walked in." He listens to something Nate says. "Yes, I agree. Okay, I'll make the arrangements. We should wait until I'm back, though, in case—of course." His lips form a disapproving line, and he holds the phone out to me. "Here."

*Is that directed toward my brother or me?*

I hold the device to my ear. "Hey."

"Don't you hey me, Lilly Ann," Nate's barked tone comes through the earpiece, and I automatically scrunch my shoulders up. "What the fuck happened?"

"Uh..." My own anger shrivels to the size of a dried raisin. Why is he so mad?

"George calls me out of a meeting with an investor, informing me that he heard a thud upstairs, and when he went to check it out, he found you unresponsive on the floor. I'm asking you again. What the fuck happened?"

I cover the speaker and hiss, "Why on earth did you have to call him out of a meeting?"

This time, George's expression does change—and not in a friendly way. "Because it took me five minutes to get you to move, let alone react. I was about to call an ambulance."

*My heartbeat seems to slow. Five minutes?*

"Oh."

"Yes, 'Oh!'" Nate scoffs on the other end. He gentles his tone. "Tell me what happened, please."

"I had another migraine," I mumble.

"But you never passed out before," my brother states, wanting confirmation.

"No."

"What did you remember?" George inserts himself, and I put the phone down on the kitchen island, pressing the speaker button. "It was about Emily and Brooks."

I recall everything, including what I saw in the café and how Emily dragged me by the arm.

"Could they just have been arguing?" my brother questions, still convinced their affair was ongoing until his mother's death.

I shake my head, not that Nate sees it. "I don't think so." Brooks's face appears in front of my mind's eye. "Brooks looked..."—I struggle for the right word—"almost desperate. Like Emily shut him down on something. I don't know, Nate. I was scared."

"Scared of whom?" George pulls my attention to his face.

I scan every inch of the man's features. Between his menacing glare and the scar, he can terrify everyone without saying a word, yet I've never felt as afraid as when I sat there between my parents.

"I don't know," I admit. "Maybe of what they were fighting about? Why can't I hear anything in these memories?"

"I will make sure to ask Lakatos that."

"Speaking of..." Nate interrupts my stare-down with George. "I want you to see a neurologist."

My gaze shoots to the phone. "What? Why?"

"It's one thing to have headaches with these flashbacks, but passing out is a whole different story. We need to make sure there is nothing...uh, missed."

Missed? Like something is not right with my brain? What else could be wrong with my head? I've already lost years of my memory. Black spots appear in my vision just as another possibility strikes me like one of the migraines itself. "You think I have a tumor?" My eyes widen in horror as my voice goes three octaves higher. They'd crack open my skull and literally rearrange everything inside, not just figuratively. What if it's terminal? I don't want to—

Nate interrupts my internal rant. "It needs to get checked out. We'll make the necessary arrangements for the day after George gets back. I want him to talk to Lakatos first. See if that is something he knows about and is...*normal*."

I cover my face with my hands.

*Why is this happening to me?*

"We should talk to Tristen."

My hands instantly drop, the panic of something growing in my brain forgotten, and I stare at the man in front of me.

"About what?" My brother vocalizes my own question.

"I never worked with Lakatos. Tristen has. He might be aware of that reaction and if it is to be expected," George clarifies.

I want to laugh at the absurdity of his suggestion. Heather would lose it. No matter what happened between all of us, I'm her little girl. She'd drag me back to Westbridge and lock me in my room in order to watch me 24/7. The fact that I'm eighteen and can support myself would be of no consequence when it came to my health. I'm so not going to tell them.

Their reaction isn't the only one that makes a pit form in my stomach. I refuse to even think about telling Rhys. I can't do that to him. I can't make him worry about anything else. I just can't.

"Let's see what we can get out of the memory doctor. Maybe he can reverse what he did." Nate sounds hopeful.

"Yeah, let's see." I don't expect anything to come from the meeting. I don't want to be negative, but I also can't bring myself to hope.

.   .   .

LATER THAT AFTERNOON, I work up the courage to call my best friend. I only type in her number three times before I finally hit the call button. Rhys talked to her, and Wes must've helped curb her best-friend-disappointment rage, because Denielle only chews me out for about fifteen minutes for packing up and *running*. She can take care of herself; let Turner try—her words, not mine. After that, she informs me that she has decided to book a flight and visit Charlie over spring break next week.

Spring break. I'm only excused from school for another nine days. What happens afterward, I have no idea. I haven't thought that far ahead, but I also didn't plan on returning to Westbridge until Nate and I have our answers and the people I care about are no longer in the crossfire of the press or stalked by a dead ex-Army Ranger. Not that Turner has physically threatened anyone, but we still suspect him to be at least involved in some of the articles. Plus, he faked his death. Who does that? And why?

I shake my head. Francis Turner is on the other end of the country. Hopefully, once he realizes I'm no longer in Westbridge, he'll leave my family alone.

*You're delusional*, the voice in my head shouts at me through a bullhorn, and I flinch inwardly.

I'm on my way to the third floor when I pass Brooks's home office and stop in my tracks. Curiosity to see the one room I haven't entered yet is making my body tilt toward the door.

Taking a deep breath, I turn to walk away but then halt again. Nate did not specifically tell me that I can't go in there. It's just that *he* doesn't enter his father's personal space.

I watch my hand reach out and clasp the handle. The metal feels cool against my skin, and I tighten my fingers, ready to push down.

"Miss Lilly!"

*Shit.*

I jerk my arm back and face George, who's jogging up the stairs.

"Yes?" My face is flushed. Did he see what I was about to do?

"Your brother wants you to call him on this number." He hands me a piece of paper.

I scowl. "Why a new number?"

"I believe he procured a second device to ensure there is no trace of you on his cell phone. It seems Miss Margot is beginning to question her fiancé's absence," he states.

I take the note and walk to the room Nate had turned into my mini NCC. Sitting behind the desk, I pull up the call function with the appropriate routine to mask the Caller ID and dial my brother's new number. A grin spreads across my face as I wait.

He answers after three rings. "George?"

"It's me," I say smugly.

"How—" Confusion clouds Nate's tone until understanding sets in. "You're getting good, sis. I'm impressed."

I chuckle. "Well, if you already have to get a second phone to erase me from existence, I might as well help with that."

"You updated the program yourself to match the parameters?"

"Yep."

A whistle comes through the earpiece. "Remind me never to let you near my computer again."

"Too late. You gave me access," I taunt.

"Ha. I did, which is why I wanted you to call me."

"Oh?" What has he planned now?

"We still need to figure out what to do with Psycho Barbie since you won't let me have George pay her a visit." He's joking about George, but the anger is apparent in his voice.

I roll my eyes even though he can't see me. George torturing her would give me some satisfaction, but it would also put me on the same level as her. "What do you have in mind?"

He gives me directions to a folder on one of the servers, and I suck in a breath at the title: Katherine Rosenfield.

"What's this?"

"This is what I pulled off her phone before I wiped it. You might find it interesting what she was up to when she was not with Rhys," Nate announces nonchalantly. "Call me when you see something you'd like to use."

*What?*

But he's already gone. I stare at the icon. I have no idea what to expect. When I finally click on it, I gawk at everything loading in front of my eyes. "Ho-ly shit!"

I scroll through what seems like over a hundred pictures with the occasional video in between. With every person I recognize in the photos and video stills, my pulse speeds up more. This is insane. Katherine has fooled everyone. At the very bottom is another folder labeled "E.S." Head slightly tilted, I let the curser hover for a moment before double-tapping on the track pad. My hands instantly fly to my mouth.

*No way!*

Fumbling with the keyboard, I redial my brother, who picks up after one ring. "You found it, huh?"

"Is this real?" I can't keep the shock out of my voice. This is a complete game-changer. It will destroy Katherine. She will no longer be the Queen Bitch—if she'd even stay at Westbridge High.

"Sure is. You recognize the other person?" Nate isn't asking for me to tell him; he already knows whose face is in the middle of my monitor. He just wants to confirm that I know who it is.

"I do," I croak.

"Soooo...any idea what we should do with it?" His voice has a sinister undertone, which is matched by the diabolical grin spreading across my face.

It's revenge time.

Tapping my index finger to my bottom lip, I ask, "How do I access someone's social media accounts?"

THE WAIT after Nate and I finalized the plan is excruciating. I am as giddy as I am nervous. They won't be able to trace it back to me, and let's face it, Katherine deserves every bit of what is coming to her, but a small part of me still revolts against being the mean girl. Katherine Rosenfield and her bitch squad have brought a whole new side of Lilly McGuire out. I still prefer to be kind to people, but some simply don't deserve mercy.

As Rhys and I talked last night, I was dying to tell him about what was going to happen in a few hours, but I bit my tongue. Him waking up to an entirely new scandal was too enticing.

So, when my phone rings at 5:22 Pacific Time, I am already sitting in front of my computer, a steaming tea next to me, and scrolling through the comments that started about an hour ago.

. . .

*MEGHAN LG: Kat, what the hell?*

*Kellan J: WHAT THE FUCK!*

*Random football player: DAYUM, that's better than porn.*

*Owen J: @Jager, you tapped that? High five, bro!*

*Lisa Bennett: OMG, she needs help. This is disgusting.*

*Random WH student: Why would anyone post that?*

*Nora Ross: @Lisa, @Meghan:: Has E seen it yet?*

*Meghan LG: I doubt it. She's going to lose it after what she did for that bitch.*

*Kellan J: Someone take that shit down before McGuire sees it!!!!!!!!*

*Nora Ross: @Jager:: Ohhhh, scared you'll piss your pants again?*

*Kellan J: Fuck off!*

I ANSWER the incoming video chat on the second monitor on my desk. "Hey, you're up early." I lace my greeting with innocence, even though I have the urge to bounce in my seat.

"That was you, wasn't it?" Rhys stares at me with a crooked grin. His voice is still raspy from sleep, hair sticking up in all directions, and he's shirtless.

Licking my lips, I trail down his chest to his muscled stomach that's peeking out from the comforter. A whole new sensation stirs inside of me, and I press my thighs together. What I wouldn't give to be able to—

"Calla!"

My eyes snap up. "Yes?"

"Up here." He circles his face but doesn't hide his satisfaction at me ogling him. "Admit it. You're responsible for this shitstorm."

I shrug casually. "If you mean Katherine Rosenfield's *coming out* announcement... Yep, that would have been me." I finally let the glee show and clap my hands like a lunatic.

Rhys shakes his head, laughing. "How the fuck did you get those pictures? And that video?" The awe in his tone makes me draw my shoulders back. Not that I had anything to do with the actual recording—that's all on the Wicked Bitch herself.

"Remember when Nate mentioned he pulled all her pictures off before wiping it last week?"

"Yeah?" He cocks an eyebrow.

"That's what he found on it."

"Oh, she is so fuuuuucked!" he sing-songs.

At that moment, someone storms into Rhys's bedroom. "Bro, wake up! Did you see—? Oh, you're already awake." Wes's voice carries through the speaker.

Rhys lazily glances past the screen at his best friend. "Good morning to you, too."

Suddenly, the camera shakes, and Wes appears at the corner of the frame. He has thrown himself down next to Rhys and is now also leaning against the head of the bed.

"Holy hell, Lil! How the fuck did you do that?" Rhys turns the phone to the side so I can see the other boy better.

Pride surges through me, and the little bit of regret is forgotten. Revenge is a bitch, and Katherine Rosenfield just fell off her throne as the reigning queen. Okay, I might have shoved her off. I brush some pretend lint off my shoulder and smirk. "It's called skill, my friend."

"It's called The. Shit! Jager blew up my phone to confess. He probably thinks telling me gives him a pass from getting his ass beat," Wes cackles.

"Nah, I don't give a fuck about that," Rhys answers, bored.

"Do we know who that is in the video?" Wes looks genuinely curious.

"Elisabeth Shaw." I throw the name out and watch the wheels in both guys' heads turn. When it clicks, their eyes nearly bulge out of their sockets.

"NO WAY!" Wes shouts.

"FUCKING HELL!" Rhys rubs his hands over his face.

I shift back to my other monitor and pull up the post I published under Kat Rosenfield's name on her various social media accounts. The announcement is accompanied by a new album I copied to each platform.

I had to make sure *everyone* gets to see it.

The one thing I made sure of was that everyone outed was of legal age, including Katherine, when the video was taken. That's the one reprieve I gave her.

.   .   .

*K*AT *R*OSENFIELD:

*I've been living a lie for the last three years, and it's time to admit to what I've known deep down for so long. I'm a nymphomaniac. I used Rhys McGuire to uphold an image I no longer can portray with a good conscience. To fill my life with everything I desire on a daily basis, I need to shed myself from the secrets of my past. In this post, I publicly admit to seducing every single one of the pictured individuals. However, none of these male objects have fulfilled my needs as satisfying as my dear friend and spiritual guide.*

U*NDERNEATH THE POST* is an album containing twenty-seven photos and one video. Each picture displays Katherine with a different guy in various make out poses: tongue down each other's throat, the dude's hand on her boob, her hand rubbing along a guy's hard-on, some even completely naked. But the video is what tops it all. I had to watch it twice before I could believe what was playing out in front of me. I expected a lot from Rhys's ex, but that was not it.

The four-minute film starts with Katherine in a very compromising position between a pair of female legs. Based on the moaning, Rhys's ex found a taste for what she was doing with her mouth, and the other person holding the phone seemed to agree. "Ohhh, yes, Kitty Cat. Just like that, baby. Mhmmmm." After about a minute, Katherine lifts her head, wipes at her chin, and wiggles her fingers toward the camera. The phone switches hands, and after some shuffling, the second star of the homemade porn appears on the screen between Katherine's thighs.

That's when I made the video stop and zoomed in on the face. Elisabeth Shaw. My former friend, Emma Shaw's, mother.

## CHAPTER ONE HUNDRED ONE

### LILLY

Even the article announcing that *Lilly McGuire went into hiding out of shame for seducing her adopted brother* couldn't undermine my satisfaction as I watched the comments multiply exponentially on *Katherine's* posts.

Every so often—whenever I came across an especially cruel remark—a pang of guilt crept in. Should I have felt this proud of causing Katherine's downfall? But then, all I had to do was lean against the back of my chair, and the still-present pain of my healing burns was enough of a reminder. Katherine Rosenfield deserved everything coming to her.

Sadly, by Saturday afternoon, someone—most likely the Wicked Bitch herself—disabled all her accounts. Another round of pride hit me, though, because it took her that long to get back in after I had changed her password and put extra authentication on it.

I wish I had recorded Denielle's reaction when she found out what I'd done. She called me immediately, and her three-minute happy dance included twerking, some very explicit cheers that would make half the football team blush, the running man, and a grand finale of *the worm*. In the end, we were both out of breath—Denielle from her spontaneously choreographed routine and me from laughing.

For the next few hours, random giggles bubble up in my throat whenever I visualize my best friend moving in front of the camera. I wish Rhys and Wes had seen it.

*I miss my friends.*

After I no longer have new comments to read through, I randomly snoop through folders on my brother's server. Maybe I can help with finding some answers. I'm three layers deep when my phone rings with an incoming video call: Rhys.

*Weird, we didn't plan on talking until later.*

I grab it from the wireless charger on the desk and swipe right. "Hey, what's—"

"Mom and Dad need to talk to you."

A pit the size of Nate's lap pool opens up in my stomach. "Why?" My voice instantly goes hoarse.

He draws in a long breath. "One of the families contacted Camden, demanding for you to be interrogated again. She wasn't aware that you're no longer in Westbridge and wasn't happy when she found out."

"What? Which family?" The hand not holding the phone begins to tremble, and I curl and uncurl my fingers in an attempt to make it stop. It's no use.

"No fucking clue. Dad just barged in here, demanding to talk to you. NOW!" Rhys exaggeratingly imitates Tristen's order.

*Shit.*

"Okay, uh...you want me to call back once they're there?" I shove my twitching fist between my thigh and the chair.

"No, I'll take the phone down. Hold on." The motion on the screen—Rhys taking two steps at a time down to the first floor—would make me seasick if I wasn't already nauseated from his news.

"Lilly is on the phone," he announces, and the device changes hands. A stern-looking Tristen sitting at his desk appears on the screen.

This is so not good.

"Sweetheart." He greets me with his usual endearment, but there is nothing pleasant attached to the word.

Tristen is shaking. What the hell? Wait. I tilt my head. He wasn't moving when he took the phone from Rhys. That's when I realize it's my nerves causing the device to literally vibrate. I clench my fingers around it tighter in an effort to stop the trembling.

"W-what's going on?" I address him just as Heather steps behind her husband and leans down to be in the frame.

"Hi, sweetie."

Unable to respond, I force myself to smile at my adopted mother.

"Agent Camden informed us that Ava Conway's father is demanding for you to be questioned further. There has been no progress on the case, and he is accusing you of protecting The Babysitter," Tristen explains.

*I'm gonna throw up.*

Oblivious to my inner panic, Heather adds, "We let Vivienne know that you are staying with family due to the incident at school, and you would be available via video conference if needed. Mr. Conway has no basis for his accusation. Ava is not a minor and has shown no interest in pursuing any actions regarding her case. From what we were able to find out, she is not even in the same state as her father."

Ava Conway was older than me when Nate...I force myself to complete the sentence...*took her*. But she's been off the radar for years. From what I found in my research, her parents have been divorced since she was a little girl. This makes no sense.

I inhale and hold the air in, forcing my rapid breathing to slow. Slightly calmer, I concentrate on the present again.

"What did Agent Camden say?" I suck on the inside of my cheek as I wait for their answer.

"Mr. Conway was contacted by a member of the press. He was told about evidence that you are faking your memory loss, and you are protecting the kidnapper." Tristen stares at me intently, and my heart sinks.

*He knows.*

At that moment, something crashes in Tristen's office, and a roar of "FUCKING TURNER!" bursts through the speaker on my end. All three of us jump at Rhys's outburst.

"Turner?" Heather narrows her eyes to somewhere behind the phone.

"Who do you think is behind that? A member of the press," Rhys mocks the wording. "Well, fuck that shit. Turner is trying to flush Calla out because he knows she's no longer here."

"Why would this man do that?" Tristen inquires suspiciously, and I tense.

*Do not take his bait, Rhys. Please, please, please.* I'm begging in my head.

There is a moment of silence until he answers, "Probably for the same reason some chick kills your cleaning lady and steals a teddy bear." He's playing the *you-have-your-secrets-we-have-ours* card.

I don't know how long we can keep this up. My phone starts shaking again, and I lean it against one of the monitors, sitting down on both of my hands this time. Thank goodness I answered on the small phone screen. The built-in camera on the desktop would have shown my whole body, revealing my physical state of panic. There would have been no hiding anything.

Heather's mouth turns to a slit before she focuses back on me. "I spoke to Vivienne, and she asked for you to come in once you are back in town. She wants to ask you some questions about both of your kidnappings."

"Okay," I choke the word out. The last thing I want is to answer any question regarding Nate.

Suddenly, the camera on their end moves violently, and I am face to face with Rhys, who doesn't look at the screen. "Now that that's all cleared up, there is nothing else to discuss." He flips around and marches out of the room and up the stairs.

As soon as he clears the threshold, Rhys kicks the door shut with one foot.

"MOTHERFUCKING COCKSUCKER!"

He knocks something off his desk, and I cringe. It doesn't sound like it was anything overly breakable, and for a moment, all I see are strands of his brown hair as he grabs fistfuls with the phone still in one hand. I wish I were there to wrap my arms around him and hold him. It becomes more and more apparent that my decision to run has made everything worse instead of better.

Eventually, his green eyes lock on mine sadly. He's back in the same position on his bed as this morning when he first called.

"Babe, this is getting out of hand."

"I know." I can't get my voice above a whisper.

I FIND George in the motor pool—calling it a garage would be like saying the Vanderbilt estate is a cute little cottage. His upper body is in the backseat of his RAM, one foot on the nerf bar, the other balancing in the air. He is maneuvering something large around in an attempt to get it under the bench.

"What are you doing?" I step behind him to get a better look.

He jerks, and the object slams into the opposite door with a clang. "Good Lord, Miss Lilly."

Unable to suppress the chuckle for actually startling the scariest man alive, I apologize behind a cupped hand. "Um, sorry."

He adjusts the large black box I can finally identify as a rifle lockbox. "More firepower? I thought you have at least two guns on you at all times." I purse my lips mockingly, remembering when Rhys told me about George's arsenal in Morristown.

"It's a custom design. I ordered it before Nate sent me to Virginia. It fits under the backseat with the opening in the front. It's connected to a button in the dashboard, which will automatically unlatch the lid, and a mechanism inside moves the rifle out. That way, I can reach for it without having to bend back."

I lean in. "That's pretty impressive. Tristen would love that setup. He has to open his *manually*," I say, exaggerating the last word with a teasing eye roll.

"Did you need something?" George steps down from the truck.

Oh yeah, the reason I came to find him. Part of me wants to ignore all of it and be a normal girl, even if it's just for a few hours. But I don't get the luxury. Turner, Camden, the upcoming meeting with Lakatos, the possibility of *something else* being wrong with my brain...none of that will go away, no matter how much I want it to.

"Actually, yes." I swallow down the burning sensation in my throat. How do I phrase this? "It seems Turner contacted Ava Conway's father, who now demands for me to be questioned. I wasn't sure if I should call Nate or not." I steady my voice, suppressing the quiver that wants to break through at the thought of being interrogated.

George snaps to attention and reaches for his phone that's

laying in the front seat. He doesn't have to wait long for my brother to answer. "We have a situation." Pause. "She is fine, but I would suggest for you to come by on the way home from the office." Pause. "That is unfortunate. Okay. Call me when you can."

After shoving the device a little too forcefully into the side pocket of his trademark gray cargo pants, George finally makes eye contact. "Nate is unable to come by. His little lap dog is glued to his side after not showing up in the office this week."

I narrow my eyes at the man in front of me, and he amends, "Hank Todd."

*Oh.*

NOT KNOWING what else to do and unable to look into Turner myself—my brother hasn't covered that aspect in his lesson plan—I aimlessly trail the mansion. The walls are starting to close in, and I've only been here for four days. George and Nate are adamant that I am not allowed to leave the property. The sudden onslaught of emotions knocks me back on my heels. What if Turner now goes directly after my family and friends? Did I make a mistake by coming here? I was so focused on my revenge against Katherine and the relief of Rhys not breaking up with me that I neglected all the other potential consequences. Why is Turner after me? What is my connection to a man that faked his death when I was just a kid?

I find myself back in front of Brooks's office. George is downstairs and won't come looking for me anytime soon. I shouldn't, but even as I'm still thinking the words, my hand reaches out.

*If it's locked, I'll go to my room.*

My fingers close around the cool metal of the handle, and it eases down without the slightest resistance. Letting the door swing inward, the hairs on the back of my neck stand like someone is watching me. There are no cameras in the house; Nate doesn't know that I'm here. Brooks was my father, too. I don't need to feel guilty.

My pep talk isn't working, and the guilt of my trespassing is taking over every cell of my body. I scan the inside from where I'm rooted to the floor. Brooks's home office does not look like the rest of the decor. Most of the mansion is bright, soft colors on the walls, light wood tones for the furniture. My biological father's personal space is... I try to find an appropriate description, and all I can come up with is 1950s Ad Agency. The walls are dark gray. The spaces around the big picture window hold identical shelves. Both pieces appear to be custom made; they're not attached but fit perfectly. Acorn boards are connected and held up by thin polished black metal bars with cabinet doors where the two lower shelf boards would have been. Centered in front of them is a massive, mid-century style desk made of the same wood. A high-back office chair behind and two low-sitting armchairs in front—all three of the softest black leather—complete the design.

I close my eyes and count to five. Nate never specifically said I wasn't allowed in here. I'm not doing anything wrong. Why do I feel like such an intruder?

*Because you are*, my inner voice sneers.

Three more breaths and my feet finally cooperate. I take one step after another until I'm in the middle of the room. The crew hired to prepare the house for my arrival must've cleaned this room as well since there is not one speck of dust anywhere. I spin in a circle and discover more identical shelves around the door. Books and different memorabilia decorate all four, while the two walls to the left and right contain large paintings that look suspiciously like the ones I found in the art studio down the hall. I wonder if Payton had a hand in decorating or if they hired someone.

I scan the books—some biographies, some business-related, no fiction anywhere. I stop at a small bronze Viking statue on a warship. The detail is captivating, and I have to force myself to move on. The more objects I discover, the more I come to the conclusion that they must be souvenirs from their travels. There is a glass with black sand, a mask, seashells, and a stand with several pipes.

When I reach the desk, I move the chair backward and slowly lower myself down. Placing both hands flat on the desk, I scan the room once more.

This is where Brooks used to work when he was not in the office. Did he read Emily's letters here? Nate's words come back to me: *I found a stack of letters and pictures in his desk at the house.*

My gaze falls to the drawers on either side of me. Swiping my palms on my pant legs, I glance back and forth between them. Screw it. I carefully slide the top right one open, unsure of what to expect. I don't anticipate finding all the answers in the first drawer I look into, yet there is a nervous flutter in my stomach.

All I discover are blank legal pads.

"What are you doing?" My brother's voice makes me jolt in the seat, and my head snaps toward the door.

"Nate." I'm like a deer in the headlights.

"What are you doing in here?" he repeats, not taking his eyes off my face. It's as if he refuses to acknowledge the room I'm in.

He wasn't supposed to come over. Shit.

"I...uh..." I stammer as I push away from the desk. When I step in front of him, all I manage is a strangled, "I'm sorry."

His eyes are still fixed on me, but his tense features soften. "I haven't seen this room in a long time."

"I shouldn't have come in. I—"

"You were curious about your father. I understand." Nate's tone is calm, yet his rigid posture screams *on edge*. This is where it all began for us, where he found out about me.

I gently place my hand on his chest and push against it. He lets me move him farther into the hallway, and I close the door on my way out. As soon as his view of the office is blocked by the wooden barrier, his stance relaxes, and he unfastens his stare from my face.

"I'm sorry," I say again, a little more confident this time.

"Don't be. I...it's..." He sighs, grasping for words. "You can enter any room in this house. I would never stop you. It's just...I..." He trails off again.

"*You* can't go in," I finish the sentence for him, and he nods.

I hope that one day, when we have our answers, things will change—that Nate can heal.

I FOLLOW my brother to the first floor where George is waiting for us in the kitchen. Sitting at the breakfast nook, I give both of them a detailed rundown on Heather and Tristen's news.

As I recall everything my adopted parents told me, Nate grips the tabletop, his knuckles turning white. Anxiety is radiating off of him, and I'm not sure if this is because of Turner or because it's the first time we're actually talking about one of the other girls.

"You believe Turner is behind it?" George looks at me for confirmation.

My gut feeling is as strong as ever. "Who else would have reason to contact one particular family—not even the family, just Mr. Conway, and cause him to raise questions?"

"Mr. Conway could simply want to seek closure, and with no real progress in the case—"

"Conway is a drunk. There is no way he came up with that on his own. He hasn't spoken to his daughter in years," Nate interrupts.

A flush of adrenaline shoots through me, and I stare at him. "How do you know that?"

My brother holds my eyes. "After you *resurfaced,* I looked into everyone. I hadn't checked on them since uh...you know. After I brought you back to Santa Rosa and you started talking to me, I made sure they were all *okay*. I wanted to know where to find them when I turn myself in."

We have never spoken about it this openly, and somehow, I didn't think Nate was already making plans for... My mind refuses to finish the sentence. I reach over and place my hand over his, needing the contact. He glances from my hand to my face and back, turning his over and interlacing our fingers.

"You know that I will make it right. You trust me?" He searches my eyes.

My throat thickens, and I swallow hard. "I do."

Nate focuses on the third person at the table but doesn't let go of me. "Conway is a useless drunk; there is no way he is doing this out of worry for his daughter. His wife ran off with another guy when Ava was three. Ava bounced between both homes until she filed for emancipation. I haven't been able to find anything on her in the last few years. She has no bank accounts, no social media, and she definitely has not spoken to either of her parents."

I'm stunned about the details he found out about Ava.

George nods. "What are we doing about it?"

"Camden agreed to delay the questions until you'd be back in Westbridge?" Nate asks in confirmation, and I bob my head up and down, tightening my fingers around his. At this moment, he's my anchor. My big brother. Who will go to prison.

"As long as she doesn't change her mind, it doesn't matter then. By the time you go back, everything else will be over as well," my brother declares.

*When I'm ready to go back, he'll have already turned himself in.*

## HER

*It took Gray two days to find a pilot willing to take my substantial donation and take us to California without putting any of the passengers on the flight manifest.*

*At this point, I have spoken to the informant seven times to get updates on Lilly's whereabouts—not that he has been able to give me anything but assumptions. Nate's socialite fiancée was of more use. Her social media post— a pouty-lipped Margot in a pool chaise, tagging Hamlin with the caption: "Fiancé on another business trip until Friday"—made it clear that he hasn't been around.*

*Brainless bimbo. Not even her non-profit work can make up for the air in her head that's only good to keep those ridiculous curls in place.*

*Gray limps after me into the beach rental my little helper procured for us. He grunts under the weight of our luggage, his leg bothering him with every step.*

*"Oh, shut up. The knife went straight through the muscle. I didn't even nick a blood vessel. You've had worse," I snap after he moans again, making his way with my bags to the bedroom I chose.*

*I dial Elise to check on my pawn. I had to leave him behind in Virginia since Doc refused to knock him out for the flight. Apparently, it could over- whelm his system with the increased dosage of paralytic drugs and anes- thetics he's received in the last few weeks. Not that I care about his body, but on the minimal chance I require him to convince Lilly to do what I want, I have to keep him alive a little longer. Such a nuisance.*

*Elise assures me he is compliant and everything is good. I confirm her statement by pulling up the cameras Gray installed for me without her knowledge before we left.*

*"Elise?"*

*"Yes, ma'am?"*

*"Why is he reading a book?" Meaning, why the fuck are his arms not in the restraints?*

*The sharp inhale on the other end of the line tells me that she did not expect me to know that.*

*I speak very slowly. "If you value your position,"—sub-context: your life —"I highly suggest that you rectify your lapse in judgment immediately."*

*"Yes, ma'am."*

*I hang up before she can say anything else and watch her hurry into the room and rip the book out of his hands. His brows furrow, and her gaze flits around the room as she mumbles under her breath. His mouth sets into a grim line, and he holds out his hand for her to tie it back down. Always the gentleman.*

*Once I am satisfied that my order was followed, I find Gray in the kitchen, popping more painkillers.*

*"Do you think that's wise with your history?" I arch an eyebrow.*

*"I wouldn't have to if you would keep your temper under control," he mumbles between gulps of water.*

*Ignoring his insolent remark, I take the car keys off the counter and toss them at him. "Make yourself useful and do recon on the Hamlin estate. I want to know everything."*

# CHAPTER ONE HUNDRED THREE

### LILLY

I am wide awake. Nate's words about Ava keep playing on repeat in my head. Hearing about her childhood—besides what my brother had done—made needles prick in the back of my throat. What happened to her?

Nate headed home around nine, after Hank started spamming his phone. My brother had given him contracts to go over so he could get away. Unfortunately, Hank figured out that said contracts had already been reviewed and started angry-texting. When Nate didn't respond immediately, he called. Twelve times.

As we watched Nate pull out of the garage, George excused himself to go to bed. Somehow, I never considered that the man requires sleep. Most of the time, he is so inhuman that it wouldn't have been a surprise to find a secret battery compartment under all his cargo gear.

By midnight, I give up. I swing my legs out of the bed, put on Rhys's old hoodie, and pat down to the second floor to my little computer room. Sitting down behind the desk, I reach for one of the laptops and press the space bar. Besides the missing wall monitors, it's an almost identical setup as at the vineyard. I love it.

I have no particular goal in mind when I open up the console, but my fingers guide me to the folder my brother mentioned earlier

—the one he added after I came to Santa Rosa. It wasn't hard to find once I knew it existed. I laugh at myself as I briefly glance at the mouse sitting next to my keyboard and then ignore it. Like brother, like sister. Who needs a mouse?

A few commands later, I'm scanning the multitude of documents Nate compiled. He has detailed information on the other four girls, and I find myself reading file after file. He didn't exaggerate. He pulled up everything down to school records to check how they're doing. Meredith and Chloe seem to have overcome *everything* without long-lasting issues—my mind refuses to use the k-word. Both have good grades, play extracurricular sports, and their home life looks...normal. Rose is the youngest and most recent. She sees a therapist regularly, but other than that, she appears to be fine as well. None of the records indicate that her experience traumatized her.

I dip my head and close my eyes, letting the relief wash over me. They're okay. I seem to be the only one who didn't make it out of this unscathed, aka lost my memory and was transplanted into a fake family. Maybe by changing his approach?...Tactic?...Routine?... Shit, I can't even think about it. What kind of person am I for wanting to be completely oblivious to what my brother has done? Audrey's face flashes in front of my eyes, and my throat thickens at the thought of what her loss did to Nate.

When I get to Ava's file, there is not much to see. She dropped off the face of the earth after becoming a legal adult. From the few records there are, her upbringing doesn't seem to have been a happy one. Her father has several DUIs and one domestic violence charge. Her mother worked one minimum-wage job after another, sometimes several at once. They lived in a rundown one-bedroom apartment in a bad part of town. The guy her mother left her father for was arrested for breaking-and-entering when Ava was eight. No mention of another relationship since.

*Where are you, Ava?*

I sit at the desk, palms flat on either side of my keyboard, and stare at the wall opposite me. Getting more insight into the girls' lives has forced me to acknowledge what Nate did. I'm not able to deny or ignore it any longer, nor what the inevitable consequences of his actions would be: Nate will take responsibility and go away.

The selfish side in me doesn't want him to leave me. The bond we've formed over the last few weeks runs as deep as if we had known each other for years. The connection was instant, which is probably why I was never afraid for my life. He's my big brother.

Pride for him making it right makes my lungs expand. He had started setting everything in motion before I even mentioned him taking responsibility. I tell myself that I'm not going to lose him forever. Having all these thoughts running through my head also brings to the forefront how little I know about my biological father.

Before I can change my mind, I push the chair back and stand up. Nate's reaction to me being in Brooks's office still has me rattled. He appears so...*normal* all the time that I forget how deep his wounds lie. But he said I can go into any room in the house. Decision made.

THIS TIME, I don't hesitate to push the handle down. Flipping the light switch next to me, the room illuminates with several small lamps strategically placed around the space, giving it a warm feel. I hadn't noticed that there's no overhead light when I was in here before.

Suddenly unsure, I turn in a circle. I eye the desk then let my gaze wander to the file cabinet under the shelf closest to me. I doubt the desk holds anything of consequence, and I let my feet carry me the few steps toward the shelf. This is the first place one can see that the house stood empty for years. The cleaning crew did a great job on the surface but neglected cleaning inside the cabinets. The little gap between the doors has let dust in over the years, and the binders are covered in a thin layer. I grab a handful and lay them out in front of me—déjà vu.

Similar to the vineyard, most of the folders are case files. Some contain more financial statements, but they are either—what I deduce—the family account or Payton's personal spending—mortgage and car payments, random expenses. Then I flip a page and pause, my fingers turning into a vise around the paper. Holy—it's the same amount. The same large sum that was deposited into Brooks's account every so often.

*He took the money from their family account?*

My heart is pounding against my rib cage. This is huge. I fish my phone from the center pocket of my hoodie but remember I can't call my brother. He messaged earlier that Margot is staying at his house tonight.

*SHIT!*

I could wake up George, but what is he going to do? I slam the paper on the floor. Damn it!

Frustrated, I stand up and move to one of the shelves by his desk, leaving the files where they are. I need to keep myself busy until I can at least call Rhys.

I open the doors to that cabinet and come to a halt once more. Photo albums. Three black leather albums. I pull the top one out, expecting it to contain some Hamlin family pictures, but instead, I stare at myself.

*What the hell?*

With shaking hands, I skip through the pages faster and faster. It's me. It's *all* me. Holy hell, Brooks has more photos of my childhood—pre-six years old—than Heather and Tristen. Cold sweat starts forming on my forehead. How is this possible? There's even a picture of Rhys and me as toddlers. We're sitting together on a blanket in the park, a ball and some snack cups between us, a set of legs on either side of us. I let my index finger glide over the photograph, stopping on Rhys's face. A flutter in my chest replaces my rapid heartbeat. I start inspecting the photo closer when it hits me: this was taken from afar, through a lens. Based on the angle and focus, I'm sure of it. Did Brooks take it, or did he have someone follow me as a kid? And if so, why? He was still seeing Emily—or that's what we've been thinking.

*Crap, I need to talk to someone about this.*

I tap the screen on my cell phone that I dropped on the floor next to me and mentally add three hours to it. It's 3:47 a.m. in Virginia. My thumb hovers over the call icon until the little clock shows 3:49, and I click the side button, locking the device again. Ugh! If I wake Rhys up now, I'll just worry him more than he already is.

A yawn slowly builds up, and I press the back of my hand against my mouth, trying to suppress it. My eyes feel heavy, and when the second yawn escapes, I push myself up. There is nothing I can do for at least another couple of hours. Resigned, I leave everything where it is and head to the third floor to give my body what it obviously demands.



*Buzz, buzz, buzz.*

*Buzz, buzz, buzz.*

"What the hell?" I dig the heel of my hand into my eyes.

*Buzz, buzz, buzz.*

*Buzz, buzz, buzz.*

It's not a text message. Peeling one lid open, I squint at my phone slowly moving across the nightstand.

*Buzz, buzz, buzz.*

*Buzz, buzz, buzz.*

What is that? Groaning, I lean up on one elbow and reach for the device before it can tumble off the edge it's getting dangerously close to. I unplug it from its charger and flop back onto the pillow. Blinking my second eye open, I stare at the screen.

ALERT: Lilly subroutine activated. Message sent.

*Huh? Oh.*

"Oh!" A rush of adrenaline hits me like a cross punch to the jaw. It worked. Holy crap, it really worked!

Sitting up, I throw back the covers and take three steps at a time down the stairs, almost running into George, who's on his way to the first-floor staircase.

"Miss Lilly? Is something wro—" His confused question drifts after me as I speed-walk with my phone still in hand past him.

I drop into my chair and pull the keyboard close. With the computers hooked into Nate's private network, I don't have to go through the same motions as when I hacked into the security feed to his LA. house. I simply open the app for the system at the vineyard and select the camera to my bedroom.

There he is. My brother sits on the foot of my bed, staring at his phone.

A broad grin spreads across my face. I did it. I jump up and down in my seat, doing a little happy dance. Yessss!

"Miss Lilly?" George's voice startles me, and my head jerks toward the door, a blush heating my face.

"Sorry," I mumble, sitting down on my hands.

George chuckles. "No need. I enjoy seeing you happy."

At that moment, an incoming call pops up with my brother's name. I peer over at the security feed, and he is now standing in front of the bed, phone pressed to his ear and staring at the camera in the ceiling. He mouths, "Pick up!" and I bark out a laugh, accepting the call.

"How did you know I'd be watching?"

Nate smirks. "You're not the only one with alerts, little sister. I got a notification as soon as you activated the camera."

"Hey, no fair," I explain in mock outrage.

"That was quite a surprise." He ignores my pretend anger.

"Well, you told me to write a routine that gets activated by a voice command," I justify myself.

"I did," my brother confirms. He looks back up and smiles. "Thank you."

Warmth floods my body, and my mouth turns upward as well. "You're welcome."

When Nate kept me busy at the vineyard, one of his exercises was a subroutine for the camera and mic in my room. I chose to write a voice-triggered notification alert for the mic. He probably assumed I'd program something and test it myself to see if it worked. But instead, I set the trigger for "little sister," hoping Nate would eventually cause the alert to go off. Obviously, I had no idea when or if it would ever happen. When the words were spoken inside my room, it would send a text message to him: **How dare you enter my room without my permission! JK, big brother. (; Just wanted to tell you that I am glad we are finally a family again. XO, your little sister. L.**

Words I felt at the time but wasn't able to admit out loud yet.

My brow furrows. "Wait, what are you doing at the vineyard?"

Nate sighs. "Margot wanted our lunch with J and Cece to be up here on the terrace, so we took the jet for the day."

"Must be nice to be rich, huh?" I say cheekily.

"You are just as rich; don't forget that," he counters with humor.

*Shit, I did forget.*

"I'll be back later tonight," he assures me, and a calmness settles inside my chest.

The corner of my mouth pulls up until the memory of last night's findings surges to the surface like an erupting geyser. The statements and photo albums with my childhood pictures are still scattered over Brooks's office floor. I gasp, and Nate's eyes narrow at the camera in the ceiling as if he can see me.

"Lilly, what's wrong?"

"I need to show you something, but I don't know if we should do this over—"

"Darling?" a female voice comes through the speaker, and Margot appears in the frame on the camera. "What are you doing in here?" She glances around, confused. Understandable since, technically, the room Nate is in is just a random guest room.

"I had to take a quick call." Nate disconnects the phone, and I watch him usher her out of my bedroom, glancing up one last time.

Crap. I wanted to confess at least where I was last night, even if we didn't have time to discuss the rest until later. It feels like every time one of us makes progress, something happens—in this case, brunch at the other end of the state—and delays things. I push back from the desk a little more forcefully.

*I should've woken him up last night.*

George is leaning against the doorframe, watching me with an indecipherable expression.

"What?" I raise my eyebrows, waiting. Does he want me to elaborate on what I found?

The corner of his mouth tilts up. "It's good to see you and Nate together."

Standing up, I make my way over to him, point my finger, and circle it toward his head. "George, you're doing it again."

It's his turn to scowl. I clarify with a grin, "You're smiling."

My bodyguard just shakes his head, turns, and leaves, but not before I see his mouth quirk up at the corner. As he walks away, I hear him calling out, "You are quite the brat, Miss Lilly."

Rolling my eyes, I follow. I can make it until Nate is back later.

---

# CHAPTER ONE HUNDRED FOUR

---

**RHYS**

"He has pictures of me!"

It's Sunday morning, and after three days and several not-so-subtle comments from Natty, I finally took a shower. So, when the vibration of my phone on the nightstand drifts into the bathroom, I drop the towel and dive across my bed to answer the call.

Thank fuck my room is on the second floor, or Lancaster would have a front-row seat to my pussy-whipped nakedness right now. My best friend would simply barge in, and Denielle is off to Georgia, getting some ass herself, which leaves only one person to call me.

"Who?" I'm confused.

"My father!" Lilly snaps like I was supposed to simply *know*.

"Which one?" I huff out with a laugh.

"RHYS!"

*Oh-kay, we're not in a joking mood.*

"Sorry, babe. I'm assuming you're talking about Brooks?" I force myself to be serious, even though I think my pun was pretty good.

"Yes, Brooks. He has hundreds of pictures of me. *You* are in some as well!" she barks.

"Me?" That gets my attention.

"I found photo albums in his office. He has more pictures of me than Heather and Tristen. I just went back and am flipping through the ones I didn't get to last night. There are so many!" Her tone pitches toward the end. She's not quite hysterical, but it won't take much more.

"Anyone else? I mean, besides me?" I don't like this. How could he have gotten these photos—Emily, a P.I., himself?

Pages turn hastily in the background, and I tap the fingers of my free hand against my naked thigh.

*I should probably get dressed.*

I picture her, sitting on the floor, surrounded by photo albums—similar to the day I found her in her bedroom. "Emily and Henry are in some. I found one with all of us at what looks like a carnival," Lilly says absently. More rustling. "Oh, my God!"

"WHAT?" Come on, woman, speak!

"Brooks!"

"What about him?" I grind my teeth. I really don't care for cryptic responses when she's across the country and I can't do shit about anything.

*Yup, I'm still bitter about it.*

"There is a picture of Brooks and me. It's when he gave me—" She cuts off, something clatters, and I have to pull the phone away from my ear at the sudden noise.

"Ahhhhh!" a scream rips through the speaker, followed by another thud and then...whimpers. "Make it stop. Please m-make it s-stop."

*The fuck—?*

My heart starts racing. "Calla?!" She's not answering. "BABE, ANSWER ME!" I'm standing butt-naked in the middle of my room, shouting into the phone.

*Fuck, fuck, fuck.*

"LILLY!" I press the device harder to my ear and tug on my hair with my free hand. "LILLY, ANSWER! Please." I'm begging more to myself than her since she's unresponsive. Motherfucker. When her moaning cuts off, so does my breathing. I can't draw any air in.

The worst possible scenario plays out in my head. Fuck. The pounding against my ribcage causes physical pain, and my gaze flies around the room as if I'd find the answers to what happened taped on my wall. What the fuck am I doing? I need to get help. I hang up and dial George, putting the call on speaker so I can cover my naked ass with the sweats I dropped on the floor earlier.

"Rhys?" he answers on the second ring.

"Something is wrong! She stopped talking and started screaming." I barely get the words out as I suck oxygen into my lungs.

"FUCK! Not again."

My stomach churns. George doesn't curse, let alone use the F-bomb.

*Wait. Again?*

"Where was she when she called?" I hear footfalls in the background.

"Brooks's office." Finally covered, I pick the phone back up and disable the speaker. I hope Mom and Dad didn't hear anything, or I'll have to answer a lot more questions.

I watch the blinking dots on my alarm clock disappear and light back up seventeen times before George speaks again.

"Miss Lilly!" Pause. "LILLY! Don't do this to me again." Another Pause. "Lilly, your brother will not be happy. Come on, wake up. Please." The last word is spoken with such desperation that my entire body begins to shake. I tighten my hold on the phone to not drop it as I sink to my mattress.

"George, what the fuck is going on there?" I try not to yell, but the rest of the house probably heard me anyway. My pulse is thrashing in my ears, and all I can do is clench and unclench my free hand, waiting.

"George?" Lilly's faint voice comes through the speaker.

*Oh, thank fuck!*

Air finally enters my lungs again, and I can feel them scream in relief.

"Yes, I'm here. You gave us quite the fright again, Miss Lilly." George's tone is gentle, a side I have not yet seen of the man.

"Us?" she mumbles, confused.

"JESUS CHRIST, GEORGE! PUT ME ON FUCKING SPEAKER!" I'm losing my shit. They must've heard me because there is rummaging, and then their voices are clearer.

"You were on the phone with Rhys. He called me when you passed out." His soothing tone does the opposite for me.

"What the fuck do you mean she passed out? Calla, are you

okay?" I press my free hand against my chest. I'm not going to make it to my nineteenth birthday at this rate. My heart will give out before.

"I'm fine." Her groggy voice manages to calm my nerves a little, but not enough to stop the trembling in my extremities.

"Miss Lilly," he warns her.

"I haven't told him," she whispers to her bodyguard.

"Told me what?" Motherfucker. More secrets? I stand and start pacing the length of my room. She's not talking to me again. The silence on the other end tells me that they are either in a standoff or somehow quietly communicating.

"Told. Me. WHAT?" I bark into the device. I'm losing my patience—with both of them.

"I passed out after my last migraine," Lilly finally admits meekly.

"YOU WHAT?" Awesome, now I seem to have developed belated puberphonia.

"I am meeting with Lakatos on Thursday. I will discuss this new...development with him. In the meantime, Nate also set up an appointment with his neurologist for the following week."

My knees buckle mid-step, and I sink to a crouch, white-knuckling the device while my other hand is back at pulling strands of my hair out. "What does that mean?" My question is not more than a barely audible croak.

"We don't know. But we want to talk to Lakatos before drawing any conclusions."

Before drawing conclusions? The reason behind my rapid pulse shifts, and I see red. "Are you fucking kidding me?" I seethe into the phone. "She passed out. TWICE! Draw some conclusions. You don't pass out from a freaking memory if nothing is wrong with you!"

"Rhys," Lilly pleads with me. She sounds better than a minute ago, but I can hear her exhaustion in my name. "I promise you that I will have it checked out. There is nothing we can do right this second. I can't check myself into the emergency room here."

I let myself fall ungracefully on my ass and drop my forehead to my knees. She's right. The press would be all over it. *Lilly McGuire Suddenly Checks Herself into an LA Hospital.* Not to mention that George's presence would cause a whole other round of questions.

*Fuuuck!*

"I get it, babe. I do. But..." I inhale for four, hold, exhale for four. "Shit. I can't sit here and do nothing."

There is silence on the other end, and I fight the urge to hang up and drive to the airport.

"What was the memory about?" I grit out the question in an attempt to distract myself from the other *topic*.

"I saw Payton."

*Huh?*

"What do you mean?" George appears just as confused.

There is rustling on the other end before Lilly speaks. "Here. I found this picture of Brooks and me in his albums. It's the day he gave me Bobo."

"Can someone please switch this damn call to video?" I don't mean to growl into the device, but I can't help it. Frustration is making my jaw clench.

"Oh! Yes, hold on." An incoming video call from Lilly's phone pops up, and I accept, disconnecting George's number. Her face fills the screen, and I take in her disheveled appearance.

*She's fine, my ass.*

I bite my tongue. I'm sick of fighting, but there will be some conversations when we're in the same time zone again.

"Show me the damn photo, Calla," I order. My ability to communicate calmly left sometime between Lilly screaming and passing out and the understanding settling in that there might be something seriously wrong with her.

The screen tilts, and a photo of a young Lilly and a blond man comes into focus. It's the first time I'm seeing Lilly's biological father. The similarities between him and his children are instantly visible. Nate and Lilly have the same light hair and similar complexion, though Lilly is on the fairer side. Since the picture was taken with a frontal view of Brooks, Lilly partially from the side and back, his hazel eyes catch my attention immediately. He is holding the teddy bear I remember Lilly dragging everywhere for years.

Lilly comes back into view. "It's Bobo, isn't it?"

"Yes."

"How does Payton fit into this?" George inserts in a tone I can't interpret.

Lilly takes in a deep breath. "I'm not sure if it was the same day. I think it was, though, because I was holding the bear, and Brooks was by my side. The more I think of it...it has to have been." She holds the picture up again. "He is wearing the same clothes. I turned toward Emily, showing her the bear, when I noticed a woman in the distance. She was partially hidden behind a tree, watching us. I've seen enough pictures of her. It was Payton."

Lilly's gaze flicks between her bodyguard and me. "That has to mean that she knew about me, right?"

"Do you remember anything else?" George probes.

She hangs her head, defeated. "No."

"Where is Nate?" I ask, suddenly wondering why no one informed him of his sister's findings or losing consciousness.

"He's at the vineyard with Margot and Julian," Lilly elaborates. "He'll be back later tonight."

Rustling indicates George has gotten up off the ground. "I will give him a call. He needs to know what happened."

"Can that wait until he's back?" Her eyes are begging the man I can't see.

"No," is his last word before fading steps come through the speaker.

We sit in silence, and I watch her stare somewhere past the camera. When her gaze settles back on me, she whispers, "I wish you were here."

My heart breaks. "Give me the address, and I'm there by tomorrow." I would be.

She sighs. "I can't. We can't risk tipping Turner off."

"Do you really think that dude won't find you? Or do something to flush you out? It's clear that he has an agenda. *You running away* will not stop him!" All restrain breaks, and I can't stop myself. "And since we're already on the topic. What's going on with finding your answers? It seems like you only have more questions. Should I assume you'll hide in La La Land indefinitely?"

Lilly's eyes grow wider the more words leave my stupid trap. By the time I'm done, I'm breathing heavily again, and tears run down her cheeks.

*Fuck.*

"I, um...I think I'm gonna check if George got a hold of Nate," she stammers.

"Cal—" But before I can apologize, she disconnects, and I'm staring at my background picture—a selfie Lilly and I took one night, lying in her bed.

My leg kicks out and connects with my chair, slamming it into the desk. My room will be an assembly of broken furniture soon.

I TURN the knob without knocking, and my father's head snaps up at the unannounced intrusion of his office. It has always been an unspoken rule for anyone to announce themselves—even Mom. However, I don't give a shit right now.

"I want you to call Lakatos!"

Dad's jaw drops, and his eyes widen. He composes himself quickly, followed by taking me in from head to toe. I haven't bothered putting on a shirt, my three-day-old sweats are stained, and my hair is a semi-dried mess from almost ripping my scalp off from finding out Lilly has kept more secrets from me. Not to mention listening to her scream in agony. My fists at my side twitch, and the motion doesn't go unnoticed.

"Who is Lakatos?" My father's tone is even and gives nothing away. He's good, I'll give him that.

"Don't fuck with me," I snarl.

He cocks his head, doing another scan. "What happened, Rhys?"

*He doesn't ask how I know the name?*

Screw it. If Lilly decides to freeze me out, I have no reason to protect her damn secrets. "Your little brain-fuck with Lilly's head is making her pass out whenever she remembers something." I'm borderline yelling.

"What is she remembering?" The question is more careful this time.

"Does it matter? I fucking listened to her scream in pain before passing out. Call that motherfucker and HAVE. HER. FIXED!" The adrenaline raging through my veins is causing the all-too-familiar body trembles to start again, and my knees threaten to buckle.

Dad slowly pushes back from the desk and walks around to

where I'm standing. His hands settle on my shoulders as he looks at me with a somber expression. My chest is heaving, and it's written all over his face that I'm not going to like his next words.

"Rhys, what was done to Lilly's mind is irreversible."

My legs give out. Bending forward, I clasp my hands behind my neck and start rocking back and forth.

*No, no, no.*

Behind my eyes, I see Lilly's unconscious body, lying on a floor, one day not waking up anymore. I'm starting to feel sick and begin to dry heave in the middle of my father's office.

"Rhys. Son!" I hear him calling out for me but don't have it in me to respond. Eventually, she'll pass out, and no one will be there to help her. She'll hit her head, or fall down the stairs, or—one scenario worse than the next plays out in my head. Another round of retching makes my stomach cramp.

Suddenly, hands grab under my arms and pull me up like a ragdoll. Dad pulls me over to the sofa, where he drops me with less care before sitting down next to me. My elbows rest on my thighs, and I bury my face in my palms. "I'm going to lose her for good." My muffled mumbling is accompanied by my eyes beginning to water.

*Fuck, now I'm also crying like a freakin' baby.*

My father's hand comes to the nape up my neck, where he squeezes ever so slightly, almost like a massage. "You will not lose her, son."

"How do you know?" My voice is hoarse.

"Because the two of you were meant to be together from the moment Emily dropped her off at our house and your mother placed her in your crib. Lilly was crying nonstop; we tried everything for hours to calm her down. You were never like that, so we were completely out of our element. In a final attempt, Mom put her down in your crib; you had just woken up from your nap. As soon this little tiny baby girl was lying next to you, you smiled at her, and she stopped. She fell asleep, and you watched her the entire time she slept."

I turn my head to see if he's shitting me, but he's sincere. At eighteen years old, I feel like I'm finally forming the bond with my father I should've had years ago.

"Why did you make me leave?" The moisture in my eyes spills over, and I swipe it roughly, embarrassment heating my face.

His expression shifts, and he's about to shut down.

"DON'T!" I order. "Don't you dare freeze me out, too."

He understands and dips his head in a fast motion. "There is a lot you don't know—"

"Whose fault is that?" Anger overtakes my senses again, and I'm grateful for the change. I don't like losing it in front of people, least of all my father.

He sighs. "I don't know how you found out about Hector, and I won't ask—*yet*. I have kept a lot from you—not just you, but also your mother—to keep this family safe. In my line of work, I've made enemies, and I was prepared for that. When my family was at risk, I handled it the way I knew how, which in hindsight was not the best solution. I..." My father swallows hard. "I pushed you away to not make you a target as well. Your feelings for Lilly made you reckless. The fact that everyone believed she was your sister was never a concern for me; that would've been an easy fix, telling people she was adopted. But I couldn't risk my son's life being threatened. It was only a matter of time before Lilly would be in the crossfire again."

"What crossfire?" He gives me answers, but at the same time, he speaks in riddles that raise more questions.

"I don't have all the facts either, Rhys. I have some, but a lot are suspicions. Some of them are probably accurate, but without confirmation or proof, I won't cause my family unnecessary panic."

"So, essentially, you're not giving me anything. AGAIN!" I bark the last word at him.

"I can give you one answer." His gaze jumps back and forth between my eyes. "I've never not cared for you. You are my son, and I would do anything to keep you safe. My methods may not have been the best, but I always knew where you were and made sure you were safe."

The steadily building rage deflates, and for the first time since being a little boy, I hug my father. He wraps his arms around my shoulders, and I feel him shudder.

I haven't gotten any answers for Lilly, but I have my father back.

## CHAPTER ONE HUNDRED FIVE

**LILLY**

NATE DIDN'T TAKE THE NEWS WELL—THE MIGRAINE-MEMORY *OR* me passing out. Again. He made up some emergency in the office and got everyone on the jet within the hour. From the moment George told me he's on his way back, I haven't been able to sit still. He is bringing too much attention to himself. What if Margot checks with Hank again? She's been annoyed for days. She could follow him here. She'd find me, and Nate would have to turn himself in sooner. My thumb won't stop flicking against the rest of my fingers. Back and forth, back and forth.

In an attempt to distract myself, I go to the theater room and turn on a movie. It doesn't work; I couldn't tell you what the movie is about if I tried. My mind constantly goes back to Rhys. Is he right? Has my running put everyone more at risk? Should I let him come to LA? We could spend spring break together, and he could get to know Nate. A flutter in my chest makes me smile. Then, a new picture flashes in front of my eyes: Turner waiting for Natty during school. But that's not where the images end: Turner running Wes off the road with his car. Turner following Rhys to the airport and coming to LA, exposing where I am. *Or* Turner hurting Rhys when he refuses to tell him where I am. Each scenario is worse than the next until I'm covered in sweat and am sitting bent forward, clutching my stomach with both arms. Inhale, exhale. Inhale, exhale.

That's all I do until my brother finds me. The door flies open, and Nate scans the room. When his eyes settle on me, he's at my side in three strides. Crouching down, he gently forces my chin up with his hand, and we lock eyes.

"Talk to me, sis." His careful tone is my breaking point.

The tears I've been holding in spill over, and I press my mouth together.

"Lilly." My name is just a whisper of a sound.

I let my lips part, and that's it. All my worries spill out. I word-vomit everything. The memory, the phone call with Rhys, my fears about Turner, and all the fucked-up scenarios I've cooked up in my head in which he kills off everyone I care about.

*I've gone off the deep end.*

Nate listens to all of it, not interrupting me once. When I'm running out of steam, he gets up from his crouch and sits down next to me.

"I'm so sorry you are going through all of this because of me." His arms wrap around my shoulder, squeezing me to his side.

My eyes flutter closed, and I lean against him. I'm emotionally drained. "I'm going to lose him, Nate," I mumble, sinking further against my brother.

"You won't," he soothes me, the words just a murmur.

I BLINK AGAINST A FLICKERING LIGHT.

*Where the hell am I?*

I try to move, but an arm holds me in place. What the—? Slowly adjusting to the brightness, I'm able to open one then both eyes and glance around. I'm still in the media room. On the screen plays a muted action movie, bright explosions being the reason for my temporary inability to see. My head is fuzzy, and my eyes burn from my crying spell. Turning my head to the side, I take in Nate's slumped form—he's out like a light. I carefully disentangle myself from his large frame and move into the hallway, closing the door behind me quietly.

I tap the screen of my phone. It's 4:21 a.m.—past seven in

Westbridge. I stare at the clock for a whole minute before I make my decision. Screw it. Before I can stop myself, I pull up the recent call log and click on Rhys's name. It rings five times, and with every beep, my heart rate increases. He's not going to answer.

"Calla?" Rhys's groggy voice comes through the speaker.

"I'm so sorry," I begin to sob.

"Wha—?" He's instantly more alert. "What happened?"

"I'm sorry I ran. I was so scared Turner would come after you. Natty can't defend herself. I kept picturing him hurting you t-to g-get to m-me—" My words break off, and I lean against the wall opposite the theater, sinking to the floor.

The silence, on the other end makes my fear become a reality. I've lost him. I've kept too much from him.

"I...I'm not sure what to say, babe. I understand why you did it. I do. But—" He exhales slowly.

"B-but?" I hiccup, pressing the back of my hand to my mouth.

"I'm...pissed. I'm not gonna lie to you. You know that's the one thing I'll never do again. It's supposed to be you and me. *Together!* But you don't talk to me; you keep hiding things from me. I love you more than anything, but I... I can't handle any more surprises. I don't want to go to bed wondering if you're still going to be there in the morning. Or be close to a heart attack every time my phone rings, thinking this time you're gone for good. When you stopped screaming yesterday, I couldn't breathe. It was discovering your crashed Jeep all over again. I thought you had died with me on the phone, and I couldn't do shit about it."

Rhys's tone is getting angrier the more he speaks, and the fear of him leaving me overtakes every cell in my body. *You left him first*, the voice in my head sneers at me. *He has every right to break up with you.*

My hands shake violently, and I can barely hold the phone up.

*What have I done?*

The door across from me opens, and Nate looks down, hair disheveled and with worried eyes. Footsteps from the other end of the hall alert me to George's arrival. I've woken them both up.

I pull my legs close and let my forehead drop to my knees, ignoring the two men in the hallway with me. "Please don't leave me," I whisper into the speaker.

"I...fuck." Rhys exhales a sharp breath. When he doesn't say anything else, I lose all self-control.

My not-so-silent crying turns into uncontrollable panic. I rock back and forth while pressing the phone harder against my ear. "I'm sorry. I'm so sorry..." I can't get anything else out other than my hysterical apologies.

"Fuck!" he curses. "Calla. Babe? Put Nate or George on the phone. Please." His tone is softer than before but detached at the same time.

*He doesn't even want to talk to me.*

I hold out the device without looking who takes it. As soon as it's out of my hand, my arms bend, and with my elbows pressing against my knees, my hands find my head, and my nails dig into my scalp.

"Yes?"

*Nate has the phone.*

Silence. "Did she sound okay to you?" Sarcasm drips from my brother's question. "Yes." Deep breath. "George did everything he could without spooking the guy. He won't meet sooner." Pause. "I get it, man. She is my sister." Longer pause. "We're taking care of her." *Since when does Nate talk this civilly with Rhys?* "This won't make it go away. You get that, right?" More listening. "Mhmm. You get four days." This is more of a warning. "Friday. We'll be in touch as soon as George is back." Sigh. "I will."

I take in the conversation on this end without moving out of my balled-up position. Four days? What's happening on Friday? Suddenly, two arms pick me up behind the legs and shoulder blades, and I'm airborne. My eyes fly open, settling on Nate's face, and a squeak escapes my throat. My body is expecting the familiar pain to set in, but after a few steps, it registers. My back doesn't hurt—not like before. With all the emotional chaos, I didn't pay attention to my healing injuries. The physical tension leaves my body, and I cover my face with my hands. This is all too much.


My brother deposits me on a barstool at the kitchen island and places my phone in front of me. I'm numb. The panic, the fear, the guilt...it's all gone. Did my mind finally break completely?

Out of the corner of my eyes, George gets busy with the kettle, and a few minutes later, a steaming cup of Earl Grey is placed in front of me. My bodyguard remains leaning against the kitchen counter by the stove while Nate sits down next to me at the island, rubbing his hands up and down my spine.

"Rhys is asking for a break, baby sis."

My bottom lip begins to quiver, yet the emotion behind it is not there. It's like the connection between the limbic system and the rest of me is severed. When I remain mute, he continues, "You and I have put him through a lot the last few weeks. I'm as much to blame. We've been selfish assholes." A non-comical snort escapes him.

The rational part of my brain still works. He's right. I've only thought of myself—what I needed.

"The guy can only take so much, and as much as I tried not to like him, I do. And I get it. He loves you. *He has loved you forever*. I would lose my shit, too, hearing what he did yesterday. Hell, I packed everyone on the plane without a real excuse and left them standing at the airport. And you're *only* my sister, *not* my soulmate." Nate pauses, waiting for me to say something.

I can't. Rhys wants a break. It doesn't mean we're broken up. He loves me. It's just for a few days.

My brother continues, "I told him we would call him Friday after George gets back. That gives him time to collect his thoughts, and it gives us four days to find as many answers as we can, including who Francis-Fucking-Turner is. Then, you and Rhys will work it out. One way or another."

"You think he'll still be there?" My voice sounds like a recording.

"He's angry and worried, but he made me promise to tell you one thing."

I turn my head toward Nate, eyebrows raised.

"He loves you, and you're stuck with him."

Those few words bridge the gap between my body and my brain. It's like a wave of emotions crashes down on me, and I'm suddenly drowning. Sadness, guilt, anger, fear, worry... I can't filter through them fast enough.

I cover my mouth with my hands in an attempt to muffle my

cries. Nate reaches out and pulls me close by the back of my head until my face is against his shoulder.

"Give him time," he murmurs next to my ear.

I nod against the fabric of his shirt.

He holds me until I regain some control and pull back. George is still in the same spot, watching me with a wrinkled brow.

"Okay. Let's get to work, then." Nate lets go of me and gets up.

AFTER FORCING down breakfast which consists of tea for me and half a gallon of coffee for Nate, he follows me to Brooks's office. He remains standing in the doorframe for several minutes before slowly setting one foot in front of the other.

Seeing him struggle to be in here, I hold my breath. I pick up a stack of paper from the floor. "Do you want me to bring everything downstairs? Or—"

"I'm fine." His words are clipped, and it's clear that he isn't.

"Nate, I really—"

"I said I'm fine!" he barks, and I jerk my head up and down. I'm not going to argue with him.

He comes over to where I piled the statements for Payton's and the family accounts, and I hand him one containing the transaction amount.

My brother scans the papers, reaching for another and another before looking up. "He transferred the money for whomever he was paying off out of the joint account he and my mother kept for the property expenses." His expression ranges from confused to pissed off.

I nod and whisper, "Does that mean Payton knew about it?"

Nate's mouth turns down. "I always assumed the family accountant took care of most of the stuff. Both my parents had their own money, and they shared a joint account for all the big expenses—properties, cars, etc. My college tuition came out of the trust my grandfather set up when I was born. Audrey had her own. After my grandmother passed away, my grandfather called a family meeting where he went over everything the Altman's own. During that, my parents also laid out to me how our family's finances were set up. But they never specifically told me who managed them. After my father..." His hands tighten on the stack he's holding. "After he died, our accountant handled everything and just handed me the papers. I never read any of them. I was too—"

"It's okay," I interrupt him. He doesn't have to spell it out. "Do the accounts still exist?"

Nate looks up. "No. Everything got consolidated into mine or your trust, which is why I didn't recognize the account number the money came from. But—" Then his eyebrows scrunch together.

"What?" I ask, unable to follow his thoughts.

"Frank knew."

"Who?"

"Frank. Our accountant. He handed me all the papers, which means he at least saw the will if not even had something to do with setting your trust up. That motherfucker. He kept that to himself all these years."

"Are you sure about that? Why would he keep that from you?"

Nate jumps up and starts moving between the door and the desk. "I will find out." He pulls his phone out of his pocket and dials someone. The other person picks up after several rings.

"Hank! I—" Hank cuts him off, and my brother gazes at the ceiling. The voice on the other end is raised, but I can't make out what he says. Nate barks, "Yes, I can read the clock, asshole." He pulls the phone from his ear and glances at the screen before holding it back up. "It's 6:23 on a Monday; you should be up by now. Stop whining. Now, what I was going to say is I need you to find me the number for Frank Hollancomp." Nate listens. "I know he retired three years ago, but since we still send checks his way, his number and address are—" The knuckles on his fists turn white. "Because I'm busy. Just do it."

Nate hangs up without saying goodbye.

"Do you always talk to Hank that way?" I ask carefully with a raised eyebrow. I've seen so many sides of my brother by now, but this one is new, and I'm not sure how to react to it.

"Huh?" He focuses back on me. "Oh. Hank's been exceptionally bitchy lately. No clue what crawled up his ass."

"You sure that has nothing to do with you?" I keep my voice low and prepare myself for another outburst. I don't want to directly accuse him of being at fault for how Hank acts; I haven't seen much of it firsthand. But Nate has been absent a lot, and I assume Hank has had to pick up a lot for him.

He shakes his head, starting to flip through the statements again. "No, it started a few months ago."

"Hmm...okay then." I'll leave it at that.

My brother gives me a hug and informs me that he'll work on tracing the money. He hasn't done anything on that end since he ran into a dead end with the last shell corporation. He tells me he'll be at his house for a bit, and I should call if I need anything. He'll be back in a few hours.

# CHAPTER ONE HUNDRED SIX

**LILLY**

THE DAYS WERE BLENDING TOGETHER. NATE WENT BACK TO HIS *keep-Lilly-busy* strategy. By the end of Tuesday, I felt like some type of accountant—forensic, maybe? Who knows. Thank goodness I like numbers. He made me go over Brooks and Payton's financial statements. All of them.

After I had left California, Nate uploaded every shred of paper from the vineyard to his servers, and I probably went through more than half a decade of Altman-Hamlin personal expenses. It gave me insight into my biological father's habits, but that was pretty much the extent of it. Besides the outgoing large—six-figure—amount coming from the family account and the smaller—five-figure—ones going out from Brooks's, everything was normal. I began to suspect that Nate was simply trying to keep me occupied, which worked during the daytime. At night, not so much.

My sleep was shit, and when I did manage to doze off, I would wake up before the sun was up, my mind instantly spiraling. I'd been replaying the previous months in my head over and over. Not just since I started remembering, but before. Rhys has always put me first. After years of protecting his parents' secrets, I forced him to keep mine. He had to isolate himself from his best friend because of me. The more my mind ran with it, the deeper the pit in my stomach became.

I couldn't fault Rhys if he wanted to continue the break indefinitely.

Grabbing my phone almost hourly, I started typing several text messages to him but deleted them all. I promised my brother I'd *adhere to the radio silence*, as he phrased it, and give Rhys the space he asked for. What was Rhys doing right now? Instead, I spent the nights tearing the place apart for more clues while Nate was busy following the money trail. Hank and Margot kept him equally busy, and he could only work on our leads when they slept. Whenever I saw him, the circles under his eyes became more pronounced. I didn't like it.

Tuesday evening, George informed me over dinner that he'd be gone most of the next morning to prepare for his trip north to meet Lakatos. He'd be leaving around five in the morning *to meet someone* (who the hell meets that early—I probably don't want to know) and then run errands. He'd be back after lunch to finish packing.

This would be the first time I was alone in the mansion. At the thought, my pulse immediately sped up. I was safe here, but the emptiness of the ginormous house—even though George was still in front of me—made my stomach churn.

*What was my gut trying to tell me?*


On Wednesday, I wake up at the crack of dawn. Surprise, surprise. Not.

I glance at the clock; it's not even six yet. George is already gone. My hands clench around the comforter. I'm alone. I slept about three hours after spending the night unsuccessfully digging through more storage bins in the basement. My eyes are burning, and even the eyedrops George handed me are not helping.

I've been here for a week, and with no specific task for today, the walls are closing in. I press my palm to my chest, but my lungs constrict even more. I need to get out of here. NOW!

That's how I end up parked, before eight—in my new, white G-Wagon—in front of Flakes, a small café the search engine spit out when I looked for a place to get tea. Not that the twenty-three flavors of assorted black teas my brother stocked the kitchen with weren't enough. I simply needed a destination—a *lame* excuse to leave the property. Driving here, I marveled at how the streets were crowded like downtown Westbridge during Black Friday. Los Angeles is so different from everything I am used to; it's hard to wrap my head around it.

Sitting in the car, I can't bring myself to get out. "Nothing to Lose But You" by Three Days Grace plays through the speakers, and the outside becomes blurry. I haven't cried since Monday morning, but the lyrics hit deep, and a sob escapes me. I sink low in my seat, wrapping my arms around myself, and let the tears fall.

After the song finishes, it takes me over fifteen minutes before I can force myself to open the driver's side door. My face is dry, and I check in the rearview mirror that I don't look too much of a mess. My brother's order to remain inside the house at all times replays in my head. He's so going to kill me when he finds out. And he will find out; he's Nate Hamlin. Maybe I should go back. I pull on the handle to close the gap again, but before the lock latches, I pause. I need this, or I will go crazy. *Crazier.* Or I'll cave and end up calling Rhys. I push the door back open.

The street is not two miles from the ostentatious neighborhood of mansions where I've been hiding. The sidewalk is busy, people on their way to wherever, passing the fancy boutiques, restaurants, and cafés lining both sides. Even if Turner were to suddenly show up, he couldn't do anything without attracting attention. And I would make sure to bring attention to myself. A woman in a business suit passes and holds my gaze. A new thought slams into me: what if someone recognizes me? My one hand that's on the steering wheel tightens, and I scan the faces passing in front of my car. Are they looking at me longer than usual?

*Shit. What am I doing?*

I release the door handle and steering wheel to cover my face and take one deep breath. No one is looking for me here. I'll be okay. Pulling down the baseball hat I found in one of the many bins, I climb out of the Mercedes. I parked close to the entrance of Flakes and am inside within less than twenty feet. My shoulders relax instantly.

Scanning the inside, I miss Magnolia's. This place is nothing like it. Where Magnolia's is cozy and inviting, Flakes looks like a space-ship stuffed with junkyard scraps. A blindingly polished gray concrete floor, shiny silver high-top metal tables, white metal bar stools, white napkin holders on each table—also metal. The artwork on the walls consists of abstract photographs. The random shapes—whatever the objects in front of the lens were—are either too close, too blurry, or too over-exposed. Between the tables are life-sized—surprise, surprise—metal sculptures made out of random...well, junkyard crap. I almost turn around and walk back out but then stop myself. I'm here for a change of scenery and tea. Who cares what the ambience is like? Stepping up to the counter, I scan the menu hanging on the wall behind it. The pastries in the display look mouthwatering, and I order my usual tea and add a chocolate chip scone to it, because why not?

Keeping my face hidden behind a curtain of my hair and the low-hanging hat, I move to the side. I wait for the barista to pour water over the teabag and place my treat on a plate. She pushes both toward me with a smile, and I reach for them. I stifle the sigh of relief when I have my order in front of me and no one has called out my name or pointed a finger at me. In my current state of paranoia, I expected to either have someone jump up, yelling, "It's Lilly McGuire," or worse, Turner himself serving me my beverage.

*Guess I'm losing it no matter what or where I am.*

I've just lifted the plate and mug when a tall, hard body slams into me from the side. My arms jerk upward, sending my food and drink flying, and I hear the impact of the plate and mug several feet away as I go down myself. I manage to brace the fall somewhat, but the same hard body lands on top of me, and all the air gets expelled from my lungs.

*Ouch.*

My initial panic when I hit the ground is replaced by confusion and...annoyance. The dude—now sprawled out on me with his head somewhere in my armpit region—begins to laugh like a hyena on crack.

*What the hell?*

He is heavy, and all I see is his shaggy blond hair. It looks like it was styled at one point, but now the gelled strands stick out at all angles. When he doesn't move and just keeps cackling, I push on his shoulders. "Hey, asshole, get off of me!"

Heat surges through me, and the annoyance quickly morphs into anger. People are staring. So much for keeping a low profile.

Footsteps come from behind us, and a female voice shouts, "Jesus-fucking-Christ! Hudson, what the fuck! I left you for two minutes to pee!"

*Hudson's* dead weight gets dragged off of me, and my lungs sigh in relief. From my position—still on the floor—I notice he can barely stand. Swaying, he leans against the bar and closes his eyes, a green tint to his skin. A hand appears in my vision, and I glance up at the girl attached to it. She is gorgeous in an innocent kind of way. Her long, chestnut hair hangs wavy over her shoulders. Her face is bare of makeup, and she is dressed in a black jogger and soft-pink V-neck tee.

"Shit. I'm so sorry. I will replace whatever my dumbass brother just ruined for you." She throws a glare to the side that would make Denielle proud. Hudson, aka her brother, is slouching with his elbow on the counter, staring at nothing, and I get my first full visual of him. He's gorgeous. He's tall, probably around Rhys's 6' 1, bronze skin, the bluest eyes I've ever seen, and high, sculpted cheekbones. His washed-out designer jeans hang low on his hips, and his black dress shirt could use a wash and an iron. But despite him being a complete mess, almost every female in this place ogles him.

I focus back on the girl and grasp her hand. As she pulls me up, I mutter, "It's okay." I don't want more attention. Peeking at Hudson again, I add, "Is he okay?"

The girl snorts. "Depends." Just as she says the word, her brother begins to tilt forward, and she latches onto his arm, whisper shouting, "Jesus, H. Get your shit together." She drags him over to one of the high tops and deposits him on the barstool where he instantly drops his head on his forearms on the table. I cross my arms in front of my chest and watch the scene.

Turning back to me, a genuine smile spreads across her face, and she holds out a hand again. "Hi. I'm Elle. I figured I have to properly introduce myself and apologize for dumb-dumb over there one more time." She tilts her head toward a now snoring Hudson.

My brows shoot up at the sound coming from him, and Elle briefly closes her eyes, mumbling, "I'm so going to rip him a new one when we get home."

That makes me snort, their relationship reminding me of my own with Nate. Not that I've ever seen my brother trashed like this.

"So..." she chirps, "what do I get you?"

My pulse speeds up. "Oh, no, I...uh—I should leave."

"Nonsense. Tell me, or I order you one of everything."

*Wha—? Who is this girl?*

"Well, um...Earl Grey and a scone?" My response sounds more like a question.

"You got it." She nods. "Do you mind making sure baby bro doesn't faceplant off his chair while I get your stuff? And some black coffee for him."

*How did I end up babysitting a drunk dude who cannot be much older than me?*

"Uh, sure?" Again, more a question.

I warily eye Hudson as I perch on the barstool next to him. This is so not how I expected this morning to go. Elle is back a few minutes later, my tea and scone in hand, and the barista in tow with two coffees.

"I didn't catch your name earlier." She seems genuine, but every muscle in my body tenses. Shit.

"Uh...Lilly." I omit the last name. If she's seen the news lately or has access to the Internet, she knows who I am.

Her eyes widen for a fraction of a second before she composes herself.

*Yup, she knows.*

I sigh inwardly and take that as my cue. "I should probably..." I start pushing off the table.

"No! I'm sorry. Please stay!" Glancing at her brother, she adds, "I'm stuck here for a while. There is no way I can drag his ass to the car. Keep me company. Please?"

"I don't know." I let my eyes wander, but everyone else has gone back to whatever they were doing.

Suddenly, a hand covers mine, and I jolt. Elle pulls back. "Listen...Lilly. Most people probably would recognize you if they knew you were here. Your name...and face are all over the Internet. You just...surprised me. I mean, aren't you supposed to be on the East Coast or wherever?"

I stare at her, my mouth dry. What am I supposed to say to that?

Then she rushes out. "Never mind. It's not important. Just... Let's chat." She shrugs, and her eyes turn sad as she looks at the boy sleeping with his head on the table.

"What's going on with him?" I whisper, feeling like I'm intruding on something private.

Elle sighs. "I wish I knew. He's spiraling, and it's mostly my fault. So, when he calls me in the middle of the night to drive to LA to pick him up at a frat party he has zero business of being at, I do it."

"He's in college?" He doesn't look like it, but I don't want to sound like a bitch.

She huffs out a laugh. "Hell no, we're both seniors. Though, H here is eleven months younger than me."

My eyes widen, and she quickly adds, "He's my half-brother. Different moms."

I nod. Who am I to judge anyone on their family history?

We chat about everything and nothing while Hudson snores peacefully beside us. I drink my tea while Elle sips on her coffee, sneaking glances at her little brother. It feels good to talk to someone who is not involved in my drama, and despite her initial recognition, she doesn't ask me anything about *the case* or Rhys. I almost feel normal—like making a new friend.

When my phone begins to buzz in my pocket, my heart stutters at the sensation. My initial thought is *Rhys*, but as I pull it out, Nate's number scrolls across the screen. My gaze skips to the top, and the clock on the screen tells me I've been sitting here for over two hours.

*Shit, shit, shit!*

I look at the girl across from me apologetically and answer the call. "I'm so sorry. I lost track of time. I'll be home in a few."

"What the fuck were you thinking?" my brother hisses into my ear. "George is not back until this afternoon, and I was on my way to the airport when I got the movement alert. Damn it, sis. We have no fucking idea where Turner is. Why would you put yourself at risk like this?"

*Airport?*

I sit up straighter, but instead of admitting that he is right, I lash out. "I've been stuck there for a week. I needed a break."

The elongated silence makes my guilt level rise even more. Finally, Nate exhales audibly. "Please get back to the house. I'm not getting on this damn jet until I know you're safe."

My eyes start to burn, and I blink several times. When the rest of his words sink in, my forehead wrinkles. "Where are you going?"

"There is a problem with one of the new hotels in Europe. Several of the local investors are freaking out, and I need to make an appearance and calm their rich asses." He sighs, exasperated.

"Why didn't you call sooner?" I keep my voice low, but it's clear by Elle's expression that she can hear my side of the conversation.

"Because you seem to be having a good time, and that Elle girl checked out clean."

*No way.*

"How do you...never mind," I trail off as I spot the camera in the corner above our table. Of course my brother hacked into the café's security feed. He probably got her name from tapping into the line verifying the credit card transactions or following her on traffic cameras back until he caught the license plate. Nothing would surprise me.

I sigh. "I'm leaving, okay?"

"Thank you, Lilly," Nate says gently before hanging up.

"Family trouble?" Elle inquires with a raised eyebrow.

I snort. "You could say that."

She smiles at me in understanding. "Hey, I really enjoyed talking to you. Why don't I give you my number, and well, uh...we can touch base when you have your stuff sorted out."

She waits for my answer, and after a moment of deliberation, I pull out my phone. Why the hell not? She rattles it off, and I put it in my contacts. I could use another friend. Worst case: I don't call her. Other than saying she has seen me in L.A., she can't do anything.

My life has taken on a status of utter insanity.

After we exchange numbers, I say goodbye, and as I walk out, I hear a slap on the table behind me, followed by, "Wake up, fucker. It's time to get on the road. I want to get back to San Diego before Hazel blows up my phone!"

*San Diego?*

# CHAPTER ONE HUNDRED SEVEN

### LILLY

I PULL INTO THE GARAGE AND SHOOT MY BROTHER A TEXT. I confirm that the roll gate is down before getting out of the SUV and making my way through the mudroom to the kitchen. I've just put down the keys on the island when my phone starts vibrating in my pocket again.

*Chill out, Nate. I would've called—*

But when I see the name on the screen, my eyebrows scrunch together. Denielle. I didn't expect to hear from her until Friday when she'd be back in Westbridge.

"Hey, D. What's—"

"HE CHEATED!" My best friend's screech makes me pull the phone away from my ear.

"Who?" I'm genuinely confused.

"CHARLIE. WHO DO YOU THINK I'M TALKING ABOUT? THAT POOR EXCUSE OF A WALKING DICK STUCK HIS MINI-SAUSAGE INTO A SORORITY SLUT!"

*Oh. Ohhhh! Well, shit.*

"Um, I am seriously speechless, D. I—"

She interrupts me with more obscenities, followed by, "THAT SON OF A—"

The phone could be at the other end of the thousand-square-foot kitchen, and I'd still hear her loud and clear.

I gentle my tone. "Den, you need to turn it down a bit. My eardrum is about to burst." If she'd been in front of me, I would've lifted my hands in an *I-surrender* gesture. Anything for her not to bite my head off. I've rarely seen, *or heard*, her this livid.

A sigh comes from the other end of the line. "I'm sorry, babe. I'm just...I don't believe what just happened."

"What *did* happen?" I glance at the clock on the stove. It's midday on a Wednesday—not the most common time to discover your long-term boyfriend is cheating.

"He went to a frat party last night, and I didn't feel like going. He's been dragging me to one party after another since I got here." My eyebrows pull together. That doesn't sound like the Charlie I know, but I don't interrupt her. "When he didn't come home, I called his friend, who told me where the party was. I just knew something was off based on how his dickwad frat brother acted on the phone." She draws in a deep breath. "So, I get to the house. It was like a mass orgy, babe! Passed out naked people everywhere."

*What the fuck?*

"I step over the, uh...bodies—some seriously going at it right there in the middle of the day. Gross. And then I start opening random doors. The third one reveals Charlie dipping his dick into some blonde bimbo with fake tits."

*Um, wow.*

My jaw drops. Literally. And I force myself to close my mouth.

"What did you do?" I'm a little scared to ask.

"Nothing there." Her reply is just a quiet mumble.

"There?" My hand tightens around the phone. This cannot be good.

"I was too stunned to confront him in front of a house full of naked asses. I walked back to his place and..."

*Uh-oh.* "And?"

"I went a little crazy on his apartment," Den confesses.

"Explain, please." My tone is careful not to set her off again. My ear just stopped ringing.

"Weeell, his entire wardrobe is in the Goodwill dumpster down the road, and so is every electronic device I could carry there. The rest..."

"Jesus Christ, Den. What did you do with the rest?" I pinch the bridge of my nose, at the same time trying to stifle a laugh. You do not want Denielle Keller as your enemy.

"I may have just thrown it out the window. At least some poor soul will benefit from this."

Good Lord. "Are you still at his place?" What if he calls the cops?

"No, I grabbed my shit and took an Uber to the airport. I'm coming to you."

My heartbeat slows before it picks up double time.

"WHAT?" This time I'm screeching into the speaker.

"I'm landing at LAX tomorrow at one. I can't get out of this shithole until tonight and then have to sleep in Chicago. Thankfully, I can get into the lounge." She sighs, exasperated.

"Den, I don't know if that's such a good idea. What if—?" My mind goes haywire with Turner following her here. And I haven't even considered what George or Nate will do when they discover my best friend in the house.

"Babe, relax. I'm almost six hundred miles from Westbridge. No one followed me here, let alone stuck around for days to watch my cheating boyfriend make an idiot out of me." There is the bitterness I expected, but I appreciate her trying to downplay my anxiety.

"Fine," I concede. The couple of hours with Elle this morning made me miss everyone like crazy. I want to see my best friend.

I give her the address, making her memorize it. I tell her to call me when she lands, and we'll go from there. It'll also give me time to confess to Nate.


AFTER WE HANG UP, I stare at my screen. Charlie cheated on her. This is...holy shit. I mean, the boys had voiced their suspicions before, but still. He adored Den from day one.

Instinctively, I pull up my most recent calls. Rhys is number three on the list, and before I can talk myself out of it, I tap his name. I know I promised not to contact him, but this morning's events, including Nate leaving not just the state but the country, stirred up a multitude of emotions. The phone rings several times before it goes to voicemail.

*"You know the drill. If I wanna talk to you, I'll call back."*

Rhys has had this greeting forever, but under the current circumstances, it's like it's intended for me. Only me. He told Nate he loved me, but he's not answering. Standing in the middle of the kitchen, I spin in a circle, taking in the empty room. What the hell am I doing here? I've lost him. What am I— I can't inhale, my lungs have closed up, and I press a fist to my chest. A wheezing sound hits my ears, and I realize it's coming from me. I need air.

My legs give out, and I drop to my knees. Wrapping my arms around my midsection, I lean my forehead to the cool kitchen floor, close my eyes, and start counting—a last attempt to prevent a panic attack. Every nerve ending in my body is charged, and a film of sweat starts building on my neck. As I reach sixty-three, the beeping of the alarm system alerts me to someone entering the back hallway from the garage. "Miss Lilly?" George's voice calls out. Footsteps come closer and then speed up.

"Lilly! What happened?" Panic laces his question.

*He's back early.*

Hands clasp my arm and pull me upright until we're face to face. I can barely make out the silhouette of him through my hazy vision. His grip tightens, and he shakes me ever so slightly. "Did you have another migraine? Are you in pain? Talk to me!"

"H-he is n-not answering," I stammer.

Reaching up, I swipe my eyes, and George's frown comes into view. "Who is not answering, Miss Lilly?"

Fresh tears spill over. "Rhys."

His mouth forms an O, but no sound comes out. He gives a curt nod and pulls out his phone. About to dial, I latch onto his wrist. "No!"

When the man in front of me cocks his head in confusion, I take a deep breath. My pulse is slowing, and my rational side takes over. "I got overwhelmed. I shouldn't have called. I'm not supposed to. But Nate was mad at me for leaving the house, and then he left. Den found Charlie cheating. I haven't talked to Rhys in three days because I've been a selfish bitch for months and he's finally had enough of me. And then I was alone in the house and—"

"Stop!" George emphasizes his command by squeezing my shoulders.

My eyes widen at the word-vomit that just came out of my mouth, and my chin dips down. Covering my face with my palms, I mumble, "I'm a mess, aren't I?"

A chuckle makes me peer through my fingers at my bodyguard.

"I wouldn't call you a mess, Miss Lilly. You've been through a lot in a very short period of time."

I attempt a smile at his words of comfort.

When his mouth pulls up in a smirk, I wrap my arms around his midsection and squeeze. George stiffens for a fraction of a second before he returns the embrace.

"You don't get hugged too often, do you?" I say before it registers that it's more an insult than a compliment.

He doesn't take it that way, though, and I hear a rumbled laugh in his chest. "No, not in a very long time." He holds me tighter for another second before releasing me with a genuine smile. "Thank you, Lilly."

I quirk an eyebrow. "Where is the Miss?"

He grins sheepishly and shrugs. "I think we're officially past it."

I can't stop myself from laughing out loud. What just happened? I was close to losing it, and this man that usually lacks any emotion —not that it's his fault, it's simply a trait his line of work brings with itself—completely snapped me out of it.

My mood sobers, and I confess in a whisper, "I don't know what would've happened if you hadn't come home when you did."

He seems to understand. After all, he has seen me through several episodes by now. "I'm glad I was here when you needed me." He looks around before his gaze settles back on me. "How about some tea, and we can go over the plan for the next two days."

WITH NATE HAVING to take the jet to Europe, George is going to take the RAM to meet Hector Lakatos. He'll be leaving in the early evening and driving through the night to make it to the agreed-upon location mid-morning. He wants time to scope out the area. After the meet, he'll check in with Nate and me, let us know what he found out, and get a few hours of rest before driving back. I ask why he wouldn't just fly—less physically draining and all—to which he gives me a stare like I've said something ludicrous. When I don't catch on, he just fans his jacket open and reveals his Glock.

*Oh.*

"Oh."

"The TSA people don't take too kindly to my security measures," he deadpans.

"You mean they don't let you bring an arsenal for a small town on a commercial plane?" I smirk.

He just winks at me.

George also is not too happy with me about taking the car for a drive. I have to swear up and down that I will not leave the *premises* while he and Nate are gone. I almost blurt out that Denielle will be arriving tomorrow but bite my tongue. I'll tell Nate later when he calls. Maybe. They'll find out eventually. A light flutter stirs in my belly. I can't wait to have my best friend here.

AFTER GEORGE and I eat dinner, I walk with him to the garage. He loaded his truck earlier, and I watch him pull out. He gives me another nod before pressing the garage opener on the visor. As soon as the gate is fully closed, an empty feeling settles in my stomach. I step back into the hallway and close the door, arming the system. A synchronous beep echoes through the house, and I clutch my cell phone in my hand.

The urge to call Rhys overcomes me again, but instead, I send Denielle a text: **Can't wait to see u tmrw.**

The response is instant. **Just landed in Chi-town. Thank fuck I'm not leaving the airport. Can u believe it's snowing here. IT'S APRIL!**

**Just a few more hours and u'll be in the golden state. ;) It was 72 today.**

The bubble pops up again. **TSNF. I'm freezing my ass off.**

I bark out a laugh, picturing my best friend at O'Hare, complaining at the poor lounge employees to bring her a blanket.

**Get some rest. Call me when you land at LAX.**

**Will do. LY.**

**LY2.**

Still standing in the hallway, I contemplate what to do. It's too early to sleep—not that I can anyway. I can't sit still long enough to enjoy a movie *or book*, and I don't feel like exploring new parts of the mansion—not while I'm the only person here.

My feet take me back to Brooks's office. The room has become oddly comforting to me, the warm colors and soft light of the lamps making the room cozy. When Nate started looking into the finances, I cleaned up what I had left on the floor, including the photo albums. Padding across the room, I open the double doors and pull the three leatherbound books out. I place all three next to each other on the desk and lower myself into the chair, pulling my legs underneath me. Sitting where my father used to spend hours on end makes me feel like I have a connection to him. I flip the first one open and start turning the pages. Not that I want to have another migraine, but there is a little spark of hope that has remained inside of me and is waiting for me to remember...everything. After an hour of scanning picture after picture, I still feel like I'm spying on a stranger's life. My jaw clenches.

*Screw this.*

I stack all three albums on top of each other and spin in the chair to put them back in their spot. As I turn, the pocket of Rhys's hoodie—which I've been wearing for three days in a row—gets caught on the desk chair's armrest. I try to disentangle myself while balancing the heavy leather books on one arm. With the weight wearing me down, I attempt a final pull. I'm free, but my force propels the chair in the opposite direction—straight into the other shelf. Books fall over, a framed picture of Brooks and Payton crashes to the floor and shatters into a thousand pieces, and as if in slow motion, I watch another row of books tilting like dominos. I watch in horror as the tipping books push the stand containing Denton John Altman II's pipe collection toward the edge. Dropping the photo albums, I reach out and watch the pipes sail past my outstretched hand.

No, no, no.

When Nate finally was past his anxiety, he told me about all the items displayed. As suspected, a lot were souvenirs from their travels, and it sounded like the Hamlin's did a lot of that.

That's my luck, ruining one of Nate's grandfather's favorite possessions. Shit!

I kneel, careful not to cut myself on the broken frame, and start picking up the antique-looking pipes. I carefully place one after another back into the stand—which, by a miracle, is still in one piece—but then suddenly halt. I turn the pipe over in my hand and inspect it carefully. This one doesn't match the rest. It's new and... I turn it again. It's plastic made to look like wood.

Taking it between both hands, I squint. Something looks weird. I twist the mouthpiece, and my eyes widen as I repeat the motion. With shaking hands, I turn and pull at the same time. My heart is hammering against my ribcage. What is this? The object slowly comes apart and—what the hell?

# CHAPTER ONE HUNDRED EIGHT

**LILLY**

I leave everything where it fell and race to my computer. It's just down the hall, yet I'm out of breath like I've just sprinted a mile. The adrenaline coursing through me puts every nerve ending on high alert. What is on this thing? Why was it hidden among the pipes? *In* a fake pipe.

I drop into my desk chair and hit the space bar repeatedly. Come on, come on, come on. It only takes a second for the monitor to come to life, but it feels like an hour.

"Finally." My voice sounds like a bullhorn in the quiet house.

With my hand wrapped around the small device, I hesitate for a moment. Uncurling my fingers, I stare at it. I should wait for Nate. No, this is important. Brooks wouldn't have hidden it otherwise.

Plugging the USB drive—*slash back part of the pipe*—into the adapter connected to my laptop, it instantly pops up in my Finder window: Nate and Lilly.

I suck in a sharp breath.

My hand is trembling as I navigate the cursor into position. I clench and unclench my hand before clicking on the device name. A single video file with the same title gets displayed on the right.

Shifting in my seat, all I can do is stare. My heart is hammering so hard I swear I can hear it. Slowly, I move the little arrow over the file.

Why did Nate have to leave town today? I have no clue if I can reach him. What time is it in Europe? Crap, crap, crap. I can't wait until he's back, though. Swallowing hard, I double click.

Oh, my God.

Brooks fills the screen, and when his voice comes through the speaker, tears begin to run down my face.

*This is my father. My dad.*

NATE. *Son. I hope when you see this, Lilly will be with you and you've already found each other.*

BROOKS'S FACE BECOMES BLURRY, and I hit the spacebar to pause the video. Seeing him—not just in a picture or one of my muted memories—actually *hearing* him, I can't contain the sob building in my throat. His voice is deep and calm. Kind. I rub my eyes with my fingers and apply pressure. Breathe. When I have myself semi under control, I continue.

*I* DON'T KNOW *where to begin.*

MY FATHER CHUCKLES and looks down for a second. Following his line of sight, I notice that he's holding a couple of photos. One hand lets go of the pictures, and he scrubs it over his mouth before focusing on the camera again.

IF YOU HAVEN'T FOUND *Lilly yet, this will be one more revelation I wish I would've had the guts to tell you, son. There is no way to sugarcoat it. You have a half-sister. Her name is Lilly Ann.*

*She looks so much like you. I truly hope you have found each other by now.*

· · ·

HIS BREATH BECOMES SHAKY, and his eyes gloss over. The emotion on his face breaks my heart, and I cover my mouth with my hands in an attempt to mute my own crying.

*It all started about seven years ago. I met a woman...Emily. Your mother and I went through a rough patch. After Audrey's birth, your mom was struggling with post-partum depression. We hired a nanny to take care of you and your sister because she couldn't.*

HE PAUSES, and his face softens.

*It wasn't her fault—we knew that—but Payton would blame herself for not being stronger. Just when she had recovered, your grandfather passed away. Payton was distraught. You know how much your mom adored your grandfather.*

*I had to take over the hotels' legal department, which was part of your grandfather's will, and I had no idea what I was doing. I was gone sixteen hours a day—sometimes even slept in the office.*

*Your mother was grieving, I was stressed, and we blamed each other for our failing marriage. We did our best to keep all this from you, and I hope we succeeded on that front.*

HE GLANCES BACK DOWN at the photos that are now flat on the surface in front of him, but I can't make out who is on them. Are those of me? Are those the same pictures Nate found? My mind starts firing questions at me, and I draw in slow breaths. I need to focus on Brooks. He recorded this for a reason.

*Emily was mysterious, energetic, spontaneous. I met her at a conference where she was visiting a friend; I forget her name. Her friend was pregnant, so Emily hung out in the hotel bar after her friend went to bed. We hit it off.*

*I'm sure you have no interest in the details...let's just say one thing led to another. After I got back to LA, we stayed in contact. We met a few more times. She lived in San Diego, and it was easy to make the drive and meet halfway.*

*We kept in touch through handwritten letters. She said they were more personal.*

HIS EXPRESSION SHIFTS, and his face becomes hard.

A FEW MONTHS INTO…THE *affair —I have to call it for what it was— Emily wrote that she was pregnant. I had planned to break it off the next time I saw her because your mother and I were finally doing better. We were working on our marriage, saw a counselor once a week, and I wanted to be there for you and Audrey—be the father you deserved.*

*Shortly before, I had also found out she was married, so of course, I questioned her if the baby was mine. We met, and she showed me proof that her husband was unable to father a child. She agreed to have a paternity test once the baby was born, and I told her that if the baby were, in fact, my child, I would be there for it. I would support her and the baby in any way I could, but the affair had to stop.*

*Emily seemed to understand and be agreeable. Lilly was born, and I got the confirmation that the little girl was my daughter.*

*BUZZZZZZZ, buzzzzzzz.*

My eyes jerk to my phone sitting next to me. I quickly pause the video, not to miss anything.

*Buzzzzzzz, buzzzzzzz.*

I want to ignore whomever it is. I need to know what else Brooks has to say. But when I glance over, the one name that could make me drop everything flashes across the screen.

*Buzzzzzzz, buzzzzzzz.*

My heart skips a beat, and my hand flies to the phone. I answer the video call immediately.

When the connection is established, the screen is entirely black. *Uh.*

"Rhys?" I say hesitantly.

"Shit. Hold on." The rustling of the comforter comes through the speaker before his bedside lamp clicks on. "Sorry."

I don't respond; I just drink him in. He's as gorgeous as ever, and my belly flip-flops at the sight. His hair sticks up in all directions as if he just woke up. God, I miss him so much.

Rhys cocks his head, studying me. "Are you okay? You look out of it. Did you cry?" His concern gives me hope.

*He still cares.*

"Yes. No. I..." Instead of mentioning the video, I say, "You didn't answer your phone earlier." I try not to sound accusing but fail miserably. I am so high-strung from my discovery that my emotions are a ginormous cluster fuck.

Rhys sighs. "I know." He's glancing past the screen, and I picture him looking at the TV on the other side of the room. When his eyes find mine again, he says, "I wanted to. Wes was here. He's been on babysitting duty since D is gone. He saw that you were calling and took my phone."

A pang hits my chest. "Why?"

*Why did he take the phone? Does he hate me, too?*

"I made him promise not to let me talk to you. I needed time to clear my head, and when I hear or see you..." He lets the sentence trail off.

Needles prick in the back of my throat, and I press my lips together. It takes me almost a whole minute before finding my words again. "I'm so sorry. I should've never forced you to keep my secrets. I was selfish and didn't think twice about the position I put you in."

I want to apologize more, but how many times can one say it before it loses its meaning?

The corner of Rhys's mouth tilts up. "I get it, Cal. And I can't really fault you for it. Think about everything you've been through."

"You're doing it again," I tell him through the tears.

"Doing what?" He's genuinely confused.

A laugh bubbles up between my sobs. "Being understanding."

"Ah, what can I say?" He full-on smirks.

"Are we——?" I start in a whisper.

His eyebrows draw together. "Are we what?"

"Are we, uh...still together?" I sound pathetic, but I can't help it.

I can't lose him. I need to find a way to tell him how much I regret my actions.

Rhys narrows his eyes at me, looking incredulous. "Did you think we broke up?"

My breath hitches. "Yes. No. Maybe?" I shrug. "I hurt you. You didn't want to talk to me."

"Babe," he sighs, "I know we haven't had the traditional dating start. Instead of fighting about where we want to go out for dinner, we argue about your secret brother, brainwashing, and a crazy stalker—two, if you count Kat. But that doesn't change the fact that we are together and will be for a very. Long. Time. If it's up to me. But we can still be mad at each other. Keeping the migraines from me and how they affected you was like a knife to the gut. The same goes for your cloak-and-dagger escape. But none of that changes my feelings for you. I just needed time to digest. We have to be better at communicating."

I hiccup a laugh between the waterfall running down my cheeks. I have no clue if these are happy or sad tears. Both, I think, based on my internal turmoil. "I promise I will never shut you out again."

"That's all I ever wanted from you, babe—to let me in. Well, maybe I also want your sexy body... No, I definitely want that as well." He winks.

"You are in. *I'm all in.*" He holds my gaze, and I add, "I love you."

"I love you, too, Calla." The A is drawn out by a yawn.

"Were you sleeping?" Is that why his hair is such a mess?

"I fell asleep during a movie. Wes just left, which is why I finally could call you back."

"I see." Hearing him say that he wanted to talk to me this entire time is like a soothing blanket. He's not breaking up with me. We're okay. He loves me.

*He's not breaking up with me.*

I keep repeating it over and over in my head.

I'm about to tell him about the video when he yawns again and rubs a hand over his face. "Shit, I'm so out of it. I haven't slept much the last few daaays." Another yawn.

As if on cue, I can feel one building up inside of me as well, and I try to suppress it—unsuccessfully.

"Why don't you go back to bed and call me in the morning?"

That way I can finish the video and tell him everything in the morning. I want to have all the information. My gut tells me there is a lot more on Brooks's video.

*You're keeping the video from Rhys immediately after telling him you would never keep anything from him again*, my inner voice accuses.

*I'm not. I want to have all the details.* I justify myself against myself. I'm losing it.

We say our goodnights, and another yawn escapes me just as we hang up. I need caffeine. With the video still paused on the screen and my phone in hand, I head to the kitchen to make some tea.

WHILE I WAIT for the water to heat, Brooks's words replay in my head, causing my adrenaline level to skyrocket again. What else is on that recording?

When the kettle signals that the water is boiling, I grab it with a trembling hand and pour the water carefully over the tea-filter.

I need to tell Nate about the video, but I have no idea where he is, if he's alone, or what. Hoping his phone is silenced, I type out a message: **Call me asap.**

Realizing how that sounded, I add, **I'm fine but found something. Need to talk to u!!!**

I place the phone down, not expecting an answer right away. I'm on my way to the trash can to throw the filter of soggy leaves away when the beeping of the alarm system chimes. I peer over to the panel installed in all the main rooms. The message on the screen makes the blood in my veins run cold. "Garage Second Entrance disabled."

I stare at the blinking notification. What the—?

"Hello, Lilly."

I spin around at the voice, sending the tea dripping from the filter spraying across the kitchen.

*No!*

**RHYS**

"Duuuude, what the fuck is wrong with you? Your aim is complete shit. I thought I left early last night so you could get some sleep and I don't have to kick your moping ass all day."

Wes is about to launch the controller at me for getting killed the eighth time in the last hour. Fucking zombies keep biting me in various body parts before I can react, which makes him lose as well.

The video call with Lilly left me wide awake until after four, and my best friend showing up here at nine sharp, like the last several days, didn't help either.

Mom stuck her head in, informing me that she was taking Natty and her friend Olivia out for a girls' day, including dinner at their favorite restaurant. That'll be good for Nat. She seems to be handling the current situation better than the rest of us, but that doesn't mean it doesn't affect her. On their way out, I pulled my little sister aside and told her that we're going to have a brother-sister date this weekend. Her face lit up like I had given her the best present ever, and my stomach sank. I have to be around more for her, get my head out of my selfish ass.

I knew that Dad was downstairs in his office, doing his secret spy work or whatever he does, but other than that, I hadn't seen him today.

I'm about to restart the game when my phone starts ringing. I peer over and see Denielle's name scroll across the screen. Why is she calling *me*? She's not supposed to be back until tomorrow. Wes told me earlier this week that she'd been bitch-texting him several times about how Charlie had turned into a serial party-drunk, but she's been radio silent since Tuesday evening. I assumed they had made up and were getting at it like the horny rabbits they are.

"Who is it?" Wes mumbles as he picks out his weapons for this round.

"It's D?" My tone makes it sound like I'm asking him.

"Huh? Why—"

The call cuts off, my voicemail probably picking up. Within two seconds, it rings again. That's odd. Maybe she came back earlier and needs a ride from the airport?

I pick up the phone and swipe to answer. "Hey, D. What's—"

"Have you talked to Lilly?" she bursts out so loud Wes glances over.

*Huh?*

"Uh...last night, yeah. Why?" I lock eyes with my best friend, who scowls at me. *Busted.*

"SHE'S NOT HOME!" Den yells into the phone.

"What do you mean? Where the hell are you?" My confusion turns into annoyance. Why can no one ever talk in complete, coherent sentences?

"I'm in LA. At her place. She's not here. Or at least no one is opening. She wasn't supposed to leave the house, so she has to be here. But she's not opening the door." She speaks so fast it takes my brain a moment to catch up.

*LA?*

My hand tightens around the phone. "What are you doing in LA?"

*How the hell did she get there?*

"Dear Lord, McGuire!" Her exasperated tone makes my blood boil. "I found my longtime boyfriend doggy-styling a sorority slut yesterday, so I jumped on the next flight to Los Angeles to see my best friend."

"And she let you?" I ask, half incredulously, half pissed. Pissed because Den is there and I'm not, but also at the way she talks to me—like I'm an idiot.

"I didn't give her a choice," she confesses. "I called her from the airport after I bought the ticket. She told me to let her know when I landed, but she didn't answer. I assumed she just didn't have her phone with her, so I took a cab. I had the address, and she must've put me on the list because this Harvey doppelganger at the gate let me through once I gave him my ID. Now I'm knocking and ringing the doorbell, and no one is answering. I can't reach G either." She draws in a shaky breath. "Rhys, I'm freaking out."

My pulse increases the longer she speaks. She's freaking out? What am I supposed to do? I'm across the fucking country. "What do you want me to do? You're there—" The phone is ripped out of my hand, and I glower at Wes, who is standing in front of me, *my* phone in one hand and the other lifted defensively so I don't clock him. I could still get a good punch in, though. His guard is way too low.

"You need to take a breath, bro. You're about to blow a gasket."

*I'm gonna show you a gasket, fuckface!*

I'm ready to launch myself at my best friend to fight him for my only connection to the West Coast when he lifts it to his ear. "D! I heard most of it. Walk around the house. See if you can find anything. Another door or something. Rhys is going to call Nate and George."

I narrow my eyes at him. Since when did he turn all drill sergeant?

"Okay," Denielle's voice comes through the speaker; he must've enabled it when he stole my damn phone.

We can hear the crunching of gravel, which I assume is Den making her way across the property.

"Rhys!" Wes snaps a finger in front of my face. "Get my phone and call George." He points across the room.

*The fuck?*

I want to break his damn fingers, but instead, I make my way across the room as ordered.

*He's so going to get a beating for this.*

While we're waiting for Denielle to tell us something, I dial the number I can recite three different ways to Sunday. It rings and rings and eventually goes to a non-descript voicemail.

"Motherfucker!" I hit end and dial again. And again. Pick. Up. The damn phone!

"Isn't he at that secret meet with the memory doctor?" D's voice interrupts my internal curse crusade against my BFF.

*Fuck, she's right.*

"He probably doesn't have his phone with him," Wes chimes in.

"Thank you, Sherlock," I snap.

"Just saying." He sounds a little less smug now, but I can't muster any remorse for my behavior. Lilly is fucking missing. A-fucking-gain!

"Oh no!" Denielle breathes into the phone.

"WHAT?" I bark, my heart instantly beating in my throat.

"The side door next to the garage is wide open," she whispers.

"Could she just be out for a walk or somewhere else on the property?" Wes tries to reason.

"I don't think so." Lilly's best friend's voice is trembling, and the saliva pooling in my mouth tells me I'm close to making a dash to the bathroom. I swallow several times before asking, "Why?" My voice sounds robotic.

"There is blood." Her response is barely audible.

I'm out the door and down the stairs before anyone can say another word. Wes is on my heels with Denielle on the phone as I push my father's office door open. It slams into the wall and bounces back, which results in me kicking it and leaving a size-twelve dent in the wood.

Dad's head jerks up. He's ready to ream me out—mouth already open—but I speak first.

"Get me on the next flight to LA!" I don't give him room for negotiation. I would get a ticket myself, but he can get me there faster with his connections.

His forehead wrinkles and he's about to say something when Wes's phone begins to vibrate in my hand. Glancing down, I recognize George's number. I answer the call before anyone else can utter another word. "SHE'S MISSING!"

Holding my father's gaze, his entire posture goes rigid when comprehension sets in.

"What are you talking about?" George snaps to attention on his end.

"Denielle is at the house. Lilly is not there. The side door is open, and there is blood," I summarize the last several minutes while clenching my hand around the device and fighting the urge to purge my revolting stomach.

He doesn't ask me why Den is in Los Angeles. Instead, he hangs up.

*What the fuck?*

"George is video calling me. Hold on," D's voice comes through the speaker. Her line goes dead.

My father glowers at me with an equally worried and murderous expression. I know I'm in deep shit, but I couldn't care less at this point.

My phone starts to vibrate in Wes's hand, and he holds it out to me. I latch onto the device and accept the incoming video chat at the same time.

Lilly's best friend, as well as George's face, fill the screen in two little squares. George is in his truck, and based on how he stares out the front, he's driving. The phone is in a car mount or somehow propped up to the side of him. Denielle looks directly into the camera, and our eyes lock. At the edge of the screen, I see her twirl a strand of hair over and over—something she does when she's upset. I've learned her tells over the last few months.

"Denielle, I want you to go slowly inside. Flip the camera around so I can see. If at any point you think someone besides Lilly is in the house, leave! Someone from my team will be there soon; I messaged him from my other device. I'm on my way but won't get there until late tonight unless I can charter a plane along the way."

"Rhys." I turn at my name. Still behind his desk but now standing with his arms crossed over his chest, my father speaks up for the first time. "What is going on?" His tone is eerily calm, yet the question holds a warning.

"Colonel McGuire, sir. My name is George Weiler. I am Lilly's bodyguard and her brother's head of security."

Dad stiffens while Wes's jaw drops. Den looks equally slack-jawed in her little square. George just told my father who he is.

"George Weiler?" Dad repeats slowly as his arms go slack on either side of him. "The George Weiler?"

*The?*

My heart skips a beat as my father addresses George. I'm taken back to the day I found out who Nate was—when I saw him holding Lilly as she had her panic attack. The shock back then mirrors what is currently going on inside of me. It's like my brain is trying to catch up with what's happening, but I'm two steps behind at all times.

"Yes, sir," George confirms, never taking his gaze off the road in front of him.

Dad moves around the desk and to my side, peering down at George. "You have been off the radar for almost twenty years."

"That is correct, Colonel."

My father stares between Wes, the phone, and me, an almost dumbfounded look on his face.

"Denielle?" George redirects everyone's attention.

"Yes."

"My associate will be there within thirty minutes. When you go inside, make as little sound as possible. I don't believe anyone is there anymore, but I want you to be careful."

Den turns the camera around, and we can see the half-open back door and a short, dark hallway behind. My free hand fists into the material of my pants. I'm holding my breath, and so is Wes from the looks of it.

Den exhales audibly and takes one step inside. When she doesn't keep moving, George starts directing her. His tone is calm, almost soothing.

"The hallway leads to the motor pool on the left and the kitchen straight ahead."

"There is blood on the floor," she whispers, her voice cracking.

My father swipes his hand over his mouth.

"Jesus," Wes mumbles.

"How much? Turn on the hallway light to the left of you," George orders.

My lungs are burning, and I force myself to let oxygen into my lungs. My free hand is now permanently balled into a fist and pressed to my chest.

"I don't know. Not much. Some drops and smears?" She tries to stay calm, but the quiver in her tone is audible. The light on her end flicks on, and we can see what she's talking about. It is not much, just like someone cut themselves and didn't have a Band-Aid. But it's blood. It doesn't matter how much or how little. Someone was hurt.

"Good, keep going."

The kitchen entry slowly comes into view. I want to yell at her to move the fuck along. I feel like someone is slowly gutting me with every snail-paced step she takes. Dad's hand lands on my shoulder, and he squeezes. I have no clue, though, if he's looking at me. I can't avert my eyes from the screen.

Den finally reaches the kitchen and waves the camera around before she aims it at a spot behind the massive kitchen island. "There is something on the floor. It looks like dried...tea? And a cup. Someone threw it."

*Lilly!*

She continues, "A broken fruit bowl." Den's breathing fast, and I can only imagine what her heartbeat is like. With mine beating in my throat, Den must be close to passing out.

She changes the angle, and we can see a large white bowl shattered on the ground—apples, bananas, and grapes on the floor.

"Is there any more blood?"

*I'm gonna be sick.*

"Oh no."

She still has the camera aimed on the fucking bananas.

"Denielle!" This time Dad directs his bark at her.

"Yes?" she squeaks.

"Don't. Do. That!"

"Please show us what you see." George is the only one able to keep his cool. He is doing his job. Dad's usual military mode went out the window as soon as the words Lilly, missing, and blood were spoken.

The camera shifts, and Denielle walks closer to an object on the floor—a small chef's knife. The blade is covered in blood.

I thrust the phone at my father, who barely catches it, and drop to all fours. Retching in the middle of my father's office, I expel the remnants of my stomach.

. . .

I DON'T REMEMBER MUCH after I saw the knife. Dad and Wes maneuvered me upstairs to my room, where I curled into a fetal position on the bed and watched Wes pace like someone waiting for his next fix and texting furiously. Dad said something about making phone calls and disappeared back downstairs.

It's 9:30, and I'm on a private plane—this time heading to Los Angeles. I have no clue how my father pulled this off. One of these days, I want to know what the man really does for a living.

Wes sits opposite me with Dad across the aisle. Mom and Natty came home around seven, and Dad ushered her upstairs immediately. I have no idea how much or what he told her. I couldn't bring myself to ask, either. Her face was blotchy, and her mascara was streaked when she watched us pull out of the garage. According to Dad, Natty was in her room, and they told her that we would be visiting Lilly to bring her home.

Nice way of wording it. He's telling her the truth, but she has no idea what it really means.

Dad props open his laptop and starts typing.

Staring out the window into the dark, I ask, "Are there any updates?" My voice sounds like a stranger to my own ears. It's the first time I've spoken since my breakdown, and their focus is instantly on me. Out of the corner of my eye, I see Dad angling his body in my direction, and I turn my head to face him.

"I've been in contact with Weiler. He called earlier to inform me that his men are at the house with Denielle." He pauses, and I scan his face. His expression is blank.

Before he can continue, I interrupt. "You knew George." I don't ask, because from his reaction, it was clear that my father had heard of the Altman head of security.

Dad chuckles. "George Weiler is a legend. He's a...ghost. He went off the grid as soon as his feet hit U.S. soil after his last mission. No one knows what happened."

*Well, well. I know something my father doesn't.*

"I do." I try to keep my face neutral but can't stop the shit-eating grin that spreads across my face. For a brief moment, I forget the reason we're on this plane.

My father raises an eyebrow, but I shrug. "Maybe he'll tell you, too."

His nostrils flare. He doesn't like that I'm rubbing my secrets in his face, but I don't care.

Wes interrupts our standoff. "So, uh...D has been saying one of the two dudes who showed up a while ago and are 'processing the scene' is almost as scary as G." He makes air quotes around the words. "The other one—"

"How is Denielle holding up?" My father seems genuinely concerned.

Wes shrugs. "From her texts, she's anywhere between hysterical meltdown and B.K."

*Bulldog Keller.*

"We should get to the address Lilly's *bodyguard* gave me around midnight local time." When I don't react, he addresses me directly. "Son?" He waits until he has my attention. "When we have Lilly back, the two of you will tell me everything. The only reason I'm not putting you into an interrogation cell is that finding my daughter has priority. The cell is still on the table, though."

He's not joking, but I just turn back around and stare out the window into the blackness.

## CHAPTER ONE HUNDRED TEN

**HER**

*G*RAY *HAS BEEN WATCHING THE HOUSE FOR THE LAST FEW DAYS. N*ATE *was going back and forth between his office, his home, and the mansion. Weiler, however, did not leave at all—until a little change in plans forced the two men to go out of town.*

*The* unexpected *complications at the new Altman hotel in Paris forced Nate to take the jet out of the country, which resulted in an extended absence of Lilly's watchdog.*

*We had two days to get everything ready for Lilly, including her accommodations. I briefly contemplated making them a little more inviting than how the pawn has been stored for the last decade, but then, why? She has a mattress and a toilet at her disposal. That's more than he's gotten for years. I have not yet made up my mind on the restraints. Let's see how the girl behaves.*

*G*OT HER. ***The little bitch stabbed me.***

*Gray's text lights up my phone at 11:53, and the corner of my mouth tugs upward. The kid has spunk, I'll give her that. The years of training that Tristen put Lilly through paid off. Too bad for her, though, that I brought some of the paralytic drugs with me.*

*I have to wait another hour before the garage door rolls up. I made sure not to wear white today; I'm still furious with Gray for ruining my new linen pants with his blood.*

*Standing in the door, I watch him get out of the SUV and walk around to the back.*

*"Did she give you any more trouble?"*

*He peers around the back of the car. "Not once I got the syringe in. Dropped faster than you can down a glass of your fancy wine."*

*"WATCH IT, Francis!"*

*He scowls at me. I haven't called him by his given name in over twenty-five years—unless he's pissed me off.*

*"Get her in the house and to her room." I turn and head straight for the kitchen. I've already gone through most of my pills, which means I have to resort to other means to calm myself. And stabbing his muscle more would be counterproductive; I need him to keep Lilly in check until I get what we came for.*

*"MAYBE WE SHOULD'VE REDUCED the dose? Or not mix it with the sedative. She hasn't moved in hours." Gray cocks his head as he watches Lilly on the monitor. It's been half a day, and I want to go back home and finally be done with this decade-long farce, but I learned a long time ago, things rarely go how you want them to.*

*"She wakes up when she wakes up. Enjoy the downtime," I say absently as I pour another glass.*

*"Christ, woman, it's not even noon." He purses his lips at me.*

*"That's rich coming from someone who gets high every chance he gets." His eyes widen. Yes, I know that he has not been as clean as he pretends to be.*

*"She's moving!" Gray suddenly exclaims.*

*I step up behind him to watch the feed, and a slow smile spreads across my face. "Good morning, Lilly," I whisper to the screen.*

## CHAPTER ONE HUNDRED ELEVEN

**LILLY**

FRANCIS TURNER IS IN MY KITCHEN. WE STARE AT EACH OTHER, neither of us moving. I blink. He's still here.

*How the hell did he get past the guard and alarm system?*

The tea dripping from the wet filter onto the floor is the only sound in the room. Holding my breath, I'm waiting for the panic to kick in, but there is...nothing. Why is there nothing? Maybe it's the shock of seeing him in front of me, in my father's house in Los Angeles. It's got to be. I'm alone with no one to contact to help me. Definitely shock.

I glance to the side, mentally measuring the distance to the knife block by the stove. Too far.

Following my gaze, he cocks an eyebrow, and the corner of his mouth pulls up in a smirk. "I wouldn't do that, little girl."

My phone is where I left it on the counter—also on the other side of the kitchen. Why did I have to go to the trash can right this second? I scan everything in my vicinity. The white porcelain fruit bowl—which probably costs more than my old Jeep—is the closest item in my reach, and I lunge for it.

Unfortunately, he anticipates the projectile and ducks to the side. The crashing sound of the bowl is equivalent to the demolition of a high-rise in the quiet house. It also is what my brain and body need to catch up with the severity of the situation. Turner pulls something out of his pocket, and my adrenaline level goes through the roof.

*Please don't let it be a gun.*

My heart beats in my throat, and I take a defensive stance. I'm trained to defend myself against almost every weapon, but no one can match a bullet. I follow his movement like a hawk, ready to dive behind the island. When he pulls out a small object, I narrow my eyes. What the hell is—a syringe? This can't be real.

Every nerve ending in my body is buzzing with energy. This asshole is not going to get me. Through his evasion maneuver, Turner is now farther from the knives than me, and I don't hesitate. I sprint around the island, swiping my phone as I pass it and clasp my hand on the first handle I can reach. What I don't anticipate is for this tall and bulky guy to be so quick. An arm sneaks around my stomach just as I pull my weapon out of the block.

"Ahhhhh!" The sudden connection sends my system into overdrive. Goosebumps erupt where he touches me, and I fight the urge to scream and thrash uncontrollably. I'm trained for this. I need to be smart—in control.

My feet leave the ground, and his other arm comes around my upper body, immobilizing me. Expelling all my air, I throw my head back, but he's too tall, and I hit his chest.

*Shit!*

"Nice try, princess," he sneers close to my ear, and his breath of stale alcohol and cigarettes penetrates my nose.

I swallow hard not to start gagging.

He fumbles with the syringe, attempting the right grip to administer whatever he has in there. Using the opportunity, I flip the handle around in my hand—blade pointing backward—but almost lose hold of it, my palms being coated with sweat. Before it slips from my grasp, I push it into the closest body part.

"Fuuuck! You little bi—" He stumbles and drops me.

I keep my fingers curled around my ticket out of here. The knife dislodges from wherever it entered his body, and I spin, holding my weapon in front of me with my other hand raised in defense. I follow his gaze down to his thigh, where his dark pant leg begins to look wet. *Blood.*

"What is it with you women and stabbing me in the legs?" he growls.

*Huh?*

Turner trains his ice-blue eyes on me, and his glare sends chills down my spine. It's at that moment that I realize I dropped my phone in the struggle. Crap, crap, crap. I flick my gaze across the floor, making sure not to take my focus off of my opponent for more than half a second.

Unable to spot the device anywhere, I take a step back to bring more distance between us. His pained expression turns into a shit-eating grin, and he leans down without breaking eye contact.

"Looking for this?" He wiggles my phone between his thumb and forefinger. My heart is pounding like a jackhammer. He lets go, and I hear it smash into the tiled floor. *No!* He glances down, back up at me, and shrugs once before he brings his heel down on the screen. I don't have to look to know that my phone has been rendered useless—the loud crack made it clear.

I'm breathing heavily, running through possible ways out of this situation in my head. Then something hits me: the alarm system. It has a button to notify the security company and most likely send an alert to Nate. The closest panel is about thirty feet away, next to the French doors to the back patio. Turner is on the other end of the kitchen, and I have a straight path to the keypad. Before I can think more about it, I push off and sprint toward help, using the coursing adrenaline to my advantage.

I'm almost on the other side, reaching out my hand, when something hits me in the back, and I go down. I try to brace my fall, but with the knife in one hand, I'm only able to block the fall with the other one which, by the force of my impact, doesn't do much good. My forehead hits the floor, and everything goes black for a moment.

*Do not pass out.*

As the darkness clears, the room is spinning from the impact, but I force myself on my hands and knees.

*I need to get up.*

My thoughts are sluggish, and I shake my head in an attempt to clear the fog. Footfalls behind me announce Turner coming closer. Suddenly, my head gets yanked back by the hair. A sharp prick punctures my neck, and I fall to the side, dropping the knife.

*Oww!*

Faintly I register that I'm lying in something wet when the smell of Earl Grey hits my nose. He threw my freaking Yeti at me. I peer up at Turner, who becomes fuzzier by the second. His head is tilted to the side as he glares down at me.

"Nighty night, Lilly."

CONSCIOUSNESS SLOWLY STARTS CREEPING into the dark void. I'm awake but unable to move. Maybe I'm dreaming. Please let this be a dream. Or a memory. I'd even take a memory at this point. Why won't my eyes open?

*The syringe.*

The visual of Turner standing over me and everything slowly turning fuzzy slams into me like a freight train. He drugged me. My heart rate increases, and so does my breathing, but drawing in the air my body demands is like running a marathon through water. Whatever he gave me prevents me from moving. No, no, no. What if, this time, there is permanent damage? What if it doesn't go away? What if I can't ever move again? I'm trapped. I try to open my mouth to scream, do something, but my body won't obey. The sound reverberates inside my head, but on the outside...I'm mute. I start counting my breaths in an attempt to calm my heart rate.

Inhale, four, three, two, one.

Exhale, four, three, two, one.

It takes several rounds, but my pulse eventually slows enough that my lungs no longer feel like they're closing up from the lack of oxygen.

I have zero sense of time. It could be days, hours, or ten minutes —definitely feels like days, though—when there is a twitch in my index finger. Instantly, my adrenaline level spikes again, and I consciously attempt to bend my finger. It's just the slightest of movements, but it's there. The drugs are wearing off. I'm so relieved I could cry.

*I'm gonna be okay. I'm gonna be okay. I'm gonna be okay.*

In an attempt to measure how long it takes for me to become fully mobile, I start counting. My brain needs to do something, or I'm going to lose it. I have no clue how accurate my seconds are, but by the time I get to 783 I can sense both my arms and most of my legs. I want to laugh and cry at the same time. By 1,341 I can consciously make my chest expand—breathing has never felt so good. I've just reached 2,127 when my eyelids snap open. At first, I think it hasn't worked, but then the faint glow from my right draws my attention. I only move my eyes, afraid to alert someone close by. There is a small gap under a door that allows light in.

When nothing happens for several minutes, I slowly turn myself to the side, taking stock. I'm on a mattress, and I'm having a hangover from hell—worse than what Nate and George pumped through my system—but I don't sense any new injuries. My clothes are in place, which is a relief I never thought I'd have to experience. Not knowing what Turner wants from me, my mind has come up with the most horrific scenarios. My back is sore, but that is most likely a result of lying on it for so long, which I am still avoiding whenever I can.

With my hands pressed into the scratchy surface of my makeshift bed, I push fully upright. My eyes have adjusted to the darkness, and I scan the inside of the room. Besides the mattress on the floor, there is one other door, but I'm not brave enough to go exploring.

A click makes my head snap toward the sound. I instinctively scoot backward until I'm against the wall and hold my breath. It slowly opens inward, and the light from the outside blinds me. Holding a hand over my eyes, I can only make out a shadow standing in the now open door, but his voice identifies him instantly.

"Took you long enough, princess."

I wait for my eyes to adjust before responding, "Well, maybe you shouldn't have used a fucking horse tranq." My words sound brave, but my insides lack the courage I'm trying to portray.

He snorts before turning his tone to ice. "I would be a little more careful about how you talk to me. I'm not your *last kidnapper*. I didn't bring you here to play family."

The hair on my neck stands, and I whisper, "What do you know about that?"

"We know everything, Lilly," a female voice comes from behind the tall man.

*What?*

He moves out of the way, and a woman enters the room. My attention is at her naked feet. Slowly, I let my gaze travel upward past the black leggings and over her dark tank top. She is slender and toned but not overly muscular. Her arms are folded over her chest, and when my eyes meet hers, I inhale sharply.

*No!*

I stare at the face I have seen in so many pictures over the last several months, and yet, my brain refuses to comprehend who I'm seeing.

"I don't understand." My words are slow, detached.

"I came to take back what you took from me," the woman explains in an equally robotic tone.

My forehead scrunches. How is this possible? Why is she with this supposedly dead former Army Ranger?

"Gray, give Lilly some water and bring her something to eat. We will continue our chat later." She turns and leaves me alone with...*Gray?*

"Who is Gray?" I ask the man I thought was Francis Turner.

He smirks. "That would be me. Francis Garrison Turner—or as she's called me since we were kids, Gray."

"Kids?" My hands are trembling, and I cross my arms in front of my chest, just to realize that that's the exact posture she just had. I quickly untangle myself again and sit down on my hands.

*What is happening?*

I follow Turner...Gray—whomever this man is—with my eyes. He walks over to the other door and opens it, revealing a bathroom. He grabs a plastic cup that, apparently, was already in there and fills it with water, only to place it on the floor, out of my reach.

"I'm not coming anywhere near you, princess. I already have two stab wounds, and I know what you've been trained to do."

My brows shoot up. How does this guy know everything about me?

He senses my unspoken question. "I've been watching you for her for over a decade, princess. I probably know you better than you know yourself."

I don't reply, and he snorts, shaking his head. "Drink water; it's the best way to get over your hangover."

"How—?"

But before I can finish the sentence, he is gone, and the door clicks shut, a lock snapping in place outside.

My entire body starts trembling, and a sheen of cold sweat coats my skin. I pull my knees close and wrap my arms around my legs, rocking back and forth. My eyes sting, and I let the tears go.

*This can't be real. I'm still unconscious. She cannot be here.*

I'm chanting the same three sentences over and over—my lips moving but no sound coming out. With every repetition, my pulse quickens, and nausea makes my stomach churn. I swallow the saliva, but it's no use. I uncurl from my position and try to stand. My knees buckle at the first step, and I end up crawling to the bathroom on all fours. Thankfully, my captor left the light in the small room on, and I don't have to search for the toilet in the dark as the bile makes its way up. I retch several times, but since my last meal was...I don't know when, there is nothing to throw up. Eventually, the sensation subsides, and I sit back, wiping the sweat off my forehead.

Too exhausted to pull myself up and wash my face, I crawl back to the mattress and curl into a tight ball.

"Wakey, wakey, princess." A not-at-all-cheery Gray pushes his foot into my back.

Facing away from the door, I arch away from the contact—not from pain but revulsion that this man is somehow associated with her. My eyes instantly gloss over, and I reach up, swiping at the moisture with the heel of my hand.

"Get up. She wants to talk to you. And you need to eat something. You've been out for almost thirty-six hours. Given the fact that you'll probably puke everything right back up, let's get the show on the road. I have more stops to make while I'm in this fucking country." He pushes me again with his damn boot.

Heat surges through my body the more he rants, and I whirl around, hook my elbow around his ankle, and use the little energy I can muster to kick both legs up. My feet connect with his groin region, pulling his leg out as soon as he is off-balance from pain.

*Fuck you, asshole.*

Gray topples over and lands ungracefully on his side. "You dirty little cunt," he yowls.

I push myself up into a sitting position and wait until his eyes meet mine before speaking. "Don't ever touch me again."

A snort comes from the open door. When my eyes meet hers, the empty pit in my stomach opens back up.

"Why am I here?"

She ignores me and addresses the curled-up man on the floor. "Get up! I told you to give her food, not get emasculated by a teenager." She kicks the brown bag I hadn't noticed before by the door toward me. When Gray doesn't move, she barges into the room and grabs him by his black hair. "I said get the FUCK UP!" She screeches the last word into his ear, and he winces.

*She is psychotic.*

She's about to turn and leave when I push myself off the mattress. My legs are still weak, but I force my spine straight and my tone calm. "Why am I here?"

She lets go of his curls, and her eyes snap to mine. "Not now, Lilly."

Her dismissive tone stirs a familiar sensation in me, but instead of cowering, I do the opposite. "Yes, now, Emily!"

---

# CHAPTER ONE HUNDRED TWELVE

---

**RHYS**

A RENTAL CAR IS WAITING FOR US AT THE PRIVATE HANGER AS soon as we arrive. With Wes in the backseat, we make our way to the address George gave my father. There are several moments where I am ready to jump out and walk—I probably could beat them there. This traffic is fucking ridiculous; it's the middle of the night.

Thanks to the WiFi on the jet, Dad has been in constant contact with George and the security staff positioned at the Hamlin Estate. Denielle has been texting Wes, who attempts to give me updates, but when I ignore him, he also leaves me alone. I have no clue what he—or my father—told Wes's parents to explain his sudden departure across the country. Don't care either. Since our one-sided chat, Dad seems to understand that I don't give a shit about what he has to say unless it involves Lilly's location and getting her back.

*Thank fuck for that. I am over talking.*

We pass a security guard, who meticulously dissects everyone's IDs before letting us enter the gated community. As we drive past the different properties, all separated from the road by various styles of walls, fences, and gates, I hear Wes mutter to himself, "Who the fuck lives here? The president?"

After what feels like years since Denielle's name lit up my phone today, we approach the wrought iron gate the nav chick directed us to. Dad opens his window and types something into the keypad like he's been here a million times.

*What the hell?*

I focus out the windshield, taking in the massive structure coming into view. In front of the house are two blacked-out SUVs and an even more decked-out RAM. Several men stand in front of the main entrance with a slightly shorter, dark-haired girl next to them: Denielle.

Arms wrapped around herself, her head snaps up as our car approaches. The men turn as well, and I recognize George instantly. How the hell did he get here before us?

Dad stops behind the farthest SUV, and Denielle takes off down the drive. Wes pushes his door open before we're fully stopped. Den jumps him koala-style and latches on. By the way her body is shaking, she is sobbing into my best friend's neck.

I exit the car a little slower, aiming straight for Lilly's bodyguard. I have tunnel vision.

George faces me as I reach the group. He's about to say something when I pull my arm back and let my fist fly. I clock him straight in the jaw, and his head snaps back. This is the only punch I get in, and the only reason I was able to make contact was the element of surprise.

I shake my hand out, even though I feel nothing. I move forward again. "YOU WERE SUPPOSED TO PROTECT HER!"

"Holy shit!" Wes exclaims somewhere behind me.

"I TRUSTED YOU! WHAT GOOD ARE YOU IF THIS PSYCHOPATH WALKS STRAIGHT IN?" My voice cracks, and tears are streaming down my face. My chest heaves, yet I feel like I am suffocating.

Two of the guys grab me by the arms and secure them behind my back, assuming I'll attack again.

"Let him go," George commands, and they instantly remove their hands. George steps closer and looks at me with such sorrow that it's clear he blames himself more than anything. Dipping his chin ever so slightly, it's like a signal. I throw myself at the man like a little kid.

George's arms wrap around me, and he says, "I will bring her back. I promise you."

Unable to speak, I nod into his shoulder. I'm losing it in front of everyone.

George shifts but doesn't let go. "Colonel McGuire. It's an honor to meet you."

I draw in a shuddering breath and step to the side, wiping my face with both hands.

My father holds his hand out. "George Weiler, how is my daughter connected to *The Ghost* no one has seen in two decades?"

Lilly's bodyguard doesn't answer his question. Instead, he says, "Let's get everyone inside and settled. Then we'll talk."

WE CONGREGATE in the living room—or one of them, as we passed two more on the way in. I scan my surroundings as I trudge after George. The money in this house is visible but not *in your face*. Everything is decorated subtly and tastefully—Mom would approve.

*Mom.* A pang of guilt hits my chest. We just left her there. I wonder what she's doing right now. If she and Natty will come to California.

I drop in the first seat available, which puts the kitchen in my direct line of sight. Two men and one woman are moving around. It looks like they're cataloging everything, taking pictures, and, as it seems, also looking for fingerprints. It's like we walked into a scene from one of those hyped-up crime TV shows, and I have to turn away. Someone broke in here and kidnapped Lilly, right there.

I avert my gaze. Den and Wes are on either side of me, with Dad standing by the door. George lowers himself into the closest armchair, and the remaining men distribute themselves in and outside the house.

"Where is Nate?" I break the silence in the room.

George's expression shifts to something unreadable, and it's like an invisible hand is choking me.

"What?" The word is just a rasped whisper.

George glances around the room before his gaze settles back on me. "Nate has been missing for over twenty-four hours."

My eyes widen. How is this possible? I open my mouth to ask exactly that but am interrupted.

"Could he be involved in Lilly's disappearance?" my father inquires in the same tone I've heard him speak in so many times on his business calls.

"No way!" I snap at my father, whose eyes widen at my outburst. I press my hand against my chest, feeling my heart beating against my palm.

"No," George replies, a lot calmer. "Nate would do anything for Lilly. He's been searching for her for over ten years."

"Ten?" Dad's eyebrows shoot up.

*Ah, he's catching on.*

No one elaborates, though, and George continues, "Nate landed in Paris around midnight local time. He texted me that he would get some sleep and be in touch in the morning before his meeting. That was the last time I communicated with him. I tried his phone and Hank's several times, but they went straight to voicemail."

"Hank is with him?" I narrow my eyes.

"Hank goes everywhere Nate goes." There is disdain in George's tone that I've never heard before.

"What about Joel?" Lilly told me about Nate's pilot.

George nods approvingly. "I contacted Joel. He went to Nate's suite at the hotel. No one was there. He alerted our local security staff and was working with them last we spoke. I've been focused on this scene since. Nate is capable; Lilly is my first priority."

My father has been typing on his phone the entire time when his eyes suddenly snap up. Something must've clicked, and he walks out of the room like his ass is on fire.

"What's up with your dad?" Wes mumbles to me, but I only shrug.

"Who the fuck knows." *Or cares.*

Denielle yawns, and I glance at the antique clock in the corner. It's almost two in the morning, and I can't stop my own yawn.

"Now that everyone is here, I am calling Joel again. Why don't you three get some rest? I'll get you if we receive any news." George sweeps our faces one by one.

*He's out of his mind if he thinks I'd be able to sleep.*

But knowing George, there's also no use in arguing. We're

dismissed—for now. We follow him upstairs, where he shows Wes to a spare room. Denielle walks past all of us and disappears inside. I cock an eyebrow at my best friend, who shakes his head at me—*don't ask*—and then follows her, closing the door.

I turn to face George, who is already making his way to another set of stairs. Too exhausted to question him why I'm not staying on this floor, I follow. I get my answer when he opens a door on the third floor.

*Lilly's bedroom.*

My eyes wander over the cream-colored décor. The bed is unmade, and clothes are hanging over the chair in the corner. I swallow over the lump in my throat as I step farther into the room.

"I'll be on the first floor if you need me." I nod, acknowledging him but not turning around. The click as the door closes indicates that I am alone.

I DON'T EMERGE AGAIN until 10:30.

After taking a shower and changing into sweats and a t-shirt, I had sat down on Lilly's bed. Falling backward, I pulled one of her pillows over my face. The remnants of the same shampoo she uses at home registered in my nose, and my eyes started to burn.

*I was so fucking sick of bawling like a baby.*

Clutching the pillow tighter, it muffled my sobs. I imagined her moving around the room, standing by the window, looking out. I want her back. This...situation makes everything else seem so unimportant.

I didn't think I would sleep, but I must've passed out eventually. The next thing I know, I'm blinking against the sunlight. My mouth is dry, and the back of my throat feels like I gargled acid—damn crying.

Not bothering to change, I pad downstairs barefoot, where I find George and my father in the breakfast nook of the kitchen. The only reason I am willing to be around anyone is that I need to know if they have news. Two laptops and three phones—one of them more remnants of one—sit between them. My stomach instantly drops, recognizing the device for what it is...was—Lilly's.

I scan the room. The kitchen appears like nothing ever

happened, which, on the one hand, is a relief—I don't think I could've handled seeing the result of the struggle—but on the other hand, it ignites a rage I haven't felt since I discovered what my psycho ex did to my girlfriend. The rational side of my brain is fully aware of how *irrational* I am. Still, with the room being this impeccable and the two former Marines lounging there like they're long-lost buddies, chatting casually over some joe, I want to take another swing at George. Or Dad. Or both. Definitely both.

Dropping into a chair on the other side of the table, I look at the two men. Like, really look at them. Some of my rage deflates at the realization that neither of them has slept a wink. Dad has dark circles under his eyes, his hair is disheveled like he ran his hands through it one too many times, and both are in the same clothes as last night.

A steaming cup of coffee is suddenly thrust in my line of vision, the dark liquid almost spilling over. As I follow the arm attached to it, an equally tired Denielle looks down at me. One corner of her mouth twitches, and I assume it's her attempt at a reassuring smile —which epically fails.

Out of the corner of my eye, Wes pulls out one of the barstools and leans against it. I take the mug from Den, not even attempting a positive facial expression, and she immediately steps back to Wes's side.

The bond the two of them have developed over the last months cause me to turn away. I want Lilly, my best friend and my girlfriend, back by my side. Seeing them so close causes a surge of jealousy that I am embarrassed to even admit to myself.

"Anything new?" Wes is the one to break the suffocating silence.

"We—" George starts when a door somewhere flies open—the front door maybe? And the noise of numerous footfalls echoes through the first floor. Every head turns as Nate stumbles into the kitchen, followed by a man in a pilot uniform and several of George's guards.

Lilly's brother is half bent forward, clutching his side, and George is out of his seat in a second. Good thing he was sitting in the corner seat, or he either would've climbed over the table or pushed my father out in the process.

"Nate, you're not supposed to be on your feet."

"What happened?"

"Where is my sister?!"

The man I assume is Joel, George, and Nate speak at the same time. Just as the words leave his mouth, Nate's legs buckle, and his pilot and head of security reach for him. George catches the brunt of his employer's large body and has to brace himself by stepping one foot back.

Nate grunts, and Joel supports him by wrapping his other arm around his shoulder. "He shouldn't be standing. Can we put him down somewhere?"

"I'm fiiineee," Nate responds in a slur.

I narrow my eyes at him.

"Dude, you don't look so fine," Wes remarks dryly, and Denielle elbows him in the ribs. "Ow." He scowls down at her.

"WHAT THE HELL HAPPENED?" George bellows, and everyone—except my father—flinches at his outburst. George doesn't raise his voice.

"He was stabbed," Joel explains with fear in his eyes as if George would hold him responsible. Maybe he does. What do I know about the inner workings of them.

*Stabbed?*

Everyone's gazes falls to Nate's side, where he's holding himself.

"How the hell did you get stabbed?" George addresses his boss, the momentary anger gone.

"Hank," Nate grunts.

"Hank? What—" Eyebrows scrunched, George turns to me as if I know what happened.

How would I know? I take a step forward, shouldering the poor pilot—who looks like he's about to piss himself any second—out of the way.

"Let me have him. I'll take care of Psycho-brother-in-law," I say, unable to stop myself from using my nickname for him. I grasp at anything that makes me not feel like floating in a dark void, and taking a verbal stab at Nate briefly does it for me. He's my connection to Lilly.

"You're funny, little brother-in-law." Nate chuckles then winces. "Fuuuuck."

"Come on, I gotcha."

Nate shifts his entire weight on me, and I brace his body as we make our way to the closest living room.

George breathes down my neck, followed by Denielle and Wes both staring like they're watching *Alien vs. Predator* about to battle it out. I guess I can't fault them for that. This is the first time I've been face to face—in person—with the guy who kidnapped Lilly. *Twice*. But as we hobble toward the couch, several things register in my brain. My anger and resentment toward this man are gone. I don't know if it's temporary or if both of us losing the one person we care most about has shifted things. We'll have to wait and see.

Panting—the dude is fucking heavy dead weight—I deposit him on the couch. Half sitting, half lying on the sectional, I take a seat close to Nate, but not too close to be in his personal space. George sits down on the small coffee table right in front of us and leans forward, reaching for the hem of Nate's shirt.

My father is standing behind George, watching the scene with a frown.

Denielle walks in with a glass of water and a pill bottle. I didn't even notice she'd left. "Joel says he has to take these." She thrusts both items at George, who inspects it closely before uncapping the lid. He hands Nate two white pills and the water.

"Can you guys stop hovering already?" Nate mumbles as he takes his, what I assume are, painkillers.

"*We* are not the ones who got stabbed," I deadpan, crossing my arms over my chest.

"Nate." George waits for him to make eye contact. "What happened?" He's running out of patience.

Nate shifts so he is more upright. "The fucker stabbed me."

"Hank?" I ask just to confirm once more.

The confusion on everyone's face is as visible as the fact that the dude is dead meat if he did what Nate claims—which I don't doubt.

Winkey-Hank won't be winking much longer.

Nate nods his head in my direction. "We were eating breakfast in my suite, as usual, preparing for the meeting. I was sitting on the couch while the little cunt, *aka Hank*, was telling me what to expect. Then my phone vibrated." Nate pauses and shifts, grabbing onto his side. "I'm going to kill this fucker," he mumbles.

"Nate." George holds a warning in his tone, trying to get Nate to focus. The crease between his eyebrows tells me he doesn't like seeing Lilly's brother in pain. George is way more than just an employee to Nate.

"Sorry." Nate groans then mercifully continues, "I picked it up, and I saw that it was a notification from the house alarm system. It was disarmed." Nate's eyes settle on George. They both stare at each other, and it seems like a silent communication is taking place between them. George's expression turns murderous, and Nate jerks his head up and down.

"Where is he?" George growls.

"No clue, man. I woke up in the fucking hospital with no ID or any way of communicating. You know my French is shit."

My pulse increases, and I'm starting to lose patience with the two. My fingers have curled inward and have left crescent-shaped indentations in my palms. "It's great and all that the two of you can, apparently, read each other's minds, but I want to know where my girlfriend is. So, *please*, tell the rest of us unknowing mortals what the fuck happened?" I glare at both men.

All eyes are on me, but I don't care. They need to start fucking talking.

Nate adjusts his position so he can address me. "The house alarm system is set to send me notifications whenever it is armed or disarmed. It's part of the system I have at all my properties. I added the protocol here when Lilly moved in. Additionally, everyone with access to my properties has their own code. No one uses the same. The message I received showed an alert for Hank's code disarming the security system in this house." He pauses and waits for the rest of us to catch on.

*Holy fucking shit!*

"You are telling me that your bitch assistant has something to do with Lilly being kidnapped?" I grind out between clenched teeth. My entire body is vibrating from rage.

Nate presses his lips together. I turn and fling the first object within my reach across the room—a small, golden elephant statue from the coffee table. It makes a decent size dent in the drywall before crashing into the glass table underneath. I can't muster any remorse for the property damage.

"What next?" My father's voice brings everyone back to the

present. He has remained silent since Lilly's brother stumbled into the house. Observing the scene.

"I told him I was gonna go take a leak. I started dialing George —fuck the meet with Lakatos. Lilly was in danger. That much was clear. The little shit must've realized that I was onto him, and next thing I know, I have a sharp pain in my side, and something hits me in the head." He inhales slowly. "I woke up in a Parisian hospital, and it took them two fucking hours to find someone fluent enough in English to get me a phone and call the hotel to find Joel. Their damn landlines wouldn't connect to a non-French number. It's like the stone age."

"I had already searched the suite when you called me." Joel stands in the corner of the room and addresses George. "Besides Nate's clothes, nothing was there. I packed everything up, and I went to the hospital. It took several more hours for them to agree to discharge him."

"We drove straight to the airport and came back," Nate finishes.

"Why didn't you call me?" George admonishes him.

"Because I had no clue if anyone else was involved, if someone had gotten into my system, or what the hell was going on. My laptop was gone, and I couldn't check the feeds." Nate is one of the best, and for him to consider someone breached his *homemade* security system—not to mention hijacking his business partner and turning him against Nate?

*Fuck.*

George suddenly stands up and turns to one of his men. "I want an APB out for Hank Todd. He is your number one priority." The guy jumps at the order, bobs his head up and down, and storms out.

"Um, shouldn't they look for Lilly?" Denielle asks, wringing her hands together.

"No, they can concentrate on the traitor. I'll find my sister. That son of a bitch is not smart enough to *not* leave a trail," Nate sneers and turns to George. "Have one of your guys go to his place and bring me everything he left. Laptop, phones, a fucking carrier pigeon if that's how he communicated with Turner. I want it all here within two hours."

His head of security nods and pulls his phone out, putting it to his ear as he follows the other guy.

Then, Nate turns to my father and pushes himself up until he's slightly swaying on his legs. "Mr. McGuire." He reaches out his hand. "I'm Lilly's brother, Nate Hamlin."

Dad looks between Nate's face and his hand. I can see the wheels in his head turning before he takes it. "Nate. Call me Tristen."

I expel a breath I didn't realize I was holding. I have no clue what I was expecting.

They both shake, followed by Nate turning to me. "Can you help me upstairs? I need to get to work."

Surprised that he wants my help, I'm momentarily stunned, but then I wrap his arm around my shoulder and slowly lead him to the stairs.

Behind me, I hear Dad tell Den and Wes that he's going to go check in with Mom. I don't know what they're going to do, but the selfish prick in me doesn't give a fuck.

Nate is here, and he is our best chance of finding Lilly.

---

# CHAPTER ONE HUNDRED THIRTEEN

---

**LILLY**

GRAY PUSHES HIMSELF UP, BUT WHEN HE PUTS A HAND ON HIS thigh for more leverage, his leg buckles, and he groans. I narrow my eyes at him—that is not the leg *I* stabbed.

He stumbles out of my room and slams the door. The familiar click follows right after, and I sink to the floor. The adrenaline is quickly leaving my body, and my hands begin to shake. Pulling my knees close, I wrap my arms around them and let my forehead drop forward.

*What the hell is going on here?*

I sit like this until the trembling in my body subsides enough to drag myself on all fours over to the paper bag without my arms or legs giving out. I'm starving, yet the thought of eating causes my stomach to churn as if someone has dared me to eat some type of insect—alive. I have to, though. If it's true that I've been here for over a day and a half, I need food. And water. The fighter in me knows I have to keep my strength up until Nate and George—oh, no, Denielle. In all of this, I completely forgot about her coming to LA.

*Shit, shit, shit!*

I gave her the address and put her name on the visitor list. She should be able to—another thought *backhands* me. How did Gray get on the property, let alone in?

My brain pulls me in so many different directions that my tired mind can't keep up. I eye the bag that supposedly contains nourishment again. Please let it be something edible.

Pulling the top apart, I could weep in relief: two plain bagels. I reach for the water that still sits in the middle of the room from...last night? Whenever Gray put it there. Gulping it down, it's like a drop of water over a hot stone. It doesn't satisfy my body's need one bit. Dropping the now empty cup, I take two large bites out of the bagel. Not a good idea. My stomach instantly begins to cramp. I clamp my mouth shut and crawl as fast as I can into the adjacent bathroom, reaching the porcelain bowl just in time for everything to make a reappearance.

Cold sweat covers every inch of my skin, and the full-on body tremors are back. I groan as another wave of nausea crashes down on me, but all that's left is bile.

"Make it stooooop," I mumble into the empty space and lean my cheek against the seat. My inner germaphobe is too exhausted to be grossed out. Gray apparently knew what he was talking about.

When my legs can support my weight, I pull myself up on the rim of the sink and rinse my mouth—what I wouldn't give for a toothbrush right now.

ON THE SECOND TRY, I know better. I take small sips of water, pick the dry bread apart, and nibble on it slowly. It takes forever to finish both, but it remains down. Win-win.

Sitting back on the mattress, I prepare myself for a long wait time but am surprised when I hear footsteps outside the door and the lock unlatches.

I'm not completely blind anymore when the outside glare hits me since I've left the little light in the bathroom on. Gray enters the room, followed by Emily. My mother.

I'm still considering that I'm hallucinating.

Both scan the empty bag on the ground, and Gray smirks. Emily is the first to speak. "I see you ate. Good."

Her tone is dismissive. Detached. She acknowledges it but couldn't care less.

Remaining where I am with my back to the wall, I stare at both of them. They are such an odd pair. Where Gray is all creep, she is put together and impeccably styled. She is still wearing black leggings, but her top is light-blue today. Her blonde hair is curled in precise waves, her subtle but professionally applied makeup making her look younger than her forty-eight years.

I steady my voice. "What do you want with me? I don't assume you want a happy family reunion."

With some of my strength returning, my attitude also resurfaces. Though, it's different than when I had faced Nate for the first time. With Nate, I somehow felt he wouldn't harm me, but I'm not so sure with these two. Gray probably would enjoy getting revenge for the stab wound and kick to the balls. I draw my shoulders back, forcing my inhales and exhales to remain steady.

*I refuse to show them fear.*

Gray leans at the wall beside the door as Emily walks closer. She squats down with her elbows on her knees and slants her head, scanning me up and down. She is far enough away that I'd have to leave my spot to reach her—a strategic move on her part.

"You grew up nicely." Her voice is cold, and the hairs on the back of my neck stand.

*What kind of statement is that?*

"Is that a compliment?" I cock my head in an identical way and mimic her expression.

She huffs out a non-comical laugh. "I see you haven't lost your attitude." I open my mouth to make a sarcastic remark, but she continues, "Heather and Tristen did a good job. Unfortunately, not good enough. I didn't plan for you to meet your brother."

*What?*

My pulse increases, but I remain mute, letting her do the talking.

"All you had to do was turn eighteen. You would've never known any of this. I had it all arranged."

*Eighteen?*

The pieces are falling into place. "This is all about the money my father left me?" I stare at her incredulously. She dumped me and went off the grid to wait her time for...money?

"What else would it be about?"

Unable to stop myself, the little girl in me speaks. "Me?"

My mother chuckles as if I've said the most ridiculous thing. "Oh, my dear Lilly, I never wanted children. Yet, fate had different plans for me." Her tone is sugary sweet, and goosebumps appear on my arms. "That's why I chose Henry; he told me on our second date that he was infertile. He was perfect. I would never have to go through that again. He was my ticket out of the life I grew up in."

*Again?* But she doesn't give me an opportunity to speak.

"We got married and moved to San Diego to be closer to my childhood friend. Life was normal for the first time. Then, I went to visit Heather at a conference and met Brooks. I didn't see him coming." Her eyes become vacant for a second before they harden again. "He made me feel."

Behind Emily, Gray shifts, and his expression becomes unreadable. I narrow my eyes at the man. She said something that made him react.

Oblivious to the change in her...partner? Accomplice? Whatever he is to her, she continues, "When I found out I was pregnant, I even considered keeping it. But then he told me he went back to his wife. He wanted to make it work with her for his children's sake." She sneers the last words, and I fight the urge to press closer against the barrier behind me.

Her face contorts. "I WAS CARRYING HIS DAMN CHILD!"

I jump at the outburst and fight the urge to wrap my arms around my midsection. *Holy hell.*

Emily stands up in a jerked motion and starts pacing. I trail her every move while keeping Gray in my peripheral vision. I cannot let my guard down with them.

"But nooo, that wasn't good enough. I wasn't a rich, stuck-up bitch. He would've lost everything if he had left Payton." She suddenly spins and gets in my face. "I had to bide my time. And if he wouldn't come to me willingly, I would at least get what I deserved another way. So...I kept you."

I press the back of my head against the concrete wall. "What you deserved?" I whisper with raised eyebrows.

But she ignores my question. "He wanted you. Did you know that? He wanted to raise you. The red-headed bitch would've taken you in as her own." The smugness in her tone makes the hair on my nape stand. "We couldn't have that now, could we?"

*Good Lord, this woman is crazy.*

"It was all fine, as long as he was paying his child support, but—"

My snort interrupts her, and her eyes snap to mine. *Shit.* I didn't mean to do that but can't take it back now. Thankfully, the anger that has slowly been building the more she rants gives my voice the backbone I need. "Child support? Are you kidding me? Twenty-five K a month is not child support. You blackmailed him!" Another puzzle piece is in its place.

Her sudden stiff posture tells me that she didn't expect me to know that fact.

My *mother* composes herself and moves on without acknowledging my statement. "He should've just kept sending the money, and everything would've been fine."

My muscles tense. I don't like where she is going.

"When Gray and Mara were in town one weekend, and Gray noticed someone following me, it was time to show your dear father what it meant to ignore my instructions. I didn't crawl my way out of the life I was born into to be made a joke out of."

I stop listening after Gray and Mara.

*Who the hell is Mara?*

"So Gray and I came up with a plan." She stops talking, which brings my attention back to Emily. She's standing in the middle of the room, hands on her hips, and looking at me expectantly. She's waiting.

Replaying what she has said so far and—oh, no. Please no! I cover my mouth with my hands, whispering, "You killed Payton?"

Her face lights up, and she puts her palm against her chest like she is proud of my deductive skills. "Well, not me, personally. I just gave Brooks the nudge to set things in motion."

Set things in motion. *What—?* I can feel the crease between my eyebrows grow deeper.

"We made Gray disappear. A dead man could not be prosecuted." She sounds almost chipper.

My eyes flick between the two people in front of me, swallowing several times. I let my gaze rest on Gray, who still hasn't moved. One foot propped against the wall, his arms are crossed over his broad chest. He'd appear bored if it weren't for him clenching his jaw.

I can't look at her, so I address him instead. My voice is a mere rasp. "Who was in the car?"

The car that went over the cliff on Pacific Coast Highway.

"My brother," Gray answers without emotion, and I choke on my saliva, coughing violently to the point of my eyes watering.

"You killed your brother for *her?*" The pitch in my tone is rising. "You both are fucking insane!"

With blinding speed, Emily is across the room and in front of me. Her hand shoots to my throat, and she pins my legs with hers. "You know nothing about me," she hisses in my face, and I can smell the wine on her breath. I'm going to be sick.

"No, I d-don't. Y-you left m-me," I croak, trying to dislodge her clawed hand from my neck.

She lets go and moves back, smoothing her hands over her top and pants. "Let's continue our chat later."

As she struts out, I gulp in all the air I can get. Watching her retreating form, I place my hand at the side of my neck where her nails dug in. Gray follows close behind, and I'm alone again. Wetness under my fingertips makes me pull the hand away again. Blood. She scratched me to the point of breaking skin.

I'm starting to feel glad that I don't remember this woman. Was she like this when I was a child? How could Henry stay married to her?

Henry! I jump from the mattress and race to the door, banging my fists against it. "EMILY!" I hit the barrier until my arm hurts, but there is no response. Exhausted, I turn, leaning with my back against the door, and slide to the ground. Tears fill my eyes, and I let them fall, uncaring if they hear me.

"What did you do with Henry?"


It's hours before I see either of them again.

I'm on the mattress, my back pressed against the wall. *Never let yourself be vulnerable in a hostage situation,* Spence's words from one of our sessions come back to me. Back then, I laughed. What hostage situation did he think I'd get in? Did he know more than he let on? After Gray's boot against my back, my trainer's advice has become like a mantra in my mind. These people are crazy. I'm in a hostage situation.

The door opens to a small gap and another paper bag projectiles in.

"EAT!" Gray's barked command echoes through the bare room, and the door flings shut again.

*So much for getting more answers anytime soon.*

Resigned, I comply. My stomach has been growling for a while, and I'm not one of those idiots that goes on a hunger strike to defy their kidnappers. Fuck that! Emily's insanity, what she said, her attack... I touch the marks on my neck. I should be more hurt that she obviously never wanted *me*. I was at first, then I remind myself that I do have a family. Two, actually. I don't remember this woman, and from what I've experienced so far, I hope I never will remember. She is a stranger. She won't break me. I'll go down fighting if I have to.

Eventually, I must have dozed off and tipped over because I'm now horizontal and staring at Emily's bare feet.

*Does this woman ever wear shoes?*

I struggle to push myself into a sitting position. *Shit.* Gray is in his usual spot next to the doorframe. His eyes are drooping, and even from here, I can see that his pupils are the size of a pinprick. Is he high?

"Darling, please excuse that it took me so long to get everything in order." Emily sounds like a doting mother.

*In order?*

"Where is Henry?" My fingers curl in. I refuse to let her distract me from the one question I want an answer to.

She places a stack of papers with a pen on top in front of the mattress. "If you sign here, everything will be rectified."

*Is she high?*

"Where is Henry?" I repeat myself slowly, purposefully talking as if she has trouble comprehending simple English. There is a buzz running through my body, a combination of rage and fear, and my fists press into my thigh.

Her nostrils flare. "I guess I was right to keep him around, after all."

My pulse speeds up. "What do you mean?"

"My *husband* is currently indisposed, but I might be inclined to let you speak to him if you sign the papers," she states sweetly.

The reason why George abandoned his position during my attack comes to the forefront of my mind, and my eyes widen as I stare at Emily. "The drugs," I whisper.

She scowls, and I elaborate louder, "The ones he bought in Virginia." I flick my gaze to Gray. "They weren't for me—at least, not all of them." I rub the spot he drove the needle in.

Emily slowly swivels on her heels and focuses on her helper. "You were followed?" Her voice turns void of emotion. Her mood swings are starting to freak me out; there's no indicator of what sets her off.

The tall man shrugs. "You have her now. What difference does it make?" His words are slow like he has to concentrate hard to form them.

"What. Difference? WHAT. DIFFERENCE?" she shrieks and is across the room in a flash, grabbing onto Gray's thigh and squeezing.

He winces but won't buckle as her nails dig into what I assume is the other stab wound.

"What else have you been hiding from me, Fran-cis?" The shrill tone has turned to an icy whisper, and I have to strain my ears to follow the conversation.

"Nothing, Em."

"What if Weiler would've followed you to the house, huh?"

"No one knows where you stashed the cripple."

*Cripple?*

My heart starts pounding, and I jump up. "What did you do with Henry?"

She doesn't turn when she responds, eyes locked with the man she's torturing with her talons. "I simply kept him in line. But one phone call from me and he will no longer be of your concern. Or mine."

White-hot rage surges through me, and I lunge at the woman

who gave birth to me. I tear her off of Gray, but she spins and back-hands me with a force that makes my head snap to the side.

"You will not touch me. I'm your *mother*!" she seethes at me, getting right into my face.

I slowly turn back to her. "You are not my mother," I grind out. My cheek is burning, but I refuse to raise my hand to the sting. "Heather is my mother. Hell, Payton was probably more a mother to me than you—and I never even met the woman." A voice in my head screams to shut up. Emily is obviously mentally unstable, but the words were out of my mouth before I could stop myself.

Instead of responding to my verbal attack, she flips around and takes two long strides to Gray, whose eyes widen at her sudden intrusion of his personal space. She pushes her hand between the man and the wall and pulls out...a knife?

Shit. I scurry backward as she approaches me like a predator advancing on its prey. "Do you want to repeat that, my daughter?"

I flatten myself against the wall and move sideways away from her, but she keeps following with the knife held low toward me. I can deflect a blade. That was one of the first lessons Spence taught me, but the shock of *my mother* coming after me with a weapon has temporarily wiped my brain of all defense moves. Before I can collect myself, Gray's arms wrap around Emily, and he stops her.

"Em, you need to calm down. If you hurt her now, she most certainly won't sign the money over."

*When did he become the voice of reason?*

She lowers the knife and stops struggling. Gray seems to know that the immediate threat is over and loosens his grip.

"Sign the damn papers, and you can have Henry. That's the only reason he's still breathing anyway," she barks out before shouldering out of Gray's hold. She spins on her heel and marches out.

Gray remains in his spot for a moment longer, eyeing me. "Piece of advice, princess. I've known your mother all my life. You need to watch your mouth if you want to come out of here..."—he pauses and quirks an eyebrow—"with a pulse."

# CHAPTER ONE HUNDRED FOURTEEN

### RHYS

Nate drops into the desk chair with a thud, and I pull another one around from the front. I keep it near the edge, not wanting to be in his way but so I can still see what he does.

His hands hover over the keyboard before he turns back to me. "I didn't think I'd like you much."

*What the—?*

"Excuse me?" I cock an eyebrow at Lilly's brother. "I just carried your heavy, injured ass upstairs and—"

"That came out wrong," he interrupts me, chuckling, and wipes a hand over his mouth. "The big brother in me was suspicious about your intentions with Lilly."

I open my mouth to tell him where he can shove his big-brother attitude, but Nate holds up a hand. "Chill, I know I'm the last person who can claim the brother-of-the-year award." He blows out a breath. "What I'm trying to say... I can see why my sister would argue about the existence of a soulmate with me. Everything Lilly told me about you two—your past. Plus, when you and I talked before and now meeting you in person... You're not so bad."

*Soulmate? He must be high from the pain meds.*

I do a goldfish imitation, no clue how to respond to that.

He focuses back on the monitors and presses the space bar. One of the monitors comes to life, and he's about to hit the other keyboard when he pauses. "What the fuck?"

Nate's face pales, and his eyes nearly bulge out of their sockets. I lean over to see what has him so unhinged and almost fall out of my chair. Brooks's face is paused on the screen.

"What is that?" I ask hesitantly, pulling myself back into the chair and scooting it closer.

Nate ignores me and hovers the curser over the play button. He closes his eyes for several inhales and exhales before they snap open, and he clicks—almost as if he didn't want to give himself a chance to change his mind.

*SHE THREATENED to tell Payton about the affair. About Lilly. She wanted me to come back to her. Said she'd leave her husband. It was like she had built this fantasy in her head about us. A relationship that never existed. When I didn't change my mind, she started threatening our daughter's life.*

HEARING BROOKS THROUGH THE SPEAKER, the fingers of Nate's hand in his lap dig into his leg. The other, still on the trackpad, begins to tremble. Then the words sink in. *She started threatening our daughter's life.* She. Lilly's mother. Emily. Emily was threatening Lilly? My stomach rolls, and I wrap one arm around myself.

*I SAW ONLY ONE OPTION. I told Payton everything. As you can imagine, your mother didn't take the news well. I had an illegitimate daughter. She left me for a few weeks. You thought your mom took Audrey to stay at your aunt's house during that time.*

*When Payton came back, we sat down and talked. We talked for days, and by some miracle, your mother forgave me. We agreed that our family would come first, and we would find a way to have Lilly be part of your and Audrey's lives. That's who your mother was. She loved and cared for every-one. None of this was Lilly's fault.*

· · ·

Tears stream down Brooks's face, and his voice cracks with every other word. A lump forms in my own throat. He recorded this video for his son. Peering at Nate, his eyes are glossed over, and his spine is rigid.

"This is why he mentioned the pipes in his will to be given to me..." Nate mumbles to himself.

"Huh?"

He pauses the video and turns to me. His tone is subdued. "I inherited everything my parents owned, which made the will pretty simple. When they read it to me, my grandfather's pipes were listed specifically, nothing else. I never thought about it. I didn't want shit to do with what's in this house—what my father cared about."

I narrow my eyes. "You think that was his hint for you to find this?" I gesture to the screen.

"Yes," he whispers.

"But why hide it?" This doesn't make sense.

Nate shrugs. "At this point, who cares? It could've been anything. Not wanting for anyone to find out before me, he could've been afraid Emily would come after him, or he was simply drugged out of his mind from the antidepressants."

*Then why didn't he hide the letters and pictures Emily sent?*

"But he didn't hide the photos and let—"

"I DON'T CARE, RHYS!" he barks, and I take that as my cue to shut up.

Without another word, Nate restarts the recording, and I focus back on the screen.

*Most of the time, Emily acted completely normal. We were two adults who made a mistake and conceived a child.*

*Then, a phone call would come, not one of her handwritten letters. She'd threaten me, Lilly, or on a few occasions, even you and Audrey. Said that if she couldn't be with me, she wanted money for raising my child. For keeping the secret from her husband.*

*The first time I questioned her about why she wouldn't come clean to him, she ended the call. Next, I received an email from an unknown sender with a picture of Lilly sleeping in her crib—nothing else, no context or message. I didn't know what it meant, but I couldn't reach Emily for days.*

*Eventually, I drove to San Diego and started following her. Everything seemed normal. Lilly was fine. She sent another handwritten letter with new pictures, and your mother and I chalked it up as a random occurrence.*

*Then, she called again. She demanded more money than we had already given her. The amount was outrageous, and when I told her so, she hung up.*

*I received another email with a picture of Lilly. This time, she was playing in the yard—again, no message. Something wasn't right, and Payton decided to contact a PI your grandfather sometimes used when their regular guy was already on a job.*

REGULAR GUY? Is he talking about George? Nate's mouth is pressing in a thin line as if he has come to the same conclusion. Did George know about any of this? Nate makes no indication to stop the video and confront his employee, though.

*WE HAD him look into Emily's past as well. The information he showed us...her childhood...it wasn't a good one. There were holes in her past. She'd disappear for months at a time until her husband came into the picture. But all the evidence led to her having...mental problems. I don't know if her husband knew about it or if she was such a good actor around people that she fooled everyone. She had fooled me for months.*

BROOKS SIGHS and clutches a picture in his hand. My heart is hammering against my ribcage. I want Nate to stop this video. I've heard enough, but at the same time, I need to know the rest.

*AFTER THAT, we looked into getting custody of Lilly. Our attorney even said we had a good chance if we could prove that Lilly was in physical danger. With Emily's husband not being her biological father or having legally adopted her, we could sue for sole custody. However, neither Payton nor I would've kept Lilly from him. Not if he was...safe.*

. . .

THERE IS such a long pause that I begin wondering if Brooks is going to say anything else.

THE NEXT TIME EMILY CALLED, *I informed her that I had looked into requesting shared custody. Your mother and I had agreed that we didn't want to spook her right off the bat with taking Lilly away; we would've accepted joint custody. Emily didn't take that...well.*

WELL? Please don't say what I think you're going to say. I'm so high-strung that my entire body feels like it's vibrating.

THE NEXT DAY, *I received an email with another picture. Lilly had a bruised eye and a split lip. S-she was b-barely a year o-old.*

I'M GOING to be sick. Tears are streaming down Brooks's cheeks as he recalls everything. Nate's hands cover his mouth, not making any attempt to conceal his crying. Someone was hurting Lilly. Nate's mother knew about all of it. My mind starts to take off on its own.

THIS TIME, *the email had a message. Either I would pay the* mother of my child *the agreed-upon amount every month on the same day—meaning the five figures Emily previously demanded—or there would be no daughter.*
*We didn't know what to do. Payton wanted to take Lilly from Emily against her will. But when we received another email with more...photos, I agreed to pay. Emily, or whoever did this to my little girl—I don't believe her husband had anything to do with it...they were serious.*
*I...I couldn't risk my daughter's life.*

MY HANDS ARE SHAKING SO BADLY I tuck them under my armpits and clamp my elbows to the side of my body. Brooks doesn't go into any details about what kind of pictures the second email contained, but I can guess. This is some fucked-up shit, and it all revolves around Lilly. How is it possible that my parents, who supposedly cared so much for her, didn't know any of this? Or did they? I want to confront my father, but I can't get out of the chair. My legs won't obey.

Nate's complexion has turned a chalkish gray with a hint of green. His leg is bouncing so fast my messed-up brain associates the tapping sound of his foot with that Irish dance-tap show Mom was obsessed with when we were kids—River-something. What the fuck is wrong with my head?

I concentrate on breathing through my nose as the video continues to play mercilessly. How much more is there?

*Payton and I met with Emily. She had Lilly with her but refused to let me hold her. Nate, she looked so much like you and Audrey. The same blonde hair, the same eye color. She was such a happy baby, smiled the entire time.*

*During that meeting, we agreed to pay Emily the sum she had demanded under the condition of regular updates and me being able to see Lilly. I wanted to be part of her life. I had to.*

*Payton cried the entire drive home, but we knew we would risk Lilly's life if we came after her in any way at this time. We hoped that if we played along and bided our time, we'd have a better chance in the future.*

I can barely see the screen. I have to untuck my arms and wipe my eyes. I have no words for what is being revealed in front of me. Has Lilly seen this? Her father loved her. He wanted her. Hell, even Nate's mother wanted Lilly. We had it all so fucking wrong.

*A few years later, we received the demand to increase the amount, and we complied without hesitation. Emily had kept her end of the deal, I visited with Lilly regularly, and our PI also kept an eye on her. From what we were able to see, she was safe and happy.*

*We wanted to wait a few more years before starting the legal procedures of getting custody. We hoped that if Lilly was older, the likelihood of her getting physically hurt was less.*

*What we didn't consider was Emily finding out about the private inves-*

*tigator. To this day, I don't know how, but she saw it as a violation of our agreement.*

ALL THE COLOR has left Brooks's face, and the blood in my veins runs cold. Nate has gone completely still. I don't think he's even breathing. Hell, I know whatever comes next will break me, and the man on the screen is not even my father.

*I* RECEIVED AN EMAIL—THE *first one in years. But instead of a picture of Lilly, it contained two photographs. One of Payton and one of Audrey. From that morning.*

FUCK.

*I* IMMEDIATELY CALLED *your mother and told her to get Audrey and go to your grandfather's vineyard. We had never been there, and no one knew about it. He purchased it not long before he passed.*

*Two hours later, the police came to my office. Your mother and sister had been in a car accident. They told me she had run a stop sign.*

*You knew your mother. She was the most cautious driver out there. There was no way she missed the sign.*

BROOKS'S SHOULDERS shake with sobs as he finishes.

*A*UDREY D-DIED O-ON IMPACT. *The car was h-hit on her side. They said your mother had s-suffocated. H-how could s-she suffocate in a car a-accident?*

I CAN'T BREATHE. My lungs have closed up, and I'm unable to draw in a breath. Nate slams his hand on the keyboard, which *finally* stops the recording of horrors. He starts retching and turns to the side, dropping out of his chair until he's on all fours. He reaches for a trash can I hadn't noticed before and pukes right into it.

Chin dipped to my chest, I wrap my arms around my midsection and rock back and forth. In addition to the smell coming from my side, a sour taste coats my tongue, and black spots appear in my vision. I close my eyes and start counting—one, two, three, don't throw up, four, five, six, don't throw up, seven, eight...

I'm waiting for someone to burst in here and demand to know what's going on. George, my father, or even Wes. But the door remains closed.

The gagging sounds from Nate have stopped, but neither of us speaks. I have no fucking clue what to do. It is clear what Brooks was saying, or rather *not saying*. Audrey and Payton's death wasn't an accident. Payton didn't die from the impact.

I turn my head in Nate's direction. One arm draped over the trash can, he lets it support his body. The other hand is holding his side, and he groans. "Rhys?"

"Yeah?"

There's a pause and another groan. "I can't get up."

*Huh? Oh.*

"'Kay, uh, hold on." Unfolding myself, I place my palms on the armrest and push myself into a standing position. When I'm sure my legs will support me and I won't faceplant next to Nate, I bridge the short distance between us. I grab him under his arms and hoist him back into his chair.

"Oof. Dude, you're not that much taller; how can you be so heavy?" I grunt.

Nate chuckles. "Itth called dead weith." His words are slurred again. He should probably rest, but I doubt this will happen anytime soon.

"Should we finish...this?" I peer at the monitor with a frozen Brooks on it. Nate remains quiet for so long that I'm not sure he heard me. Suddenly, he hits the space bar, and we watch Brooks trying to regain control.

. . .

LILLY, *if you are with your brother, I am so sorry that I never got the chance to come for you. Please know that you were always on my mind. On Payton's mind. And that all we tried to do was keep you safe.*

HOLY SHIT, this video was for Nate and Lilly.

NATE, *if Lilly is already part of your life, take care of your little sister. If not, please find her. You deserve to have your family in your life.*

*I'm sorry I wasn't a better father to either of you. I will never forgive myself for being the reason my wife and daughter died and that my son went to a mental hospital for something I caused. I'm so sorry. Please forgive me.*

NATE, *I never said it enough, but I'm proud of you.*
*I love you both with all my heart.*

## CHAPTER ONE HUNDRED FIFTEEN

### RHYS

I have no fucking clue how long Nate and I stare at the black screen once the video cuts off. So many thoughts assault my brain at the same time, and I dig the heels of my hands into my eyes. I press so hard until it hurts, but nothing stops the onslaught of emotions and new information needing to be processed.

*The affair didn't go on for years.*

We were wrong.

*Nate's mother knew about Lilly.*

Admiration for the woman's compassion and understanding makes warmth spread through my body.

*Emily was blackmailing Brooks for money.*

A bucket of ice douses the warmth.

*Emily hurt her own daughter. Over fucking money.*

Rage slowly begins to course through my veins. Lilly as a toddler flashes in front of my eyes. I've seen so many photos of her as a little girl, always laughing and smiling. But instead of remembering those good times, my brain alters them, inserting injuries into the mental pictures. One worse than the other. The sound of her crying reverberates in my ears, and I want to clamp my hands over them.

*Nate's mother and sister were killed. Murdered.*

My heart is beating so fast I feel dizzy.

*Brooks wanted to take care of Lilly. He was a good person who made a shitty mistake during a weak moment.*

"I blamed him for everything," Nate mumbles, interrupting my inner rampage. I remove my hands, glancing at him. His gaze is vacant, still on the monitor. "I told him at the funeral that I hated him. I refused to take his calls. He tried to visit after my arrest, but I made the staff send him away." He turns to me. "My father wanted Lilly to be part of our family. He didn't have an affair all those years." His gaze flips back and forth between my eyes.

"I..." Fuck, what do I say? "You couldn't have known. He didn't tell you any of that."

"I didn't let him. He probably tried," Nate bursts out, and I jump at the sudden shift. "He *killed* himself."

"None of this is your fault, Nate." George's voice makes both of us jerk around. Neither of us had noticed the door opening. He remains in the threshold.

"Did you know?" I grind out between clenched teeth.

"No." George steps inside and closes the door. "I came to check on you. I heard...sounds, then your father's voice." He tilts his head toward the computers. "I knew your family had someone else they worked with occasionally when I was busy, but never what cases they put him on. It wasn't my place to ask."

"Emily killed my mother. She didn't die in the accident. There *was* no accident." Nate looks like a little boy as he peers up at George, and my chest tightens.

George steps closer, pulling Nate up and wrapping his arms around him. Both men stand like this for several minutes, Nate's shoulders shaking silently. Averting my eyes, I stare at the floor.

When Nate regains some control, he moves back but instantly sways on his feet. Both of us jump into motion and latch onto him before his legs give out.

"You need to rest." George's tone is commanding yet laced with worry.

"I need to find my sister," he pleads after he lets us guide him back into his chair.

"Dude, you are no good for anyone if you collapse," I snarl. *Shit.* I didn't mean to sound like an asshole. "I—" I'm about to explain when Nate waves me off. He gets it, and a sigh of relief escapes me. I can't handle much more.

With George, Nate starts the video over, and we conclude that Lilly must've watched the beginning but got interrupted—by whoever *took* her.

She would've told someone otherwise. She would've called me.

When we get to the part of Brooks recalling Lilly's abuse—there is no other way to say it—I fly out of my seat. "I, um...I'm gonna get some coffee for, uh, you. And me." There is no fucking way I'll listen to this one more time.

SEVERAL HOURS, and even more cups of coffee later, everyone in the house was up to speed. As per usual, my father remained mute. I wanted to punch the answers out of him. There is no way he didn't know about at least part of this. The man has eyes in the back of his head, for fuck's sake. How could he have missed Lilly being used as a punching bag by her psychotic mother? *My mother's* best friend.

I wanted to rip my hair out.

Denielle had burst into tears, and Wes dragged her to their room for her to calm down. Dad disappeared with his phone plastered to his ear before I could confront him. A need to be with Nate while he looks for Lilly kept me from searching for my father.

Sitting back in my chair, with my arms folded over my chest and my ankle crossed over my knee, I watch Nate at work. The guy is good—and fast. His hands are flying over the four different keyboards on the desk. And Lilly is on the fast track to being at the same level—at least that's what Nate said to her. Lilly. Fuck, where are you, babe? Please be okay.

I squeeze my eyes shut. "You need to work faster."

"I work as fast as I can," Nate responds without pausing what he does, not taking my stab personally. He's better equipped and smarter than any authority we could've brought in, but at the same time, it's not fast enough.

There are still so many questions, but after Brooks's video, I'm convinced that everything is connected to the affair. It was the start of everything. Hell, Lilly has been saying it for weeks. I wonder if she has memories that were buried under the fake ones but were not fully erased—that, subconsciously, she knew.

Emily killed Payton and Audrey. She had an innocent woman and child murdered and then disappeared off the face of the earth. If she's involved now, what is the purpose? What does she want? My mind shifts. If she took Lilly and she had no problems harming an innocent child—two if you count Lilly *and* Audrey—I don't want to think about what she would do to someone who is an actual threat.

*I need to get my ass out of this rabbit hole, or I am going to lose it. Again.*

I focus on Lilly's brother instead. Nate switches between typing on the two wireless keyboards and the laptops simultaneously. On one, he pulls up information about Hank, aka the traitor, which looks like his personnel file based on the Altman logo. Two monitors show command line windows, and I quickly zone out of those. The last one is the security feed for the property.

I move closer to get a better look. Nate pulls up the video from Wednesday night, right before the alarm system got disabled, and we watch the outside view to all the entrances.

"I don't have any cameras inside this property," he murmurs as he fast forwards. George gave him more pain meds, and the three cups of coffee seemed to have done the trick. He no longer sounds drunk or looks like he's about to pass out. He's jittery, but I blame the caffeine for that.

We watch the feed until a dark SUV with tinted windows pulls into the drive. Nate switches the vantage point to another camera. "It's a rental."

Scrunching my eyebrows, I glance between him and the screen. "How do you know?"

He points at a sticker in the window.

Just then, we watch a tall man get out: Turner.

No. Fucking. Way!

"Motherfucker!" I feel like someone just kicked me in the junk. Fucking Turner works with (or for) Emily—if she's behind this. And so does Hank, the bitch assistant.

*It's all connected. Every-fucking-thing. How?*

"He disguised the license plate." Nate's voice is detached, and I eye him warily.

I follow his line of sight and scan the car. The plate is smeared with something reflective to the camera, and I curse under my breath.

We watch Turner leave the frame, and with no camera's inside, all we can do is wait. Nate skips ahead thirty seconds at a time until we hit the nine-minute mark. Turner reappears, carrying Lilly over his shoulder, and throws her in the backseat—literally throws her.

*No!*

I want to scream. Destroy something. He hurt Lilly. She's unconscious. What if she's seriously injured? My hands begin to tremble, and I clench and unclench my fingers.

Oblivious to the havoc raging inside of me, Nate keeps watching then zooms in. "Intelligence level of a damn amoeba."

That snaps me out of it. "Huh?"

"Hank got them the car. The moron used the company we hire for all the out-of-state board members' rentals. They have built-in GPS tracking."

I snort. "I didn't take him for that dumb." We can track her.

Nate pauses then starts typing again. "It's too easy. He'd know I'd find that trail in less than thirty minutes."

*Fuck!*


NATE IS CORRECT. One of George's men finds the SUV abandoned in a less desirable part of town—keys in the ignition. Turner switched his mode of transportation, and with where he did it, there is a zero chance of finding a reliable witness. It is a fucking miracle the car is intact. George sends it for processing, but even if we find fingerprints, we know Turner is involved, so I have no clue what the purpose is.

Later that afternoon, George comes in with a single laptop, declaring that it was the only electronic device left in Hank Todd's apartment.

"It's questionable if he had any intention of returning when you left for France or if he never had anything of value in the place," he tells Nate as he hands the computer over to me.

Something registers in Nate's brain. "I've never been to his place." He locks eyes with his head of security, then me.

George doesn't show any reaction, but I squint at him. "How

long have you known him?"

"Long."

"You think he's been spying on you this entire time?"

"At this point, I wouldn't rule it out." He blows out a breath. "Let me see how far back I can search his bank account. His business cell phone was clean, but he could easily have a personal device I don't know about. And if he uses a burner, there is no way for me to find that without a receipt."

"So, we're back to square one." I grind my teeth. The urge to throw something makes my hands twitch.

"Not yet."

AFTER WATCHING Nate for another couple of hours and learning that his curse vocabulary is as extensive as my own—if not larger—my patience is wearing thin.

He has run into several roadblocks, and Hank's laptop was useless. All it had was company documents—which Hank was supposed to have—and porn. A lot of porn. To the point where even the guy in me who wants to jump his girlfriend every possible occasion had to cringe.

I yell at Lilly's brother to work the fuck faster and to suck it up since his stab wound didn't hit any major organs. To which George tells me to go cool off for a while.

*Whatever.*

My ass is asleep anyway, and I need to move.

Entering the kitchen, the clock on the stove shows it's past seven. Den and Wes are—I do a double-take. "Are you guys playing Monopoly?" I stop next to the kitchen island, rubbing my eyes.

My friends turn, and Wes shrugs. "We found it in one of the cabinets in living room number two. It seemed like a better option than watching a movie." He tilts his head toward Denielle. "This one wouldn't sit still, and it was driving me nuts."

"Fuck you, Sheats," D murmurs while rolling the dice.

I take in the board. Each of them has a whole battery of houses and hotels and an even bigger chunk of multicolored money in front of them.

"How long have you been playing?" I raise an eyebrow.

"Dunno, man." My best friend taps the screen of his phone. "About three hours."

I bark out a laugh then sober. "Listen, uh... I'm sorry I've been holed up with Nate. I—"

"Rhys." Denielle brings my full attention to her. "We get it. We do. I'd take my mother's entire stash of benzos right now if I had access to them."

I hold the air in my lungs until my chest begins to burn, and I let fresh oxygen into my body. My gaze swivels between my two friends before I pull Den off her stool and wrap my arms around her. She instantly returns the embrace and buries her nose in the crook of my neck.

Her shoulders shake, and she hiccups. "Just bring her home."

I cup the back of her head and hold on just as tight as my gaze locks with Wes. "She'll be home soon."

I have no clue if my words hold any truth, but I have to believe that between Nate, George, and my father, they will find Lilly.

We talk a little longer. My father informed both of their parents that Den and Wes are in LA, visiting Lilly with us. Denielle had to come clean to her parents about Charlie, who immediately agreed to let her stay with us. Her dad chewed her out for jumping on a plane without telling them, but the mass orgy her long-time boyfriend was involved in quickly overshadowed her father's anger for her purchasing a first-class ticket across the country. Mr. and Mrs. Sheats already knew where Wes was since Dad had cleared it with them before he got on the jet with us.

*Dad.*

"Where is my father?"

Wes is about to take half of D's cash after she landed on one of his streets with three hotels. "Haven't seen him in a while."

WHEN THERE IS no trace of my father on the first floor or the second, I try the third. He's nowhere to be found.

*What the hell?*

I make my way back down and walk past my friends who are bickering about how much *play* money one of them has to fork over to the other. At least this way they're distracted.

I find the basement door ajar and hadn't even considered looking down there—I was on my way to the garage to check if our rental was still there.

Opening the door all the way, I take two steps when I hear my father's muffled voice. His tone is...tense. I slowly make my way down, conscious of minimizing any sound that could alert him to my eavesdropping. I'm at the bottom step when I can hear him clearly. I flatten myself against the wall and stay out of sight.

"I'm positive, yes." Pause. "I don't know, honey." He's talking to Mom? "I promised I wouldn't keep anything from you anymore, but you need to stay calm."

From the shrieking that I can even hear from my hiding spot, my mother is anything but calm. "Heather." More yelling. "Heather! Stop!" Dad uses his command voice, and it shuts Mom up. "We need him. He is our best chance of finding our daughter." *Who—?* "I don't like it either. The father in me wants to bash his head in, not even hand him over to the authorities." *Fuuuuck.* "But for one, we don't have any proof. Yet. And two, he seems to truly care about her. I'm not sure what to make of it. And we don't know how much the kids know." He listens again. "I will. I haven't been able to be around Nate much; Rhys has been with him the entire time. He seems to trust him." Pause. "I agree." Another pause. "Okay, I'll keep you posted. Please try to stay calm. We'll get her—" Mom doesn't seem to like his last statement. "As calm as you can, honey. For Natty's sake. How is she?" Dad is quiet, and I've heard enough. Tiptoeing back up the stairs, I halt outside the basement door.

Dad knows—or at least suspects that Nate is The Babysitter. FUCK, FUCK, FUUUUUCK!

I HIDE for the remainder of the evening, an easy feat since everyone already waits for me to lose my shit and doesn't question my behavior—like, at all. I could run through the mansion in the blowup unicorn costume the team forced on Owen during last year's Homecoming prank, and no one would bat an eyelash. Well, maybe George, but he still would remain his stoic, lovable self.

Lying on Lilly's bed, I've gotten well acquainted with the ceiling over the last several hours. There is a tiny cobweb I want to remove tomorrow once I find a broom or a ladder. And some type of water stain I need to mention to Nate. But besides coming up with a maintenance list for the bedroom, I have no fucking idea what to do. Telling Nate about Dad is out of the question. He needs to concentrate on finding Lilly. I'm a selfish prick for that, but there is no way I'll let him get distracted.

By one in the morning, the walls are closing in. Not that I mind being alone. Besides watching Nate work, I prefer it that way. The pity looks everyone tries *not* to give me—and fails epically—make it impossible not to go apeshit. Nate's the one with the ability to find her when the big bad Marines can't.

I keep picturing my father changing his mind and having Nate arrested or taking it into his own hands. I don't think he would do it here—with George and his men around—but my mind has played out more scenarios than Denielle has shoes. Eventually, I swing my legs off the bed.

*I need to talk to someone.*

I pat down to the second floor. The lighting in the house is muted, the hallway fixtures dimmed, and most doors closed. It's eerily quiet after the commotion all day. The only room lit is Lilly's office. When Nate first dropped that tidbit of information on me, I choked on my water. Because despite being aware of her newfound affinity for the digital world, imagining her sitting behind this desk with all the screens, command line windows, and her hair up in a messy bun with her glasses gave me an instant hard-on. So inappropriate for the current situation.

*So. Inappropriate.*

I peer into the room, and my eyes widen when I see Nate's head resting on his forearms, asleep. My jaw clenches, and I want to shake him, yelling what the fuck does he think he's doing? But the momentary surge of heat is quickly replaced by understanding. The guy got stabbed, flew across the world, and has been in this room for twelve-plus hours.

With a sigh, I ease back out and pull the door closed.

On the first floor, I come to an abrupt halt when I find George sitting in the kitchen, a laptop and a mug in front of him. He looks like shit—like, the pile someone stepped in and then tried to smear it across the sidewalk to get it off their shoes.

His eyes flick to mine, but he doesn't show a reaction otherwise.

"Have you slept at all since Wednesday?" I ask as I sink down opposite him. He sure doesn't look like it, and Lilly went missing almost thirty-six hours ago.

"Some." He leans back and folds his arms over his chest, waiting.

"Where is my father?"

"He took the spare room next to Weston and Denielle. He said to get him if we find anything new."

I nod, avoiding direct eye contact. I scan the kitchen, focusing on nothing in particular.

We sit in silence for several minutes. I keep glancing back at the man across from me several times, but he just raises an eyebrow, his scar pulling the corner of his eye up with the movement.

"My father knows about Nate," I blurt out when I can't take it anymore.

"What exactly would that be?"

*I want to pound the calmness out of him.*

"That he's The Babysitter." I drop the bomb, but George doesn't seem surprised.

"I'm aware." He places his hands flat on either side of the computer.

"You're aware?" My head rears back in disbelief.

George dips his chin once. "Your father has quite the reputation of his own, and despite my focus being on Nate, I've watched him closely from the moment they were both in the same room. He was suspecting something."

This is all kinds of fucked up. "But you didn't know what?"

"There is not much it could have been. Nate is well known, and your father can easily pull up his past. Nate's...breakdown was well documented by the press. The timeline between his discharge and Lilly's disappearance, in combination with his parents' tragedy...your father is a smart man. Especially after we informed him about the video." He says it all with such a lack of emotion, I grind my teeth.

"And you're not worried he'll call the authorities?"

"No. Tristen is fully aware that Nate is Lilly's best chance. Plus, he's not putting all his cards on the table."

My eyebrows pull together. "What do you mean?"

"There is something he's keeping from us."

My jaw is starting to cramp, listening to his monotone report.

"Is this, like, a thing you do?"

He just cocks his head.

"Both of you act like this is one of your secret spy missions." My voice rises. "This is Lilly's LIFE!" I shout the last word at him.

"That's exactly why we are doing what we're doing. Lilly is our number one priority. If your father had the facts that would help bring her back, he would share them."

AFTER MY LITTLE chat with my BFF, I go back upstairs. I want to pound on Dad's door, demanding answers, but him spilling his secrets is about as likely as getting *him* to wear the blowup unicorn costume. I watch the blinking dots on the alarm clock until my eyes start to droop around five in the morning.

*Bang. Bang. Bang.*

What the—?

"Dude! Get your ass downstairs!"

Wes's voice jolts me upright.

What time is it? One of the worst head rushes I've ever experienced makes me squeeze my eyes shut. Slowly blinking them open again, I glance to the bedside table—2:34 p.m.

*Holy fuck, I passed out for over nine hours.*

I jump up and pull the door open. My best friend is standing with his hands in his pockets in the hallway. His blond hair is a mess, and he hasn't shaved since we got here. He stares at me with a grim expression.

"What?" I know this guy better than myself half the time. "Spit it out."

His eyes harden. "Nate's got something."

I tear past him without waiting for more information.

Voices lead me to the office, and I find Nate, George, and my father behind the desk, with Den in front of it. She's chewing on her thumb, a gesture I have never seen on the always-confident Denielle Keller. Wes moves past me into the room and takes his spot next to Lilly's best friend.

All eyes are on me, and Nate breaks the silence. "I found her."

## CHAPTER ONE HUNDRED SIXTEEN

**HER**

M*Y DAUGHTER IS AS DEFIANT AS SHE WAS AT SIX YEARS OLD. A TRAIT* *that made me want to throttle her back then and, apparently, still does. If Gray hadn't interfered, she would also have a few holes in her legs.*

*Never go for the vital body parts; that's what growing up where I did taught me. I rub a palm over the outside of my right thigh, remembering that particular incident. I was fourteen and had to make up excuses for weeks about why I couldn't join Heather at the pool and skipped P.E. One more reason he got what he deserved in the end.*

*I pour another glass as Gray walks in.*

*"If my husband is not enough incentive for Lilly to sign over what should've been mine long ago, we will take other measures." I don't turn as I speak.*

*"Yours?" His question makes me clench the bowl of the wine glass.*

*"Ours," I correct myself. I really can't deal with one of his tantrums right now.*

*He lets it go and switches gears. "Have you heard from your little bitch?" Hank—the informant—Todd.*

*"No. He is still in Paris with Nate." I neglect to tell Gray that Hank should've given me an update yesterday, but my messages have been unanswered.*

*I need to speed things up.*

*Facing Gray, I tap my index finger to my lips. "How many paralytics do we have left?"*

*His eyes shoot up, and he opens and closes his mouth a few times. "You want to paralyze her?"*

*Why is he so shocked? We both have done worse over the years. Well, mostly him. That's why he's here.*

*I pull up one shoulder. "Just her legs. She might be more inclined to comply if she thinks she is in mortal danger."*

*"Is she?" He eyes me skeptically.*

*Heat surges through my body. "What do you care? It's not like you can claim the father-of-the-year award. When have you last spoken to either of them?"*

*Gray's nostrils flare. He doesn't like when I bring them up. After all, he left them behind for me.*

*"Get the drugs," I bark at him.*

*After a moment of hesitation, he turns and storms to his bedroom. Spineless idiot.*

*I face the sliding glass door and take in the ocean. It's not as blue as at home, but good enough for the few days I have to endure this place.*

## CHAPTER ONE HUNDRED SEVENTEEN

### LILLY

It doesn't take long before the door opens again. Besides a five-second pee break, I haven't abandoned my spot on the mattress. My birth mother has proven by now that she is certifiable, so there is no way I'll turn my back on her.

Emily stalks toward me with Gray close on her heels. I crane my neck to see their faces as they stop in front of my makeshift bed. Taking in my mother's expression—or lack thereof—my pulse increases to an uncomfortable level.

Her eyes are dead, and she looks at me like one examines a bug right before squashing it. My gaze flicks to the man behind her, and he appears almost conflicted, which scares me even more. What's going to ha— I see her hand move out of my peripheral vision, but before I can react, I feel the sting in my thigh.

"Ahhhh!" I jerk my head around and stare in horror at the syringe sticking out of my leg.

"Now that this is done"—she pulls the needle out and holds it up for Gray to take—"we'll chat when you're back."

*Back?*

Still thinking the word, both of them turn fuzzy and then—

. . .

Voices register in my brain, but it's hard to concentrate on them. I feel like I'm lying on a merry-go-round with my eyes closed. What. The. Hell is going on? My forehead wrinkles as I'm straining to make out the words. Slowly they're starting to make sense.

"—been out for too long. How much did you put in?"

"The same amount the doc always gives."

*Slap.*

"Did your drugs finally reduce your IQ to the single digits? She is half the size of him. We wanted her unconscious for a few hours, not an entire day. The addict in you should know that you need to adjust the dose based on body weight."

*Another slap.*

"She'll be awake soon. Why are you in such a rush? Your fucking wine and beach chair aren't running away." Gray's tone seeps annoyance.

"What's the rush?" she barks followed by a grunt.

"Stop slapping me, Em," Gray growls.

He stops her from making contact a third time.

With the dizziness slowly subsiding, I peel my eyes open, and the white ceiling comes into view. I take inventory—how many freaking times have I had to do that in the last six months? I'm on the mattress. Okay, they didn't move me. Turning my head, I notice that the door to the room is open, and Emily and Gray stand out in the hallway. They don't pay me any attention. Their guard is down, which is...odd.

I wiggle my fingers then my toes. Where are my toes? I can't feel my toes. I bolt up—or more like attempt to, because from the belly button down, there is nothing.

Instant panic sets in. "Oh, God!" I exclaim before I can stop myself. I scramble up onto my elbows, one arm buckling once before I can steady myself and stare at my lower half. They're there, physically, but there's no sensation in either of my legs. Or my butt.

My stomach revolts. I feel sick. Quickly, I turn to the side and heave, but nothing comes up.

"You're back!" Emily's cheery tone makes the hair on my nape stand. She talks like I just came home from school. This woman is insane.

Lifting my gaze from the floor, I choke, "What the hell did you do to me?"

"Nothing permanent—yet," she chirps.

*Yet?*

Gray remains at the other end of the room, watching both of us closely.

Emily picks up the plastic cup I had put down next to the mattress and holds it to my lips. I want to refuse her offer. I don't want her anywhere near me, but my body demands the water. I greedily gulp it down, though it's not nearly enough.

*I'm not going to ask for more.*

"So, my darling daughter." I focus on Emily, who's still squatting in front of me.

"Why did you send me to Heather and Tristen?" I interrupt her before she can get to the point: *her* money. The question has been on my mind since the day I found out who I'm not.

"They wanted you," she answers simply without a pause, and I read between the lines: she didn't.

"You could've just left me with Nate." The words are a mere whisper, and I speak them as they pop into my head.

"Oh, I was planning on that, but your idiotic brother, despite his intellect, also doesn't know how to administer sedatives properly." She throws a glance over her shoulder. I follow her gaze and notice Gray scowl. Why does he let her talk to him like this?

"Anyway"—her conversational tone gives me the creeps—"when he brought you to the hospital, and you told them your name, I had to be the relieved mother, didn't I? Though, Nate's messages worked in my favor; everyone thought he was a threat." She rolls her eyes. "Henry was not at all for Tristen's idea. Why Tristen came up with that plan, I have no idea, but you don't look a gift horse in the mouth, right? They wanted you, so why fight them?" She smiles, but it doesn't reach her eyes. Her eyes are dead, and I have to avert my gaze. The longer she speaks, the harder it gets to breathe. Her confession gives me the answers I wanted, yet with every new word, my heart breaks a little bit further. No child wants to hear how her mother didn't want her. Emily continues her story without seeing or acknowledging what it does to me. "Did you know Henry even wanted to run with you? The silly man." She laughs. "I convinced him that it was in everyone's best interest for you to go with Heather and let her raise your bratty behind. That mouth on you as a child..."

"You really had Brooks fooled," I mumble more to myself.

Her eyebrows shoot up. "Brooks?"

I meet her incredulous gaze as needles prick at the back of my throat. I force myself to speak over the pain. "He left Nate and me a video. I found it the day he"—I dip my head toward Gray—"broke into my house."

"Your house?" Emily cackles. "Child, did they brainwash you again?" She shakes her head. "Oh well, none of that is important now. I was astonished to hear your father had the sense to change his will beyond the trust I knew he had set up for you. He was so out of his mind in the end. It was a pleasant surprise when I got the final number a few weeks ago."

My shoulders and neck start to cramp, but I force myself to remain propped up. The emotional tidal wave drowning me in everything from unimaginable sorrow to white-hot rage about who this woman is and what she has done is draining me fast.

"Let's talk about you putting your signature on the dotted line." She switches back to the topic that matters most to her. "If you do so now, this will be your only dose, but if you keep refusing, you may end up like my dear husband."

*Henry.*

My heart skips a beat at thinking his name, and I'm briefly distracted from her tirade.

"What did you do to him?" My voice is barely audible over the pounding in my ears.

"He's alive, if that's what you want to know."

Tears well up in my eyes. She hasn't killed him.

"But that can easily be rectified," she amends with a grin that I've only ever seen on a villain of a horror movie. She is pure evil. How can this woman be my mother?

"Where is he?"

*Is he here? In this house?*

Her expression turns smug. "He is in Westbridge."

*What?*

"I had to leave him behind after your little disappearing act, but I'll gladly hand him over—if you give me what belongs to me."

"Are you delusional?" I look between her and Gray. It sinks in, too late, that my words could have been interpreted as a refusal to give her the money, because that's exactly how she takes it.

Emily's hand shoots out, pushing me back into the semi-soft surface of the mattress. Her perfectly manicured nails dig into the flesh around my trachea again, constricting air from reaching my lungs. Choking seems to be one of her go-to torture methods. I latch onto her wrist, but I'm too weak to put any force behind it.

"I can't—" I rasp, barely audible.

"Em." Gray's warning tone penetrates the rushing in my ears, but she doesn't ease up.

Instead, the pressure remains, and she leans down, hissing in my ear. "*I* was meant to be at Brooks's side. He was supposed to leave the rich whore for *me*. ME! Which was the only reason I didn't run to the next clinic when I found out about you. But he wanted you. Only you. He cast me aside like trash."

Tears run down the side of my face, and black spots begin to form in my vision. In the back of my head, I know I won't stay conscious much longer. My eyes flutter closed, and my hand loosens around her arm, dropping to my side.

"Emily. You're choking her," Gray's voice gets louder.

He has come closer.

"If I couldn't have him, he couldn't have you," my mother hisses. "But he would pay. I was going to take everything from him and finally have the life I deser—"

The pressure around my neck disappears, and I suck in as much oxygen as I can. I'm faintly aware of shuffling, raised voices, and then a door slamming shut, but my entire focus is on breathing. I have no idea how long it takes before I open my eyes and come face to face with the man who has given me the creeps since the first time I saw him at Magnolia's.

"Princess, I told you to watch your mouth if you want to come out of here alive," he chastises me as his gaze moves down my legs then up to my face. "Or walking."

He doesn't mean it as a threat. It's a simple fact. He said he'd known my mother her entire life. She would paralyze her own child without a second thought.

"She can have the money," I croak, lifting a hand to wipe my stinging eyes.

I don't care about that. I only had it for, what, a week? I never planned on being rich. I was going to go to college on a partial scholarship and get a job. All I want is to go home to Rhys and my family. Fresh tears start to fall. *Rhys.*

Gray nods, no sympathy for my current state visible on his features. "Good. I'm gonna leave the contract here." He lifts it and glances down, stiffening. His eyes narrow, and he flips the pages. His nostrils flare, but he smoothes his features. Placing everything within my reach, he locks eyes with me once more. "You have quite the amount in your name." He pushes himself up, and with one last glance down at me, he leaves.

I REMAIN on my back for a long time after Gray leaves. Emily's words replay in my head over and over. It never crossed her mind that her words could hurt me—her daughter. It's like she has no feelings.

Eventually, I force myself to stop letting her verbal slap to the face break me further. I have a family. I have a mother, a father, and a sister. I have Rhys. And I have Nate. This woman means nothing to me. I repeat those words over and over in my head until Emily's slowly begin to lose their meaning.

Gathering the little strength I have left, I attempt to maneuver myself into a sitting position against the wall. With still no feeling in my legs or butt, this simple task is the equivalent of a two-hour sparring match with Spence. I'm drenched in sweat. I topple over twice due to the lack of sensation in my lower half, and frustration makes me slam my palm into the mattress until my hand hurts.

I. *Smack.* Refuse. *Smack.* To. *Smack.* Give. *Smack.* Up. *Smack. Smack. Smack.*

"Arrrrrrg!" With one last push, I am finally upright.

I eye the cup in front of the mattress. Out of my reach. *Shit.* I need water, but it's empty anyway. And there is no way for me to refill it myself. Fuck!

I glance at my legs and poke a thigh with my finger. Nothing. A pit opens in my stomach, and it feels like a hummingbird took residence in my chest—and not in a good way. What if Emily was wrong and it is permanent? She said Gray gave me too much. I poke the other leg. There has to be a way to make the numbness go away. I reach behind one knee and pull the leg up, but as soon as I let go, it flops to the mattress. I keep pushing into the muscles, no idea if it'll do anything, but I have to try something. Stay busy.

I'm on it for who knows how long when the door suddenly flies open, and I whip my head in the direction of the noise.

"What did you do?" Emily is standing in the door, legs apart, her arms hanging at her side. Her tone is so low and void of emotion that the alarm bells in my head immediately go off.

"W-what do you mean?" My heart starts pounding as my mother stalks toward me. I notice that she is holding something in her hand. Gray's knife. It's not hard to recognize, given the fact it's a KA-BAR. Tristen has several of those, and I've even seen some in George's arsenal.

"Where is Gray?" I press my hands into the mattress and my back further against the wall.

"*Gray* is sleeping off whatever he shot up his veins this time. Now, tell me, what did you do?" she snarls.

"I have no clue what you're talking about." Fear settles in my bones. Has she completely lost her mind?

"I can't reach Elise." Where I sound like a hysterical mouse, her tone is calm and monotone.

"Who the hell is Elise?" I press sideways as she takes a step closer, but it only makes me fall over again.

*Fucking damn it!*

"Elise was supposed to watch Henry while I took care of you."

I remain mute, focusing on pushing myself away from her as she continues her prowl.

"She didn't give me the usual update, and when I called, her phone went to voicemail. The doctor isn't supposed to be back until tomorrow, so I'm asking you again...what did you do?"

"I've been here the entire time, you crazy bitch. What do you think I did? Pulled out my magic phone and called the police in Westbridge, sending them to an unknown location where you're hiding my not-father?" Apparently, her drugs have also paralyzed my rational thinking because the words are out before I can stop them.

Of course, my outburst pushes her over the edge. Emily loses it and attacks.

"WHO DID YOU CALL A BITCH?!" I see the knife go in, but I don't feel a thing.

Eyes wide, I stare at the hilt sticking out of my thigh.

Oh. God. Oh, no. No, no, no. I'm going to be sick, and I manage to turn sideways before it comes up. She pulls out the blade, and my pant leg begins to turn dark red. Emily holds the handle in one hand and pokes her index finger with the bloody tip of the blade.

"Did you know that my father, your grandfather, stabbed me in the exact same spot once?" She peers down at my leg with an unreadable expression. "Gray and I were out with Ronnie, Ronnie wouldn't drive me home when he was supposed to, and Daddy lost his temper. He never liked when he didn't get his dinner on time." She goes on as if I'm not bleeding in front of her. "When I blamed Ronnie for what happened the next day, he slapped me then laughed and made Gray take me to the hospital to get stitched up." Her eyes are vacant, lost in her memory. "But that wasn't the only time I got acquainted with his knife. See."

My breathing is labored. If from the shock of what just happened, from the pain I cannot feel, or from the entire situation...I'm not sure. It doesn't matter anyway. All I can do is stare at the woman who gave birth to me as she keeps going on.

Emily holds out her free arm, turning it so I can see the inside between her biceps and triceps. A jagged scar, about three inches, is clearly visible. "Ronnie also didn't like when he didn't get what he wanted."

*Who the hell is Ronnie?*

"Maybe we should try your arm next—the one you don't need to write, that is." Emily is now on all fours on the mattress next to me.

"You can have the money," I croak the words out before she can inflict more damage.

She doesn't hear me; she is too far gone. She lifts the blade and pokes the tip against the skin of my upper arm. I fling out my other one to deflect her weapon, but it's no good. Between the drugs, the exertion from sitting up, and now the blood loss, I have the strength of a malnourished stray kitten. All I accomplish is cutting my palm on the blade.

"Ahhh!" I can't stop the scream, nor do I want to.

Suddenly, there is a loud bang somewhere outside the room followed by shouts and footfalls echoing through the house. Emily doesn't seem to notice any of it. She pokes the end of the knife just underneath my ribcage, twisting it until it breaks skin.

A whimper escapes me, and tears run down my face.

*I don't want to die.*

"STEP AWAY FROM HER, EMILY!" The command penetrates the room, and both of our heads snap to the door.

---

# CHAPTER ONE HUNDRED EIGHTEEN

---

### LILLY

THE BLOOD LOSS IS MAKING ME HALLUCINATE. BLINKING SEVERAL times, I wait for the two blurry shapes to disappear, but all they do is slowly enter the room and spread out, circling us from both sides.

Emily shifts to straddle me, moving the knife at lightning speed to my neck. "Tristen, what a surprise," she chirps as if she ran into her long-lost friend in the grocery store. Then, her gaze swivels to the other man. "And George Weiler. I did not expect you two to ever join forces." She cocks her head.

"And why is that?" George mimics her expression, unfazed.

"Well, would you expect Lilly's father"—she chuckles, smiling sweetly at Tristen—"excuse me, adopted father, to work with the man who is his daughter's kidnapper's accomplice?"

*No, no, no.*

Unable to move in more ways than just being paralyzed, my gaze flicks back and forth between the men. Tristen and George are going in and out of focus, and I'm blaming my current physical state for that. What I do see, though, is that neither of them shows an emotional response to the bomb Emily dropped. Does Tristen know? My mother adjusts her position on top of me, pushing the knife deeper into my flesh.

"Ahhhh," a high-pitched gurgle comes out of my mouth.

The pain receptors in my upper half work perfectly because the intrusion of the metal in my skin sends a searing sensation through my body. My heart rate has exceeded any acceptable rhythm and has moved to an unhealthy, call-an-ambulance-immediately pace.

*It fucking hurts.*

This is the first time George and Tristen acknowledge me. They scan me from head to toe and settle on my leg. It's mostly covered by Emily sitting on it, but they see it. The blood must've seeped through my pants and into the mattress. Their eyes narrow, and both lift their arms simultaneously. Until now, I hadn't noticed their guns. George's Glock 19 and Tristen's Sig P365XL are both trained at my mother.

"Get off my daughter," Tristen commands in an eerily calm voice. He locks eyes with me, and just then, everything blurs again. Ugh. Squinting, I try to focus on the scene in front of me, but it's no use.

"Not until she signs the papers." Emily's response is just as calm. She reaches back with her free hand and squeezes my injured leg. I can feel her torture. My stomach flips; the sedatives are wearing off. Unfortunately, my relief is short-lived. That also means I can feel the agonizing assault of my wound. Make it stop.

A whimper escapes me, and I clench my jaw not to scream out loud and distract George and Tristen from their target: my mother.

George jerks a step forward at my pained sound, but Emily expected one of them to react, and she digs in deeper. Every cell in my body is suddenly on fire, and I can't stop myself. A gut-wrenching cry erupts in my throat.

"Ahhhhhhh!"

At that moment, all hell breaks loose.

"CALLAAA!" Three sets of eyes jerk toward the door as Rhys bursts into the room.

"Rhy—" I can't finish his name before my voice gives out.

He tries to get to me, but George moves lightning-fast, dropping his gun and wrapping his arms around him, pinning him in place.

Rhys struggles against the hold, George having a hard time keeping control over him. Rhys is losing it. "LET ME GO, YOU COCKSUCKER! I'M GOING TO KILL YOU, YOU CRAZY

BITCH." He's screaming at George and Emily at the same time, his eyes blazing, never leaving mine.

I want to soothe his pain.

I don't like seeing him like this.

*Please don't let him get hurt.*

*What is he doing here?*

My thoughts are all over the place; I can't concentrate. This is all too much.

Tristen flicks his gaze to his son before focusing again on his target. "Emily, if you don't let go of my daughter immediately, you will not walk out of here."

But instead of complying, she starts laughing hysterically. "You are such a joke, Tristen. What are you going to do? If you so much as twitch that finger, I will slice her open so George's face decoration looks like a beauty mark. Tell *my daughter* to sign over the money, and you can have her. Hell, you can have all of them. I'll give you Gray on top of it. He's the one who killed Payton anyway. I had nothing to do with that."

"No, you cunt, you only physically abused your child, gave her up, and now kidnapped her. For what? Money that the man who didn't want *you* left to *her*?"

"RHYS!" Tristen barks at his son's outburst.

"FUCK THIS SHIT. SHOOT HER! You're faster than this crazy bitch!" Rhys rears his head back to slam it into George's face. Rhys is trained, but George has years on him, and he turns his head at the last second. All I can do is watch, tears streaming down my face.

*Please don't hurt him or let him get hurt.*

"That's enough!" George roars in Rhys's ear and somehow gets through. Rhys stops his struggle—or that's what he makes everyone believe. As soon as George relaxes his arms, Rhys lets himself drop and goes for the abandoned Glock.

"Noooooo!" The scream bursts out of me, and I try to buck Emily off my body, but she is already gone.

Both men follow Rhys's abrupt movement, not realizing that Emily anticipated the action and dived for it a fraction of a second faster. My mother and Rhys both grasp for the gun at the same time.

I can't see who reaches it first. They're in a tangle of arms and legs when a gunshot makes everyone freeze. George and Tristen are staring with wide eyes at the two slumped forms on the ground, and I register something splash across my face.

*Oh, please, no!*

Time is frozen. I can't breathe. Someone do something! I want to crawl over, but as soon as I shift, the pain in my leg immobilizes me. I need to get to him. *No, no, no.* I wipe my eyes. But the tears are falling faster than my weak hands can remove them. Then, everything springs back into action, and both men dive toward Rhys, who is buried underneath Emily. Pulling my fingers back, I see the crimson color on them. My face is not only wet with tears.

"RHYS!" Tristen roars.

The world fades away, my eyes glued to my fingers. Red. Blood. I can't lose him. The thought repeats itself over and over in my head. I can't lose him. I don't pay attention to anything that's happening around me. I can't lose him.

A shadow appears above me, and my focus changes.

Gray.

My surroundings turn silent. Everything besides Francis Garrison (Gray) Turner is on pause. He peers down at me, his eyes briefly flicking to the side before returning to me. He squats down, and for the first time, I let my head turn toward the center of the room. I still can't make out what's going on. My eyes are burning. Tristen kneels on the floor, his back blocking most of my view. All I see are Rhys's legs and part of my mother sprawled on the ground. My face is grabbed by the chin, a rough hand forcing me to look back up at the man who broke into my house and kidnapped me. Something in his expression changes, but I don't understand what.

He leans down further until he is close to my ear. "No one betrays me. Our paths will cross again, but until they do...take care of her."

He shoves something into the pocket of my pants before he stands back up and disappears.

*Her?*

It's as if someone has pushed play again, and sounds filter into my brain. Rhys! I attempt to turn myself over once more, but the agony shooting through my leg is unbearable, and I whimper. The paralytics must be completely gone because the pain is worse than the blade to my neck, worse than the shoulder injury after my car accident, or the burns from the shower attack.

I manage another gurgled cry before everything goes black.

*Too tight* is my first thought after I come to. Someone is holding onto me—no, not holding on. Focus. I'm nestled in someone's lap, arms wrapped around me. Whoever is cradling me is rocking back and forth. Saliva pools in my mouth, and I swallow down the nausea. My body doesn't like the motion. I want to tell whomever it is to stop when something wet hits my face from above.

More noise registers. Commotion to the side of me. Someone barking orders. Feet shuffling. More commands. A hand comes to my face, and I lean into it—a touch as familiar as my own.

"Open your eyes for me, Calla," a voice begs between sobs. I know that voice. *I love that voice.*

With an excruciating amount of strength, I peel my eyelids back.

Green eyes dulled by tears find mine. "There's my girl," he breathes.

My stomach flips. "Rhys." I can't muster more than a whisper, and my lids want to close again, but I force them to remain open.

"Hey, babe." His thumb brushes the moisture under my own eyes away.

"You're here."

He chuckles. "Where else would I be?"

I attempt to turn toward the noise, but he cages me in. "Don't."

My forehead scrunches.

"Let me see," I whisper, my pulse increasing with anxiety. What is he hiding?

Rhys slashes his mouth, his gaze flicking to something beyond my peripheral vision.

"She can handle it," George says from somewhere close by.

Rhys's grip loosens, and he helps me shift to a half-sitting position leaning against his chest. I can see the entire room—my prison cell.

There, in the center, is a body in a pool of blood. Emily's body.

My mother. I feel nothing. I don't remember her being my mother, and after everything I've learned the last few days, I don't want to remember. I no longer fault Tristen for what he did. I let my gaze linger a moment longer, scanning the room. Tristen is talking to a man by the door, and George is next to us, but his focus is also toward the other men.

I turn back to Rhys. "You shot her?"

Rhys shakes his head. "No. She got to the gun first."

My mouth parts.

"She was on top of me, the gun against my side, but she didn't get the safety off fast enough. Turner killed her."

*Wha—?*

## CHAPTER ONE HUNDRED NINETEEN

### RHYS

*THREE MONTHS LATER*

THE DAY HAS COME. The day everyone has been working toward since I carried Lilly out of that house. The sun is slowly coming up, and the outlines of the buildings around the original Altman Hotel in Los Angeles are morphing into actual structures—we never closed the blinds last night.

I yawn and peer down at Lilly's naked body sprawled over my chest. Her hair is fanned around her face and down her back. Scanning every inch visible above the massive down comforter, I swipe away a strand that fell over her eyes. I haven't been able to get any shuteye in days. The last two, I've been solely surviving on the constant stream of caffeine Wes has provided for me.

Every time I close my eyes, I relive that day. See the blood. Hear her screams. And today, nine months after the fateful homework assignment, everything comes to a close.

Wes and Denielle, together with my parents and Natty, came a few days ago. Lilly and I never left Los Angeles.

We finished the school year on the West Coast. Lilly refused to set foot into Westbridge High again, and I wouldn't leave her side.

There had been yelling, tears on Lilly's and Mom's sides, scowling from Dad, but in the end, we're eighteen. Mom and Dad *agreed* to let us stay under the condition we finish our coursework online—not that they could've forced us back east anyway. But I preferred the amicable resolution over another family shit show.

No fucking clue how Mom pulled everything off with the school, but she did. After what happened to Lilly in the locker room, they probably would've said yes if we had asked for our diplomas without finishing the year.

Lilly and I moved into the Hamlin mansion permanently, and George stayed at the house with us because Turner, aka Gray, being on the loose had everyone still on edge. Mom, Dad, and Natty flew in every two weeks for a *check-in*—the perks of suddenly having a private jet at our disposal.

Every time my mind wanders to those few days after Denielle's phone call, it's still a miracle to me how Nate found Lilly. Despite his injury, he worked himself into the ground. The only time he slept was that night in the office, and he had literally passed out from exhaustion.

Because of Nate, I can hold Lilly in my arms today, which is one of the reasons my preconceived psycho-kidnapper opinion changed. He's still a criminal, but that's just one of his many sides—most of them are actually pretty tolerable. He also handed me the keys to the R8 a few weeks ago. What idiot would say no to that?

While I was passed out in Lilly's bedroom that night—or day—Nate had dissected Hank's personal life down to the color of his dishtowels. When the bank accounts showed nothing out of the ordinary, Nate started digging. Deep.

Hank's credit history listed several joint and active cards linked to his mother. The same Mrs. Todd who had been in an assisted living home for over a decade and had not used a debit or credit card for just as long. Nate shifted his focus to her, and after finding several domestic accounts through various banks all over the country, he tracked down an offshore account with a *considerable*, multi-figure balance. Money Hank did not earn with his job for the

Altman Hotels, nor his mother, who was the primary account holder.

Whoever helped set all this up knew their shit, and if it were anyone but Nate, we probably would've never found Lilly in time.

He followed the deposits to Mrs. Todd's offshore account back to one containing a sum that was suspiciously close to one Brooks had paid Emily over the years. Said account was with a bank in South America, not too far from where Nate ran into a roadblock when tracing his father's transfers. He had lost the trail when the entire amount was withdrawn on the receiving end, and the account was closed.

The amount was obviously not exactly the same anymore, but close enough. The living expenses in that region were not very high, and one could afford a decent lifestyle from the interest alone and accumulate more.

Don't ask me how he did all this. I probably don't want to—or shouldn't—know.

This also solidified our suspicion that Hank worked for Emily Sumner.

Nate then convinced one of the tellers at the financial institution to identify the account's owner who was supplying Hank with the funds. The helpful employee received a check that will support her family for years to come and immediately picked Lilly's biological mother out of the stack of pictures Nate emailed to her.

To not just provide her one option, he attached pictures of my parents, the Kellers, and Mr. and Mrs. Sheats—none of whom the lady obviously recognized.

And with that, we had the proof. Turner kidnapped Lilly. Hank provided Turner with the vehicle for the abduction. Hank received money from Emily Sumner, Lilly's mother. Emily and Turner were linked.

Mrs. Todd's credit history also listed a brand-new lease for a bungalow on the Pacific Ocean. With Hank's passport still not back on U.S. soil—again, not asking so I don't have to plead the fifth if it ever comes down to it—George and Dad agreed that the house was most likely where Turner took Lilly.

All of this developed while I was sleeping on the third floor. Initially, I was pissed that no one woke me up, but it was probably better in the end. I wouldn't have been much help with my impatient nature. I can admit that now.

While the two were talking strategy, Nate pulled up the CCTV around the location. Between Turner breaking into the Hamlin estate and how long it would've taken him to get to the beach house, taking into account that he switched cars at least once, Nate narrowed down a time window. He recruited Denielle and Wes to watch the feeds with him, and Denielle was the one who spotted another dark SUV on the camera closest to the beach property.

The license plate to this one was not covered, and with some more *information seeking*, Nate soon had a close-up security camera picture of Francis Turner renting the car, though the name on the agreement was Ronald Turner, Francis's brother who had not been seen in—have a guess—almost twelve years.

MY RECOLLECTION GETS INTERRUPTED as Lilly begins to stir, and I look down. Her eyes are moving rapidly under her lids. The nightmares are another outcome of everything she went through. She admitted that it's always the same but won't elaborate on the details. I suspect it has something to do with Emily, but what? No clue. I pull her close and wrap both arms around her body. She stills instantly, which makes warmth spread through me.

I watch her steady breathing for several minutes, counting each inhale and exhale. Something I've come to do after preventing a nightmare from fully taking hold. It calms me enough to usually go back to sleep myself—not today, though. My thoughts carry me back to that day.

AFTER THEY FINALLY WOKE ME UP, George had been on the phone with his team while Dad and Nate went over more details of the property. The ins and outs, closest neighbor, and whatnot. Watching my father in action was new to me. He had talked about his job before, but seeing him focus on a mission was as impressive as it was intimidating.

"When are we leaving?" I asked as George got off the phone.

Both men looked at me expressionless yet as if I had asked to go skydiving without a parachute.

"You are going home. I've already contacted Joel. He will take the three of you back to Virginia."

I stared at my father incredulously. Was he fucking serious? He couldn't be. He was.

*FUCK!*

Anger started to build deep in my core and spread throughout my body. "I'm not getting on the damn plane!"

"Yes. You are," he stated as he checked the chamber of his P365XL.

"The fuck?" I ripped the gun out of his hand.

In hindsight, that was an irresponsible and completely dumbass thing to do. I mean, it was a loaded fucking gun. But the chance of keeping my temper in check was about as likely as jumping out of the previously mentioned airplane without the parachute and surviving. No chance at all.

If they seriously believed I would get on that damn jet while Lilly was held hostage by her psycho bio-mom, they were more delusional than my ex thinking I'd come back to her.

Dad stared at me with a murderous glare, not just for ignoring every gun safety rule, but for interfering with his mission. And bringing Lilly home had become his mission.

"I'm not having you anywhere near the place when we go in. We have no idea what to expect. We don't know if it's just the two of them or if there are more. Henry is still missing, for Christ's sake," he barked at me.

*Henry. I completely forgot about him.*

"You think he is involved?" I narrowed my eyes at Dad.

"No." My father's response came so quick and convinced that I paused.

We stared at each other, and then it clicked. "She did something to Henry."

This time, he didn't answer, which was everything I needed to not hear. George had told Dad about Turner's visit to the warehouse district and what he most likely procured there.

Dad and George ended up letting me stay with Nate, but Denielle and Wes were put into a car to the airport with George's guys. They were going home—Den kicking and screaming. Even Wes couldn't calm her and, eventually, had to step back. George's men caged her in and deposited her in the SUV by her hands and feet. It was not a pretty sight, and I don't think she has forgiven George since.

Nate was to watch me which, let's face it, was fucking hilarious —I didn't point that out, though. What was the guy gonna do? He could barely keep his eyes open, let alone stand straight between his exhaustion and his stab wound. He'd been avoiding the pain killers after he fell asleep because he didn't want his brain to turn all fuzzballs again. But once Dad and George were ready to move out, he finally agreed to self-medicate.

It only took five minutes for Nate's eyes to droop, and I was off. The keys to Lilly's G-Wagon hung with the rest of the cars in the entrance to the massive garage. I put the address I had memorized from earlier into my phone and was no more than maybe ten minutes behind the rescue operation.

Looking back, following them was, by far, the most reckless shit I've ever pulled. I'm fully aware that I would've died that day if it weren't for Francis Turner.

Turner had been Emily's lapdog since they were kids. But we didn't know that until my mother arrived in Los Angeles.

The moment I walked into the house, all I had to do was follow the screaming—Lilly's screams. My pulse was pounding in my ears as I crept along the hallway toward the noise. A lot of what came next was a blur.

Should I remember it? Process what I saw? What happened with Emily and the gun? Maybe. Okay, probably. But I have no desire to hash that shit out with the therapist Dad has had me see once a week since. Lilly is alive. I'm alive. The bitch is dead. Moving on—or pretending to. All I want is to get through today, and I know we'll move past it eventually. Dr. *How-Do-You-Feel-About-This*  is not going to be part of that progress.

I do think about everything that followed Lilly coming back to consciousness, though, and it sends me into a fucking tailspin every single time.

*Maybe I should open up to Doctor McShrink?*

George had stayed back at the house of horrors with his men, securing the scene and dealing with the authorities.

*I bet that was an interesting conversation.*

Dad tried to take Lilly from me so she could get medical attention, but as soon as he reached for her, every muscle in my body locked. I braced my legs, my arms tightened around her, and my hands curled into fists, clutching her clothes. Even if I had wanted to hand her over, I couldn't. The thought of losing contact with her in any way had my chest constricting, and I felt like someone was choking me.

We made it to the G-Wagon, but the events are distorted. Skipping. It's like my brain has blurred it all out of focus.

*Self-preservation?*

Lilly was in the hospital for three days. Dad took her to a clinic that catered to the privacy of its patients. They whisked us into a room upon arrival. It was not a traditional hospital room. It was a full-on hotel suite with a queen bed, sitting area, and a spa-like bathroom.

Lilly was examined, cleaned, and her leg got stitched up. They ran a gazillion blood tests, gave her multiple transfusions, and monitored her for side effects. By some miracle, the psycho bitch didn't hit any major blood vessels.

A lot happened on the outside during those three days, but I didn't give two shits. My focus was on Lilly and making sure she was okay. I ignored my phone—let it die—and the only people I spoke to were the ones that came to us: Nate, George, Dad, and the medical staff.

Lilly and I didn't talk much either. I mostly held her, needing the constant contact. No one blinked an eye when they discovered me under the covers with her. The first time she was able to go to the bathroom by herself—with the help of crutches—my hands started trembling, and my entire body was covered in a sheen of sweat. After that, I made it a habit to follow her and wait outside the door.

The attending physician's main concern was monitoring her bloodwork. The amount and combination of sedatives and paralytic drugs her body had to process caused her to lose sensation in her legs twice more in the first day and a half. When that happened, my pulse would pound in my ears, and my entire body shook like I was the one experiencing the possibility of not being able to feel my extremities again. I would yell at whomever was in the room, go completely ballistic, followed by George or Dad having to restrain my ass before I lost it on the poor nurse checking Lilly out.

Nate's neurologist also paid us a visit. Having money apparently makes the medical professionals come to you, not the other way around, but I didn't complain. He ordered a CT scan as well as an MRI followed by several hours of more exams. The helplessness as we waited for the results was as excruciating as watching the nurse check on Lilly's numb legs and not knowing if the sensation would come back this time. When the neurologist informed us that Lilly showed no signs of a tumor or brain injury, everyone in the room, including the two big bad Marines, had tears in their eyes.

No wonder my brain turned the events into a distorted movie. Who the fuck would want to remember all that in vivid detail?

One particular conversation, though, keeps replaying in Technicolor. And every single time, my chest feels heavy, as if someone has put a hundred-pound weight on it. I was sitting next to Lilly on her extra-wide bed, Nate in a chair to her left, Dad in one to her right. George had just returned and stood at the foot of the bed. It was day two, and Dad had let us know that Mom and Natty would be arriving in LA the next evening. Natty got excused from school for two weeks and would complete her work online—no issue there. She'd probably finish the entire school year in those two weeks if she had all the materials.

Arms folded across his chest, George eyed everyone in the room one at a time.

"G, what has your cargo panties in such a twist?" Nate smirked, hands interlaced behind his neck and legs propped on the bedframe.

Lilly's brother actually has a decent sense of humor once you talk to him about more than stalking reporters and rescuing his sister from her birth mother. Another trait that made me like him.

Lilly had a good day, no more losing the feeling in her legs, and we were all in a decent mood.

All eyes were on my BFF, and I was about to add an inappropriate comment when he blurted out, "Lakatos agreed to try and reverse Lilly's memory loss—as long as it's at a location of his choosing. I've been negotiating with him over the last few days."

*Wha—? Dad said it was impossible.*

Nate leaned forward in his chair, dropping his feet to the ground with a thud, and even Dad's entire posture stiffened. Did he know there was a possibility and lied to me back in his office, or did Lakatos tell his clients it was a one-way street? George's meeting with Hector Lakatos was a week ago, but no one had mentioned it since. We all had other things on our minds, which is why this felt like a punch to the gut. How could I have forgotten?

"That's okay." Lilly's soft voice came from the side, and every head turned to her.

I arched an eyebrow, and she whispered, "I don't want to remember."

"Are you certain? He said he has never done it, but he would try." George's question was filled with concern, which was mirrored in Nate's eyes when I let my gaze wander to him.

"I am."

I wanted to demand why, but her tone was stern, and it was clear that she wouldn't discuss it further. Not at the time.

My father pulled me aside later that day and assured me that Lakatos always said it was impossible—it was even part of his contract—and that he didn't lie to me. He knew my mind had gone there.

We've talked about it several more times over the last few months, especially after my parents' confessions a few days later, but Lilly has remained adamant. She says the only thing she regrets about her choice is that she may miss a memory of Brooks, but with everything in his video message, Emily herself, and what my parents revealed to her, Dad did the right thing.

Her forgiveness had my father bawl like a baby the day he and Mom told us the rest of the story—the day we learned more unnerving facts about Emily.

# CHAPTER ONE HUNDRED TWENTY

### RHYS

THE WEEKEND AFTER LILLY WAS DISCHARGED, WE WERE IN sitting room number three at the Hamlin estate. Number three was the one with direct access to the backyard. Wes and I had numbered all the duplicate rooms after missing each other twice when we were going stir-crazy waiting for Nate to find his sister, and '*I'll meet you in the living room*' was a one-in-four chance.

Natty, Lilly and I, together with Nate, had been playing board games all afternoon. It was something we used to do a lot before everything went down the shitter three years ago, and having Nate join us was one of the most bizarre experiences of my life—not counting the whole kidnapping and almost-dying thing, of course.

Nate had left a few minutes earlier. He was all vague and secretive about his whereabouts and whispered something in Lilly's ear that made her eyes bulge and hug him tight.

He placed a kiss on the top of her head. "I'll be fine."

Lilly didn't look convinced, though. "Call me after."

He nodded and walked toward the garage. She could read the guy as well as she read me.

"What was that about?" Mom, who sat in one of the armchairs, scrunched her eyebrows.

"He is going to end it with Margot." Lilly sounded...sad.

*Oh.*

"Why?" I couldn't stop myself from asking. Not that he had spent any time with his fiancée, nor had he answered her calls in days. Hell, he barely left the house. He even slept here instead of his own mansion the size of a medium-sized apartment complex.

"It's not my place to tell." She smiled softly at me. Her loyalty to her brother was admirable. But that was Lilly. When she loved someone, she loved fiercely and never betrayed the person's trust.

Mom asked Natty to help George make dinner—the man could actually cook like a Michelin Chef—and then turned to me. "Can you two meet Dad and me on the back patio?"

*Uh.* A hollow sensation settled in my stomach. Sending Natty to George and asking us to come outside...not good.

Lilly was right behind my parents, but I followed at a slower pace. Much slower. Maybe if I took my time, they would forget whatever they wanted to say. Unlikely, but worth a try. Subconsciously, I already knew that I wasn't going to like what I was about to hear.

"RHYS!" my father's bark assaulted my ears.

*Fuck!* "Coming."

I sat down in one of the cushioned wrought iron patio chairs surrounding the matching eight-person table—Lilly and me on one side, Mom and Dad across from us. The whole scene felt like we were in one of Mom's court proceedings.

When the prolonged silence turned beyond uncomfortable, I reached over to grab Lilly's hand. She squeezed it in return, just as my mother announced, "We know who Nate is."

Mom's words were like a bucket of ice in the face followed by several precisely executed uppercuts. I mean, we sorta knew, or at least suspected, but no one had said a word since I overheard Dad's phone call in the basement. Lilly's fingers turned to a vise around mine, and I, unsuccessfully, stifled a grunt as two of my fingers cracked under the pressure. "Argh."

"He's going to turn himself in," Lilly rushed out, not letting go of my hand.

*She's going to break my damn fingers.*

"We know," Dad inserted himself.

My eyes widened, the pain in my hand forgotten.

*Holy fuck? How did that happen?*

Mom took one deep breath before explaining. "Dad found out while you were still...missing." She looked at Lilly with a pained expression. None of us talked about those days unless we had to. I wasn't the only one in avoidance land.

"The moment Dad told me, I dialed Agent Camden on the house phone," she declared. "I was furious with your father. How could he not turn him over immediately?" She took a long breath and stared at her folded hands on the table. "But then he convinced me to hold off."

*Convinced her?*

Lilly's grip loosened—thank you, Jesus—and I peered over at her. She was completely unmoving, not averting her eyes from my mother.

"If it hadn't been for Natty, I would've been on the next flight out. Dad kept me up to date." Her voice cracked, the guilt from not being with Lilly when she was in the hospital written all over her face.

My heart was jackhammering as I waited for her to continue.

"I honestly had no idea what to expect. For one, we were talking about Nathan Altman. I looked into his case as soon as Dad gave me his name. He almost killed a man in college." Her voice got louder, and Dad placed a hand on her thigh.

"He paid for—" Lilly came to Nate's defense, but Mom lifted her hand to stop her. She kept shifting between lawyer- and mom-mode, and I was getting whiplash.

"He has, but that's not my point. He has a media focus that makes the one you previously faced look like an interview with the high school's newspaper. When your relation to him comes out, you'll be in the same spotlight as Nate. Not to mention what he'll be charged for."

*The kidnappings.*

I swallowed several times against the sudden overproduction of saliva. Another topic everyone had been avoiding—until now. Lilly's bottom lip began to tremble, and I scooted my chair closer to wrap my arm around her shoulder.

"He'll come forward and go to jail," Lilly whispered as the first tear ran down her cheek. We'd known for weeks that this was the inevitable outcome, yet seeing Lilly like this broke my heart.

"He told us."

My eyes flew to my father, who had Colonel McGuire on full display. I wondered if he needed this *side of his personality, his life,* to deal with the situation.

"Nate, Mom, and I sat down last night. Over the last week, I've gotten to know him in a way that I will never be able to repay him. Without him, Emily would've killed Lilly. I'm not under the delusion that she would've just sent her home after she got what she wanted." He looked at his adopted daughter. "Emily was...*ill*."

"Ill?" My forehead scrunched. What the hell did that mean?

"I met Emily in kindergarten. Back then, her name was Emily Kaczmarek. Did you know that?" Mom's tone was low, and Lilly and I shook our heads at the question. Nate dug further into Emily's past, but with everything else, he hadn't had a chance to tell us what he found. It seemed my mother was going to fill in some of those blanks.

"We attended the same schools all our lives since Lake Robertson only had one for each grade level." Mom grew up in a relatively small town in the Midwest, but when she left for college, our grandparents moved as well, so we've never actually seen where she grew up.

She looked at a spot behind us as she continued. "We were close. Emily had been my best friend from the day we were put at the same table in school, but there were things I never knew about her. I've asked myself many times over the last few weeks if I was too self-absorbed with my own life or if I didn't want to see it." Mom wiped under her nose. "She would come to school with bruises. One time, in middle school, she didn't show up for a week. When I asked her about it later, she gave vague answers that made no sense. She never let me come to her house. Maybe if I had...if I had just shown up, things would have been different. I could've helped her," Mom's voice turned desperate.

"Honey." Dad forced her to focus on him. "We've talked about that. There was nothing you could've done."

She nodded and then leveled us with a serious expression.

"Emily was always around two brothers when she wasn't with me. Their names were R.J. and Gray."

*R.J. Ronnie. Turner's brother. Holy shit.*

Lilly sucked in a breath, and I could feel her beginning to tremble. I tightened my hold around her shoulder, wanting to reassure her that she was safe and ignore my own inner turmoil at the same time. It was easier to manage when I focused on Lilly rather than what my parents were revealing.

"I didn't put it together until Dad told me what Emily called Turner in front of you." She looked at Lilly. "R.J. was a few years older. He gave me the creeps. As the years passed, the rumors around him started. He was the local dealer, and his little brother functioned as his runner. I confronted Emily once, but she lost it on me. Yelled at me to mind my own business and that my rich ass had no idea what I was talking about." The corners of Mom's mouth turned down.

*Rich?* My grandparents were maybe upper-middle class—at most. Anger against Emily flared in my chest, even though all this happened years before I was even born.

"Her behavior became erratic. She would have mood swings, be her normal sweet self and then start yelling for no reason. At the end of our junior year in high school, Emily disappeared. She would call every few weeks but refused to tell me where she was—said she needed a change of scenery. I was too busy with myself to question her further. We had grown apart when her behavior changed, and I was already focused on getting into college—the future. We would still talk occasionally, but I didn't see her again until I was already at Georgetown. She came to visit and wanted to repair our friendship. Thinking about it now, maybe she had gone into a rehabilitation facility?"

Mom trailed off. I glanced at Dad, and he picked up from there. "Mom and I met during sophomore year, as you know, and Emily would come to visit a couple of times a year, but that was it. It was usually short visits, a long weekend, but even during those times, she would have moments where her behavior was...unpredictable and, at times, inappropriate for the situation."

*What the fuck did that mean?*

I scowled at my father but clamped my mouth shut, afraid that if I interrupted, the hour of truth would be over.

"Shortly after I started my position at Pendleton, she moved with her fiancé to San Diego. We met Henry once before, and he was a good guy. She seemed better. Then she got pregnant. You"—Dad made eye contact with me—"had just been born, and your mother was so excited for our children to be so close in age." He glanced over at Mom sympathetically. She picked at her pantleg, avoiding the three of us, and dread filled me with what would come next.

"But Mom was taking care of our newborn son and didn't see the changes in her friend," he continued. "It wasn't your mom's fault. Not by a long shot."

Huh? What wasn't—?

"Lilly was born, and Henry adored his little girl, but he had to travel a lot during the early years for his job."

"What did he do?" Lilly interrupted, speaking for the first time since the topic had switched to Emily. She still didn't know much about Henry.

"He was the lead architect for a national construction company. He would be onsite for a couple of weeks and then commute back and forth. That left Emily alone with Lilly a lot. She would drop her off with us every other day, sometimes leave her overnight."

"I loved having you, so I never questioned her for it. I should've..." Mom interjected fast, and Dad moved his hand from her leg to cover her hand on the table.

"Honey." He addressed her, and her shoulders slumped. He turned back to Lilly. "Mom always saw the good in people, so she would've never suspected anything being wrong with your biological mother." He emphasized the bio part. "You were at our house more days than not when Henry was gone. You were about a year old when you started having bruises that didn't add up with the stories Emily gave Heather. One day, you were around five, and you had a split lip. She said you had slipped after your shower and fell on the tiles in the bathroom. That was when I consulted with an associate about it. I didn't tell Heather about it at first. I didn't want your mom to worry or, worse, act differently and tip Emily off. You can't just accuse someone of child abuse without valid proof. My associate, Hector Lakatos, specialized in mental illnesses and, as you know, other areas of the brain." Dad paused, letting us digest all the information. Lilly's chest was rising and falling as if she had just run a couple of miles at full speed, and I didn't feel much better. I had the urge to jump up and pace the entire length of the estate.

"Hector owed me a few favors. He had me keep a log of Emily's behavior. I made a point to invite her and Henry over. We would meet them or make day trips together—anything that would allow me to study her. I cataloged every little thing and handed it over to Hector. One day, he asked me if any mental illnesses ran in her family, and I started digging into her past. There was not much to find, though. Emily's mother was institutionalized for endangering herself and her family when Emily was a toddler. She died a few years later. Her father was mostly unemployed and eventually dropped off the face of the earth when Emily was a young teenager. Hector managed to get a look at her mother's medical files somehow and concluded that Emily may have a form of Schizoaffective disorder."

"What the fuck is that?" I burst out.

God, I needed to get out of this chair. My leg started bouncing of its own volition.

Mom pulled her hand out from under Dad's and clutched the arm of her chair as she explained, "It's a mental health disorder. The person displays a combination of schizophrenia symptoms, as well as mood disorders, such as depression or manic behavior."

*Motherfucker.*

"Do I have that?" Lilly squeaked, her gaze ping-ponging back and forth between my parents.

"No. Hector didn't find any indicators when he...treated you," Dad reassured her.

Treated. *Brainwashed.* I closed my eyes and counted backward. Five, four, three... When I opened them again, I found my father staring at me with furrowed brows. He was expecting me to lose it, flip the table or something similar, and he wasn't too far off. I was working hard on controlling my anger, though.

I let out a breath I didn't realize I was holding.

"When you disappeared and she wouldn't do anything about it, Henry was beside himself. Emily refused to go to the authorities.

She acted like you were…visiting someone," Mom added with tears running down her face.

"That's when I filled your Mom in on what I had been doing," Dad admitted with a sigh.

"I was horrified that I had been so blind. All the signs were there when Dad laid them out, but I didn't see them." Mom was full-on sobbing at that point.

"You turned back up in Santa Rosa, and I saw it as the right time to suggest for you to stay with us for a while. I meant to fill Henry in on my suspicion and hoped we could get Emily to seek help while we took care of Lilly getting past her…experience. But I never got the chance to talk to Henry in private. Emily heard Mom and me discuss it in the hospital and instantly agreed. She said she would speak to Henry and, shortly after, came to us saying he also thought it was a good idea under the circumstances. We never saw Henry after that. According to Emily, he had to leave to go to another job site."

"We should've questioned her further. Henry wouldn't have just left you. But we were so focused on you, worried because of the messages Emily kept getting," Mom pleaded with Lilly. She blamed herself for what Henry went through. "I just wanted for you to get bet—" She broke off, covering her face with her hands.

"Honey, please." Dad wrapped his arms around her, and she sobbed into his shoulder.

I was shocked to realize how much guilt my parents were carrying around—misplaced guilt. They made mistakes, no question there, but what Lilly's psycho mother did should not have been part of that.

After my parents filled us in about their knowledge of Emily's past, and Mom had somewhat calmed down, we sat in silence. Lilly flicked her thumb against the fingers of her hand when she suddenly stopped.

"So, you had Lakatos wipe my memory because of Emily, not *just* Nate?"

*Huh?*

"Something happened while you were, uh…gone." Dad didn't use the word kidnapped, and Lilly and I both noticed it—her tick stopped abruptly.

"We never figured out what. We talked about it last night. Nate was 100% transparent with us on everything that happened while you were with him. Whenever Emily would come near you in the hospital, you would start crying, cringing away. Even scream. You would cling to whomever was near—Henry, me, your nurse," Mom whispered. "It was heartbreaking. Nate couldn't tell us, either, what the trigger may have been. You were scared and wanted to go home, but there was nothing that would explain why you reacted toward your mother the way you did. You were terrified."

"I informed them what Hector would be able to do," Dad redirected the conversation before Lilly could get too worked up over what her mother may have done. "Emily agreed without a second thought." Dad scrubbed a hand over his face. "In hindsight, she probably wanted you to forget. I'm starting to suspect that your reaction in the hospital had something to do with what she did to you."

"She never wanted me." Lilly's words were barely audible, yet it was like she shouted them at us. My mother gasped and jumped out of her chair, rounding the table.

"Oh, sweetheart." She wrapped her arms around Lilly.

"You helped her by taking Lilly away," I told my father, who nodded solemnly.

He blinked slowly. "I never anticipated her being that—"

"Psycho?" I supplied with a raised eyebrow.

Neither of my parents contradicted my statement.

Lilly wrapped her arms around Mom, and they both lost their battle against the waterfall of tears. When Lilly calmed down enough, she disentangled herself from Mom and pushed off the chair. She rounded the table to where Dad was sitting and sank down in the empty chair next to him.

Placing her hand on his on the table, she said, "Thank you." Her face was still wet, and a fresh tear ran down her cheek again.

Dad's eyebrows drew together in confusion, and she smiled. "Because of you, I got a childhood I will *never* forget. You and Mom"—her gaze swiveled to my mother—"are the best parents I could've wished for. So...thank you. For everything." She peered over at me with glossy eyes, and her meaning was clear. They also brought us together again. Who knew what would've happened if

Lilly had stayed with Emily? I was sure Henry would've done his best, but we'd never find out—which I was fucking glad about.

Emily visiting my mother during that conference had set a chain of events in motion no one could've ever anticipated.

By the time Lilly finished her sentence, Dad was bawling and hugging her to him. I stood up and opened my arms for my mother, who dived in and clung to me, her shoulders shaking.

It took a long time before anyone was calmed down enough for me to ask the question. I wasn't sure if Lilly forgot about it or didn't want to ask, but I had to.

"Are you going to turn Nate in?"

Lilly flipped in my direction in shock, but I kept my eyes on my father.

"No," my mother spoke up, and I jerked my gaze to her.

"You aren't?" Lilly was as surprised as I was.

"No," Dad confirmed. "Your mother and I spoke about it at length last night after Nate approached us."

*He came to them?*

"Nate will turn himself in. He laid out his plan to us but left it up to us whether we would give him the time he needs to get everything in order."

AND HERE WE ARE, three months later, in the penthouse suite of the Altman Hotel.

A HAND TOUCHES the side of my face, and I'm pulled out of the memory. I dip my chin. My girl is awake, and her hazel eyes look at me with concern.

"What are you thinking about?" Her thumb moves over my cheekbone.

I lean into the contact, loving the feeling of her skin on mine.

"Just remembering."

She understands the meaning behind my vague answer and nods, continuing her caress. I don't insult her by pretending it's all good. That's not who we are. We've been through too much to disrespect one another by putting on a façade.

"The alarm hasn't gone off yet," she states.

I loosen my hold and trail my hands down her arms, letting my gaze follow the motion. Goosebumps erupt where my fingers make contact with her skin, and seeing her reaction to me stirs a flutter in my chest. Reaching her elbow, I tug until she's on top of me. Her breathing increases.

"No, it hasn't," I confirm, locking eyes with her again and brushing my lips over hers.

The memory is forgotten. All I see is her. The now. The future.

She pulls back slightly, scanning my face. Her eyes darken, and I know what's going through her mind. My dick knows it, too, and stands at instant attention. No matter where in my fucked-up headspace I am, what situation we're in—or with whom—one look, one touch, and I lose all control over my body (part).

In those moments, we're like your typical couple in a new relationship—horny all the time. Lilly can feel my response as well. She rocks into me, and I groan, regretting that I had put on briefs after the last time she sat on top of me just a few hours ago.

*You could already be inside*, the voice in my head whines.

As if reading my mind, her mouth quirks at the corner. "I told you not to get dressed."

We haven't spent a night apart since we found her on that bloody mattress, and I don't intend on being away from her anytime soon. I no longer have panic attacks when she leaves the room, but the need to be close to her—and inside of her—is as overpowering as ever.

Lilly leans in and bites at my bottom lip, followed by her tongue soothing away the sting. Heat shoots to my toes. "Fuck, Calla."

She knows exactly what this does to me but enjoys the torture. She starts trailing kisses down my neck, over my torso, until she reaches the unwanted barrier between us. My chest heaves as Lilly continues her exploration. She studies me through her lashes, a devilish grin spreading across her face.

"Babe?" I prop myself up on my elbows, tilting my head.

Her fingers curl into the waistband of my briefs, and she tugs on them until my cock springs free. She pushes the fabric down until it reaches my ankles, and I kick it off hastily. Trying to rid myself of the damn thing, I also kick the comforter off the bed in the process —*I swear I'll go commando from now on.*

Lilly crawls toward me on all fours until her face is level with my —fuuuuck.

She's on me before my brain fully comprehends what's about to happen. My eyes roll back inside my head at the sensation of her mouth on me, and my arms give out—I drop back into the pillow.

The mattress shifts, and a hand grips my painfully hard length in addition to her mouth. Holy fucking hell. She bobs her head. Whenever her lips near the crown, she swirls her tongue around my tip before sinking back down. She continues mercilessly. My chest is heaving as I lie on the bed, letting her do to me whatever she wants.

"Fuck, babe." Every nerve ending in my body is on fire, and I have to fight the urge to thrust into her, not wanting to choke her. The combination of her stroking my dick while her mouth works me...I bite the inside of my cheek not to blow any second.

"You...need...to..." Eyes still closed, my hands fumble for her until I find her hair. Her tongue is pressing against the back of my cock as she continues to suck on me. My body has a mind of its own, and my hips jerk. I hit the back of her throat, but Lilly doesn't let up. She moans, and the sound alone is enough to push me almost over the edge. With all my willpower, I tug on the strands of her hair, signaling for her to stop. I raise my head off the pillow and peer down at her.

*What a view.*

Lilly takes mercy and glances up, eyes twinkling with mischief. "Something wrong?" She licks her bottom lip, and I groan.

"If you don't sit down on my dick right this second, I will bend you over that chair over there and show you what's wrong." I smirk, dipping my head toward the armchair next to the bed.

A picture of me fucking her from behind on said chair while smacking her firm ass conjures in my head, and I want to follow through with my threat.

We can always have a repeat on the chair later.

Lilly tilts her head as if considering the idea as well. Please say yes! I raise an eyebrow in challenge.

Pressing her mouth together, she stifles a laugh before scooting up on the bed. She straddles my waist but remains up on her knees as I let my gaze trail from her beautiful face, over her gorgeous tits, to what's now perfectly aligned with my one body part that probably loves her more than the rest of me.

She leans forward, placing her hands on my shoulders, and our eyes lock, all playfulness gone. We don't need pretty words anymore. Even though we've only been together for just about six months, we know each other better than most couples after years.

Lilly sinks down, never breaking eye contact. She moans, biting her lip, and I can't wait any longer. Grabbing her hips, I pull her down until I'm all the way inside.

*So fucking tight.*

*Mine*, a growl echoes in my mind.

Sitting up, I let my tongue swipe over one of her nipples before sucking it into my mouth, my hand palming her other breast. Her fingers dive into my hair, nails scraping over my scalp, and I gently bite down, having learned over the last several months that this is something she likes—a lot. She arches her back, giving me better access, and I oblige, tugging on her skin.

"Yesss, just like—" Lilly rocks herself into me, creating more friction over her clit. My girl knows what she wants and doesn't hesitate to take it. Another reason she's perfect for me.

My hand, the one not already occupied, finds her ass, and I press her further against me, thrusting up in the process.

"Oh, God," she breathes next to my ear before starting to kiss right underneath it—my weak spot. A shudder of pleasure runs down my spine.

"Babe, I..." I'm so fucking close. It's embarrassing how she can make me come in less than ten minutes. Thankfully, it never takes long before I'm ready again, or my ego would be shot by now.

Lilly starts increasing her speed, and I meet her every move. The only sounds in the room are our ragged breathing and the sound of flesh on flesh. I release her nipple, and her mouth instantly finds mine, opening up. My tongue tangles with hers, and she purrs.

*The sounds that come out of this girl.*

Both my hands move to her back, pulling her to me until we're flush together. She moans as my fingers dig into her back, and I feel her walls tighten around me.

"Come for me, Cal." I watch her fall apart in my arms with my cock buried deep inside of her. The look of ecstasy on her face is enough to push me over the edge. I groan as my cum releases inside of her, biting down on her shoulder. Thank fuck we're past the condom stage.

*Still need to send a letter to whomever invented oral contraceptives.*

Once our breathing evens out, she places both hands on either side of my face and puts our foreheads together. She looks at me, and I tilt my head, our lips brushing together.

"I love you." Her tone is soft.

"I love you."

## CHAPTER ONE HUNDRED TWENTY-ONE

**LILLY**

I STAND IN FRONT OF THE DOUBLE-SIZE MIRROR IN THE BATHROOM of our hotel penthouse. Of course, we don't just have a room; we have one of the two penthouse suites on the top floor—Nate staying in the other—with my friends and family one floor underneath in the *slightly* smaller suites.

My wet hair hangs down my back, and my stomach clenches as I'm debating the appropriate hairdo for today. Curls, straight, up, down, French twist...how should one look coming out to the public as the illegitimate heir to a billion-dollar empire? Not to mention the other news that will drop today. My pulse increases, and my fingers tighten around the edge of the vanity. I close my eyes, taking a deep breath.

"Calla?"

Rhys's voice startles me, and my eyes snap open. He's standing in the doorway—butt naked. I let my gaze trail his body. Rhys has bulked up over the last three months. He's been training with George every day, and it shows. Every muscle in his body is toned. Between his bulging biceps, defined pecs, and ripped abs, heat pools in my core, and I have to clench my thighs together.

*Hell, he just gave me a mind-blowing orgasm not twenty minutes ago.*

He chuckles. "Don't do that."

"Do what?" I ask innocently, meeting his eyes. I'm fully aware of him noticing my shift in stance. And I can certainly *see* how it affects him.

"We don't have time." His face turns serious. "G called. Henry landed."

*Henry.* My heart starts pounding. Henry is in Los Angeles.

HENRY HAD BEEN in a hospital in Virginia when Heather and Tristen filled Rhys and me in on everything they knew or had suspected about Emily. From there, he went straight to one of the best physical rehabilitation facilities in the country. Nate took care of the logistics, and I couldn't have been more grateful to him. At first, it was debatable if he would ever regain full functionality of his legs after years of paralytic drugs. The doctors labeled his one almost-escape a fluke. He shouldn't have been able to stand on his legs, but he did—one time.

Henry got the best therapy, and because of that and his hard work, he's regained 75% of his leg mobility over the last few months. He still relies on a wheelchair, but his right leg is stronger than his left, and on a good day, he can move around on crutches for a little while or stand in one place on his own.

It took me almost a month before I found the courage to call him. Whenever I put in his number, my hands started sweating, and I'd become nauseated. The guilt about Emily's actions was eating my insides. Everyone kept reassuring me that none of this was my fault, and deep down, I knew they were right. After all, I was a kid when it started, but still. He was trapped by her for years—because of me.

I confessed my feelings to Heather during one of her visits to LA. We were in the kitchen, preparing dinner at the time, with Natty doing her online schoolwork at the breakfast nook. Heather wiped her hands on a dishtowel, placed it on the countertop, and walked over to the island where I was chopping onions. I don't remember if the tears running down my cheeks were from the vegetable or from the deep-rooted feeling of being the reason my father...stepfather—we still hadn't defined his role—was partially paralyzed for years. She hugged me before pulling back and placing both palms on either side of my face.

"My sweet Lilly, I'm going to repeat myself as many times as you need to hear it. None of this is your fault. None. Henry is not upset with you. Quite the opposite."

"But I still haven't talked to him," I interrupted her reassurance. My hands started to shake, and I had to let go of the knife's handle.

"He is processing himself, sweetheart. Tristen and I have been in touch with him. We feel just as guilty because we didn't see Emily's...problems either. Not how sick she really was. Henry is working with a therapist to move past his guilt of not noticing Emily's mental issues before it was too late, letting his daughter get physically abused and later not being able to protect her from his wife's plans."

"But he couldn't have done anything about it." Sudden anger makes my cheeks heat.

"Exactly. And neither could you. Both of you were victims in a game that used you as pawns." She placed a kiss on my forehead, and when she pulled back, I nodded at her. She was right, but there was no saying how long it would take for me to truly believe it.

"Did you know that Henry spoke up for Emily's employees?" I asked Heather. Nate had informed me the night before that Henry gave a testimony that the maid, Elise, and the medical staff, who were charged as accessories, had all been threatened or blackmailed by Emily and Gray.

"Yes, I heard about it. The court will have to decide how to proceed with that." She directs an apologetic smile at me. She wouldn't give me any more answers on that topic. Her professional side never gave any predictions on a legal matter. We would have to wait and see on that one.

Heather was just moving back to the stove when I swiveled on my heels.

"Mom?" Heather had become Mom again. She was my mother. My anger toward her for keeping me in the dark had long since been replaced by light. She had cared for me since I was a baby, even when I wasn't yet her daughter.

She turned back around while continuing to stir the sauce. "Yes?"

"Do you remember what you said to me at Hill Crest?" The hospital where George dropped me off in Nebraska.

Her eyebrows rose. "We said a lot while you were there." Her expression turned pained for a fraction of a second, but she smoothed it out just as quickly. "You have to be a little more specific."

I drew in a deep breath. It'd been nagging on me for weeks, months, but it'd never been the right opportunity to bring it back up. "After I told you that I knew about me not being your daughter…biological daughter," I correct myself, and she smiled softly at that. "You said to me, '*No matter what you know or think you know, you are my little girl.*' What did you mean?"

Heather—Mom scrunched her forehead and looked up at the ceiling. When she found my gaze, she opened and closed her mouth several times before speaking. "That was a very emotional day. Dad had just confessed to me about his suspicion that Henry was not your father. Yet, I didn't know how much more there was."

"Hannah and the cameras," I finished, and she nodded.

It was the other bombshell that Tristen confessed to Rhys and me when Heather first came to LA. He had kept the extent of the home surveillance to himself for years to not scare his wife and children. He didn't understand why Emily would come after our housekeeper—after no communication from her since I had moved in with the McGuires—and steal my teddy bear, of all things. Was it because Brooks had given me that bear? Was it her way of making a point? That she could get to me if she wanted to? Or was it simply part of her mental illness, and there was no real reason? Hannah was most likely a victim caught in the crossfire. We may never know. Not unless Francis Garrison (Gray) Turner shows back up. He'd been missing since the day he shot Emily, and we could only speculate about his motive. I repeated his words to my family. *No one betrays me.* But none of them could make sense of it either. *Did Emily betray him?*

Heather's eyes were shining with love as she explained, "You were confused about who you were, and I wanted you to know that you will always be my daughter, even if I didn't give birth to you."

This time, I walked over to her and hugged her.

. . .

ARMS CIRCLING my stomach bring me out of my memory. Two thumbs caress the spot underneath my belly button, and I let my vision come back to focus and face Rhys in the mirror.

"Where did you just go, babe?" He cocks his head and studies my face.

"Just thinking about Henry."

He nods and pulls me tighter to him, his erection pressing against my back. One hand moves upward and cups my breast, his mouth peppering my neck and shoulder with kisses.

I lean into him, tilting my neck, and close my eyes. "Mhmm...didn't you just say we don't have time?"

He blows out a resigned breath, and the cool air against my neck causes goosebumps on my arms. "I did, didn't I?" he murmurs, placing another kiss on my shoulder.

He loosens his hold and steps back, his gaze moving down to my butt. He sighs dramatically, and I bark out a laugh.

"Go take a cold shower, big boy."

He smirks, and I add, "Alone."

Rhys gives me a one-sided shoulder shrug before he turns on the spray. "Not my fault I have the hottest girlfriend."

The hornets in my stomach go haywire at his words, and I shake my head. Then, I meet my reflection in the mirror again, and the hornets turn to dust, a black hole opening up in my stomach.

IT'S TIME. With my hand safely secured in Rhys's, we make our way from our penthouse to the elevator down the hall. I knocked on Nate's door, but there was no answer. He must've already gone down.

When we arrived yesterday, Kevin, the hotel's bellhop of forty-two years, informed me that the top floor is reserved for the Altman family. No one else is allowed to stay there unless Mr. Nate —or now I—gave permission.

When I looked at him with confused eyes, the gray-haired man smiled. "You look like your father and brother."

My mouth dropped open, unable to form words.

"The second suite has been empty since Miss Payton and Miss Audrey left us. Mr. Nate always stays in his grandfather's suite," he said with a bowed head as the elevator ascended, and I fought against the lump in my throat.

Rhys, who had remained quiet, wrapped his arm around me and pulled me into his side. He saw that this friendly man's words had almost caused me to break down.

*My biological mother was the reason why the penthouse had been empty for over a decade.*

Now standing in the elevator, my heart rate is increasing. My palm is getting damp in Rhys's, and I focus on our reflection in the mirrored doors. Rhys is dressed in dark-gray slacks and a white button-down shirt. His short hair has the perfect amount of gel in it. I shift to myself. I decided on a navy-blue pencil skirt with a white cap-sleeve blouse and nude heels. After blow-drying my hair, I twisted it in a low bun, letting a few strands hang loose around my face. I want to look put-together but still like myself. When my gaze lands on my free hand, I snort, which draws Rhys's attention back to me. I was flicking my thumb against my fingers and didn't even notice.

*I am more nervous than I want to admit to myself.*

LATE LAST NIGHT, Nate and I met in the grand ballroom to go over everything one more time. Rhys patiently waited for two hours, sitting in one of the chairs on the stage. Today's announcement would only take thirty minutes. George and I, along with Agent Lanning, Agent Camden, and Doctor Stern, would be onstage together with Nate. We would need law enforcement, and after several heated discussions between myself, Nate, Heather, and Tristen, we all agreed Lanning and Camden were the best choices. Both were shocked, to say the least, when we flew them out to LA and introduced them to Nate. It took some convincing from Heather and Tristen to give us two more weeks to finalize the plan.

We also have several members of the hotel's security team, as well as George's own team, standing against both walls. George took charge of that. Everything is planned meticulously, down to the most superficial detail. Where Nate just wanted it all over, George and I refused to leave anything to chance.

That's how it happened that the first two rows are reserved for the families of *the girls*. I personally called each of the parents and asked them to be here today. They knew who I was—obviously. We took care of their travel and accommodations, but none of them knew the true reason why they were summoned. I only told them that it had to do with the case, and it'd be important for them to attend in person.

We were at the vineyard during that time, and before the first call, I had a complete panic attack. Rhys almost called 911—if he would have known how to navigate Nate's NCC set up. He almost tore the door out of the hinges, yelling for Nate.

The third row is for the board members, and the fourth will be occupied by my family. Rhys was pissed that I wouldn't let him be onstage, but Heather sided with me on that. "She needs to do this alone. She'll be safe."

He hasn't left my side in months. Wherever I go, so does he. I see the looks Heather and Tristen give him, and he probably should work with his therapist on his fears, but I'm also selfish. I don't want to be without him as much as he doesn't want to be without me.

We have time to deal with the past when today is over. To heal.


WE ARRIVE on the second floor where the ballrooms are located. My heart is beating in my throat, but as the doors open, we're greeted by a familiar face, and my nerves calm a little. Marcus has become my shadow—as Rhys and Wes call him—whenever George isn't with me.

Between Gray and Hank both missing, I have a 24/7 security detail. Hank still has not returned to U.S. soil, and Nate lost his trail after he left the hotel and got into an unmarked car.

Marcus is one of George's men and is around Nate's age. He was personally trained by George for years, which was why he was chosen for the role.

He dips his chin, and without a word, he falls into step slightly behind me. We make our way to the side entrance, avoiding the press waiting in the back by the main doors. Rhys's hand never leaves mine, and I know he won't let go until the last minute. He's my anchor. He is worried, and if I'm honest, I am too. Not for my safety, but for how the audience will take what we have to say.

The press conference is to start in ten minutes, and the room is already buzzing. I stop abruptly when I step onstage and notice that the block of chairs has been moved back twenty feet. My eyes find Nate's, who's standing next to an uncomfortable Doctor Stern, and he slowly moves toward us. He is dressed in a custom navy suit, white shirt, no tie. We look like we color-coordinated.

"George and the hotel's head of security decided to put distance between us and, uh...the families."

*Oh.*

I bite my bottom lip and look between my brother and the first row. Before I can say anything, Rhys speaks up.

"Good." He nods at Nate. "We have no fucking clue how this will go down."

I bite harder. They are right, but I can't help the guilt that's settling in my stomach. We are about to turn these people's lives upside down as much as we will give them closure.

*As much as we can after what my brother did.*

I scan the room, and most of the seats are already taken. I'm met with nervous glances as well as glares from the first two rows. I should've expected that after everything that went down when I *reappeared*. I see almost everyone, except Ava Conway. Her mother is there with a woman that must be her sister. But neither Ava nor her father, who had demanded my interrogation, are present.

Ava's mother meets my gaze, and I avert my eyes, my mouth going dry. In the fourth row, I spot Heather and Tristen quietly talking to another man. *Henry*.

As if he senses my stare, he turns his head, and it's the first time —that I remember—I see him in person. He does a double-take, and I swallow against the needles in my throat. I squeeze Rhys's hand, making him follow my gaze.

Leaning closer, he whispers, "Go to him."

I jerk my head around. "I...I can't." The nervousness I felt entering this room is replaced by the imminent fear of facing the man who was held hostage for a decade because of me. My free hand finds my lower abdomen.

*I feel sick.*

"Well"—Rhys glances back toward the audience—"he's coming to you."

Every muscle in my body tenses, and I slowly swivel in the same direction. Henry is in his wheelchair and slowly approaching the podium. As if giving me an out, he doesn't avert his eyes from mine. One signal, and he'd turn around.

When he is right in front of the stage, my feet slowly move toward him. There was never a question of me stopping him. A multitude of emotions causes my stomach to somersault. I'm glad that I skipped breakfast today.

With Rhys on my heels, I descend the four steps and come to a halt in front of—

"Daddy?" my barely audible voice breaks. I feel my insides shatter like a crystal chandelier plummeting to the ground, breaking into a million shards and pieces. My hands fly to my mouth as I take in every inch of his face.

Henry's eyes spill over, and he pushes himself out of the wheelchair. Rhys steps to his side for support, but he shakes his head. Fully upright, his arms fall to his sides, and I launch myself at the man I only consciously know from my migraines. Subconsciously, a deep-routed sensation starts spreading through me. He was my father for my first six years. He is still my father. I never got to meet Brooks, but I have Henry and Tristen. He wraps his arms around me, and I squeeze his midsection.

"Hey, honey." His voice is deep and smooth. I can feel his chest rise and fall against my cheek while his hand cups the back of my head. I don't remember him, yet I do. It makes no sense, and at the same time, it makes perfect sense.

"I'm so sorry, Daddy." I'm sobbing, ruining his light-blue dress shirt and most definitely my makeup, but I don't care.

"Shhh," he soothes. "You have nothing to be sorry for." He pulls back and searches my face. "We have all the time in the world to talk. I'm not going anywhere."

I nod, wiping with one hand under my eyes. Glancing to the side, Heather is mimicking my motion under her own eyes, and so is Denielle. A hand touches my shoulder, and I turn, facing George.

"It's time."

*Already?* I look back at Henry, suddenly unsure and feeling like a little girl.

He gives me an encouraging smile. "I'll be right over there." He tilts his head toward the edge of the fourth row.

I nod hesitantly, unable to form words. My knees feel weak, and I'm not sure I can make it back up the steps to the stage.

Rhys retakes my hand and squeezes it. "You sure you don't want me with you?"

*Yes, please stay with me.*

"I have to do this alone," I tell him with as much confidence as I can muster, given the pit that has rooted itself in my stomach and my voice cracking.

"Ok." He kisses me on the cheek, and I expect him to follow Henry, but instead, he levels George.

"If anyone harms her, I will hold you responsible. I don't care that you make everyone shit their pants just by looking at you. If anything happens, you jump in front of her, or I will come after you with your own gun. I know the combination to your safe; don't forget that." I am shocked at the menace that rolls off Rhys's tongue but equally touched by it. He loves George. The two have a bond that none of us understand, but he is one hundred percent serious.

George bows his head. "I will." He doesn't say anything else, but there is also no need for more words. We all know that this man would put anything on the line for Nate and me.

With one last squeeze of my hand, Rhys lets go and walks past the first three rows. He positions himself next to Henry's wheelchair, not moving into the row to sit down.

The sudden loss of his contact makes me almost double over. My anchor. Before I can change my mind and race after Rhys, begging him to come back, I turn and follow George.

I make my way to my assigned seat between Agent Lanning and Doctor Stern. The poor man looks like he's going to pass out any second. He probably never expected to be in this situation, but his testimony is prudent.

. . .

THIS IS where we wait until George taps the microphone on the podium in front of us. "If you would please all take your seats. The press conference is about to begin." I scan the room and take in several sets of wide eyes staring at the man who just addressed them. It's almost comical how intimidating he is despite being dressed all professional in a pressed suit.

## CHAPTER ONE HUNDRED TWENTY-TWO

**RHYS**

I STAY NEXT TO HENRY IN THE AISLE AND CROSS MY ARMS IN front of my chest, focusing on the stage. Out of the corner of my eye, Mom gives me a disapproving glance. She wants me to sit down but knows why I've positioned myself here. I want a direct line of sight to Lilly and to be ready to move at any moment. Several of George's men, including Lilly's shadow, are closer than me, if it came down to it, but I don't care.

Lilly's eyes find mine from her seat between Lanning and Nate's doc. Holy fuck, the guy's face is all kinds of green. Guess he should've paid more attention to the shit he prescribed to his patient. If the situation weren't so serious, I'd laugh my ass off.

There is movement in my peripheral vision. Denielle shuffles past my parents and stands behind Henry, followed by Wes, who stops behind me. I glance back without losing sight of Lilly on the stage. She is nervous, flicking her thumb against the rest of her fingers.

"She'll be ok," Denielle whispers.

I'm not sure who she's trying to reassure or if she truly believes it. Hell, I have no clue what's going to happen in the next thirty minutes. This whole thing is fucking insane. I thought Lilly having her memory erased was the craziest thing that I would ever experience in my life. Never in a million years would I have expected to find myself here, in the fanciest hotel in freaking LA, after Lilly—*and I*, thanks to being the reckless idiot I am—almost got killed by her biological mother, now waiting for Lilly's brother/first kidnapper to admit to his past crimes.

*I couldn't make that shit up even if I wanted to.*

GEORGE APPROACHES THE PODIUM AGAIN, and I hear several intakes of breath behind me from the press rows. It's hilarious that this scary-ass guy with a massive scar across half his face is like a doting father to Lilly and Nate. I remember the night he stepped out of the shadows in Den's backyard; I almost pissed my pants.

"Ladies and gentlemen..." The room goes eerily quiet, and all eyes are to the front. Lilly, however, is looking directly at me, and I give her the slightest nod.

*You got this, babe.*

"Mr. Hamlin has called for this press conference for several reasons. One is to announce a change in ownership for the Altman Hotels. However, the main objective is for him to inform everyone in attendance of the truth in the disappearance of the five girls that went missing and reappeared *unharmed* over the past ten years."

Instantly I hear chairs scrape against the floor, flashes go off, and reporters behind me start shouting questions. "What does that mean?" "What do the Altman Hotels have to do with a string of kidnappings?" "Why are we here?" "Who is the man next to Miss McGuire?"

*I recognize that voice.*

I glance over my shoulder, and sure enough, Lancaster is front and center. The dude will cry like a baby after losing his life's sole purpose today.

George ignores all of them and taps the mic again. When the press realizes that he will not answer their questions, they slowly sit back down one by one.

*Shit, this guy is good.*

"My name is George Weiler, and I am the head of Mr. Hamlin's personal security." I notice how he purposefully neglects the fact that he is also Lilly's security. They probably don't want to use her name until Nate and Lilly announce who she is.

"The press conference will proceed as follows. Mr. Hamlin will address you first, followed by several other speakers who will comment on what Mr. Hamlin is about to tell you." Again, he doesn't mention any names. "We are asking all of you to remain calm and seated the entire time. We will *not* allow questions during *or after*. The objective is for all of you to receive the same information at the same time. Any questions can be submitted in writing afterward and will be answered by the Altman legal representatives and the assigned authorities. Anyone who disrupts the press conference, does not remain seated, or attempts to approach the podium will *immediately* be removed by my security staff." George nods to both sides of the room, and it's almost as if everyone just now notices the men standing against the walls. Several gasps are audible throughout the large room, amplifying the sounds.

"Does anyone have an issue with the rules?"

*Nothing.* Not one sound. I'm pretty sure the entire room is holding its breath.

"Very well. Mr. Hamlin will address you first." With that, George steps to the side, and Nate slowly moves forward. He looks at Lilly before taking the last step, and she gives him a tight smile.

It's written over her entire face how much she loves *and supports* her brother. She has forgiven him for what he has done to her and what she went through because of his actions. Not many people would be capable of that. As scared as I am for her and for what is to unfold in the next few minutes, I am even more proud to call her mine.

"LADIES AND GENTLEMAN," Nate's voice rings through the ballroom. "My name is Nathan Altman Hamlin. My legal name is Nathan Hamlin; however, since taking over the Altman Hotels, I have used my mother and grandfather's name to conduct my business affairs. The two names have allowed me to live *two* separate lives, but this will come to a close today." Nate pauses and looks down at his notes. Where he sounds calm and collected, Lilly's posture is rigid, and even from a distance, I can see the white knuckles of her clasped hands.

My entire body is tense, and I fight the urge to march up there and throw myself in front of her. Denielle must've noticed the shift in me, because she gently places her hand on my lower back, keeping me in place. Behind me, hasty typing and the clicking of cameras is audible, and I assume the press is also holding up microphones. I don't turn around. My focus is on our current speaker and his sister behind him.

"As my head of security has already mentioned, we will not accept any questions. However, I am aware that some of the information I am about to share will be unsettling and upsetting to you, but I have to ask you to remain calm, or we will not be able to continue. Please let all the speakers finish."

Taking a deep breath, Nate turns one last time to Lilly, who locks eyes with him but doesn't show any expression. I haven't seen this blank mask in a long time. I don't like it, though I get that it is the face she has to put on.

"You were wondering who the people behind me are, and I will explain each of their roles to you in a moment. Most of you"—this is directed toward the press—"are aware of my past: my mother and sister's fatal accident, my father's suicide, and my altercation with another student, resulting in his hospitalization and my stay in a psychiatric facility. Doctor Stern"—he nods toward the small and, by now, extremely sweaty man in the farthest chair—"has been my therapist for the past *ten* years and will explain the medical aspect of this to you.

"On the other side, you have Agents Lanning and Camden of the Federal Bureau of Investigation. You may have heard their names over the last several months." He's alluding to the case without saying it directly. "Agents Lanning and Camden are here to ensure that the appropriate legal measures are taken once this is over."

A murmur runs through the crowd, and I almost expect someone to speak up, but George moves forward, and everyone quiets.

*Fascinating.*

"Before introducing the last person onstage, I would like to express my deepest apologies to the four families in the first two rows. I now understand what you have been put through, and there are no words that can ever erase the pain you experienced...through my hand." This is it. My adrenaline level shoots through the roof, not that my blood pressure wasn't already in the unhealthy range.

Flashes go off, people behind me jump up, and from my angle, I can see the shocked expressions of the parents in the front. Slowly the information sinks in. The women all sit with covered mouths, some crying, some in their husband's arms. One man jumps up and attempts to reach the stage when two security guards stop him.

"YOU MOTHERFUCKER! YOU TOOK MY BABY GIRL!" the man is shouting, and I feel Denielle behind me cringe at his words. The woman next to him starts crying harder and pulls on his arm, trying to tug him backward.

I force myself to remain rooted in place. Lilly is not in danger. I inhale and exhale through my nose, watching George slowly make his way off the stage and quietly address the man. I have no idea what he says to the outraged father, but all of a sudden, his shoulders slump, and he lets the security guard guide him back to his seat.

*I did not expect that.*

Focusing back on the stage, I realize that Lilly stepped up next to Nate and has her hand on his forearm. Glancing around, others have noticed the same gesture and are now looking at the two with a mix of curiosity and contempt. They know who Lilly is—at least part of it.

Nate covers the microphone while Lilly quietly talks to him. He shakes his head vigorously as she keeps addressing him. Her entire focus is on her brother; she has tuned everyone else out. Where Nate looks pained, she is serious, and knowing Lilly, there is no negotiation. George joins the two, and after Lilly seems to bring him up to speed, George places a hand on Nate's shoulder, nods at him in his typical no-bullshit fashion, and slowly guides him toward the chair Lilly vacated. I hold my breath as she takes the podium.

*She is not in danger.*

I curl my toes inside my shoes to keep myself in place. As soon as she stands behind the microphone, everything goes quiet.

"Ladies and gentleman of the press, Mrs. Conway, Mr. and Mrs.

Scagliotta, Mr. and Mrs. Lynn, and Mr. and Mrs. Ashbaugh, thank you all for coming today. I would like to introduce myself first before continuing with the rest of the information Nate was about to share with you. My name is Lilly Ann Hamlin."

A collective gasp goes through the room, and I expect someone to speak up, but no one does.

From my angle, I can see Lilly clutch the notes Nate left behind. Lilly takes a deep breath before looking straight at the people in the first two rows. "I am Nate Hamlin's sister and his first"—she pauses for what I count seven breaths—"victim." Lilly's chest is heaving, and I know the signs. Unless she can calm herself, she is going into a panic attack. I take one step, and her eyes find me instantly. I halt, waiting for her cues. She looks at me, and I hold her gaze. I don't know how long we stare at each other when she finally dips her chin and faces the parents again. She's back in control. I expel a sigh of relief.

"My apologies. This is still hard for me, as well. As I said, I was my brother's first victim. My biological mother had an affair with Nate's father, Brooks Hamlin. Neither Nate nor his mother or sister knew about me, nor I of them. After Audrey and Payton Altman's death, Nate found out about his father's affair through a number of letters my mother had sent to him. At the time, my brother was in a very dark place. He had just been released from his stay at the hospital and was highly medicated. Medication that impacted his judgment and thinking to a point where—"

"ARE YOU MAKING EXCUSES FOR THIS FREAK'S CRIMES?" the man from earlier shouts in the first row.

*Fuck. This is getting ugly.*

I'm ready to storm to the stage; Marcus is already front and center.

Lilly faces the man with a sad smile. "No, Mr. Lynn. I am not. My brother needs to account for his crimes. I have told him that from the day I found out who I was and what he had done to your daughters and me. There is no excuse for that." Someone else is standing up, about to say something, but Lilly holds up her hand. She looks like she does this every day, and my chest swells. I'm even a little turned on.

*This is so not appropriate right now.*

"Please let me finish. I understand that this is hard for you, and I promise you will get the answers you need. I have had time to come to terms with what has happened to me and worked alongside my family and my brother to deal with the past."

"Why didn't you come clean when you reappeared last March?" Lancaster shouts.

*So much for no questions.*

"Mr. Lancaster, please let me proceed. As our head of security has informed you, we will not allow questions."

I can't help myself and glance back at the guy who had camped out on our front lawn for weeks. His face is a mixture of surprise and shock, and I grin to myself. I wonder how many times he's been told off by an eighteen-year-old.

Lilly continues. She tells the room everything. Every detail that led to today. With some topics, she's vague, like how she lost her memory. With others, there is uncensored explicitness, like Emily's blackmail and abuse. When Lilly mentions Henry, all eyes are on him, but he only focuses on his daughter. At Lilly's recollection of Turner breaking into the Hamlin Estate and what Emily did to her to get her inheritance, a collective gasp goes through the room. One of her hands leaves the podium and rubs over the scar hidden underneath her skirt. She does that whenever someone brings up those few days.

"The reason I am telling you all of this is for you to understand why it took so long for my brother and me to hold this conference. The Altman board of directors was notified last week of my existence and that I will take over for my brother, effective immediately. While I continue my education, I will rely on the board's experience and guidance to make sure my family's business is handled appropriately. Upon completion of my degree, I will take on the official role as the president of the Altman Hotels until my brother returns."

"Returns from where?"

*Fucking Lancaster.*

Lilly ignores him and focuses back on the parents of the four girls. "My brother has given his statement to Agents Camden and Lanning of the FBI. Upon finishing this press conference, he is voluntarily checking himself into a facility specialized for this type of disorder. At the same time, his attorney will collect the testimony of the pharmaceutical companies, Dr. Stern, who prescribed the medication that caused his impulsive and erratic behavior, and any witnesses before taking the case to trial. During his treatment, my brother will learn how to cope with his actions and—"

"THIS IS FUCKING RIDICULOUS. THE BASTARD NEEDS TO GO TO JAIL!"

Lynn is losing it, and this time, neither his wife nor George can calm him down. His yelling becomes louder, and when he takes a step toward the podium, George's men are on him, grasping his arms. Marcus has positioned himself directly in front of Lilly, making her peer around his large frame. The guys drag Chloe's father to a side entrance while his wife stands there staring after her kicking husband.

Suddenly, Lilly moves around her shadow and down the steps. Marcus says something, but she waves him off.

*What the hell is she doing?*

The only reason I'm staying where I am is that Marcus is right on her heels. She approaches the woman, who now stares at her with wide eyes. Lilly has her hands clasped in front of her body and quietly speaks to Chloe's mother. Mrs. Lynn keeps nodding, covering her mouth with her palm as she wipes her eyes with her other. Lilly gives her a genuine smile before she climbs the stage again, and Mrs. Lynn takes her seat.

"My apologies, ladies and gentlemen. Mr. Lynn will remain outside until the press conference concludes. However, I would like to say that his reaction is justified given the circumstances. I appreciate the rest of you following Mr. Weiler's instructions, and we will finish as quickly as possible."

Lilly takes a step back, and a shaking Dr. Stern approaches the podium. Instead of sitting back down, she remains at the side of the stage, flanked between George and Marcus. She studies Nate with furrowed brows, who has his gaze trained on the floor. His lips are pressed in a thin line, and—is he flicking his thumb against his fingers?

My attention gets redirected as Stern introduces himself, followed by giving a brief explanation of the medication Nate received over the years. He only states facts and doesn't go into the many side effects these drugs can cause. I guess that'll be part of the trial. Agent Camden is the last to speak and updates everyone on how this impacts the case. When she finishes, Nate stands from his seat, and Lilly and Camden turn. Agent Lanning reaches behind him and pulls out a set of handcuffs.

*Why the hell did no one tell me that this would happen?*

Lilly stands stock still, and George places a hand on her lower back as they watch Nate placing his hands together and Lanning putting the cuffs on. Tears are streaming down Lilly's face, but she doesn't make any move to remove them. Nate lifts his eyes to his sister, and before the two agents lead him back toward the other side entrance, he mouths, "I love you."

*It's over.*

## LILLY

*Six Years Later*

It's been fifteen months since I last saw my brother face to face, and my body is buzzing with nervous energy. We're approaching the small airport in Northern California, and I'm trying to get some notes to my assistant before shutting off the computer for the next week.

After finishing my degree, I took over the Altman security department. Thanks to Nate beginning my intensive training before he went *away,* and my education, I turned the Altman Hotels into one of a kind. People all over the world choose our hotels for their security measures and privacy.

"Babe, how long is that damn email going to be?" Denielle barks at me from her seat across the aisle.

I flick my gaze to her before returning it to my screen.

"Leave her alone, D. You know if my wife doesn't get her work done, we won't see her for the remainder of the trip."

I glare at Rhys over the top of my laptop, but he just smirks and winks. He'll never let me live it down for disappearing during our rehearsal dinner to fix a bug that one of my developers built into the custom system at an offshore location. I was still in college but had already started taking over parts of the business.

Instead of snapping a retort at him, I concentrate back on my screen. The sooner I get this done, the faster I can focus on what's important for the next seven days.

Typing, I listen to the conversations around me. Heather and Tristen are in the front, murmuring to each other. Natty is sitting in the other seat in the front row, reading a book. She's attending an online high school, which allows her to move between West-bridge and L.A. every few weeks, or in this case, fly to the vineyard with us.

"How was the beach?" Hudson asks Wes behind me. Hudson and Elle were able to make it; the others would fly in tomorrow.

Wes snorts. "Oh, you know. The girls played in the ocean until they passed out from exhaustion, and then I had to take care of myself—even cook my own dinner." *Smack*. "Ouch! Woman!" I glance over my shoulder and see Wes rubbing his arm, glowering to his right.

Grinning, I turn back around.

"You guys never learn," Elle laughs. "Don't antagonize the women who feed you."

Her voice gets closer, and she squats down next to my seat. "Hey, girl."

I smile at my friend. "Hi."

Who would've expected that the day she drove to LA to pick up Hudson and ran into me while I was escaping my gazillion-square-foot hideout would result in a friendship that will last a lifetime? We've visited each other a lot over the years, especially after Elle moved to Colorado for college and offered to give me free ski lessons. I dragged Rhys to the jet that same week, and after that, it became a tradition that brought our two groups of friends and family closer together with every visit.

"I just wanted to say that we're excited to be here for the big occasion. Too bad not everyone could make it today. Hazel was livid she couldn't be on the jet with us today and has to fly commercial. You know how she is." She laughs then chews on her lower lip, and I cock an eyebrow, waiting.

"Has he met her yet?" she asks carefully.

I avert my eyes as butterflies take hold in my stomach. "Not yet."

Rhys watches me closely.

"I'm not going to have a panic attack," I snap at him but immediately regret my unwarranted reaction. "Shit, babe, I didn't—" I cover my face with my hands. There is a high chance I will have a meltdown, and we both know it. I haven't had one in years, but I've been a mess since we found out about Nate's early release date and that it would fall close to this week. Nate was officially discharged three weeks ago, but besides a handful of phone calls, I've spoken to him less than the years he was in the facility.

Fingers clasp around my wrists and pull until I let my hands drop away from my face.

I lock eyes with Rhys, and he interlaces our fingers on top of the table that's separating our seats.

"Everything will be fine," he reassures me calmly.

Not letting go of him, I stand, and Elle moves out of the way to let me out. I step to Rhys's side, and he tilts his head. Without a word, I straddle his lap and wrap my arms around his neck.

"Ahem..." Elle clears her throat. "I'll take that as my cue." There is laughter in her voice, and I know she's not offended.

I brush my lips over Rhys's and whisper, "I love you."

He pulls me closer, his mouth less than an inch from my ear. I feel his breath on my skin as he replies in a murmur, "I love you more," and a shiver of need runs down my spine.

Closing my eyes, I move my hips, but Rhys stills me, chuckling. "Do you really want to do this on a jet full of people? In front of my parents—*your in-laws?*"

Heat surges into my cheeks. *Dear Lord, how could I have blocked them all out?* I hear a snicker from across the aisle—Denielle—and I bury my face in Rhys's shoulder.

He's shaking underneath me with silent laughter. After all these years, I still can't get enough of this guy.

"We'll make sure to get some alone time later," he says in a low tone, full of promise, and the heat spreads to other parts of my body as well.

Joel's voice comes over the intercom for everyone to take their seats, and I reluctantly move back to mine and buckle in. Across from me, Rhys is adjusting his pants and throws me an accusatory glare when he catches me watching. I shrug, and his eyes crinkle.

"Tonight," he mouths.

Two LARGE SUVs wait for us in the hangar, and I spot George instantly. He leans against one of the vehicles but pushes off as soon as we step off the jet.

Initially, he was supposed to accompany us on the flight since it was Marcus's week off as well. Then, last Friday, he called, saying he'd be staying at the vineyard with my brother, and Marcus would be in charge during the travel. Something was off, and my mind immediately started coming up with all kinds of scenarios in which Nate was not okay. But when I asked, George kept assuring me that Nate was fine. That man was, and still is, a closed vault. If he doesn't want to talk about something, there is no way to get it out of him. *My shadow* was kept in the dark as well. He has never kept anything from me, no matter how bad the news was—and there have been many instances over the years. The media is ruthless.

Marcus has become like a second big brother and one of Rhys's closest friends. Even when he isn't on duty, he always hangs around. Marcus is also George's second in command when it comes to our security, which made me worry even more that he had no clue what was going on.

"Lilly." A huge smile turns George's mouth upward, and some of the tension leaves me. If it were something serious, I have to believe he'd tell me—warn me. *Nate is fine.* Everything will be okay.

I hug the man who's become an integral part of my family. "Hi, George."

"G-man." Rhys comes around me and gives him one of his usual clasp-hands-side-shoulder-man-hugs.

*Oh, how things have changed.*

"How was the flight?" George looks over my shoulder where Heather is carefully maneuvering down the stairs.

"Great, slept almost the entire time." Rhys puffs up his chest.

George's grin turns wider, and I snort.

"I don't need your help." Den's growl echoes through the hangar, and I sigh before turning around. My best friend and Marcus are standing on the top step, and she's tugging ferociously on the handle of her suitcase he is attempting to carry for her.

"Dude, just let go. It's not worth the tongue lashing she'll give you if you take Louis away from her," Wes shouts from the back door of the second SUV where he's waiting for his turn to climb in.

"Fuck off, Sheats!" Denielle barks at him, but Wes only grins wider and blows her a kiss.

"Fine. Whatever. I'm done," Marcus snaps before disappearing back inside the airplane.

Rhys bursts into laughter, and even George can't hold back a chuckle. I shake my head and stroll over to Heather. This week will be interesting.

WE PILE into the two cars. George is driving ours with Rhys in the passenger seat, Den and me in the middle, and Heather in the third row. Tristen and the rest went into the other SUV.

"Henry called right before we took off," Heather announces, and I turn in my seat.

"He did? Is everything okay?" I had spoken to him just this morning, and the jet is going to pick him up two days from now. He isn't able to make it earlier due to his current project.

After his recovery, Henry moved to Virginia, and Tristen helped him get an architect position with a well-known builder in the city. Whenever Rhys and I visited, I would make sure to spend a few days at Henry's as well, and over the years, we've been able to grow our relationship.

Besides the few migraine memories of Henry, I never remembered anything else prior to being six years old. But between him, Heather, and Tristen—their stories, as well as all the photos—I could picture it. That was how I wanted to remember my childhood, and not once have I regretted my decision to not meet with Hector Lakatos to let him try restoring it.

"Everything is fine. He was just asking if he should bring any of the travel toys you left at his house last month," Heather explains.

*Oh.*

I sigh in relief. The anxiety that instantly shot through me disappears, and I glance down at the middle seat where George expertly strapped in the baby carrier. My heart skips a beat. In just two days, this little one will be one year old. She rubs her eyes and slowly blinks them open.

"Good morning, sleepyhead. Did you have a good nap?" I coo at her, caressing her cheek with the tip of my index finger.

Her big green eyes slowly take in her surroundings, and Rhys twists in his seat.

"How is my princess?" Hearing his voice, she immediately gets antsy and tries to reach for him.

When she can't see or touch him, her fussing gets louder. Whenever Daddy is near, no one else matters. "You need to wait a few more minutes. Then you can go to Daddy," I try to soothe her, and Den chuckles.

I glare at my best friend, and she makes a zip motion across her mouth. Denielle thinks this is hilarious.

George also laughs in the driver's seat, and my daughter's undivided attention switches to our head of security. Yup, I'm officially in third place; she prefers our bodyguard to me. I can't be mad, though. The men in her life adore her and spoil her rotten. Who wouldn't want that all the time? I smile down at her little round face, and the image of an old baby picture instantly appears behind my mental eye. I blink a few times. This is not the time to cry.

WE PULL straight into the garage, and I let George and Rhys get out while I unbuckle our daughter. I barely have her out of the car seat when she reaches for Rhys, who has just opened my door.

"Here you go. There is your da—" is all I get out before she dives into his arms.

He grins down at her proudly and hugs her to his chest, placing a kiss on her blonde curls. "I missed you, too, princess."

I climb out of the car and grab the diaper bag. My pulse increases as I scan the motor pool. His car is here, but why is he not coming to say hello?

"Where is he?" I address George, who's already halfway through the door leading to the east wing. Turning, he first looks at Rhys then at me. "He is in the kitchen."

Heather steps to my side. "You go on. I'll make sure everyone gets situated, and then we'll meet you in a little bit."

I hug her absently, my gaze not leaving the now empty doorframe to the house. "Thank you."

She is starting to direct everyone to their rooms.

With shaking legs, I step from the garage into the hallway. The smell of garlic tomato sauce drifts into my nose, and I'm instantly taken back to one of my first meals here so many years ago.

So much has changed since then.

Nate has spent the last several years in a psychiatric facility, taking responsibility for his crimes. He was taken off medication for the last three and solely focused on therapy. I'm so proud of him for what he has accomplished.

Rhys and I finished college, got married, had a baby—not to mention what went on in our friends' lives. Life was never...ordinary.

Rhys places his free arm around my waist, smiling down. "Let's go. It's time he meets his niece."

My stomach is in knots the closer we get to the kitchen, and my feet are moving slower and slower until Rhys begins to herd me. I don't know why I'm so nervous. Maybe it's because I haven't seen him in so long, or because we've barely spoken the last few weeks, and I'm worried something is wrong.

Slowly, I push open the door and pause. Nate is standing at the stove, his back to us. His hair is longer than I remember, and he is wearing faded blue jeans and a white long-sleeve shirt.

"Nate?" I call out hesitantly.

He whirls around, and our eyes lock. My throat thickens. I've missed him so much this past year. I was on bed rest for the last few months of my pregnancy and then didn't want to leave my daughter overnight. Rhys and I also were extremely overprotective of her. We avoided everything that could bring her to the attention of the media. Hence, we didn't take her to see Nate.

I can't stop myself and run over, wrapping my arms around his waist and holding on as tight as I can. He returns the embrace and places his cheek on the top of my head.

"I missed you, too, little sister," his voice cracks.

His words make me squeeze him even tighter, and a sob bubbles up in my throat. We stand like this for several minutes until a tiny squeal alerts me from the door that there is someone else my brother needs to greet.

I disentangle myself from him and wipe at my eyes. Still keeping one arm wrapped around him, I guide Nate away from the stove while Rhys slowly walks into the room. When we are only a few feet apart, Rhys turns our daughter in his arm so she is sitting on one arm, and he secures her with the other against his chest.

Nate's gaze moves from my face to his niece, and he sucks in a breath. His free hand flies to his mouth. With tears in his eyes, he glances between my daughter's, Rhys's, and my face.

"She looks so much like..." a hoarse whisper comes from my brother. Our little girl's eyes fly to her uncle's, and she immediately starts grasping for him, opening and closing her tiny fists, squirming in Rhys's arms until he can barely contain her. He looks at me for help on what to do. Feeling the moisture in my own eyes spill over, I simply nod, and my husband hands our baby girl over to my brother.

Nate cradles her like she is the most precious treasure in the whole world. She peers up at him, and her small hand tries to pat his face.

With my arms now wrapped around Rhys's waist, I wait for my brother to meet my gaze before saying, "Nate, meet your niece, Audrey Hamlin McGuire."


THE END

Make sure to check out the acknowledgements
in this book for a few more secrets that will be revealed **soon**.

But first, keep reading for an exclusive preview of
**Because of the Dark**, Book Four in The Dark Series.

## KEEP READING

**Because of the Dark
(Prologue)**

## WES

MY HARLEY STREET BOB VIBRATES UNDER ME AS I WAIT FOR THE light to turn. I'm still in disbelief about how Kai finished the entire bottle of Patrón and was still standing upright when I walked through the door of our shared townhouse. The guy has a capacity for liquor I've never seen before and is still fully functional. But of course, I'm stuck replacing it once we run out. Allowing him behind the wheel of his Rover—functioning or not—is not something I can do with a good conscience. Thankfully, this task has become easier since June, when I turned twenty-one, and I no longer have to rely on a fake ID or bribes.

The red finally switches to green, and I'm moving again. Two more blocks until The Moose's Head. After almost twenty-four long-ass (and most of them cold as fuck) months, I'm still dumb-struck by the names of bars, restaurants, or local shops. You'd think just because we're in the Treasure State, surrounded by mountains and wildlife, we'd still have something like Whole Foods or Binney's. No, we have *The Farmer* and *The Moose's Head*—TMH for the locals.

Turning off the ignition in front of the liquor store, I take in the decked-out Jeep MOAB next to me. The car screams badass. Matte black, five-percent tint all around, black rims, light bar, chrome tube steps—that's what I call a sweet ride.

I take a step toward the double doors when a familiar ping sounds in my wireless headphones.

"Message from Rhys McGuire."

*Fuck me. As if my day isn't already bad enough.*

"Wes, bro, you can't avoid us forever. It's been two years. We know you got the invitation. Calla misses you. Call us," the robotic female voice reads me the text from my former best friend.

*You bet your rich ass I can keep avoiding you.*

They're the reason my life turned into this dumpster fire. I don't bother pulling out my phone. Seeing the words will only result in me sending it flying, and I can't afford a new one. Instead, I walk into The Moose's Head and veer toward the aisle with the hard stuff.

After this, I really need to replenish our stash. Thank fuck I brought the hiking backpack. That way, I can load up triple time.

Getting everything I need, I add a pack of Big League Chew to my liquid purchase—never heard of that shit until arriving in Podunk, Montana, but it's addicting, and now I buy it whenever I come here.

I head back to my bike, bottles clinking together on my back despite the layers of paper bags I ordered the flannel-clad clerk to wrap around them. My gaze sweeps over the Jeep. After the text, I forgot all about it.

*I wonder who owns this baby.*

I'm standing at the light right off of TMH's parking lot, waiting for it to turn, when I see the Jeep pull out of its spot in my side mirror.

*Weird. I didn't notice anyone leaving the store behind me.*

"Radioactive" by Bullet For My Valentine blares through my headphones as I drive down 19th to our house on the south side, near the university. I approach another intersection just as it turns red, and I slow the bike down. Almost stopped, I glance in the mirror and spot the Jeep speeding toward me.

*What the—?*

I'm about to abandon my Harley to save my ass, when the driver hits the brakes and brings the car to a standstill about a foot from my rear tire, leaving skid marks on the asphalt.

Adrenaline is pulsating through my body, and my hands tighten around the handlebar. This dude is asking for it. Still riled up from the text, I wouldn't mind planting my fist in someone's face. I'm about to get off my bike to march toward the MOAB when the light switches, and the jerk beeps at me.

*Lucky motherfucker.*

I've never been a hothead. Rhys used to be the one who tended to lose his temper in our friendship. Not that I was a pussy; I simply didn't have the desire to pick a fight. I was the jokester—the person no one took seriously—until everything was ripped from under me. The day I punched my best friend across the face...that was when I changed.

The Jeep drives behind me with less than the mandated safety distance, and I clench my jaw.

*Give me a reason, fuckface.*

I switch lanes as I approach Bear Court, where I have to turn left—yup, even the streets have ridiculous names here. The dick navigating the Jeep follows suit and comes even closer. Fast.

At the last moment, the Jeep moves back into the right lane and halts next to me. The light turns green, but neither of us moves. I glower at the blacked-out driver's side through my visor—equally tinted—when the window suddenly lowers about halfway. My heart stutters when a girl with wavy, dark-blonde hair comes into view. Wayfarers cover half of her face that's visible, and despite not seeing her eyes, I can feel her gaze on me. Somehow, I know that she is stunningly beautiful. My body is instantly buzzing with...recognition?

*Have I seen her before?*

I hold my breath as something in her expression changes. She is smirking. The crinkle around her eyes is noticeable even though most of her face is hidden from me. Lifting a hand, MOAB Girl salutes and takes off with screeching tires.

Stunned, I remain at the intersection until I can no longer see her lights down the road.

I have no idea what just happened, but the thudding beat of my heart tells me that it was the most exciting thing since exiting the plane two years ago.

Born and raised in Germany, Danah moved to the US, where she met her husband, eventually trading downtown Chicago's city life for the northern Rockies.
She can be seen hanging with her twin girls and exploring the outdoors when she's not arguing plot points with the characters in her head.
But it's that exact passion that has produced *The Dark Series* and continues to keep her glued to her laptop, following her dreams.

Scan the below QR code to sign up for my newsletter and be the first to know about upcoming releases, sales, and new arrivals.

Add me on Facebook
www.facebook.com/authordanahlogan/

Follow me on Instagram
www.instagram.com/authordanahlogan/

Visit my Website for more content
and other places to stalk me
www.authordanahlogan.com

Or scan this second QR code for all the links:

# ALSO BY DANAH LOGAN

**The Ghost**
*The Beginning.*
A Dark Series and Davis Order Novella
(George & Lou)

**The Dark Series**

**In the Dark**, Book 1
**Out of the Dark**, Book 2
**Of Light and Dark**, Book 3
(Lilly and Rhys)
A Dark, New-Adult, Romantic-Suspense Trilogy

**Because of the Dark**, Book 4
(Wes and King)
A Dark, Hidden-Identity, Romantic-Suspense Novel

**Followed by the Dark**, Book 5
(Denielle and Marcus)
A Dark, Enemies-to-Lovers, Age-Gap,
Romantic-Suspense Novel

**I Am the Dark**, Book 6
(HIM)
A Dark, Age-Gap, Romantic-Suspense Novel

# The Davis Order

**Rezoned**, Prequel
(Ethan)
A Dark, Hate-to-Love, Second-Chance,
Romantic-Suspense Novel

# ACKNOWLEDGEMENTS

I can't believe this is the end of Rhys and Lilly's story. I can't tell you how many times I've cried toward the end of this book. I've lived with these two in my head for three and a half years. They've grown with me, and I've learned from them.

Never in a million years would I have expected this journey to be such a wild ride. Lilly, Rhys, Den, Wes, Nate, George, even Natty...they all have become a huge part of me.

Certain scenes, especially in this book, were extremely challenging and emotionally exhausting to write for various reasons, but in the end, I am glad I worked through them. Because of those moments, you get to experience Lilly and Rhys in their rawest and truest form. Every character in this series has their own strengths and weaknesses. They are selfish yet loyal to a fault for the people they love. And when they love, they love fiercely.

Even though this concludes Lilly and Rhys's story, this is not the end for them. **You've met several characters in these three books that will make a reappearance** in future books in The Dark Series, as well as get their own books or even series.

I'm aware that there are still some **unanswered questions**, but I can promise you, **they will be answered**.

- Where is Gray? Why did he really shoot Emily, and what was on the note he gave Lilly?
- Make sure to add ***Because of the Dark***, Wes's book, to your TBR on Goodreads.
- What happened to Hank after he stabbed Nate? Good question. I have a vague idea on that part but have to have a few more conversations with Hank on that. ;-)
  What I do know: he will be back.

With that being said, Wes has been *yelling* in my head for over a year and a half, and Denielle's story has slowly been forming, and even Nate and George have more to say. I hope you are as excited for Wes as I am. If there are any other loose ends that you would like to know when they will be tied up, message me. I'd love to hear from you.

The list of people I need to thank has been growing over the last few years.

First and foremost, I need to thank my husband. His endless patience and support made this possible. He gave me an office, he put up with me when I was in one of my characters' headspaces and my emotions would run wild (aka, my crazy side took over), and he accepted that, for the past year, I've barely cooked (besides for the kiddos) and he had to fend for himself.

D., I love you. This book is for you!

Abbi, who is the reason I started this journey. Thank you for believing in me and pushing me to do something I never thought I could.

Sammi (S.J. Sylvis) and Eleanor (Aldrick), my amazing and wonderful author friends, who took time out of their busy schedules to read my books and give me valuable feedback.

Maria, for your help on all the legal questions that came with this book.

Laurin, for taking my random text messages day and night and answering medical questions.

Mary, who started as my beta for *In the Dark* and has become not only my alpha, beta, and proofreader, but also one of my dearest friends. I can't wait to come up with more plots with you. And I'm sorry, but you still can't take residence in my head, munch on popcorn, and watch the stories unfold. There are already too many people in there. ;-)

Lyndsey, my side chick and beta, who shares my love for books and has endless conversations with me about the characters as if they're real. I mean, they are, right? Don't tell me they're not. :-P

A big thank you to my editor, Jenn Lockwood, who had to deal with my constant schedule changes and also re-edited books one and two multiple times until I finally stopped adjusting the plot.

Pantser all the way! (Note to self: Not great when you write a continuous trilogy.)

And of course, THANK YOU, THANK YOU, THANK YOU to all the readers, bloggers, and reviewers! Without all of you, none of this would've been possible.

Wes, let's do this!

xoxo,
Danah Logan